MW00583081

# ATLANTIS

## INSPIRATION FOR THE FUTURE

ATLANTIS INSPIRATION FOR THE FUTURE

First edition

All rights reserved.

Copyright  2005  by Walter F. Laredo


This book or parts thereof, may not be reproduced in any form,
without prior written permission from the author.

Laredo Publications
ISBN  0-9629148-0-0


Printed in U.S.A.

# Contents

WALTER F. LAREDO

# ATLANTIS

## INSPIRATION FOR THE FUTURE

Tales of Everyday
Life in Atlantis

# Paintings and Drawings

## 8 Color Plates follows this page

## 32 Ink Figures follows the color plates
These ink figures includes maps, road to Chapare, hiking in the jungle, ancient dreams and life in Atlantis.

Former road to Chapare

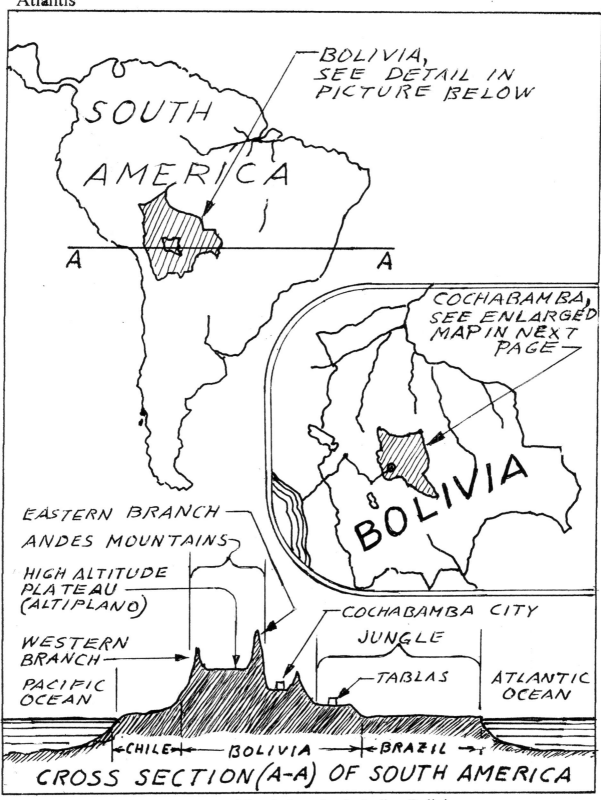

Figure 1.   Map of South America including Bolivia

Atlantis

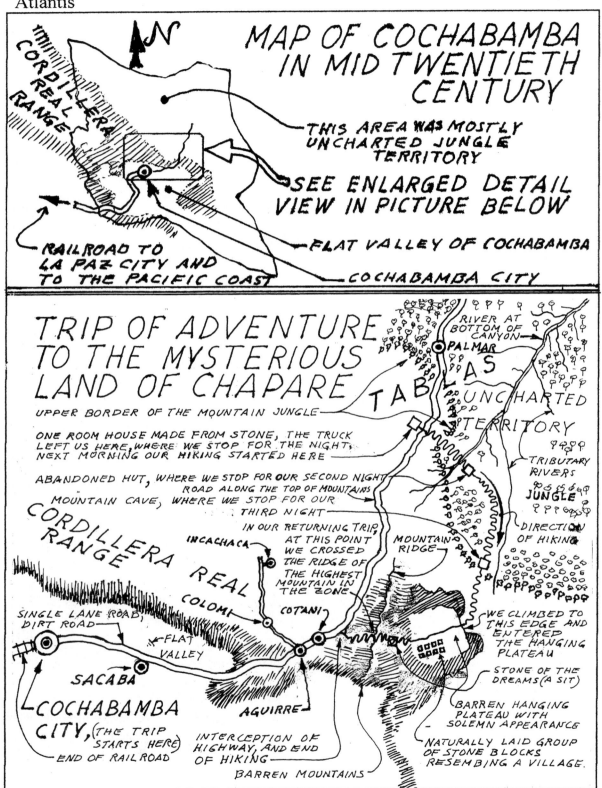

Figure 2.   Map of Cochabamba and Chapare

Atlantis

Figure 3.   A dangerous road to Chapare, where accidents happened often
as the collapsing of road segments into the cliffs.  For each
fatal accident a wood cross was put at the road edge.

Figure 4.    Crossing at the opposite side of the gorge, by walking through a falling three trunk.

Atlantis

Figure 5.   Angels guided children to the celestial gathering where all
prophets from the universe were present.

Figure 6. Angels served children and prophets at a heaven gathering, dinner.

Figure 7.    UNDERGROUND ATLANTIS CHAMBER. The Custodian
Monks, which modern headquarters is shown at the top of
picture, discovered that eons old Atlantis Chamber.

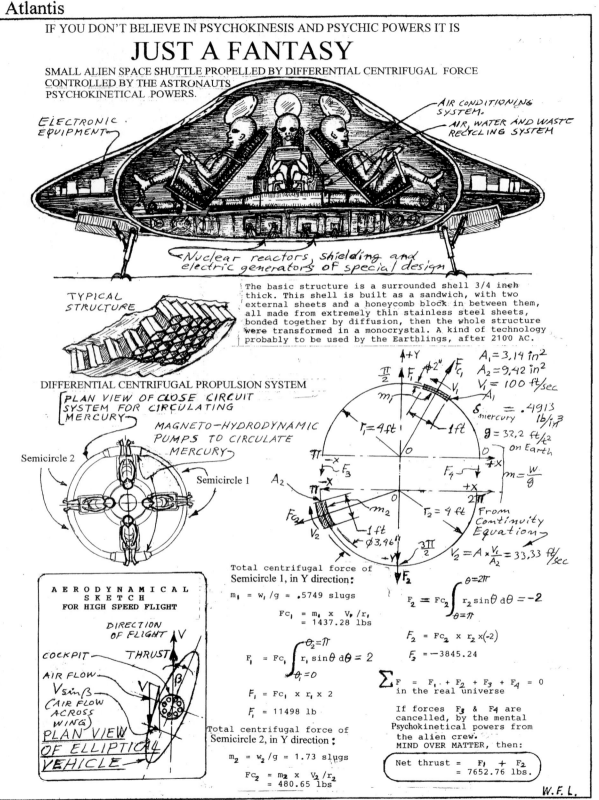

Figure 8. An alien spaceship of the imagination.

Atlantis

Color plate 1.  Short stop on the old road to Chapare

Color plate 2. Resting during a return hiking trip, hallucinating of flying saucers, and
looking at a group of naturally arranged boulders that mimic a one street village.

Color plate 3.  Temple of Poseidon in Atlantis' Acropolis,   as depicted by Plato

Atlantis

W.F. LAREDO
-1966-

Color plate 4.   Paradise, according to one of the Atlantis religions

Atlantis

Color plate 5.  The triumph of good over evil according to an Atlantis religion

Color plate 6.  Krill helping Meya to climb the mechanical horse

Atlantis

Color plate 7.   Costume ball in Atlantis

Atlantis

Color plate 8.  Photograph of a water fountain and Nereid in the front of a home in
Kent, Washington.   Sculpture by W. F. Laredo

Figure 9.    Atlantis nears the end of the ice age.

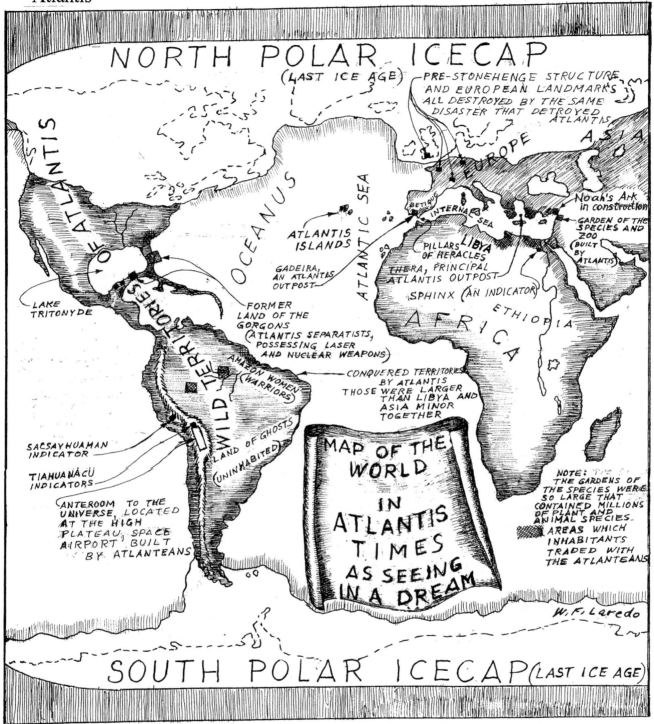

Figure 10.   Ancient map of the world.

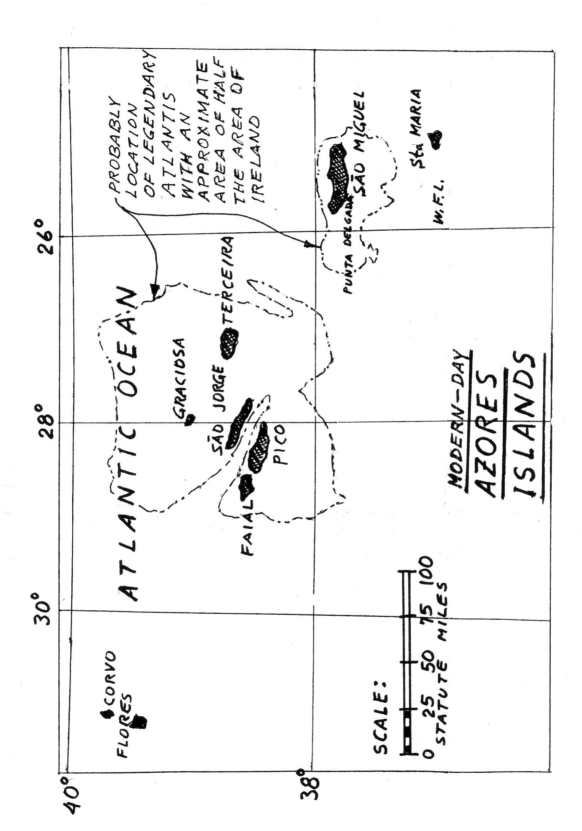

Figure 11.  Map of the Azores islands.

Figure 12. Map of the Atlantis islands as it was in 9600 BC.

Atlantis

Figure 13.   200,000 BC, Alien base on Earth, including a genetic
engineering laboratory installed by the Entarian
extraterrestrial in order to create man from
primitive hominid animals.

Figure 14. Adam and his hominid cousins watching the departure of his creators alien geneticists (incomplete mission, man will remain imperfect).

Figure 15.   Dawn of agriculture.

Figure 16.    Manual primitive fabrication of mud bricks.

Atlantis

Figure 17.    10,600 BC.  View of Atlantis Acropolis, by Plato's description. Eons later, after the aliens left the Earth and their memories vanished the Atlanteans took over the complex and changed it into a place of pagan worshiping.

Figure 18.    Temple of Poseidon in Acropolis, Atlantis

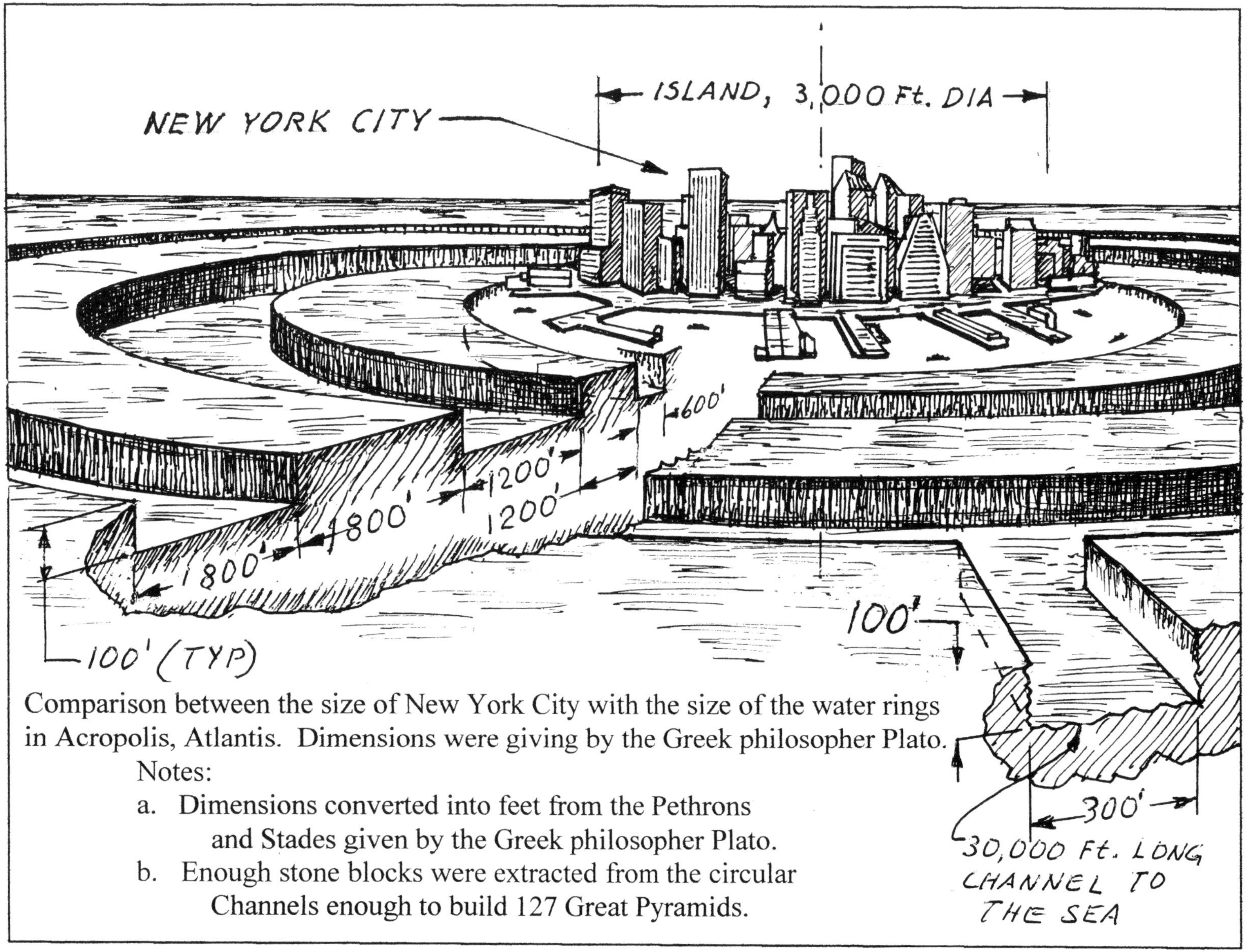

ATLANTIS

NEW YORK CITY

ISLAND, 3,000 Ft. DIA

100' (TYP)

600'

1200'

1200'

800'

800'

100'

300'

30,000 Ft. LONG CHANNEL TO THE SEA

Comparison between the size of New York City with the size of the water rings in Acropolis, Atlantis. Dimensions were giving by the Greek philosopher Plato.

Notes:

a. Dimensions converted into feet from the Pethrons and Stades given by the Greek philosopher Plato.

b. Enough stone blocks were extracted from the circular Channels enough to build 127 Great Pyramids.

Figure 19.   Comparison in size, New York city  vs. the water rings of Acropolis

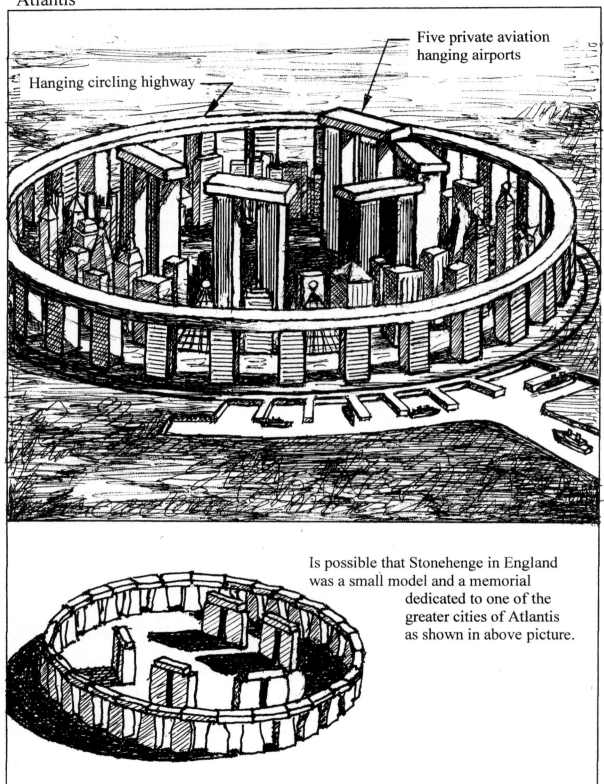

Five private aviation
hanging airports

Hanging circling highway

Is possible that Stonehenge in England
was a small model and a memorial
dedicated to one of the
greater cities of Atlantis
as shown in above picture.

Figure 20.  Stonehenge

CITY OF BRASEA (9600 B.C.)
BUILT IN THE MODERN TIMES OF LEGENDARY ATLANTIS

Figure 21.  City of Brasea (9600 B. C.) Build in the modern Atlantis times in order to move the capital of Atlantis from the ancient Acropolis to modern Brasea.

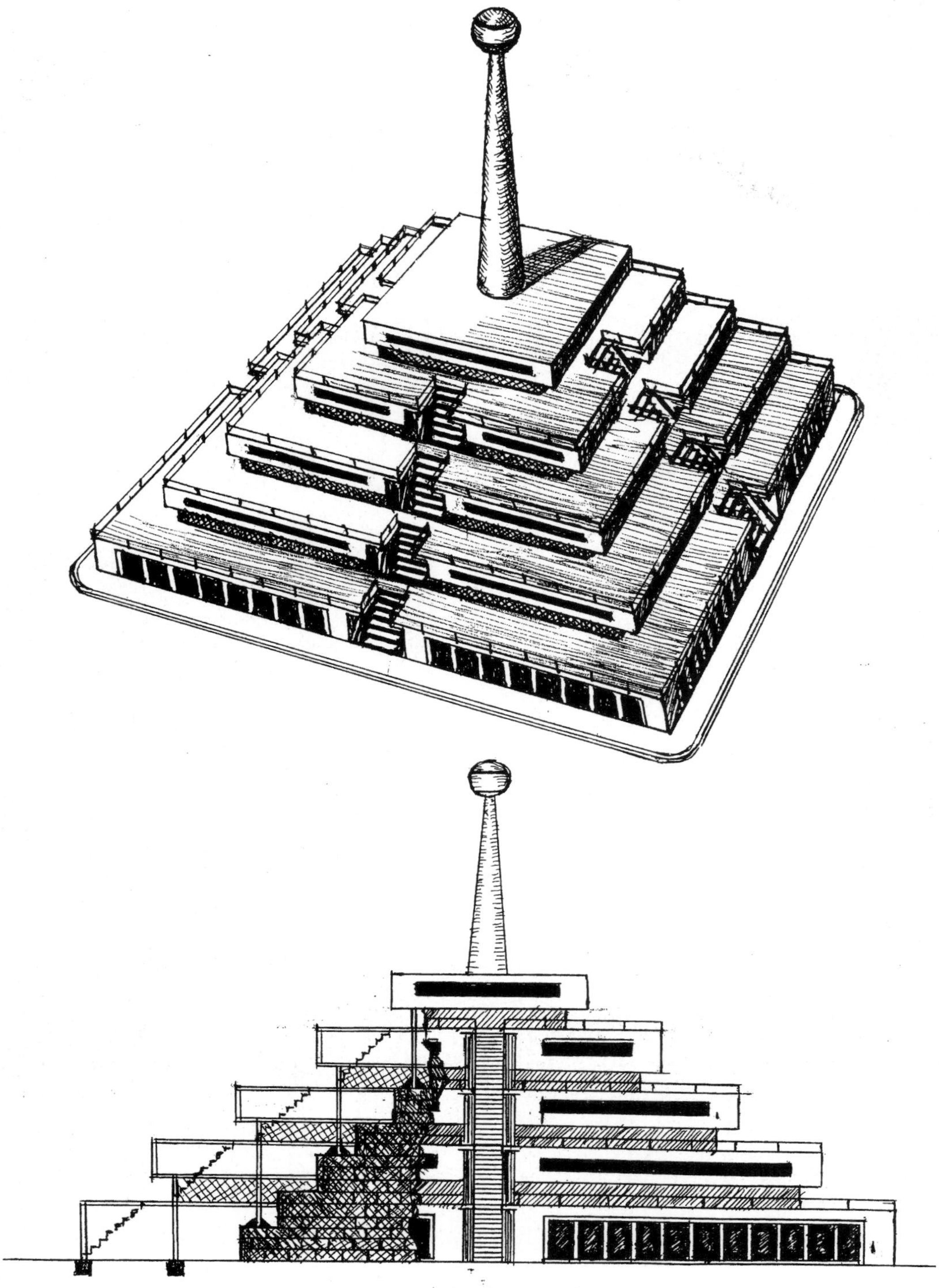

Figure 22.   A modern building built over an abandoned pyramid

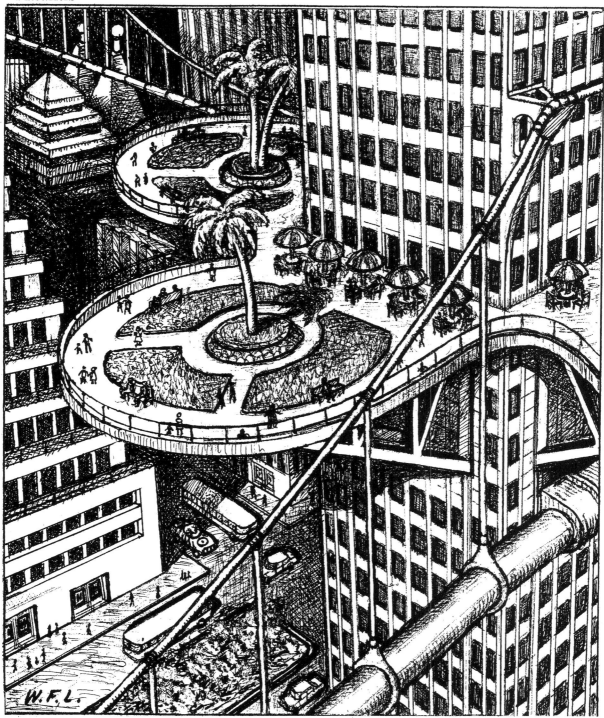

Figure 23.    A restaurant in a building high floor with hanging
                gardens in the form of a four-leaf clover, at lower
                right is shown the tube of a hanging urban train.

Figure 24. Atlanteans contemplating their space base located at a high altitude plateau in South America.

W.F. LAREDO

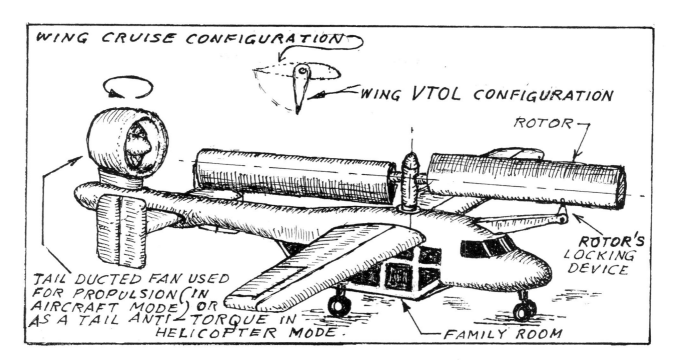

Figure 25.   FLYING CAMPING VEHICLE (VTOL),
Krill a toddler feels safe behind the unbreakable glass.

Figure 26.   Garden of love and romance, Atlantis

Figure 27.    Encounter with Doctor Re and Commander Ore
extraterrestrial from planet Entar.

Figure 28.    Captain Cronos approaching the killer comet.

Figure 29.    An Atlantis astronaut monk watching through the spaceship windows to Saturn and its rings.

Atlantis

Figure 30.   Interstellar beacon, operating once every six months, is
            located in the Bermuda triangle, its function is to indicate
            the location of invisible Earth to other distant advanced
            civilizations somewhere in the universe.

Atlantis

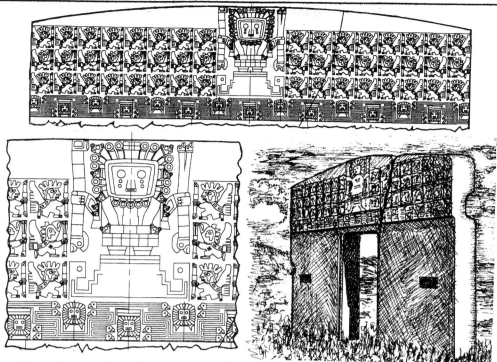

Meeting between God and his congregation of uspars (similar to quarks), before the birth of the universe with the Big Bang. In the meeting God weep, because he knew that in creating goodness also would be created evil. Event that was carved in the upper portion of the "Gateway of the Sun" at the ruins of Tiahuanacu in Bolivia, as shown in above picture and its details.

Verse 2, (Genesis, Chapter 1, Holy Bible, King James Version).
And the Earth was without form, and void; and darkness was upon. And the spirit of God moved upon the face of the waters. Interpretation: God's active force (also called the fifth interaction, anti-gravity force or universal mind) was moving to and fro in an ocean of uspars (similar to quarks). All this super-dense energy, which also included the spirit of God, was contained in the primal universal black hole. Outside which there was nothing of anything.

Figure 31. Greatest drama, instants before the creation
of the universe.

Figure 32.  Pantheist Temple in Atlantis, located at an idyllic place dedicated to meditation and contemplation of nature.   Built as a slow rotating steel structure with glass walls and a dome with darkened glass.
    Pantheism was considered the religion for the intellectuals.

# INTRODUCTION

It all started with a cardboard box. While organizing and cleaning my garage, I happened to open the box and came upon an old manuscript I had written a long time ago. It was a story about an advanced civilization from the past and had been stored in that box since the time I lost interest in editing it. I took out the manuscript, blew off the dust, and went to work.

This book is the result of that original manuscript and describes the wonders of Atlantis, a great civilization that, whether real or legendary, is an inspiration for the future of our civilization. Engineering designs included in the appendices of this book are presented to illustrate how we may benefit from the vast knowledge that the Atlanteans possessed.

The story began when my father, a businessman who enjoyed climbing and hiking, and I embarked on a trip more than 40 years ago into a jungle that has remained unchanged for more than a million years. My father had been asked to do a feasibility study for prospective investments in coffee plantations and cattle breeding. Our journey took us into an area that had barely been explored -- the mysterious rain forest of Tablas, near the center of Bolivia. Before leaving, my father hired a porter to carry our luggage on his shoulders during the long walk. (Unknown to us, the porter was a superstitious man and often believed he saw UFOs!)

For days in advance I dreamed about this adventure. I was as excited as a Boy Scout before his first trip away from home. I knew I would experience things that I had never encountered before. Finally the big day arrived.

Before we could reach the rain forest, we had to cross a series of tall and barren mountains. We wound down long valleys and crested tall, cold mountaintops. My binoculars were a constant companion, as I didn't want to miss a thing.

On the first night of our trip, we stayed in a one-room stone house. After leaving there, we began a long descent into the tropical rain forest. The second night, which was one of continuous rain, we stayed at an old abandoned hut. The next morning, we realized we had not seen a single human being or any trace of civilization along the way.

My father did not find anything useful for his study in this part of the jungle, so we began our return trip. We had a long climb up a rocky mountain and found ourselves tiring quickly. As we passed by a jagged outreach, we discovered a shallow cave and decided it was a good place to stop and spend our third night. This was where I had my first dream (in a series of many) about the mysteries of Atlantis, upon which this book is based.

In this first dream, I encountered several historic figures--philosophers, artists, men of science, prophets, and even Christ. I also met other young people like myself. Christ told us we had been brought together to hear a message that was vitally important to our planet, Earth. He told us that sometime during the first century of the third millennium, a comet was going to strike the Earth and would wipe out all living beings on this planet. It would be a disaster like no other ever witnessed by the human race. He said the only way to save the world from this coming cataclysm was to destroy the comet or divert it from its course by using the same wisdom and science that the people of Atlantis had used against the comet that had struck their world many ages before.

He went on to say that to gain this wisdom, it would be necessary for one of us to travel to the past and then return to the present with the secrets of Atlantis. This would happen when one of us sat on the "Stone of Dreams," a stone that the people of Atlantis carved eons ago into the shape of a chair. Inside the stone, Atlantean scientists had placed electronic equipment that would act as a virtual reality machine and allow a person to actually experience events from the past.

This was where my dream at the cave ended.

The next day we ventured into another region, different from the one we had traveled the day before. This hike took us through a cold and barren hanging valley, and finally to the highest mountain in the area.

As we walked, I thought about my dream and remembered it was the year before that I had first read about Atlantis. It was in a chapter from an old book that was written by Plato, the Greek philosopher. He had said the people of Atlantis existed about 9000 BC (long before Egypt, Mesopotamia, the Minoans, the Indus Valley, or Greece) and was a civilization that thrived while the rest of the world lived in the Stone Age. Although originally a violent people who set out to conquer the world, over time their attitudes changed and they evolved into kindly protectors of the planet Earth. From then on, they searched only for truth and knowledge and their wondrous creativeness led them to make amazing scientific discoveries and introduce great technological achievements, some of which remain unsurpassed to this day.

As we began to hike up the very steep and perilous mountainside, my thoughts of Atlantis slipped away. It was a rugged and dangerous climb and I was glad when we came upon a level area where there were lots of rocks and boulders. It was a perfect place to take a few minutes to rest and catch our breath. We each found a boulder to sit on to regain our strength. My choice was an inviting, well-contoured stone that cradled me and felt tailor-made for my body. I immediately drifted off to sleep. As I thought back later, it was almost as though the stone had emitted some sort of narcotic effect on me.

I immediately began to dream again. This time I saw strange-looking creatures digging a tunnel in the side of a hill. An engineer explained to me that they were building vaults to store the wisdom and science of Atlantis so future generations would have the knowledge they needed to save the Earth from the comet their astronomers had foretold. I wanted to know more, but before I could ask any questions, I felt someone violently shaking me.

It was the porter who wanted me to drink some hot tea from his Thermos. He explained it was made from dried coca leaves and for thousands of years, the natives had used it to prevent altitude sickness. I reached for the thermos and had no more than swallowed down the hot liquid when the drowsiness returned and I once again began dreaming, only this time the dream was much different. It was intensely real and seemed to last for a very long time.

In this dream, I was a young boy living in Atlantis. I had an uncle who was an engineer; he also was an elder in the Atlantean government and he showed me many wonders of Atlantis. Because his business kept him very busy and he often had to travel, I spent much of my time with Godin and Gofreigga, an Atlantean family who lived near my uncle. They had a grandson named Krill and I remember that we became close friends, along with another boy named Crom.

Krill was an explorer at heart and one part of the dream I especially remember was when he set off on an adventure to see things no other Atlanteans had seen. It was on this journey that he met and fell in love with a beautiful girl that lived in a remote and primitive area, far from Atlantis and its engineering wonders.

As the dream continued, I became a young man and even had a girlfriend named Mila. I was a chief engineer at an aerospace facility where they designed interplanetary ships and developed other space projects. One night, Mila and I attended a dinner at Godin's and he told about meeting two extraterrestrials named Captain Oren and Dr. Re. It was a fascinating story that I remember to this day.

My dream changed after that. Atlantis seemed to fade away and it was as though I could see myself resting on the stone chair, although I knew I was still sleeping. Suddenly, some mysterious-looking monks walked up to me. After explaining that they were part of a secret organization whose duty it was to protect the world and the Atlantis scrolls of wisdom, they took me with them in a strange flying machine to a huge cavern where they had built modern barracks. They said they were going to share many secrets with me.

One particular monk became my host and took me on a tour through the barracks. As we walked, he related many wonderful stories about God, the history of the world, and the history of Atlantis. He also took me to a library where there were hundreds of books, film recordings, scrolls, and gold plates that contained information on what happened before, during, and after the creation of the universe.

We then visited a large chamber hidden in the center of a mountain, not far from the barracks. Inside this chamber was a huge vault where many ancient treasures were stored, such as sparkling jewelry, magnificent pieces of art, and life-size statues of solid gold. It also held Atlantean intellectual riches, including the history of their arts, sciences, and technologies.

Shortly after this, my visit ended. The monks returned me to the stone where they had picked me up. I tried again to wake up, but I was very tired and couldn't seem to open my eyes. It was as though I was in some sort of trance. This time, a message seemed to form in my mind.

It was a desperate plea from the ancients of Atlantis to us, the people of their future. They knew their part of the world was doomed and their one wish, when humanity recovered from the great comet cataclysm, was for the welfare and prosperity of the survivors. Knowing that history repeats itself, they were certain a new race of humans would begin again as hunter-gatherers in a new Stone Age. Because they so loved the grandeur of their civilization and wanted to perpetuate it past the cataclysm, they wished to pass on their knowledge, their wisdom, and their immense riches. They did not want their accomplishments to be in vain.

I was told that everything about them was stored in seven treasure vaults (including the one I had visited) to show future generations how the Atlanteans had built their great civilization. The final part of the message was that my dreams would go on and in them, I would learn more about the inhabitants of Atlantis.

Finally I awoke. My father and the porter were stretching and yawning and commenting how deeply they had slept. We all agreed that it seemed like we had slept for hours, yet our watches indicated only 20 minutes had passed.

Storm clouds were fast approaching from the low valleys, and I sensed my father was frightened because there were no caves around for shelter. In a few moments, the downpour began and as we rushed to find shelter, I quickly forgot the dreams and visions. It wasn't until much later, when we had returned to civilization, that we found out a whole day, not just 20 minutes, had gone by. My father said, "This is very strange. If we skipped an entire day, where were we during the missing time?" But then he never again mentioned the strange occurrence.

***********

As I grew older, I thought often about these strange and mysterious dreams and wondered if they were just a result of my active imagination. I remembered being captivated by Plato's story of Atlantis, as well as Journey to the Center of the Earth by French writer Jules Verne. Or perhaps the dreams were a result of being at an altitude of 18,000 feet, fatigued by the climb, and my brain starving for oxygen.

I also pondered the stone chair on which I had rested. Did it truly have the power to communicate with my mind? Did the people of Atlantis leave it there? Or perhaps it had been positioned there by extra-terrestrials? Did it have a higher purpose? Was it, as Christ had said, some sort of time machine to transport the mind to a distant past where dreams become virtual reality? Was there a type of transmitter imbedded inside that bridged the gap of knowledge and experience between our creation and recorded history?

As the years passed, I eventually stopped thinking about the dreams and moved on with my life.

Then one day, the dreams returned, at first, only occasionally; but sometimes I would have them as often as once a week. They were always so real, so vivid and rich in detail. In fact, when I awoke, I frequently felt as though I had been living actual events in the great past civilization of Atlantis--a civilization magnificent beyond my understanding. In one of my more recent dreams, I again received the cold warning about the returning comet and the cataclysmic disaster that will happen in modern times, and this has caused me some distress.

I have written this book to share these dreams with you, dear reader, because I cannot get away from the belief that they contained an underlying message to the people of Earth.

Moreover, I believe that much of mythology is, in reality, our prerecorded history. The history of Atlantis and its splendor has been disputed by many, yet much of the vocabulary is still with us today. Names such as Atlas, Oceanus, Heracles (Hercules), Thor, Odin, Kronos, Poseidon, Nereids, Cyclops, Acropolis, Inti, Viracocha, Kukul-kan, and Amazon have survived through the millennia, even though more recent cultures, such as the Greeks, the Incas, the Norse, and others have taken these names and used them as their own. There are many hidden mysteries in the story of Atlantis.

\*\*\*\*\*\*\*\*\*\*\*

One final note: In the Appendices at the end of the book are drawings of designs inspired by the engineering wonders of Atlantis which, if not a historical fantasy, may very well have been a real civilization. Although the general concepts of these drawings originated in my dreams, some driving force urged me to develop them into actual preliminary designs by using twentieth century state-of-the-art technology, the laws of physics, standards, specifications, and scientific information used today in laboratories and industry. Engineers and scientists of today will find those designs fully suitable for use in actual engineering projects.

# CHAPTER 1
## Trip of Exploration

Many years ago, when I was 14 years old, my parents, younger siblings, and I went to live northwest of Cochabamba. Located in the center of Bolivia, it was the second largest city at that time with an approximate population of 70,000. We settled into a residential area where the homes resembled American architecture.

The train we traveled on to reach our destination was pulled by a steam engine and took us from the Pacific Coast through the dry, hilly land of Peru. Finally arriving at the foot of the western Andes range, we started a zigzag climb to the top of the mountains. From there, we crossed a mountain pass, then descended onto the Altiplano Plateau where Bolivia is located.

The Altiplano Plateau is approximately the same distance in length as San Diego to San Francisco in California. It is like a dusty, dry desert without dunes. In fact, it is so flat that a small plane could land anywhere on it. Usually by 10 in the morning the plateau becomes a remarkable land of mirages, looking more like a lake with the surrounding snow-capped mountain peaks reflected in it upside down.

Heading east, the train crossed the plateau and then started climbing up the eastern range of the split in the Andes Mountains. After reaching the crest, we began a long descent through a series of mountains and canyons -- a sharp contrast to the barren terrain we had just traveled across -- and began zigzagging our way down, just like on the way up. As the train descended into the lowlands, we began to see small agricultural plots and Indian homes.

We then crossed a beautiful and serene valley of picturesque farms. My father explained that landlords (or land barons) ran these farms and lived in huge homes with elaborate gardens. Orchards of oranges, peaches, apples, and other fruit trees and vineyards surrounded the homes. In the barns were prize horses and other farm animals. The landlords also owned extensive fields of crops, most of which were grains.

In contrast to all this luxury were the peasants who worked the farms. Equipped with only hand tools, they lived with their families in one-room mud dwellings with dirt floors and no windows. Outside the houses, I could see small pens of sheep and goats. These peasants received no pay for their labors and were bound to the land for their very existence, however meager. I was greatly disturbed by these sights and was glad when lunchtime finally arrived.

We walked to the restaurant car, which was located at the very back of the train. My parents and I sat at a booth for four, and my four siblings sat at another booth next to us. The car was so crowded that another passenger asked to join us at our table. We agreed and he began to talk with my parents. He spoke of the land barons and told us how they often sent their children away from Bolivia to be educated at the finest schools in places like London, Paris, Buenos Aires, and San Francisco. He said that although Bolivia was known as a democratic society, in practice it was still in feudalism and had been governed and controlled by these elite families for many generations. He told us that the peasants who lived on the farms were forced to give half of their yearly production of crops and animals to the landlords. Some of the landlords were so rich they had more than a thousand peasants working on their land.

The stranger continued his story by telling us about the "Right of Pernada," a barbaric, 400-year-old tradition still practiced by some of the land barons. He explained that this is where young maiden daughters of the peasant workers are required to spend the first night of their wedding with the landlord, who is known as the "Patron." Should the Patron be unable to perform because of impotence, the maiden is then passed on to any of his sons. After that first night, some of the girls, who had been viciously and repeatedly raped, ended their torment by committing suicide.

When we stopped at the next small village, the stranger bid us goodbye and got off the train. Two hours later we reached the end of the line and our destination, the city of Cochabamba.

After getting off the train, I looked to the northeast and could see a distant mountain range. I knew that behind those distant mountains was the Amazon jungle, which extends over most of Brazil, parts of Bolivia, Peru, Ecuador, Colombia, and Venezuela -- an area larger than the continental United States. My father had told me that the only way to reach the jungle from Cochabamba was to cross the mountains on a single road that had been hand-built by Bolivian prisoners from dirt and rocks.

That afternoon, I took a walk on a short street that had some retail stores and coffee shops. I hadn't gone very far when I saw a warehouse building with a sign that said "Exports." At the very moment I passed by, the doors opened wide and a truck with a rear platform drove in very slowly. It was carrying two piles of what appeared to be thick cardboard sheets piled as high as two feet. Then I looked more closely and realized that the piles were not cardboard sheets. They were flattened wild animal skins! I could see that one of the piles consisted of hundreds of flattened jaguar skins with their claws still hanging at the end of the skin that was once their legs. Another pile consisted of caiman skins, a South American crocodile. As I was staring at this macabre sight, two tourists walked by and I could tell they were very distressed by what they saw.

I walked up to the security guard standing at the warehouse door and boldly told him that this uncontrolled hunting of wild animals was going to make them extinct. For a moment, he didn't answer and just looked at me. Then he explained that some indigenous people from the jungle had recently turned into poachers and were selling the skins at incredibly low prices to the businessmen in charge of exports.

A few weeks after getting settled into our new home, my father invited four of his friends over for dinner -- an English explorer, a Czechoslovakian entomologist, a German entrepreneur, and a Swiss social drinker. We had previously visited the entomologist's home and he had shown us his giant collection of dead insects. What looked like millions of bugs were carefully mounted and displayed inside shallow boxes with glass covers. Each specimen was labeled with its scientific classification. He told us he had discovered hundreds of new species in the jungle and had had the honor of naming them. He said he exported many of his insects to various museums in both Europe and the United States.

At dinner, the German gentleman had the most to say. He spoke enthusiastically about the ranch he was building near the edge of the jungle. My father said he wanted to explore the region (known as Tablas) located in the jungle of Chapare at the beginning of the Amazon basin. The Englishman, with typical aplomb, informed us that he had already visited the region several times and was, as far as he knew, the only civilized man to travel there. He said that because there were no roads, he had traversed the whole area on foot. He captivated us with his descriptions of crystal streams, magnificent wild orchids, butterflies of every shape and color, and birds that could only be described as flowers with wings. The Czechoslovakian told us he, too, used to hike into the jungle for long periods -- sometimes being away from his family for several weeks at a time.

It was only a few days after this dinner that my father, who was in the business of importing agricultural machinery and vehicles, came home with two large maps rolled up under his arm. He had a big smile on his face as he enthusiastically unrolled the maps and hung them on the wall. It seems that after hearing the tales of the explorers, my father couldn't resist seeing Tablas for himself. He was an avid climber and hiker, but his motives for this trip were strictly business. Some 30,000 acres of land was available at the cost of $1 per acre and he wanted to bring back soil samples to analyze and determine if the land was suitable for coffee plantations and cattle raising.

Being a curious teenager, I rushed over and began to intently study the maps. One was of South America and showed the long Andes mountain range, which runs along the west coast all the way from Colombia to the southern tip of Chile. To me the range looked like a thin snake with a fat rat in its stomach because about halfway down the continent, it split into two ranges that later joined together again. Where the ranges separated is a flat land known as the Altiplano. Although on the map the Altiplano resembles the very fertile lowlands of the San Joaquin Valley of California, in actuality, it is a freezing cold and barren plateau that is 13,800 feet above sea level. I learned later that the Altiplano is the second highest plateau in the world -- only Tibet in Asia has one that is higher.

I moved to the second map, which showed Bolivia and covered far more detail than the first map. I saw that Bolivia is located on the Altiplano. I could also clearly see the mountains, valleys, and rivers, as well as the railroad tracks that had brought us from the Pacific coast of Peru to Bolivia.

I asked my father if I could accompany him on his exploration trip. Since I was on vacation from high school, I said there was no excuse for him not to take me along. He accepted.

I was overjoyed! I knew this was going to be a great adventure. We would be hiking in uncharted territory and the only thing awaiting us was the unknown. Every moment we would have an opportunity to experience the expected. We might even be risking our lives in these threatening territories!

Since I wanted to learn all I could about our trip, I went to the library and did some research. I excitedly read a story about some ancient and abandoned cities in the depths of the jungle that were said to have secret vaults filled with gold and other treasures. I also read about mysterious blonde men and women who lived in the jungle. Reportedly, they were descendants of German and American pilots who had crashed in the jungle many years ago.

One day before leaving on our great adventure, my father and I were taking a walk through Cochabamba when we passed a crowded coffee shop. Inside we could see a man waving at us. It was the German explorer, beckoning us to join him for a cup of coffee. After being seated, my father told his friend of our upcoming trip to Tablas.

"What route are you planning to take?" asked the German. When we told him, he cautioned us. "That road is not safe for cars. It is very rocky and only trucks with mountain tires can travel it. I'm leaving in two days to do some work on my land and if you are interested, I'll take you along and drop you off at the stone house at the top of the mountain. A man and his wife live there and I'm certain they will put you up for the night. I'll also be carrying some tourists who want to see that part of the world." He smiled and winked as he said, "It puts a little extra money in my pocket."

We accepted his offer.

My father said we would each carry our own backpack on the trip and would not be taking any climbing equipment. The only safety gear my father planned to carry was his revolver. I planned to take an old Winchester rifle and a small pick to excavate any Inca treasures I was lucky enough to discover. My father hired an indigenous porter to carry our luggage. His English friend had recommended the native, telling us he was as good as a Tibetan sherpa. (What he had not told us, however, was that the man was very superstitious and often thought he saw UFOs.) The porter also was bringing along an old flintlock musket that he said had been in his family for so many generations that he could no longer remember its origin. Along with the gun, he carried black powder and lead shot which he had made himself. I noticed the shots were unevenly sized and not perfectly spherical, which would greatly affect the accuracy and dependability of his firearm.

Two days later as he had promised, the German stopped by our home to pick up the three of us. We were a bit surprised when we saw our mode of transportation. Where we had expected something like a bus to carry passengers, what we saw was nothing more than a flatbed truck with an open box-like structure on the back. It was about three feet high and consisted of wooden railings along the sides, some of which slid up to allow access inside. Seating was on long, narrow wooden planks that had been placed parallel to the back of the truck and secured by lashing them to the wooden railings. There were also three drums of gasoline immediately behind the driver's compartment. The porter and I reluctantly climbed aboard to join the tourists. My father somehow managed to talk his way into the seat inside the cabin next to the driver. As the truck departed, my mother and siblings wished us good luck and waved good bye to us from the porch.

We left the city and began traveling on the dirt road across the flat valley. Dust continually blew in my eyes. The wind from the moving truck blasted my face, neck, and shoulders, and the hot sun beat down upon my skin. Occasionally I would enjoy a brief respite from the sun as we passed under a canopy of woven branches and leaves from willow trees that lined the road. However, some of the trees had become so overgrown that we were continually ducking the low hanging branches to avoid being decapitated.

After more than two punishing hours of crossing the valley, we finally reached the mountains. I looked up and could see the long, narrow, one-lane road winding its way to the top with sharp, switchback curves. I was relieved that we would finally get out of the dust and sun but unbelievably, I found the trip up the mountain even worse! Carved out of bare rock, the road surface was so irregular and uneven, it resembled roughly finished steps. The tires took such a beating on the sharp edges of the rocks that I knew they would only last one round trip. Any time we met an oncoming vehicle, we had to pull off on a recess carved into the mountainside. These recesses were only every two kilometers so I was glad there was little traffic.

After being beaten and bounced for hours, we finally crossed the first lower mountain and arrived at a small plateau where the village of Aguirre, an enclave of Indian agriculture, was located. Aguirre was composed of eight mud houses with rough wooden doors, no windows, and roofs covered with dry straw. Bonded with mud at the corners of the roofs were long-horned ox skulls. Feeling sorry for us, the driver decided to stop here for awhile so we could stretch our legs, eat some sandwiches, and drink some coffee. All too soon, it was time to leave. This was the last village we would see on the way to our adventure.

The steep road began to climb an even higher mountain than the one we had just crossed. The road was extremely narrow and ran along the side of a steep cliff. I was riding on the left side of the truck -- the cliff side. As I looked down, I nervously saw that the truck was getting far too close to the side of the road. I sucked in my breath as I noticed the outside rear twin wheel was resting on nothing but thin air and below us was a half-mile drop to the canyon below. "Oh my God!" I screamed in horror. Fortunately, as we rounded a curve, the tire settled back on solid ground. I decided that although I had not enjoyed the hot sun and dust, riding in an open truck was much better than in a closed bus. At least I could jump onto the road if the truck started to fall into the canyon. A little farther along, I could see many twisted and burned vehicle frames at the bottom of the gorge next to the river. Not everyone had survived this perilous road.

The truck labored more and more as the altitude and steep climb took their toll on the engine. Our speed decreased to that of a slow walk. An opaque emptiness surrounded us and we all put on sweaters, raincoats, and hats as the cool air enveloped us. I could see low clouds touching the mountaintop, covering the road in a thick blanket of fog. Soon all points of light disappeared except for the high beams of the truck.

After about an hour, we had climbed high enough to emerge above the clouds. The visibility was breathtaking and the thin air was refreshing. Night had settled in and our roofless truck allowed us to look straight up and see the breathtaking dome of the night sky and the millions of shimmering stars. Above us, from one horizon to the other, the Milky Way stretched like a long band of sequins against a jet-black, velvet blanket. It was the grandest spectacle I had ever seen. It made me feel like I was in outer space. Everything was so clear that it seemed as though there was no atmosphere between the stars and us. I could see Sirius, the Southern Cross, Orion, Sagittarius, and Scorpio. There were clusters of stars that looked like patches of fog across the sky, but which I knew were nebulae. The biggest thrill was watching shooting stars as they drew lasting lines across the heavens. I wondered what my fellow passengers thought about this beautiful display. Some of them were indigenous people who still became frightened whenever a comet and its brilliant tail crossed the nighttime sky.

In later years, I realized how lucky I was to have been in the Andes Mountains at that wonderful time. The small human population in the interior of South America was in perfect ecological equilibrium with nature. There were no fires being used to clear the Amazon jungle. I had the opportunity to see the sky with a sharp clarity that people today will never enjoy because of the terrible pollution that covers our planet.

We rode in the truck all night. Early the next morning, the driver informed us we were close to the highest point in the road, some 15,000 feet above sea level. From such a height, it felt like being suspended in air -- like riding in an airplane. We rode along the ridge of a chain of mountains, switching sides in between peaks. After crossing what seemed to be the top of the world, we began descending. The only sign of life at this alttitude was mostly lichens, with a few bunches of brown grass poking through patches of snow.

Finally we arrived at Casa De Piedra, "The Stone House." It was a one-room dwelling made from rectangular blocks of stone and mortar. The driver stopped just long enough to allow the three of us to get out of the truck. "You're on your own now," he said and drove off.

We stood in silence on that cold, barren mountain. From our present altitude, we could see far into the distance -- perhaps 50 or 60 miles -- to where the foot of the mountains blended into the tropical plain. Looking through my binoculars, I could see a small coca plantation next to the road. The Indian porter told me that when the coca leaves are dried, they produce a mild narcotic effect. He said the biggest consumers were the peasants who did the heavy manual labor on the farms. He sighed as he added, "It helps them get through their days of drudgery and the hopelessness they feel working on the Patron's plantation."

The only humans in this lonely region were the man and his wife who lived in the stone house. The man was a "road-watcher" and his whole job was to report road conditions from time to time to the maintenance office. They graciously invited us to spend the rest of the day and night in their humble home. They told us they were grateful for the company as they only saw a vehicle every two days or so.

The road-watcher motioned to my father and me to sit down with him at the hearth in the center of the room, close to the fire. Fed with straw, the fire produced more smoke than heat. As we relaxed, the man began to tell us a series of stories. The first was a tale about how ancient Indians had buried many riches and gold somewhere nearby. Then he told us about the hut where we could stay the following night and the tale of the hermit who had lived there. He said that after descending the mountain from the house, towards the end of our day's hike, we would find the dwelling. He felt certain it was still in good condition because it had been only three years since a jaguar had devoured the hermit. I shivered inside.

The third tale was a warning from our superstitious host. He cautioned us to watch for strange and mysterious beings that were said to live in inaccessible mountain caves. Nobody had ever actually seen these beings up close, but at a distance, they appeared to be humans. He also told us to be alert for unidentified flying objects. I was filled with questions, but our host would say no more.

The rest of the day was spent looking at maps and planning the next phase of our journey, which would be on foot. We decided that on our return trip, instead of back-tracking to the stone house, we would travel a long circular path that would take us through unexplored territory and eventually bring us back to civilization.

We were tired from the long rough truck ride and the cold mountain night air made us sleepy. The road-watcher's wife provided us with warm sheep hides for warmth and comfort and we immediately drifted off to sleep.

By the next morning, we were well rested and anxious to get started on our new adventure. We packed up and my father gave the road-watcher some money as a present. He told us that it was unnecessary, but it was clear from his smiling face that he was happy to receive it.

Our hike immediately took us away from the road onto a rocky path with little vegetation. We had walked no more than a quarter of a mile when the path abruptly came to an end. Not only the path but it seemed the whole world had ended as we came to the edge of a cliff and stared into the abyss below. I sucked in my breath. The pathway down reminded me of a balcony with no railing. Although beautiful, it was also a very frightening sight.

The gorge below was perhaps a mile deep and as broad as the Colorado Canyon. At the very bottom was a silver ribbon of a river. Looking down the river, I could see the green hills gradually decreasing in size until they blended with the flat, tropical jungle that extended all the way to the Amazon. We were so high it was easy to distinguish the different colors of vegetation for each climate and level. On the opposite side of the canyon, I could see smaller ravines with tributaries running to the main river. Our objective for the next day was to cross the river and reach a particular ravine that was to the south of us.

We had to carefully watch our footing because the pathway down to the canyon was quite slippery. As we descended, the temperature gradually increased and we noticed the snow-covered rocks with lichens and short straw give way to small shrubs. The cold forest we entered became more temperate as we inched our way down. We traveled about a mile and a half farther and finally reached the canyon bottom.

All around us was a hot and humid rainforest with tall trees, wild orchids, and brightly-colored birds. We saw parakeets, parrots, and noisy macaws. Butterflies flashing wings of blue, yellow, and gold fluttered around us. In all directions in front of me I could see insects, snakes, and small lizards running through the grass. The funniest sight was the hyperactive monkeys who were constantly jumping from tree to tree above us. I couldn't help but think how wasteful they were as I watched them pull a fruit from a tree, take one bite, and then throw it away.

It was noon when we finally stopped walking. We found the hut that the road-watcher had told us about and planned to spend our second night there. Our Indian porter decided he would hunt for an animal to use for our lunch. I watched as he put the butt of his musket on the ground, holding the muzzle almost vertically. He loaded a half cubic inch of black powder through the muzzle and it fell to the bottom of the barrel. He then placed a small piece of newspaper on the muzzle. He removed the ramrod (a long rod attached to the musket under the barrel) and used it to tamp down the powder and newspaper wadding. Then he took less than a cubic inch of tiny, lead shot pellets and dropped them down the barrel. Lastly, he took another piece of squeeze paper and compacted it into the barrel with the ramrod. Then he was ready.

A short time later, the porter returned with two ducks, which he barbecued. We enjoyed our tasty lunch next to a beautiful crystal clear stream that was flowing nearby.

Early the next morning, not wanting to stay in any one place very long, we quickly packed up and resumed our trip. We crossed to the opposite side of the main canyon by walking on a tree trunk that had long ago fallen across the river. The map confirmed that this was our area of exploration, so my father went about his business, snapping pictures, sampling the soil, and taking vegetation for later analysis. While my father worked, I started my own project. All went well until our porter cast a superstitious cloud over my father's efforts. He was deeply disturbed that we had violated the gods by not pouring the customary bottle of rum into the ground. Apparently, the Earth Goddess, or Pacha-mama, lived below and had a taste for rum. The porter told us our trip was doomed and the land would never be fertile again -- all because we had forgotten our bottle of rum!

When my father finished his investigations and gathered all the information and samples he needed to determine if the land was suitable for coffee plantations and cattle breeding, he came over and asked what I was doing. I told him I was using my pick to excavate gold. My father got very upset with me. He said I was desecrating the ancient and abandoned graves that were in the area. I stopped excavating immediately.

With my father's exploration work completed, we began our journey home. This part of the trip would be across totally unfamiliar territory. All we had to guide us was a red pencil line we had traced on our map. We hoped that within three or four days, we would be able to complete the circle and rejoin the road we had come in on.

We followed one of the secondary canyons that branched off from the main canyon, walking along a tributary stream. My father looked at his compass and pointed to a large boulder in the distance. He said we should reach that boulder sometime that evening and there would most likely be a shallow cave there where we could spend the night. As I looked at the tangled forest growth in our path, I seriously doubted his timeframe.

Our pace quickened as we hiked on the rocky side of the river. Rounding a bend, we came upon a magnificent waterfall tumbling down from a very high vertical rock wall. As the water splashed against the rocky ledges on its way down, it created a misty spray that brushed against our faces. My throat swelled as I realized how fortunate I was to be here in this beautiful, isolated part of world that few people, if any, had ever seen.

Not far from where we were standing, perhaps no more than 200 steps to our left, a large animal was lying on a rock. I grabbed my binoculars and saw that it was a puma (also known as a cougar). In spite of the distance, its sensitive hearing alerted the animal to our presence and he cautiously watched us until we left the area. I was filled with excitement, as this was the first time I had ever seen an animal like this in the wild.

Finally, as my father had predicted, we arrived at the large boulder and sure enough, there was a shallow cave where we could spend the night. It was in this cave that my strange dreams began.

# CHAPTER 2
## Close Encounter with God and the Prophets

I snuggled down into my sleeping bag and quickly fell asleep. It seemed I had only been sleeping a short time when a ray of light crossed my face. I thought it was the morning sun, but as I opened my eyes I saw that it was still dark outside. Then I noticed a man standing at the cave entrance. I asked him what he wanted. He replied that he was an explorer and was puzzled why we had come to this isolated region. I told him of my father's research. He said he was familiar with the area and asked if I would like to take a little hike and he would show me around. I agreed and we left the cave.

We began walking up a hill along a narrow pathway. As we approached the top of the hill, we entered a heavy fog bank and the only thing that was visible was the path in front of us. I asked the explorer where we were going, but he didn't answer. I turned my head to ask him again, but the man was no longer there. In his place was a beautiful, slender being wearing a white robe and on his back was a pair of shining silver wings. I sensed immediately that this was a real angel. I was confused and a little worried. Had I died? Was I being taken to heaven?

We continued walking and soon the narrow dirt road turned into a shining marble walkway. Down the center was a long strip of golden carpet. Then before I could blink, the pathway had turned into a narrow bridge that was suspended in space. There were no suspension cables above or supporting columns below. And there were no handrails! On either side was a dark and forbidding abyss. The angel finally spoke and said, "This is the pathway to heaven."

Far ahead I could see a gigantic temple with silver domes. As I moved forward, a mist began to surround the temple, becoming thicker and thicker as I approached. Soon the temple disappeared and all I could see in front of me were two giant doors standing open. I peered inside at an enormous hall that was lighted by millions and millions of tiny lights. I looked around, but I could not see any walls. It was as though the room just went on and on to infinity. In the far distance, I could see a glowing bluish sphere that looked like a fiery, shimmering star as bright as the sun. Encircling the sphere was a ring that looked like it was made of pearls. All around the sphere and the ring were millions of sparkling lights that reminded me of fireflies. The angel that had accompanied me said,

"The brilliant sphere that you see in the center is God, the Only One. God is pure energy and does not have a form like humans or animals. Only the holy men and prophets can stand in the presence of God. All others who are not spiritually prepared are instantly incinerated."

I turned to the angel and asked why I was here. Was this heaven? Had I died? The angel replied tenderly, "You are indeed in heaven but you are not dead. You are very much alive and well."

Behind me, I heard the sound of many voices. I turned and saw hundreds and hundreds of children coming in my direction, traveling on many pathways, not just the one that had led me here. I saw that some of them were very young and some were teenagers like myself. An angel was guiding each of them. Soon everyone was gathered at the entranceway to the grand temple.

Suddenly a gruff old man with long white hair, a flowing white beard, and wearing a white gown and sandals appeared at the gate. "Stop!" he cried. "You are all wrongdoers and cannot see God without being spiritually prepared. Here! Put on these divine headbands." With that, he brought out a silver tray loaded with narrow silver headbands trimmed with silken ribbon. As he passed around the tray, he continued, "The souls of mortal visitors must be purified or they will suffer instant death when they look upon the radiance of God. These bands will protect you and keep you safe. They will also enhance your comprehension so that you will be able to understand all conversations in all languages."

The angel who had accompanied me explained that this was the first time in the history of these heavenly celebrations that a group of humans from planet Earth had been invited. He said the celebrations are held every 2,000 terrestrial years and include a great reunion of spirits from all corners of the universe. Generally the only ones present are the spirits of holy beings and prophets that lived in ancient times. They all come to be in the divine presence of God. He went on to say that each of the children was picked at random and that none of us had any special qualities; we were just average mortals. "In fact," he added, "some of the children are nasty, rebellious, and a bit spoiled. Many of them have no idea how to appreciate the good things of life."

After putting on our headbands, we were divided into small groups and each person was given a "floating carpet" -- a small square of cloud -- that immediately whisked us to the bright light that I had seen when I peeked inside the gates. As we drew closer and closer, I could see that what had previously looked like millions of fireflies surrounding the sphere were actually shining angels. And what I had thought was a circle of pearls turned out to be thousands of tables aligned one behind the other, and at these tables were seated seemingly limitless numbers of beings.

The angels brought us to a table with a sign in the center that read, "Reserved for Planet Earth." Many people were already seated, with empty seats on each side of them. We were told to sit in these spaces so we would have an elder on each side of us. As I moved towards the table to choose a seat, my angel pulled me aside and said, "Come with me. I will take you for a tour around the table and introduce you to some of the famous guests."

The first guest I was introduced to was Buddha, the Enlightened One and Wise Teacher. As he turned to greet me, I recognized him immediately because of his round face and round belly. He smiled and said, "Be sure to collect as many merits as possible through good deeds and continuing education so you will reach Nirvana, the ultimate goal."

The next person I met was Confucius and he said, "By living in this high place, I have been able to observe humanity for more than 2,000 years. I have witnessed its advancement in the sciences, as well as its decline in morality. However, what has made me most happy is that modern scientists are making new discoveries that are in tune with my teachings. In ancient times when I was living on Earth, only a small number of people could understand what I taught. Today I observe that humanity is finally developing new concepts related to cosmology and the mysteries of the universe that are linked with religion. The modern scientists have given these concepts new names, but they are very similar to Taoism."

· Next to Confucius was a Shinto priest who had been carefully watching me. He said, "I agree with Confucius that there are many new advancements in science by the latest generations of humans. I wish to add my advice to the people of Earth and tell them to also venerate the beauty of nature and believe in the power and will of themselves."

We moved on to the next individual, a man dressed in Greek garments and holding a glass of what appeared to be wine. He turned towards me as I approached and said, "Let me introduce myself. My name is Plato. I was a philosopher who lived in Greece around 400 BC After I died, my spirit went first to purgatory, then I came here to heaven. From here I can see and hear what people on Earth are saying and doing. As a matter of fact, I am aware of all the things that have happened on Earth during the twentieth century."

He continued, "I also know that many people are confused and upset with my writings about Atlantis because they felt I was amiss in my dimensions. I would like to correct some of those errors by saying that Atlantis was not a continent, but a group of small islands. The largest one was twice the area of today's Puerto Rico. In my writings, I had said that Atlantis was larger than Libya and Asia combined, but I was not talking about dimensions. I was speaking of the economical and military power of the Atlantis Empire. In actuality, it was greater than the entire world."

The angel and I resumed our tour around the table. As we walked, I couldn't help looking at the food that was being served. My angel noticed and chided me, "Don't stop. Let's continue with your introductions. You will have plenty of time to eat later."

My host angel told me that the next person I would meet was one of the earliest Asian prophets of the world. He lived in a time so ancient that there is no history, long before the times of the great empires. I noticed he was eagerly eating some type of salad and when he saw me he said, "You should find a seat and try the salad in the big blue bowl. It is considered a delicacy by the ancient kings of Asia." My stomach growled.

After he introduced himself, I asked him to repeat his name. It was a very complicated-sounding name and I could barely pronounce it. He then went on to say that many thousands of years ago he had lived in the area where India is now located. He said he was a teacher of philosophy and was born 54 years after the great disaster of Atlantis. He took another bite of salad, then continued. "Do you know about the great civilization of Atlantis? It consisted of a group of islands located near the center of the Atlantic Ocean. In the Sanskrit literary books that were written by pre-Hindu people, it was known by another name. Atlantis was inhabited by a fantastic race whose scientific discoveries have never been surpassed, even to this day. It may surprise modern man to know that the peak of the human brain evolution didn't happen in modern times, but in the times of Atlantis. In fact, since then the evolution of the human brain has suffered some regression."

He paused as if remembering then went on, "The disaster happened so fast that the people of Atlantis were unable to transfer their wisdom or to share the beautiful things they had created with the rest of humanity. This caused many saints and spirits of the universe to weep. God was moved by the tears of the many spirits in heaven and promised that sometime in the future, some of the great people who had lived in Atlantis would return to Earth so they could reproduce some of the splendid works they had once created. This happened a few centuries before and after the birth of Christ. Among the reborn were great composers and artists, including sculptors, painters, and architects, as well as philosophers and scientists. Many of their names are recorded in modern history books."

The gentleman leaned back in his chair, no longer interested in his salad. "I am like all humans--my spirit is several centuries old and I have gained great experience and knowledge since the dawn of mankind. I have been reborn many times and witnessed the birth and death of scores of civilizations, many of which existed before history was recorded. I find it sad that many of these ancient nations, such as Atlantis, are not remembered by humanity. It is because they used the more advanced construction materials like metal, plastic, and wood, which do not endure through the millennia and thus leave no visible evidence behind. Fortunately, the military and commercial outposts of Atlantis were constructed of more durable materials such as stone, cement, and bricks so there is some evidence of their past existence. Some of their clay jars and pots also lasted through the centuries."

"After the disaster, the Atlanteans were forced to evacuate to other lands. Over the millennia, as they intermarried with their more primitive neighbors, nearly all of their knowledge and skills disappeared. A few individuals retained some of the wondrous genes and were able to create beautiful art paintings on the walls of their cave dwellings." The prophet shook his head sadly.

Then he continued, "I recall in one of my lives on Earth -- I believe it was in one of the pre-Hindu civilizations -- I used to teach philosophy. I taught that after death humans continue to exist in spirit form until they are reborn into another body. Death is merely a transition from one life to another and depending on the deeds we perform, we may return to a better life or a worse life. But in every life, we gain experience and wisdom. Here in heaven, I have a book of records where I have recorded every past life lived by the people on Earth from 100,000 years ago to the present."

He abruptly turned and looked straight at me as he asked, "Did you know that locked deep inside your subconscious mind are the memories of all your former lives?"

Before I could answer him, he went on. "Every person you see as you walk down a street has most likely died several times – often under very brutal conditions. Because we were at one time all savages, our deaths were often tragic and cruel. Most of us died by middle age because competition for survival was extremely difficult and nature was unforgiving. Our many deaths have come through being devoured by big cats, bitten by poisonous snakes, bleeding to death after being attacked by gangs of baboons, wild dogs, wolves, or bears, or while hunting mammoths, big ox, or woolly rhinoceros. Quite often, we died in tribal wars in which we were hit by rocks and sticks, or even by being bitten by another human being. Later, as our ancestors evolved, our deaths came by the use of spears and bows and arrows."

Then he waved us on as he said, "But I talk too much. I apologize. Better try to find a chair so you can sit and eat before the food gets cold."

The next person I met was Muhammad, who was sitting next to the magnificent archangel, Gabriel. Muhammad proclaimed there is only one God, whom he referred to as Allah. He explained that this God is the creator of all things, the divine force of the universe, and is without form or body. He pulled me closer and said, "You should pray to Allah five times a day and perform good deeds so that after your death, when you stand in judgment, your soul will be sent to paradise where you will enjoy many pleasures. You will be able to savor such things as the wonderful food that you see on this table and be in the company of the virgins of paradise." I nodded and told Muhammad that I would try very hard to follow his advice.

I was getting hungrier by the minute. I turned to my escort angel and asked if the introductions were now complete because it seemed we had walked a complete circle around the table. He smiled and told me to be patient because there were still a few more famous personalities from the past and even some from the present that I should meet. He explained that besides the children, many other composers, philosophers, poets, and sculptors had been invited to the feast. He said these included Homer, Phidias, Michelangelo, along with such great scientists as Darwin, Planck, Newton, and many more.

As we moved along from person to person, I recognized many people whom I knew were still living. Each of them was wearing the same silver headband as the children to protect them from the overpowering radiance of God.

One of these people was Frank Lloyd Wright, whom my escort said had previously lived as a famous architect in Atlantis. During that lifetime, he had helped shift the nation from the Imperial Classical era to the Modern era using much of the same contemporary design work that he was noted for in his present life. I commented that he was very old, and my escort predicted that many of the older visitors would soon be passing on to a better life.

Although I had never had much interest in the important people of the past or the present, I found that information about these great people was constantly being transmitted to my brain through the silver headband. I presumed some microscopic electronics were concealed within the strands of ribbon.

Finally we reached a vacant chair and my angel escort motioned for me to sit down but before I did, I turned to him and said, "Thank you so much for bringing me here. I must admit that at first I was drawn by the smell of the food and beverages, but now I'm so grateful for the opportunity to be in the company of these great guests." The angel smiled knowingly and moved away.

After settling into my chair, I looked at the individual on my right. He had a fair complexion, well-trimmed beard, looked to be in his 30s, and was wearing a white robe. On my left was a more mature man, although not what I would consider old, and he was wearing a brown garment. Beyond him, I could see three other persons that looked to be priests or some other dignitaries. Each was wearing a luxurious garment with gold symmetrical designs woven throughout the material.

I couldn't help but wonder why I had been invited to this grand event with all these notable figures. I was like any average teenager trying to avoid responsibility and concentrate my attention on the more pleasurable aspects of life. Even on those occasions in my life when I had met great and holy men, it hadn't changed my attitude. Yet, in this place, I felt somehow different. The angels especially fascinated me. I couldn't help but wonder if they were male or female.

My thoughts were interrupted as one of the serving angels set down a plate full of warm food in front of me. The wonderful scent reminded me again of my hunger. I was anxious to start eating but before I could pick up my fork, the person seated to my right leaned over and said, "Welcome, young man! Let us pray before we start eating." I bowed my head as he offered a brief prayer and then finally took my first bite of food.

The same gentleman started up a conversation by asking if I could see all the distant tables in the gigantic ring. I told him all I could see were tiny dots of bright lights. He nodded and said, "This ring is so enormous that the seating capacity is well over a million to accommodate all the prophets and holy beings that come to this celebration from all corners of the Universe. Did you know that the glowing light in the center of the ring is no other than the awesome Spirit of God?" I confirmed that my escort angel had identified God earlier. The young man continued, "And have you felt the divine vibration of God in your heart and spirit as we all have at this extraordinary gathering?"

I stopped eating for a moment and realized that I was indeed experiencing an immense peace and joy within. It was an ecstasy that I had never before felt. I stared in awe at the shimmering light of God and tried to determine how far away he was. I noticed that my perception of distance was distorted. One moment it seemed God was as close as the length of a football field but in the next instant as far away as the stars. One thing I did know for certain: This was a moment that I would never forget, for I knew I was seeing the Grand Master of the Universe, the real and eternal God.

The man on my right added, "You are present at a very momentous occasion in the universe. The billions of people here all share a special bond in that they are all spiritual leaders on their planets. This holy congress is a celestial tradition that takes place once every 2,000 terrestrial years and has been carried on for billions of years after the formation of the second generation of galaxies."

The gentleman resumed eating and I anxiously returned to my meal.

Between courses, I glanced at some of the distant tables and saw several beings that looked very strange and horrific to me. I assumed they were aliens from other planets and galaxies and asked my dinner companion about them. I was particularly interested in a being that had a very heavy physical structure and looked much like a human with two arms and one head, but walked on four legs.

"Those are prophets from the Centaur race," he explained. "They are quite intelligent and come from a very advanced civilization that has mastered space flight. Their planet has a higher gravity than Earth, which is why they have developed four legs to support their bodies. If you were to visit their planet, your weight would be about one-and-one-half times heavier. It is said that in ancient times, Centaur astronauts visited Earth and encountered people of the Stone Age. Many centuries after the Centaurs returned home, some cultures created the mythological creatures that you read about in your books of ancient stories to describe these ancient astronauts."

Then he directed my attention to another table farther away. "I don't know if you noticed, but the creatures at that table are from a planet with less gravity than Earth so you will notice that their physical structure is more like regular humans, although much skinnier." He turned to me and chuckled. "I suppose the strangeness of these beings frightens you, but let me assure you that their horrible appearances are only skin deep. All of them are spiritually beautiful because when they lived on their planets, they were known for their kindness, compassion, and love of God. They helped many people in need and often sacrificed themselves for the welfare of their people. Here in heaven, there is no discrimination between the species. At this gathering, we are all brothers and sisters who love God."

The face of my friend then became very somber as he confided to me some startling news. "Although this is a grand occasion, it is also one in which we prophets from Earth's past must share some bad news with the mortals who are present. It is about a terrible catastrophe that is going to happen in the third millennium if humanity does not change their ugly and corrupt ways." I shivered from the sense of foreboding in his words.

Yet I felt very safe with this man. He reminded me of an uncle that I especially liked. In fact, I thought it would be nice to call him "uncle," so I asked for his permission to do so. He gently thanked me for the thought, but said he would prefer for me to call him by his real name. "And what is that?" I asked.

"My name is Christ. You may have heard me referred to as Jesus the Christ. I was born in Judea, east of the Mediterranean Sea more than 1,900 years ago. I lived as a human on earth for a little over 30 years, and I remember my experiences there so vividly that they seem as though they happened only yesterday."

Before I could say anything more, Christ stood up and asked for silence. Immediately everyone ceased talking.

"The time has come when our guests must be told why they have been brought to this gathering." He looked around at the many children seated at Earth's table. "Each of you was randomly selected to be an official ambassador from Earth and will be given special assignments concerning the future of your planet. Of necessity, your stay at this place must be short. It is imperative that you return to your world and begin to carry out your assignments as soon as possible."

Christ continued, "Because humanity has lost its respect for Earth and for each other, God issued a declaration that life on your planet is to end by a cataclysmic encounter with a comet from space. It is a comet with a million times more destructive power than the one used to destroy Sodom and Gomorrah. This disaster is set to occur sometime in the first part of the twenty-one century."

All the children looked at each other with fear in their eyes.

"All the former prophets and I were devastated by this declaration and implored God to reconsider. We reminded God that although there are many people on Earth who are cruel and uncaring, there are billions of others who are innocent and upright and don't deserve to die. Fortunately, after much pleading, we were able to sway God's decision … although only slightly.

"The comet will be allowed to continue on its path, but God removed the decree of final destruction. Instead, without any divine assistance, the fate of the planet Earth has been placed in the hands of the people of Earth. In other words, only humankind can save the world.

"Please understand. This does not mean your future is hopeless. However, you must realize that because you are the citizens of tomorrow, your planet's final fate is in your hands. It will take abundant ingenuity and resourcefulness to devise a way to destroy or deviate the comet to prevent total destruction.

"Each of you must recognize the seriousness of your task and be in tune with the signs that will come to pass. You have all been imbued with special talents and the necessary skills to carry out your assignments. Once you leave here and return to Earth, I urge you, in the name of my fellow prophets and myself, to become educated in the sciences, such as astronomy, physics, and chemistry so you can help humanity in their moment of truth.

"During the coming years, you will live a normal life. However, your brains have been programmed so that as the time approaches when the comet is due to strike the Earth, your subconscious will awaken. This is when you will need to call upon the knowledge you have gained and begin building rockets and other devices to prevent the comet from striking and destroying Earth.

"I realize this is a very serious and heavy message that I have conveyed to you, but God in his omnipotent power will be with you."

## Encounter with Noah

It seemed only moments had passed when I realized I had become an adult and was now sitting with a group composed of Christ, Noah, and a barely visible spirit of Isaac Newton.

Christ spoke, "Humanity is not getting any better and although there is still a chance for the people to save Earth from the great comet, it is my suggestion that you should be prepared for the worst in case all attempts to divert the disaster fail. It would be a tragedy for humankind to cease to exist. Therefore, we are presenting you with an additional project."

Noah began speaking. "You will build a modern ark to save Earth's species. It will be a giant interplanetary spaceship designed to travel to the planet Mars. One hundred human couples will travel as passengers. In cryogenic containers, you will place thousands of human embryos, plus genetic material that has been extracted from thousands of men and women, animals, and plants. Ideal conditions would dictate that the human embryos be implanted and carried by surrogate mothers, but since the number of passengers must be limited, bio-engineers and bio-material scientists will develop special artificial reusable uteruses where, once on Mars, the fetuses will grow. These uteruses will be made from a unique plastic and transported in regular boxes.

"While construction of the ark is being carried out, robots will be sent ahead of you, as well as remote-control vehicles and equipment. The robots will prepare the terrain and set up self-sustaining living quarters for you. They will also construct transparent plastic greenhouses to house your crops and orchards.

"In a specific location on Mars, where it is permafrost, there is a natural pyramid-shaped hill with a large cavern leading to an underground chamber. Inside this chamber, you must erect giant plastic containers as this will be the storage area for the embryo cryogenic receptacles and their systems. The thick walls of the pyramid-hill will protect the bio-materials from the destructive cosmic rays and other kinds of space radiation. To vent the radon that naturally emanates from the ground, you must drill narrow inclined passageways from the inner chamber to the outside. This is where the genetic materials must stay until the first immigrants to Mars have settled and installed modern genetic engineering laboratories.

"During the time of Atlantis, similar pyramids were constructed to preserve the bodies of their rich owners in hopes that someday in the future, science might be able to clone that person by using the DNA that remained intact. The people of Atlantis used special substances to embalm the bodies so the DNA was not damaged. They removed the brain, blood, and some of the viscera from the bodies because they decompose rapidly, but stored some of the viscera in separate containers to increase the chances of preserving more DNA."

I asked Noah how it would be determined whose DNA would be extracted for the trip to Mars and he replied that God would make that decision. Then I asked, "Who will design and build the ark?"

The figure of Isaac Newton responded, "This is a project that you and the other children that attended the celestial gathering, plus many other people on Earth, will carry out. Noah and myself will assist you by sharing our past knowledge and offering advice." He smiled broadly as he looked at Noah, "I can give you a fine reference for Noah since he has several thousands of years of experience in building ships, most of them to save species throughout the universe from various disasters. His first project was the ark he built for the people of Earth in which he saved himself, his family and friends, and many animals from the great flood that is mentioned in the Bible."

I looked at Noah, who was nodding in agreement.

Isaac continued, "Do not be concerned about how all this will be accomplished. You will find that in a time of despair and catastrophe, the people of Earth pull together. You will receive all the cooperation and assistance you need from the space agencies and most of the world governments. And don't worry about the cost. Everything will be taken care of."

Christ then added, "In addition to these tasks, I have decided to give you one more. This one is to be carried out after Earth's dangerous moments have passed without major consequence and humanity has resumed its normal living.

"You will be responsible for the construction of a new Atlantis. It is to be one of the most beautiful places on Earth as it will be the home of the Messiah and a huge congregation of angels. It should be located on a piece of land on a peninsula – not on an island that will sink – that is still wilderness. It is to include two of the most important cities of the original Atlantis – Brasea, a city of skyscrapers and modern buildings made of steel, glass, concrete, and plastic -- and Acropolis from the classical era of Atlantis history. The buildings of Acropolis are to be made of marble, copper, and gold and will house the magnificent arts and classical splendors of its time."

I suppose I must have looked completely overwhelmed because Christ added, "Do not worry. I promise to send the spirits of the great architects and sculptors that built the first Atlantis to share their advanced technology and scientific knowledge. They will help the modern people of Earth to design the wonders of the New Atlantis. All the necessary technical information shall be provided through these masters and the knowledge will be transmitted through the Stone of Dreams."

"The Stone of Dreams? What is that?" I asked.

"It is one of many stones throughout the world that is carved in the shape of a chair. The person who sits in this rock-chair slips into a trance-like state and all kinds of visions and information related to the creation of the New Atlantis are transferred to that person's mind.

"It is important that you tell everyone about the New Atlantis because it shall belong to the entire world. When the Messiah of the Bible returns to transform Earth into a place of peace and prosperity, Atlantis will be his sacred home, along with thousands of materialized spirits. If anyone asks you who will be chosen as the Messiah, tell them only God knows."

I was surprised to suddenly see the spirit of Max Planck, the scientist, appear and begin speaking. "From my place in heaven, I have watched Earth and the gradual progress of humanity. I have also watched many other worlds in the Milky Way Galaxy and witnessed hundreds of them, mostly those with great scientific civilizations, suddenly disappear. Each one suffered the same fate."

"What happened?" I asked.

Max went on, "In order to deepen their knowledge of the mysteries of the microcosms, each of these civilizations built gigantic atom-smashing machines, which they used continuously. One day I witnessed a great catastrophe, which happened as a microscopic black hole was created by these machines. It was a billion times smaller than a grain of sand, but black holes are horrible predators of matter and energy and in approximately six hours, the entire planet was devoured and became a black hole with the same original mass as the former planet."

I shivered at the thought as I wondered aloud, "Could the same thing happen to Earth?"

The spirit of Max Planck noticed my anguish and said, "Don't worry, humans would not be able to build such as a machine to create microscopic black holes for at least the next million years. By then, I will return to Earth and warn humanity to act with caution when using this kind of laboratory equipment, to prevent the same kind of accident that happened to other worlds."

Abruptly, I realized my meeting with Noah and the others had ended and I was now back in the enormous dining hall. Christ was speaking.

"Children of Earth, you have little more than 50 years to accomplish your mission to save the Earth."

One young boy looked very annoyed and spoke up, "Hey, we're just kids. We don't care about missions or assignments."

Christ shook his head as a sign of disapproval, but did not reprimand the boy. Instead, he said, "Let us pray to God for understanding and wisdom."

After a lengthy prayer, many of the guests resumed talking among themselves. I overheard one angel talking to another one, "After dinner, we shall be returning our guests to the place where we picked them up. Our presence must ever remain close to them to ensure they learn the engineering sciences and acquire real world experiences that will help them build aircraft, space vehicles, and nuclear devices. They must also learn how to develop weapons of mass destruction, not for use against other humans, as is their inbred nature, but to use against the killer comet. As time passes and they become adults, we must see that all of them band together to fight against this common enemy by using all the knowledge they shall gain about nuclear weapons during the Cold War of the twentieth century. We must guide them to see that this material can be used as fuel to propel multinational spaceships across the solar system but more importantly, to destroy the comet."

More and more I was beginning to understand the magnitude of our assignments. I turned to Christ and asked, "What happens if we are unable to save the world – either by destroying the comet or by diverting it from its course? What if we are not advanced enough to build a spaceship that will transport humans and other beings from Earth to Mars or some other safe planet in the galaxy?"

Christ answered, "I understand your concerns and will share with you one other small possibility. If the people of Earth are open to it, they can obtain knowledge through encounters with extraterrestrial visitors – hundreds of whom are much more advanced than the residents of Earth. Nearly all of these beings are willing, even anxious, to share their wisdom and experiences. But the people of Earth must recognize the signs of their visits and act upon them."

"And there are no other solutions?" I asked.

Christ paused, then responded, "Yes, there is one more possibility to obtain the knowledge you will need and that is by traveling back though time to the advanced civilization of Atlantis. These people also faced destruction from a comet and though they were unable to save their own nation, they did develop powerful tools to prevent the comet from destroying the Earth. For this to happen, a person living in your time would need to travel to the past and be reborn as an Atlantean."

"But how would this happen?"

"Remember I told you earlier about the Stone of Dreams?"

"Yes, I remember."

"The Stone of Dreams is a virtual time machine. This means that although your physical body remains in the present, your mind and soul are released and you are able to travel back 11,000 years ago to one of the Atlantean outposts in the Mediterranean Sea. You are reborn as a baby that once existed during the time of Atlantis. Your mind and his fuse and you become that child. You grow up on the Island of Thera to learn the ways of the people, then when you become a teenager, you travel to the capital of Atlantis on a freight sailboat."

"Could I be the one to travel back in time?"

"If you are the one who was picked up from a cave in the Andes Mountains, then you are most likely the one that will travel to Atlantis."

I could feel chills going down my spine. "Yes! That is me! I was picked up at a cave! Can you tell me more? What will it be like? Will I know who I am?"

Christ smiled at my eager questions. "Yes, I can tell you more. After your arrival at the fabulous and splendid island of Atlantis, you will meet and go to live with your Atlantean uncle. There you will grow up as an ordinary Atlantean boy, attending regular schools, and becoming a member of the local Explorers Club and a sports club. No, you will not be aware of who you are or that you came from the future. All your memories from your life in the twentieth century will fade away. But you will enjoy life because you will be living with your rich relatives and will have the opportunity to learn about the arts and sciences, and particularly engineering. Later you will become an apprentice and gain experience in the Atlantis aerospace industry. You will be an important citizen in the nation of Atlantis."

"How will I return to my real life?"

"Ten days before the comet strikes Atlantis, you will join other evacuees on a ship to Europe that hits a rock and sinks. Everyone will perish, including you. It will be at that moment, due to psychological pressures, that your mind and the mind of the Atlantean will split. You will instantaneously return to the present and your sleeping body. When you awaken, you will not be aware that the Stone of Dreams has transferred the knowledge you gained while in Atlantis into your subconscious mind. Instead, it will all seem like a dream to you. Nevertheless, in due time, sometime at the beginning of the next millennium, you will begin to remember, in great detail, your past life working as an engineer and designer in Atlantis. Most of these memories will come to you in vivid, life-like dreams."

Christ added more information. "The comet that I have warned you about is the same one that was on a collision course with Earth many thousands of years ago. At that time, the Atlanteans used their advanced weapons to break the comet into pieces. The largest piece veered away from the Earth, but one of the pieces fell into the Atlantic Ocean and produced the earthquake and giant tidal waves that sank Atlantis, and also produced Noah's flood. Now the piece that remains is going to complete its huge orbit around the solar system and head back towards Earth."

Nothing more was said for several moments. I thought about all that I had heard and even though it all sounded exciting and fantastic, I began to have doubts and I blurted out, "I don't believe a time travel machine exists that can take anyone to another time and back again!"

Patiently, Christ replied, "As a matter of fact, there are seven time travel machines on Earth. They were placed by the Atlanteans months before the comet hit the earth and are proof of Atlantis' past existence. Each one is called the Stone of Dreams and its only function is to transfer wisdom and knowledge to help future generations survive the disaster that will result from the returning comet."

I remained skeptical.

Christ added, "Perhaps I should not call the Stone of Dreams a time travel machine since your physical body does not travel through time; it only creates virtual trips into the past. It manipulates your mind so you believe you are actually existing in a different space and time and also transmits recorded ancient thoughts. Although it looks like a rock, it possesses electromagnetic powers generated by concealed ancient solid state electronics. You might be interested to know, however, that real time travel machines do exist in many other parts of the Universe."

"Why haven't humans been able to create real time travel machines?"

"The human mind has not reached a point in its evolution in which it can comprehend the principle of time travel. Time machines operate in a higher space-time dimension and this is a concept that will not become clear to humans for many thousands of years. At present, the human mind is trapped in a tri-dimensional universe and is not aware that many universes of higher dimensions exist concurrently. Each one is occupied by beings whose level of intelligence corresponds to a particular dimension. At the very highest level of the universe, only one being exists and that is God."

Christ fell silent again and I was left to mull over all that he had said. I hadn't eaten much during the time he was talking and now reached for a piece of meat that looked like a turkey thigh. After my first bite, I knew it was not from a turkey. It had a strange taste, but I found it appetizing.

Soon, Christ spoke again. "For two millennia, I have observed your world from here in heaven. I remember when I was living as a man on Earth, I told my disciples that my words would last approximately 2,000 years, but no longer. I knew that after the twentieth century, the corrupt morals, the greed and the total disregard for others would eventually overtake the hearts and spirits of humankind and they would either destroy themselves or be destroyed. But I have always loved humanity with an unconditional love and it is my goal to keep them always safe."

"Christ, I have two questions that I would like to ask you. The first one is that I have heard people call you the son of God. Are you?"

"Humans often call themselves the children of God, but all humans and animals are creatures of God."

"I guess you're pretty close to God, so I'd like to know if you are as intelligent as him. If not, how many times more intelligent is God than you?"

Christ chuckled quietly. "My child, your question is not very well worded, but I understand what you are asking." He thought for a moment, then said, "The word intelligence doesn't have a simple meaning, but I would say God is about a billion times more intelligent than I." He reached over and patted my shoulder, then rose from his chair and, with a sign of his hand, said goodbye to everyone and left to join the multitude of saints and prophets who were leaving their tables and moving towards the brilliant presence of God.

A few of the prophets remained at Earth's table where I was seated, and a prophet from the planet Entar walked over and joined us. He sat down next to me and began to describe a visit that he and some other Entarians had made to earth nearly a million years ago.

"We loved your planet Earth. It was like a beautiful paradise with more breathtaking scenery than any other planet in your solar system. We delighted in the forests and thick vegetation that covered the continents. Seldom did we see any type of desert or barren areas. Everywhere was an abundance of plant and animal life. However, there was one thing we couldn't understand. How could a planet so full of life and beauty not have one intelligent species with whom we could communicate. The most complex creatures we encountered were some primitive bipedal animals that roamed the savannas and all they did was make grunting sounds. We were terribly disappointed and returned to our planet with heavy hearts."

The Entarian looked at me with a brief sadness in his eyes, then continued with his story. "It wasn't until several years later that one of our chief scientists came up with a solution. Apparently, God had told him in a dream that we should return to Earth, capture several of the bipedals we had seen, and genetically accelerate their evolution. We were to create these creatures, which God told us to call 'humans,' in our likeness but in God's spiritual image. Although we knew it was a massive undertaking and would involve centuries of work and experimentation, we excitedly moved forward.

"Finally after hundreds and hundreds of years, we were able to develop a specimen that we felt possessed acceptable characteristics and attributes to become an intelligent creature. But we were not yet finished. We now had to implant this species on Earth and make sure that it would grow and thrive."

"A laboratory was set up on Earth on a group of islands in the Atlantic Ocean. There our scientists continued to mold and develop the human over several more centuries. At last, they succeeded in producing three 'males' and three 'females' so the species could reproduce and multiply."

The Entarian turned to me and remarked, "You're probably aware that one of these couples was named Adam and Eve, but what you probably don't know is that the other couple was Poseidon and Cleito, the ancestors of the people of Atlantis. The third couple was a brutish human subspecies, called a Neanderthal in your modern times, but it has been extinct for thousands of years."

"Poseidon and Cleito? No, I've never heard of them. But then, you're telling me many things that I've never heard before."

The Entarian smiled and nodded.

"Once these three couples were complete, the scientists closed the laboratory and returned home. Over the next several centuries, we made regular trips to Earth to monitor the humans' progress and became very familiar with your ecosystem, geography, and of course, your history, which included information on Poseidon and Cleito. Interestingly, we found that through the millennia, the stories of this couple became distorted and today they are considered as nothing more than mythological creatures.

"Anyway, two of our esteemed leaders, Captain Oren and Dr. Re, made one of the last visits to your planet and they were pleasantly surprised to find that the many years of hard work by our genetic engineers had been successful. The primitive humans left behind had now evolved and were living in a highly developed technological society, which even included occasional interplanetary space trips. They called themselves Atlanteans, and Captain Oren and Dr. Re were thrilled when they were welcomed and invited to stay and teach about our sciences."

"I have heard much about the Atlanteans since I've been here. I wish they were still living on Earth in my time." I said longingly.

The Entarian smiled broadly, patted my shoulder, then moved away to talk to some of the other guest children. As I glanced around the table to see who was still present, I saw a figure that looked familiar although I was quite sure I had never seen him before. I studied him intently and soon he looked my way. He smiled, got up, and walked over to me. As he approached, he stuck out his hand and introduced himself as Moses.

"Mr. Moses ... sir ... you ... uh ...," I stammered. "I'm ... uh ... extremely happy to meet you. I never imagined that I would ever have such a wonderful opportunity in my lifetime."

Moses chuckled at my discomfort, then sat in the chair next to me. "I'm very happy to meet you, too."

"Mr. Moses, could I ask you a few questions?"

"Certainly, my son."

"Well, I was wondering if you think our group will be able to accomplish all of the assignments that Christ gave us? I mean, we're just ordinary kids, but we're being asked to save the world."

"Don't worry," Moses assured me. "By the time the world will need your help, you will all be mature, educated adults. In addition, approximately one year before the predicted cataclysm, a group of angels will visit many millions of people in their dreams and tell them that humanity must unite to defeat a common enemy. Everyone will be urged to support the building of the necessary machines and equipment to destroy the comet, as well as the spaceships that will be used to carry the special human cargo to the planet Mars."

I felt relieved to hear these words coming from such a great master of the Bible. I began thinking back about how, when I was very young, my grandmother used to read chapters from the Bible to me, particularly the Book of Genesis where Moses had played such an important part. I also thought about my trips to the school library where I read the story of Atlantis that was written by Plato in Critias Dialogue. I mentioned to Moses how much I had enjoyed reading about this advanced civilization. Suddenly it occurred to me to ask Moses how the books of Genesis were created and he began telling me a story that I found to be totally fascinating.

"When I was Prince of Egypt, I was given wondrous opportunities to learn and grew up to be very well educated. Egypt had some of the best libraries in the world and much of my time was spent reading all kinds of books, both old and new.

"One book that I remember in particular was said to be the oldest book in the world. It was called The Great Atlantis Book of Genesis, found in a cave by an Egyptian soldier returning from an exploration trip. Although it was written in the Atlantean language, some priests who could read Atlantean were able to translate it into the Egyptian language. Like you, I learned many things about Atlantis in this book, but I also learned many other mysteries. Did you know there are millions of advanced civilizations throughout the universe?"

I shook my head and Moses continued, "Each of these peoples has written their own version about how the universe was created and the stories are as varied as the species who wrote them. But today, I am going to tell you about the Book of Genesis that you are familiar with and how it came to be.

"Our Milky Way consists of more than a hundred billion suns. It is a spiral galaxy with several branches and one of the smallest branches is called Orion. In this branch are billions of stars, including our sun, and many of these stars have solar systems. In one of these solar systems existed a very old super civilization, and they are the ones who wrote the first version of the Book of Genesis more than a billion years ago.

"Thousands of copies of the Book were delivered to the Galactic Confederation of Advanced Planets. It was their duty to distribute copies of the Book to advanced civilizations as they appeared in the cosmic neighborhood. Since many planets in the galaxy were inhabited by nothing more than unicellular organisms, the GCAP would have to wait many eons before more complex forms of life evolved and became ready to receive the Book. Unfortunately, the people of Earth never reached a stage of advancement that would allow them to receive a copy.

"However, the Entarians, who had taken a vested interest in the humanoids on Earth, did receive a copy. Knowing that humans had difficulty dealing with the sciences, such as mathematics, tri-dimensional geometry, and physics, they wrote a simpler version for the people on Earth.

"You see, the Entarians, like any other advanced extraterrestrial, had the capacity to visualize complex space-time concepts concerning universes of four and five dimensions. They understood that, depending on the circumstances, a biblical 'day' of creation could mean a span of time of several different durations. For example, they recognized that a day could be just one Earth day or it could consist of several billion Earth years … or some other span of time. These things, however, were far beyond the comprehension of the people of Earth."

Moses paused, then looked me straight in the eye as he said,. "To give you an idea of the difference in advancement between the Entarians and humans is to compare yourself with a chimpanzee. I think you can see why humans would never be able to comprehend the Book of Genesis as it was originally written." I nodded as I considered the comparison.

Moses glanced over towards where the Entarian prophet was seated and then continued with his story. "During their last visit to Earth , the Entarians presented the simplified version of the Book of Genesis to the Atlanteans. The people of Atlantis were fascinated by it contents and published many copies so everyone would have a chance to read it. They also made one special copy from materials that wouldn't degrade with time and buried it in a cave that was located in a barren area of North Africa. There it remained for several thousands of years until it was rediscovered by the Egyptian soldier I spoke of earlier."

"Were the stories in this book the same as the Book of Genesis that my grandmother used to read to me?"

"No," Moses answered. "Not entirely. Much of the book was about cosmology and other sciences that were familiar to the Atlanteans, but the people who lived in other parts of the world would never have understood many of the stories; for example, the creation of the universe. There was a detailed description about how the universe was born with a huge explosion and how its expansion will continue for billions of years. It included precise explanations of the creation of universal forces and physical laws. It also told how the galaxies, the stars, and the solar systems were formed, and how the planets, such as Entar and Earth, were brought into being. Finally, there was an explanation of how primordial life, including microorganisms, was created and how, by natural selection, it evolved into plants and animals, and humans as you see them today."

"What happened to these parts of the book?"

"Well, when I was leading the exodus of the Israelites through the desert, it came to me that I should rewrite the Book of Genesis so it would be easier for the average person to understand." Moses paused and his face became very serious as he added, "Besides, I felt people needed to learn a more spiritual and humane approach to life.

"Anyway, I deleted almost 500 pages of the Atlantis version. I removed the scientific explanations of creation and only briefly described what took place. I did not include the parts about other planets and just wrote about Earth and, indirectly, without mentioning it by name, Atlantis. I left out information relating to evolution, and changed many verse sequences to reinforce what I felt would be helpful to people."

I told Moses that his efforts had been worthwhile because his version of Genesis is a very revered part of the Judeo-Christian Bible. He seemed pleased to hear this as he reached for something to drink.

An individual in monk's clothing approached the table and greeted Moses. Then he looked at me and said, "Have you been boring this young man with your tales?"

Moses looked over at me and laughed. "Well, he may have been a little bored, but he's hidden it well."

I squirmed in my seat. I wanted to defend myself and tell him I wasn't bored at all, but I was too embarrassed to say anything.

Moses stood up and said he was going to visit some other guests. "But I'll return later and bring my book of Genesis with me so we can talk some more." He motioned to the monk to sit down in his vacant seat.

"Hello, young man," the monk said as he reached out to shake my hand. "My name is Soar. I was once a priest on Atlantis. You've probably heard a great deal about this wonderful place since you've been here, but I hope you will allow me to tell you a bit more. It is too bad that you were not able to live during the time that Atlantis flourished on Earth. From here in heaven, I have been able to observe how things are on Earth today and it's certainly no longer the paradise that it was during the time I lived there." He shook his head sadly.

"Are you aware that Atlantis was located on a small group of volcanic islands near the center of the Atlantic Ocean? The scientists of Atlantis knew that the geological structure of these islands was not stable and that someday a natural disaster would cause them to collapse under their own weight. Believing they had plenty of time, however, they did nothing. Unfortunately, they were wrong and disaster struck when the great comet hit. The only thing that remains today of this great nation is the small island fragments called the Azores.

"Many people in your time believe that Atlantis never existed. But one day a tool will be invented that will allow humans to see through sand and water. When this happens, they will discover the evidence that Atlantis did indeed exist and is now buried at the bottom of the Atlantic Ocean under hundreds of feet of sediment.

"Of course, if the people of Earth were more observant, they would see many signs of this past civilization. There is remaining evidence of many of Atlantis' outposts throughout the world. For instance, one is on the island of Thera, which is located in the Mediterranean Sea; another is in the Bahamas near the United States, and there are areas in Europe and North Africa where evidence can be found. Moreover, there are many megalithic structures that were constructed as markers to trace the underground chambers of Atlantis. Although eroded by the ravages of time, remains of these can be found in South America, Europe, and Asia."

The monk reached for a glass that looked like it contained some kind of juice, took a swallow, and then continued with his story.

"Would you like to hear about the terrible comet disaster that destroyed Atlantis?"

I nodded my head enthusiastically.

"Many thousands of years ago, our astronomers saw that Earth was in the direct path of a giant comet. They estimated that it would strike the planet within one year. The government leaders of Atlantis immediately met with our top scientists and engineers to try to come up with some way to prevent this impending disaster. It was decided that Captain Cronus, one of our finest astronauts, and his crew would travel to the comet and place nuclear bombs under its surface in hopes that the explosion would break the comet up into harmless pieces. Unfortunately, the plan did not turn out quite as the scientists had expected.

"After Captain Cronus left in his spaceship, everyone on Atlantis prayed that he would be successful. Finally, after several months, scientists received word that the captain had been able to break the comet up into several pieces with the largest one headed away from Earth.

"Of course everyone was relieved and happy and life soon returned to normal. Then several months later, we began noticing seismic activity among the islands of Atlantis. Earthquakes were occurring more frequently and old volcanoes started erupting. Many people considered it a divine sign of impending doom and began evacuating to other parts of the world.

"It seems these people were right because one evening an astronomer with a powerful telescope discovered that some smaller pieces from the original comet, leftovers after the nuclear bomb explosions were going to be caught months later by Earth's gravitational pull and would head straight for Earth.

"When these comet fragments hit the Earth, they landed in the middle of the Atlantic Ocean. The impact shook the ocean floor and the main islands of Atlantis collapsed and sank into the sea. Volcanoes on Atlantis that had lain dormant for years were reawakened and began erupting and spewing forth fiery lava. Ash from the burning forests and volcanic dust filled the air and covered the sun. Huge tsunamis wiped off the surface of the surviving islands. Great quantities of steam rose to the heavens and later turned into massive amounts of precipitation that brought torrential rains to the planet, causing floods all around the world, including Noah's flood."

"What happened to all the people? Did everyone die?"

The prophet shook his head. "No, thankfully, some people were able to evacuate in time."

"But where did they go?"

"Well, since the shores of Europe were the closest, many settled there. Others traveled to more primitive areas of the world where they were regarded as gods or kings. In fact, some even had structures erected in their honor."

I was puzzled. "But if some of the people were able to survive, why aren't they living on Earth today? I know some smart people, but they sure don't compare with everything I've heard about the people of Atlantis."

The prophet sighed deeply. "Unfortunately, the people on the lands where the Atlanteans settled were not as intellectually advanced, so after generations of interbreeding, most of the special qualities of our people had all but vanished. However, some of their genes survived in all of today's humans, in particular those with dominant right brains. The people you know today as the British, Germans, and Scandinavians fall into this category."

I must have looked confused because the prophet asked me, "Do you know about right and left-brained people?"

"Uhhh, I think so. I think I might have heard something about that in one of my classes at school."

The Atlantean chuckled quietly at my embarrassment, then continued. "Let me give you a quick lesson on left-brain and on right-brain thinking. Humans with dominant right-brain capabilities generally gravitate to the sciences, creativeness, and to logical thought. They like to build things and plan for the future. This was a common trait among the Atlanteans. By contrast, people whose left brain is more dominant tend to be dreamers, poets, actors, opportunists, gamblers, and lazy, Machiavellian politicians. These traits seem to be more common among the descendants of Adam. In other words, the people of today."

Neither of us said anything for several moments. My thoughts began to drift and in my imagination, I could see that piece of rock falling from the sky. I could hear the terrified screams of people as they ran for cover.

Just then, the prophet started speaking again. It startled me, but I was glad to have that awful scene erased from my mind.

"The Atlanteans were the product of a lucky gene mutation that occurred when the Entarians were creating us. It enhanced our brain development and skills, which allowed our civilization to evolve in an extremely short period of time. In fact, it took a little less than 1,000 years. While the rest of the world was still in the Stone Age, we had progressed to the Space Age. This evolution continued for many eons even after the Entarians left the earth.

"During the period of history known as the Bronze Age, my people were intent upon becoming conquerors of the world. Over generations, however, attitudes changed. We began to seek peace and harmony and no longer wanted to intervene in the affairs of other peoples. Except for commerce and the construction of space ports in the Andes Mountains and the Himalayas, we remained to ourselves and became advocates for preserving the world ecology."

"What were the Atlantean people like?" I asked. "What did they believe? How did they live?"

The prophet leaned back in his chair and looked upward, as if deep in thought. After a few moments, he began to talk. "During most of the history of

Atlantis, people were honest and upright. There was little need for government rule. In fact, there were very few laws – the ones we had would have fit into a small book. This was because the Atlanteans used good common sense and logical thinking in their everyday lives.

"Of course, we still had certain issues to face that not everyone agreed upon. For example, many discussions were held on the topic of abortion. Overall, abortion was allowed before the fetus was two-and-one-half months old; however, there were general rules that governed the act. There had to be justifiable circumstances present, such as saving the life of the mother or the fetus was known to have brain or body abnormalities. In most cases, the final choice rested with the Atlantean mother. In cases where biological problems weren't discovered until three or four months, the mature fetus was always anesthetized to ensure it did not suffer any pain during the abortion.

"Another topic that was sometimes contentious was euthanasia. In most cases, euthanasia was voluntary; however, there were restrictions. It was only allowed when the possibility of recovery was remote and the patient was suffering from physical pain beyond what that person could bear with dignity. If each additional second brought intolerable suffering, euthanasia would be permitted. Sometimes, patients would carry out the act themselves by pressing a button connected to equipment that would kill them.

"One of the times that euthanasia seemed most acceptable was when dying patients were repeatedly subjected to resuscitation efforts. There were stories that the cruelty of life support equipment created horrendous physical torture for the patient. What was unfortunate is that many of the sufferers were unable to communicate the agonies they experienced. Those that could tell of these experiences spoke of feeling as if they were being burned alive, drowned, or even eaten by a predatory animal. They said it was like being in hell and that the doctors and nurses were sadistic partners of Satan."

I shuddered inside as I listened to the prophet's descriptions.

He continued. "The only other time that euthanasia was permitted was if a baby was born highly deformed or with considerable brain damage. In such cases, it had to be done before the baby was four days old and then only with the permission of the parents. If the doctors waited any longer, the baby would become self-aware and its brain would start to program itself to the experiences of the outside world. If this were to happen, euthanasia would have been considered murder.

"Some individuals were never candidates for euthanasia, such as the mentally disabled, parasites that fed off society, persons with extremely low IQs (idiots), incapacitated seniors, or patients suffering from Alzheimer's disease. Instead, these individuals would be sent to the proper institutions to be cared for since the Atlanteans preferred to preserve life rather than end it. In fact, health care was universal on Atlantis, although rich people often didn't use the system since they had the money to choose the care they desired."

"What about the death penalty," I asked. "There are a lot of people on earth that argue over that all the time. What did the Atlanteans believe?"

"In early Atlantean times, it was believed that forced labor was worse than the death penalty. In later times, Atlanteans felt the death penalty was more appropriate for the most dangerous and incorrigible criminals, although there was considerable debate over the most humane way of execution. For awhile, we used a type of guillotine; however, doctors discovered that the shearing blade of the guillotine caused the veins and arteries of the separated head to momentarily seal, keeping the head alive for several seconds. They found it could hear, think, and move its eyes. It was quite hideous. Of course, once the blood vessels opened and the blood was allowed to escape, the head ceased any activity. Most people felt this was a shocking way to end someone's life, so the method of choice was changed to lethal injection. The deadly drug that was injected created an almost immediate state of sleep and the individual died in comparative peace."

"I'm glad they did away with the guillotine. What a horrible way to die!"

"Yes, lethal injection was much better," the prophet nodded in agreement. "Now I'll tell you a little about the schools of Atlantis. Would that interest you?"

"W-e-l-l-l-l-l, I guess. School isn't one of my favorite subjects to talk about."

The prophet smiled knowingly, then continued with his narration. "The Atlanteans believed that learning was very important and all students had to attend school for at least 10 years. The main courses of study were science, mathematics, and the humanities. Unlike your schools, in order for elementary and high school students to move up a grade, they had to take a mandatory exam to be sure they had a good understanding of what they had been taught."

The prophet stopped talking for several minutes while he nibbled on some type of plant food that was on the table. When he continued, his voice became almost ominous as he said, "You and all the other children who were brought to this gathering must realize how important it is to be well prepared in the sciences and technology. Not only will this knowledge help you protect the Earth from the coming comet, but you will need to call on all your educational resources when the Ortusian aliens attack the Earth."

"The what?"

"The Ortusians -- a highly advanced race that considers itself the only species worthy of respect. They are evil, flesh-eating predators and of all the living beings in the galaxy, they are the only ones considered highly dangerous. Many years ago, a galactic general assembly exiled the Ortusians to an isolated and lonely planet on the edge of the galaxy. This did not stop them, however, from constantly moving about space in convoys of over a thousand ships looking for new planets to conquer and decimate. There have been many occasions when they have sent scouts to Earth, searching for food. Have you heard about cattle being killed and gutted with extreme precision? This was the work of the Ortusians. Unfortunately, the animal population of Earth doesn't agree with their systems; they prefer human flesh and the soft part of the human brain."

I could barely breathe. My heart was thundering in my chest and my skin turned cold and clammy. "What ... how ... we ..." I stammered.

"I know this is very upsetting, but it is something that you must know and be prepared for."

I nodded slowly and swallowed hard. Taking a deep breath, I urged the prophet to go on with his story.

"Several people, mostly children, have been abducted by the Ortusians over the years. After analyzing their brains, they would put them in a hypnotic state and teach them that it is evil to practice birth control. Once they were certain this belief was imbedded deeply into the children's subconscious mind, they would release them to spread this doctrine among the people of Earth. You see, the goal of the Ortusians is to increase the human population so there will be plenty of food for them."

I interrupted the prophet and asked, "Sir, does this mean that the Ortusians will make the planet Earth as their home?"

"Oh, no! They're nomads by nature. What they will do is slaughter all the humans and preserve their remains in cans and bottles and other forms of containers. Then they'll put this bountiful food supply into a gigantic net, which they will tow behind their spaceship. You see, space is a great natural freezer, so their "food" will last them for at least 10,000 years as they travel around the galaxy."

I swallowed hard. This story was beginning to have a very unpleasant effect on my stomach.

"Listen carefully. There is more that you need to hear. Although the threat of the Ortusians is incentive enough to control the world's population, there is an even more crucial reason -- and that is the devastating effects that a population explosion will have on the ecological equilibrium of the planet. As the number of humans increases, the natural habitats of animals, fish, birds, and other living creatures will be overrun. Plant life will slowly be obliterated as billions and billions of hungry humans fight to sustain themselves. People will become angry and violent and fight among themselves, even to the point of nuclear war. Disease and plagues will prevail. That is why it is so very important for you and the other children to be sure that the human population is kept under control. One way you might do this is by paying couples with two or more children to submit to sterilization. You may find other solutions, but you must consider this a high priority to ensure the safety of the planet Earth."

I felt totally overwhelmed with the burden of responsibility. I looked around at the other children. How would we be able to do all that was being asked of us? But then I remembered what Moses had said -- that we would be given the resources we need. I still felt very nervous, but I had to trust this great man of history. Suddenly, a question about the Ortusians came to mind.

"Sir, is there any way that the people of Earth can fight the Ortusians?"

"Oh yes. To stop them from coming to your planet, Earthlings must band together and declare a global space war against this appalling enemy. Humans must use every resource at their disposal to stop the Ortusians and protect the Earth."

As he finished speaking, one of the angel hosts walked up to the prophet and momentarily distracted his attention. As they were talking, I tried to visualize a space war against the Ortusians. Instantly, I remembered something I had read in an encyclopedia at my high school library. It was in the Mahabharata and the Ramayans, two ancient Hindu epics, and told about colossal wars that took place in the heavens between gods and demons. Defenseless humans could only watch these wars from Earth and pray that the gods would win.

After the angel had moved away, I commented on these stories to the prophet. He nodded his head and said, "Yes, I know about those epics from Hindu culture. What you need to know is that the gods they spoke of were actually kindly extraterrestrials and the demons were scouts of the alien Ortusian predators. But enough of wars and Ortusians. Let me tell you more about the Atlanteans. Let's see, why don't I tell you about their religious beliefs?

"Much like the people of your time, there was a diverse mixture of religious practices. In my particular religion, we believed there was a constant struggle between two gods, the god of good and the god of evil. In our drawings, a good-looking young man with long hair wearing a simple white robe represented the god of good. The god of evil was always a dark, foreboding figure with black bat wings, a pointed chin and ears, and the horns of a ram."

"Those descriptions sound very similar to what we call 'God' and 'Satan,' only most of our drawings picture Satan in red with horns and a tail."

The prophet nodded in understanding, then continued. "Something else that may sound similar is that we believed that when people died, their spirits went either to hell or to paradise, depending on whether they performed good or bad deeds during their lifetime. If a person went to paradise, his or her spirit would be transformed into an angel with brightly colored butterfly wings with many designs. Paradise was like a beautiful garden full of birds and flowers and all sorts of glorious sights.

"Another religion that was practiced was a combination of sun worshipping and pantheism. Pantheists identify nature as God. Since it would be impossible to worship every animal or plant that is part of nature, they chose the sun as the representative of God and worshipped it. They believed that this ball of nuclear fire truly symbolized the power of God. Their temples of worship were circular in design, with tall slender marble columns and no walls. Covering the temple was a transparent dark glass dome that allowed them to look directly at the sun without injuring their eyes. These places of worship were erected in some of the most beautiful places on Earth so the pantheists could feel in close connection with their nature-god. Some philosophers believed that pantheism was the most logical of religions."

The prophet pushed back his chair and stood up. "Well, my son, it is time for me to go. I enjoyed speaking with you and I hope I was able to convey some of the wonders of the Atlantic nation to you, as well as the importance of being prepared for Earth's future." He reached out and shook my hand, then moved towards the brilliant light of God, along with all the others who were still seated at the table. A nearby teenager stood up and stretched and said, "Well, it seems this conference is over." I agreed.

As I arose from my seat, I was surprised to see Moses walking towards me. "Wait, boy! I've brought you the two books that I spoke about before. Here, this thick one is the Atlantis Book of Genesis and includes facts about cosmology and the sciences. This thinner one is the book that I wrote when I was leading the exodus of the nation of Israel. I would suggest that you read them both and make comparisons."

"Moses, sir, there's no way I can read these books! I've never in my life read so many pages and besides, I don't know anything about science. I couldn't understand the Atlantis Book of Genesis even if I did read it."

"Son, you forget about that special band around your head. The micro-electronics that are woven into it will allow you to read each page in about three seconds and to understand everything you read. Try it and you'll see."

I opened the thick book and sure enough, in a matter of seconds, I had completed reading several pages and was fully aware of what I had read.

"Wow! This is great! I wish I had something like this on Earth."

Moses grinned and patted my shoulder. "It is time for you to leave now. Go in peace."

I looked around and saw that the host angels were assembling everyone together for the return to Earth. I turned back towards Moses to say goodbye, but he was gone. In his place was a bright light that kept getting brighter and brighter by the minute. Then I heard a loud voice.

"Come on! boy. It's time to get up. You've had enough sleep. We have to get moving."

I opened my eyes and saw sunlight flooding the cave. My father was rolling up his sleeping bag and gathering up his belongings. I sat there for several minutes in a daze. Strange images floated across my mind. Had I been dreaming? Somewhere in the back of my mind, I remembered seeing Christ and being told about a coming comet, but everything was all mixed up and I didn't understand any of it. My father nudged me and said to get up and get dressed. He wanted to get moving so we could hike as far as possible up the mountain while there was still light. I climbed out of my sleeping bag and within minutes, had forgotten all about the dreams.

[Editor's Note: Chapter 16 includes a re-creation of the Atlantis Book of Genesis. It describes the eternal triad as being made up of God, gravity, and the primordial basic particles. Also included are answers to the big questions that man has asked since the dawn of mankind.]

# CHAPTER 3
## Back to Reality

After getting dressed, I grabbed my rifle and went hunting for some breakfast. I shot a viscacha, which is a rodent about the size of a hare. Although the caliber of my rifle and the bullet were far too powerful for game this size, our Indian porter skinned it anyway and we had a good breakfast.

We gathered up our things and then crossed the river by jumping from rock to rock. Once we were on the other side, we began an uphill climb. The river began flowing faster and faster, singing to us as it danced over the rocks and ledges in its path. Looking back the way we had come, I could see the green, tropical forest we had left behind hours before.

As our route took us higher and higher, my father commented that we probably should have brought the climbing gear. Little did we know how treacherous this part of the journey was going to be. I began to have very mixed feelings about the rugged beauty that was all around us, fearing instead for our safety. I became especially scared as we began crossing a cliff horizontally. The pathway was so narrow that our chests rubbed against the mountain.

Because the terrain was precariously steep, we had to walk like spiders, extending our fingers as far as possible. I even stretched out my toes in my shoes. We all knew that if we were not very careful, we could easily fall thousands of feet into the abyss below. What made it even scarier was that a layer of clouds obscured our view so we could not even see all the dangers below. Adding to this was the roar of the river rapids as it rose up through the clouds and filled our ears.

My father warned us, "As you climb, always be sure your hands wrap around at least three bunches of grass. Some will have solid roots, some will be rotten, and some will fall out from under you, so test each handhold and be very careful." Just as my father finished his warning, I reached for a handful of grass above my head and it came loose. Luckily, my feet were planted on some solid bunches of grass or I would have gone tumbling to my death.

Finally we reached a ledge and as we stepped up on it, we were surprised to discover that the upper part of the mountain was missing. It was as though it had been cut like a slice from the top part of a cake. In its place was a long valley that extended far off into the distance. My father said it was a hanging plateau. Whatever it was called, I felt like I was standing at the entrance to another world. I looked behind me at the deep canyon, then in front of me at this new solemn and silent landscape.

As we began our trip through the valley, I could see a row of hills on each side with a high mountain at the far end. Our porter told us that this mountain was the highest one in the region and the last one to climb before we returned to civilization. He said, "I have never been in this zone before. The explorers that hire me to carry their packs are not attracted to this range because the mountains are not as tall as they are on the Eastern Range. Climbers require peaks of at least 20,000 feet before they get excited." He went on to tell us that while we were traveling in the truck, he had seen the backside silhouette of this mountain so he knew the road we needed to intersect with was several kilometers behind it.

Crossing the arid plateau made me think of being on the surface on another planet. Every time I looked around with my binoculars, all I saw were vultures and condors circling high above us. There were no other signs of life. We had to travel slowly because of the thin air and I couldn't help but wonder if this was what attracted the scavengers.

Even though my father was a healthy man and experienced at hiking and climbing, he was experiencing chest pains because of the high altitude. His discomfort reminded me that in an emergency, there would be no help within a thousand square miles. Certainly the porter would not be able to carry both my father and me out of the area. It felt like we were the only people in the world. I could only pray that we would have the energy to cross the mountain that lay in front of us.

The signposts of those who didn't make it off this plateau began to appear. First we saw the bleached bones of llamas and mules, probably baking there for half a century. A kilometer ahead, we found the cracked and sun-bleached bones of a human. They were lying across the broad, flat top of a low rock that had apparently been his deathbed. "This place is cursed," I thought to myself. "Whoever visits here leaves their bones as a warning to others of the consequences of Sorojche!" (Sorojche is the Indian word for mountain sickness.)

My father interrupted my thoughts as he commented that the boots and exploration gear on the skeleton looked like he might have been a European explorer from the turn of the century, possibly looking for the "Dorado Treasure." I wondered if he had died of the thin air? Or had he run out of food and water? Suddenly, I realized how tired and thirsty I was. I shook my canteen to see if there was any water left, but it was empty. I feared we might suffer the same fate as this poor man.

I was immensely relieved when we saw what appeared to be an Indian village in the distance. I was starving and looked forward to being able to stop and eat. As we moved forward, I thought I heard dogs barking. I knew it was common for villagers to have dogs and, of course, they always bark at strangers. As we got closer, we could see square, gray, windowless dwellings arranged in two lines, with a street down the middle. But as each step took us nearer, we began to realize that these were not dwellings at all. They were large square boulders topped with tufts of dry grass that looked like moth-eaten toupees. And there were no people … which meant there was probably no food or water. The idea that we had seen a village was pure hallucination. We all felt extremely frustrated.

Approaching the boulders, we noticed they were laid out in a very neat and orderly pattern, not randomly and scattered as one might expect. We wondered among ourselves how this could be. It seemed highly unlikely that the pattern had occurred naturally, and we knew of no single crane in the world that could have lifted any one of the stones. I began to imagine that perhaps they had been placed here by an ancient and intelligent society. But then I told myself it must be altitude sickness playing games with my mind.

We moved slowly away from the boulders and soon reached the far side of the plateau to begin our final ascent. I knew we were close to finishing our long journey. Before many more days, we would intersect the road and be picked up by the first vehicle returning to the city. However, between where we stood and that road was the tallest mountain in the area. We began to climb. After we had gone only about 500 feet, I was already feeling tired and weak. I was hungry and there was nowhere in this dead world to catch any fresh meat.

We continued to make our way up the mountain. We passed a recessed area where there was a pile of rocks. My father declared, "Let's stop here. We can all use a break. It's 3 o'clock now, so we'll rest for half an hour. We need to keep moving so we can make some time before the sun sets." Each of us chose a stone to sit on and relax. Surprisingly, they made comfortable seats. We ate some sandwiches made from canned meat -- the ideal food for explorers -- and drank some coffee that our porter had made that morning. We needed to regain our energy for the final climb across the ridge and the descent to meet the road and our return to civilization.

The stone I chose was perfectly contoured for my body. I settled into the smooth cavity and put my head into a recessed area that resembled a helmet. I felt very relaxed as I gazed at the plateau below. In the distance, I could see a small group of clouds moving swiftly towards us from the large canyon. They passed by very quickly and as they did, I could see six perfectly shaped clouds directly in line with one another. Each one resembled two bowls that had been placed edge-to-edge. My father saw it as well and exclaimed, "What a strange weather phenomenon!" Our porter had other ideas. To him, these strange clouds were messengers from space. "I have seen these kind of clouds before," he said. "They floated over me once when I was exploring with an Englishman in another virgin zone, far north of this one. They always seem to come from this area. People say they are space vehicles and are responsible for the disappearance of many."

The idea of extraterrestrials and UFOs was exciting to me. The only science fiction story I had ever read was by Jules Verne, but the idea that clouds might be space vehicles fascinated me. My father said nothing, but I knew he didn't believe the porter's remarks.

I began to feel very drowsy. I looked over at my father and saw that he was yawning and about to fall asleep. Suddenly everything around me turned dark, but it didn't feel like I was asleep. Maybe it's a solar eclipse, I thought. No, that doesn't make sense. It wouldn't happen so quickly. I began to feel like I was spinning. In my mind's eye, I could see myself drifting towards a whirlpool.

Just as I was about to be sucked into the swirling eddy, I could hear the porter exclaiming loudly, "Don't fall asleep at this altitude! You must make every effort to stay awake or you will get Sorojche, the sweet death, and never awaken."

But I couldn't help myself.

# CHAPTER 4
## 11,600 Years Ago

Within moments, the darkness returned. Then without warning, it lifted and I realized I was still seated in the stone chair. But when I looked around, I saw my father and the porter had disappeared. Where were they? What was happening? I felt very uneasy, but then a thought seemed to enter my mind from nowhere. It told me that the stone I was seated on was no ordinary stone. It was actually a mechanism that members of a superior human race had left in this place eons ago, and it was now transporting me to a distant past when neither my father nor the porter exists.

In front of me, I saw that the landscape was the same yet many of the details were different. I looked back at the plateau and saw the large cubic stones that we had previously thought were houses. I was surprised when I saw that there were only two of them; the rest had disappeared. All around the stones I could see ghostly beings moving around. As I stared in amazement, each one gradually materialized into a human. Then more humans appeared on the plateau. About a quarter of a mile away, I saw other humans climbing some mountains to the right of where I was sitting. Halfway up the mountain, I could see a tunnel and excavation workers were going in and out of the entrance.

As I watched these workers, a gigantic beast that resembled a dragon appeared from inside the tunnel and deposited some gigantic chunks of rock just outside the tunnel entrance. From the valley below I saw another extremely large creature, similar to a giant ape, climb up the mountain. It went directly to the massive rocks left by the dragon, picked the rocks up with its bare hands, and then carried a load of them back down the mountain. Gradually, two rows of stone that exactly duplicated what we had seen earlier were put into place.

I was so intent on watching these beasts that I nearly jumped out of my skin when I saw movement from the corner of my eye! I spun around and saw another huge ape. This one was lying on the ground and a group of people were moving around and working on it. I couldn't help but marvel at the immense size of the creature. It looked to be as big as a 10-story building. It had hairy legs and one eye, the size of a house window, in the center of its face. It reminded me of the creature in Greek mythology named Cyclops.

At first, I thought the people working on the ape were veterinarians and the ape was ill. Then I realized they were removing and replacing mechanical parts.

This was no ape! This was a mechanical robot that only resembled an ape. Apparently it was used as a beast of burden in large-scale construction projects.

I looked more closely at the people. I knew they weren't natives because there weren't that many inhabitants living in this area. They were most likely relocated workers or immigrants from another continent. They didn't appear to be slaves, as they looked well fed and happy. They had the physical features and garments of modern-day Mongolians. I wondered if they might be the ancestors of the South American Indians. What appeared to be the supervisors resembled Northern Europeans. I found it interesting that they wore skirts and shirts similar to those worn by ancient Egyptian nobility, except that these garments were made of silk.

I saw the lead mechanic looking my way. He put down his tools and walked towards me. "Don't be alarmed," he said. "I don't know who you are, but I know you come from the future and you have been transported 11,600 years back in time. That bulky stone seat you're sitting on is the source of all you're seeing and experiencing. The people of Atlantis put it there for a purpose you will understand later. I know you're curious about the ape robot. Later I'll share the engineering plans with you and show you how it works. But first, I have some explaining to do."

Although I knew the Atlantean was speaking in his native tongue, I was able to understand everything he said. Somehow I understood that his thoughts were being transmitted to me by electromagnetic waves stored in the stone chair. The decoded words and images traveled directly to regions of my brain cortex where the actions of thinking and planning and emotions are executed. This was possible because there was no need for the thoughts to first pass through the mapped sensory areas and the areas of preliminary decoding of the brain cortex.

The mechanic sat down on the ground next to me and continued. "We know the great comet is nearing our world of Atlantis so several groups of engineers and builders, similar to this group, have been sent to seven different locations around the world to build vaults to store our treasures. Our group has come here to the Andes Mountains to bury the Scrolls of Wisdom, on which we have recorded our complete knowledge of art, philosophy, and technology. We hope that someday these treasures will be found so we can share our wisdom with the humanity of your generation. We know that centuries will pass, perhaps millennia, before our vaults will be discovered."

He went on, "We also know that the man of the future may be unable to find our vaults, so we have made additional preparations. Before the comet impacts Atlantis, a small band of astronauts will leave the Earth. After a few thousand years have passed, their descendants will return to Earth and help their primitive brothers to build a new civilization in the image of our incredible nation."

The mechanic stood up. "I must go now. These projects must be completed before the comet comes so we are working as quickly as we can. We will talk more later."

My mind was filled with questions. What was I doing here? Had I really been mentally transported back in time to when Atlantis ruled the Earth? Who were these people? Why was I being told these things? I wanted to know more! I started to get up from the stone chair to look around but before I could get to my feet, I felt someone shaking me. I opened my eyes to see the porter handing me his thermos.

"Here, drink this. It is hot tea made from dry ground coca leaves. It will help prevent altitude sickness and keep you awake. My ancestors have used coca leaves for centuries so we can work in the land barons' fields for endless hours without rest. We believe coca is a gift from Pacha-mama, the Earth Goddess. It is part of our religion that we inherited from the Incas."

I reached for the thermos and took a swallow of the hot tea.

# CHAPTER 5
## Simple Lad Goes to Atlantis

Within seconds after swallowing the hot liquid, I felt myself drifting back into blackness. I seemed to hear a voice coming from inside the stone that said, "Several Atlanteans have recorded their thoughts and experiences in this stone. You are here to live their experiences. We will transfer your personality into theirs and only a few minutes of your time shall pass."

I then saw a bluish light begin to glow, gradually increasing in intensity. In the center of the light appeared an old man with gray hair, a moustache, and beard that were heavily flecked with silver, and wearing a blue robe and golden sandals. He said, "I am the image of Luzaire, an Atlantean who lived a long time ago, and I am your uncle. After you arrive in Atlantis, I will be your host and guide. Because you are exploring this inaccessible, barren plateau and because the stone has chosen you to receive this message, we assume you are young and in good physical condition."

He continued, "In the stone are recorded the thoughts of a modest boy of humble origins. He is not from Atlantis, but coming to Atlantis has been the goal of his dreams. He is a temporary helper on a sailboat coming from Thera near the North Shore of the Internal Sea. It is near what you know today as the country and waters of Greece. Your mind and his will blend into one and you will become that boy. His name is Kappa."

The old man continued, "Kappa was born to two Atlantis missionaries who lived in the northeastern region of the Mediterranean Sea. They believed that the spirits from good people who die become angels with colorful butterfly wings and the spirits of bad people suffer for awhile then disappear forever. It was their mission to convert the people of the area to their beliefs. However, when Kappa was very young, his parents, along with his brothers and sisters and many others, died from the great plague. I tell you this so you will understand, but Kappa has no memory of his parents because he was so young when they died. A native couple whose children were about the same age adopted him. They are shepherds and hunters of small game, and are poor, but happy.

"Often while tending the sheep and goats, Kappa enjoys making small clay animals and toys that resemble little carriages with four wheels. One day, a neighbor noticed the clay toys and said, 'I'm going to tell you something that no one has told you before. The reason you are skilled in making these carriages is because you are of Atlantean blood. You were adopted by the people you call your parents, but you are, in reality, a son of Atlantis. Only in Atlantis do these carts with wooden wheels exist.'

"Kappa was shocked to discover that he is adopted, but was even more amazed to learn that he is an Atlantean. He has never seen the people of Atlantis before, although he has often fantasized about going there. He has always imagined that they are giant people of fame who live in the most powerful nation on Earth. Now that Kappa knows about his real background, he has a burning desire to see the great Atlantis for himself so he joined the crew of an old ship. They soon set sail from the rocky coast where Kappa lives."

As if by magic, when Luzaire finishes talking, I become Kappa. I find myself in a rough-hewn boat that is poorly caulked with pitch and driven only by a crude sail. I feel cold water around my feet and a rough garment chafes at my skin. Four men dressed in ragged clothing are constantly bailing water from inside the boat using large shells. Their sandals are tucked inside their rope belts. Looking down, I discover that my attire matches theirs, although mine seems a bit more tattered.

"Where..." my voice is weak and my tongue feels thick with disuse. I swallow. "Where are we going?"

"Hey! The bonehead can talk!" exclaimed a tall, bearded man. Breathing hard from his bailing efforts, he says, "We're going to the land of the god Poseidon to sell our goods and be damn rich for awhile. Now get back to work and bail this blasted boat before we all sink to the bottom of the sea. If I have to tell you again, it will be with my fist." This warning came with his fist shaking vigorously in my face. I began scooping water as fast as I could.

The next morning, I'm greeted with a swift kick in the ribs and told to get up and get busy bailing. As I scoop and pour, I look towards the horizon but all I see is the sun glaring off the blue sea.

We sail for several days and then cross the Pillars of Hercules. The work never stops except for brief respites for food and sleep. I lose track of time as I must stand watches in both daylight and darkness. After several days pass, I can see a silver ocean liner moving rapidly across the horizon. It is very modern and moves gracefully across the water, like something out of the future. I can't help but wonder why we're in such a miserable leaking tub when a ship like that exists. Just then one of the crew notices the ship as well and shouts to the rest of the group. Everyone stops bailing to watch the ship.

"Boy", the captain says reverently, "that is a magic boat belonging to Poseidon. Bow your head." No one spoke while the ship was in sight.

A few days later, gulls come screeching around the boat. "We're nearing land," one of the grimy crew members comments. "We're almost there, thanks to the gods of the sea." My aching body receives this news with grateful anticipation after so much hard work.

The next morning, dawn brightens the sky and I see a large island with low, rolling hills. Coming towards us from the direction of the island is a polished sailboat rigged with glistening white sails. I can see that the men on board are wearing brightly colored clothes and the women are clad in scanty swimsuits.

They are all laughing and seem to be having great fun. Some of them are embracing. I wonder if these are people from Atlantis.

One of the coarse sailors takes a step towards me. I duck just in time to escape a blow from him that was aimed at my head. "You'd rather sightsee than work?" he bellows. "Keep your head down before the gods sink us! We're close to our mark now, so get to work." I returned to the backbreaking task of bailing out water. To me it was a miracle that this ship was able to stay in one piece.

Then I see another boat approaching us. Someone on board calls loudly to our captain, "Ahoy! You have a boy on your ship. His uncle sends a message to the boy that he will meet him halfway to the end of the channel. You are to stop at the narrow stairs that are carved in stone on the side of the channel and let the boy off."

As we sailed close to the shoreline, I was awestruck by the handsome people swimming, surfing, and sailing in the shallow waters. Farther back from the shore, I could see turreted castles. They had multi-colored towers decorated with silver and gold. I had never seen such beauty. In the sky, I spotted ultralight aircraft that were adorned with dragons, giant butterflies, and winged horses. I couldn't help comparing the magnificence of the island and the dirty, old, ugly boat that I was on. But soon I would be able to get off this wreck and meet my uncle.

"What island is this?" I asked.

"This is a group of islands," the skipper replied. "This one closest to us is the ancient and magical island of Poseidon. Its buildings, temples, and palaces are made of marble. We're headed for the next island. It's larger and more modern." He chuckled as he added, "And there's more money there." He lowered his voice as if telling me a secret. "The people that live on the next island are called demigods because they know everything there is to know in the world."

Once we were past the beach resort, the coastline became rocky and the sea grew choppy and rough. The wind kicked up and whistled around us. Dark clouds began moving in. As I stood watching the menacing sky, I suddenly felt dizzy. Then all of a sudden I saw the clouds forming the image of an old man's head and heard a voice say, "I came with the wind and I shall go with the wind." I looked around but no one else on board seemed to be paying any attention. I shook my head, thinking I must be hallucinating. Then the image faded. "I must be suffering from heatstroke," I said to myself.

Up ahead I could see two immense statues flanking the channel we were headed for. They were each holding a lantern in one hand and beckoning with the other. As we passed the statues, the normally raucous crew became very still and solemn. Then one of the crew members -- probably the only literate one -- read an inscription from the base of one of the massive statues. As he spoke, the rest of the crew bowed their heads. "Welcome to all. We invite the people of the world to visit Atlantis."

After entering the channel, I noticed that the walls of the canal were smooth and perfectly engineered. Way in the distance, I could see what looked to be a modern city made completely from crystal. The buildings were so tall that they seemed to rise into the heavens. One of the men turned to me and said, "Most people that sail to Atlantis bring exotic materials and metals, as are we. Others bring gems and crystals."

I could hardly contain myself as I realized that I was finally about to see the city of Atlantis. As we drew closer, I saw that graceful bridges connected the tall buildings I had seen earlier. I longed to walk on one of those bridges. I imagined how magnificent it would be to see this city from the air.

"That is Brasea, the most modern city of Atlantis," I heard one of the crew comment to another.

The boat moved closer to the smooth wall of the canal and I saw the stairway where I was to get off. The captain steered close to the dock at the base of the stairs. "This is where you get off, lad."

"But … but," I stammered. "We're … the city …" I complained, pointing to it in futility. The crew wasted no time in helping me off the boat.

At the top of the stairs, there was a broad path that crossed green fields and led straight to the city. Horses and cattle grazed nearby. Ahead of me, I could see three people walking on the trail. They were all clad in white. I followed them.

Pretty soon I spotted a bearded man approaching me on the pathway. As he got closer, I recognized him as the face that had appeared to me in the clouds. Like the others, he was dressed all in white, except he had a golden belt around his waist. He smiled as he came up to me.

"My dear nephew. I am Luzaire, one of the ten elders of the government of Atlantis. Your mother was my sister. I am an engineer and physicist, and many people call me the Wizard. But I am no more a wizard than you are." His eyes twinkled.

"You need to understand something. While I am talking to you, I am also talking to a person who is here from the future. That person is now sitting on the Stone of Dreams and is sharing your spirit and your thoughts. We are linked through time by the great concealed helmet inside the Stone. Although it appears you are living in Atlantis, in truth you are still asleep. Your mind is receiving a message from the distant past. At the time you are receiving this message, I have long since died and my lovely city of Atlantis has not existed for thousands of years."

I gasped at the thought of talking to a dead man. As if reading my thoughts, Luzaire smiled at me. His teeth were white and even. He went on with his explanation.

"The boy whose body you now occupy is identical to you in mentality. I've chosen him because it will make the blending of your minds more compatible, making it easier for you to share his experiences of living in Atlantis."

The part of me that was asleep on the stone asked, "Why am I here?"

The old man ignored my question and continued speaking. "In a span of time of no more than 1,500 years, the people of the Atlantean civilization have progressed six times faster than any other civilization in the world. They have gone from the Copper Age, through the Age of Technology, and into the Space Age. This happened because of their natural tendencies toward science. Living in these modern times, you will experience the pinnacle of the Atlantis culture."

We started walking along a concrete pathway that ran along the top of the channel. It was lined by a steel railing along the canal side. Approaching us were two beings. Amazingly, I sensed three minds in their two bodies. I looked down at the water. I could tell it was extremely deep. Moving through the canal were several big ships, some of them heading towards the internal harbors and others departing for the open sea.

Just then something whizzed by me and I jumped.

"Watch out for the cars," Luzaire laughed. "They're self-propelled boxes with wheels that transport people and baggage across land."

We passed by a fenced-in green field. Luzaire stopped and put his fingers to his head as though deep in thought. Then he said, "There's not enough time for us to go to the city today. Let us sit down here on this bench and I'll tell you more about Atlantis.

"The Atlantis nation is made up of two islands and several islets. The island we are on is the largest one and is called Island of the Sun. Its largest city is Brasea, which is the one you see in the distance. The people who live there are practical, modern, and busy most of the time. More than 50 years ago, this island was nothing more than wilderness. The government built all the cities entirely from scratch. Today it is dedicated entirely to science, technology, and industry. Economically, it is the most powerful place in the world.

"When we leave here, we will go to where I live. It is a smaller island, not too far from here, called Poseidon. Although Atlantis is now a magnificent nation, for 2,000 years Poseidon was its home. I am proud to have my residence there." Luzaire looked over at me and smiled. Then he continued.

"In contrast to the people who live on the Island of the Sun, the people from my island are highly conservative. Most of them wear togas, like what I am wearing. We are a society devoted to philosophy, the arts, the humanities, and meditation. Our island is the home of the old gods. Their temples, which have beautiful golden domes and walls of orichalcum, were long ago converted to museums of art for tourists to enjoy. There are many mansions on the island, and most of the buildings are of classical architecture. Fine marble statues are scattered throughout the many gardens on the island."

Without any warning, my uncle Luzaire stood up and said, "Follow me." We walked a short way and then went through a gate that opened onto the green field.

"This is an airport. The objects you see that look like mechanical birds are called airplanes. They carry people and baggage like the cars you saw, except airplanes move through the sky. The red one up ahead is mine and it is what we will take to reach Poseidon."

I told Luzaire how I had often watched birds with envy and wished I could be one of them.

"Now you will get to live your dream, and you'll be able to see the grandeur of Atlantis from the air."

So much had happened to me today! I was surprised that I wasn't exhausted. But instead, I felt exhilarated and excited. I was learning so much.

Luzaire started the airplane engine. The noise was very uncomfortable at first, but then I got used to it. We climbed inside this great mechanical bird and lifted into the sky. We flew low and followed the canal in the direction of the sea. On either side of the canal, I saw there was a line of pyramids. "What's the purpose of all those pyramids?"

"When the canal was excavated, the material that was removed was piled outside the city in the shape of pyramids instead of dumping it in an ugly heap. The people of Atlantis are very well-organized, even in simple things. Actually, the pyramids have no real purpose, although sometimes architects use them as sites to build apartment houses on top and on the sides. And some eccentric millionaires have been know to buy them to use as their own private burial place."

As we reached the end of the island, we started to cross a strait of water. Suddenly Luzaire said, "I've changed my mind. It is too early to go home. Let's turn back and I'll show you more of Atlantis."

As the great mechanical bird turned, I could clearly see the city of Brasea. What a marvel it was with all the tall buildings made of glass and metal. The idea that it could have been built by extraterrestials crossed my mind. Just outside the city limits, I saw that the canal we had walked along intersected with another canal that formed a semi-circle around half the city. Big ships were docked here and there.

"We're now approaching the downtown area of Brasea," my uncle said. "I'll fly around the city at a low altitude so you can get a good look."

I studied the skyscrapers and saw that four of the tallest ones were identical to each other and stood at the four corners of the main square. Luzaire explained, "Those buildings you're looking at are 100 stories high. As you can see, on top of them there are two long platforms that look like bridges. These connect the buildings and are runways for small aircraft and helicopters. People who live in the suburban areas outside the city but work downtown use these aircraft. We call them commuters."

"What are those thick ropes suspended from the skyscrapers to the lower buildings on the edge of the city" I asked. "The whole thing looks like a tent without a canvas."

"This will have to be your last question, my nephew. We are approaching heavy air traffic and I must concentrate on my flying. Those are not ropes. They are actually hollow tubes of aluminum and they act as suspended tunnels for rapid speed trains. We call them sky trains. I'm going to move out of the city now for the countryside."

I was completely in awe at this powerful sight. What great power this civilization has!

We soon left the city and began flying over plains that were divided into enormous squares. My uncle continued his descriptions.

"Most of those squares you see are used for agriculture. You will also see a number of farms scattered about. Irrigation channels have divided the land, with the wider ones being used as waterways for navigation. A variety of crops are grown here. Atlanteans also raise cattle and horses, using some of them in the traditional sports of Atlantis."

Luzaire took the plane to a lower altitude and I could see barbed wire surrounding a large area. Inside were elephants, mammoths, bison, oxen, and wooly rhinoceros. My uncle pointed to the animals and said, "This is a specially designed park for endangered species that we bring in from all over the world. Our laws protect these creatures from being destroyed. We have other areas, which we call zoos, where there are no fences and the animals roam free. People are allowed to walk among them in tubes made from unbreakable glass."

"What's that?" I asked, pointing excitedly to my right.

"Oh, that is an Atlantis spaceship coming in for a landing," answered Luzaire.

I watched in fascination as the flames from the tail of the ship illuminated the ground below it.

Finally, we left the large island and headed for the island of Poseidon. I felt safe and warm in the comfortable seat of the airplane. The old man was so kind.

Soon I could see our destination. My uncle, the wizard, commented, "Isn't it beautiful? It draws many artists and philosophers who want to immerse themselves in the solemn beauty that existed before the death of the gods."

As we started our descent, Luzaire told me that he would soon be going overseas on a business trip and I would be staying on the island with his neighbors, Godin and Gofreigga.

"They are good people. Ovald and Ada, their son and daughter-in-law, along with their grandson, Krill, live with them. I'm sure you will like everyone. When I return, I will take you to my home, which is only a city block from Godin's house. I know you will be happy here on Poseidon. I have already picked out several places for you to visit while I am gone."

# CHAPTER 6
## Godin the Ingenious

After landing at a small airport, Uncle Luzaire took me to a lavish mansion. To get to the entrance doors, we had to walk through lush green gardens with stunning marble statues. Along the way, my uncle told me a short story about his friend, Godin. "Ever since he was young, Godin has been a man of dreams. One of them was to become rich and build a magnificent, platinum palace for himself. As you can see, he attained this dream. He also told me of another dream that he had when he was single. In this one, he saw himself carrying his girlfriend away on a powerful horse. They would go faster and faster until the horse would sprout golden wings, lift them into the sky, and take them to a dazzling crystal palace."

Just them, my uncle pointed ahead of us and I could see two people standing on a porch.

"Welcome, welcome! You must be the nephew of our good neighbor, Luzaire. I am Godin and this is my wife, Gofreigga. Come inside." He opened the ornately decorated door and ushered us into the entryway.

Gofreigga looked at me knowingly as she said, "You must be hungry. Dinner is almost ready." She pointed to a room just ahead and added, "You may wash in there."

As I walked to the washroom, I looked down at my ragged clothing. I felt very much out of place in this stately home, but no one had seemed to notice. As I washed my hands and face, I realized that Gofreigga was right. I was hungry. My stomach was growling like a wounded bear.

The meal was a feast! I couldn't identify any of the foods, but I ate heartily nevertheless. Everything tasted excellent. I couldn't help but compare it with the awful food we'd had to eat on the rickety boat that had brought me to Atlantis.

Godin and Luzaire talked enthusiastically with each other during dinner. It was obvious they were good friends. I listened attentively, but said little. From what I was able to gather, Godin was the head of a design team at a robot factory in western Atlantis.

When everyone had finished eating, Luzaire, Godin and I moved into another room. Godin was reminiscing about his single days. "Ah yes, I remember how I used to ski and sail and fly. And the parties! What grand parties we used to have. But did you know that as hard as I played, I also had my quiet moments when I wrote sonnets?"

I could see Uncle Luzaire's eyebrows raise.

"Many of the sonnets I wrote were for Gofreigga. When I met her at the snack shop near where I worked, I knew right away that she was the one for me. Oh yes, I know everyone was surprised when I married her. No one thought I was ready to settle down, but Gofreigga was very special to me from the first day we met."

He turned to me and said, "Soon you will meet Ovald and his wife, Ada. They are guides with the Department of Tourism and should be home soon. And you will like their son, Krill." Godin's eyes shone with pride as he talked about Krill. "He has grown into a tall, adventurous young man. Sometime back, he decided he wanted to become independent, so he moved to Brasea and started working five-hour shifts as a mechanic repairing industrial robots. He spent many of his evenings enjoying the city nightlife but after about a year, he decided the frenetic life in Brasea was not for him and he returned home. I think he longed for his family and the quiet life here on Poseidon. In any event, I was happy to have him back."

Just then, Ovald and Ada entered the room. "Ahhh, here is my son. Come, Ovald, I want you to meet Kappa, Luzaire's nephew." We shook hands and Ovald introduced his wife to me. Godin told them that dinner was still warm and waiting for them, but they said they had eaten in the city.

The couple settled into one of the plush couches. The conversation drifted to Ovald and Ada's upcoming vacation.

Ovald mused, "We want to go to a campsite that's away from the populated areas but every time we do, we often find ourselves being honored as gods by the primitive tribes. Some of them have even erected shrines to honor what they consider to be our magic. We don't like confusing people's beliefs, but if we want to get away from the polluted areas of the big city, we have no other choice." He shook his head and added, "It's interesting that although Atlanteans want to preserve the ecological equilibrium of this planet, they do very little to keep pollution on their own island under control."

Everyone was silent for a few moments, considering Ovald's comments. Then Gofreigga joined us, having completed her chores in the kitchen. She apparently had heard Ovald talking about their vacation because she said, "Godin, do you remember when we first married? We often went camping and you always took along your ravens." She looked at me. "Godin had trained the ravens to ride on his shoulders and to obey his commands. He created quite a stir among the natives. There was no doubt that they thought he was a god. And he enjoyed every minute of it!"

I looked over at Godin, who had a big smile on his face. Then he turned to me and said, "You're a very curious person, aren't you? I've noticed how you've been observing every detail of this house. I think you would make a good engineer. Why don't you come with me to my studio? I'll show you some engineering drawings."

Godin and I left the others. When we reached his studio, he pulled out a package from one of his desk drawers and handed it to me. "Here are designs of the wonders of Atlantis. I believe you are going to develop a strong interest in engineering while you are visiting us and I want you to learn to appreciate the great achievements we have accomplished."

As I studied the drawings, I knew I was seeing them through the keen eyes of the boy whose body I occupied and I could feel his interest in engineering being kindled. In my own body, I felt a great respect for the creativity of the Atlantean people.

# CHAPTER 7
## Krill's Romance

I had been living in Atlantis for several months now. I attended school regularly and was learning all the nuances of the Atlantean language. I had become quite close to Krill and his friend, Crom, and people often referred to us as the "gang of three."

On this day, I was walking along a sandy beach. The bright, spring sunshine glistened on the breaking waves. The songs of birds filled the air and butterflies glided from flower to flower, taking nectar from each variety. Up ahead I saw a ball game in progress between two teams of young explorers and I stopped to watch. I could see Krill and Crom were playing. As I watched, I could see that the object of the game was to get the ball to pass through two large holes in the net. If it did, that team scored three points. If the ball went over the net, they only scored one point.

Suddenly the ball swooped through one of the large holes in the net, heading straight for Krill. If he missed returning it, the opposing team would gain a crucial point. He lunged at it, his dark eyes flashing, and the ball sailed over the net. Just then a dog ran through the players on the opposite team, tripping the boy who was getting ready to return the ball. The ball fell to the ground and Krill's team won the final point.

"No fair! Canine interference!" shouted someone on the other team.

"We won! We won!" Krill and his teammates were jubilant.

Joggers passing by on a ribbon of highway near the shore waved at the winning team. Just then, three sand buggies came racing down the beach. They slammed to a stop when they reached the group of players and several young people started unloading ice chests and radios. Someone switched on one of the radios and couples began to dance. Others drifted away to go swimming or to rest in the sand.

Krill and Crom started to walk down the beach and motioned for me to join them. They were talking excitedly about going on an expedition to distant, uncharted lands. I knew that both of them burned with a desire to see the lands beyond the ocean, and how they yearned to do something that would gain them recognition.

I smiled as I looked at my two friends. Both were tall and thin, but Crom had blonde hair in contrast to Krill's black hair. Both were 19 years old, enjoyed sports, and spent many long hours on the beach. They also frequently attended dances and parties, some of which were organized by the Young Explorers' Club. Crom earned his living by fixing sports cars. Krill, on the other hand, was a young man who had everything so he had quit his job and spent all his time pursuing good-looking girls. He owned one of the most expensive sports cars in the city. Krill loved his independence, which is why his grandfather, Godin, had allowed him to live in a private apartment located in a corner of the mansion grounds. It was a frequent gathering spot for friends to come and drink beer and listen to music. Krill especially liked to play music that incited romance and sex. He also used to borrow his grandfather's large sailboat and take his friends with him on sailing trips. Sometimes they would be gone for days, continuously partying and drinking.

As they continued their conversation about their dream expedition, Krill said, "Who knows what strangeness might be out there? Even if we tried to guess, we would probably be wrong. All we know is there are unmapped lands just waiting for us. Crom, we were born to be explorers. It's our destiny!"

"You're right," Crom agreed, his blue eyes dancing at the thought. He then turned to me. "Kappa, would you like to go on an exploration trip with us?"

"Only if it was while I was on vacation from school," I replied.

Krill passionately continued, "Life is too easy here. It's too shallow. We've taken our life of wealth and ease for granted. Most people aren't interested in something that might make them uncomfortable. They wouldn't travel anywhere without their FCVs."

"Yeah, their oh-so-safe flying camping vehicles," said Crom disgustedly.

Krill went on, his anger growing. "They would rather remain in Atlantis, tramping about year after year on Poseidon. I can't believe there are actually people who don't believe that seeing the world and learning about other cultures broadens and enriches our lives."

"You know," Crom reminisced, "I remember when I was a kid, we used to take the train and travel all around the island. I loved it! I would be riveted to the window the entire ride, watching the constantly changing scenery and wondering what I would see next. Yesterday, I bought a geographical magazine that had an article about some anthropological work that's being done in northern Europe near the Arctic Circle. Would you like to see it?"

"Sounds good to me," Krill replied. "Bring it over to the house tomorrow. I've got to get going now. See you at the Explorers' Club!"

I realized it was getting late. The air on the beach was getting cooler by the minute, so I decided to head for home also.

The next day, after washing his car, Krill picked me up and we headed for an Explorers' Club meeting. When we arrived, we heard Kania, one of the members of the club, excitedly telling everyone about the tour that she and her boyfriend, Barus, were going to take with seven other people. They would be gone for several days and would cover the entire coast of the Mediterranean. Her blond hair bounced as she enthusiastically shared her hopes of learning new words from the different people that she would meet. Kania was a firm believer in learning languages by fully immersing one's self in the culture.

"We're going sailing on a 55-foot yacht!" she exclaimed. "It's owned by a man who just joined the club and has a fiberglass hull and the latest in navigational systems. It will be soooo comfortable. I can't wait to explore and get to know people outside my own race."

Someone turned on some music and most of the members started to dance, but Krill sat in a corner brooding. I could tell he resented that others would have the chance to taste the adventure and danger that he wanted so badly.

A couple of weeks later, Krill invited me to another meeting of the Explorers' Club to hear about Barus and Kania's recent journey. They showed slides and told everyone how they had landed on the beach near the Pillars of Hercules, then hiked north for five days before they realized their navigational device was malfunctioning.

"We were beyond the protective range of any Atlantean base and utterly on our own," Kania reported. "It forced us to rely on our training to survive. What started as a five-day journey turned into a three-week trek. Every day, we had to learn new words in foreign languages and dialects so we could communicate enough to get food and shelter from the tribes that live in the area."

Barus added, "We were lucky that the people we came across were hunter-gatherers. If we had been any farther north, we would have been in the middle of the warlike, nomadic tribes. We didn't want to think about the reception we might have received from them."

As the presentation droned on, I saw Krill starting to nod off. Then Crom leaned over and whispered, "Krill, I think it would be much better if we went on a trip by ourselves instead of going with a tour group. I hate feeling like a bunch of cattle."

Krill's eyes flew open. "Yeah, I agree. Besides, I'd rather go to the gray areas of the map that are marked 'unexplored.'"

"There's plenty of them," exclaimed Crom.

"We'll go places where no Atlantean has ever been!"

"Except for the FCVs," Crom said pessimistically.

"I don't think even the FCVs have been where we're going," Krill asserted.

It was fun listening to Krill and Crom and their bold plans.

Crom continued, "We'll have to travel on foot. It's the only way for us to gain recognition for the discoveries we'll make."

"That right," Krill agreed. The National Geographic Society doesn't give full credit for travel made with FCVs. That's one of the best rules they have!"

"It's also easier to walk up and meet someone instead of making your first impression by buzzing by them in an FCV."

"I want friendship, not worship," said Krill.

Crom plucked at his shirt. "We'll leave our clothes behind and wear animal skins and carry a spear. Or maybe bows and arrows! And we won't take our pistols or radios with us."

Krill got caught up in the excitement, "And we can use animal skins to disguise our backpacks!"

"All we would need are our sleeping bags, mini-tent, tools, and a medicine kit," declared Crom.

"Yeah, and our knives and canteens," said Krill, completing the list.

Crom spoke soberly, "Krill, we have to prove that haven't lost our innate abilities to survive. We have to show others that modern life doesn't have to kill our natural instincts."

"You're right! Let's do it!"

I couldn't help but smile as I enjoyed the eagerness that was passing between my two friends.

"Where should we go?" Crow asked. "I've always wanted to explore the warm areas along the Mediterranean, beyond the Pillars of Hercules. We could travel on towards the Atlantis base on the Island of Tremors. There's a beautiful village there. We could have a blast!"

"Hey! I know that village," I exclaimed. "It is called Thera. It's where I'm from and I agree it's a beautiful area."

"That sounds great," said Krill, "It will be the ideal place for us to make our discoveries. The weather in the Northern Territories doesn't agree with the Atlanteans so they never go there. Besides, I've wanted to explore that area for at least five years."

"Hmmmm ... and have you heard about the women along the Mediterranean?" asked Crom with a twinkle in his eye.

"Yeah, yeah, I know. But Crom, there are beautiful women all over Atlantis. I want something new. I want adventure. I want danger!"

The two of them talked some more about where to go, but were unable to reach a unanimous decision. Finally Krill presented Crom with a challenge, "Let's each go our separate ways and when we return, we'll see who had the greatest adventure." Crom agreed.

Krill set out to plan his journey. He located some friends who were planning to go ice diving among the icebergs and they offered to drop him off along the northern coast. Their plans were to camp for about three days and then head for the ice packs. Krill would be taking a different route.

Two weeks later, I said goodbye to Krill as he set sail with his friends. Crom would be leaving on a merchant liner heading for the Pillars of Hercules in another week. By then, Krill would have already reached his point of departure.

When Krill returned, he shared his adventure with me. Here is
## KRILL'S ACCOUNT OF HIS ADVENTURE.
The first leg of the trip was uneventful. Different members of the crew took turns at the rudder. There was plenty of leisure time for listening to music, fishing, and reading. The skipper gave lessons to those who were interested on how to orient themselves using celestial navigation. I learned how to use a sextant, a skill I knew would come in handy when I landed. I'd be able to find my

position at night by looking at the polar star and during the day by looking at the position of the sun.

A week after departing from Atlantis, the sailboat arrived at a primitive port with no village. I said goodbye to my friends on the boat, then headed north along the coast. It was pretty exciting to know that I was finally on my own.

Just before nightfall, about 500 feet from the shoreline, I set up my tent, built a small fire, sat down on a nearby log, and started writing in my diary.

## THE DIARY

Day 1: Everything went smoothly today. I found a nice spot along the beach to spend the night. I didn't see a living soul all day. After eating, I sat on a log for awhile and stared out at the ocean and thought about how long the trip will take me. I'm going to hike all the way to the Atlantis Air Base on the edge of the polar ice cap.

Day 2: I got a great night's sleep last night. This morning I packed up my belongings and stuffed them into my backpack. It took awhile to get everything to fit because nothing ever goes in the same way it comes out. When I finally got underway, I was a little panicked when I couldn't find any of the trails that were so neatly drawn on my maps. Everything was completely overgrown with plant life. It made the woods seem very dark and foreboding. But I'm on my own. At last. I'm going to experience the danger and adventure I've been wanting ... even if it is more than I had originally planned. I thought about Barus and Kania and how they had lost their way under even better conditions than what I was facing.

All through the day, I had to frequently check my compass since the sky was cloudy and I was unable to check by position of the sun. Thank goodness, I was able to confirm my position by the stars when night came.

Where will I go tomorrow? The maps I brought aren't very detailed. I should have brought some aerial maps. The ones I have only show a few rivers, forests, plains, and hills ... and the scale is far too large to help me on my walk. If I continue to follow the same direction all the map shows are a couple of streams for reference. How am I going to keep from getting lost? Perhaps I should have been better prepared.

Day 3: I awoke to the sounds of dogs barking way off in the distance. It was so dense in the forest, I couldn't tell how far away they were and the sound seemed to bounce off the trees so I couldn't even determine the direction. My biggest and most immediate concern was that the dogs might smell my food and come after it ... or me! I had no way of knowing if they were wild dogs or not. I quickly ate my breakfast, packed my gear, and set off. I decided to leave a few morsels of food for the dogs to fight over while I made my escape.

Before long I came to a clearing and saw a house a few yards ahead with a pen full of sheep. I wondered if the sheep were what the dogs were barking at. Maybe they routinely raided this pen. I worried that the owners might mistake me for a dog so I stayed out of sight and inched my way closer.

I jumped as I heard a noise behind me. It was very close. I slowly turned and could see the bushes moving a few feet away. I reached behind me and retrieved an arrow with a razor sharp steel tip. I knocked it on my bow and gingerly stepped backwards, pacing myself so as not to fall and impale myself with my own arrow. I froze as a twig broke under my foot.

Whatever I heard was moving closer. I took another step back and realized I was up against a tree. I felt the chill of sweat and my fingers were slippery as they pulled back on the bowstring. I worried that I might release too early and not have time to rearm. The sound was getting closer. All too soon I would face my opponent. Then a small fox trotted out from the brush with a hare in his mouth. I let out a deep sigh as I derided myself for being so afraid.

I finally reached the end of the forest. Unfortunately, I had also reached the end of the map. From here on, I knew I would have to rely on my instincts. Unlike my colleagues, I would now become a true explorer.

I never again heard the dogs. In the afternoon, I came across a trail of human footprints. Not knowing who they might belong to and wishing to avoid contact, I changed direction. All the walking was making me very hungry so I started looking for a good place to hunt and a safe place to camp for the night. I found a small rise, put an arrow in my bow, and waited. After sitting very still for several minutes, I saw a rabbit poke its head up from its underground home. Still I waited. The rabbit wiggled out of its hole and looked around. I waited an instant longer to make sure that it was comfortable with me being in its field of vision and then I let my arrow fly. The rabbit never knew what hit it -- which is just what I had hoped for. I walked over and thanked the spirit of the rabbit for allowing me to take it for my dinner. It was a very good dinner!

Day 4: I awoke when the first rays of sunshine hit my face like a warm slap. I was now traveling through grasslands and the pollen made me sneeze almost continuously. But at least I could see farther and would know if any danger approached.

Around midday, the weather started deteriorating. The billowing white cumulus clouds quickly darkened and threatened rain. In the distance, I spotted some low hills and made my way towards them. I managed to find some cover and pitch my tent before the rains came. The hours passed slowly as the wind howled and roared and torrents of rain battered against my flimsy quarters. Thank goodness I had made sure it was securely fastened to the ground. All I could do now is wait. At least there was some consolation in knowing that predators were also waiting for the storm to pass.

I feel pleased with myself. My training from the Explorers' Club is proving most useful. I'm still alive and doing quite well under the circumstances.

Day 5: The wind was so strong last night that I couldn't sleep. I was certain it was going to blow away my tent. The lightning and thunder also kept me awake. It was so close, it was scary. Thankfully, about sunrise the storm finally eased up and I was able to fall asleep. I didn't get up until noon. I made some tea and decided that this was a good location. I think I'll stay here for a couple of days.

Day 6: I shot a deer today. It was not more than 100 feet away when I shot it, but I had to stalk it forever, approaching it one step at a time and remaining absolutely motionless for several minutes between each step. I was lucky and my arrow pierced it right in the heart so it only ran a few yards before it died. I butchered some of the meat and left the rest there. I had plenty to eat for dinner and even had some left over to take with me.

Day 9: I passed a small village today. The houses were rock and mud with roofs made of straw and grass. Nearby, I saw mammoths grazing so I decided not to stop. Sometimes these creatures have bad tempers.

Two days ago, I knew I had reached the land of the Alpernians because I saw a human skeleton pierced with spears and tied to a tree. I remember reading an article in the Atlantis Geographic magazine that the people in this area believe that being a brave hero and great warrior got them a seat in Valhalla, the warriors' hall, after they die. To them, dying a warrior's death is their door to immortality. This has made them bloodthirsty fighters for ages. Grandfather told me he used to visit this region often when he was young and single because he was impressed with the beauty of the Alpernian women. Fortunately for him, the natives thought he was the god Odin.

Day 11: I feel my body getting stronger living in the outdoors. I'm able to walk faster, farther, and longer each day. Last night, I heard a pack of wolves howling nearby. I lit a fire to keep them away. I'm tired today after keeping the fire going all night. I still need to hunt. I've run out of provisions. Game has been scarce here, but I still have to eat. I'm really very hungry. One of mom's home-cooked dinners would really taste good right now. I'm also still in danger here. I have several more days to hike before I'll reach the northern Atlantis air base.

Day 16: This morning I was abruptly awakened when someone kicked in my tent … and my ribs in the process. Before I could react, four big natives dressed in sheep and goatskins grabbed me and dragged me outside. I was quite sure there were Alpernian hunters. They rummaged through my belongings and divided everything among them. Fortunately, this diary was in my pocket.

Pointing their fingers and motioning, they made it very clear that I was to march in a certain direction. If I even hesitated for a moment, they poked my shoulders with their long spears. I began to feel blood dripping down my back. Before long, we arrived at their village and everyone came out to look at the new prisoner -- me! My captors took me to their chief, who was surrounded by four chained wolves. They shoved me forward to stand in front of him and I promptly fainted from hunger, loss of blood, and exhaustion.

When I woke up, I was lying on a hard bed of logs. I had been stripped and wrapped in a blanket of skins. I could see my clothing hanging on a nearby rope. Apparently it had been washed as it was dripping water. The room was dark and I was not fully alert, but I felt someone move the blanket off my back and begin to treat my wounds. I lay very still until the person moved away. When I raised up to look around, I saw that a clay bowl of hot soup had been left for me. It tasted wonderful after so long without eating.

Day 17: Today a man, woman, and boy came into the room where I was being held. I pulled the blanket of skins around me as I glanced towards where my clothes had been. They were gone. Behind the family was another person, out of my line of vision, but I sensed this might be the person who treated my wounds. I rolled over to get a better look. At that moment, she walked across a shaft of sunlight that was shining through the open door. What I saw was one of the most beautiful girls I have ever seen--more beautiful than any girl on Atlantis. She had blonde hair and deep blue eyes--and the most heavenly smile. She looked like a golden-haired angel that I had once seen painted on a mural in a church in Brasea. I remembered thinking when I had first seen the image that I would search the world for a girl who looked like this angel. And here was the girl!

As she approached me, I asked, "Am I dead? Are you an angel?" She answered me, but in a language I couldn't understand. Nevertheless, even if we couldn't communicate, I knew I was in love. But then other thoughts interrupted my daydreams. Why was I here? Was I going to be used as a sacrifice? Or perhaps a slave?

Day 20: I'm completely recovered now and nothing bad has happened to me. I spent the day with the lovely daughter of the family who nursed me back to health. I still don't know her name, but we're trying to learn each other's language. We spend a lot of time laughing and smiling at each other.

She brought me some seeds to eat. I ate a few and then went outside and planted the rest of them. She looked at me with confusion before I realized her people were hunter-gatherers and didn't know about agriculture.

Her father is a good man. He recovered my belongings and my clothes from the warriors. I'm very grateful as I did not want to walk around naked in front of this exquisite girl.

Day 21: Today my gorgeous friend taught me her name. It is Meya. What a beautiful name. Meya. Meya. I want to write it again and again. I'm learning more of her language every day.

Day 22: Today I got to leave my quarters and go for a walk with Meya. We went to the hills around her village and gathered wild fruit and roots. She was very playful, running ahead and hiding behind trees, then jumping out to scare me. As we walked through a stream, we began splashing water on each other and before long, it turned into a real water fight. Meya is so great.

In the afternoon, I helped Meya herd the family sheep and reindeer to the fields to graze. Then we went back to where I had planted the seeds and watered them. We are communicating better and better each day. Today I held her hand. I was nervous, but she didn't pull away. I can tell the other boys in the village are jealous of me.

Day 25: Meya's brother feels that I should try to escape from the village and run away. He said the hunting and fishing hasn't been good for several days and some of the tribe members think it's because of me. Although I couldn't understand everything that Meya's brother was telling me, I picked up enough to know that the village offers human sacrifices to pacify the gods when things aren't going well. I could tell that he and Meya were very upset.

Meya explained that sacrifices are done one of two ways. Sometimes the person is thrown into a pit of wolves. Other times the tribe butchers the individual on a sacrificial altar. I could see panic in Meya's eyes. Ever though the thought of being sacrificed was completely terrifying, my heart swelled because I knew that Meya cared about me. How could I die now? I had found the girl of my dreams. I decided I would escape and take her with me. But how could I do that? All I had was a sleeping bag and a one-person tent. How would I provide for her?

Day 27: This morning, three men stormed into my room and grabbed me. They took me before the tribal chief. Thank goodness I didn't faint this time. Although I could barely understand what was happening, I knew it wasn't good. It was pretty obvious, even to me, that the chief was going to have me sacrificed to the gods. I had to think fast. Meya was there and I had her tell the chief I had magic that I would share with him and his people. He was reluctant, but finally agreed to give me a chance to show him what I could do. I knew I had to be good. My magic was going to be the art of cultivation.

I started building a plow that would be pulled by two oxen. I modeled it after the ones I had seen in the museum in Brasea. I knew I had to work fast because they could come for me at any time. My nerves were a wreck, but I was certain I would have it finished by tomorrow.

Day 28: The plow is finished! I made it with two tree sticks. The short one will be used as a tow bar that is held to the long bar with leather thongs. The rear end of the long stick has a natural bend that will act like a hook to open up a ditch in the ground. The chief provided two bulls for my demonstration; however, they didn't like what was going on because they had not done anything like this before.

I showed the chief the plants I already had growing. Meya swore that I made the plants grow at my command. Thank goodness for Meya! If it hadn't been for her, I might be fertilizing the plants instead of writing this in my diary. Now everybody in the village thinks I can sprout anything from the ground, so I'm off the hook for now. I wonder about the bulls, though. Will they be tame enough to use later?

Oh! I almost forgot. Meya was able to convince the chief to return my bow and arrows. She has been a real lifesaver.

Day 30: Meya and I went to get water from the stream and sat and talked for quite awhile. I've learned about 30 words of her language. Her dreams are so simple. She wants a larger, more comfortable home. She wants two pretty puppies and a kitten. She wants protection from the wolves for her family and their sheep. She wants some magic arrows and a magic bow like mine so that her father and brother will have the only steel arrowheads in the land. She also wants a bracelet and necklace like the chief's daughter wears. I told her that enjoying nature, being able to travel, and meeting her has brought me more satisfaction than great wealth. She blushed and smiled shyly at me.

We held hands and watched the clouds. Meya said she had always dreamed of flying like a bird so she could swoop and play over the hills and soar though the canyons. I shared with her how I've always wanted to be an eagle, floating and circling on the thermal air currents and looking down at everything far below.

Overhead, we saw a long, white wake of an Atlantis aircraft. Meya thought it was Odin. I tried to explain that it was just an airplane and the god Odin was my eccentric grandfather, Godin. Meya angrily told me she didn't appreciate my disrespect for her gods. I reached up and ran my fingers through her golden hair and told her how beautiful she was and how I was so glad I had met her. She immediately calmed down. And then I kissed her! It was wonderful.

Day 31: A hunting party left the village today with a big send-off. It was a break for me because most of the party was made up of the guys in the village who are jealous of me being with Meya. The chief's son, who's the most jealous of all, led the hunt. Ha!

Day 32: Today I told Meya how much I love her. She is so sweet, so pure, so innocent, not at all like the girls in Atlantis. They're all too modern and practical. Every time I look at her lovely blue eyes, I feel something stirring deep inside of me. Just hearing her voice makes my heart leap. I told her I wanted to take her back to Atlantis with me.

I'm writing this with sadness because Meya told me her parents would never agree to let her leave. They believe that over the horizon from their village there is a land of demons, cannibals, and other horrors. In a way, they're right. There are tribes outside the village that aren't too friendly. But once we got past them, things would be different. Of course, her parents would never understand this.

Day 33: I overheard Meya's father and mother talking to her about marrying the son of the chief! It seems the chief helped the family when they lost everything during a recent storm. Also, the chief is rich and could give Meya a good life. Meya told her parents that she didn't love the chief's son.

Later, I talked to Meya alone. I tried to tell her not to marry someone that she doesn't love. This was when she looked straight into my eyes and told me she loved me! Me! She loves me! I love her and she loves me back!

Day 35: The hunting party returned today. There was great rejoicing in the village because the party was successful, bringing back several animals to be butchered and skinned. They also brought back new prisoners to be used as slaves … or as sacrifices to the gods.

Later on in the evening, there was a big party. Two reindeer were roasted in pits and served with a fermented beverage that I decided not to drink. But the chief's son drank it and got very drunk. He started chasing Meya and tried to drag her into his hut. I knew what he was after and I exploded. I went after the beast and socked him hard across his jaw. I guess because he was so drunk, it didn't seem to faze him and he slammed me into the wall. We wrestled on the ground for several minutes, but the fiend finally got tired and passed out. Meya was able to escape while we were fighting.

Day 36: The chief's son questioned Meya about me. He really hates me after what happened last night. Of course, he didn't like me all that much before. He told Meya that I was a spy for enemy tribes. Meya argued that I was an explorer from another land and pointed out that I didn't look anything like the people in the area, but the son wasn't convinced. Then he accused me of being in love with her. Is it that obvious? How grand! I want the whole world to know that I love her!

But I must be careful. I'm in a dangerous situation here. I can't put the woman I love in more peril than she already is by betraying my feelings. I must protect her at all costs.

Day 50: Meya told me that the chief's son was planning to accuse me of being a spy from the enemy tribe to the south. I guess he wants me dead so he can marry Meya. Just the thought of him touching her makes me want to kill him! But I know that according to Atlantean regulations, I cannot disturb the flow of progress in this primitive society. It would probably be better for everyone if I just escape and go back home.

But I don't care about regulations! I want to be with Meya. I want to take her with me. And I know she wants to go with me, even without her parent's permission. How my heart sang when she told me that. But what can I do? Logically, I know it would be too dangerous for her. Better that I leave her here.

I have a plan. I know the chief's son cannot touch her until after their marriage, so I will leave and come back for her.

I spent the rest of the day getting ready to leave and continue my journey towards Atlantis Base North.

Day 51: It was very hard to tell Meya that I am leaving. As I held her close, she told me that her family had sealed the agreement to give her to the chief's son in marriage and that they don't want me to come around her anymore. The ceremony has been set for two full moons from now. I must come back for the woman I love within that time or that monster will have the right to defile her in unspeakable ways.

When I explained to Meya where I was going, she thought I was going to the temple of the gods where the shining birds lived. I realized she couldn't understand because she had never been beyond the village boundaries. I told her I would be back to get her, but she thinks I am poor and she will never see me again. She is resigned to her fate because the alliance will bring wealth to her family. I must prove my love for her and return in time to save her from marrying the despicable son of the chief.

Day 52: Before dawn this morning, while the people were still sleeping, I left the village. I hiked all day. I miss Meya more than I could ever imagine.

Day 54: Last night I checked my course by the stars. I seem to be going in the right direction to the base. As far as I can tell, I should reach it in three more days if I keep up my current pace. I've been making pretty good time so far. I sometimes wonder if the chief's son arranged for a war party to hunt me down. I'd rather not find out.

Day 57: It's been cloudy for the past three nights so I haven't been able to check the stars. This afternoon I reached the spot where I thought the Atlantis base would be. All I found was an empty plain. I'm tired, discouraged and worried. What will I do if I can't find the base?

I decided to camp here tonight and try to decide what to do in the morning when my head is clear. I regret now that I didn't bring a radio transmitter with me. I can't help but think how my parents must feel. They've probably given me up for lost. What about Meya? If I don't return for her in time … I don't want to think about that.

Day 58: Finally -- Atlantis Base North! After it got dark last night I was able to see the glow of its lights on the eastern horizon. I couldn't walk fast enough across the flat plain to the outpost. A guard stopped me when I reached the fence. After I explained that I was from Atlantis, he let me pass. Once inside, I relaxed and thought how good it was to be in a modern and comfortable base like this. Especially one made from steel that keeps everyone safe.

The commander of the base welcomed me and I called my parents to let them know I had made it. I could tell my father was very proud of me. My mother was relieved. The rest of the day I spent eating and sleeping in comfort. It was quite a change from life in the village.

Day 59: Today, between meals and naps, I went to the recreation room and played games with off-duty personnel. One of the men stationed at the base told me I was very lucky I didn't stop at any of the villages that I saw along the way. He said they don't like outsiders and I probably would have been killed.

How I miss Meya. I want so much to look into her warm blue eyes, run my fingers through her lovely, soft hair, and touch her smooth skin. I must get back to her in time.

Day 60: Today I head for home. It will be wonderful to see my family and friends again. But my heart is broken because Meya isn't with me. I must start planning now how to save her.

**\* \* \* \* \* \* \* \***

When Krill arrived in Atlantis, I went with his family to meet him. His grandfather accompanied us. As soon as Krill saw him, he exclaimed, "Grandad! You're going to laugh at what I have to tell you. I was in Valhalla -- the same area you used to land in with your helicopter when you were young. Do you remember how you told the people you were a god? Well, they still think you are, only now they mispronounce your name and call you God Odin." Everyone laughed.

After a couple of days of resting, Krill invited Crom and I to his grandfather's mansion to spend the afternoon and share stories of their travels. As we walked across the mansion lawn, Krill came out to meet us. The two friends hugged each other and both began talking at once.

"It's great to see you," said Crom. "How did you survive the cold and snow in the Northern Territories?"

"I survived by my wits. It's a great story. How about you? How was your trip to the desert?"

"You'll never guess what happened," said Crom. "I ended up going on a tour with some members of the club in a quick ship. We visited a few villages and returned to Atlantis practically as fast as we had left. It really wasn't much of an adventure. I spend most of the time you were gone at home relaxing. But … I did meet the most beautiful woman in the world on the trip. She's a new member of the Explorers' Club and has the most fascinating cat eyes."

Krill rose to the challenge. "Sorry, but I met the most beautiful girl in the world. Her name is Meya and she has hair that shines like pure gold and eyes that are bluer than the deepest sea."

I listened while my two friends compared their new girlfriends, their travel ordeals, and their accomplishments.

A few days later, Krill made a presentation to the club. The members were all quite impressed by his feats. However, when the girls learned he had given his heart to a primitive native woman, they became very upset.

"How could you be so stupid as to fall in love with a girl from a barbarian world," one complained. "What's wrong with the women of Atlantis?"

Another girl added, "Don't you know that Atlantean women are the best women for Atlantean men?"

Krill replied, "When a girl from the outside world loves you, it's real love. It's not tainted by any other conditions. This is the kind of girl I've always looked for."

The girls at the club weren't the only ones that thought Krill was wrong for having a girlfriend outside of Atlantis. On the first night he was home, I was asked to join the family for dinner. When Krill announced he was in love with Meya, every member of the family turned and looked at him.

His father sternly pointed out that Atlanteans were the greatest builders and designers of the world. "You can't possibly ignore that we are one day going to reach the stars and become the great protectors of Earth and the solar system."

His mother was aghast and exclaimed, "You can't choose an outsider. We're the descendants of Poseidon and Cleito, not from Adam and Eva. Even though Poseidon and Adam were cousins, we must maintain the purity of our race. Go back with your former girlfriend or find another Atlantean woman."

Then Godin chimed in, "On the contrary, I agree with my grandson. In my humble opinion, foreign girls make good wives." He gave Krill a sly wink and added, "When we're through eating, I'll tell you some stories of my youth."

After dinner, Godin, Krill, and I moved into the living room. As we settled ourselves into the richly upholstered living room furniture, we saw Crom drive up to the mansion in his flashy car. He quickly crossed the splendid gardens and bounded onto the porch, pausing at the wide, carved doorway.

Krill called out, "Come on in, Crom."

As Crom entered the room, Krill said, "Grandpa was just going to tell me about when he was young and in love with a foreign girl."

"Yes," Godin confirmed. "It was when I worked at Drago designing robots, long before I won the Atlas prize for engineering. I remember we had one model that looked like a giant insect. The natives called it The Scorpion and were terribly frightened by it. Another one was bipedal and looked like a giant ape. We used these for construction. We also built submarines that we used to explore the bottom of the ocean." He chuckled as he continued, "Over the past 30 years, these robots have given rise to all kinds of legends among the local primitives."

"Grandpa!" Krill exclaimed. "You were going to tell us about the foreign girlfriend."

"Yes, yes. I'm getting to that. Anyway, did you know that I used robots to build this mansion? I designed it to look like a ship being pulled out of the bay by the statue of Poseidon. Machines that I designed also carved the statues. I built this mansion as a shelter for a woman who, at the time, existed only in my dreams."

Crom interrupted, "Why do the primitives call you Odin, God of all Gods?"

"Ahhh, yes. I suppose it was wrong for me to encourage that. But it's not our fault that other people in the world consider us as gods. It's most likely the only way they can describe us since Atlantis is so much more advanced than any other country. As for the name, I suppose that since they thought I was a god, to them I was God Odin." He paused as he reminisced. "Some of the tribes invented some very elaborate myths about me. That's why I can no longer travel to those regions. I'm not a god and it is no longer amusing to me to be considered one." He shook his head. "I shouldn't have led them on so."

"But grandpa--what about the girlfriend?" prompted Krill.

"Oh, yes. Well, I was very successful when I was a young engineer. I loved to throw parties here at the mansion. When guests came, they were always impressed by all the opulence, especially the young women. They saw me as an eligible bachelor. What they didn't know is that I had given my heart to a beautiful, auburn-haired woman I had met on an adventure similar to yours, Krill. I promised to go back for her, but my work kept me too busy. I feel very bad that I had to break my promise." His aged eyes wandered about the room.

We were all very intrigued and eagerly waited to hear his next words.

"I wanted to build a special transportation device that I had imagined. It was a winged horse that could run like the wind and soar through the clouds. I began secretly building it in the basement. It was to be the vehicle that I would use to abduct my beauty and take her away from her fierce tribal people." He sighed deeply, then continued. "When the horse was half finished, I got sidetracked. I met a girl in a snack shop. She was an artist and musician and I found myself quite attracted. I ended up marrying her and never went back for my first love."

"Wow! I never knew about all this," said Krill, fascinated by his grandfather's romantic side.

Godin's spirits seemed to pick up as he went on with his story. "I did go ahead and finish the winged horse, even though I no longer had a mission for it. It's the only one of its kind. I remember when I made my first test flight. I flew up the coast and circled over a boat loading laborers returning to their homelands. I decided to land nearby, but as soon as I touched ground, the laborers all fell on their knees and started praying. One of them shouted and asked if I was a god from heaven. I told him no, I was just an ordinary man and my name was Godin.

Then I galloped down the beach and flew away." Godin's eyes twinkled as he remembered this excursion.

"Anyway, since I had already married an Atlantean woman, it was no longer important for me to return to my love. I became very involved in my work and her memory slowly faded away. And now the horse is stored away. I'm too old for such things now."

Then Godin put his hand on Krill's shoulder. "I'm giving you the greatest gift possible. I'm giving you my flying horse."

Krill's eyes lighted up with excitement.

"The horse carries two people, Krill. Make your dreams your reality. When do you want to start your flying lessons?"

"Gee, Grandpa, I can't wait. Let's start tomorrow morning! I never knew you had a mechanical horse. Can we see it now?"

"Of course," said Godin. "It's stored in my basement workshop. It's been covered with canvas since that first test flight."

We all got up and descended the stairway leading to the basement. The horse was in perfect condition. It was shiny and clean, as if it were built only yesterday. Krill could barely contain his excitement.

Over the next few days, Crom and I watched Krill as he learned to fly and effortlessly maneuver the flying horse by himself. Upon landing after his first solo flight, Krill told Godin that it felt like he had descended from the heavens. "This is the best thing you've ever created, grandpa. It's truly an engineering masterpiece."

We could tell Godin was very flattered. Then he said, "Tomorrow all the family is going on vacation for several days to the Isle of the Sun. You will be in charge of the mansion. Don't forget to lock it if you go to Europe again." He winked and smiled broadly at Krill.

At that moment, my uncle Luzaire (the Wizard) walked up to where we were standing. "Come with me, Kappa. You can stay at my home while the family is on vacation." As we walked towards his house, he asked how I was doing in school. I told him I had already learned how to read. He smiled, put his arm around me, and patted me on my shoulder.

A few days later, Krill left in the flying machine to rescue Meya. This is the story he told us when he returned.

********

After I left Meya, her parents went ahead with the arrangements for her to marry the chief's son. It was a difficult time for her because she longed to be with me, and besides, she was afraid of the son. He was known to be violent and cruel. She said she was sad and melancholy all the time and spoke little to anyone.

One day she took her parents' sheep to a new pasture that was far from the ranch. She said she was enjoying the sunshine and gathering wild flowers. She even said she wrote a song about me that told how handsome and strong I was!

But then the chief's son appeared. Somehow he had found her. He got very rough with her and tried to pull her close to him. She screamed and kicked, but the beast just laughed at her. Finally she was able to writhe away from his grasp, picked up a sharp stick from the ground, and stabbed him in the neck and arms. He was furious!

He called her a bitch and slapped her so hard she fell to the ground. He told her she would pay for what she'd done. Her dog must have sensed something was wrong because he came running from the far side of the flock and immediately lunged at the brute's face, biting him on the shoulder.

Fortunately, he decided not to fight both of them and retreated. He shouted back at Meya that one day soon she would be his and then he would do as he wanted with her. Meya said she hugged her dog and prayed that I would return soon.

The next day, while Meya was again watching the sheep, the chief's son came up to her, the scratches and cuts clearly visible. Meya pulled her dog close in case she again needed protection. She said the dog growled and the hair on his back stood up as the son drew close. What happened next makes me sick to my stomach even to this day. Before she even realized what was happening, the monster knocked an arrow to his bow, aimed, and shot directly at the dog. The poor mutt yelped, then fell dead with a plaintive whimper.

Meya was in shock. She began to weep for her best friend, but even as she did so she knew the same fate could be hers if she wasn't careful.

It was then that I showed up. Of course when they saw the winged horse, they thought I was a god. I could see the chief's son moving towards the forest, panic written all over his face. But Meya stood very still. She said later that she would rather face one of the gods than to have to marry that tyrant.

I cleared a landing space by clearing away the brush with my laser, then circled down and gently landed near Meya. I dismounted and walked over to her. Her eyes were wide as she asked me, "Are you a demon or a god?"

As I removed my helmet, I replied, "Neither." Meya was still looking at me with terror in her eyes.

"Don't you recognize me, Meya? I'm Krill. I've come back for you. I've returned for the love of my life just as I said I would." Meya started weeping and fell into my arms.

It felt so wonderful to hold her close again. I kissed her hair, I kissed her face, and I kissed her soft lips again and again. I didn't realized how terribly I had missed her. "I thought about you constantly, Meya. I'm so happy to be with you again."

My heart soared as she reaffirmed her love for me.

We sorrowfully buried Meya's dog and then sat down to rest on the soft grass. We shared everything that had happened to us while we'd been apart. I was concerned that the chief's son might have abused her. She said he hadn't but he had become more and more aggressive over the last few weeks.

I couldn't contain myself any longer. "Meya, my love, I want to be with you forever. Will you marry me?"

"Oh Krill! I love you so much. How can I say anything but 'yes, yes, yes!'" I wrapped her in my arms and we sat there for a long time, enjoying the warmth of our bodies as we clung to each other.

After several minutes, Meya's attention was drawn to the winged horse and she asked, "Is that a toy or an animal? It looks like a horse, but it's the strangest thing I've ever seen. Would it be all right for me to sit on it?"

I helped her climb up on the tall horse. She looked so innocent and pure as she sat on the gold and white winged creature. Every part of my being quivered as I stood there, gazing at her lovely face. Finally, I urged her to get down and take the flock home so we could tell her parents of our plans.

After Meya left, I checked everything on the winged horse to be sure all was in order, replaced my helmet, then lifted up and flew towards the village. As I circled above Meya's house, every living being in the village came out to see this strange flying object. The animals all scattered and hid. The natives held each other in fear.

When I landed near Meya's hut, the people all bowed down in awe … except Meya. She came over to me, took my hand, and led me to her parents. Removing my helmet, her parents quickly recognized me and greeted me warmly.

Her father shook his head in amazement, "We thought you were poor. We do not understand."

I couldn't wait a minute longer and I blurted out, "I want to marry your daughter."

Her mother quickly responded and said, "Oh no, we need her to tend our flocks and help with the work. We are very poor."

I walked over to the winged horse, removed two bags, and presented them to Meya's parents. "Here are some bows and arrows, cooking pots, knives, and axes -- all made from steel. You won't be poor any longer. Now you are wealthier than the chief. All I want in return is your blessing. I will take your daughter to my people and she will live like a queen in a large, beautiful home."

Meya's father studied me for several minutes, then pointed to my laser. "I would also like to have that."

"Impossible," I told him. "This is a laser weapon," and I shot the trunk of a small tree. It exploded and everyone ran in all directions, including the chief and his son who had been quietly moving towards Meya.

Meya's father looked at me in wonderment, then he said, "We love our daughter and we want what's best for her. I see the glow in her face as she looks at you and I know there is love in her heart. You have our blessings."

My heart was beating so hard, I thought surely my whole body was shaking. I turned to Meya and said, "I have a gift for you." I walked to the horse and pulled a package from the saddlebags. "This is something that will protect you from the wind and the rain while we travel to my land."

Meya's eyes widened with delight. She reached for the package and opened it excitedly. She gasped as she pulled out a shiny blue jumpsuit that was identical to mine. She rubbed it against her face. "Ohhhh, it is so soft."

"It will keep you warm at the high altitudes where we must fly. Now go try it on."

Meya turned and ran into her family's hut. In a few moments, she returned, transformed into the most radiant beauty I've ever seen. The jumpsuit fit her like a glove and I could barely contain my passion. She was so lovely. Like a princess. And I was her prince who had come to take her to my castle.

"Let us slaughter a sheep!" Meya's father exclaimed. "We will have a farewell feast to wish my daughter eternal happiness and joy."

The natives quickly set about preparing food for the celebration, and the banquet lasted far into the night. I enjoyed the lavish feast, but most of the time I was kissing and hugging my lovely bride-to-be. Finally, everyone disbursed and a place was made for me to sleep in the family hut.

The next morning, everyone slept late. After breakfast, Meya's mother prepared food and beverages for us to take on our journey. The family hugged and kissed goodbye. Then we all went out to the mechanical horse.

We climbed in and I started the horse running in preparation to take off. Meya laughed and giggled as the wings spread and we lifted from the ground. I circled above the tribe so she could wave goodbye to her family one more time. The primitives were staring at us in awe. I felt certain they thought I was a god.

Traveling low so Meya would be able to have a final look at her homeland, I watched her golden hair blow and swirl around her lovely face. Her blue eyes glittered with happiness. Suddenly she cried out, "Oh look! There is the village of our enemy. Kill them with your magic weapon."

"No, no, Meya. Violence is wrong. War is caused by lack of understanding. We must not harm others just because we don't like them. When we get to Atlantis, you will learn more peaceful ways of living."

After leaving the primitive areas behind, I maneuvered the flying horse high into the sky, playfully soaring in and out of the clouds. Then I showed off a little and swooped down to a plain where some deer were grazing. Of course, they immediately scattered and we both laughed. I skimmed just above a stream and the horse's hooves splashed in the water. Meya giggled gleefully and said, "This is the most wonderful thing that has ever happened to me."

I couldn't help thinking how limited her world had been … and how different she would find Atlantis. But I knew that it wouldn't take long for her to adapt. She was a fast learner. I was overjoyed that she had come to love me and trust me.

Overhead I saw some sea gulls and swooped up to chase them. They scattered in all directions, startled and confused. Meya cried out, "Oh! We're flying higher than the birds. And look … the ground is all covered with weeds."

I smiled and replied, "No, those aren't weeds, my love. Those are trees. They just look like weeds because we're up so high. You're not afraid, are you?"

She snuggled closer, hugging my waist, and putting her lips to my ear, "Not when I'm with you, my prince."

"And you are my princess, Meya."

"You spoil me, Krill. And I love it!" She paused a moment and then asked, "By the way, doesn't your horse need a rest? Maybe we should go down and let it eat."

I almost laughed out loud, but I didn't want to make her feel bad, so I told her gently, "No, my sweet, this is really a machine. It just looks like a horse. And we can fly a long ways before we'll need to 'feed' the machine."

"When will we arrive in Atlantis?"

"It will take us two days. Tonight we'll stay at Atlantis Base104 in Tartessos, and tomorrow we'll fly across the ocean."

"What's an ocean?"

"Oh my dear, sweet Meya. You have so much to learn. An ocean is a very large body of water. It's so big that when we fly over it, you won't be able to see land in any direction. If we get to the base early enough, you'll get to see a little of it tonight."

"Oh, look at the sunset! The sky is all red and orange. I don't think I've ever seen such a glorious sunset."

"And look at the wings, Meya. The sun is making them look red as well. Doesn't it seem like we're riding on a fiery steed?"

"Krill, I have no words to describe everything I'm seeing. I wish my family could be here."

I realized that we were nearing the base, but I couldn't see any lights. I had been so taken with Meya, I wasn't paying enough attention to my flying. "Meya, we'll be landing soon. Help me look for the lights of the base."

"There they are," she said, pointing to the landing lights in the distance.

I called the traffic tower and requested permission to land my grandfather's special flying craft. The tower gave me the go-ahead and we started our descent.

"Hang on," I cautioned Meya, although I really didn't need to say anything. She had never really loosened her grip around my waist the whole trip, despite a seatbelt firmly holding her in place.

The runway stretched out in front of us with lights on either side to guide our path. The horse flew lower and lower until its hooves touched the ground with a slight bump, then it broke into a gallop. Gradually, it slowed to a trot and I folded the wings against the sides. We reached the doorway to a large building and I helped Meya dismount.

The base commander came out to greet us and looked admiringly at my passenger. "And who is this lovely lady?" he asked.

My chest swelled with pride as I introduced Meya as my future wife. She blushed and smiled sweetly at the commander.

"She seems quite happy at the prospect. You know, as base commander I'm authorized to perform weddings. Would you like to be married now?"

His idea was perfect. I preferred a small and cozy wedding instead of the gaudy and lavish affairs that were usually held in Atlantis. Besides, I wasn't sure how my parents were going to like the idea of me marrying Meya. Better to do it here and now and be done with it. I asked the commander if he was available later that evening. He said he was and suggested we finalize the rites after dinner.

Since all we'd eaten on our trip were a couple of sandwiches, his plan sounded great to us. We were both starving.

Walking towards the base dining room, I couldn't help watching Meya. She was taking everything in with child-like wonder. This was her first time to see such large, clean buildings. As we reached the door, she paused before stepping gingerly onto the tile floor. Another new experience for her.

I pulled out the chair for Meya to sit down and she immediately picked up a plate and started examining it. She ran her thumb over the fork and spoon. Then, spying the knife, she grabbed it and stowed it in the bodice of her dress. To her, a good knife was quite an asset.

"You need that to eat with," I tried to explain, but she would hear none of it. The knife was too valuable.

The server brought the soup and had no more than set her bowl down on the table when Meya picked it up and started noisily slurping the contents. When she had finished, she reached over and grabbed the bowl of the woman next to her and started gulping it down as well. The woman was flabbergasted and fixed an icy stare on Meya, who immediately responded by waving her new knife in the woman's face.

"Do you have a problem?" Meya challenged. The woman quickly looked away and returned to her meal.

Soon the meat and vegetables were served. I tried to show Meya how to cut the meat, but she wasn't interested. Instead, she grabbed the piece that was placed on her plate and started gnawing on it. She had no use for utensils. I was embarrassed, but I knew this was the way she had always eaten her food. How could I expect her to act any differently at her first civilized meal time? I shook my head in frustration and announced to the people at the dinner table, "She has much to learn."

Seeing the impression that Meya was making on the diners, the commander asked if I was certain that I wanted to marry her. I assured him that I was and the sooner the better. We finished our meal and then followed him to a small church where the décor could easily be changed for use in all kinds of religious rites, including those that were part of my beliefs. The ceremony was brief and then we retired to our sleeping quarters.

Meya was fascinated by the soft bed and bounced on it like a child until she finally grew tired. I led her into the bathroom and showed her the shower. She couldn't understand why we didn't just bathe in a waterfall like she did at her home. I explained the use of the faucets and she turned them on and off several times, marveling at the feel of the hot water.

Finally, we went to bed. I was trembling with passion. I pulled her close to me and kissed her again and again. I was dizzy with the sweet scent of her body. I ran my hands up and down the curve of her breasts and then over every part of her body. She responded by pulling me tightly to her and enfolding my body with her strong, slim legs. When I could stand it no longer, we made love.

The next morning, we arose early and packed some provisions. I fueled up the winged horse and checked the incredibly complicated mechanisms that made it fly. When I had finished my inspection, we both climbed aboard it and the mechanical steed started trotting down the runway. It quickly broke into a gallop, building up speed, but it was so heavily laden with fuel it barely had enough momentum to lift off the ground. As we headed out towards the ocean, we were only a few feet above the swells.

"Is this as high as we're going to fly?" pouted Meya.

"Only for a little while," I said and explained to her that some of the fuel had to burn off before we could climb higher. "Besides," I told her, "it gives you a chance to see the ocean close-up."

"It looks like a huge lake."

"Except that the water is salty."

At last the horse was able to gain altitude. Meya was awed that above her was blue sky and below her was nothing but blue waters. I pointed out some clouds ahead that looked like islands in the sky. "Let's try to land on the closest cloud." Meya squeezed my waist.

As we passed through the puffs of white, I told Meya to imagine we were following a white road that was twisting between ivory towers and cotton castles. She worried that we might fall through the clouds, but I explained that we were safe.

The morning wore on and the winged horse was able to move higher and higher. Meya's fascination with the ocean soon faded. When the sun reached its zenith, I pulled out our food and drinks and we had a romantic lunch in the sky. Meya again declared her love for me ... and then added that she had also fallen in love with flying.

I was bursting with happiness. Not only did I have the most beautiful girl in the world as my wife, but she also shared my passion for flying. I knew I had made the right choice.

"Did I tell you my grandfather built this horse and it's the only one of its kind?"

A frightened look crossed Meya's face as she whispered, "Your family must be gods." I smiled but didn't say anything.

We were now at a point in our trip that I could put the horse on automatic pilot and devote more attention to my exquisite bride. Of course, she went into a mild panic thinking we were going to crash. I tried to explain the radio guidance system that was now flying the horse, but quickly realized it was too much for her to understand.

In the meantime, we were nearing the Island of Poseidon. Below us were many sailboats and Meya wanted to know all about them. After my unsuccessful efforts to tell her about the automatic pilot, I avoided her questions and instead told her the tales about my eccentric grandfather and how he had come to build the winged steed we were riding on.

The first red streaks of sunset were filtering across the sky by the time we reached Atlantis. The people below all stopped to stare at us as we flew by. I pointed out some of the sights of the city and told Meya how the statues at the entrance to the channel were the works of great masters of art. The golden roofs especially fascinated her.

I pointed ahead of us. "Do you see the house with the marble stairs emerging from the bay? See? It has gardens with statues and a pool beside the house? Do you see it?"

"You mean the one by the water with the long line of columns?"

"Yes. That's my family's home. It's where we will live."

We circled downwards, approaching from the seaside, passing above the colonnade, and gently landed in the back garden.

"Welcome to your new home, my princess," I said as I gently helped her down from the winged horse.

Meya was completely taken in by everything. She walked over to one of the statues and touched it, then she wandered over to the bright array of flowers and smelled each one of them.

"Wait here for a moment, my love. I have a surprise for you." I'm not sure that she even heard me, she was so absorbed in her new surroundings.

I went inside -- the house was still empty, the family hadn't yet returned -- and went directly to my storage room. I got out all the life-sized robot toys that I've received for birthday presents every year from grandfather Godin and placed them in the living room. I stood in the crystal doorway that led to the outside patio and noticed that Meya was gathering flowers just as she had done when she tended sheep.

I called to her. "Come in, Meya, the surprise is ready … and we're alone." She walked over and took my hand as we entered the house.

A mechanical voice spoke as we crossed the doorstep, "Welcome to Atlantis. I am Ku, chief of the dolls."

Meya jumped and said, "Krill! I thought you said we were alone."

"We are. Come and see," and I led her to the living room. "These are mechanical dolls, Meya. They're called robots. The one you heard was Ku, she was a present from my grandfather for my tenth birthday."

Meya was awestruck. "But they look so real. How can they not be alive?" she exclaimed.

One of the dolls curtsied. "This one is the queen of the fairies." I turned and looked straight into her striking blue eyes and said, "But you, Meya, are the queen of my heart." I took her in my arms and kissed her. It was hard to believe that she was finally here with me in my home.

All the dolls lined up in two long lines. The musician dolls began playing the Atlantis Wedding March, as I had programmed them to do. Then I guided Meya down the center and introduced her to each doll in turn. I pointed out the Atlantis duck, the mischievous dog, the clever rabbit, the acrobatic monkey, and the mermaid in her carriage. As we came to the end of the line, all the dolls said in unison, "Welcome, highness. We wish you eternal happiness."

Then I took Meya to a doll that was standing apart from the others. "This robot girl will be your very own personal maid and she will do anything you ask."

Meya reached out and ran her fingers down the arm of the doll with wonder in her eyes. Then she turned and smiled at me, her blue eyes sparkling.

We enjoyed the next three days by ourselves. Meya was totally enchanted with everything. On the third day, my family returned. Godin was completely taken with Meya and insisted we have a party to celebrate. My mother was not as happy. She pulled me aside and urged me to send Meya back. She wanted me to get back with Helga. She went into minor shock when I told her it was too late, that the commander had married us at Atlantis Base 104.

Godin overheard me telling about the marriage and was elated. He immediately started calling family and friends and inviting them to a party.

**\*\*\*\*\*\*\*\*\*\***

Just as Krill finished his story, someone called for a toast to the happy couple. Everyone was talking and laughing and having a great time. An orchestra was playing the latest Atlantean hits and Meya was dancing with her new father-in-law. Crom walked over and pinched Krill on the arm. "Great choice," he said as he looked admiringly at Meya. "She's truly as beautiful as you said."

"Yes, she is," Krill said proudly.

"How did it go with the flying horse?" Crom asked.

"Wonderful! No problems. Of course, the natives all thought I was a god," Krill laughed. "Say, how about you? Any plans to marry the love of your life?"

"You bet. I can't get her off my mind."

Over the next few months, Krill, Crom, their wives, my new girlfriend, and I got together during the weekends to catch up on what was happening in our lives. Krill and Meya never seemed to lose the glow of true love.

# CHAPTER 8
# Encounter with Extraterrestrial Beings

Ten years have passed. I have matured and moved from my island of gardens, classical sculptures, and marble architecture to the modern and busy Island of the Sun full of modern industry and steel structures. I'm now working as chief engineer for an aerospace group and our engineering department is located in a skyscraper in downtown Brasea.

I live in an apartment located in a residential suburb not too far from work. It's a modern building made from glass and steel and is surrounded by other similar buildings, all of them shaped like stepped pyramids. This design, with its broad base and narrow top, gives the buildings greater stability in case of earthquakes or strong winds. One of my neighbors said that living in these pyramidal apartments gives him the feeling of living on a hillside and is ideal for people who are frightened of heights. Around and outside of each floor is a projecting balcony with flowerpots on the railings. The view is of the residential area known in Atlantis as the Hanging Gardens.

Living in Atlantis, I enjoy a life of comfort. On weekends, my girlfriend, Mila, and I go to different places in my beautiful turbine sports car. We both love driving at high speeds.

One afternoon while my girlfriend and I were tanning ourselves on the terrace of my apartment and listening to the popular music of the time, I began to think back on my days when I first came to Atlantis as a simple and illiterate boy. I remembered how I was in such a hurry to get educated. I worked my way through high school in record time, then went on to the University and completed a five-year engineering program in three years. Even though I was only a part-time student and worked full-time during the day at Godin's factory, I found myself faced with the same engineering problems at the factory that I was given in my homework assignments. It allowed me to do my homework and factory work simultaneously so that when I graduated as an aerospace engineer, I already had plenty of practical experience in the real world of the industry.

My thoughts drifted to Krill and Crom, who continued to live on Poseidon, the quiet Island of Gardens. They were happy there, content with their wives and children.

Just then, the telephone rang, interrupting my lethargic sun tanning. It was Uncle Luzaire. He said that Godin and his wife were hosting a small gathering in their mansion that evening and Mila and I were invited. They were preparing a special meal with salads and vegetables that Krill had brought back from his last overseas vacation. Two of Godin's old friends, a popular university professor and his wife, had also been invited.

I eagerly accepted the invitation and Mila and I immediately got cleaned up and dressed. We hopped on an air taxi and flew to Poseidon, landing at the small airport three blocks from Godin's home.

When we arrived at the mansion, we went upstairs to the end of a broad overhanging terrace where everyone was gathered. We extended our greetings to those present, including Krill and Crom and their families, then moved to a long table that was filled with all kinds of exotic food. We hungrily served ourselves and then joined the group dining at a nearby round table that was shaded by a large umbrella. The food was excellent and we both complimented Godin and his wife on their cooking talents.

As we were finishing the first course, Godin explained that this gathering was to commemorate a historic day that the Atlantean people should never forget. "Forty years ago," he said, "Atlantis was visited for the first time by alien voyagers called the Entarians. It was their highly advanced science that allowed us to create the mighty nation of Atlantis. When we have finished eating, I will explain this wonderful event in more detail."

As we finished dessert, Godin prepared to tell his story but before he could begin, Krill and Crom said they preferred to go swimming in the pool on the other side of the garden. They invited Mila and me to join them, but we declined, as we wanted to hear this fascinating story. We promised to join them later. As I watched them depart, I admired the lovely view of the marble colonnade at the edge of the garden with the beautiful blue ocean behind it. I could see several surfers and many luxury boats were docked at the nearby marina.

Godin cleared his throat, then began his story. "Many years ago, when I was a young professor, I hosted a large party in my country home that was located on a green prairie on the Island of the Sun. The party was to celebrate my first job promotion at the university."

Uncle Luzaire exclaimed, "I remember that party as if it were yesterday! In fact, it was a party I'll never forget. I believe it was mid-spring in Atlantis and I chose to drive my red convertible. It was a beautiful evening. The sky was clear and I can still feel the cool breeze that blew through my hair and rippled the grasses on the plain. I remember as the sun went down, I could see the distant lights of Brasea being turned on one by one."

Godin nodded and smiled. "Yes, it was a perfect evening for a party. Some guests pulled up in their vehicles with turbine engines, while others arrived in their quiet electric cars. I remember one gentleman pulled up in his aero-car and caused a fright among the ladies, but the men--ah--they were quite caught up with this innovative mode of transportation. It was the latest Anchor II and you could tell the owner was quite proud of it.

"We turned our entire home into a party hall. A band played in one room, in another we had a large, thin-screened TV that was broadcasting a ball game by satellite, and ... "

Uncle Luzaire interrupted, "Do you remember who was playing?"

"Hmmm, let me think, I believe it was between the Galaxies and the Quasars." He looked over at my uncle who nodded in agreement.

Godin continued, "Outside on the patio I was barbecuing over an open fire. Several guests hovered around, helping me where they could. When the meat was done, I put the word out that dinner was served. People immediately flocked around the long tables and piled their plates high with the ample supply of meats, salads, and fruits. As everyone was eating and talking, one of the children suddenly shouted, 'Mama, look!' He was pointing towards the night sky. 'That shooting star was falling but then it just stopped.' Of course, everyone looked at where he was pointing, but no one saw anything until finally, I noticed what appeared to be two bright stars hovering just above the northern horizon.

"Everyone immediately started offering ideas on what we were seeing when suddenly, one guest pointed out that one of the stars seemed to be moving towards us at a very rapid speed. Everyone stopped eating and stared at the advancing bright light. Abruptly, the object froze in mid-air and we saw three legs drop down from its belly. I knew immediately that what we were watching was a spacecraft. It was circular and about the size of a football field. There were two rows of windows all around it and they emitted a soft green glow. It began to lower itself and finally came to rest in an open field about 200 yards from my house.

"Everyone became very quiet. Some of the children were whimpering and clinging to their mothers. I told everyone not to panic and to remain calm. Several minutes went by and then we saw a doorway open and a stairway dropped to the ground. One of the guests had gone to his car and retrieved a pair of binoculars. He began to describe what he saw. 'Something's moving near the door. Oh look! They're humanoid! And two of them are walking towards us.' Our dog began to frantically bark, but as the beings neared, he became strangely quiet.

"The guests began commenting on the appearance of the beings. One pointed out that they were shorter than most humans and very slender. As they drew closer, another noticed their eyes and commented that they looked 'alert, yet different.' Another said their heads were too large for their bodies and someone else remarked that their mouths and chins were tiny. As the two beings drew closer, we could see they had on silver suits and I noticed their faces were white and pasty looking.

"This was an extremely exciting moment for me because I had always believed that intelligent beings existed elsewhere in the universe. Naturally, I hoped they were here on a friendly mission; nonetheless, I cautioned the guests to move slowly and not to do anything that might frighten the beings. Everyone stood very motionless and quiet.

"My family and I moved closer to the low fence surrounding the grounds. The two aliens came towards us and stopped only a couple of feet away. One lifted his hand in an apparent greeting and then said in a rather strange-sounding voice, 'We come from the planet Entar and are here on a mission of peace. I am

Oren, captain of the ship, and this is Dr. Re, my physician. Our planet is in the solar system Mank, which is located 16 light years from here.' The captain pointed in the direction of the Milky Way. 'Our system is located in the same spiral branch of the galaxy as yours. It took us 68 of your Earth years to get here. We are about half way to our destination and are scheduled to stop on your planet for only a few days. Then we will proceed to our destination near the outer edge of this galaxy where we will visit a solar system whose people are more advanced than ours.'

"I could scarcely contain my excitement as I realized I was actually speaking to an extraterrestrial. I asked them how they knew our language and how we measured time and space. Captain Oren said they had detected our radio transmissions about half a terrestrial year ago and their computers had deciphered our language. He said their progress in learning more about us was slow because they had no data to go on. Then one day, they were able to detect more radio signals, plus they began receiving television images. He commented that they were quite amazed at our appearance because we looked very much like their ancestors did thousands of years ago. He also pointed out that we have five fingers on each hand, instead of four as they did. They were able to conclude from this that we used the base ten numbering system, whereas they used base eight.

"The access to television allowed them to observe our planet and people and study our customs and languages so they had accumulated considerable information about us by the time they arrived at our planet."

I was in total awe of what I was hearing. I realized I hadn't moved a muscle since Godin had begun his tale and now shifted my body to a more comfortable position.

"Captain Oren explained their landing craft was a shuttle and the mother ship was still in orbit high above the Earth. He also told us they had visited our planet many times previously and found that it was mostly populated by animals and some bipedal creatures. They were pleased when they saw that we Atlanteans had evolved so rapidly and looked forward to visiting us. He added that many of the people on Entar believed that life here was still primitive, or even extinct, because of brutal bombardments by meteorites in ancient times. The captain warned us that this would again happen in about 13 million years.

"Dr. Re began speaking then and told us the crew consisted of geophysicists, anthropologists, and archaeologists who wanted to visit Earth to obtain new data and compare it to the older data in their files. They had also planned to refuel here because they knew uranium was available. Suddenly, Captain Oren interrupted him and reported he was receiving telepathic calls from their ship and they must leave to rendezvous with the mother ship. He assured us that they would return the next day and meet us at this same location.

"As they returned to their ship, I remember one matronly guest gushed, 'How charming.' Other guests commented that they seemed very polite." Godin laughed quietly to himself as he said, "In my mind, I was reflecting on how *logical* they were and began planning my next thesis."

Several of the guests smiled at each other, knowing this was Godin's passion. I asked, "And did they come back as promised?"

"Oh yes," replied Godin. "As well as several of the guests from the party, plus a number of historians came armed with cameras and recording devices of all kinds. We also invited the elders of Atlantis and they sent some representatives.

"This time when the aliens arrived, I escorted them into the living room. My wife offered them some tea and cake, but they politely refused. Captain Oren then began to speak at length. He told us the main ship would remain in orbit around the Earth for 20 days. During this time, 12 of their landing crafts would be coming and going, carrying personnel to conduct research on Earth and to obtain needed supplies. He said they would be stocking their ship with minerals from our planet, such as lithium, tritium, and deuterium for their nuclear engines, gold (which they used as an anti-corrosive on their mechanical structures), and silver and platinum for various other uses in their spaceship.

"Someone asked Captain Oren if they would be returning to their own planet after they completed their mission on Earth and he said no, they were going to continue on to the planet Iris, which was 34 light years from Entar and 18 light years from Earth. Dr. Re said that the Iris civilization was more advanced than the Entarians and they hoped to study and learn from them. He told us they communicated solely by telepathy.

"This prompted another person to ask our visitors if they knew of any advanced civilizations that were evil. I remember Captain Oren nodding very slowly and becoming very serious. He told us that from their studies of more than one million civilizations in the galaxy, they had found only one that had a belief system based on malice and evil. He said they were called the Ortusians, and they had no respect or regard for any other species except those they considered more advanced than themselves. Humans, in particular, were looked upon as no more than animals to be used by the Ortusians in any way they saw fit."

I shuddered as Godin continued with his story.

"According to Captain Oren, the practice of the Ortusians is to land on technologically inferior planets. They appear to be friendly and kind by offering devices that can cure disease or help the people in some other way. Once they have gained the confidence of the inhabitants, they offer to show them the inside of their ship and take them on sightseeing tours around the Earth. At the beginning, the passengers are treated very well and made to feel comfortable. Then the Ortusians start luring small groups of 10 or so into a special room. It is there that they slit the throats of the passengers and then gleefully watch as they run screaming and spurting blood from their jugular veins. Apparently, the Ortusians consider it great sport to listen to the terrified cries for help and see the wounded and ever-weakening bodies collapsing around them."

I looked around the room and saw I wasn't the only one who was feeling a bit squeamish about Godin's story.

Godin continued. "Yes, I know this is unpleasant, but you haven't heard the worst. After the blood-stained floor of the spaceship is covered with corpses, the Ortusians gather the bodies and send them to the protein processing plant that is part of their convoy of ships. It is there that the remains are converted into food for the wealthy of their species."

Several of the people in the room gasped.

"Captain Oren then told us that the Association of Advanced Planets, who had a strict policy against killing, tried to put a stop to this practice by exiling the Ortusians. Unfortunately, the beasts had already ravaged three planets, leaving them desolate and empty. Nevertheless, the association hoped that by sending them to the uninhabited parts of the galaxy, it would keep the rest of the planets safe.

"Then Dr. Re presented us with some bad news. He told us that the trajectory of our planet Earth would cross the path of the Ortusian starships in about 12,000 years! Of course, we were all quite shaken by this news, but then Captain Oren assured us that at the rate we had been developing and prospering, we would be well prepared to defend ourselves when that time came. It was then I decided to ask the captain and doctor if they would be interested in lecturing at the University of Brasea while they were visiting. I was absolutely delighted when they agreed.

"About that time, a committee of Atlantean elders approached the two alien visitors and requested an interview. Of course, a television crew immediately rushed up and began focusing their cameras on the group. I think Captain Oren was a little surprised, but he remained polite and composed and agreed to answer questions."

"What kind of questions did the elders ask?" I wondered aloud.

Godin stroked his chin as he contemplated my question. "Well, let me see if I can remember. They wanted to know if the Entarians had visited our planet before. Captain Oren said they had been visiting Earth regularly for approximately the past two million years. The elder asked their reasons for the visits and the captain explained they had come to observe the evolution of the planet. He also commented they had seen the planet in their voyages through the galaxy and had named it Paradise because it was such a beautiful place.

"But then Captain Oren gave us some terrifying news that I'll never forget. He said that on this latest trip to Earth, they had crossed the path of a huge comet heading straight for the sun. He said the astrotechs on their ship had made some calculations and discovered that the comet was due to cross Earth's orbit in approximately the next 30 years. Then he solemnly added that there was a very good possibility it was going to collide with our planet and, due to its great size, the devastation would be tremendous. Very few of Earth's inhabitants would survive.

"Of course everyone was shocked at this news and I recall Captain Oren was very saddened that he had to bring it to us. But he offered encouragement by saying that as the comet drew closer, our astronomers would be able to make more accurate calculations and perhaps discover that it would bypass the Earth. He also offered an invitation to the people of Atlantis to move to Entar if the cataclysmic event appeared inevitable. He told us that the gravity, atmosphere, and biology were nearly the same so we would easily adapt. He also told us that

Entar was a peaceful planet -- their last war had occurred over one million years ago.

"The elders profusely thanked Captain Oren for the warning as well as the invitation, then asked if he could be present at an assembly of elders that would be held on the following day. Captain Oren agreed. I was also invited."

One of the guests asked, "What happened at the assembly?"

"After introducing Captain Oren to the group, the elder leading the meeting told everyone that astronomers had checked the calculations and found they were completely accurate. He then accepted the invitation that Captain Oren had extended saying the people of Atlantis would be pleased to move to the planet Entar. He made it clear, however, that it would not be a permanent move. Descendants would be urged to return to Earth in 12,000 years to rebuild and again establish the Atlantean nation.

"The next day, as promised, Captain Oren and Dr. Re arrived for their presentation before the university members. Their spacecraft touched down in the stadium and as they exited, many of the students and faculty were visibly awestruck. Understandably, the auditorium was full and overflowing. It was a momentous occasion."

Godin looked around the room. "I have the transcript of their presentation. Would you be interested in having me read it?"

Everyone nodded vigorously. I looked around the room and could see that everyone was as excited as I was. Godin stood up and walked over to a nearby desk where he retrieved a large packet of papers. As he settled back into his chair, he turned to the first page.

"Dr. Re was the first to address the crowd." Godin looked down at the papers in front of him and began reading.

" 'I am from the planet Entar, the fourth planet from the sun in the solar system of Mank. In our system, the first two planets have no life. Planets three, four, and five are inhabited. Planet six is a large gas planet and has two large moons. It also has 11 miniature moons where we have constructed bases for extracting minerals. Entar has two moons that were excavated long ago. Today they hold several underground facilities. We also have two artificial moons. Originally, they were metallic asteroids where we installed mining bases and smelted iron and nickel into sheets. These sheets were then fastened together into pressurized spheres and divided into apartments and sanitation plants for the miners. We also erected hospitals, shopping centers, and schools. After the asteroids were completely mined, we used the remaining material to construct our artificial moons. Many people still make their homes there.

" 'Life in the universe is very scarce. That is why we try to protect it and encourage people on all planets to cooperate in this effort. Our civilization is more than two million years old, whereas your Atlantean civilization is less than 2,000 years old. The civilization of Iris, where we are going next, is also several million years old. In our galaxy, there are planets with civilizations that are nearly a billion years old. We are going to Iris to learn from them, as you are learning from us. Their inhabitants are so advanced intellectually that they seem like walking libraries to us. They have mental control over matter and use telekinesis to move objects. Telepathy plays an important role in their daily communication.

" 'Lately, members of our Institute of Interplanetary Anthropology and Archeology have been concerned about the state of the human race on Earth. Since it had been several centuries since our last visit, we were not sure if you had perished or survived your competition with wild animals. We speculated that if you had survived, you would now be nearing the end of the Stone Age. Imagine our surprise when we arrived and observed cities and other signs of an advanced civilization. We never imagined that you would have already passed through the industrial phase, the first atomic era, and automation in such a short time. We were especially amazed that you have begun interplanetary travel. The Atlantean people are to be commended.' "

Godin paused and said, "I remember one of my fellow professors interrupted the doctor and pointed out that most humans living outside of Atlantis were still in the Stone Age, with only a few having progressed to the Bronze Age. Dr. Re told him their equipment had detected that anomaly." Godin then returned to reading from the transcript.

" 'The reason we took such a particular interest in Earth is because long ago, when our ancestors first visited your planet, they felt this was one of the most beautiful planets in the universe. At the time of this visit, they found a few primitive species were beginning to prosper. Future visits, however, revealed that the evolution process was periodically being hampered and many forms of life were becoming extinct. Fortunately, because of the beneficial environment of Earth, life was able to recover quickly. On other planets where conditions are not as hospitable, this is not always the case. But then, many of these other planets do not suffer from the meteor showers that repeatedly pommel Earth, so once their civilizations become established, they rarely perish and some have existed for millions of years.

" 'It is a different story on Earth. In fact, it was the meteorites that destroyed the dinosaur species that once lived on your planet. It was a particularly devastating time when your solar system passed through a sector of the universe that is called HELL. After this event, because we knew that Earth life periodically regresses after these natural disasters, some thought an intelligent life form might never appear on Earth.

"'Then one morning, a quite revolutionary thing occurred. A genetic engineer arrived at his laboratory highly excited. He told his colleagues that God had appeared to him in a dream the night before and had commanded him to organize an expedition to planet Earth. The goal was to create a being in the physical image of the Entarians with the spiritual attributes of God. These beings were to be called humans and were to take control over the destiny of Earth. Of course, the religious Entarians believed this was an authentic revelation from God and they immediately started pushing for a voyage to Earth to carry out God's will. The non-believing atheists of Entar said such messages from God were merely hallucinations from an unbalanced mind. They did, however, support a mission to

Earth because from a scientific viewpoint, they believed it to be a fantastic opportunity.

" 'I feel it is important to say at this point that subjects related to the existence of God are highly controversial. Not only for the people here on Earth, but for all civilizations in the galaxy from the most primitive to the most advanced. Nonetheless, word of our project quickly spread to Mank's neighboring solar systems and even to the Galactic Confederation of Advanced Planets. Everyone wanted to participate and we were provided extensive scientific information on space travel.

" 'Finally, the day came when the scientists and engineers were to depart. The Galactic Confederation of Advanced Planets bestowed on them the honorary title of Astronaut Keepers of Worlds. It was quite a celebratory event.

" 'On their first expedition to Earth, the Entarian scientists were unsuccessful in locating a species from which they could create the first humans, even though they explored the whole planet. However, on their second voyage, while they were investigating a region that you know as Africa, some geneticists spotted an animal running on two legs, instead of the usual four as the other animals. They also saw that it had what appeared to be hands, which they believed had the potential to become dexterous. They noticed its shape was similar to the Entarians and it was able to produce many sounds, indicating that it had vocal chords. The creature was hairless and the scientists determined it had a brain about half the size of modern man. Everyone felt this was the ideal specimen for the project.

" 'One other thing the scientists noted was that this animal seemed to be handicapped for survival because it had no claws or fangs and, although it was able to move bipedally, it moved much too slowly to escape its predators. Because of this, they determined it was doomed for extinction unless we intervened in its future. Therefore, several of these hominoid species were gathered up and returned to Entar. The group also brought with them several other small animals and many kinds of edible plants.

" 'A specially equipped laboratory had been set up just for creating the first humans, and a group of elite scientists began work almost immediately. The project itself took several generations as much experimental genetic engineering and selective mutation was necessary and, of course, we had to observe the effects of the accelerated evolution on these primate species and their descendants. It was a long, but rewarding, undertaking and, in the end, we were able to create six humans in our image, three male and three female. All had brains nearly the size of modern man. It was an astounding accomplishment.'"

Godin paused, placed the document on his lap, and looked around the room. "Well, what do you think so far?" Not one person spoke up. In fact, it seemed that everyone was in a sort of trance as we digested what we had just heard. Godin nodded knowingly, picked up the document from his lap, and resumed reading.

" 'At one of the final meetings before the new humans were to be returned to Earth, the chief scientist pointed out that although they were not yet perfect, over the years they would keep evolving and eventually become all they were designed to be.

" 'A return trip was scheduled and the humans were put into hibernation so they would not age during the 62 terrestrial years it would take to reach Earth. Over the lifetime of the project, several entomologists had also developed a fruit tree that had extraordinary nutritional benefits for the humans and several seeds were also packed for the space journey.

" 'Once the ship arrived in Earth's orbit, the scientists analyzed and studied the atmosphere and geography, searching for an area that would be conducive to the development of new humans. They looked for a place that would offer a mild climate, preferably surrounded by timbered mountains to protect the area from harsh winds. They wanted it to be rich in minerals and metals for mining in order to produce all kinds of alloys, like Orichalcum. The ground needed to be fertile so the humans could grow their own food.

" 'Beyond this, they also needed to find a place where they could build their facilities, living quarters, genetic engineering laboratories, and space ports as they would be carefully monitoring the evolution of these humans and performing additional genetic engineering mutations for many hundreds of years to come. They also had to locate a source of geothermal energy to supply the large quantities of electricity that would be needed to power their energy-hungry facilities.

" 'Finally, they found a group of volcanic islands in your mid-Atlantic Ocean. The largest island was rectangular in shape and measured about 100 by 150 miles. The next largest was a circular island about 25 miles in diameter. When the scientists saw that the circular island had two natural streams of water in the center, one cold and the other warm, they chose it immediately.

" 'Once they landed and became accustomed to the gravity on Earth, our people began their assigned tasks. There were 64 members in the group, including engineers, physicists, biologists, genetic engineers, and physicians. Our people called this group the Elhim.

" 'Part of the crew explored and mapped the entire planet, looking for minerals to be mined. During their exploration, they reported seeing many huge mammals, including mammoths, oxen, bear, wooly rhino, herds of elephants, and saber-toothed tigers, but did not see any of the bipedal primates like those that had been captured and taken to Entar generations before. As we had suspected, it seemed apparent this species had been unable to survive in the wild and competitive environment. Incidentally, this is why the missing link that your people talk about has never been discovered. The only remains of the true human missing links are found in the genetic engineering graveyards on the Planet Entar. Our advanced alien technology is what enabled us to bring the species back to Earth as full human beings.

" 'Other crew members began setting up temporary barracks and erecting laboratories and other buildings to house supplies and equipment. Still others planted orchards to provide crops the year around.

" 'Five engineers were assigned the task of constructing a giant system of concentric rings of water, as wide as lakes, on the island. They started at the center of the island and cut a circular channel that was approximately one kilometer in diameter. This formed an artificial island in the center and this is where the permanent buildings and laboratories were erected because we wanted them to be kept separate from the rest of the island.

" 'After completing three circles of water, the engineers then cut a straight channel that extended to the sea. Large transoceanic ships were built and they used this channel to bring food and other supplies to the inhabitants from around the world.

" 'You might think it amazing that only five engineers worked on this project, but they had several giant steel robots that extracted and removed more than a million huge, rectangular stone blocks, each weighing about 90 tons. You see, under the rich soil of the island were thick layers of volcanic rock. White-colored blocks were extracted from the upper layer, red-colored rocks came from the next layer, and black rocks came from the layer closest to the channel bottom. Since black became the natural color for the bottom of the channel, this allowed for maximum absorption of solar energy that was released in the form of heat throughout the night. This kept crops from freezing during cold weather.

" 'Instead of blasting through the rock as modern humans do, the Entarians carved the rocks like pieces of art using high-pressure water equipment that shot a supersonic jet of water through an extremely precise and small nozzle, thinner than a needle. We had discovered that this was much more efficient than any steel saw or pneumatic hammer because it made straight, deep cuts through the rock.' "

Godin stopped reading and again looked around the room. "I remember it was about this time that the doctor took a break. It stuck in my memory because he had reached into his pocket and pulled out what looked like a toothpaste tube, put it in his mouth, and squeezed. We could only assume it was a form of food or nourishment, but we were all quite fascinated. He then took a bottle of sterilized water and drank all of it before continuing. I couldn't help but wonder if the water and the substance in the tube worked together somehow."

Godin seemed to ponder his own statement for a moment or two, then resumed reading.

" 'You may wonder what happened to all the massive rocks that were extracted. Some of the stones were fragmented and used to build bridges, buildings, walls, and fences around the contours of the artificial circular islands. Other rocks were used to building beautiful, truncated pyramids on nearby plains. One such pyramid was constructed north of the central complex and was a huge, stepped structure with a rectangular base about a kilometer long. The top of the pyramid was so high that clouds sometimes covered its cusp. It was built for the sole purpose of supporting a high tilt steel runway for launching our heavy crafts into space. The runway started at the foot of the pyramid, curved up its face, then upon reaching the cusp, it aimed straight for the heavens. The humans were so impressed with this wonder that they often climbed trees and rocks to get a better view and stare in awe at its magnificence.

" 'On the center artificial island, the Entarians developed a very special area and named it the Garden of Eden. This was where the humans and the Entarians lived together for many years but, after a time, the scientists felt it might be better to separate the six humans. They noticed that the development of the three couples had progressed at different levels and they were concerned there might be interbreeding. Also, the couples had started fighting among themselves more and more frequently. So they moved the human they had named Adam and his mate to the ring of land immediately surrounding the artificial island. The less developed couple was placed on the next outer ring, and the two humans that were the most evolved, Poseidon and his mate, remained on the center island with the Entarians.

" 'It was some years later that the mate of Adam died and the Elhim group grew concerned that Adam was getting bored. Although they agreed he needed another mate, they also knew that it would take generations to create a compatible human. Then one of the group members had an idea. Why not surgically remove some of Adam's cells, and somehow stimulate that its sex chromosomes' would change, from XY to XX and create a female clone? This they did and shortly thereafter, presented Adam with his new mate, whom he named Eve.

" 'Finally the day came when the Entarians felt it was time to return to their home planet and allow the humans to proceed in their natural development. They were especially pleased with the progress of Poseidon and his mate because they seemed ready to embark into the Space Age. As they were preparing to complete some final experiments and close the laboratories, something went terribly wrong. The couple known as Adam and Eve defiantly disobeyed one of the major rules the Entarians had given them for their continued survival.

" 'You see, the genetic engineers had created a tree that bore the perfect food for humanity. It supplied all the required nutrients, accelerated wisdom, and kept humans in perfect health. But it was only one tree and needed to blossom and put forth seed that could be used for planting more trees, so the humans had been instructed not to pick the fruit until a full-sized orchard had been planted.

" 'Eve was unable to overcome temptation. She wanted to taste this fruit and experience its benefits now so she climbed the fence around the proposed orchard and picked and ate the fruit. Then, to make matters worse, she gave some to Adam, who also partook of its goodness.

" 'When the theft of the fruit was discovered, the scientists were devastated. All their long and arduous years of work were gone in a moment. All their efforts to create a species that would be perfect and rule the planet and the solar system went up in smoke. They were so disappointed and angry that they decided to leave Earth immediately. The humans would have to fend for themselves without any further help from the Entarians.

" 'Before they left, they banished Adam and Eve to the other side of the planet to a place located near what is known as the Euphrates River. The less evolved couple was moved to the area known as Europe. Poseidon and his mate, the most advanced of the humans, were the Entarians' biggest concern. After living their entire life in a civilized environment, the scientists knew the couple would not be able to survive in the wild. Some of the group felt the couple should be taken back to Entar, but others disagreed. Finally, a poll was taken and it was decided the couple should be allowed to remain on the central island and have full access to the surrounding islands.

" 'Once that decision was made, the Entarians packed up and left Earth.

" 'As the milleniums passed, we knew that you humans would gradually forget your genesis, which is part of the reason we are here today. We want to reacquaint you with the Entarians, your creators. We have long since forgiven those first humans for their actions and consider you all as our beloved creatures.'"

Godin laid the papers aside and looked around the room. One of the guests, as if thinking aloud, said, "I wonder if the Entarians believed in God." Godin immediately leaned forward in his chair and said, "That's a very good question – and one that was asked by one of the students that attended the lecture. Dr. Re told him that he believed in God, but that he didn't speak for the rest of his people because there were many thoughts and opinions about the reality and existence of God. The student then commented that from the story that Dr. Re had told, it appeared God was not the Creator of humans as had been taught for many years. Dr. Re responded by saying that, according to his personal beliefs, God created the Entarians and so everything the Entarians created with good intention was done in the name of God.

"Dr. Re answered several other questions, then finished his time at the podium by telling us that the Entarians had much to teach us humans. He said they had been able to increase their life span by five times over what it was a thousand years ago and now lived to be approximately 480 of our terrestrial years. He told us that most of this was due to their diligent attention to nutrition and the removal of all carcinogenic and harmful substances from food, water, and the air. He also said they had learned to control stress in their lives and used natural herbs to keep their veins and arteries in good shape and clear of cholesterol."

Godin sighed. "It seems we still have not learned what the Entarians tried to teach us."

"Did Captain Oren also give a speech?" I asked.

"Oh yes," Godin replied. "In fact, I had to make a mad dash from the lecture hall where Dr. Re was so I could at least hear part of his discourse. Would you like me to share what he said as well or are you getting tired?"

Everyone excitedly assured Godin they were not tired and definitely wanted him to continue with his narrative. He crossed the floor to his desk, rifled through some files, and finally pulled out a brightly colored folder. As he walked back to his chair, he flipped through several pages, then continued his reading.

" 'Our cities are highly functional and we live in comfortable apartments and homes. Most of us have at least two robot servants to do the menial work, like cooking and cleaning. We have extremely modern transportation systems.

" 'Since it appears we have arrived on your planet at the height of your progress, it will not be difficult to teach you our advanced principles of science and technology. Using our engineering drawings, you will quickly be able to create interstellar spaceships designed for long voyages throughout the universe. Spaceships many times faster than what you humans use today. We will show you how to power the ships with fantastic thermonuclear fusion propulsion that will make them many times faster than any ships you have today. With similar technology, you will be able to generate unlimited electric power to light your cities. In no time at all, you will have the same technical knowledge as some of the most advanced civilizations in the galaxy.

" 'Over the years, you may have suspected that your planet has been visited by other beings in the galaxy. You were probably correct because thousands of years ago while we were in the process of creating the first humans, we also constructed giant beacons and installed them on the ocean floor at five different locations on the Earth. One of them is located close to the western continent, an area you have named the Bermuda Triangle. Twice each terrestrial year, these beacons are automatically activated for a few minutes. They give off electromagnetic signals of great intensity that broadcast Earth's existence to other advanced civilizations and alien astronauts throughout the galaxy. It was these signals that helped us navigate to your planet since not even our best telescopes on Entar allow us to see Earth. As we approached the orbit of the planet Neptune, we could see Earth as a tiny gray dot with our ship telescopes, but without the beacons, we would not have been able to create a flight plan. In the coming years, if your civilization doesn't die out and the beacons remain in working order, you can expect more visits, both from us and other advanced peoples.

" 'There is one thing I must, however, caution you about the beacons. When the signals are scheduled to broadcast, it is important that all ships and aircraft stay out of the area. The signal is very strong as it has the energy of a hydrogen bomb and will boil the waters of the surrounding ocean. If you have had reports of missing sea vessels and flying machines, it is most likely because they were in the area when the beacon was transmitting.'"

Godin stopped reading and sighed deeply. "This was where Captain Oren told the attendees what he had told us the day before – about the impending collision with the comet. He emphasized that the devastation of Atlantis would be total if the comet landed anywhere nearby, which their predictions indicated it would. He said the many dormant volcanoes that cover our island nation would erupt and, of course, there would be terrible floods and most likely, Atlantis would eventually sink into the sea.

"Captain Oren repeated the invitation for the people of Earth to move to Entar. He also mentioned that although we were welcome at any time and without any previous notice, because radio transmissions are not instantaneous, it would take several Earth years to travel to Entar. The one encouraging thing he did say was that the engineering drawings he was leaving us would show us how to build a convoy of gigantic interstellar space arks, and each one would be capable of carrying thousands of people."

Godin looked up from the pages in front of him as he said, "Captain Oren concluded his speech by offering his gratitude for being allowed to replenish their supplies. He told everyone that he and Dr. Re would be leaving in a few days and that after they returned to Entar, they were going to nominate Earth for membership in the Galactic Association of Advanced Planets. Then he turned to our chief elder and presented him with what he called a symbolic golden key to the heavens.

"Shortly after that, the captain joined Dr. Re for their departure. Everyone went outside to watch the spacecraft, as it, slowly rose vertically, then rapidly accelerated in a straight line until it was out of sight.

"Naturally, there was a flurry of interest in all the technology that the Entarians gave to our scientists. One thing I found particularly interesting was that a few weeks after the Entarians left, a physics professor published a paper stating that the Entarian's warning about the comet was incorrect--that there was not going to be any collision. This pleased the worried populace of Atlantis and the dire predictions of Captain Oren were quickly forgotten. But personally, I could not shake the feeling that what he had said was true."

Godin closed the report and smiled at everyone. "Enough doom and gloom for today! There's still plenty of good food left."

Mila and I stood up, stretched, and started moving towards the balcony. As we walked, Mila said, "I found that totally fascinating. How about you?"

"I agree. And I have to say that I can't help but agree with Godin about the comet. I tend to believe the aliens. It's not a pleasant thought, but with their advanced knowledge, I can't see how they could be wrong."

By then, we had reached the table and saw that a large broiled bird had been added to the fare. I recognized it as being one of those that are often brought from Europe and Africa to the Atlantis food markets. Mila reached for a breast and I took a wing and leg.

After finishing, we decided to join Krill and Crom in the swimming pool. Later, as we returned to our apartment on the Island of the Sun, we talked about all that we had heard and agreed that we had been very fortunate to learn about this incredible event in the history of humankind.

# CHAPTER 9
## Wise Monks

I turned to Mila to say something, and she was gone! My surroundings had abruptly changed and I was back in the stone chair. Atlantis and all its glory were gone. My friends, the beautiful city, the flying horse ... all gone. The realization washed over me that it had all been a dream. Just a dream. But it had seemed so real.

I felt strangely sad.

Suddenly, I heard a noise behind me and turned to see an ugly, yellow and red-striped insect coming in my direction. It looked like a colossal centipede – the size of a truck – and it was dragging itself in and around the rocks. When it was about 100 paces from me, it stopped. Then I heard another sound – a buzzing noise. I looked up and saw a giant gray dragonfly. It flew directly over me and landed on a nearby boulder. My heart started pounding so hard I could hear it in my ears.

As I fearfully watched these two creatures, I saw the skin from the torso of the centipede begin to tear open. The monster was shedding! But then I realized that what I was seeing was a door opening, and from inside this ugly insect, two humans wearing garments that resembled Tibetan monks emerged. Before I could comprehend what was happening, I saw the dragonfly's torso also rip apart. This time, the two humans that stood in the doorway were wearing silver jump suits and looked like pilots. They threw out a rope ladder and descended to the ground.

The two monks approached me. I wanted to get up and run, but felt completely paralyzed. One of the monks spoke and said, "Hello, young man. Don't be frightened. We are here to tell you more about Atlantis. You see, we are called the Custodians of Planet Earth. We belong to a secret philosophical society and our duty is to keep unbiased records of the true history of the world. We have been doing this since the time that Atlantis disappeared into the waters as a result of the great comet.

"The founders of our society were descendants of the few surviving Atlanteans. Through the years, others have joined our organization and we are now a blend of many peoples who believe in the same principles and rules that were set down many hundreds of years ago."

"I know our arrival frightened you because our vehicles resemble giant insects, but they are actually our modes of transportation. The centipede is, in reality, an off-road vehicle with several mechanical legs and no wheels. The dragonfly is a special helicopter that can land anywhere with its long joining legs. It can even perch on high cliffs. The designs for these vehicles were copied from the golden scrolls left by the Atlanteans."

My thoughts started racing and I said excitedly, "The golden scrolls! Yes, I remember hearing about them. It was when I was in Atlantis. At least I thought I was in Atlantis. I don't know. It seemed so real, but it must have been a dream."

"Yes, to you, it was a dream and will always seem that way. But in truth, it was much more than a dream. It was a virtual reality in which your thoughts were transported to another time."

"Why are you here?" I asked the monks.

"We are here because as soon as you sat on that Rock of Wisdom, also called the Stone of Dreams, your brain waves became tuned with the electromagnetic waves emanating from the stone. When this happened, an alarm went off in our nearby quarters where we were working. We came right away to find you because you are the first to ever sit on the stone. We have some very important information to share with you. Now we must return to our headquarters. Please go with the pilots."

I looked past the monks and saw the two pilots walking towards me. I started to get up from the stone chair and move away, but one of the pilots reached out and touched my arm.

"It's all right. We are not going to harm you. In fact, you will be our guest."

"I'd ... I'd ... rather ... not," I stuttered.

One of the pilots reached into his pocket and gave me a gold pen. The other one handed me a miniature radio that was playing some kind of strange music. I wondered what else they had for me. I decided to go with them to find out.

We entered the dragonfly helicopter climbing by the rope ladder and the main pilot started the engine. As we ascended, the other pilot handed me a black hood and said, "Please put this on to cover your eyes. We don't want you to see where our secret base is located." I pulled the hood over my head as instructed. The pilot continued to talk with me.

"Besides being the Custodians of Planet Earth, we are also the keepers of one of the secret Atlantean chambers, which is located inside the center of a mountain not far from here. We reach the chamber from our barracks, which are also below the surface, by walking through a long, narrow tunnel. It was our parents who discovered the chamber and constructed the barracks and the tunnel, so the facilities are fairly new.

"Stored in the chamber were some gold tablets that told of six other hidden chambers, but no location was given. There was only a cryptic message that said the person who sat on the Stone of Dreams would reveal the locations. That is why the monks were so excited when they heard the alarm."

"But I don't know where these chambers are," I exclaimed.

"Ahhh, but you will," the pilot assured me. "After we show you around, we will return you to the stone so you can receive more communications."

After the pilot stopped talking, I realized how quiet it was inside this strange flying machine. There was no sound of propellers or engine noise. I wondered how much further we had to go. It seemed like we had been flying in circles for quite some time. Then I heard the pilot telling me to remove my hood. I quickly pulled it off and saw that we were flying inside a deep gorge. Suddenly the craft banked right and headed straight for the rocky face of the huge mountain. I gasped and opened my mouth to scream. But before I could make a sound, two doors that were disguised as a part of the rocky formation opened and we flew inside.

As my heart slowly returned to a normal beat, I could see we had entered a large subterranean passageway that opened into a large cavern. Up ahead the underground small town surrounded a heliport. After we landed and disembarked, we entered a very modern building. It was illuminated by scores of fluorescent tubes and there were several other unusual-looking flying machines parked here and there.

The pilots walked me to the outside plaza and told me that one of the monks would join me shortly. While I waited, I looked around and saw people hurriedly walking back and forth. Many were dressed as monks and pilots, but there were others dressed as business people, medical personnel, and some that looked like scientists.

One of the monks approached me and said, "Welcome. Let us sit on this bench. I'm sure you are very curious about us, so let me explain. We make everything we need right here. We gather our resources throughout the planet, discreetly of course, to draw as little attention as possible. We still have some of the gold bars that the Atlanteans left in their treasure vault. We make exchanges for currency with them when necessary because our scientific research is very expensive.

"Our duty is to be observers of the events on Earth and keep a written record of important happenings without comment, prejudice, or bias. Our ancestors started this practice after the big hammer (comet) hit and it has continued for hundreds of generations. We have seen many unsettling events, but never have we done anything to alter or change the course of history. Until now.

"You see, when we saw the explosion of the first atomic bomb on Earth, we realized that humans had become capable of destroying themselves and their world. We all agreed that we must intervene and prevent a nuclear war. Therefore, some of our members have secretly been living and working in the outside world as teachers, scientists, and researchers. Others are serving on the board of directors for many large-scale businesses and some are acting as advisors to those in high political arenas. This is being done in hopes of influencing the thinking of people to live peacefully and in harmony. I myself am working as an aerospace engineer in Europe." The monk glanced at his wristwatch and exclaimed, "I'm sorry but I must leave now. I have an appointment to keep. One of the other monks will join you momentarily. Goodbye, young man."

I watched as he hurried to the heliport and climbed into a strange, shiny flying machine. As it lifted off, another monk who was dressed as a Buddhist priest approached me. "I imagine you are wondering about the aircraft you have just seen."

I nodded.

"It is a stealth flyer with special geometry. It is built from radar-absorbent materials to avoid detection when our pilots cross borders. It is important that our operations remain undiscovered by the outside world." The Buddhist monk started walking and motioned for me to come with him.

"Our methods for observing the events on Earth are based on a process that the Atlanteans used many eons ago. The Atlantean people knew they were much more advanced than the rest of humanity, but they were curious about how other people lived. They didn't want to interfere or frighten the primitives, so they created spying birds-- noiseless miniature helicopters that carried tiny television cameras inside. These so-called birds resembled sea gulls or white doves and were remotely controlled by radio transmitters. Fortunately, when Atlantis was destroyed, this technology didn't die and it was passed on to our ancestor monks.

"There is a story that on one occasion about 2,000 years ago, our ancestors used a helicopter shaped like a white dove to witness the baptism of Jesus by John the Baptist in the Jordan River. It was said that the people from that time thought they saw a halo as a circle of light around the white dove when it stayed still in the sky watching Jesus. People never realized that really there was no halo, but a couple of counter-rotating propellers attached to the back of the mechanical dove.

"These mechanical doves are still in use today in many areas of the world because they are so non intrusive. No one gives them a second thought."

Another monk approached us. He exchanged greetings with the Buddhist monk, and then turned to me. "Hello, young man," he said, "My name is Fred and I'll be your host during your visit to the complex." The Buddhist monk touched my shoulder and wished me Godspeed and moved off around the village.

Fred and I started walking along one of the many walkways. "You are very fortunate to be the one who sat on the Stone of Dreams, but you definitely have your work cut out for you."

I wondered what he meant by this statement, but I felt it would be impolite to ask, so I didn't say anything.

Fred continued, "Before we begin our tour of the barracks, let me tell you a little more about our secret order. Originally, our organization was made up of the descendants of the surviving Atlanteans, but now people from all over the world have joined us. Most are highly trained specialists in their field who are looking for intellectual freedom. About a third of us have families outside the facility, but they do not know anything about this place. They just think we work in companies that require overseas travel for a few months each year.

"Our membership includes a small number of gifted design engineers from America, Europe, and Asia who were forced to use their talents during the Second World War to develop aircraft and armaments to kill other human beings." Fred paused, then shook his head as he added, "I find it amazing that they were able to achieve so much by using nothing more than slide rules to do their calculations. Anyway, after the war was over, they were disheartened and disillusioned with the evils they had created and were looking for a way to redeem themselves.

Fortunately, at about that same time, we were looking for intellectual giants to join our group. We contacted each of them and once they became familiar with our organization, they became members. As a condition of membership, they had to symbolically renounce their citizenship and sever links with everyone but their family, but they were all more than willing to do so. Of course, these men are very old today, but they still spend their time creating wonderful new inventions. In fact, I have something to tell you that I think may come as a big surprise."

He leaned towards me as though he were about to tell me a deep, dark secret. "You're probably familiar with all the stories about UFOs that people claim to see in the heavens?" I nodded. "Well, about half of these aircraft are not of alien origin. They are the creations of these elderly scientists and engineers. The technology they use comes from the information stored in the Atlantean chambers."

After walking around the barracks, we entered a building. I noticed that it was quite cool, but comfortable. There seemed to be a faint smell of chemicals, but the odor wasn't disagreeable. There was no dust anywhere. Everywhere I looked was spotlessly clean.

We approached a huge door that looked to be made of oak. With no little effort, Fred pulled it open and we stepped inside. I was immediately awestruck. Everywhere I looked, I saw shelves filled with hundreds of books. Along one wall, I saw stacks of film cans.

Fred made a large sweep of the area with his arm and said, "This room not only holds all the knowledge of the ancient Atlanteans, we even have the originals of books that were lost in the fire in the ancient library of Alexandria in Egypt. You will see that many of the books are made of thin gold plates. We also have some scrolls made of gold. The ancient Atlanteans knew materials such as paper, leather, and wood would eventually turn to dust, so they wisely used gold for the most important information."

"What are those?" I asked, pointing to some black, rectangular boxes.

"Those are the movies and documentary files of all the world events. Many took place before the great hammer and Noah's flood. We record everything on a nearly indestructible plastic, not yet discovered by the people of your time."

Fred tugged at my sleeve and said, "Come. We'll now go visit the chambers."

We left the library and Fred pointed to an opening at the far end of the underground village. "That dark hole is the entrance to the chambers. We will travel a long, dark, and narrow tunnel that goes deep into the ground. When the Atlanteans knew their civilization was not going to survive the great comet, they desperately wanted to preserve the culture and achievements as a gift to people of the future. To keep their priceless treasures safe, they dug massive chambers in the center of mountains throughout the world. Then they activated the Stone of Dreams so one day future generations would be able to benefit from their extensive knowledge."

"So, tell me. What do you think of our barracks?" Without waiting for a response, Fred continued. "They were built by our parents around 1900. The only thing that separates us from the outside world is the entrance in the side of the mountain where you came in and its couple of heavy steel doors at ground level. Both doors are well concealed by rocks and plants and are impossible to detect from the outside. They are hydraulically controlled; only members of the Order can open them with remote transmitters."

As we got closer to the tunnel's narrow entrance, my curiosity increased. "What's in the chamber?" Fred turned and looked directly into my eyes. "What you will discover in the chamber are the most breathtaking and magnificent marvels that human eyes have ever seen.

"Less than a year before the comet collided with Earth, Captain Cronus, the best astronaut from Atlantis, went after it in his spaceship. He blasted it into two large pieces and many small ones. This accomplishment saved the world but not Atlantis. Two large chunks of ice continued their course to Earth. The larger one barely missed the Earth, while the smaller one fell in the Atlantic Ocean near Atlantis. The impact activated many dormant volcanoes on most islands of the Atlantic Ocean. The comet impact also generated huge tidal waves, causing more destruction.

"The scientists were right. Today the skeletal remnants of the islands of Atlantis are the Azores. The rest of Atlantis disintegrated along with everything on it, and lies just as sediment at the bottom of the ocean.

"I am going to tell you the truth about Noah's flood. Most people believe it was the whole world's flood. The truth is that several local floods occurred almost simultaneously in the world. It was a consequence of the cataclysm that destroyed Atlantis. The comet impact produced huge quantities of steam that rose to the sky. This got mixed with the soot from the burning forests around the Atlantic coast. Then gradually this steam condensed in dark clouds and precipitated as torrential rains, flooding many places in the world. This event was called the Universal Flood, recorded with different names in holy books from different ancient cultures around the globe. The Judeo-Christian Bible calls it Noah's flood.

"In the last pages of the Atlantis history books, it explains that Noah built his ark near the largest garden where most species of the world dwelled. This garden was located in Asia Minor and was one of three zoos sponsored by rich Atlantean protectors of wild life. At the time Noah built his ark, he worked there as a zookeeper and sometimes as a carpenter. Noah was a person who loved humans and animals. When he knew that a flood was going to happen, he wanted to save them. As a carpenter it was not hard for him to build an ark. When it was finished, he collected animals in couples from the same zoo and put them in the ark. The ark embarked on the floodwaters.

# CHAPTER 10
## A Journey to the Center of the Mountain

Fred said, "I will take you on a journey to the center of the mountain. You may get the impression you're going to the center of the Earth."

As we stroll by a path, we approached the entrance of a narrow tunnel that made me feel claustrophobic. Fred explained how the monks had found the chamber. "We were really quite lucky. We had been exploring several geographical areas around the planet when we came upon some megalithic stone landmarks. We found the first ones in the broad Andes Mountains, in a zone extending over Peru, Bolivia, Argentina, and Chile. The stones were all cut with amazing precision, most likely with laser or possibly high-pressure supersonic jets of water. We quickly realized the indigenous people did not build these structures. To our archaeologists, these stones were proof left intentionally by a previous advanced civilization, most likely the Atlanteans. These monuments were originally designed as indicators or pointers to help the people of the future find the Atlantean treasure chamber."

I spoke up excitedly. "I've heard of these stones! My father mentioned the ones at Machu Picchu and Ollaytaytambo in Peru, but no one can explain them."

Fred nodded. "Yes, over the years, various cultures have discovered them. Most of them thought those were no more than gigantic rocks. Later cultures converted them into places of worship, astronomical observatories, and fortresses to protect them from their enemies. More recently between 700 B.C. and 800 A.D. the Incas and many other indigenous civilizations took them over and added more structures which were made from smaller and more crude stones quarried locally. Also, the Incas built agricultural terraces around them.

"After we discovered our chamber, we learned more about the stones and how and why they were built. It seems that the Atlanteans constructed mammoth robots to be used as workers or as mechanical beasts of burden, to move and transport gigantic boulders from nearby quarries. We saw pictures of these robots. They looked like mechanical Cyclops with a big eye in the center of their faces."

I interrupted. "I saw creatures like those in one of my dreams...or my virtual trip...or whatever it was."

Fred smiled, "That's not surprising because I'm sure the Atlanteans wanted to share as much of their history as they could through the Stone of Dreams. Anyway, at the beginning of this century, our custodian monks were impressed with the complicated and perfect assemblage of those stones. Cut with great precision, they fitted exactly together as in the megalithic Fortress of Sacsayhuaman in Peru, left by the Atlanteans as a landmark for some purpose. From the air its huge zigzagging stone walls, built one behind the other, appeared as the representation of the bolt thrown by the right hand of the god Poseidon.

In the traditional design of their temples and buildings, the Atlanteans sometimes used rectangular and other times, trapezoidal doorways--designs that could be found in ancient structures around the world such as Sacsayhuaman, Tiahuanacu, Stonehenge, and other locations in Malta and in Crete. A stone temple of beautiful simplicity, which was much older than the pyramids was excavated not too long ago, near the sphinx of Giza.

"The top portion of the Peruvian Ollaytaytambo fortress is a megalithic structure built on a mountainside. It is built with six pink rectangular stone columns, erected side by side, making up a cyclopean wall. The surfaces in between these monolithic stone blocks matched so perfectly that a pin could not be inserted between them. Mortar wasn't necessary; the stones were fastened to each other at the top with heavy, metal, locking clips. Over time the clips rusted and disappeared, but the carved grooves remained. Each of these pink stones weighed approximately 30 tons. It is possible that this monument was also built as an indicator to locate the treasure chambers of Atlantis.

"Giant stones were brought from a distant quarry located in a nearby mountain. A gorge separated both mountains. After the stones were extracted, they were carved into monolithic rectangular thick columns. Mechanical Cyclops workers transported them first down the hill, then up the side of the next mountain, to the site where those were erected to form a symbolic wall which remains today as an unfinished structure. On the side of that mountain you could see several similar stones that never reached their destination and were abandoned along the steep side of the hill. Probably the builders realized that the day of total disaster was coming sooner than expected. It was easy to notice that the broad surrounding structures were of poorer workmanship, just additions from later cultures, among them the Incas.

"In the last days of Atlantis, most news was bad news. However, once in awhile there was good news, as when Noah finished building his ark. This project was so large he had to cut down all the trees from a nearby forest to build it. The ark was ready for the flood and got finished about a week before Atlantis disappeared."

As soon as Fred finished this story, he began another," Tiahuanacu's ruins in La Paz, Bolivia, were well preserved for thousands of years because it was built on a high, barren plateau, where rain and erosion were minimal. Unbelievably, most of the damage to Tiahuanacu occurred in the first half of the twentieth century when the site was not protected. Stones with precision carvings, some weighing as much as four hundred tons, were fragmented by dynamite and reused as building material for the construction of modern buildings and homes in Bolivia.

"Among the surviving Tiahuanacu ruins is the 'Gateway of the Sun', it is a monolithic structure. The central higher figure is Viracocha, the god of creation, who radiates some kind of energy from his head. The god was surrounded by anthropomorphic figures with bird's heads. The god holds two sticks, each with the head of a snake, probably some symbolical representation of the chords of gravity, which the god neutralized for an instant in order to produce the Big Bang, and with it the birth of the universe.

"It seems that the 'Gateway of the Sun' was not an indicator of hidden chambers; instead some thing higher, it was a cosmological instruction using symbolic carvings. The scientists of Atlantis intended it as a memento for the physicists and astronomers of the future, perhaps of the twenty-first century. Perhaps, someday humanity will be able to decipher these petroglyphs.

"The petroglyphs of the 'Gateway of the Sun' depict the drama of the last meeting between God and the buspars, just before the Big-Bang. The buspars are the ultra-small particles of the primeval soup that appeared in my dreams. They are analogous to the modern definition of quarks. The buspars are eternal and continue to exist before and after each Big Bang.

"With each dawn and each sunset, the stone of the 'Gateway of the Sun' represents the rebirth and the death of this pulsating universe. The carving of the stone shows the dramatic moments of the last communion between God and the super-compressed particles inside the infinitely dense primeval black hole, moments before its release for the birth of the universe with a big bang. This interpretation was taken from the story of the creation, written in the Genesis from the Great Book of the Atlantis religion.

"The Atlanteans also built, several monolithic monuments throughout Europe as indicators for other hidden vaults. However, simultaneously all of them collapsed by the same disaster that sank Atlantis and produced Noah's flood. The stones remained scattered over fields for ages and their flat surfaces eroded beyond recognition.

"Originally built as a model, Stonehenge represented the downtown area of the modern city of Brasea in Atlantis. Each column represented a skyscraper and each horizontal lintel above them a hanging runway, an air terminal linking the top of twin buildings. Millennia later after the general collapse of the monuments appeared other cultures, including the Druids with their magician Merlin, who was more a physicist than a magician. The Druids used the same monolithic stones already lying there for a millennium to build a new monument, perhaps a calendar or an observatory. Every time the Atlanteans built monuments in areas of the world covered by ice, they transported the large, monolithic stones on ice sleds to the chosen site, from which the ice had been removed. They erected their monuments with the help of giant robots, the same ones used around the world to perform different tasks. (For additional technical information, see the appendices part of this book.)

"The total collapse of the ancient European monuments was not recorded in history because at the time, the European population was small and living in the Stone Age. Half of Europe was still buried under many feet of ice, the last vestiges of the Ice Age.

"In South America, neat designs of objects, animals, geometrical figures, and hundreds of straight lines were traced on the surface of the perfectly flat Peruvian desert next to the town of Nazca. Those designs could only be seen from the air from hot air balloons or aircraft. These pictures probably represented sky constellations as seen from the Southern Hemisphere or huge signs and images, warning extraterrestrial visitors by showing them the images of the poisonous and dangerous animals that existed in South America. They are still admired today by tourists and archaeologists.

"Long trapezoidal and rectangular shallow depressions are found in the same desert. They are about the width of a road and are sunk a few inches deep into the ground surface. They look like giant's footprints or belly prints left by huge, alien spaceships. They had to be the size of mountains weighing thousands of tons. The trapezoidal belly supported their full weight, which sank a few inches into the flat, desert ground. It seems that huge alien spaceships from different civilizations used to land and takeoff from special, flat barren areas. This happened eons ago, when our ancestors were already a little bit smarter than chimps.

"Near the end of the ninetieth century, our monks found a stone slab with carved symbols in Tiahuanacu, Bolivia. The stone was not big; two persons could lift it. The same monks that found it were able to decipher those hieroglyphs. It read that two lines, traced on the ground of two different deserts, intercepted with each other far to the north, at the top of a mountain located at the center of South America. Under this intersection could be found a buried Atlantis chamber. It was in times so ancient that there were no other designs on those deserts, but only the two traced lines. Today we can see hundreds of these neat designs in the Nazca desert, some of them of more recent times, designs that still remain a mystery. Our grandfathers observed them secretly from high-altitude hot-air balloons. Our monks were only interested in one or two old straight lines, the ones traced eons ago by the Atlanteans, lines that are fading today.

"One barely visible ground line became of particular interest. It started from Nazca desert in Peru and stretched northeast for more than a thousand miles, ending at the center of Bolivia. There it intersected with another similar line, which started in another desert located north of Chile. Both lines intersected at a point above this mountain. At that point, we excavated a hole several feet deep towards the center of this mountain, until we reached a hard surface, like reinforced concrete. After cutting a hole there, we discovered it was hollow underneath. We found a mysterious ancient treasure chamber, by perforating its dome.

"Following this discovery, our grandfathers began to excavate a long tunnel to reach the chamber from the deepest corner of this natural cavern. Luckily a few months later, our grandparents found this natural cavern at one side of this mountain, and built barracks inside it. Finally after so much dusty work excavating that tunnel, they reached the chamber of wisdom. Once we had a tunnel, we no longer needed the hole from the top of the mountain, so we plugged it with rocks and dirt.

"That is the end of this story. I apologize for talking always so much with my guests; sometimes I can't stop. Perhaps now you'd like to retire to your assigned room. We will talk later at the time we will walk inside that tunnel, if you want to hear more about Atlantis."

I told him, I definitely wanted to hear more of those tales. But I repeated again that I had nothing to do with this strange business of Atlantis; I was just an ordinary teenager. He didn't answer me, instead he said, "I'm going to show you this place right away. We built these barracks not too far from the treasure chamber to guard it from the outside world. At the same time we learned some of the wisdom kept there and later we moved most of the prehistoric library from that ancient chamber to our barracks, to have all those books at hand." I told the monk that all this sounded very interesting. The monk said, "After we have visited the underground chamber and returned, we will walk directly into the library here in our barracks. There you will see clay tablets, golden scrolls, documents and ancient movies from Atlantis." I was beginning to trust these people.

A very old monk joined us at the barracks, main walkway, and we walked to the deepest corner of the cavern. There I saw a black hole, the entrance to the claustrophobic tunnel. I thought it might lead to the center of the Earth. I lost my trust again and I became apprehensive of these monks. Perhaps they were really demons taking me to Hell, a place of eternal torment ruled by Lucifer. I couldn't take another step forward. I wanted to leave their facility, escape from these demons, and wander through the mountains, searching for my father and the porter. The monks told me not to be apprehensive. I was going to see what no ordinary man had ever seen, not even in his wildest dreams. Finally they convinced me that I should trust them.

I was still trembling when I entered the tunnel. It became darker and the two monks turned on their flashlights. We walked through the long, narrow tunnel for half an hour before we reached its end, deep at the center of the mountain. I had not noticed how long we had been walking because their stories entertained me, from the moment we started our march.

Fred began to tell a story, "Incidentally, the boost of a new Earth civilization will coincide with the return of a small group of half aliens, the true descendants of the Atlanteans. Our brothers will arrive soon from Entar after thousands of years of absence. We know they will be kind and beautiful. They will cause no harm to the present population on Earth. They are the descendants of the kindly Atlanteans who once were the protectors of Earth.

"Modern human societies must come to know about our order and the return of our brethren who will come to help us prevent polluting the world and the suffering from nuclear fallout. They will also prepare the new humanity to counteract any attack from the ugly Ortusians.

"A long time ago, a few days before the destruction of Atlantis, they quickly built seven underground chambers then permanently sealed their entrances with clay and rocks. Then the workers returned from overseas to their beloved islands to undertake on what was going to be their last project. The interstellar exodus, it was a project undertaken because of the pessimistic assumption that the coming comet would not only partially damage Earth, there was a possibility it might decimate all life on the planet. As a precaution against the worst-case scenario, in order to preserve our species and the species of animals and plants from Earth, the Atlanteans wanted to send various living specimens, including humans, to some other planet able to sustain life in the galaxy. It needed to be a planet similar to Earth, with the hope that eons later their descendants would return to repopulate an Earth that probably got decimated.

"In the last days of Atlantis, a small group of rich Atlanteans decided to send 500 Atlanteans to planet Entar in the solar system Mank, located in the Orion constellation of this galaxy. The Atlanteans remembered that 50 years before, at the time when the Entarians visited Earth and Atlantis, the kindly Entarians invited them to visit their planet at any time in the future and without previous announcement. By journeying there, the Earth tourists would learn from their extraterrestrial wisdom.

"Going back to the topic of the construction of the spaceship, the Atlanteans realized that it would be impossible for humans to build a ship similar to those of alien technology. For this reason they used extraterrestrial blueprints to build and assemble it in outer space. These were the plans the Entarian aliens had given them as a present on their last visit to Earth. The ship was assembled and moored with long cables to the Atlantis space station. Space shuttles and space planes made hundreds of trips to carry the delicate mechanisms, systems, and people. The prefabricated, heavy structural components of a ship weighing as much as a skyscraper was not sent in the flimsy space shuttles. Instead, man-made volcanoes, with holes resembling volcano shafts, were used as cannons to violently shoot the heavy components to be assembled into a spaceship in orbit, a cheap, crude but practical way. Several man-made volcanoes were built around the rocky perimeter of the beautiful, classical island of Atlantis. As the man-made volcanoes blew up, so did the island. This island was sacrificed along with its temples, palaces, and marble statues all in order that those 500 interstellar travelers could survive.

"The holes or shafts of the artificial volcanoes were also called rocky cannons, which were slightly tilted towards the rising sun. The cylindrical heavy rock blocks to be shot into space didn't rest directly on the flat bottom of the hole but on four blocks supporting their weight, forming a gap or a cavern underneath. To launch all this into space, a small nuclear bomb was installed in that cavern, which later was flooded with seawater. The explosion of the nuclear bomb turned the underground lagoon into super-heated steam that violently catapulted the bullet all the way into an orbit around earth. The temperature of the explosion was so high that it vaporized the rocky bullet's lower half. The cargo was sent into orbit by strapping it down with chains and cables to the top of the rocky bullet. Normally the pollution and nuclear fallout would be abhorrent to the environmentally conscious Atlanteans. However, they were not even considerations for a world soon to be destroyed.

"Meanwhile crew and passengers were already living for 30 days in that crowded space station. It was like a big hotel. From their windows passengers could contemplate the gradual completion of their ship as the materials and components were shot up from Earth.

"Three weeks before the comet hit the Earth, an order was given to fire all rocky cannons at once, so that all the remaining components necessary for the final assemblage would arrive simultaneously and in the neighborhood of the space station. The shock of the explosion of the 100 man-made nuclear volcanoes collapsed the geologically unstable island of Poseidon, which is lying today as thick sediment at the bottom of the ocean. The other islands still remained intact. Day after day the comet was getting closer. The population of Atlantis had already evacuated, except for a few heroic volunteers with important assignments who remained there until the end.

"All great works of art were abandoned on the island of Poseidon, except the huge statue of the god Poseidon, a statue four stories high, of him standing in his chariot pulled by six steeds. The statue was moved more than 1,000 kilometers south and placed on the top of a deep submarine plateau. Seawater protected the statue from natural disasters and erosion.

"There was some hope for the ancients, that someday the statue would be rescued by the people of the future, when they were advanced enough to discover it by learning first to communicate with some dolphins that know many secrets of the sea. The discovery of this statue would add evidence to the past existence of Atlantis. However, nobody knows if the statue survived the disaster.

"Once all the spaceship components were in orbit, it took only two weeks to assemble the huge, interstellar ship weighing millions of pounds. At the space station travelers looking to Earth, saw the sad view of the destruction of the island of Poseidon. Eight days later appeared the frightening view of the approaching comet high above in the sky. Two days later it fell into the Atlantic Ocean, destroying not only the rest of the Atlantis islands, including the Island of the Sun, but also devastating the shores of nearby continents. The impact caused fires, smoke, steam, and brown clouds that gradually covered the blue Earth. A chain of natural events, including awakening volcanoes and tsunamis contributed to the destruction.

"Crew and passengers assigned to the exodus had to be young in order to endure the 60-year voyage traveling at one quarter the speed of light. All passengers and crew boarded the space ship before it got untied from its moorings for the journey to planet Entar. As the ship departed, the passengers could feel the gentle thrust of the nuclear fusion rocket engines. Many thousands of years have passed since that voyage. Hundreds of Atlantean generations have lived on Entar as a welcome minority. Most of them forgot their earthly roots in the same way we have forgotten Atlantis.

"According to our calculations, the descendants of the exodus are due to return in our lifetime. The first expedition has already arrived. Unfortunately their journey ended in tragedy." The old monk bowed his head in sorrow. Fred the monk went on, "Boy, you wouldn't believe who is the other Custodian walking next to you in this tunnel. He is really an alien monk. We call him the Far-born. Although he is human, Far-born was not born on this planet. He is 122 years old and still in good health." Incredible as it seems, he walked at the same pace we did. He wore sandals and a simple robe and looked like the other friars.

At last the alien monk spoke, "My name is Toroid and you are the only outsider who will hear my stories. I am the only survivor from the first group of travelers returning to this planet. We came eager to find our roots and to help in everything for our human brothers. People on this planet consider me an ordinary man even though I was born on Entar. Our voyage from Entar ended in June of 1908 in Siberia, north of Asia.

"This is what happened. Less than two centuries ago on Entar, a librarian lady with Atlantean ancestry discovered in old, dusty archives, the origins of our race and our immigration to Entar. She learned of a long forgotten planet called Earth, a beautiful blue planet. In the same file, she read that sometime in the future the evil Ortusian race might pass by and invade Earth.

"A popular movement spread through one group of Atlanteans who advocated that the time had come to return to Earth, thus fulfilling the prophecy. We wanted to arrive in time to assist our Earth brothers to develop new technology for a possible war to defend the planet against the Ortusians. After a few peaceful demonstrations, the kindly Entarians understood our reasons for returning to Earth. On Entar the helpful Entarians promised to build, free of charge, two ships for our return voyage. Upon completion, the ships would depart one at a time, approximately 110 earth years apart.

"The first ship left Entar in the middle of your nineteenth century. We were in the first group of returning Atlanteans. I was only a small child traveling with my parents. They later died of old age before we arrived. As we approached the blue Earth, its beauty, more beautiful than Entar and many other planets in this galaxy amazed us. I never forgot that view. We knew from our old records that at this time the Earth atmosphere would turn clear from the soot and dust produced by that forgotten comet's impact. We assumed that not all humans perished; some had to have survived the disaster. A month before our arrival, we made our first radio contact with the custodians. It was at the beginning of the twentieth century. They were the only ones in the world able to receive our radio transmissions. We were greatly relieved to hear their voices because it meant positively that humans had survived the comet 11,000 years ago.

"As we approached the Earth, we studied its atmosphere and many other details we needed to know before landing. At last we arrived and parked in a polar orbit, and turned off the engines. A tremendous celebration took place inside our ship. Those were our last happy moments." I could see in his eyes that the old monk was lost in his memories. "We wanted very much to communicate with the custodians, in spite of some language problems. As last we tried to communicate in the ancient Atlantis language. Fortunately the monks had learned it from the scrolls. We learned it by studying from old recordings.

"In June of 1908 we identified ourselves to the order as the returning ones. From then on we were in full contact with every custodian station around the world. Our crew was busy with the last calculations searching for an appropriate landing site. If there were not an ideal place, then at least a cold area with adequate water would be better than a desert. The custodian monks warned us that the gravity on Earth must be many times stronger than the artificial gravity we had inside our Entarian ship.

"I was sent to Earth in a personal landing craft as a test. The rest of the passengers were to follow in a larger craft. I landed safely on the north face of the Himalayas but was quickly overcome by Earth's gravity. I couldn't stand up. I wasn't used to this and had to rest until the Custodians living in the area rescued me.

"An enthusiastic young monk greeted me saying, you just arrived in time to stop the escalation of hostilities between nations. He said that the coming of the First World War was imminent.

"After the happy celebration, all 540 passengers who had shared the trip for 61 years walked to the front section of the cabin which was designed as a huge landing capsule. When all the people got inside the capsule, its doors were closed. The rest of the ship was no longer needed so it was going to be abandoned in space. Then something unpredictable happened. The landing craft failed to separate from the main ship. From the ground with my small telescope I watched my helpless countrymen circling the Earth once more before plunging into the atmosphere and exploding over a cold forest in the Soviet Tunguska region." The old man wiped a tear from his eye.

"During their last orbit one of our astronauts talked with me by radio. 'We don't have a chance. We know we are going to die because of a big mistake. This is my last report, my Earth brothers. Be ready for the arrival of the second group of Atlanteans who will arrive sometime in the next century. The cause of our tragedy was a contact of metal to metal between the landing capsule and the rest of the ship structure. In the vacuum of space, you should lubricate or at least put a piece of paper in between metallic surfaces; you cannot allow metallic parts to touch one another for long periods of time because they get welded. After removing the bolts from all the spaceship supports, two supports could not get separated. Nature welded the two structures, by being exposed to the vacuum of space during the long voyage. The engineer responsible for periodic inspections of the ship exterior was also in charge of lubricating all metal surfaces that were in mutual contact. He failed to do his job. He became senile during the latter part of the voyage after neglecting to wear the heavy, lead helmet to protect his brain from the cosmic radiation outside the spaceship. He felt the helmet was uncomfortable and underestimated the effects of cosmic rays on the human body.'" Before finishing his story Toroid said, "Today people in Russia and the world don't realize that explosion was a spaceship, not a comet. Its explosion wiped off a huge extension of the Tunguska region of the Siberian forest." The monk became sober and sad.

# CHAPTER 11
## Entering the Chamber

My apprehension subsided while walking down the long dark tunnel, hiking with the help of a flashlight all the way to the center of the mountain. When we arrived to the end of the tunnel, a monk opened a wardrobe box lying against the rocky wall. Inside it, there were several sets of diving equipment. He handed a set to each of us, and then took one for himself. Each set had a mask with a glass face and a tank of oxygen to be strapped to the back of the person. He explained that anybody that wants to enter the chamber must wear this equipment. The chamber contained no air and no oxygen, just an atmosphere of inert gases including helium. The Atlanteans intentionally filled the chamber with these gases in order to prevent bacteria infestation, fungus, and corrosion, protecting forever everything stored there, including the masterpieces of art, scrolls, and books made from gold and plastic, and a variety of machines stored in the lower floors.

As Fred touched the rocky wall, he turned on a concealed switch, illuminating simultaneously the end of the tunnel, a small anteroom, and some of the bright lights inside the vault. The door to enter the small anteroom was not located in front of us; it was a hatch on the floor because the anteroom was located below, in between this tunnel floor and the vaulted ceiling.

Again I began trembling with apprehension. I thought probably I was entering hell to see where Lucifer and his fallen angels dwelled. Fred said, "Please move aside, you are standing on the round hatch flush with the floor. It is the only entrance to the chamber below." The latch had odd handles. Fred pulled it up and opened. Then we descended one after the other by a vertical ladder to a small anteroom, which was also an airlock. Fred, who was the last to descend, closed the latch above him, so nobody coming by the tunnel could fall through the hole. The same modern monks who had excavated the tunnel and built their barracks a century ago had, also built this airlock.

In the floor of this airlock we saw second access hatch to descend to a still deeper room. Fred opened this second hatch and we descended as before through this second hole and by another ladder. As before, Fred was the last to descend, closing the hatch above his head. We found ourselves in an well-illuminated chamber, this time as wide as a hotel lobby. I looked back to the last hatch through which we had descended and realized that hole was cut on the ceiling of the huge vaulted chamber.

The old monk still had the energy of a young man, climbing ladders without a problem. We found ourselves inside the upper basement floor of a huge chamber. It was like visiting a department store of many floors. I could not figure why a structure so large was built at the center of the mountain. After a moment of silence, Fred confirmed we were standing on the upper basement floor of the treasure chamber and ready to initiate our tour by descending floor by floor. The ceiling and walls were beautifully lined with stainless steel plates. What a great civilization!

I wondered again if this was the entrance to Hell or Heaven. Anyway, I was excited and exclaimed, "How luxurious! This empty floor looks like an unfurnished palace."

In order to keep some of the objects from this floor on hand, the monks had already moved most of it to their barracks and private library. The exceptions were some scientific charts, with physics and chemistry formulas, still hanging from the vault walls. My host said those formulas represented the most intimate secrets of the universe, which may take them years to decipher.

The Atlanteans built this egg-shaped chamber with its longest axis set vertically. Each floor was a wide gallery, with a huge circular cutout at its center. Handrails all around served as a balcony. We were standing, on the top floor with the domed ceiling above us. The illumination was superb. Everything there was shiny and clean as if brand new. We descended to the second basement floor; it was like an art gallery, while the rest of the floors resembled museums of science and industry. Fred explained that the Atlanteans had not intended to create an art gallery or a museum, just a storage unit built for eternity. In their grief the Atlanteans wanted to conserve their culture for posterity.

Our host continued with his narration, "We call this top floor the floor of the intellectuals, because it is here where most of the educational material, including golden scrolls, clay tablets, maps, and films were stored. Then at the beginning of the twentieth century, our monks moved most of it to the library in our headquarters. Ever since, we've dedicated most of our lives studying contents. Now we will descend to the second lower floor, what I call the floor for the artists."

We descended and I saw many thin aluminum partitions standing in the floor, which were used for hanging paintings. The monk explained that this floor was full of sculptures, engravings, and drawings from different Atlantean periods showing various artistic styles created by great artists who were already forgotten. Again as before Fred said that the monks had removed some of the pictures hanging from the partitions to their barracks. However, on the right side of the same floor still remained some works of art from the Atlantis Classical Period, when the people believed in Poseidon, Zeus, and the other gods. It is interesting to observe that millennia, after Atlantis disappeared, the Greeks adopted the same gods with some slight change of behavior, with Zeus as the principal god.

Still hanging there were some paintings, some displaying the favorite sports and games of the Atlanteans, including ball games. Most Atlanteans were fanatics with traditional games involving bulls and horses, which, although dangerous for the performers, didn't hurt the animals. Paintings and drawings representing old traditions and customs had survived through a period after their mythology had been transformed into folklore.

On a table I saw several small shining statues, some of pure gold representing old gods, old kings, and sacred animals. Two full-sized bronze statues standing on the floor particularly caught my attention. One was of a bull and the other of a nervous horse.

Hanging there was a particular painting representing Paradise, as depicted by one of the modern Atlantis religions. At the center of the painting were a couple of angelic lovers, with shining, colorful butterfly wings, flying perhaps no more than a few feet above a spring of crystal clear waters flowing in between the round rocks. In the painting background was shown a forest with some playful cupids. The members of this sect believed in an afterlife. They believed when a good person dies his or her spirit goes to Paradise, to be transformed into an angel with colorful butterfly wings. Next to this painting there was another, representing another Atlantis religious belief. It displayed the final battle and victory on Condemnation Day, where the god of good kills the god of evil.

The monk pointed out the resemblance that existed between the modern and the old Atlantis classical art with the old European and the modern American. It seemed as if history repeats itself.

We walked to another section of the same floor. It was full of glass cabinets displaying jewelry and fancy objects with the crowns from the ancient kings of Atlantis, with bracelets and pendants of silver and sapphires that belonged to their wives. In another cabinet were luxurious garments that once belonged to foreign kings, princes, and princesses that often visited Atlantis. I saw diamonds larger than a man's thumb inserted in intricate gold and platinum settings. I saw necklaces laced with rubies and emeralds and rings of pure platinum and gold.

"Come closer and take another look, if you aren't afraid of heights," said Fred. The monk invited me to approach the ornate hand railing from the circular balcony. I looked down into the vast, round empty space. It reminded me of the interior of a great cathedral. It was also like looking from the top gallery near the dome of an opera theater to the floor below. For a moment I imagined I was looking down into an abyss to the center of the Earth. After a while, I felt more relaxed. At the very bottom of the building, standing on the marble floor, were strange shining, flying machines. I was awed at the sight.

Suddenly I was struck by a thought. Who are these people? Maybe they are demons. Am I being led to Hell, as was Dante? Or maybe it's another race of sentient beings, possibly non-human, maybe dangerous? I shivered at the thought. "Are you the devil?" I blurted out. My host began to laugh. He held his belly and guffawed at the idea. Showing such human emotion, he didn't seem like much of a devil.

"No, no," the monk struggled to reply. "No, I'm not the devil. That is a good one though, very funny. My boy, there is no Heaven or Hell. There is only this chamber -- it is our Heaven and Hell, "Relieved by his lighthearted response, I let my concerns pass and continued to pursue my special interest in the artwork.

I was puzzled and inquired of my host how the Atlanteans brought all these objects and large machines into this underground chamber. He answered that at the beginning of the project, the Atlanteans began excavating a large, deep hole from the mountaintop. At the bottom of the hole, they built this storage chamber. It is a building in the shape of an egg. Before they covered it with a huge lid, it looked like a pot. All this structure was made from reinforced concrete. The Atlanteans used a giant crane to lower those objects through the large opening on the top of the mountain. Once the chamber was full, the crane lowered the huge vaulted lid to cover and seal its top for eternity. To conceal the chamber, the excavated hole was filled all the way to the top of the mountain with rocks and dirt.

Before I finished examining the gallery from this floor, the monk called me to accompany him to the next floor below, which was a fairyland of small models. He led me to a miniature bronze statue inside its temple. He said, "This is a replica of the statue of Poseidon." I saw an energetic, muscular man riding his chariot. His massive right arm held the rein of six sinuous horses their manes and tails flying, eyes wide and nostrils flaring. It stood about a foot tall. "The actual statue is four stories high," the monk explained.

The roof of the small temple model was removed, allowing a view of its interior. Each column, each lamp, each statue was reproduced exactly in miniature. A large water fountain at the center of the temple represented the sea. Poseidon was standing on his chariot, and the entire statue including the horses protruded above the water of the fountain.

Fred continued the tour, "On the back side of this floor, miniature replicas of the main cities of ancient and modern Atlantis were represented. You can find exact streets, homes, public buildings, parks, and universities." A model representing the city of Acropolis that once stood at the center of the ancient island of Poseidon was now standing on that table. While this Acropolis model was small, the Poseidon temple seemed massive. The wide courts were carefully tiled with marble. The green grounds were sprinkled with white statuary.

I could have spent many days just studying in this floor, or maybe just studying this single tabletop model of the ancient classical city. I felt like I could live my entire life in this chamber and never get bored.

"Is this Earth?" I asked the monk, pointing at a globe in a different area of the same floor. It was not the globe I was used to seeing. This was Earth in times of Atlantis, before the Great Hammer (comet impact). The North Pole ice extended south covering large parts of Europe, Asia, and America, glacial vestiges of the last Ice Age.

A relief map made of plaster stood on a nearby table representing the green islands of Atlantis. The surrounding ocean was decorated with miniature ocean liners and idyllic sailboats on the blue seas. Next to this relief was the model of modern Brasea, the largest city in Atlantis. The Acropolis and its temples had been demoted to a historic city and a museum. Brasea by contrast was a super-modern city of skyscrapers and great transportation systems. Many tubes hanging in the air from skyscraper to skyscraper looked as ribbons. In reality those were skyways and hanging trains. We kept walking by the gallery and arrived in another area that looked like an enormous toy store, with more glass cabinets. Inside this were miniature models of cars, buses, planes, spaceships, and ocean liners.

Just before descending to the next floor, we met a small group of young monks wearing oxygen masks as we were. They were probably on their way to conduct some advanced research. When I asked Fred who they were, he replied, "They're just a group of our custodian brothers. Every day a group of us come to investigate the artifacts in this chamber. You could spend 40 years visiting this chamber and never learn everything. You can find here the most advanced technology that any power in the world could imagine."

One of the monks approached me and said, "You will be awed when you visit the rest of the lower floors, where is stored scientific equipment and instruments; medical equipment; remote-controlled robots, some are smaller than an ant used in microsurgery. Also you will see there a bionic eye created for the blind, and an artificial heart made from a special material, not to be rejected by the human body. Next to the heart you will see a golden scroll explaining its design." In this chamber we found a variety of incredible industrial machinery and breathtaking transportation systems. There was a model of a supersonic aircraft shaped like an arrow, designed to carry 100 passengers across the Atlantic Ocean in only one hour.

We left the group of monks and moved down to the third level. "What are the walls made of?" I asked, admiring their smooth, non-reflective surface.

"Reinforced concrete," answered Fred. "However, the entire chamber is lined with bare plates of stainless steel. Our ancestors wanted this place to last for an eternity," Fred said, smiling.

"Wow! Look at this!" I shouted with delight upon seeing a red and silver sports car. I ran to jump on it.

"Stop! Don't touch it," Fred bellowed. I jerked to a stop. I had forgotten his one and only rule. I hadn't touched the car, but I still felt guilty.

"Oh, I'm sorry. I forgot," I apologized.

"It's okay," said Fred, as he placed his hand on my shoulder. "I understand your excitement. Pardon me for yelling at you, but it is of the utmost importance that you touch nothing. Protecting this cache of treasures is my mission in life." We were friends again, perhaps even more so than before, as I saw the human side of my austere host.

"This vehicle that you call a sports car is powered by a small turbine engine that dwarfs your greatest internal combustion engine. This car was actually owned by Krill Godinson, one of the richest and most famous men of the last days of Atlantis. Soon you will hear more about him, much, much more," Fred explained. Then he turned and walked away. I followed him, although I was still drawn to the fiery, dynamic car. On this level I could see more beautiful sports cars which belonged to rich Atlanteans. In the same gallery on various tables were miniature models of a super-fast train, four different models of sailboats, and a small yacht.  Fred said that electric cars were not expensive, but very practical in Atlantis, because electricity was very cheap.  Some electric power plants were able to tap free energy from underground geothermal sources.  Atlantis had a lot of them.

The monk led me down to the fourth floor.  He said, "Here you will see two kinds of huge robots, some like dragons and others like the Cyclops.  The dragons looked like shining dinosaurs made from durable metals.  They were built for mining and excavating tunnels and to extract mineral ore.  The Cyclops were like giant apes, anthropomorphic robots with one eye the size of a house window.  They were used as construction workers to transport heavy objects.  In the Atlantis language and later in Greek, the word Cyclops meant, wheel.

That part of the gallery wasn't too dark; still I could see much detail.  Then Fred touched a spot in the wall and bright light filled the area.

Confronted by the huge, armored, ape-like Cyclops, I jumped, startled.  I explained to Fred that this was the same monster I had seen in my dreams back on the mountain.  I couldn't believe this time it was real, and not part of a nightmare.  I was close to the mechanical ape and could see every detail of it.  I calmed down and observed the motionless robot outstretched, with the light glinting off the polished metal of its upper torso.  Its ugly legs were sparsely covered with stiff hairs, as seen on some insects.  Actually these one-inch diameter hairs covering its feet and calves were electrical terrain sensors.  The signals from its legs and from the robot's laser eyes were transmitted to the robot's electronic brain for a variety of terrain mapping computations.  All this happened at great speed before the robot could move each leg to advance one more step.  The robot had additional laser eyes located under its belly, to look continuously at the ground evaluating the shape of the terrain before its foot would step on it.  "Don't be frightened," said Fred.  "This robot was used to grab and transport tree trunks and huge blocks of stone. Some of them weigh more than a hundred tons, transporting them through valleys, plains, and mountain ranges. "At that moment it looked like a grotesque, sleeping ape to me.  It was so big that the only way it could fit inside the vault's floor was horizontally.  Slowly we walked its length.  The monster lay as if asleep on a timber cradle laid on the platform of a heavy truck trailer with so many wheels I couldn't count them all.  All the tires were flat; over the eons the air had leaked out. The ape on its trailer occupied most of that floor.

A dragon robot set on another timber cradle had a long, shining, silver body and hydraulically operated legs attached to its sides.  Wheels built under its belly showed it was a machine, not a dinosaur.  Fred said, "The ancient name for this machine was 'dragon.'  When it was working, sparks flared like acetylene torches. Crushed rocks glowed from its carbide cutting blades.  This spawned ancient legends about monsters that snorted flames from their mouths and threatened to eat the sun.  These legends are still alive today."

Changing the subject, Fred said, "This is a critical moment for humanity.  We are not sure yet if today humanity is mature enough to receive this legacy, the wisdom enclosed in this chamber, which could be used either to build a great civilization, or to destroy this planet." As we moved down to the fifth level, Fred asked, "Tell me, Walt, do you know the moment a civilization becomes so advanced that other great civilizations from the galaxy become aware of its existence?"

Try as I might to come up with an answer, I drew a blank.

We walked a few steps and the monk put his hand on a large, cylindrical machine. "Well, I'll tell you. This is what makes a civilization great. Thanks to this device, several advanced civilizations from the galaxy accepted Atlantis culture as the Earth culture.

"This is a thermofusion nuclear reactor. It is a clean source of boundless energy that works, as long as there will be water in the oceans. Eleven thousand years ago two types of reactors were created in Atlantis: one to provide limitless quantities of electricity for the cities, the other to propel spaceships throughout the universe on voyages lasting for years. This was the greatest Atlantis accomplishment. We hope that today's humanity can develop a similar device for the future."

On the fifth lower level there were a variety of aircraft and three kinds of helicopters. The monk pointed to a relatively small passenger jet, similar in design to modern commuter jets. He said, "Walt, this was the most popular aircraft sold in Atlantis. It outsold every other plane on the market. It was of simple design and a practical passenger commuter for flights between the islands. There is an interesting story behind it. In Atlantis an airline needed this kind of aircraft, and at the same time its executives were eager to promote education for young people. So they gave a grant to a high school to organize a group of eager, talented teenagers to design and develop this small jet transport. Less than a dozen students were chosen, mostly because of their ability to design by using computers. They developed it under the supervision of an experienced engineer, working after school hours."

Still there were two more floors below to explore. After descending to the next floor, I saw a vast expanse of strange flying machines, including Unidentified Flying Objects (UFOs), stored there since Atlantis times, all of them shining as if new. "The gilding is due to an anticorrosive coating made of gold, which is actually only a few molecules thick," Fred explained. I wondered if he could read my mind. He seemed to anticipate my questions. An oblong object attracted my attention. It glittered like gold and stood on three legs. Fred said it was an extraterrestrial-flying vehicle used to shuttle goods to and from Earth to the alien giant mother spaceship operating in a low orbit. This vehicle was left by the Entarian aliens as a token of friendship to the Atlanteans on their last visit to Earth.

He said, "I shouldn't do this, but for you I will make an exception." He opened the vehicle door and we stepped inside it. Once inside the vehicle, I saw a short column at its center. Around the column four reclined seats were arranged in a cross. They were small seats built for people the size of twelve-year-old children. "Look at the headrests," said Fred. "They are for big heads, perhaps for brains one-and-a-half times larger than humans, good enough for telepathic communications and to memorize entire encyclopedias and scientific information about the universe.  They didn't need to bring bulky libraries with them.  These aliens also used their brains for telekinetic mind over matter purposes, in a manner we cannot comprehend, mostly to propel their own space vehicles through the universe."  Fred pointed to a small box and said it was the recycling system for air, water, and waste.  Then he pointed to another box saying it contained many mini-computers.  One of its purposes was to maintain a cool environment inside the vehicle, useful for long flights lasting for years.  There the crew would hibernate; meanwhile, the vehicle would fly just by inertia and sometimes controlled by its autopilot.  The cabin had eight windows for full visibility. In front of each astronaut, controls, monitors, and dials were flush with the interior wall. Fred never told me how the aliens dealt with the damaging effects of cosmic radiation.

Fred said, "You should know that there is only one kind of energy in the universe that can repel or neutralize gravity, and that is the telekinetic power from the mind of God and of course also the mind of other superior beings, like the alien astronauts. Every time the aliens wanted to takeoff and fly in their machine, the thing they did first was to fall into deep meditation, enhancing their telekinetic powers, in order to be able to repel gravity and levitate to some height, perhaps a height of a quarter mile high, then they started to fly their vehicle in the direction they wanted, pulled by the partially disturbed centrifugal force produced by a rotating machine. In the beginning when this machine started to run, by the laws of physics in a three-dimensional universe, the system of forces is in equilibrium and the resultant (vectorial sum) of the forces is zero.  Then some of the forces that maintained that equilibrium were cancelled not by physical means but by the telekinetic power from the mind of the same astronauts.  The new resultant force from the disturbed group of centrifugal forces prevailed in a particular direction, and the vehicle was propelled in that direction. Those vehicles or flying saucers had infinite range.  This concept of propulsion definitely defies the laws of physics in our three dimensional world, but not in higher dimensions.  Humans never will be able to fly this vehicle, because humans doesn't posses the extraordinary telekinetic powers that extraterrestrial do.  Humans can't even lift a pencil one hundredth of an inch high above the top of a table."

> (For additional information see REALITY OR FANTASI,
> CHRONICLE OF ALIEN VEHICLE ANALYSIS
> at the end of this chapter.)

I never understood this UFO propulsion system, because until today probably nobody has found reliable proof that psychic powers of the mind, including telekinesis, exist.  Who knows?

I looked appreciatively at the alien space vehicles as we walked to the stairs to descend one more floor to the sixth, the lowest of the building. There I saw a piece of an Atlantean space station. Also, another fantastic nuclear fusion engine built by the Atlanteans, in some way similar to the one I saw before, but it was not used to supply electricity for the cities, but instead was of a special design to propel large spaceships for long voyages through the solar system.

Fred said, "Underneath this marble floor there is a small basement with locked doors nobody can open to see inside. We assume that inside it was the environmental control system and the electrical power source that illuminates the whole complex, which had been working without failure for more than eleven thousand years."

We were at the bottom of the building; I walked freely to the center of the marble floor and looked up through the round open space all the way up to the domed ceiling. The whole thing looked like a pantheon of gods. I thought I would weep as I looked into awesome space. It was like the interior of a huge cathedral dedicated to greatness. "To get the idea of the height of the dome," said Fred, "look at those bronze statues near the ceiling that seem to be only a foot high. They are actually six feet tall. This is the end of our tour. Let's go."

"I was so impressed with the tour, I didn't realize I was pushing you for more information," I said, apologizing to Fred.

"No, it's okay. I didn't even think about your exhaustion. Come with me," said Fred. We climbed the stairs all the way back to the upper basement floor, then up by the same ladder we came in, through a hole in the domed ceiling. From there on, we began our long march returning by that long dark narrow tunnel to the monks' barracks.

## THE SECRET LIBRARY AT THE MONKS BARRACKS

Everything looked too good to be true. Perhaps it was all just a dream. I remembered that in high school I was reluctant to study my history lessons. However strange as it may seem, I was now getting educated by the monks in their cave high in the Andes Mountains, learning about some kind of weird world history, and strange ideas about the origin of the earth. Perhaps it was from beings that were hybrids of alien and human origin. I asked myself, should I trust that this history is true? Of course I should. It came mostly from the advanced Entarian aliens who taught the Atlanteans during their last visit to Earth.

After leaving the vault, we walked again by the same claustrophobic tunnel. To make our trek easier, the monk told some jokes and decided to start another narration. It was certainly time for one; I was eager to hear more stories. This time the story was with reference to a famous, ancient, secret library in Northeast Africa, which in the past was only open to a few, an elite group of wise men. Fred began his new story, "We believe that the largest of the seven underground chambers is located somewhere near the Nile delta in Egypt. We suspect it remains hidden under the floor of a small ancient adobe house. This house was a secret ancient library where were kept some of the ancient dusty scrolls of Atlantis. The illustrious wise men that frequently visited this library in different times never knew that under its floor was hidden a huge underground chamber with the greatest treasure of the world. The library's exact location no longer is known," Fred said. "To give you some idea of the dimensions of that underground chamber I will tell you a little bit more about this. Once upon a time, most of the stone blocks extracted by excavating that chamber went to build the three pyramids of Giza."

Fred continued, "Incidentally, this underground cavity was created by extracting millions of rectangular stone blocks, most of the same size and shape, and deposited not too far from there. The organized Atlanteans hated disorder, so deposited them not as heaps of rocks, but as a broad terrace. For seven thousand years this giant platform remained untouched. That was until three generations of Pharaohs, who considered themselves to be gods, used this material as quarry to build their own tombs in the shape of pyramids. There were not enough stones to complete the last pyramid. So the Egyptians extracted and cut more stones from their local quarry to complete it.

"Someday, someone will discover that chamber, which is bigger than ours, and has more gold than anyone could dream. The future explorers who enter that chamber for the first time will feel surrounded by all kinds of objects and inventions; some still in good working condition in spite of the passing millennia. Those explorers will be just as astonished as you were when you explored our vault."

I asked the monk what he thought the estimated total value of the contents (mostly scientific and industrial secrets stored in that particular chamber would be. He replied "Enough to pay the entire debts of many countries." (Near the end of the twentieth century, perhaps a trillion dollars.)

Fred said, "On top of that buried structure was a small anteroom of cheap construction, called the secret library of wisdom, mentioned in some contemporary books. After Atlantis disappeared, the existence of that treasure chamber was forgotten, but not the existence of the library. Spanning thousands of years, many great thinkers from all races have passed through this library: philosophers, holy men, spiritualists, prophets, alchemists (known in modern times as nuclear physicists), mathematicians including Pythagoras and Archimedes, men from biblical times like Moses, King Solomon, and Jesus Christ from age twelve to thirty. All of them acquired their wisdom by studying scrolls, perhaps of Atlantis origin.

"Sometime later in the first millennium after Christ, a Greek engineer and a group of his intellectual friends, realized that humanity was not mature enough to receive such a huge amount of knowledge. A knowledge that could be use as a double-edged sword to do good or harm, to make from Earth a Hell or a Paradise, depended on the principles and morals of who acquired this knowledge. They decided it was too big a risk. With such dire prospects, the Greek and his friends moved the contents of the library against its back wall, which was a shallow cave, and by using sand, mud, and rocks sealed it forever. Then they took a sacred oath, binding them all never to reveal the location of the library, and to carry that secret with them to their graves. Since that time nobody was able to find this library and the chamber location. There is hope, however, that the location of the library with its treasure chamber underneath it can be retraced again by interpreting some of the ancient stone indicators that still exist. Megalithic structures like the Sphinx are good candidates.

## SPACE ABDUCTIONS

Fred's stories were so entertaining while we had finished walking through the tunnel, I forgot its claustrophobic effect. We were back to the small plaza in the barracks, walking on a paved pathway to the monks' library. A young busy monk, coming from the opposite direction, passed by us then turned his head and looked at me. Suddenly he stopped and said, "You look familiar. I think I saw you somewhere. Now I remember, it was long ago when you were just a small child. I saw you at a weird children's school, where all the kids brought there were kidnapped. You were only about four. Please, try to remember." I answered that I was never kidnapped. But somehow I could barely remember that once I had been in a large kindergarten. I had not paid too much attention as I assumed it was just an ordinary school.

At his insistence, I tried hard to remember what I did when I was four years old. I could remember that every year after the school year ended, we spent our vacation at my grandparents' farm. It was like a reunion with many kids of different ages including friends and relatives. My grandmother with the help of her domestic women employees was in charge of us; our parents remained working in the city. These were in Victorian times, where good morals abounded. On the farm, we the children were completely free. If one of us didn't appear at dinner, most likely the child went to play with some other kids at any of the nearby farms, and when it was late, kids were invited as guests to stay for the night. It was a relaxed traditional life. I could remember we used to be in touch with our parents by means of a decorated, antique telephone without a dial. The telephone operator made all the connections. Our telephone was powered by two large batteries made of transparent glass, kept in the lower shelf of the same telephone table.

One day I bought a sling and a whistle from another kid and I ventured out not too far on the prairie. I played with my sling, hurling gravel and stones at trees and rocks, scaring birds and mice. Then I saw a silent helicopter in the sky. I don't remember if it had a rotor and if it was reality or a fantasy. For most four year olds both are the same. The helicopter landed close to me. Then a smiling pilot stepped down from his machine and asked me if I wanted to go to see a school with a lot of children the same age as myself. I was curious but not suspicious. I accepted the ride.

The flying machine kept ascending until I saw through its top windows that we were approaching from underneath a yellow, approximately quarter-mile long, diamond-shaped object that appeared motionless in space. I didn't knew what it was called, so I gave it the name of whistle, because it had the same shape and yellow color as my whistle, which hung with its string from my neck. Perhaps I fantasized or dreamed, but the spaceships did look like my yellow whistle. As we approached the huge object, there was a moment when it seemed as big as a world, covering most of the sky. Then, a couple of doors opened from underneath and we flew inside. I was too young to be scared; I assumed everything was normal. After landing we walked into a large classroom full of kids. I assumed it was just an ordinary kindergarten class. Kids from all races spoke all kinds of languages; there, the teachers smiled all the time. But there was something strange about their faces, which looked like they were wearing smiling masks.

At recess I played with a girl about my own age. I grabbed her and kissed her. I didn't know why, but when I tried to kiss her again, she screamed; so I beat her up. One of the teachers saw me and said, "It is obvious humans are just another animal species and should be treated just as the rest of the animals from this planet." Another smiling teacher approached me and said, "You are a very bad boy, the worst in the world." I believed it for a while, but not for long, because the following year when I attended a normal kindergarten, I realized I was not as bad as most of the kids there, hyperactive naughty kids fighting most of the time; I thought they were crazy.

I was relaxed in that cheerful atmosphere of kindergarten. Suddenly I noticed the teachers became excited. One of them looking outside through the window screamed in his language and said something to the other teachers. Several kids approached the windows and saw that someone stole one of the small landing vehicles and returned home. A few minutes later, the scared teachers brought most of us back to the same place where they had picked us up. I myself found nothing extraordinary about this experience. I took everything for granted and I forgot about the whole thing. My grandmother asked me where I have been all that time. I replied simply that I was in a big school with lots of kids.

The young nervous monk, who talked to me at the barracks, said he was one of the oldest kids that had been taken there. He was the one who stole the landing vehicle and escaped. He said it was very easy to fly; just moving a lever did every maneuver. "I fled after I saw a macabre spectacle," he explained. "As I walked by the aisle in the ship, I peeped inside a small room through a door left partially open. I saw a large transparent container full of arms, legs, cut-off heads, and other human organs, ready to be disposed." The young monk continued, "A teacher surprised me and asked what I was doing there. He was excited and got to close to me. I was so scared, to defend myself I removed his smiling mask and found he was a horrible monster with the dark face of an insect. Immediately I realized these monsters were not friendly; they just pretended to be by wearing those smiling human masks. I was old enough to realize it was not a school but some macabre place. Later as the years passed by, I learned it was a lonely scout ship, belonging to the Ortusian predatory race, traveling one Earth century ahead of their huge convoy. These scout spies are the same evil ones that once in awhile land on Earth to kill and mutilate domestic animals. With precision surgery they extract their organs and carry them to their ship, probably to do some kind of experiments."

The young monk said. "You cannot imagine how many people from all over the world have been abducted, mostly young children living or camping in the countryside. Once abducted, they were randomly distributed into two groups.

"The ones from the first group were brainwashed, hypnotized, and implanted with artificial memories. They were well indoctrinated then returned to Earth. As they grew up, they became moral advocates against birth control, preaching for the limitless reproduction of the human race. All this was well planned, so when the day arrives when the Ortusians will invade Earth, they will find mostly one species, the human. They don't enjoy eating the flesh of animals as much."

The young monk paled, trying to recall what he saw there, and continued with his narration. "I witnessed the horrendous experiments they conducted on the second group of people, impressions that ruined my life forever. To forget them, I tried to keep myself busy. One day I was doing my college homework in the library of my hometown. I was lucky to meet an old custodian monk from this institution who went to that public library looking for some strange books. We had an interesting conversation, and he enrolled me in his institution. Since then I have worked and studied at this facility." The young deranged monk left.

Who knows what kind of mental problems plagued this young neurotic monk perhaps he confused reality with fantasy. His insinuations stimulated my own teenaged mind. Probably he made me believe things that never happened such as that fantastic idea of been kidnapped by aliens. Fred didn't say anything either approving or denying what the young monk said.

\*\*\*\*\*\*\*\*\*\*\*\*\*

The following supplementary information is furnished so that the reader may drawn his own opinion as to reality or fantasy regarding my visit to the fifth lower floor of the underground chamber.

## CHRONICLE OF ALIEN VEHICLE ANALYSIS

The vehicle structure was simple, resembling a giant eggshell with no frames. Fred said the shell was from a honeycomb sandwich structure. The material was very thin, almost transparent, very strong, made from some unknown alloy.

The honeycomb sandwich panels from this structure were built by bonding simple components, bonded not with glue nor brass as used in the modern aircraft industry, but by using instead diffusion bonding. This is when the areas of the parts to be welded are put in contact and welded but without using welding materials, just joined between themselves by diffusion of their own molecules. This procedure made it possible to build very light and at the same time super strong structures that also could withstand high temperatures.

## UFO PROPULSION

Inside the vehicle the monk touched two vertical rings fastened face to face, rings made from hollow tubes. He said, "This is the centrifugal propulsion system, controlled by the telekinetic powers (mind over matter) of the alien astronaut. The rings are filled with mercury, the heaviest liquid at ambient temperature. Electric pumps circulated this mercury at great speed inside the tubes of the rings. The pipe diameter in the upper half of the ring was smaller, hence the mercury circulated inside it at greater speed than at the opposite side of the same ring, generating in the upper half of the ring greater centrifugal force than at the opposite side. The mercury inside each of the two vertical rings installed facing one to the other, counter-circulated in one ring in respect to the other.

"When the system operated under the laws of physics in the three-dimensional universe, the system of forces was in equilibrium, and the resultant (a vectorial sum) equals zero. So, when there was no dominant force prevailing in any particular direction, the resultant propulsive force was zero. However, when the alien astronauts wanted to fly in some particular direction, they just applied their telekinetic powers to cancel some of the system forces, disrupting the equilibrium of the total system of forces. The forces to be cancelled were located at the couplings where the tubes of different diameter were joined to each other. Then the dominant centrifugal force, from the ring segment of tube where the mercury flows at the highest speed, prevailed and pulled the vehicle in the direction they wanted to go. This is a propulsion system that only works if telekinetic forces are real. I don't know what to believe because I don't have proof that psychic powers exist, so I leave to the reader to decide if this type of propulsion is real or just a dream of fantasy."

# CHAPTER 12
## More About Extraterrestrial

After relating those stories related to space abductions, the neurotic monk, left as quickly as he appeared. We entered the library and my host wanted to show me a series of ancient movies and documentaries that no outsider had ever seen.

As my host prepared the movie projector, he explained, "In our vast galaxy there are billions of worlds, some about the same age and with similar atmosphere as Earth. In some of them life manifested at approximately at the same time. However, in the last billion years, Earth suffered periodic global catastrophes caused by impacts from meteors and comets, causing mass extinction of thousands of species, including the dinosaurs some 65 million years ago. In those more fortunate planets with no periodic global disasters, intelligent beings had the opportunity to evolve without periodic interruptions, reason enough for them to be way ahead of us in evolution.

"When Earth was still in its Triassic Period, many highly advanced civilizations already existed in the galaxy, which prospered and evolved to the point that they even attained interstellar flight and the ability to use antimatter to propel their spaceships. They began exploring the galaxy; occasionally they collected specimens and recorded details from each planet they visited, including Earth when it was still primitive. Huge amounts of collected information were shared between intellectual cultures that belonged to the same club in this galaxy from events that happened long before man came into existence. It seems unbelievable, but for hundreds of millions of years Earth was continuously visited by extraterrestrial. Only three of them left proof of their visits, filming themselves in some videodisks. It was millions of years before a copy of them reached the archives of Atlantis, and from there somehow to the files in our library. We kept the records of three species of extraterrestrial including the Gatoxins, the Entarians and the mysterious humanoids that have not shown their faces in that ancient film.

## MYSTERIOUS HUMANOIDS

"A mysterious alien race from an old civilization used to explore this galaxy for long periods of time. On their first visit to Earth, which happened millions of years ago, they filmed a documentary; it was in that time when the dinosaurs reigned. This film was made out of a material, which if protected, would not degrade, and should last for a billion years. They made hundreds of copies from this documentary; mostly to give as a present every time they met inhabitants from another advanced civilization, including the Gatoxins and the Entarians.

"Walter, a quarter of a billion years ago, alien astronauts from different places in the galaxy often visited Earth and we know nothing about them, except the Entarians and Gatoxins who left those records.

## FILM ONE

"You are very lucky, Walter," said Fred, as he prepared to show me the film from the mysterious humanoids  "The film you are about to see is a true documentary from Earth's prehistory. A much older race than the Entarians and the Gatoxins made it. We may never know who made this film or what they looked like, because they did not show themselves on the film and left no clues."

Fred turned on the movie projector. A jungle scene filled the entire screen, showing the dense vegetation from ancient Earth times. I saw giant ferns and trees, and giant insects like one-foot-long dragonflies. I could hear the strange cries of unseen beasts. The camera was carried by a walking humanoid, yet it was made long before humans existed. The film had the quality of a home video. I wondered what the filmmaker looked like. The camera kept moving forward into the clear flat top of a low hill. Lizards scampered away. All of a sudden, a small dinosaur, the size of a dog, turned back and froze. It looked ready to spring into the camera operator, baring its pointed teeth menacingly. A second later, half the dinosaur's head was blasted away. I glimpsed a small but powerful weapon held by a four-fingered hand in a silver glove.

"Are you sure this is Earth?" I asked Fred.

"Although what you see is not familiar to you, it is indeed Earth - millions of years ago," Fred assured me. The camera started to move again towards the shallow hill. On top of the hill, a large spacecraft stood on three tall legs. The camera carrier reached the top of the hill, but did not stop there. It passed beneath the elliptical ship, which was different from the Entarian ships I had already seen. Passing under the spacecraft, the camera carrier descended to the opposite side of that hill, approaching a swampy lake where huge dinosaurs waded and gnawed on aquatic vegetation.

Suddenly, a roar coming from nearby trees interrupted the quietness of the scenery. I saw a huge head rising above the vegetation. It was a hungry beast with menacing teeth--today known as Tyrannosaurus Rex. It burst from the jungle and charged a slow moving dinosaur that was leaving the swamp. I noticed the T. Rex behaved like a giant chicken, hyperactive with quick automatic reactions as a machine, but not necessarily intelligent. It was a monster with a small brain, but a bloody killer that relied on brute force and bursts of violence. It lacked the efficiency of today's modern predators who seem to plan first, then attack their victims at their most vulnerable parts. The T. Rex tore its helpless prey violently. Shreds of flesh hung from its bloody jaws. It struck again and again inflicting more and more bloody wounds on its prey. Finally the victim tumbled over, quivering in the throes of death, while its assailant gnawed the flesh of the still living animal.

"The mysterious aliens who made this documentary distributed copies throughout the galaxy. Eons later a copy reached the Entarians who made more copies by themselves and on their last visit to Earth brought one and gave it as a present to the Atlanteans. That is the copy you have just seen," Fred explained as he set up another film in the projector. Then, he said, "The main reason to see the next film is to observe how some advanced civilizations artificially stimulated the evolution of living beings, creating from them new races and new subspecies at a much faster rate than may normally happen."

## FILM TWO

There was a short intermission between films. A female monk brought a cup of tea for each of us and one for herself, then sat next to us to watch the next movie. Fred said, "This is a narrative film, which we brought here from the secret chamber of the ancient Atlanteans. It narrates a chapter from the history of Gatox, an advanced alien civilization from a quarter billion years ago, a civilization also located in this galactic branch of Orion."

As the film started, a man wearing ancient garments appeared on the screen and began talking in his native Atlantean language. Fred translated as follows at incredible speed, "About two hundred million years ago, the Gatoxins found it necessary to expand the range of their galactic explorations. They realized the only possible way was by creating a specialized race of astronauts, which could be done by using genetic engineering. This was to be a new race able to endure long space voyages, some lasting for hundreds or thousands of years. For this project the Gatoxins requested volunteers. The volunteers and their offspring were subjected to an extraordinary mutation project of genetic engineering. The experiment lasted for several generations until finally a totally different subspecies with different anatomy was created. This new subspecies met the required physical configuration needed for space voyages lasting for thousands of years. They became a new race of intelligent humanoids, known as the gatherers of universal data, because every time they returned to their home planet, they delivered the collected data to their compatriots in order to enhance their knowledge.

"Most of the times after these humanoids returned home from a long voyage, several centuries had passed, and the people they knew no longer were around, so they met only their descendants. To avoid emotional involvement, the social circle of these interstellar travelers was limited only to their loved ones, friends, and their fellow humanoids with whom they traveled. They relinquished all emotional attachments with the rest of the people from their world.

"From the concept of four-dimensional space-time continuum of the special theory of relativity, we can deduce that time slows down for the crew on a ship approaching the speed of light. For the astronauts traveling near the speed of light, only a few years passed and they aged slowly, while from the point of view of the creatures left on their planet, or in other celestial bodies from this galaxy (external observers), millions of years had already passed.

"Due to their specialized anatomy to endure long trips, gradually they had become a different subspecies of the Gatoxins. They were about five and a half feet tall, baby faced, with large oval eyes, very thin bodies, arms, and legs. They had brains twice the size of a human being, but arranged in such a way that each hemisphere was encased in a separate skull located side by side. Each of the skulls was similar to a flat oval capsule, looking like the ears of modern day Mickey Mouse. Every time these ingenious astronauts visited Earth, to avoid scaring people they covered their heads with plastic helmets concealing the two parts of their skulls.

"Their special anatomy, with thin body cross sections, enabled them to quickly cool by cryogenic freezing, without damaging their tissues and cells, and not causing death. Freezing massive bodies such as the human body is slow, it produces ice, which destroys the cell membranes and causes death. Another interesting feature of these aliens was that their blood contained natural antifreeze, enabling the humanoids to hibernate during their long voyages throughout the universe; hibernating for hundreds, even thousands of terrestrial years without getting old. Their frozen bodies remained dormant inside cryogenic capsules. Their ship traveled at approximately ninety per cent of the speed of light, under the control of the astronauts on duty and the ship autopilot. Astronauts took turns controlling the ship, getting defrosted and awakened for duty."

The film ended and Fred continued, "The first Gatoxin visit to Earth took place during the time of the dinosaurs. However, on their last visit, millions of years later, the aliens found that Earth had changed. There were no longer dinosaurs. They remembered that in ancient times there was only one continent surrounded by the ocean; after their return, they saw that the only continent had broken into several, which were slowly spreading out. Forests and other green areas got reduced in size; Earth looked like a different planet, with mammals as we know today and with intelligent beings already living in the Stone Age. Humans began to control the planet and multiplied into millions. This magnificent alien visit occurred not too long ago, although a long time after Atlantis had disappeared. It was at a time coinciding with the birth of the Egyptian civilization.

"Each time these ancient astronauts visited foreign planets, including Earth, they wore helmets to conceal the shape of their horrible double skulls. Attached on each side of their helmets, just behind the astronaut's ears, they had plastic triangular outward extensions full of microelectronics. These amplified even the weakest sounds and determined their direction to alert astronauts when they explored the wilderness. The helmets extended down to the back of their necks, like the headgear of an Egyptian pharaoh--though at this ancient time, neither Egypt nor pharaohs had come to exist.

"Before the time the Egyptian empire existed, a group of these alien astronauts landed and met with people living near the Nile River. The people thought these aliens were gods.

"These early settlers on the Nile wore an imitation of that strange head gear used by the Gatoxin astronauts.  They considered this headdress a symbol of prestige and status.  It became a tradition that lasted for centuries and was passed down through several generations of pharaohs.

"The civilization of the kindly Entarians was much younger than the Gatoxins. After the Entarians finished creating man, about two hundred thousand years ago, they left Earth. A big chapter of history drew to a close.  The world was ready for a new beginning. Without the protection of aliens beings, humanity survived.  However, a question remained whether man would have concern for the welfare of the other species. Would man be a real protector of the world? Or would he become an evil, wasteful predator, destroyer of other species, which would eventually lead to his own extinction?"

# CHAPTER 13
## History of Atlantis

As soon as each film episode ended, Fred the monk kept changing films to the next episode. He told me I was going to see a historic film about ancient and modern Atlantis, made by a quick compilation of a series of short stories.

## ANCIENT ATLANTIS

As Fred turned on the projector, an Atlantean man appeared on the film, narrating something in his native language. As in previous films, Fred began translating quickly what the man said. That man from the film was standing next to a map hanging from a wall. It was an ancient map exactly as the world used to be at the end of the last Ice Age 11,000 years ago when the northern ice cap covered large areas of Europe, Asia and America.

Fred began translating, "From the time of Adam, humanity had evolved into the many races we see today. We Atlanteans are nephews of Adam, not his direct descendants. During Atlantis times, the human population had multiplied and spread over most of the continents. Atlantis is today at the apex of its civilization, while the rest of humanity still remains in the Stone Age living as hunters and gatherers. Our earlier ancestors knew nothing from their past and remained isolated in these islands knowing nothing of the outside world.

"At the dawn of civilization, Atlanteans had already forgotten everything related to the origin of man, and his creators, the Entarian aliens. They also forgot that the Entarian aliens were the ones that had carved the navigable rings of water to build their alien genetic laboratories they called Paradise Number One. To explain the creation of such mysterious wonders of engineering that they knew nothing about, including the rings of water, the Atlanteans created their own mythology and gave credit of these works to their mythological god Poseidon.

"After a long period of no progress, called by them the Dark Ages, the Atlanteans rose again but this time by themselves and without the help of space aliens or gods. It was as if they awoke suddenly with great projects in mind, ready to build the great projects from their dreams. So the Atlanteans began cleaning the ring of water and the rings of land of wild weeds and plants to make room for the temples and palaces they was going to build. Also they scraped the rusted metallic ruins, remains of their ancient buildings and alien genetic engineering laboratories, lain dormant for the eons, used by the aliens to create the first humans from inferior animals. However, as hard as they tried, the

Atlanteans never could figure out the real purpose for the existence of those ancient building remains.

"The islands were fertile with good soil, covered with superb vegetation that supported a variety of wild animals. The mountains were covered with tall forests, used to produce a great variety of timbers. Survival in primitive Atlantis was not difficult because the islands, privileged by nature, remained a paradise of eternal spring, producing abundant natural food. Atlantis had several springs of both hot and cold water; it also had some geysers.

"Small villages could be seen everywhere, in the plains and in the mountains. Early Atlanteans practiced primitive agriculture and bred herds of domestic animals including cattle, sheep, and horses. With their dexterous hands unlike the rest of the humans, they made copper tools like axes, spear tips, and knives. As hunters they hunted wild animals such as mammoths, woolly rhinoceros, giant oxen, and deer. It happened that thousands of years before, the ancient Entarian astronauts brought these animals from other continents.

"After the first humans were abandoned by their alien creators, Atlanteans began their decline — from their high standards living as spoiled children of the aliens, to a primitive Copper Age. However they never degenerated all the way to the Stone Age as did the rest of their cousins. It is clear that the creators were more interested in their genetic creation than in educating them for their survival.

## MYTHOLOGY AND THE OLD ATLANTIS CLASSICAL ERA

"To explain the creation of those mysterious ancient works of engineering and ancient remains left on their islands, the Atlanteans created their own mythology, the oldest of the world, with Poseidon (known as Neptune by the Romans) as their principal god, the god of the seas, earthquakes, and horses. He was credited with the creation of Atlantis and its wonders. Poseidon's brother, Zeus, (later known as Jupiter by the Romans) also was worshipped as the second in importance after Poseidon, although several centuries later for the Greeks reversed this, with Zeus becoming their principal God.

"Poseidon the First, one of the first humans created by the aliens and brother of Adam, eventually died of old age. Several generations of his descendents passed, until one day a young drunk man, called Poseidon the Second, proclaimed himself to be a living god, reincarnation of Poseidon the First. Even he himself believed this was true. He was young, strong, and sharp. He fell in love with Cleito, the most beautiful woman of the islands and the only child of a kindly couple living in a nearby forest. This was during the times when everybody lived happily on the island. But bad times came. An epidemic decimated most of the population, including Cleito's parents. Poseidon the Second, who began calling himself just Poseidon, took Cleito as his wife, and united the survivors from the surrounding tribes. Poseidon and Cleito had five pairs of twin sons. As they grew up, each became a king with a piece of land. The island was divided into ten pieces; the largest one was given to Atlas, the eldest son. Poseidon named the whole group of islands Atlantis, after his eldest son Atlas, who in term named the round and highly inhabited island Poseidon, in honor of his father.

"Plato the philosopher described Atlas from Atlantis as different from the Atlas of the Greek mythology. Perhaps there were two different Atlases. The entire Atlantis population used to live just on the island of Poseidon, second in size, while the largest one remained a wilderness for centuries. During their Bronze Age, the Atlanteans began building small boats to navigate in between the group of islands. A thousand years later they built large sailing ships to sail east and discover Europe, when they set foot on the coast of what today is Portugal. Savages attacked them with spears, killing some of the Atlanteans. The ship returned with bad news. Because of this first bad experience, the Atlanteans changed their attitude from seafarers and traders to warriors, looters, and conquerors, terrorizing continents on both sides of the Atlantic Ocean. The conquerors became the men of fame, as they were named in the Genesis from the Judeo-Christian Bible, and were known by the rest of the world as the evil race from the sea.

"As the Atlanteans grew richer, they began to develop their artistic skills, becoming great painters, sculptors and architects. They transformed the alien built rings of land into a religious center, by building pagan temples, fully decorated with beautiful works of art. The name of this group of concentric rings, originally named Paradise Number One by the Entarian aliens changed millennia later. Atlanteans called it Acropolis. At the center of Acropolis was the central circle of land also called the internal island, which could be reached by crossing bridges built over the existing channels. The main entrance of the Royal Palace was aligned first with the bridges, then with an ancient road coming from far away in the countryside. In the internal island the old classical Atlanteans build two temples, one dedicated to Cleito and Poseidon, surrounded by a tall wall, and another temple, the largest and most magnificent of the whole world, dedicated solely to Poseidon. Inside this last was the gigantic statue of Poseidon, whose head almost touched the ceiling. The statue was made of marble, ivory and gold. It was standing on his chariot, and the chariot was inside a huge water fountain symbolizing the sea. It depicted Poseidon riding a chariot on the sea, pulled by six immense horses and holding a trident in the right hand.

"The royal zone of Acropolis with buildings of incredible beauty and splendor were built during the Atlantis Classical Period, at the time when the ravaging Atlantis warriors dominated the world through terror.

"The Acropolis was surrounded by a rectangular country plain. On one side the plain extended all the way to the sea, while on the other three sides to the foot of the mountains."

## MODERN ATLANTIS ERA

Fred went on translating what the documentary said, "The Atlanteans during their modern times changed their attitude. This civilization had become so advanced in the sciences and the arts, to the extent that the Association of Advanced

Civilizations from this part of the galaxy became aware of planet Earth's existence and named Atlantis as the planet's cultural representative.

"As the Atlanteans moved into their modern times, their mythological gods were demoted and the religious center of the island of Poseidon changed from religious to a historic place and a museum dedicated to the arts, poetry, and history. Outside Acropolis were built suburbs with residential areas for the rich, some of them facing the sea with a nice beach. The island of Poseidon became a place of gardens and parks, dedicated to beauty and splendor. Then came the time when its population began to grow so fast that its excess began moving to the neighboring large, rectangular island, called the Island of the Sun, which up until then was a wilderness. In the island of the Sun, a different Atlantis culture began, a modern and advanced civilization concentrated on science and technology. The contemplative and meditative style of life of the conservative Atlanteans changed to a busy one, inclined to business and technology. Engineers and architects became active, designing modern functional cities with tall skyscrapers made from steel, glass and plastic. No longer were historic decorative architecture and impressive columns and obelisks built on this modern island. Marble was no longer the material of choice.

"The modern Island of the Sun grew into a great industrial center with great economic power. Their skilled inhabitants created modern systems of transportation, including fast trains, electric cars, modern airports, spaceports for Atlantis spacecraft, and spaceships of extraordinary complexity, to travel to the other planets. Waterways and a grid of irrigation channels divided the countryside into squares of land of approximately five kilometers per side. Many automated farms occupied those squares. In an exceptionally large square was the zoo, where all kinds of wild animals roamed free, including mammoths and saber-toothed tigers. In one corner of the square terrain was a reservation, where more than a dozen survivors from a very primitive human subspecies lived. There were called in the modern twentieth Century Neanderthals.

"By the time the Atlanteans had become the only power of the world, they also became the kindest people on Earth. They felt sorry concerning the nasty behavior of their ancestors in the past, boasting and showing off how powerful they were by oppressing the rest of the world. They dissolved their armed forces and organized voluntary groups of young explorers, like our present day Boy Scouts. Atlantis had become so peaceful that most primitive people in the world began to forget about their existence; some had never met or known about the Atlanteans.

"While most of the world remained in the Stone Age, Atlantis was already in its Space Age exploring the solar system. Some islands and some small coastal areas of the Mediterranean Sea were in their Copper Age and became trading posts for the Atlanteans, including the island of Thera, strategically located for commerce.

"A gifted race of designers and creators, the Atlanteans could mentally visualize complex geometrical shapes. Most possessed great manual dexterity from the early age of four. Kindergarten children enjoyed building their own toys. With this early training, they grew up to become great surgeons, design engineers, and architects.

"Atlanteans enjoyed a variety of sports, including sports played with ball. Some sports were traditional remnants from old Atlantis. At the fairs one could often see spectacles where acrobats played with bulls and horses. They also held a kind of Olympiads, with games displaying great strength, skill, endurance, and speed.

"Intellectually they appreciated literature, philosophy, visual arts, the theater, music, dancing, and some kind of opera; they also enjoyed visiting museums. During their modern period, Atlanteans organized industrial shows with the participation of different industrial companies, displaying science and their newly developed products, mostly competing for government grants.

"After splitting into two enemy nations that almost went to war, Atlantis got unified into one peaceful country. Every year they celebrated an important holiday, which lasted for two consecutive days, commemorating this national consolidation. On this holiday, people enjoyed going to various fairs. One of the most popular was the air show at an airport located near a broad beach, with its runway parallel to the shoreline. Wood bleachers for thousands of spectators faced one side of the runway. The fair began first with the strange parade of giant robots, which looked like giant apes, used by the industry as construction workers; with the help of these giants, Atlanteans built wonders overseas. Robots the size of buildings, each weighing around 100 tons, marched in front of the spectators. The ground shook under their tremendous weight.

"After the robot parade was over, the air show began, first with parachutists, followed by a flock of slow ultralight aircraft flying above the public, who appreciated the beautiful designs in full color on their silky wings, some imitating birds, others colorful butterflies in flight. On the ground some people strolled, looking at the different types of aircraft on display. The show lasted almost the whole day and as the last number and the most dangerous number, thundering fighting aircraft appeared in the sky, performing dangerous aerobatics and performing mock combat between two flying teams. Each team flew its favorite type of fighter, all of them developed during the Atlantis cold war, before their consolidation.

"The pilots finished their demonstrations in the show, and landed not too far in front of the spectators, parked their planes next to the runway, then walked to the bleachers to join with the rest of the spectators. While on the field, a group of busy mechanics brought two robots dressed as dummy pilots, and secured each of them to the seat of the same aircraft that had flown with human pilots. The same planes took off again, but this time piloted by robot pilots. Since robots and planes were expendable, this demonstration allowed them to enact real air combat. An impressive display as the last show in the evening, it was somewhat dangerous for the spectators. I remember in a similar air show I saw two years before, a duel took place between two of the most advanced fighters in Atlantis. One of them was a delta (triangular) wing fighter with delta canards loaded with conventional weapons and built by the eastern Atlantis block during the cold war.

The other was a more sophisticated aircraft made of carbon fibers and resin, loaded with laser ray weapons, built by the western Atlantis block. Both planes fought to death with their robot pilots, until one of the aircraft was shot down, the falling debris hurting some spectators.

"In spite of the possibility that burning parts of the destroyed aircraft could fall over them, the public was fanatical about this kind of dangerous display. They accepted danger as part of the game.

"The government encouraged this exhilarating entertainment displaying real war between fighting aircraft because other than entertainment, it had another purpose, which was to find out which aircraft manufacturer did the best design. It was assumed that the company that designed the winning aircraft had the best technology to offer and it won the government grant to continue the research developing more projects for the next year.

"As Atlantis split, they also divided the world. The rebel leader was from western Atlantis, a group of islands located not too far from the eastern coast of today's United States. These were small islands that are today entirely covered by water due to the rising ocean level after the end of the last Ice Age.

"During the escalation of hostilities, the two warring factions of Atlantis had developed sophisticated armaments. "After the rebel leader died of natural causes, both sides were reunited again into one nation, and their armed forces, dissolved. For eternal peacetime, military equipment was no longer needed. Some of the aircraft were sold to amateurs and others flown in air shows exhibiting air combat. (For additional information see preliminary design drawings of two different types of fighter aircraft in the appendices section of this book.)

"After the consolidation, normal happy life resumed. But not for too long, because after a mild earthquake, a small volcanic islet, full of bird nests,luckily with no people, collapsed and disappeared under the waters, spreading its soft, rocky material as sediment at the bottom of the ocean. With this collapse, Atlantis geophysicists discovered the tragic fact that the entire group of islands comprising Atlantis had the same unstable geological structure as the small island that had just disappeared. Atlantis was a paradise of volcanic islands rich in minerals and nutrients excellent to grow many crops a year. The gentle slope from its beautiful beaches extended for some distance under the water, suddenly ending at the edge of a submarine cliff. The geologists predicted that strong earthquakes might trigger their collapse, perhaps leaving only narrow cores with their tops rising like masts above the sea level as small islets. They predicted that after collapsing, soft, rocky material would lay at the bottom of the ocean as rubble and thick sediment. This would destroy all the evidence of temples and other wonders the Atlanteans built.

"The elders of Atlantis, rulers of that nation, were alarmed with the bad news, then decided that sometime in the future they should move the entire population to Atlantis' western territories. However, most Atlanteans hesitated to leave their paradise. These western territories are known today as the Americas. This is the territory that Plato referred to when he wrote saying it occupied an area larger than Libya and Asia Minor.

"Atlantis was governed by ten elders who sat around a round table, each elected for a term of ten years. The chief elder position rotated every two years, so during each administration, only five elders would serve in this position.

"Years passed and the possible threat of destruction by earthquakes faded from the Atlantean mind. Atlanteans continued to prosper and live happily. One day, astronomers received a faint radio message from Atlantis astronauts, traveling near the outer limits of the solar system. By looking through their spaceship telescope, they had rediscovered the same comet mentioned earlier by the Entarian aliens during their last visit, which at that time was not taken seriously. The Atlantean astronauts communicated to Earth the bad news that there was a possibility that sometime later the comet might hit the Earth, the impact awakening dormant volcanoes around the world, producing huge tidal waves, then triggering the collapse of the Atlantis islands.

· "This collective apprehension persisted until the day Captain Cronus, chief astronaut of Atlantis, blew up the comet."

# CHAPTER 14
## Captain Cronus, Hero of the World

Fred continued. "Suddenly bad news alarmed the Atlanteans. The scientists decided that there was but one option to save the world and it was by blowing up the menacing comet; however there was no guarantee it would be successful. A report was presented to the elders. They accepted the idea and assigned Captain Cronus the mighty mission to intercept the comet then destroy it with nuclear bombs.

"Captain Cronus, his crew and his son who also an astronaut began to prepare for the trip. Two days later, Cronus, his wife, and, son departed from Brasea in a fast airplane, flew all night across the Atlantic Ocean, and early next day arrived at the second highest Atlantis space port in the world, second only to the one located in Tibet. This aerospace port was built on a high altitude-hanging plateau, located in the Andes Mountains between today's Peru and Bolivia. The base including its building were all made from prefabricated materials, everything brought from Atlantis.

"The next night, the base commander organized a formal reception for the travelers at the Atlantis hotel not too far from the space base. There in the reception he introduced Captain Cronus to the rest of the guests at dinner, and delivered a long speech. He said, 'Captain Cronus has had a brilliant career. After he graduated from the Space Academy, he became a member of the crew for the Atlantis Spaceship No. 1. In this ship he made extraordinary long voyages through our solar system, making important discoveries. Cronus worked his way up the ranks, gaining experience, and with time, ultimately became a captain. He won various awards for valor. One for what he did more than 20 years ago, while crossing the asteroid belt between Mars and Jupiter, when he saved his ship from total disaster. The ship was hit with an asteroid the size of an orange. In just a fraction of a second, the asteroid went through the body of the ship, and out the other side, disappearing in space. The asteroid perforated walls and destroyed equipment. Part of the equipment caught fire and was consumed. From one room, all air escaped and its occupants died of suffocation. Cronus saved many lives from the other compartments by plugging the holes perforated by the asteroid with everything on hand (plastic sheets, blankets, pillows and glue). During the long return trip to Earth, this temporary repair 2could last enough time, so that the maintenance crew could weld the holes and repair the rest of the damage.'"

"The commander continued with his long narration. Now Captain Cronus is about to embark on the most important task of his life. He has been assigned the mission to save the Earth from the killer comet.' The base commander finished his introduction, and sat down to begin dining with his guests. There at the dinner Captain Cronus met several of the guests, among them a recently married couple who introduced themselves as Tucan and Oca. They told Cronus they were students of astronomy and had won the year's science prize for the paper they wrote about meteorites and comets. The prize was a round trip voyage for both of them through deep space as tourists. They did not have any kind of astronaut's training. Cronus replied, 'Don't worry, as tourists you really don't need it. You are welcome to travel with us to the outer limits of our solar system. It will be a great experience for both of you. You don't need to be fully trained for space travel because the ship was designed with artificial gravity, which is none other than centrifugal force. You will feel as if you are traveling in an ocean liner. However, you should be aware that this voyage is not an ordinary one. We are on a special government mission. We are carrying nuclear bombs to blast the threatening comet.'"

## THE VOYAGE

Fred began translating the story as if through the eyes of Tucan the tourist. "'Captain Cronus was a tall man with Nordic features. His shimmering, gray hair topped a neatly tailored, military style tight uniform of white silk. It had beautiful silver and gold designs on the shoulders, chest, and back. At the base dinner the passengers chatted on a variety of topics with the captain and his wife. Then after the reception was over we left for the night.

"'Early the next day we joined with the rest of the travelers at the hotel lobby, where a bus arrived to transport us to the space terminal. We got in it, and just before Captain Cronus stepped in, he kissed and hugged his wife saying, "Don't worry, we'll return alive from this mission." The bus rode by the cold barren plateau. We enjoyed looking at the strange flat scenery and the breeze of the pure thin air on our faces. The sky was clear and visibility superb. In the distance along the outskirts of this high altitude plateau we saw mountains peaks covered with glacier ice. Their light blue blended with the blue of the sky. A passenger said that we were going in the direction of the mountains with the highest peak.

"'It was a short ride. We arrived at the terminal building, which was located near the foot of the mountain and next to the beginning of a runway used for takeoffs. The runway was tilted and looked like a continuous straight bridge made from steel. It rested against the steep side of the mountain, supported all along by a series of short columns. A steel tower built on the top of the tallest snow-capped peak supported the far end of the runway aiming to the heavens.

"''There at the beginning of the runway was parked a space vehicle resembling a giant airplane. It was ours, it was awaiting us, already full of fuel. On its back it carried a smaller spacecraft for passengers, like carrying a baby on its back.  The small piggyback airplane was the one that would take the 36 of us to the Atlantis space station, which orbited around the Earth for years.

"' Once we all got aboard, we secured our belts.  The giant vehicle carrying our Space Shuttle started its engines and began to roll first slowly, then faster and faster.  Strange as it seems, it was not only moving by its own power, but also pulled by long continuous catapults, attached to the runway, such as the ones used in the aircraft carriers, but by far much longer.  Our craft accelerated all the way up the steep runway and left it, flying directly into the heavens.  Two minutes later or so, the large plane carrying our vehicle got disengaged from us and glided back to the base.  A couple of seconds later, our smaller craft fired its own rocket engines, and we felt a push, as we kept climbing higher and faster.  Looking through the window, I saw the black sky and the bluish curvature of Earth.  Finally we reached orbit, and after some hours we could rendezvous with the space station.  As we approached, it looked like a round floating building in space.

"'We approached the station very slowly until our entrance latch got connected with a tube extended sideways from the shaft of the space station.  This tube was used as an aisle for the passengers.  The access latches were opened.  Passengers and crew rushed through the tube tunnel with no gravity.  They moved just by grabbing the handrails and reaching the shaft of the station and from there the main circular lobby of the station, which rotated with the main body of the station to produce centrifugal artificial gravity.  My wife and I caught our breaths as we looked at the floating building's enormous size.  My wife said she felt just like being in a large airport terminal, crowded with travelers, some on their way to their own destinations, while others were just arriving.  Patiently we waited to board our spaceship that would take us on a three-year mission.

"'There, in the lobby, we made the best of our long waiting hours, by enjoying light meals or by strolling from window to window.  From one of the windows I saw the beautiful, blue curvature of Earth in the blackness of space and above the imposing view of the Milky Way.  I moved to another window and saw a white structure moored with cables and connected to the tubular tunnels from this space station.  It was a ship; its main structure made by two round metal bodies, like fat wheels or huge donuts, each the size of a building, counter rotating the one with respect to the other, both mounted on a common long shaft.  The whole thing looked as if it were floating in space.  Black letters painted on its surface read Atlantis 2.  There was no doubt it was our spaceship. Later I learned that Atlantis 1 was dismantled because it was very old.

"'My wife and I went to the cafeteria and drank some hot tea; we sat next to a window and from there I saw another docked Atlantis ship that recently had arrived. A man sitting at the table next to us eating his breakfast said that he had just arrived from Mars on that ship along with other passengers. They were waiting to board the space plane that would take them back to the surface of the Earth. I realized he meant to the same vehicle that had brought us from Earth. It was a relaxing environment.  Then the loudspeaker announced we would be delayed for another day.  I approached the window and found the cause of our delay. Space workers were securing some heavy cargo at the middle of the 250-meter long tail's boom of the spaceship. This cargo included a tractor to excavate tunnels, and four boxes. Each box carried a printed warning--HANDLE WITH CARE, NUCLEAR BOMBS.

'"The next morning, after breakfast, our group met at boarding gate 5, located close to the station's shaft. Captain Cronus was waiting there to instruct us how to board Atlantis 2. Inside the boarding tunnel whose far end reached to the spacecraft, there was no artificial gravity. We floated and by grabbing the handrails we pulled ourselves forward, one after the next, until we reached and entered our spaceship. When all of us were aboard, a crewmember closed the latch, and Atlantis 2 was disconnected from the space station tunnel. Our ship was free. Captain Cronus assigned each of us our rooms. Ours had the comfort of a modern studio with an artificial window on one wall. Actually this window was a very thin flat television embedded in the wall. It gave us the illusion of looking at the universe outside the ship, as if through a real window. In the room we also had a standard television to see programs from Earth and from the Atlantis bases on Mars, depending on which celestial body was the closest. Once in awhile we watched videos borrowed from the entertainment room.

'"As the ship began moving, we felt a gentle push. Captain Cronus explained over the microphone that our ship got separated from the station and now was pushed away by two space tugs, small vehicles with rocket engines, in some way similar to the tug boats which push departing ocean liners out of the harbor to the open sea. When we were approximately twenty kilometers away from the station, the space tugs returned. Captain Cronus slightly rotated the ship, and ordered to start the nuclear fusion engines. The people we left at the space station communicated by radio. They said they saw a light brighter than the sun radiating from the rear end of our ship. The engines were mounted at the tip of the ship's long scorpion tail. After an hour or so, the space station was just a speck in space. Captain Cronus explained. "If we had started the nuclear engines at the station, the ship's radioactive exhaust, and the radiation would have killed everybody there."

'"Our three-year voyage to the outermost limits of the solar system had begun. The ship accelerated for three orbits around Earth, gradually gaining speed to escape Earth's gravity. For long voyages, artificial gravity inside spaceships is important for trained as well as for untrained travelers. Centrifugal force caused by the counter rotating donut shaped bodies acted as artificial gravity. We enjoyed the view of Earth, perhaps for the last time. Two days later we crossed the orbit of the moon. From then on we were surrounded by the blackness of space, except the views of Earth, the sun, and the stars. As time passed by, looking through the window became boring, just stars and more stars. The ship continuously accelerated for two months, then its engines were shut down. From then on, the ship traveled just by inertia. From that distance Earth looked like a blue baseball ball and the moon looked like a yellow marble."'

We had many things to do inside the spaceship. I wondered if the busy crew and the rest of the passengers felt the same way as I did. We were no longer bored, and we no longer needed to approach the windows to see the same black space day after day. Nothing extraordinary happened for months. We had the impression the ship wasn't moving at all, even though it was moving at tremendous speed. We use to spend our spare time socializing; it was like living in a small village. We organized parties and dinners. The entertainment room was often crowded with people, some of them playing computer games. The rooms for sports and physical fitness were also visited. The rooms closest to the ship's axle were the ones with the least artificial gravity, and were used by some of the tourists the ones wanting to be trained as amateur astronauts. For travelers interested in education there were courses and lectures at the theater; also anybody could borrow videotapes from the library.

"One day, half way to Mars, we saw a dot of light in the distance. It grew larger. The object looked like it was coming head-on. It was Atlantis 4 returning from Phobos, one of the moons of Mars, where some years before the Atlanteans had installed a base. That ship on its way back to Earth passed near us, blinking its lights as a salute. One day Captain Cronus made a happy announcement. Our ship was going to pass by Mars, although we were not going to stop there.

"'As we passed Mars, we observed the red planet for about half an hour. Captain Cronus was in constant contact with Mars and Phobos. We left Mars behind, and we returned to the same routine and the same view of dark space again.

"'To distract the passengers from boredom, Captain Cronus invited everybody to the theater, and told some stories, the first about the first human exploration to Mars. The main mission had been simple, the astronauts had to survive there for two terrestrial years; after that when they returned to Earth, they were to bring some rocks from Mars. They survived by melting and extracting water from permafrost, and by creating inside their inflatable chambers an atmosphere for breathing. In another inflatable chamber they cultivated a small orchard, with the quinua seeds they had brought from a high altitude zone from the Andes Mountains on Earth. This nutritious food grew easily on Mars.

"'Captain Cronus continued with the story. Half a century before, long before the first human explorers landed on Mars, the Atlantean Space agency had been sending probes, robots, and satellites to obtain the necessary data from the red planet, including locations with water, preferable in zones with plains and some small hills. Prior to send the first astronauts to Mars, a lightweight robot tractor was sent to excavate three round short tunnels at the foot of a hill. The robot tractor was operated by remote control from Earth.

"'When the first astronauts arrived, the three tunnels were already there. What they did first, was to inflate a long cylindrical and transparent plastic bag inside each tunnel. The bags were inflated with air from pressure bottles to a pressure equivalent half the air pressure at sea level on Earth. The first long bag was used as their living quarters, the second for their laboratory and recycling equipment, and in the lower part of the third bag, they installed their hydroponics garden to grow vegetables for their survival. A quarter-mile away from their headquarters in a small crater the astronauts installed a small plutonium nuclear reactor to provide electricity. Electric power was used all the time and for almost everything.

"'The four purposes to install the environmental plastic bags inside tunnels was that the tunnels protected against the cosmic rays, sun flares, sandstorms and provided better temperature insulation. As Captain Cronus finished his presentation, we left the theater, and it was already late and after a few minutes most of the ship's internal illumination was turned off automatically; this illumination was synchronized to match the days and the nights of Atlantis.

"'With time we became friends with the ship astronomers who often invited us to join them at the observation deck. We shared their telescope located inside a glass dome mounted on the observation deck. We also enjoyed seeing with our naked eyes, the billions of tiny stars in the Milky Way, while from Earth because of the atmosphere all that we could see at night were only a few stars, and a blurred Milky Way. The spherical head of this ship had three floors, which were on the top of the observation deck where we saw more stars by looking up and also down through the transparent floor of the observation deck. The next floor below was the bridge, with its walls full of dials, screen displays, and navigation instruments. Captain Cronus sat on his tall chair behind his crew, the crew faced the front windows, and each of them operated his own controls.

"'When our ship was halfway between Mars and Jupiter, I was in bed watching videotapes, which reminded me of my life on Earth. Then I shifted my attention to the artificial window. In the distance I saw two asteroids looking like small pebbles. As we approached and passed by them, I realized those were no pebbles but the size of mountains. Two days later we heard the blaring of the emergency sirens, followed by a general announcement from Captain Cronus. He said, "We are crossing the asteroid belt. Here the size of the asteroids ranges from a grain of sand to the size of a small world. However, the largest one in our particular pathway will not be larger than a brick. Even so, these can be worse than cannon projectiles. The impact of a meteorite the size of a grain of rice can puncture the wall of the ship. If not repaired, air could leak out. If an asteroid the size of a chicken egg hit the ship, it probably would not produce an explosive decompression of a compartment, because the outer shell of the ship was constructed with integral shallow thick ribs, called stoppers of progressive cracks. On the other hand a meteorite larger than a brick would probably prove catastrophic."

"'After this announcement Captain Cronus called to my room by phone, saying he needed help from everybody including tourists. He assigned me to report as a gunner to one of the gun stations, to operate one of the weapon systems. It consisted of radar to detect incoming asteroids, and the weapon to destroy them. The weapons included either laser or elementary particle beam guns. The ship also carried missiles with nuclear warheads of different sizes, which were used only to shoot down large asteroids. The ship's six gunners, including myself, shot and blew up several small asteroids.

"'Finally we finished crossing the asteroid belt without problems. Captain Cronus explained that our spaceship was not a warship. but for exploration;

however, it was provided with the most formidable weapon system any warrior or ruler of the world could dream of. Its highly efficient weapon system could detect incoming asteroids and destroy them before they could hit the ship at more than 100 times the velocity of a cannon projectile. However, the ship's defenses were limited mostly to destroying relatively small asteroids. For asteroids larger than ten meters, the only defense was avoiding them when they still were thousands of miles away.

"'The next day, at dinner, Captain Cronus explained the advanced weaponry system of the spaceship. He said that it was the same one that was developed during the cold war, at the time when Atlantis split into two powers. Now just as a reference I want to mention that years later after I wrote the manuscript of this book, this weapon system was similar to the Strategic Defense Initiative (SDI or Star Wars) developed in the twentieth century by the United States. It was a defense system, not too practical and not too effective against incoming missiles in an actual war; however, very useful for the further development of the sciences by stimulating new discoveries. This was a program that also created employment and training for thousands of unemployed engineers and scientists.

"'In a hypothetical advanced civilization where wars are not known, the knowledge gained from a program similar to the American SDI would be very useful to design weapons to be used as defense by their space ships, where the enemy is not living beings but debris from space. The same idea applied to the Atlantean spaceships.

"'Going back to the topic of the long voyage, we enjoyed the pleasant narration of Captain Cronus, then after crossing the nasty asteroid belt, we relaxed and the days passed. Next we crossed the orbit of planet Jupiter. The planet was not close. By looking sideways through the window, the giant planet appeared only as a distant small ball, with its moons as points of light.

"'Everybody resumed his or her own activities on the ship. Some people worked in the hydroponics gardens, others on a variety of technical and intellectual projects. In our free time some of us played ball games, and many were active in social activities. One day Captain Cronus announced over the speakers that he was going to turn the ship around, making it go in reverse, and to turn on the engines full power, not to return to Earth, but to slow down the ship, which was traveling too fast. This time the main engines were used as "thrust reverses" or brakes. The ship had already built up tremendous speed and it would take several days to slow down traveling tail first.

"'More than a month had passed since the ship started to slow down. Saturn had become the largest object in the sky. It looked like a polished ivory ball; a resplendent jewel in the blackness of space. As we approached, we passed close by two of its moons. The view of Saturn was breathtaking. By that time it looked about forty times the size of our moon, as seen from Earth. For most of us the view was wonderful, only a few found it scary. The ship engines were turned off.

"'Carefully our ship approached and docked on a nearby space iceberg, made mostly from dirty ice. It was a moonlet looking like an iceberg not larger than a mile across in orbit around Saturn, still away from the edge of the rings. My wife and I went to the bridge and paid a visit to Captain Cronus. I asked why we hadn't docked in any of the ice blocks inside the rings. He answered, "We must not come any closer to Saturn than what we are now, in order to prevent exposure to its dangerous magnetic field that could kill all of us." From there the captain pointed out from the window to the moonlet's iced surface, and explained, "We just landed, as you can see, teams of workers in their space suits. They have already moved their equipment to the surface of the moonlet. One of the nearest team is operating a machine that melts down chunks of ice, purifies it, and pumps it directly into the ship reservoirs, so we could have enough drinking water for the duration of the trip."

"'For hours I kept looking through the window, as the busy space workers operated their equipment. In the same icy arena, further away I saw another team operating what looked to be very complicated equipment. A sign painted on the machine read "HEAVY WATER SEPARATOR." It was the equipment where heavy water was extracted by very complicated means that only this advanced people could understand and pumped it into special tanks inside the ship.

"'Later Captain Cronus said, "Once we depart, we will continue our voyage to intercept the comet. We will have plenty of time to operate continuously our electrolysis equipment, where the heavy water will be separated into its basic elements, deuterium (hydrogen's heavy isotope) and oxygen. The oxygen will be stored in aluminum bottles to use later in our breathable atmosphere inside the ship. The deuterium gas will flow into a special machine, to be synthesized with pulverized lithium, to become a powder of lithium deuteride. Another machine will encapsulate this powder into millions of miniature pellets.

"'""These pellets containing lithium deuteride and covered with special coatings are going to be stored in a special container. These pellets constitute the actual nuclear fuel for the ship's fusion engines. We will have enough fuel to last for the rest of the trip. "

"'On our last day at the space iceberg, most of the equipment was packed back and brought up to the ship. The ship still stood on its three crab-like legs, grasping the huge ice block with its mechanical claws. The legs were slender and light for an environment of very low gravity. Once everybody was aboard, a bunch of small rockets attached to the spaceship's belly ignited at the same time, kicking and separating the spaceship from the ice block. Captain Cronus said, "Good, we are free, and ready to start the main fusion engines." Our ship began moving and accelerating on a broad orbit, turning just once around Saturn. Upon reaching escape velocity, we left the orbit and continued our journey into deep space. And we were getting away from Saturn, our sun looked only one-tenth the diameter, as it was seen from Earth. We continued our nonstop travel to the outer limits of the solar system to intercept the dangerous comet. It would take a year or so.

"'As our space voyage proceeded, we crossed the orbit of Uranus. The planet was not too far to our left. We appreciated its beauty, a bluish jewel in the sky. Months later we crossed the orbits of Neptune and Pluto. These last two planets were not visible from either side our ship. However, every time we crossed the orbit of a planet, Captain Cronus organized and celebrated the event with a formal party where everybody attended in formal dress.

"From that distance the sun still appeared as the brightest of the stars, brighter than Sirius and perhaps brighter than planet Venus when seen on a clear night from Earth. One night while my wife was looking through our window, she noticed a weak dot of light, perhaps it was a new planet she had just discovered and should be named after her because she saw it first. Suddenly Captain Cronus' voice came over the speakers. "Please everybody move close to your windows. The dot of faint light you see in front of our ship is the killer comet. It is still millions of kilometers ahead of us. Everybody please relax on your seats or beds. We are going to repeat the same braking maneuver as we did before to reduce speed. That will allow us to approach the comet very slowly and dock on it as we did the last time with the space iceberg."

"'Later at the ship cafeteria, my wife inquired of a fellow passenger, why we just didn't blow up the comet by shooting it with nuclear missiles? Why did we need to approach and land on it? The reason was that nuclear missiles could only peel away the surface of the comet. We would need to land there and drill deep wells, then drop a nuclear bomb at the bottom of each. When the bombs exploded, they would blow it up into small fragments. We were satisfied with the answer. Our ship kept decelerating for days until it slowed down enough to match the same speed of the comet. We were getting close to the comet. It looked like a small world of ice, about 40 kilometers in diameter. Its collision would certainly have made Earth one more dead and barren planet in our solar system.

"'Our ship was already in orbit around the comet, moving slowly and no more than a kilometer high above its surface. It decreased its speed and finally landed. We could observe the comet frightening scenery through our window. A latch from our ship opened and some space workers rushed to the comet's surface. Some walked to the tail of the ship to retrieve the well drilling equipment and the four boxes each holding a hydrogen bomb. For hours they dug four holes on the comet's surface, each about a kilometer deep, and placed at the bottom of each a hydrogen bomb. Long electric wires connected each bomb to a radio receiver left on the comet's surface. The bombs were to be detonated by remote control. When all work on the comet was done, everybody returned to the ship. After the digging equipment met its purpose, was abandoned on the comet's surface.

"'The fusion engines started, and the ship lifted off from the comet. We departed for our return trip to Earth. We had traveled already for no more than three hours and we were at a safe distance from the comet. Captain Cronus took his microphone and addressed the ship. "I don't want any of you to miss this spectacle." Then he exploded the comet by remote control. A bright light was produced, but because of the great distance, it just looked like no more than a strong flashlight. This event was celebrated with joy in the ship. Captain Cronus communicated the good news to Earth. Atlantis, and its various outposts around the world, celebrated the great event.

"'The next day, two astronomers, my wife, and myself were on the observation deck, happily discussing the destruction of the comet. Captain Cronus peered up through the telescope and said, "It seems that the comet was not completely shattered, but I am satisfied with the results, thanks to everyone's help." The waiter brought us cocktails in special glasses designed for a low gravity environment. One of the astronomers asked me to hold his cocktail glass so he could peer out the telescope one more time. He said, "The comet has broken into countless chunks of ice spreading in all directions." Suddenly he became scared and yelled, "Bad news! Two big chunks are still moving along the same pathway as the original comet was. They may still collide with Earth, who knows when." The astronomer rushed to communicate the bad news to Captain Cronus who at the moment was celebrating with his guests. The astronomer suggested to him that we should turn back the ship and destroy each of those two chunks of ice, but this time using missiles.

"'The Captain replied, "It is unlikely that the ice chunks will follow the same exact path as the original comet. Maybe you have had too many cocktails. Also, we don't have large enough missiles to blow them up. There is nothing we can do at this time, but to proceed with our return trip to Earth."

"'My wife and I could remember that for half a century before the discovery of this comet, the Atlanteans felt rumbling deep beneath the ground followed by tremors. Also we found out about the geological instability of our islands. Some of the elders had planned in advance to move our civilization to the western territories of Atlantis (today the Americas), a huge continent with almost no human population. Anyway we were not in a hurry to leave our paradise. We knew that cataclysms could happen anytime; it could take days or be millions of years in the future.

"'As we headed nonstop for Earth, the long trip gave enough time to the ship's astronomers to prove if a collision between the comet fragments and Earth was imminent. Finally we arrived back on Earth. It was at the time when the last boats and ships were departing with different destinations, today know as America, Africa, and Europe; however, most went to Europe.

"'A small group of pessimistic Atlanteans believed it was not worthy to get evacuated to any other place of the globe, and that anyway the whole planet was going to be destroyed by the comet's fragments. They believed their duty was to save as many creatures as possible, including the human species. They organized themselves into an engineering group to construct an interstellar spaceship capable of traveling at 25 percent the speed of light for a voyage to planet Entar. But in order to develop such a sophisticated space ship, humans needed to evolve for a hundred thousand years more, before they could think of getting involved in such a project. However, the Atlanteans were lucky; they were going to use the plans and the technological information left to them by the Entarian aliens. The Entarians had left it as a token of friendship during their last visit to Earth. This was going to be a spaceship ten thousand times more efficient than the ones built by humans. The Atlantean spaceships were only designed to explore but not beyond the outer limits of our solar system.

"'Another helpful event was that during the same visit to Earth, the Entarian aliens gave the Atlanteans an open invitation to send a delegation of Earth scholars to Entar, who should stay there for a couple of years or so, learning their customs, their wisdom, and their advanced science. So when they returned, they could use on Earth what they learned in Entar in order to help their own species. This open invitation from some years before was a great opportunity for the Atlanteans living in their last days, to send several chosen individuals to planet Entar. However, this time not as visitors or students but as immigrants to perpetuate the human species, because there was the possibility that a cataclysm should destroy all life on Earth. Most of the chosen travelers were children, who, by the time they reached Entar would have grown into mature individuals. The adults who traveled with these children were the best teachers and tutors that Atlantis could offer. The computer chose travelers for this interstellar voyage, so nobody could argue with the choice.

"'Both comet chunks kept moving menacingly toward earth. Meanwhile, Atlanteans overseas were busy day and night trying to finish the construction of the secret vaults, then filling them before the disaster. At the same time a group of engineers were trying to finish the construction of the interstellar ship for the voyage to Entar. This ship was so big that it could not be sent into space as a whole. It had to be sent up as separate components to be assembled in orbit and in the vicinity of the space station. The problem was how to send up millions of pounds of equipment and structural components into an orbit in space. To assemble the spaceship would require at least a hundred space shuttle flights, flying day and night. Another problem was that to build so many space shuttles on such short notice would be impossible. So at the last moment, the Atlanteans devised a more economical and crude way to send cargo up into space, by excavating some of the artificial volcanoes as explained earlier.'"

Tucan left the screen; it was the end of the last documentary. Fred the monk turned on the lights of the auditorium and commented, "The elders were already aware of the coming catastrophe, and there was nothing anybody could do except to evacuate from the unstable islands.

"Amazingly in the last days of Atlantis, the weather was so wonderful that the elders declared a national holiday that actually lasted for three consecutive days. They recommended everybody who still remained in Atlantis to forget all their problems and dedicate those days to enjoying life. The beaches became crowded with people in swimming suits. From the beach we could see some ships leaving while others were arriving from different places of the world, bringing back Atlantean workers from overseas. Among the returning ones were who had already finished filling and sealing the treasure chambers, and others who finished the construction of those megalithic indicators left on each continent.

"On the TV evening news from the last holiday, an astronomer announced that the largest chunk from the comet would miss the Earth. Everybody felt relief for a moment. The astronomer continued and said, however, the second piece would collide within 23 days. He even indicated the time and the place where the impact would occur; it would be in the middle of the Atlantic Ocean.

"Half a year before, a large number of worried Atlanteans began evacuating because the frightening news about the two comet fragments. Without losing time the elders organized the last massive evacuation of the people still remaining in the islands."

Fred the monk said, "Walter, when you were Kappa the Atlantean engineer, you evacuated to Europe in one of the last boats. As the boat approached the European shore it hit a rock and sank. Everybody died, including you. However, it was only a virtual death in a virtual reality of the past. It looked like your spirit got separated from Kappa, then was rescued and brought back from the past by the same Stone of Dreams where you were taking a nap."

Fred said, "Boy, I hope you enjoyed this documentary about captain Cronus and your visit to our place inside these mountains. Now there are no more films or time left; we are going to take you back to the same stone from where we picked you up. Your father and the porter are still dozing back there, each lying on a separate rock. You will join them; from then on the stone's strange powers will take care of you; you will fall asleep again and start receiving its most important message. It is for that message the Atlanteans built the stone. No more fancy dreams as you have experienced before from that world that also was a paradise. The stone will resume its final transmission by bringing you back once more into the virtual reality of Atlantis, this time only for a quick trip, long enough to learn some data and some facts. It will include, a visit to the schools of Atlantis, in order that the people from your time could appreciate the Atlantis educational system with students of all ages, from the age of toddlers to graduation from university.

"At the University of Brasea, you will visit the schools of aerospace engineering, medicine, and so forth. You will have the opportunity to meet famous professors. Also in this second trip to Atlantis, you will have the opportunity to read in the Atlantis Chronicles the sciences, the technology. In the medical field you will find the Atlanteans were conducting extensive medical research concerning the extension of human life, the cure for cancer, and the discovery of a new material for the construction of nonrejectable bionic parts for the human body, featuring an artificial heart. However, from all, that you see and hear, the most important part of the message will be revealed to you near the end of the stone transmission. The revelation is of the three greatest secrets, given as a present by the Atlanteans to that humanity eons in the future. With this wisdom humanity will be able to defend itself from that returning comet fragment and from the nasty Ortusian invaders.

"As you awaken, you will forget for awhile everything you have seen and heard, including your encounters with prophets and with us, the monks. Also you will forget your visit to our great chamber, our headquarters, and about Atlantis. It is too late, you should leave now before the weather worsens. I wish you, your father, and the porter a good journey returning to your home and civilization. Be careful climbing those mountains; there are no emergency services for hundreds of miles around."

I asked Fred my last question. Why haven't you shown your hidden chamber to the world?"

He replied, "Humanity is not mature enough to receive such an enormous legacy.

"Years will pass by, then one day you will feel surprised, when you will start to remember those dreams, by dreaming them over and over again, every time with more clarity than the time before. Even you will believe you had actually lived in Atlantis, as its last living citizen.

"You will remember their great ideals, their mentality and the strange objects and machines you have seen, some still in perfect working condition after 11,000 years of storage. You will even remember menial details, as when you walked by the streets of Brasea counting the number of floors of the tallest buildings or when you were in the underground vault, touching and looking at the strange rivets and rare bolts from airplanes and spaceships. Today is the day the mysterious stone will reveal also to you a variety of Atlantean plans and engineering drawings, the ones that were used for the construction of spaceships, modern cities, and many other amazing engineering, architectural, and bioengineering tasks; a revelation for the benefit of mankind. The only question is if the humanity from your time will use all these for good or for evil."

I told the monk that the stone committed a great mistake by choosing me. I'm just a boy, more interested in parties, sports, to be with friends, a boy free of responsibilities. But the monk was sure that the stone was a miracle machine for anybody sitting on it and turning it on. The stone would transmit telepathically the thoughts and living experiences from people that lived in the past, directly at incredible speed into the mind of whoever sits there to receive their message.

The monk gave me his last recommendation. "Near the end of its transmission, the stone will reveal the three great secrets that may change the world of your time forever. Two of them were used not only by the Atlanteans, but also for thousands of years by the greatest civilizations from this galaxy, those concerned with the creation of clean fusion reactors to produce cheap electricity for modern cities. Similar fusion reactor design was also used as the propulsion system to propel spaceships during their long journeys through the universe. The construction of these nuclear fusion reactors was considered the most important technological threshold for any civilization that wants to gain respect from all the other advanced, alien civilizations of this galaxy.

"One day when the galactic aliens become aware that the people from Earth created their nuclear fusion reactor for peaceful purposes, they will reactivate Earth's membership in the galactic fraternity, which was active in times of Atlantis.

"Being a member of this galactic association has its advantages. Valuable data in all disciplines, generated by advanced civilizations of the universe, are available free of charge to the members of the Galactic Association. Saving the members many resources, since they no longer need to duplicate expensive experiments and research already conducted by some other alien civilization.

"Fred the monk was tired of so much talking and I was eager to leave at once and go to sit once more on the mysterious stone to receive its last short transmission, the most important part of the message, concerning the greatest secrets of the universe.

I was not aware that this dream could be interrupted. When it was, important technical information was lost (see chapter 15). I got awakened prematurely into reality and the dreams ended abruptly. My father awakened me because we had been dozing longer than expected and the weather began to change becoming stormy. It was necessary to continue hiking and climbing those barren Andes Mountains to return to civilization. Minutes before I was awake I could remember an old man with a white beard, who began to explain me some blueprints laid on a table, plans designed by the Atlantean industry which were used to build nuclear fusion and ion propulsion systems for long voyage spaceships. The old man had a lot of patience when he tried to explain me the purpose of those highly detailed construction plans.

The old man dressed as a monk told me that eons ago several advanced civilizations from this galaxy, in order to explore the universe, began to develop nuclear fusion engines and ion propulsion systems for this spaceship.

Just recently I became aware that in our modern twentieth-century Earth, our civilization has already expended more than a billion dollars doing research in order to create fusion nuclear power plants, and already more than thirty years have passed and it seems there has not been too much progress.

In the appendix section of this book are recreated engineering drawings from the dream, including preliminary designs for the construction of a spaceship designed for long voyages through the solar system. In the drawing zone of the nuclear propulsion system is blurred and blank spaces representing the missing information. I am hoping that someday somebody could rediscover it.

(For additional information see SPACESHIP ATLANTIS 2 in Engineering Chronicle II from the Supplementary Chapter and in the appendices section from this book.)

# CHAPTER 15
## Back to the Stone of the Dreams and the Great Revelation

A helicopter was waiting for me. I ran and I climbed into it. Then I looked for the last time at the giant cavern. Fred was waving his hand and yelling good-bye and good luck. The pilot asked me to put the same hood as before on my head to cover my eyes, just like on the way in, so that I should never recognize the area where their base was located. We left, and after a short flight, we landed on the rocky side of the mountain. I recognized the terrain and I saw my father and our guide still dozing on their respective rocks. I could not tell if in this adventure we spent only a few minutes or days. I left the helicopter, and sat back on the same mysterious stone from where the pilots picked me up before. The pilots waved their hands and left. I was getting sleepy, I tried to stay awake, but I couldn't resist the power of the stone. Anyway I fell asleep and my dreams began with my second virtual visit to magnificent Atlantis, but this time just for business.

As I awoke not in this world, but in Atlantis, my real memories and the fact that I came from the twentieth century vanished. It was my second trip back in time, but I appeared not in the Atlantean times I used to be in, but in another different time. I didn't know how, but I suddenly appeared dining with my Atlantean girlfriend at a place well known for its excellent seafood and wines. Old memories sprouted in my mind. I remember I had two friends, Krill and Crom. After they got married, each moved with his wife to different towns. Krill was Godin's grandson and I remember he got married to a girl he brought himself from the European wilderness by crossing the ocean in his mechanical flying horse, a horse designed by his grandpa. Once in Atlantis he got formally married in the temple of Poseidon, a temple that also doubled as a place of ceremonies, the same temple that in modern Atlantis got converted into a museum, after the mythological gods became just folklore.

I also could remember from another ceremony that took place, in the same temple of Poseidon, in Godin's honor, when he was awarded the Great Atlantis Prize as the "Atlantis Design Engineer of the Year." He received a gold medal, a box full of gold coins, and two vacation packages, which included two roundtrip tickets for him and his wife, to a new resort built on the moon for space tourists. Godin was eager to go, but his wife didn't like flying, so instead her ticket was given to their grandson Krill, who appreciated it and said, "Great, I always wanted to visit that underground Atlantis tourist resort at the moon.

It was strange, moments before the departure, Krill had the premonition that something bad was going to happen on this trip. Godin remained smiling. The space vehicle departed, and they traveled through deep space for several hours. As the vehicle approached the moon, the pilot announced over the speaker, "We got hit by a miniature meteorite. We have problems with the heater and the air conditioning; inside the cabin is getting cold. Please be patient, we are going to land at any moment." The pilots' hands were so numb that they could not grab the controls, and the vehicle made a rough landing. It broke into two parts, killing half the passengers and all the crew. Luckily all passengers were wearing space suits, which reduced the number of deaths by depressurization.

Godin still was alive, although a heavy beam fell and crushed his body and vital organs. Krill died instantly; the same beam that hit Godin crushed his head. Both were picked up in an ambulance and brought to the moon's hospital. Both bodies were almost frozen. In the hospital, Godin's head and the upper part from his body were kept alive by a complicated life support system, a heart lung machine. Krill's smashed head was removed. His heart was still beating and his headless body was kept alive by another life support system, for possible organ donations.

But then, I was living in a modern apartment in Brasea. Once in awhile I used to fly to the island of Poseidon to visit my Uncle Luzaire, his family, and old Godin. This time it was urgent; I flew to express my grief for Krill's death and Godin's traumatic condition. I began remembering my early years when I came to Atlantis the first time; they were my first friends. I remember after finishing high school, Godin gave me a part-time job in his factory. At that time I also got enrolled in the school of engineering at the University of Brasea.

Like most students, I had some spare time to enjoy sports, vacation trips, hiking by the wilderness, visiting museums, and going to concerts. I enjoyed going with Mila to dancing and parties. As most Atlanteans, I also enjoyed going to the circus and the traditional Atlantis games, where acrobats, bulls, and horses displayed a good show, an Atlantis tradition for more than 500 years. Atlanteans always were fanatics for these games where bad-tempered bulls were teased but not hurt; however, sometimes performers were hurt or killed if they weren't careful. Each town of Atlantis had a coliseum dedicated to traditional games.

Another kind of entertainment I never missed was the air show held once a year on a broad field, close to the popular beach from the Island of the Sun. This air show was a new kind of entertainment created in modern Atlantis times.

My new return to Atlantis in my second dream began with the sudden appearance of three young foreign teachers, who came from a small kingdom north of the Internal Sea. They were chosen by their king to visit Atlantis and were thrilled at the prospect. They would be given an opportunity to observe a society with a superb educational system where almost every mediocre student could be transformed into a genius. The three teachers had already heard of the wonderful Atlantis educational system, mostly by commentaries from returning visitors and merchants who traded minerals, metals, and crystals with Atlantis.

At the time of their departure, their king spoke to them: "I am sending you to Brasea, the greatest and most modern city of the world, to observe their educational system. Upon your return, you will advise us what improvements we can make here in our own houses of learning."

It was a long slow sailing. Finally the teachers arrived in Atlantis, where they met and stayed for a few days with Professor Kriton, a foreign affairs man from the Office of Education. My girlfriend, Mila, was his polyglot secretary. "Welcome to Atlantis," said the greeting professor.

"I can hardly believe we are finally here," said the foreign woman teacher.

"Well, you are," said the professor, "Now, right this way please. You'll be staying in my apartment, which is located in that brown skyscraper two blocks ahead. My office chose me to be your host because I speak a little bit of your language."

Mila asked Professor Kriton if she could bring her boyfriend with the tour. She meant me. He agreed, so I went with them.

Our first visit started with a visit to the school for toddlers and young children. Another professor approached us and introduced himself, "I am Dr. Kunkun from Asia. I'm a specialist in early childhood education, ages two to five. Please follow me." We walked into a classroom. Doctor Kunkun said, "As you can see, the geometric skills of these five-year-olds are already well developed. Some of them are drawing patterns on white cardboard, then cutting them out and assembling them with glue. These children are building the toys from their own imagination. They are making paper horses, dogs, dolls, houses, trucks, airplanes, merry-go-rounds and many other things they could imagine by themselves.

"In the Atlantis educational system," Dr. Kunkun continued, "there are seven years of elementary school and three of high school, a total of ten." He walked us across the well-kept grounds of the primary school. He went on, "The same program of studies applies with some exceptions to all students. However, they are free to advance at their own pace with no pressure. The gifted ones meet no barriers; they could complete the same study program in less time, just by requesting in advance to take their final grade exams in any month of the year. There is no age discrimination for final grade exams; age doesn't matter. There were cases when highly motivated students did the ten years' program in only three.

"Most children of the world do not enjoy compulsory education; all they want is to play full time. The children think of these games as entertainment. But they don't know that behind those games are concealed educational material, created by good educators. As they play, they are learning languages, art, mathematics, and the sciences. All this happens incredibly fast and with no pressure. Some of them become addicted to education."

We walked into the elementary classroom where children were absorbed their own activities. Some of them were watching the screen of a magic box called a video recorder in the twentieth century; others were at their computers, and it seemed they never got bored. Doctor Kunkun said, "By the time the average, self-motivated child is ten, they will have completed all short courses pertinent to general education: language, world history, art, geography, and government. The courses of mathematics and science are given priority."

I realized there was not too much recorded history for the Atlantean children to learn, other than a few wars among savages and some peaceful encounters from them with the Atlanteans. In times of Atlantis, the rest of the world was a wilderness, where people organized themselves in simple tribes. Geography was equally simple. Most of the world was uncharted territory and there were not too many names or places, including plains, mountains, or rivers to learn. Similar simplicity happened with the course of government, considering that most Atlanteans were logical people and were happy with their simple government system, with a small but highly efficient bureaucracy. Most courses of general education were short; the world from that time was so simple that children graduated from elementary school with a general education diploma already well prepared to start high school.

## HIGH SCHOOL EDUCATION

Dr. Kunkun continued his narration, "There are three years of high school. As before, it is up to the student to complete it in less time. The Atlantis race has more tendency to science and technology than to letters and humanities.

"Some highly motivated high school students in their senior year, are taking additional courses after school hours in engineering or medicine at the university level. Those programs are sponsored by grants given by the industry, allowing them to graduate simultaneously with two diplomas, a high school and a semi-professional degree. After graduation, if they prefer, they may work for companies at a modest professional level. However, to work in more advanced projects, they prefer to hire people with university degrees. "

The most interesting part of this tour was our visit to two different classrooms, both dedicated to research and development. Each class had a team of only a small number of students, who were chosen from among several candidates, all of them in their last year of high school, who after regular classes walked to their corresponding classroom, where they performed real life projects. In those rooms we saw students each working on a computer doing their research and developing their assigned project, all in order to get additional school credits, and at the same time they were well paid, enough money to save for their university education.

We walked into one of these special classrooms. There we met with our new host, a professor in aeronautics, and the group leader. He was pleased to receive us and said, "This particular group of 16- and 17-year-olds are working on a real-world project, supported by an airline grant. By getting involved in real projects, the students learn to trust themselves, becoming trustworthy leaders for the future and able to make responsible professional decisions by themselves. This time, we got an interesting task. It is to design a small commuter aircraft for the airline that gave the grant. This airline makes daily flights in between the Atlantis islands and once in awhile to Europe. The design consists of a small, commuter twin-engine jet, with a capacity for 30 passengers."

I saw each student working on his or hers computer. I asked the professor what kind of pictures and calculations they were doing. Our host smiled and said, "This is a group of seven students. Each of them is working in their own specialty. To encourage these children, we gave each of them a temporary title as a specialist engineer." Our host acted as chief project engineer while his students acted as his assistants. He said that we were lucky to visit them at this time when most of the construction drawings for the airplane were almost completed.

(For additional information, see "DESIGN OF A MEDIUM RANGE TWIN JET TRANSPORT" in the Engineering Chronicles from the supplementary part and the appendices from this book.)

We left this room, but our tour to the high school was not over yet, there was one more class to visit. We walked into a different class from the previous one, it was a bioengineering laboratory. At this place we met another host, a bioengineer who also acted as project chief. He explained to us that his group had received a government grant to design an artificial heart, to be permanently implanted into the patient body without the danger of being rejected.

The professor introduced us to his students who were about the same age as the students designing the airplane. As before, these students were chosen from among many volunteers because of their design ability. Our host continued, "You have arrived just in time to see the mechanical heart in its final stage of design. It is about the size of a normal adult heart. Practically speaking, this is no morethan a pump actuated by hydraulic power."

Our new host asked us to follow him into the school auditorium where he would show us a medical documentary. As the documentary progressed he explained the series of steps his students accomplished in order to develop the artificial heart. These medical students working in this project were as well paid as those designing the airplane. In the film appeared the same host, and the same students we saw in the class. On the screen the professor explained to his students that before starting with the design of a real artificial heart, they should first get some training by designing a simple ordinary double pump for water, actuated by inflatable diaphragms. It was mainly a closed box made from transparent plastic with two tubes and two valves. The box was divided into two compartments by a central partition. The compartments were full of water, and at each side of the central partition was mounted a rubber diaphragm. Every time the diaphragm got inflated, it expelled the water from the compartment through one of the tubes. The pump was a crude representation of the artificial heart. The pumping membranes were inflated by high-pressure hydraulic fluid that came through long hoses from a remote power system.

After this short training period, the students were ready to start with the design of the real mechanical heart. At the end of our visit to this class, our host gave each of us a medical brochure which explained with great detail the design and the development of this artificial heart. In the last pages of the same brochure was the description of another type of heart design, a hybrid, half-living and half-artificial. The lower part of this heart constituted by the ventricles was the living portion, the tissues of which were stimulated to grow from living heart cells. The brochure also explained that depending on the needs of the patient, the cells were stimulated to grow either way, for a whole heart or only part of it.

By applying the practice of tissue engineering, undifferentiated cells were turned into heart cells, and stimulated to growth, either way, by implanting it in the patient's abdomen or in a tube in the laboratory. For the case when this living heart grew in the patient's abdomen, this fully-grown organ, still in a dormant state, was removed and minutes later transplanted into the thorax of the same patient. In the other method where the heart cells were stimulated to grow in laboratory tubes, growing only as simple heart components, the heart ventricles or heart valves were transplanted into the same patient with no risk of rejection, since these organs were produced from cells extracted from the same patient.

When scientists tried to clone a whole heart, most of the time it grew with defective valves, so the upper portion with its defective valves was discarded. This upper portion was cut off and replaced with an artificial one.

We left the high school, impressed with the skills of those students who were able to develop such great projects.

(For additional information, see "DESIGN OF AN ARTIFICIAL HEART" in the Medical Science Chronicles from the supplementary part of this book.)

## THE UNIVERSITIES OF ATLANTIS

We were really tired with the extensive tour, and two days later Professor Kriton took all us for a four-day camping trip to enjoy the sunshine, the good weather, the countryside, and specially the green hills far away from the city. It was a good idea after those tiring urban tours. With the camping trip, the foreign teachers had recuperated enough to resume with their indoctrination. It was already night when we arrived at Brasea, the streets as always well illuminated. Professor Kriton parked his car and said, "Let's take a walk through the Main Street and enjoy looking at the fancy windows of several stores."

We were hungry and decided to enter a popular restaurant, which served domestic as well as international food. Our table was located next to a large window. From there we could contemplate the beautiful buildings of the modern city of Brasea, buildings built from steel and glass, able to withstand the frequent earthquakes. The city of Brasea was designed with concentric avenues looking like rings, crossed by another set of straight avenues, radiating out from the main City Square like the spokes of a wheel.

The next day, Professor Kriton took us in his wide car to visit the campus of the University of Brasea. The campus occupied one third of the ring of land next to the fifth circling avenue.    As we approached the campus, our tourists were impressed by its twenty towering skyscrapers, all facing the curved avenue, and with their backs facing the broad campus and sport fields. "In this university we will visit three schools," said the professor,   "the schools of architecture, medicine, and aeronautical engineering.  Let's hurry up because I made an appointment with Professor Oca at the School of Architecture." We arrived to the university and walking by the lobby, we met professor Oca who was already waiting for us.

Oca and Kriton engaged in a menial chat.  "Did you have any trouble finding the School of Architecture?" asked Oca.

"No," said Kriton, "the campus is large, and well marked."

"Did you come in by sky train?" asked Oca.

"No, I drove my hydrogen-powered car," said Kriton.

"Oh.  Indeed, you came very fast."

And you, professor what kind of car do you have?" asked Kriton.

Oca answered, "I have an electric car.  It isn't as powerful and expensive, as yours isn't.  However, it is an economical and nonpolluting vehicle.  Electric cars are practical for countries like Atlantis, where the cost of electricity is low.  In Atlantis there are several power stations, which tap geothermal sources of hot underground steam to produce electricity, a great blessing from nature to Atlantis. Electric cars are great, as long you don't forget to, recharge the batteries at night. Hydrogen cars are also clean and nonpolluting, but the power stations that produce hydrogen use fossil fuels, contaminating the environment as any common power station."

Professor Oca guided our group into a room arranged like a fair of small models. A highly detailed miniature model of one of the three identical modern cities of Atlantis was laid on a large table.  All three cities were built from the same plans.  As a preview, professor Oca narrated some old history. "During old classical times, the population of Atlantis was limited to the small island of Poseidon, while at the same time the larger Island of the Sun remained a wilderness.

"When Atlantis entered into its new age, the island of Poseidon became overcrowded.  It was in the time when people began moving to the Island of the Sun, where the government had created new designs for modern urban and rural areas.  The Island of the Sun became a good place for agriculture, industry, technology, and science, well suited for a modern civilization.   The broad wilderness provided plenty of space for land development, followed by the construction of three identical cities with modern skyscrapers, including the city of Brasea.

"In downtown Brasea, most buildings except for a few tall rectangular ones, had the shape of slender stepped pyramids, where the perimeter of each floor was surrounded by a terrace which had plants, called hanging gardens.  The architects found that buildings with the shape of pyramids have better stability in seismic areas with frequent earthquakes than the vertical ones.  This was not the only reason.  The principal architect of Atlantis had a fear of heights, and wanted the dwellers from those buildings to feel as if they were living on a stepped hill, not in a skyscraper." After Professor Oca finished his narration, we thanked him. Our tour for the day was over and we left. However, we would return the next day, this time to visit the School of Medicine.

## THE SCHOOL OF MEDICINE IN ATLANTIS

Perhaps this part of my dream was stimulated by some of the impressions I got as a teenager. My uncle, then a medical director from his own clinic, tried to encourage me to study medicine. He and his colleagues frequently invited me to see a series of different kinds of operations usually performed in all areas of the human body except the head, and in total perhaps I saw more than seventy. Finally after finishing high school I told my uncle the sad news that I felt more inclined to study engineering.

Going back to the topic of Atlantis, the next day I went with Mila to meet again with Professor Kriton and the foreign teachers. We met at the lobby of the apartment building where the professor lived. Professor Kriton came down and took us in his big car as usual back to the university. After we arrived at the lobby of the School of Medicine, Professor Kriton told the receptionist we had an appointment with Dr. Nubis for a tour of the university hospital. Before the clerk could answer, a smiling young doctor came from somewhere and greeted us.

"You must be Professor Kriton," said the young, Oriental man. "Dr. Nubis sent me to welcome you. He is attending an emergency case. As soon as he will be available, he will come." Meanwhile this man told us, "I am a native from the backside of the world. Atlantis is a generous land that encourages foreign students to come and get educated, so they could return to their homelands with knowledge and experience to serve and help their own people. In Atlantis there is no discrimination against foreign professionals. Foreign-born doctors are as efficient as the Atlantis doctors are mostly for cases related to internal medicine or when performing simple routine operations. However, advanced surgery is another matter. Only skilled surgeons are permitted to do such operations, most likely the Atlanteans. They have a slightly more dominant right brain hemisphere than ordinary humans. This enables them mentally to visualize complex shapes in three dimensions. With their sentient sense of touch, surgeons could mentally visualize the shape and location of organs and other objects inside the human body."

"Is my young colleague helping you?" asked Dr. Nubis, walking up just as the young intern finished talking. "I am Dr. Nubis, head of the School of Medicine. I enjoy showing our hospital and explaining our new programs to foreign visitors. After graduation, our young doctors begin to work on a variety of different tasks to become aware of their own aptitudes and capabilities. After this period of rotation, they can decide whether they want to become surgeons or pursue internal medicine. The students that want to become surgeons practice their first operations not on cadavers, but in much cleaner way, on sophisticated dummies which are made from special plastics mimicking very closely to the human body.

(For additional information, see "ATLANTIS SURGERY PRACTICED BY MEDICAL STUDENTS ON PLASTIC DUMMIES," in Medical Chronicle No 2, from the supplementary chapter of this book)

Then, Dr. Nubis took us to the cardiovascular department and introduced us to Dr. Quetzalco, the head of the department, who became our new host. We followed him down the aisle and stopped for a few seconds in front of a glass cabinet inlaid in the wall. Several artificial hearts were on display, including one of the latest designs.

## VISIT TO THE NEUROSURGERY DEPARTMENT

Dr. Quetzalco guided us to the Department of Neurosurgery. There he introduced us to Dr. Wascar, an outstanding neurologist who took over the tour. Dr. Wascar said, "The medical sciences in Atlantis have advanced in giant steps; transplant of organs, implantation of bio-medical body parts, and the adoption of computer-powered prosthetics have become routine." The group murmured in awe. The doctor continued his lecture.

"This is the largest medical school in Atlantis, with several small hospitals around the world to provide free medical services for the poor. Also we have a new hospital outside planet Earth. It is an underground medical facility on one of the Atlantis moon bases to provide medical service to our lunar explorers, workers, and miners living there. In the laboratories of that facility we take advantage of the low gravity to produce pharmaceuticals that cannot be duplicated on Earth. Our hospital on the moon has several rooms, laboratories, libraries, cafeterias, and living quarters, all of them inside chambers pressurized with air.

"Among the operating rooms, there is a round room used only for extremely complicated operations, where several surgeons could operate simultaneously on one patient; each one in his own specialization performing the operation from his own office, but by remote control. At the operating room before the operation the patient already anesthetized will be lying inside a shallow box made from glass. This box will be on top of the operating table, surrounded with life support equipment, miniature television cameras, and robots of different sizes, but no humans will be around. Surgeons and auxiliary personnel, depending on their specialty, are located in nearby rooms or offices. Each surgeon will be responsible for a specific surgical assignment to perform on this patient. The surgeons operate by remote control, by looking an extra-large television screen that occupies one of the office walls. The huge screen displays a close-up of the patient's body area to be operated on by a particular doctor. In that view, magnified several times, the ant-size mini-robots could be seen as big as dogs, and the patient's spinal cord as big as the cross-section of a sequoia tree trunk. The operating room is full of automated equipment, there are mini-robots performing micro-surgical operations, remotely controlled by surgeons, who push buttons and manipulate levers from their independent offices."

Later Dr. Wascar took us to the hospital's auditorium, used also for presentations and display of medical documentaries; it had a large curved screen. In that place Dr. Wascar showed us a documentary of the greatest operation performed in the moon's hospital. He started narrating a sad story. He said, " Probably some of you already know this story, which happened more than a year ago. Engineer Godin and his grandson Krill went on a round-trip tour to the moon in one of our spaceships.

"As they were about to land on the moon, the ship crashed. The body of Godin and the head of Krill were badly damaged in the wreck. There was no hope to save them. However, they removed the head of Godin, which was still alive, and the headless body of Krill. Both incomplete bodies were kept alive, each by a separate life support system. The head remained anesthetized, with a recently invented anesthesia that could be used for months without causing brain damage."

After the sad announcement, Dr. Wascar began projecting the documentary on the screen and said, "We, the Atlanteans, didn't want to lose Godin's brain because humanity still needed his scientific knowledge. So we decided to rebuild a new body by joining Godin's head to the strong headless body of his grandson. Prior to the operation, all tests verified that the blood and tissues from both persons were compatible, decreasing the chances of organ rejection." Doctor Wascar continued, "Here on the screen you are going to witness one of the greatest operations ever performed, a historic operation performed simultaneously by more than 40 surgeons on one patient. The operation started immediately after Godin's and Krill's relatives sent a telegram approving the operation."

As the film began, a narrator appeared on the screen, explaining to the audience, "Nerves grow very slowly. The patient should not move and should rest in one position for as long as six months or more, sleeping for months under the effect of a special anesthesia that doesn't destroy brain cells. Bedsores and deterioration are minimized because the patient's body is pressed slightly against the soft supports inside the glass box, where the patient's body remained at rest. The low gravity of the moon was an advantage for long term operations. On the moon the weight of a person is only one-sixth of what it is on Earth.

"It took six motionless months for the severed spinal cord and neck to heal. This healing and restoration took place by transforming neutral cells, into the cells of the various tissues in that area, mostly into nerve cells, letting those cells reproduce and grow across both cross-section surfaces of the severed spinal cords to be spliced, letting each nerve fiber splice with its counterpart. The nerves from Godin's neck spinal cord got stimulated to grow with the help of some complex substance invented by Atlantean scientists. When the head of Godin and the body of Krill were joined, a new human was created by means of a number of operations performed during six months in the neck area. After the spinal cord and the joints of the peripheral nerves were already healed, a sequence of surgical operations began. Some of the previously removed cervical vertebrae were saved then brought back to their original position and secured in place with supports that gradually, would be reabsorbed by the body. Procedures followed that stitched up ligaments, muscles, blood vessels, esophagus, larynx and trachea.

"A new man with the old face and brain of Godin and the young body of Krill was created. The new person was also called Godin, who awoke from his six-month coma. After his release from the hospital, he went into rehabilitation training, where he learned everything all over again, including how to walk, talk, and read. His brain rewired and reprogrammed by itself, mostly in order to compensate for the many inaccuracies and wrong contact joining between the thousands of corresponding nerve fibers in their process of healing. A large number of new growth axons from Godin's head group made wrong functional contacts with their counterparts from Krill's body. Other nerve fibers followed wrong tracks inside the other person, and nerve fibers will continue to grow. It was too much for the mind of the old genius; his brain could not rewire satisfactorily because he was an old man. He never fully recuperated. Mentally he remained a gentle moron for the rest of his life."

(For additional information, see "RECREATION OF A NEW HUMAN BEING BY USING ORGANS FROM TWO DEAD PERSONS" in Medical Chronicle No. 3 from the supplementary chapter of this book.)

## BIONIC EYES FOR THE BLIND

We were impressed with all that we saw and heard that day. We wanted to return home, but Professor Wascar asked us to visit one more office in the same medical building. The Professor guided us to the Vision Center and he said, "What you are going to see will impress you for the rest of your lives." We walked into an office where an ophthalmologist was removing the medical instruments that surrounded a patient's head. We were awed at what we saw; the doctor was examining what could be an extraterrestrial monster that looked a little bit human. It had a deformed head with a bony ridge growth under the scalp on the left side of the skull. The ridge started above the left eye socket and extended all the way to the back of the skull. When the monster left, the doctor introduced himself by shaking hands with each of us.

The doctor said, "My patient, who just left, is an ordinary person who used to be totally blind. He suffered from detached retinas in both eyes, retinas that were already dead. We thought we could give back some of his eyesight and we operated him several times implanting inside his eyeball a bionic eye. This patient sees mostly in black and white, with a slight mixing of colors. Really this bionic eye is a marvel of microelectronic engineering."

(For additional information, see "DEVELOPMENT, DESIGN AND IMPLANTATION OF A BIONIC EYE" in Medical Chronicle No. 4 from the supplementary chapter of this book.)

## THE SCHOOL OF AERONAUTICAL ENGINEERING

In our last day as tourists, we were back with Professor Kriton at the University of Brasea and walked to the School of Aeronautical Engineering. Professor Condory, who was the dean of the school, came to meet us and became our new guide. As an Atlantean engineer, I was going to enjoy this tour. Dean Condory said, "Most students graduate from our engineering school at age 20, and many of them have jobs already waiting for them in the industry or in the Space Agency."

Dean Condory told us a little bit of his life, including the story that once he was in charge of the design of a huge freighter aircraft powered by nuclear engines. Only two of these transports were ever built. These transport aircraft flew day and night, crossing all oceans of the world.

## SEA AIRCRAFT WITH NUCLEAR PROPULSION

Flying monsters, weighing hundreds of tons, were actually flying cargo boats, which could fly with a nuclear propulsion system for more than ten continuous years without getting refueled at all. The aircraft were called "geese" because of their canard shape. The vehicle had a long, thick hollow neck, which was in reality the cabin, for cargo and passengers. The head of the bird was the cockpit, which had good visibility for the pilots. The bulky rear end of the aircraft contained the nuclear reactor and its engines.

(For additional information see "SEA AIRCRAFT WITH NUCLEAR PROPULSION" in Engineering Chronicle No. 3 from the supplementary chapter of this book.)

## A VISIT TO THE AEROSPACE ATLANTIS AGENCY

I was not sure if the foreign visitors understood everything that was said. We began walking across the campus grass field towards the building of the Space Agency. Half-way in our hiking we reached and stepped on a long walkway with a marble floor flanked on both sides by marble and bronze statues. One of the tourists asked what the statues represented.

"There are 84 statues," explained Chief Engineer Wiracocha. "Each statue is twice actual life size, representing a rich Atlantean who contributed to finance the creation of the Atlantis Space Agency, the pride of Atlantis, an institution which made possible travel to the planets and the other celestial bodies of our solar system. The name of this walkway is "The Avenue of the Benefactors, for the Voyages to the Stars. To have a statue here is one of the greatest honors of our time."

As we approached the entrance of that building, Wiracocha said, "It is the famous aerospace building where all the spaceships from Atlantis were designed, including the spaceship commanded by Captain Cronus. The interior of the building is like any ordinary one, with large offices and laboratories full of engineers and scientists. The exterior was made from brick and cement, but imitating the shape of the first Atlantis spaceship that made the first long voyage."

The rear end of this round building was connected to a decorative structure resting on the grass. Although it looked like a steel fence, it was not a fence at all, just an imitation of the ship's long tail, at the far tip of which was bolted decorative round boxes, imitating faked atomic engines. In the real world the nuclear engines pushed the spaceship by its rigid tail during those long space voyages. However, in this campus all these were not for any other reason other than to be artistic works of modern architecture which also decorated the campus. After admiring for a couple of minutes the round exterior of the building, we walked inside and visited different offices, including the large design room crowded with engineers.

Engineer Wiracocha remarked, "In Atlantis there are no technical secrets; everything is created for humanity. Foreigners have the same rights as Atlanteans. As you can see, some of them are working in this office. However, in a smaller office, on the floor above this, you will see only a small number of selected engineers, all Atlanteans, who are working on advanced projects for the future. Atlantis engineers possessed high mental concentration, and a natural gift for 3-D mental visualization of complex structures and machines that at the beginning of the project only existed in their minds. They could mentally visualize the intricate geometry of a complicated engine or mechanism, with all its parts, just inside their minds before they could express their idea in the form of plans and blueprints. Atlanteans have a good sense of justice; every time a foreign designer with the same skills as the Atlanteans was discovered, although a rare case, this person was received with open arms.

"Some old designers working here hated computers, and preferred to do everything the old fashioned way, using only their brains, pencils, and triangles. They express their ideas by sketching quickly on a piece of paper, before starting the real design."

My surroundings gradually became darker, as in an eclipse. The sightseeing, the surroundings, and all the people next to me faded out. I realized that everything was just a dream and I relaxed; however, a point of light flared in the darkness and gradually increased in size and in brightness, and a new chapter involving a new dream began. I could hear a voice coming from behind the fog. I recognized it as the voice of Luzaire, the Wizard of Atlantis. He said, "I am satisfied that you feel proud to be an Atlantean, as if you have lived your entire life in the greatest nation that ever existed on Earth.

"Atlantis, a nation privileged by God and nature, was also privileged by being visited by the Entarian aliens in times when we needed most from alien knowledge in order to reach the peak of our progress. The Entarians used to visit Earth approximately once every fifteen thousand years. In their last visit, they granted Atlantis advanced scientific information including the most intimate secrets of the basic building blocks of the universe. So, in this way the Entarians saved us billions in money. There was no need for us to continue building expensive laboratories, equipment, and atomic supercolliders to discover what some other civilization from this galaxy already did; all this information was available to anybody else in the universe who needed it. The Entarian aliens provided us the necessary data to create complex projects, including cheap electricity for our cities and nuclear fusion engines required to propel our spaceships in their long voyages through our solar system."

Luzaire's voice vanished and I fell asleep again. I awoke not into reality, but in another dream. I realized I was in the last days of Atlantis. I saw a multitude evacuating to Europe and I found myself among them, evacuating in one of the last boats. After sailing for days we approached the coast of Europe, then the boat's bottom crushed against a rock and we sank. I noticed something strange begin to happen to my own personality. Under psychological pressure it split quickly into two different persons: Kappa and myself. I realized I was no longer Kappa, the Atlantean, who died when the boat sank. I was confused--for a moment I got back my old personality. I was again the same teenager from the twentieth century that enjoyed adventures, sports, and parties. But still I had the dreams of a series of events, produced by the telepathic transmissions from a computer concealed inside the mysterious rock on which I sat by accident, then a virtual reality today of events that happened more than 11,000 years ago.

I suspected the Stone of Dreams was playing tricks with my mind, turning it on and off, shifting my mind for different dreams each from a different Atlantean time, and finally using me as a recording machine.

I thought Uncle Luzaire was gone; however, somehow he appeared and spoke. "This is the last time I am going to talk with you, this time not as my nephew Kappa but as our guest from the future. The stone is near the end of its transmission; its most important information was saved for the last. Before the stone stops forever, it will transfer and download into your subconscious mind or any person resting on it, its last message, which was really the main purpose for what the Atlanteans built it."

Uncle Luzaire said, "From now on, no more fancy dreams as you experienced before, which in reality were not too important. The last transmission is going to be a grant from our civilization to yours, in order to create a new Earth civilization using ours as a model. You are going to receive real facts about the sciences and the technology of Atlantis, which includes the two great secrets used by most of the advanced civilizations from this galaxy. Finally, as a bonus, the stone will reveal the exact location for each vault of wisdom buried around the world. So, you could tell it to the world office of your time (perhaps he meant the United Nations of the twentieth century), in order that they will take possession of all vaults, including their treasures.

"This stone contains five recorded chapters of dreams. The first four are the fancy ones you have already seen, which in reality are not too important. The last chapter is the only one that is really important because it contains the necessary data to build a new great civilization, using Atlantis and its ideals as a model, by promoting ideas of freedom, the pursuit of happiness, living in harmony with each other, as well as with nature. It is with the wish Earth would become again the same paradise that it once was.

"Humanity should grow in spiritual and intellectual quality, not in quantity. The leaders of the world should encourage that Earth's population should not pass two billion inhabitants, approximately the same as the Earth population was in the year 1,905, which is ideal to maintain the ecological equilibrium of the planet, and to reduce pollution.

"You should not care what language the Stone of the Dreams speaks, since all the scientific and engineering information will be transferred directly into your brain, already decoded in the form of final elaborated ideas.

"Young man," Luzaire concluded, "I must leave now, this time forever. I wish you good luck. From now on the Stone of Dreams will take care of you. Get ready for the most important message. Good-bye."

As I relaxed by stretching myself on the stone without realizing what happened, I felt sleepy again, then I began receiving clear, telepathic transmissions, and started dreaming again. Suddenly I found myself in a long room, standing in front of an oak table with tilted top used to support wide books. I heard a noise coming from the far end of the room. I turned around and saw that a door opened, and two persons walked in. One of them looked like a holy man with white beard and a white robe; the other was a young man also with a white robe. Both brought a heavy book, a book with large pages, and put it on the oak table. The old man said to me, "Come in. In this book there are several construction plans, all draw by Atlantean engineers. I knew you are curious, you may browse it." So I did, and as I turned the huge pages, one by one, the man with a white beard kept explaining to me the purpose of each drawing. It was strange, I was neither bored nor tired as I was supposed to be, but relaxed. I could not figure if to see all of them took me minutes or days.

I remember seeing a series of technical Atlantean drawings, used for the construction of a variety of engineering projects, Industrial machinery, heavy equipment, robots, bridges, crafts for sea, land, and air transportation, space stations, space shuttles, interplanetary spaceships, advanced fighter aircraft, super-fast trains, and many other projects of advanced technology.

(For additional information about them, see engineering drawings in the Appendix section of this book.)

Not only I did see mechanical drawings but also artistic plans for the construction of beautiful mansions. The Stone of Dreams kept downloading more ideas into my subconscious mind as if I was a recording machine. Who knows how long took this downloading took, perhaps it was a few hours, or perhaps only a few seconds. What was the purpose of all this? Suddenly the old man stopped me from turning more pages and said, "In the last pages of this book will be revealed, the two greatest secrets of Atlantis and also other advanced civilizations from this galaxy. Be patient, all this will be recorded into your subconscious mind with maximum detail. Also will be revealed to you a message that you should deliver to the office of the world of your time concerning the exact location from each one of the secret underground vaults of wisdom around the world.

"After the revelation, the stone's purpose will be fulfilled and it will turn itself off forever, becoming one more dead rock.  The introductions of such revelations are:

"Revelation I--Display of detailed construction plans with instructions to build nuclear fusion engines, to propel space ships through the universe.  Also plans for the construction of similar engines but stationary ones, to provide limitless quantities of inexpensive electricity to the energy-hungry cities of Atlantis.

"Revelation II--Simplified mathematical formulas to understand better the microcosmos and the macrocosmos of the physical universe, including mathematical revelations of how the universe was created and what will be its future.  Then the most important and most complex of all revelations, which concerns how advanced civilizations visualize the mystery of God's true identity and his role in the universe."

## THE GREATEST REVELATION OF ALL, LOST

I was eager to receive the revelation of the great secrets that made Atlantis great.  Then, instead, I felt a pull on my left arm.  Then more pulls.  How inopportune; I heard a voice saying repeatedly,  "Wake up, wake up."  My dreams got interrupted as I awakened back into reality.  I had not received any of the great revelations, and dreams and fantasies all vanished.  A different kind of landscape appeared in front of me; it was not Atlantis, but one of tall mountains.  Gradually, I began recognizing the dead barren landscape from the upper region of Tablas, quite different to the jungle of low Tablas in the tropical Chapare.  This region was approximately located at the center of Bolivia.  I forgot all about the dream, just as prognosticated by Atlantis Uncle Luzaire.  However, I was deeply upset as if I had lost some important message, perhaps from a divine source, but from whom?   I couldn't remember; probably from beings that communicated by dreams.

Then I recognized the voice of my father as he again pulled on my arm, "Wake up."  Then I said,  "I am already awake."  He said,  "It is strange, we were supposed to take a nap of only 15 minutes on these boulders and we haven't heard our alarm watches.  What I know is that a storm is coming and at this altitude without proper equipment, with no caves around, our lives are in danger."  After consulting with the Indian guide my father said to me, "We have no other chance, let's climb quickly to the crest of this mountain before the storm catches us, and descend its back side."

I forgot all about dreams.  At that moment it was more important to depart as soon as possible from that desolate place, and keep hiking up the mountain as fast as we could, while there was still daylight.  Finally, after we reached and crossed the crest of the mountain we descended its backside.  What a relief, the most difficult part of our trip of exploration was over.  Two more days of hiking and we were back in civilization.

For years I forgot all about those dreams until one day I gradually began remembering them, segment by segment and in successive dreams.


# THIS IS THE END OF THE TRIP AND END OF THE MYSTERIOUS ENCOUNTERS.

# CHAPTER 16
# The Creation

## GENESIS FROM THE GREAT BOOK OF ATLANTIS

I resumed my normal life and I forgot all about Atlantis, the dreams and the related stories. Then, not too long ago, many years after the dreams stopped, I found a King James version of the Bible in the attic of my home. As I began reading Genesis, my fade'd memories from my strange dreams returned, in especially about meeting Moses and talking about the Book of Genesis (see Chapter 2).

I began to imagine that the first seven chapters from the book of Genesis were the most important of the Judeo-Christian Bible, because of its possibility as a source of prehistoric hypothetical information and the way that hypothetical advanced civilizations might think. I felt an urge to write a long article using as guidance those chapters concurrently with new discoveries in modern science, also with the help of the available history, and by putting myself in the shoes of the average person of an advanced society. In short, creating a version of Genesis as if the Atlanteans would write it.

## INTERPRETATION AND COMPARISON OF THE GENESIS FROM THE GREAT BOOK OF ATLANTIS WITH MOSES' BOOK OF GENESIS (KING JAMES VERSION)

It should be considered that Moses wrote his Genesis for the people of his time, uneducated and superstitious. For example, in ancient times the majority of people believed the Earth was flat. This concept changed centuries later to the belief that the Earth was a sphere but located at the center of everything. Moreover, in the time of Moses, names such as galaxies, solar systems, and universes were unknown.

The sequence of some verses in Moses' Book of Genesis doesn't coincide with the cosmological Great Book of Atlantis. Assuming that the people from Atlantis were so advanced their use of terms and descriptions of events was foreign to Moses. In order to assist the reader, I have provided the following interpretations of words, concepts, and names used in the King James version of the Bible, by using modern science and the available history.

Note: the King James version of the Bible has been used for the purposes of this comparison and analysis.

# GLOSSARY

**Earth:** Depending on the circumstances in old times, the word Earth could have any of the following meanings:

a. The planet Earth.

b. The primeval black hole before the Big Bang.

c.       In Verse 1, Chapter 1 of the King James Bible, the word Earth means Universe. During the time of Moses, the word "universe" did not exist. It should also be pointed out that Earth was created after the universe came into existence.

**Waters:** Depending on the circumstances in old times, the word Waters could have any of the following meanings:

　　　a. The primeval sea.

　　　b. The primeval soup filling inside of the cosmic egg.

　　　c. The primeval black hole before the Big Bang.

　　　d. In Verse 6, Chapter 1, the word waters could mean universal forces.

**Light:** For advanced civilizations, either from the past or the present, the word light could also have the following meaning:

　　　Radiated energy in all frequencies and in all directions from the center of the Big Bang explosion.

**Heavens:** A space-time universe.

**Firmament:** May mean either:

　　　a. An expanse.

　　　b. An expanding young universe.

**Chariot:** In modern times, this word could be interpreted as any of the following: a coach, a wagon, motorcycle, automobile, train, and any vehicle moving on wheels.

**Chariot of Fire:** Today, this word could mean a flying vehicle such as an airplane, helicopter, or a UFO.

**Whale:** The big fish, as mentioned in the King James version of the Bible, like the one that swallowed Jonah, did not exist. Large fish, even whales, do not swallow people or other animals. It was more likely a submarine left by the Atlanteans and restored by the ancient ancestors of the custodian monks. It is possible it was a submarine designed for ecological research and fitted with a huge mechanical mouth to trap sea specimens. In that mouth Jonah was trapped for three days.

**Giants** (Nephilim): Defective cloned humans, giants that were despised by Atlantean women who left Atlantis to find wives overseas.

**Moses' Book of Genesis. King James version of the Bible.** Chapter 1, Verse 2: "And the earth was without form, and void; and darkness was upon the face of the deep. And the Spirit of God moved upon the face of the waters."

(Compare this verse 2, which corresponds to verse 1 of the Atlantis Book of Genesis, as shown below)

**Atlantis Book of Genesis**

Verse 1: Three eternal entities existed before the Big Bang. The mysterious sea constituting the primeval black hole was peaceful and was of uniform density. Outside was complete darkness, the absolute nothingness of nothing. No energy, no matter. God was moving to and fro, inside and on the surface of the sea made of uspars. These ultra small particles were held together by the force of gravity. Uspars (Ultra Small Particles similar to today's quarks), were the basic stuff from which the universe was made. Then, from his relaxing state and for reasons only known to Him, God decided to create a new universe. An assembly with the uspars was called. In that place God said, "The eternal triad is constituted by myself, the force of gravity, and you, the uspars. You are the sea that fills this primeval Black Hole. We all three are eternal, with no beginning and no end. Nobody created us and nothing could destroy us."

**King James Version.** Chapter 1, Verse 1:
In the beginning God created the heaven and the earth.
Note: This short, one-line verse is equivalent to an entire chapter of The Great Book of Atlantis, a chapter related to the creation of the Universe as is shown as follows.

## GENESIS FROM THE GREAT BOOK OF ATLANTIS

Verse 2: Then God went on to say, "Let us start a new beginning, a new Universe, new adventures with times of happiness and times of sadness." As He spoke the word sadness, God wept.

Note: There is an eons-old monolith that portrays this cosmic drama, which takes place moments before the Big Bang. Carved on the upper part of a stone, carved by the unknown people from the mysterious Tiahanaku culture in Bolivia, there is an interpretation of this last meeting between God and his congregation of uspars. At the end of this meeting God wept. This stone today is known as the "Gate-way of the Sun."

> IN THE GENESIS OF THE GREAT BOOK OF ATLANTIS,
> THE THEORIES OF CREATION AND EVOLUTION ARE NOT
> OPPOSITE, INSTEAD THEY ARE COMPLEMENTARY WITH
> EACH OTHER, AND WITH A THIRD THEORY IN BETWEEN,
> CALLED THE THEORY OF SELFTRANSFORMATION.

In The Great Book of Atlantis the three theories apply to three sequentially arranged periods of time, those are:

Period 1.　Creation of the universe by God, using existing material (uspars).
Period 2.　Self transformation without the help of God.
Period 3.　Creation of life followed by the evolution by natural selection without the help of God.

## THE CREATION OF THE UNIVERSE

The main two purposes for the existence of God are the moment of creation and the moment of death of the universe.  The period in between these two events is the period of self-transformation which also includes the evolution of life.  It is during this period in between that the universe doesn't need God or help from gods.

God continued with his speech to the congregation of Uspars, "I am going to create a new universe by letting you free to fly in all directions. You will embark upon a journey that should last for billions of years. During this time, you will be allowed to create, by yourselves and without my intervention, billions and billions of galaxies. Now, for an instant of time (figure of speech because time didn't exist yet) I will neutralize the force of gravity that restrains you, then you will disperse in all directions and a new Universe will born (the event of the Big Bang).

## GOD, ONE OF THE COMPONENTS
## OF THE ETERNAL TRIAD

GOD, THE USPARS, AND GRAVITY ARE THE ETERNAL ENTITIES THAT CONSTITUTE THE ETERNAL TRIAD.　NOBODY CREATED IT AND NOBODY CAN DESTROY IT.

We live in a cycling universe. Each cycle begins with the birth of a new universe and ends with its death, life cycles that repeat forever. God is the ruler and the architect for each new universe. The basic stuff from which each universe is made (uspars) is indestructible and eternal, as is God.  This basic stuff will be used over and over again for the creation of new universes.

Intelligence and the consciousness that engulfs the whole universe are called God.  God is aware of everything that happens everywhere – from the smallest event such as the jump of a flea to a major event such as the collision of galaxies. Because God is part of all things in the universe, everything that exists has some sort of self-awareness. A grasshopper will have more self-awareness than a grain of sand, and a human being will have billions of times more self-awareness than a grasshopper.

Gravity is the force that holds the universe together. By using the telekinetic power of his divine mind, God can reduce, cancel, or increase the force of gravity at will; thus creating new universes as well as letting old ones shrink and die. Some physicists consider God to be the fifth universal force of the universe, which they believe is the force that activated the Big Bang, and also the force that concurrently with gravity, will restrain the universe from expanding forever.

As the universe ages, it expands and constantly transforms itself. To prevent from expanding forever, sometime during its cycle God will start reversing it. God absorbs the kinetic energy from this expansion until finally the universe contracts and dies in a Big Crunch.   This absorbed energy is stored in God himself, to be used later, to create again the next new universe.

Many believe that space is empty; in reality, God is the "ether" (the old ether theory) that fills the vacuum of space. Observing two identical beams of light traveling together in the same direction can prove this. If one of them is out of phase by half a wave from the phase of the other, they will cancel each other and seem to disappear. But this is not possible because energy cannot be created nor destroyed,  only transformed. Something must remain there – the ether of space (also part of God).

## ANOTHER WAY THAT GOD WANTS TO PROVE HIS OWN REAL EXISTENCE TO HIS CREATURES.

God wants to prove His existence and His infinite power to some of His creatures in the universe, including humans. He wanted His creatures to admire the universe as His greatest creation. Rays of radiant energy including light coming from distant places in the universe, as from the stars and the galaxies, must cross the vast space between them, which is definitely not empty.  Most of space is filled with rarefied hydrogen gas.  So the light coming from a distant star or galaxy, after traveling for millions of years through trillions of atoms from that rarefied gas, logically should become scattered in all directions.  To make matters worse, that beam of light will change direction due to local variations of gravity in the universe. So light coming from distant places of the universe should arrive fuzzy to Earth.

In a clear night sky, we should not be able to see most of the stars in the Milky Way, not even other galaxies with the best telescopes.  The Milky Way should appear to us as a long white cloud with no stars, and we should not be able to contemplate the work of God beyond some distance. Only a few of the closest stars would be visible.  The spirit of God was annoyed with the idea that His creatures that populate the universe would not be able to admire His creation and appreciate the glory of God by looking at the mighty universe. So God decided to make an exception to Himself, by going against His own rules and the laws of nature, by constantly performing a miracle.  A miracle consisting of aligning, straightening, and reorganizing those rays of light coming from different places in the universe, into the reorganized ones that would reach the retina of billions of His creatures, including man; also the rays of light and other energies that reach our telescopes.  So God used this realigned light as a tool for everybody to see His creation.

God was active during the period of the creation, which lasted no more than a few seconds (figure of speech because time and space did not exist yet).  A short period of time that started with the Big Bang to the time when all forces and all universal laws were created.  Then God relaxed and said, "I have created my new universe, now it is my seventh day, I am going to rest and remain contemplative until the end of time.  I don't want to contradict the laws of physics I created.  I don't want to interfere with my universe's self-transformation and evolution. From now on, in this seventh day this universe becomes autonomous.  I will not perform miracles to help any of my creatures in the universe. For example, if in an earthquake a building is falling on you, even when you pray for help to me, you may die anyway. Very seldom and only in exceptional cases I may decide to overcome my own laws of physics.  Such events is what you call miracles."

## GRAVITY, SIBLING OF GOD

GOD DID NOT CREATE GRAVITY, IT IS HIS SIBLING.  GRAVITY IS ONE OF THE THREE ETERNAL ENTITIES OF THE UNIVERSE.

In the dream about that celestial gathering (Chapter 2 of this book) when I met with prophets, Christ, and other important people from the past, a monk approached me and said, "My name is Pierre Gassendi.  I was a French priest and philosopher.  In 1624 I wrote a scientific book, which included the theory of gravity.  After my death my spirit kept evolving and learning more about the mysteries of the universe.

"Gravity restrains all the subatomic building blocks that make the universe. After the Big Bang gravity slowed them down from flying too fast in a universe that expands. The pulling forces of gravity always remains active for eternity, even before the creation and even after the death of the universe.  The exception is at the instant of the Big Bang, which happens when God neutralizes gravity by using his telekinetic powers generated by His own will and mind."  The priest proceeded with his narration, "In the seventeenth century when nobody knew that dimensions higher than three existed in the universe, my theory of gravity failed to explain celestial motion.  After my death, my spirit kept learning.  Now I could explain the nature of gravity from the point of view of a hyperdimensional universe, a concept of gravity you should call, the modified theory of Gassendi's with straight strings in a multidimensional space, this is independent and have nothing to do with the theory of Superstrings that somebody from your 20th century is going to create.  Ramsey, a mathematician from your modern times, never knew that his mathematical theory was in reality the essence of gravity.

"Each uspar can be considered as a tiny block with trillions of elastic strings or cords attached to its surface; each of these strings of gravity is grossly analogous to a rubber string.  The number of these elastic strings that exist in the universe is the mathematical expression of   $(1/2)\,(n)\,(n-1)$   where n is the total number of uspars (ultra small particles) that exist in the universe.

"An uspar from any place in the universe is linked by means of a straight elastic string to any other from the rest of the uspar that constitutes the universe. It doesn't matter how far or how close they are from each other.  My strings of gravity that link each pair of uspars could stretch from one end to the opposite end of the universe. Those strings could cross millions of galaxies, without noticing their presence and could bend just a little by the gravity from local zones with concentrations of mass that happen in many places of the universe. Each elastic string is infinitely thin and its length is equal to the distance between two uspars attached to the same string. This distance could vary from infinitely small to a distance the size of the universe. Strings stretching trillions of kilometers have extremely weak force.

"The strings of gravity are always straight, never tangled and never interfere with each other. They do not behave like ordinary elastic strings and springs, where the pulling force is proportional to the longitudinal deflection. However, the pulling force of these mysterious strings of gravity is inversely proportional to the square of their length, a concept that only could be visualized in a hyper-dimensional universe.

"Each string links only two uspars and ignores the rest of the uspars in the universe and other strings, as if those don't exist. For a particular string, the effect of the pulling force from any other strings across it is equal to zero.

"An individual string doesn't tangle with the trillions of other strings that it crosses. Strings can extend across anything, including atoms, without touching anything. Nothing in the universe can cut a string, except the mind of God.

"Gravity is one of the universal forces of the universe. It may be considered also as a sensory system of God. It makes God aware of any big or small event anywhere in the universe, like the dancing of a bee or a supernova. God is like the invisible classical ether mentioned in the old books, an ether filling the universe for the propagation of electromagnetism including gravity waves.

The only energy that counteracts gravity is the telekinetic force from the mind of God, every time he wants to produce a big event like the Big Bang explosion. A similar assumption, but on a smaller scale would take place when a guru performs levitation by using the telekinetic force from his mind. Nobody knows if this last assumption is true or not, because levitation never was proven.

It seems that our human species has not evolved intellectually enough to understand the essence of gravity.

**King James**, Chapter 1
Verse 3: And God said, Let there be light: and there was light. (Compare this with verse 3 of Atlantis book, shown below). Note: In above verse, the word light means not only visible light but all kinds of radiated energy in all frequencies and in all directions from the Big Bang explosion.
**Atlantis**
Verse 3: And God proceeded to say, "Let there be a Big Bang explosion, that will blow up this primeval black hole, which contents will be thrown out, most converted into radiant energy and some portion into billions of miniature black holes, called galactic seeds. With the eons each seed will attract the surrounding matter which was formed later, mostly hydrogen, to form a galaxy. In this way billions of galaxies will forms."

God saw that this energy release from the Big Bang was good; then He was satisfied.

**King James**, Chapter 1

Verse 6:   And God said, Let there be a firmament in the midst of the waters, and let it divide the waters from the waters.

(It corresponds to verse 4 of the Atlantis Book, shown below.  For interpretation of words in above verse, see glossary from this chapter.)

**Atlantis**

Verse 4:   And God went on to say:  "With a Big Bang I will create a space-time four dimensional universe, plus other parallel universes of higher dimensions.  The Big Bang explosion will release out and in all directions the contents of this primeval egg, also known as a primeval black hole.  This event will generate the rebirth of a new universe, which from then on will remain expanding for billions of years to come.

A short time after the birth of this universe, a division will occur to create three more universal forces in addition to gravity and God.  After God restrained the cords of gravity for a very short period of time, in order to produce the Big Bang, gravity was reinstated immediately.

The universal force of gravity, God, and the uspars remained as the three entities that form the eternal triad.

NOTE:   The name of uspars came from one of my dreams at the mountain. Uspars are supposed to be indivisible, eternal components of subatomic particles that constitute the whole universe (similar to what today are known as quarks).

Nothing could destroy any of the eternal entities constituting the eternal triad.  It continues to exist forever, in spite of the periodic rebirths and deaths of this pulsating universe.

**King James,** Chapter 2

Verse 1:   Thus the heavens and the earth were finished, and all the host of them.

Verse 2:   And on the seventh day God ended his work, which he had made; and he rested on the seventh day from all his work which he had made.

Verse 3:   And God blessed the seventh day, and sanctified it: because that in it he had rested from all his work which God created and made.

(These three verses correspond to verse 5 from the Atlantis Book, as shown below).

**Atlantis**

Verse 5:   Thus the young universe including its universal forces was finished in the seventh symbolic day, and continued transforming itself, into the many random shapes made of gas. This was the turning point in time, when the universe no longer needed God.  Then God said, "I am satisfied and I am going to rest from all the work I made, to the end of time, until Judgment Day, when I will awake to judge all the creatures of the universe."

This long period of the universe without the intervention of God is called the period of self-transformation.

After the Big Bang explosion, billions of years passed and the universe became autonomous. In space, locally concentrated forces of gravity generated by the cosmic seeds or miniature black holes, which kept attracting and concentrating the surrounding gas. This gas later became the galaxies, each constituted by billions of stars. Most of the galaxies turned around a galactic black hole or seed.

Shortly after God created the universe, He also created the universal forces and the laws of physics, which began controlling the universe. At dawn of the universe existence's, all the matter consisted only of hydrogen and some helium. God was satisfied when He saw that the universe had become autonomous, ready to control itself without His help. That is when galaxies began to form.

God knew at that time that sometime in the future primordial life would be created on billions of planets. Every time this would occur only by pure chance, to be destroyed later by the same nature, until one day, some organism could adapt to its environment, survive, then multiply. This was the turning point of prehistory when by proxy the process of evolution by natural selection began. Then for eons some of those microorganisms would evolve into more sophisticated forms, countless species of plants and animals, and much later the creatures that can think and reason.

In the Atlantis Book of Genesis, the length of each day during the seven days of the creation was not the same, but of different lengths. For example, the duration of the first and second days was equivalent only to a fraction of a second. The third day was equivalent to a thousand terrestrial years; the fourth around a million, the fifth and the sixth equivalent to billions of terrestrial years.

The seventh day is the longest, and today humanity is still living in God's seventh day. This is the day that will last for several billion years until the end of time, when this universe will end in the Big Crunch.

God said, "On this seventh day, my work is complete and I will retire to rest and to began a contemplative existence of dreaming. Then God said, "All of you will exist in my dreams. When I will not be dreaming I will be contemplating and enjoying the changes and events that will happen in a universe that is continuously recreating by itself. From now on, the universal forces and the laws of physics I created will take over by proxy to control this self-transformed universe and the evolution of life. From now on, the universe is autonomous and there is no need for gods." And in saying this, God fell asleep and began his long dream. However, even asleep God is aware of everything that happens everywhere.

The history of the universe with still a lifeless Earth ends here, from now on, a new topic only concerning Earth history will be narrated.

## ATLANTIS BOOK OF GENESIS
## RELATED TO PLANET EARTH

The universe was already created and was in an autonomous process of continuous transformation. God relaxed on the sacred seventh day. He no longer wanted to intervene, just enjoy watching how several solar systems, including ours, were gradually created by no others than themselves. In our solar system, the sun, the earth, and the other planets were formed from the same disk-shaped cloud of gas. In those early times the whole universe, including Earth, was still a dangerous place for the creation of life. Millions of meteorites and comets stroked the planets continuously. The Earth's surface was red hot and in some places melted. For the next billion years the fierce impacts from meteorites and comets decreased and the Earth's surface began to cool. Clouds appeared and precipitated in the form of rain. Seas were formed; however, the atmosphere was still poisonous.

**King James**, Chapter 1:
Verse 9.   And God said, Let the waters under the heavens be gathered together unto one place, and let the dry land appear: and it was so.
Verse 10.   And God called the dry land Earth; and the gathering together of the waters called the Seas: and God saw that it was good.
(Compare these two verses with verse 6, shown below)
**Atlantis**
Verse 6.   Nature brought the waters under the skies together into one place allowing dry land to appear. And it came to be so.
    The dry land made up one big continent (pangea), surrounded by waters, called seas, forming one big ocean.

**King James,** Chapter 1:
Verse 16.   And God made two great lights; the greater light to rule the day, and the lesser light to rule the night: he made the stars also.
Verse 17.   And God set them in the firmament of the heaven to give light upon the earth,
(Compare these two verses with verse 7, as shown below)
**Atlantis**
Verse 7.   After the big continent and the surrounding ocean were created, dark clouds of noxious gases shrouded the planet for eons. These clouds didn't allow the light of the sun, moon, and stars to shine through. But gradually the atmosphere cleared and the sky became transparent. The image of the sun appeared followed by the moon and later, the stars. Then came the day that the expanse of the heavens became visible from the Earth's surface.

**King James**, chapter 1

Verse 14.   And God said, Let there be lights in the firmament of the heavens to divide the day from the night; and let them be for signs, and for seasons, and for days, and years:

Verse 15.   and let them be for lights in the firmament of the heaven to give light upon the earth: and it was so.

(Compare these two verses with verse 8, as shown below)

**Atlantis**

Verse 8.   The luminaries of the heavens, the sun, the moon and the stars, make a division between day and night, and serve as signs for the seasons, for the days, and for the years.

## EARTH READY FOR THE CREATION OF PRIMEVAL LIFE

As Earth's environment improved and its temperature became favorable, some areas of the planet became ready for the creation of primeval life. Countless suitable areas with the proper environment and nutrients appeared in the big ocean.  Primeval life was created and evolved by pure chance from unanimated matter, not only once but thousands of times.

For millions of years in those suitable areas, simple microorganisms appeared countless times, every time by pure chance, to be destroyed again by nature.  Every time there was a small change in the environment, they perished. Nature is a patient experimenter and also inexorably, when ruling by natural selection.

Nature's countless trials of creation and destruction of primeval life continued, then once upon a time, who knows when, a microorganism created by pure chance evolved into a stable life form able to survive and reproduce. An organism simpler than a bacterium was able to reproduce and survive and was able to get adapted to small environmental changes.  This was the greatest event in the history of Earth, the turning point, when evolution by natural selection took over from then on.   Similar events happened in other planets too.   Natural selection is a proxy from God, who had retired and remained at rest on His seventh day, His longest day until the end of time.  God didn't intervene in the creation of life and its progress.  God is only needed for two great events, the instant of creation (Big Bang) and the death (Big Crunch) of the universe.

## EVOLUTION BY NATURAL SELECTION
## TOOK OVER ON EARTH

The surface of the Earth cooled enough to hold water in liquid state, small areas with the proper environment and nutrients to sustain life appeared, and there the first microorganisms were created just by pure chance, as explained early in this chapter.  For the next three billion years, the primeval microorganisms evolved into several kinds of one-cell organisms. This long period of time for the creation of life approximately ended six hundred million years ago when another period took over, where some of those unicellular organisms evolved into countless multicellular living forms, including sea plants, sea animals, and much later on land plants, animals, and finally man.

In chapter 2 from this book is described the creation of man on earth.

**King James,** Chapter 1

Verse 11.   And God said, Let the earth bring forth grass, the herb yielding seed, and the fruit tree yielding fruit after his kind, whose seed is in itself, upon the earth: and it was so.

Verse 12.   And the earth brought forth grass, and herb yielding seed after his kind, and the tree yielding fruit, whose seed was in itself, after his kind: and God saw that it was good.

Verse 20.   And God said, Let the waters bring forth abundantly the moving creature that hath life, and fowl that may fly above the earth in the open firmament of heaven.

Verse 21.   And God created the big whales, and every living creature that moveth, which the waters brought forth abundantly, after their kind, and every winged fowl after his kind: and God saw that it was good.

Verse 22.   And God blessed them, saying, Be fruitful, and multiply, and fill the waters in the seas, and let fowl multiply in the earth.

Verse 24.   And God said, Let the earth bring forth the living creature after his kind, cattle, and creeping thing, and beast of the earth after his kind:  and it was so.

Verse 25.   And God made the beast of the earth after his kind, and cattle after their kind, and every thing that creepeth upon the earth after his kind:  and God saw that it was good.

Verse 26.   And God said, Let us make man in our image, after our likeness: and let them have dominion over the fish of the sea, and over the fowl of the earth, and over the cattle, and over all the earth, and over every creeping thing that creepeth upon the earth.

(Compare these 8 verses with verse 9 of the Atlantis book)

**Atlantis**

Verse 9:     For billions of years life on earth consisted of one-celled organisms.  Later some of them evolved into countless multicellular living forms, (from the Cambrian explosion to the beginning of the Quaternary period), first on the ocean and later on land.  Multicellular creatures like animals, plants, insects, flying creatures and many other kinds of living forms began to multiply.  Man didn't exist yet.

Then God began to dream about the creation of intelligent creatures that could become the caretakers of this world.  God restrained Himself to intervene with nature, but in dreams expressed His desire to the Entarian aliens to create man on Earth, by subjecting inferior animals to artificial accelerated evolution.

The creation of the first six human beings, including Adam and Eve, is explained in more detail in the corresponding chapters of this book about Atlantis.

**King James,** Chapter 6

Verse 1:   And it come to pass, when men began to multiply on the face of the earth, and daughters were born unto them.

(Compare this verse with verse 10, shown below)

**Atlantis**

Verse 10:   Humans started to multiply in large numbers on earth.

**King James,** Chapter 6

Verse 2.   That the sons of God saw the daughters of men that they were fair; and they took them wives of all which they chose.   (Compare with verse 11 of the Atlantis book)

**Atlantis**

Verse 11:   The sons of God, who were the gigantic Atlantean clones, began to notice the females were good-looking.  These men began to take wives for themselves, namely, all whom they chose.

**King James,** Chapter 6

Verse 3.   And the LORD said, My spirit shall not always strive with man, for that he also is flesh: yet his days shall be an hundred and twenty years.

(Compare with verse 12 of the Atlantis book)

**Atlantis**

Verse 12:   God said: "My spirit shall not protect man indefinitely in that he is also flesh.  Accordingly, his span of life shall decrease by nature to a hundred and twenty years."

**King James,** Chapter 6

Verse 4:   There were giants in the earth in those days; and also after that, when the sons of God came in unto the daughters of men, and they bare children to them, the same became mighty men which were of old, men of renown.

Interpretation of some words in the previous paragraph:

a.   **Giants,** also called **The Nephilim**  mean the great Atlanteans.

b.   **The sons of God** mean cloned giants from Atlantis, defective because
                of their large size.

c.   **The daughters of men** mean the daughters of common men of the world.

d.    **Mighty men, men of renown,** also called **men of fame** mean the intelligent but greedy sons of the Atlantean clones with common women.

(Compare verse 4 with verse 13 of the Atlantis book)

**Atlantis**

Verse 13:   In those days the Atlanteans became famous all over the Earth, they were the wisest and most powerful race on the planet, known throughout the world as the great ones.  They were wise in the arts and the sciences, including the knowledge prohibited by God.

In Atlantis' last days, cloning became common practice. Some wealthy Atlanteans chose to be cloned repeatedly four to five times, until they got an exact copy of themselves. Usually this took an average of four times to clone a successful, perfect replica of the donor. Some old donors used to think of their clones as their own partial reincarnation in a young body and called them their favorite child. Deformed clone babies were terminated by euthanasia. Clones born without a brain were kept alive as organ donors. Killing a clone that could think and was self-aware of his or her own existence was considered a premeditated murder. Some clones were as intelligent as the average Atlantean, but physically giants. This was a problem; because of their size they were considered defective by society. No Atlantean women wanted to marry these seven and a half feet (2.25 meters) giants, called the sons of God.

In frustration the giants left their native islands and emigrated to other places around the world. They had relations with the daughters of common men who bore children to them. The descendants of the giants were as smart as their fathers, but their thoughts were only evil.

**King James**, Chapter 6
Verse 5. "And God saw that the wickedness of man was great in the earth, and that every imagination of the thoughts of his hearth was only evil continually."
(Compare with verse 14 of the Atlantis book).
**Atlantis**
Verse 14. Consequently God saw that the evil in men was abundant on Earth. Every inclination of their thoughts and feelings of their hearts were always evil.

**King James**, Chapter 6
Verse 6. And it repented the LORD that he had made man on the earth, and it grieved him at his heart. (Compare with verse 15 of the Atlantis book).
**Atlantis**
Verse 15. And God felt regretful that he had made men on Earth, and his feelings were hurt.

**King James**, Chapter 6
Verse 7. And the LORD said, I will destroy man whom I have created from the face of the earth; both man, and beast, and the creeping thing, and the fowls of the air; for it repenteth me that I have made them. (Compare with verse 16 of the Atlantis book)
**Atlantis**
Verse 16. And God said, I will destroy man whom I have created from the face of the Earth, also I will destroy animals including beast, birds and insects, because I feel repentant that I have made all them.

**King James**, Chapter 6
Verse 8. But Noah found grace in the eyes of the LORD.
**Atlantis**

Verse 17. "Noah was half Atlantean and half common. He met a rich deranged Atlantean that enjoyed making friends in foreign nations, who befriended Noah, and once he told Noah, "You, Noah, have found favor in the eyes of God and I know He instructed you in your dreams to build an ark. So, start building it as soon as possible." Later this Atlantean, who came from a race called "The people of The Sea," became Noah's technical advisor for the construction of the ark. The flood and Noah's Ark were explained in Chapter 2 from this book.

----

# ANSWERS TO THE BIG UNIVERSAL QUESTIONS
## LAST CHAPTER FROM GENESIS OF THE GREAT BOOK OF ATLANTIS

### 1. Who is God and what is the purpose of His existence?

Answer: The main purposes for the existence of God is to be the fifth universal force. This is the force that initiates the birth and also initiates the death of each of these cycling universes. Perhaps for respect it should be called not the fifth, but the first force of the universe.

If there are other purposes for God existence, those are only known by God Himself.

### 2. What is the purpose of the universe?

Answer: Universes are created and destroyed by God in cycles, but the materials from which they are made are eternal and indestructible as God Himself.

The universe is God's greatest project, a creation God feels proud about, the universe is His companion; he entertains Himself by observing its continuous self-transformation. However, God only knows the principal purpose of the existence of the universe. Not even the most advanced beings that populate the universe comprehend the real purpose for the existence of the universe.

### 3. What is the purpose of the existence of humankind?

Answer: There is no special purpose for mankind's existence, it is just an accident of evolution, the same that also applies to the other creatures, which are just a product of evolution by natural selection. Its serves the same purposes as animals, plants, and bacteria. All these creatures have the same right to exist. God doesn't discriminate among any of the species or prefer a particular form of life with respect to the others. Each form of life keeps evolving at its own pace for the survival of its own species.

Humans are social animals, hence they are important only to other humans. In general all beings are only important to the individuals of their own species. Humans are not important to less advanced species, except the dog and the horse, which consider them partners. Sometimes in order to survive, we kill and eat the other species, for example, cattle, in the same way long ago predatory animals frequently ate our ancestors.

Man is just an advanced product of evolution. However, among the billions of species that populate the universe, some are by far more evolved while others less than humankind.

### 4. Is a man a special being for God? To God is man more important than a dog or bacteria?

Answer: In the eyes of God, man is equally important as is the dog or a bacteria, even if some bacteria could kill humans. God doesn't discriminate among species, regardless of how primitive, advanced, or dangerous they are. Man could be defined as the product of a half billion years of evolution starting from an ancient microorganism, similar to a bacteria, or as the product of four million years of evolution from an ape-like creature, take your choice.

### 5. Is consciousness a universal attribute or only an attribute of intelligent beings, as the human?

Answer: Consciousness is universal and covers the entire universe, there is no place without it. Universal consciousness as a whole is also the mind of God, who is assumed to be everywhere. In some places consciousness appears tenuous as happens in the intergalactic open spaces, in clouds, in rocks, grains of sand, in plants and in most animals, while very apparent in human beings and perhaps less apparent in some apes.

As an example we could assume that a grasshopper has a billion times more consciousness than a grain of sand, and a human has a billion times more consciousness than a grasshopper.

### 6. Other than matter, perhaps his mind, his consciousness, his soul or some kind of unknown energy could be eternal in a man? Or when man dies, is he totally gone like an animal?

Answer: It is a question without an answer for a long time to come, perhaps for the next ten thousand years in the future, until someday man could comprehend universes of higher dimensions.

Someday in the future, we may get the answer by encountering extraterrestrial beings that are wiser than we are. Until then this question will remain unanswered.

### 7. Does God love humans more than other beings, including animals?

Answer: God doesn't love one species over the other. His love for humans is the same as for animals and other creatures. If God loved the human species over all the others, then there must be a mysterious reality behind all this that nobody knows. An improbable assumption would be that we humans were demigods, members of the family of God, companions of God, divine demigods with incredible powers to move mountains. But we humans committed some transgression that offended God. So God stripped us of our powers and memories, and sent us to live for some time in a penal colony, the place called planet Earth where we were sent to be born, grow old, struggle, and die. Depending on the life humans lead on Earth, their spirits will die eternally or would return to heaven, and God would restore their great powers, as they had before they were sent to Earth. Each demigod who was once a human would become again God's helper in the universe. Today nobody knows or remembers anything about a former life or the transgression and this punishment.

If this speculation is true, then God's love for humans is above His love for animals and other beings. However, from what we know today, it seems logical to assume that the love of God for humans is the same as His love for the other species, considering that humans evolved from inferior animals.

# SUPPLEMENTS

I.   **Atlantis Medical Science Chronicles**
II.  **Atlantis Engineering Chronicles**

# SUPPLEMENT I

## ATLANTIS MEDICAL SCIENCE CHRONICLES

**Contents**

# CHRONICLE No. 1
(BIOENGINEERING)

## DESIGN OF ARTIFICIAL HEARTS FOR PERMANENT IMPLANTATION IN THE HUMAN BODY
(Also see Chapter 15)
(Project presented in April 17, 1998, by Walter F. Laredo to NASA for its review)

In the school's auditorium, was displayed a medical documentary. In the documentary a professor explained the different steps his students accomplished to develop an artificial heart, a heart to be permanently implanted in a patient's thorax without being rejected. The students working in this project were well paid as those designing the airplane we saw before.

On the film the professor explained to his students that before they start designing the real artificial heart, they should first get some training by designing a simple double pump to pump water, a devise consisting of a box divided into two compartments by a central partition. At each side of this central partition was bonded an inflatable rubber diaphragm membrane, every time it got inflated, it pushed the surrounding water out through a hole in the wall of the box, a hole mimicking the aorta artery. The hydraulic fluid coming through long hoses from a remote hydraulic power system which inflated sequentially the diaphragms.

After building that crude water pump, the students had enough training to start the design of the actual mechanical heart. At our visit to the school ended, our host gave me a medical chronicle brochure, which explained with great detail the design and the development of this artificial heart.

## BROCHURE CONCERNING THE DESIGN OF AN ARTIFICIAL HEART

Practically speaking, this heart is a pump, actuated by a remote hydraulic power system. This artificial hearth is light enough to be supported and held in place in similar way as the living heart is, at the top supported by the same group of main veins and arteries of the old heart, its outer surface is supported by the pericardial membrane.

The power package is a separate unit that supplies power to the mechanical heart and is located at a different place and is constituted by the four following components: a hydraulic pump, an electric motor, an internal battery, and the electronic control. This power package is installed not in the thorax, but inside the lower abdomen, tied to bone extensions of the hip bone, which were artificially stimulated to grow by a pre-operation, months before the actual open heart operation. This power system provides hydraulic power to the artificial heart through a long, 3/8-inch diameter, flexible plastic tube in which interior runs two flexible hydraulic lines (thin hoses), each to actuate each of the ventricle's artificial membranes. The outer plastic tube runs through a special fitting in the person's diaphragm.

During its development, this artificial heart got redesigned four times, mostly because its complex shape and cross-sections, went through four stages of design metamorphosis, becoming each time smaller more efficient, more compact and more refined than the time before, finally became small enough to fit inside the pericardial cavity. The heart surface was covered with a soft coat of antirejection material. Further refinements were performed without reducing its blood pumping efficiency.

At that moment, Dr. Quetzalco entered the room and greeted us saying, "The human body is so compact, from top of the head to the toes, that is difficult to implant large artificial organs inside it. Same concept applies to the pericardial cavity where there is no room for large, artificial hearts."

In the documentary was shown the sequential steps his students followed to develop this heart. These teenage students were well paid for their work.

The professor in the film was also the Heart Chief Project Engineer and went through an extended presentation. A transcript of this documentary was made available to me, and it is as follows:

## Transcript
## DESIGN AND DEVELOPMENT OF AN ARTIFICIAL HEART

This heart was designed for an approximate blood pumping capacity of five liters per minute, and an approximate frequency of 70 beats per minute.

## DETAILED DESIGN OF HEART COMPONENTS

EXTERNAL SURFACE. The superior external surface of the mechanical heart is from titanium, and is designed with the same complicated contours as an exact copy of the corresponding one of the living heart. Short segments of tubes made from titanium protruded out from the top surface of the mechanical heart, to be coupled with the patient's major blood vessels, after the patient's sick heart was removed and disposed. The connections between the protruding short tubes of the artificial heart with the major blood vessels were made using a new safe connection method that the body will accept without rejection. Inside the superior part of this titanium heart are the two auricles. In the living heart, auricles are flexible and act as small pumps. In contrast, for this mechanical heart they are rigid and are used only as blood reservoirs.

HEART VALVES. The design of mechanical heart valves for a life span of 30 years, equivalent to a billion beats of continuous operation without failure was a real challenge. In the design of the valves of an artificial heart are encountered similar engineering problems as in the valve design system from most ordinary machines, as compressors, pumps, and engines. For example, one way to increase the power of a gasoline engine, without increasing its size, is by increasing the size of its valves, or increasing the number of valves in order to let more air pass through for the combustion.

If in a mechanical heart in development is doubled its number of valves, the volume of blood flow would increase without increasing the size of the heart. But this kind of design will turn the laminar blood flow next to its internal surfaces and internal cavities, into turbulent. When blood flows over irregular surfaces creates internal hydrodynamics problems as turbulence, and at some locations producing reversed blood flow, causing oxygen deprivation and mechanical damage to the blood cells, and worst of all, blood clots.

DESIGN OF AN INDIVIDUAL HEART VALVE. In this section will be considered the design and development of an individual valve. The simplest, most reliable and efficient valve is the popular and familiar one-way ball valve, which was used for years. This is acceptable for patients requiring the replacement of one valve only. A natural heart, using four of these mechanical valves would be too massive to be practical. Unfortunately the same idea applies to an artificial heart with four ball-type valves--it will occupy more space, beyond the size of the patient's pericardial cavity, and will require the removal of part of a lung to make more room to locate this heart.

A flexible flap type of design for a valve similar to the ones from a living heart would be ideal, but artificial valves made from nonliving material are not self-repairing like the valves of a living heart. Hence its flexible material subject to bending will not last long and eventually will fail by fatigue. However, this design is acceptable for a heart that will last no more than few months, ideal for patients waiting for a living heart transplant. In the illustrations of the mechanical heart, is shown that all four valves are of the flap type. These are of a special design, for a heart that should last for thirty years. In the illustrations could be seeing the gradual development of these valves, from concept to final.

PUMPING DIAPHRAGMS.   The central partitions that separates the two titanium rigid ventricles of this mechanical heart support on each of its faces an inflatable flexible membrane called a diaphragm which is supported by circular frame. There is a narrow space that separates both membranes. Hydraulic fluid, under pressure, coming from a remote electric pump, is injected inside that tight space under each membrane, forcing them to expand outwards as inflating balloons, pushing out the blood contained inside the rigid titanium ventricles. The·blood pressure will open and will flow through the valves to the aorta and to pulmonary arteries. This pumping will not happen simultaneously on both ventricles, but sequentially, controlled by a hydraulic sequence valve, from the remote power unit, and all this process is controlled electronically.

Temporary artificial hearts for short life spans doesn't have sophisticated valves system as the one previously explained, those are of much simpler design, made with especial rubber pumping membranes.   For each cycle of expansion, the rubber membranes stretch radial and tangentially simultaneously.   After a few months, its material of limited life, would fail by fatigue.

The special design of the long lasting pumping membranes minimizes material fatigue by decreasing the membrane tensile deflection in all directions; the secret is that mostly bending deflects each minute element of the membrane.  These membranes are built with plies, each from a different material; the ply that doesn't touch blood is built from a special, durable, metallic alloy material called tireless devil, because of its great resistance to fatigue. The smooth surfaces that touch blood are coated with a special material that doesn't allow the formation of blood clots; it doesn't allow blood to adhere to it.   The smooth surface of the pumping diaphragms doesn't mechanically damage blood cells.

## POWER SUPPLY FOR THE ARTIFICIAL HEART

The internal power system is permanently implanted inside the lower abdomen of the patient.  This power pack includes batteries, an electric hydraulic pump, a sequence valve, and electronic controls.  All these components are enclosed in a container the size of a grapefruit.  The power pack and the artificial heart are connected by a flexible plastic hose system, which is coated, it is two feet long and its interior contains another two smaller diameter hoses.  The hose system is routed in between organs like a snake, passing through a special grommet implanted on the diaphragm at a location where it doesn't affect the deflections of the moving diaphragm. Each of the two tubes inside the larger hose supplies hydraulic power to each of the diaphragms of the mechanical ventricles.

The internal batteries from the power unit located inside the abdominal cavity are recharged by connecting them to a portable pack, carried externally and strapped to the patient's body with a harness. The portable pack weighs about three kilograms, The external battery has a short cord with a connector which can be plugged or unplugged into the patient's plug, which is an electric bony socket permanently implanted into the skin of the patient's abdomen. This electric bony socket protrudes from the abdomen skin, just as the horns of an animal protrudes through the skin of his head. When the portable power pack is plugged into the patient electric socket, it transfers electric power to the body's internal rechargeable batteries. Now in the case the patient wants to take a shower or go swimming, he could unplug his pack from the electric socket in his skin. But never should remain unplugged for more than four hours, which is the maximum safe time that the internal batteries inside the body can remain charged and still keep the patient alive.

Four months before the patient receives his artificial heart, previously is subjected to a pre-operation in the lower part of his abdomen, which purpose is to stimulate the growth of four small bony protrusions from the pelvis ilium bones. Each protrusion looks as the ears from a small tea cup, through which holes will pass the artificial ligaments to support the power supply.

The whole procedure is a lengthy process, which began with the slow growth of those bony protrusions by installing first a scaffold for each of them. The scaffolds establish the shape of what will become the bony protrusions. The scaffolds are made by using fibers from a biodegradable polymer, then implanted on the edge of the hipbone. With time the scaffold will disappear leaving in its place new bone as if it grew from the hip bone itself.

Four months later the principal operation was schedule to be performed for the implantation of the heart. Two teams of surgeons operated simultaneously on the patient. One team was in charge of the artificial heart implant inside the thorax, and the other team in charge of the implantation of the internal power system inside the lower abdomen. The team working in the lower abdominal cavity implanted the internal power system, which was secured to the artificially grown bony protrusions as hooks with artificial ligaments. The ligaments were implanted in such a way that neither, the ligaments nor the power system interfered with the other organs. Finally, the abdomen was closed and sutured. The surgeons inserted a specially designed seal, a grommet at the location where the long hose system went through the diaphragm. This is the hose system that provides hydraulic power to the heart.

## ANOTHER ALTERNATIVE, A HYBRID HEART

The last part of this chronicle describes another type of heart design, a hybrid, half-living and half-artificial. The lower part of this heart corresponded to the living portion which included the ventricles. The ventricles' tissues were stimulated to grow either from extracted or from modified living heart cells, temporarily implanted in the patient lower abdomen, there those cells will grow into fully developed ventricles. Later at the time of the operation the ventricles were removed from there to be implanted in the proper place, inside the patient's thorax.

The living portion of this heart, constituted by the two ventricles and its respective coronary blood vessels, are made from actual heart tissue. The muscles from the ventricles have the same three functions as in any living heart which are 1) a contracting motor acting as a pump, 2) an electric power source just in itself and 3) self repairing. A pacemaker contributes to control its operation.

The upper part of this heart is artificial. It includes the valves and the nipples to couple with the large vessels. There are also small nipples to be coupled with the coronaries and bypass blood to the living ventricles. The artificial portion of this heart could be made either from a special plastic or from titanium. The surfaces of the artificial portion of this heart should be treated with a special inert coating, on the inner side of the lining, endothelial cells are stimulated to grow cells from the same patient would multiplied and attach there by themselves.  This inner lining made from protein deposits covers all the internal surfaces of the artificial part of the heart to avoid direct blood contact, avoiding blood clothing.

Other alternative would be, by applying the practice of tissue engineering, undifferentiated cells are turned into heart cells, to growth in laboratories, then used to create heart ventricles and heart valves.  Since these organs were produced with cells extracted from the same patient, there was no risk of rejection.

When scientists tried to clone a whole heart, it grew with defective valves, so this upper portion was discarded, and replaced by an artificial one, as was described before.

# CHRONICLE No. 2

## MEDICAL STUDENTS OPERATING ON PLASTIC DUMMIES
By Dr. Nubis from Atlantis
(Also see Chapter 15)

Long ago, our students used to practice surgery by dissecting and performing mock operations on cadavers, a nauseating process because the foul smell.  Today they practice the same operations on full-size dummy patients. A mannequin manufacturer began mass-producing them as full-size dolls, made from various soft plastic materials mimicking different human tissues.  The anatomical complexity of the dummies simulated very close to the real human.  The dummies have body systems with similar anatomy as the real human body; systems as the skeletal, the muscular, the circulatory, the digestive, the nervous, etc, all made from different kinds of plastics. The dummies' internal organs made from different kinds of materials, were perfect copies from those in the human body.

Thick red liquid circulated inside the mannequin blood vessels, mimicking the same consistency and ability to coagulate as real blood.  It circulated by means of a small electric pump.  During mock surgical operations, the dummies bled like a real person and the cut veins were cauterized.  The dummies even could get a transfusion of fake blood.

Some models resembled humans afflicted with different kinds of diseases and health problems.  For the medical students was less intimidating to practice simulated surgery on dummies then real operations on real people.  To work with dummies was much cleaner than with cadavers.

Concurrently with the courses of mock surgery was a much less scientific course, but important, it was the suturing of different kinds of organs, a pragmatic technical course to improve surgeon's manual dexterity.

Do you know that in suturing, some surgeons were more skilled than tailors were? The most advanced course in suturing was microsurgery performed with the help of a microscope by using remote controlled microrobots.

"We have also partial anatomical models, used for mock surgical operations of some particular part of the body, some for the head, others for the limbs, or the trunk and so on. Thorax models are very popular, our students practice all the time open-heart surgery on them. After the models got old and damaged by being operated several times, they were thrown in trash boxes to be recycled. Young doctors before they perform their first surgical operation on real people, they already had experience by performing hundreds of operations on those dummies.

# CHRONICLE No. 3

## RECREATION OF A NEW HUMAN BEING BY USING HUMAN PARTS FROM TWO DONORS WHO DIED IN A CRASH
(Also see Chapter 15)

## THE DOCUMENTARY
A spaceship brought passengers from Earth, among them Godin and his grandson were about to land on the Moon, and crashed. In the wreck Godin and Krill were badly hurt. Their space suits were deformed but still retained oxygen. There was no hope to save them. Once at the moon's hospital the head of Godin and the headless body of Krill were kept alive, by separate life support systems. Godin's head remained anesthetized, with an anesthesia recently invented in Atlantis and useful for months without causing brain damage.

After the sad story, Dr. Wascar began narrating the medical part of the story. While projecting a documentary on the screen he exclaimed, "We, the Atlanteans, didn't want to lose Godin's brain because humanity still needs his knowledge of science and his capacity to invent. We decided instead to rebuild a new person by joining Godin's head with the strong headless body of his grandson. Prior to the operation, all tests verified that the blood and tissues from both persons were compatible, decreasing the chances of organ rejection." Doctor Wascar continued, "Here on the screen you are about to witness one of the greatest operations ever performed, a historic operation performed simultaneously by more than 40 surgeons on one patient. "

As the film began, a narrator appeared and explained, "Nerves grow very slowly. The patient should not move and should remain at rest in one position, sometimes for as long as six or more months, sleeping for months in one position, under the effect of a special new anesthesia that doesn't destroy brain cells. When the patient's body is resting motionless in one position, bedsores and deterioration are minimized when the body presses only slightly against the soft supports inside that glass box. The low gravity of the moon has an advantage for long-term operations, because the moon's gravity is one-sixth of the Earth's gravity, resulting in a lower force of gravity on the patient."

The cameraman filmed as he walked through several rooms in the moon's hospital. In most rooms we saw a couple of surgeons and their assistants, but no patients. The surgeons were looking at an extra-large television screen that covered a wall. The doctor's assistants pushed buttons and levers, that remotely controlled miniature robots, which actually performed the microsurgical operation in the distant operating room. The huge screen showed a magnified view clearly showing the miniature hands, clamps and small tools of the miniature robots. Forty surgeons were involved in this operation, each doctor from his own office contributed in his own specialization. What finally emerged was a human body rebuilt in the like of Frankenstein.

The cross-section image of the human neck was projected on the huge screens, in each room. The cervical vertebrae of the spinal cord were shown, clearly displaying the spinal nerves and surrounding tissues. The view of the spinal cord appeared as large as the cross section of a Sequoia tree trunk. After the filmmaker walked by the different rooms while filming the surgeons, he moved to the solitary operating room located in the center of the building. There the camera scanned highly complicated equipment containing dials, tubes and instruments. A pair of life-support machines was already in full operation. At the center of the room, on top of a table, was a long, glass box, and inside was the prospect of a new man in the process of being rebuilt from other human parts.

The face of sleeping Godin was pale, but recognizable. The ends of the two spinal cords were already in the process of being joined. Miniature and microscopic equipment surrounded the neck area. During the long operation, the head and body were full of tubes containing circulating blood and other fluids and connected to various blood vessels. There were bundles of thin electric wires, some thinner than a human hair, connected to an army of miniature robots which were controlled electrically at a distant location. Three bundles of fiber optic scanners were placed no further than one centimeter from the operation zone, transmitting images that were enlarged hundreds of times and visible on the huge screens in each of the surgeons, offices.

Dr. Wascar said the spinal cord belonging to Godin's head was in process of being attached Krill's body. Months later after the spinal cords were joined, and the peripheral nerves were healed, it was time to start a different series of sequential operations with the other organs and tissues, reconstructing and stitching the rest of them in the neck area. Starting with the neck bones--the cervical vertebrae that were removed in small pieces at the beginning of the operation were stored in a cool place, then brought and restored to their original position. This was followed by other operations to reconstruct additional organs, including the suturing of ligaments, muscles, blood vessels, esophagus, larynx, and trachea.

There was special electromagnetic devices surrounding the spinal cord in the neck area, stimulating the axons of the neurons to growth from one person head into the tubes of myelin sheaths belonging to another person, consequently resulting in the death and disappearance of the original axons. A growing procedure lasting six months.

Also there were devices for the injection of adult stem cells ready to transform by themselves into neurons contributing this way with the healing and restoration of the new human spinal cord..

The severed surfaces in mutual contact should match perfectly and should have no gap, allowing Godin's nerve fibers to align with Krill's myelin sheaths.

A group of micro-robots were precisely matching both ends of the spinal cords prior to being spliced, and reducing the gap as much as possible in the neurilemmal sheath so that the Schwann cells on either side might begin growing together.

Veins and arteries still remained clamped at the ends ready for their final reconnection. In the neck area, sectioned muscles and skin originally belonging to the head and to the body still remained separated. The scar tissue was trimmed off before these organs could be joined and sutured together. At this point the most complicated part of the operation was completed. Still there were more steps to perform with the other organs, therefore surgery resumed. The whole process took over six months to complete.

The later series of operations involved joining the rest of the tissues in the neck area, including the conjunctive, muscular, skeletal, blood vessels, and organs such as the larynx, esophagus, and trachea. Before the organs were joined and sutured, miniature robots trimmed off the scar tissue that formed at the edges of the sectioned organs.

The space available to perform an operation around the neck area is very limited. Surgery in this area is further complicated by the presence of other organs and surrounding equipment, which block the view. I suspect that what I was seeing was only a dream or nightmare caused by the strange powers of the stone where I was resting, it was during our returning hiking trip, at high altitude in the Andes Mountains.

Special cradles supported the head of Godin and the body of Krill, each kept alive by a separate life-support system, including heart/lung machines. In the same close-up view the ant-size mini-robots looked as big as dogs. The view was enlarged to such a degree that the view of gray and white matter from the spinal cord filled the entire screen. Thousands of axon fibers were visible. Some of the miniature robots were reorganizing these bundles of fibers, which looked like thousands of microscopic telephone lines. Concurrently, other micro-robots performed micro-neurosurgery on other nerves.

Dr. Wascar said that most of Krill's spinal cord axons would die. However, the axons regenerated from Godin's head would grow inside the tubes of sheath cells previously occupied by Krill's original nerve fibers, which would die and vanish. The newly grown fibers would eventually reach the other end of the sheaths to synapse with the living fibers, for functional contact of the nerves. In this way, Godin's nerve fibers were targeted with the corresponding nerve fibers from Krill, which had not yet deteriorated.

In this series of operations, the spinal cord was the first organ to be treated. The rest of the organs were grafted at a later date.

After lying with its respective life support systems for six months on the cradles, both spinal chords got joined and healed, and step one was finished.

The next step included a series of operations performed by surgeons of other specialties. One procedure involved the restoration of previously removed vertebra, followed by suturing of minute veins, arteries and other tissues in the neck area with the help of another group of micro-robots. All operations were performed by remote control from several offices and the complex series of surgical procedures lasted for six months with the aid of 40 surgeons and 90 nurses. A special long-term anesthesia that doesn't kill brain cells was discovered and used.

Two years of rehabilitation were required allowing time for the brain to self-reprogram itself, mostly in the motor and sensory areas. Since not every axon will synapse correctly, the self-reprogramming brain will correct those errors at a later time.

Awaiting the operation at the round central room, the patient head's was anesthetized, and laid inside a shallow glass box, resting on the operating table. There he was surrounded by several pieces of equipment, including life support equipment, miniature cameras for closed circuit television, and robots of different sizes, but no human beings.

The team of doctors observed their patient for several months while he laid in a coma. It was exciting to see the rebirth of a new man with no name, a new man with the old face and brain of Godin, and with the young strong body of Krill. After this person awoke from his six-month coma, he was again named Godin,

After his release from the hospital, he went into rehabilitation, in order to learn everything again, including how to walk, talk, and read. His brain had to reprogram itself. A young patient's brain could tolerate this better than the one of the old genius which was unable to reprogram in a satisfactory way. He never recuperated completely, and remained a gentle moron for the rest of his life.

# CHRONICLE No. 4

## BIONIC EYES FOR THE BLIND
(Also see Chapter 15)

This patient used to be totally blind," said the doctor. "He suffered from dead, detached retinas on both eyes. We operated on his left eye several times to provide him with a bionic eye. Although the patient only sees in black and white, this eye is a marvel of microelectronic engineering.

"Inside the outer structure of the emptied living eyeball (choroid) was implanted a small, plastic ball with a lens in the front. Back inside this bionic eyeball there is a smaller, artificial retina with the shape of a miniature cap, made up of 10,000 special micro-photoreceptors. The artificial retina is divided into two semicircles, the left and the right. Each corresponds to half of the retina and is made up of 5,000 special micro-photoreceptors, most of them concentrated in the artificial fovea, where more acute vision is needed. Each minute photoreceptor is connected to a long conductor, a wire from gold, thinner than a human hair, acting as an artificial nerve fiber. The wires coming out from the bionic eyeball are arranged into two bundles of 5,000 each. Each bundle is connected to one half of the artificial retina, two bundles together constitutes the artificial optic nerve."

The doctor said that the patient's living eyeball, including its cornea, was not removed. The sclera and the choroid were modified to support inside the permanently implanted bionic eyeball. The aqueous humor, the crystalline lens, and the vitreous body were removed to make room for the spherical bionic eye. The living choroid maintained its highly vascular blood vessels.

It took years to develop special materials to be used in the construction of the bionic eye, and also a special external coating, so that the bionic eyeball would not to be rejected by the body. Two flexible bundles of wires began behind the eyeball, inside the eye socket. The bundles or bionic optic nerves were flexible enough to bend and allow eye movements. The bionic optic nerve did not follow the usual internal routing as in the living optic nerve, which passes by the optic chiasma. The bionic optic nerve made by thin gold fibers first was routed to outside the skull through a hole drilled in the lower left frontal bone along the left side of the skull. To avoid infection by external exposure, the external optic wires, also called bionic optic nerve, were covered along their entire length with a long ridge of new bone, which was artificially stimulated to grow from the skull bone but under the scalp. To do this, the patient's scalp was opened and the bionic optic nerve was laid and extended in contact with the left side of the skull, all the way back to the occipital area of the head.

He continued explaining that each of the two bionic optic nerves or cables ended in a contoured, flexible plate installed inside the occipital area of the head, each plate supported five thousand minute probes. The material from each flexible plastic plate supporting the probes was able to breathe, because it was full of tiny breathing holes. The plastic plates looked like brushes with tiny metal bristles. These plates were attached to the corresponding bionic optic nerves. To bring these plates inside the occipital area of the skull, and put them in direct contact with the brain, a rectangular portion of the occipital bone, with part of the arachnoid, the dura matter and the pia matter membranes had to be removed. These parts were saved and restored at the end of the operation. Each plastic plate was flexible enough to be extended and laid like a miniature carpet and fit over a mapped, visual sensory area of the cerebral cortex of the brain.

These rectangular plastic plates were specially molded for each patient so that they could match exactly the convolution surfaces of the occipital part of that particular patient's brain. Those were molded quickly in a laboratory located in the same room, it took no more than a few minutes to the technician. The plates were pressed smoothly against the brain so the microscopic pin probes would pierce the corresponding surfaces of the convolutions of the brain, penetrating the outer surface of the primary visual cortex. This was all done without damaging tiny veins and arteries. The illustrations from this chapter shown that plastic plate have a pin guidance device that doesn't allow pins to buckle at the time of their insertion on the brain. The microscopic probes were so small that their penetration produced negligible damage to the brain cells. For the areas of the brain where there were some small arteries and veins, the plates, surfaces were flush and had no pins.

The patient could move his bionic eye without problem, because it was implanted inside the hollowed living eyeball, for eye motion is used the same muscles attached to the original living eye structure. After the operation was finished, the patient went through many months of rehabilitation. A lengthy process that allowed his brain to reprogram itself, learning to decode and interpret what it saw with the new eye, similar to what happens with babies who are two months old and trying to see the world. The bionic eye has a rigid lens designed to focus better on objects that are at a distance of one meter. The patient carried two monocles with him, one for reading and the other for long distance vision. The patient could read only large print. The quality of his restored vision was not perfect, but it was satisfactory for his condition.

# BIOENGINEERING  PLATES
## 15 plates follows this sheet

Mechanical Heart, plates 1 through 11

Bionic Eye, plates 12 & 13

Reconstruction of a new human being,
By using the head and the body from
two different persons,  plates 14 & 15

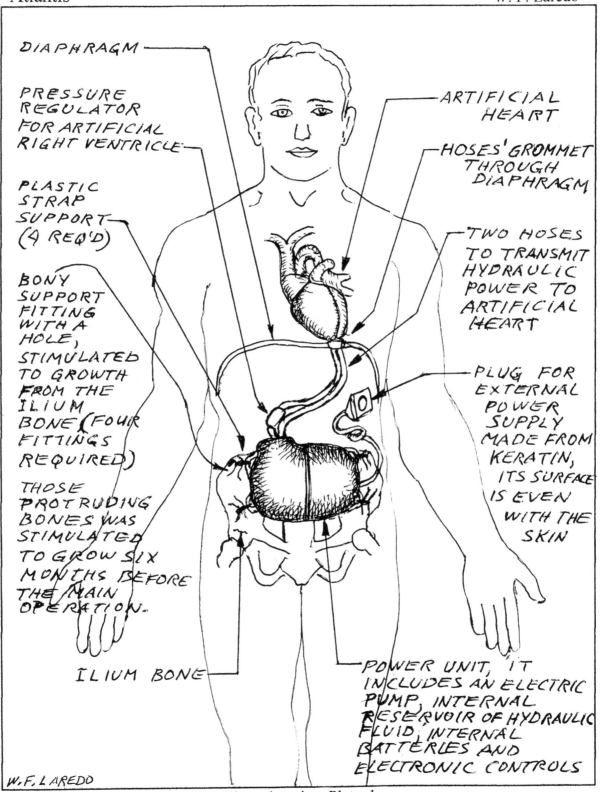

DIAPHRAGM

PRESSURE
REGULATOR
FOR ARTIFICIAL
RIGHT VENTRICLE

PLASTIC
STRAP
SUPPORT
(4 REQ'D)

BONY
SUPPORT
FITTING
WITH A
HOLE,
STIMULATED
TO GROWTH
FROM THE
ILIUM
BONE (FOUR
FITTINGS
REQUIRED)

THOSE
PROTRUDING
BONES WAS
STIMULATED
TO GROW SIX
MONTHS BEFORE
THE MAIN
OPERATION.

ILIUM BONE

ARTIFICIAL
HEART

HOSES' GROMMET
THROUGH
DIAPHRAGM

TWO HOSES
TO TRANSMIT
HYDRAULIC
POWER TO
ARTIFICIAL
HEART

PLUG FOR
EXTERNAL
POWER
SUPPLY
MADE FROM
KERATIN,
ITS SURFACE
IS EVEN
WITH THE
SKIN

POWER UNIT, IT
INCLUDES AN ELECTRIC
PUMP, INTERNAL
RESERVOIR OF HYDRAULIC
FLUID, INTERNAL
BATTERIES AND
ELECTRONIC CONTROLS

W. F. LAREDO

Bioengineering Plate 1

## NATURAL HEARTH FOUR-PHASES PUMPING CYCLE

**DIASTOLIC PHASE, THE EARTH RELAX**

**ATRIAL SYSTOLE WITH VENTRICLE STILL IN DIASTOLE**

**VENTRICLES CONTRACT, VENTRICULAR SYSTOLE**

**ATRIA EXPANDS AND FILLS WITH BLOOD (CYCLE REPEATS)**

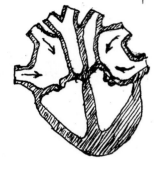  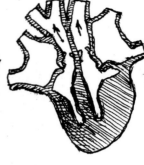 

MUSCULAR INTERVENTRICULAR SEPTUM

## MECHANICAL HEART TWO-PHASE PUMPING CYCLE

INFLATABLE MEMBRANES

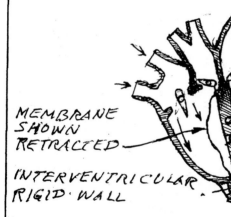
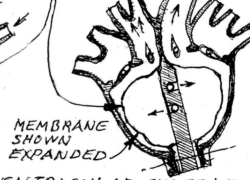

MEMBRANE SHOWN RETRACTED

INTERVENTRICULAR RIGID WALL

DIASTOLIC PHASE THE CHAMBER INSIDE THE RIGID VENTRICLES EXPANDS AND FILLS WITH BLOOD.

MEMBRANE SHOWN EXPANDED

VENTRICULAR SYSTOLE, THE BLOOD IN THE CHAMBERS IS COMPRESSED BY THE INFLATABLE MEMBRANES AND ENTERS THE AORTA AND THE PULMONARY ARTERY.

## PHASES OF OPERATION
## COMPARISON BETWEEN THE NATURAL HEART AND THE MECHANICAL HEART

W.F. LAREDO

MECHANICAL AND HYDRAULIC SYSTEM TO TEST
THE MATERIAL OF THE VALVES AND THE
PUMPING DIAPHRAGMS

SYSTEM'S
COMPONENTS
MIMICKING
ARTERIES;
VEINS,
CAPILLARIES
AND A CUBIC
HEART WHICH
INCLUDED
ATRIUMS,
VENTRICLES,
VALVES AND
DIAPHRAGMS

LUNGS

AORTA

PRESSURE
GAGE

W. F. Laredo
January 1997
Rev. Dec. 2004

RIGHT
VENTRICLE

LEFT
VENTRICLE

RESTRICTION
VALVE
MIMICKING THE
FLOW RESTINCE
BY THE HUMAN
CAPILLARIES IN
THE BODY AND
THE LUNGS
(4 REQID)

ELECTROM
MECHANICAL
PRESSURE
CONTROL
DEVICE FOR
THE RIGHT
VENTRICLE

ELECTRIC
PUMP

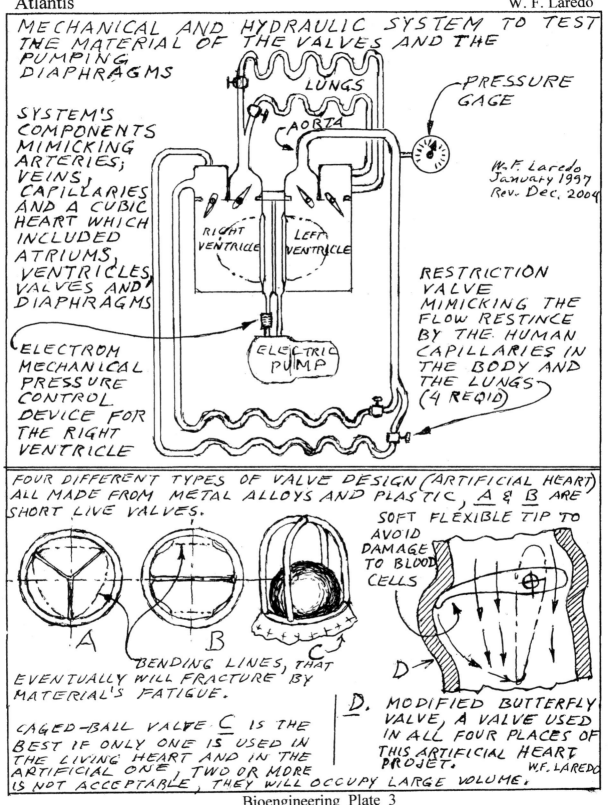

FOUR DIFFERENT TYPES OF VALVE DESIGN (ARTIFICIAL HEART)
ALL MADE FROM METAL ALLOYS AND PLASTIC, A & B ARE
SHORT LIVE VALVES.

SOFT FLEXIBLE TIP TO
AVOID
DAMAGE
TO BLOOD
CELLS

A                    B                    C

BENDING LINES, THAT
EVENTUALLY WILL FRACTURE BY
MATERIAL'S FATIGUE.

D

CAGED-BALL VALVE C IS THE
BEST IF ONLY ONE IS USED IN
THE LIVING HEART AND IN THE
ARTIFICIAL ONE, TWO OR MORE
IS NOT ACCEPTABLE, THEY WILL OCCUPY LARGE VOLUME.

D. MODIFIED BUTTERFLY
VALVE, A VALVE USED
IN ALL FOUR PLACES OF
THIS ARTIFICIAL HEART
PROJET.          W. F. LAREDO

Bioengineering Plate 3

ARTIFICIAL HEART MADE FROM TITANIUM WITH
RIGID EXTERNAL WALLS, IT IS IN CONTRAST TO THE
LIVING HEART WHICH HAVE FLEXIBLE WALLS.
THIS MECHANICAL HEART USES ITS ATRIUMS AS
BLOOD RESERVOIRS AND THESE ATRIUMS ARE
SMALLER THAN IN THE NATURAL HEART.
ALL EXTERNAL SURFACES ARE COATED WITH AN
ANTI-REJECTION SUBSTANCE WHILE THE INTERNAL
SURFACES IN CONTACT WITH THE BLOOD ARE
COATED WITH AN ANTI-CLOTHING SUBSTANCE.

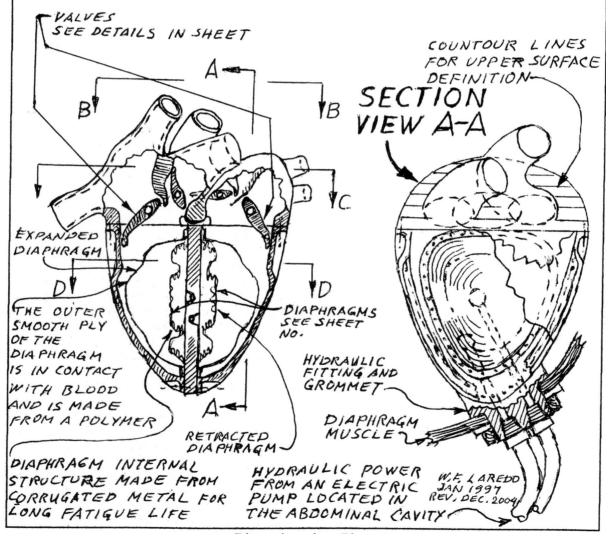

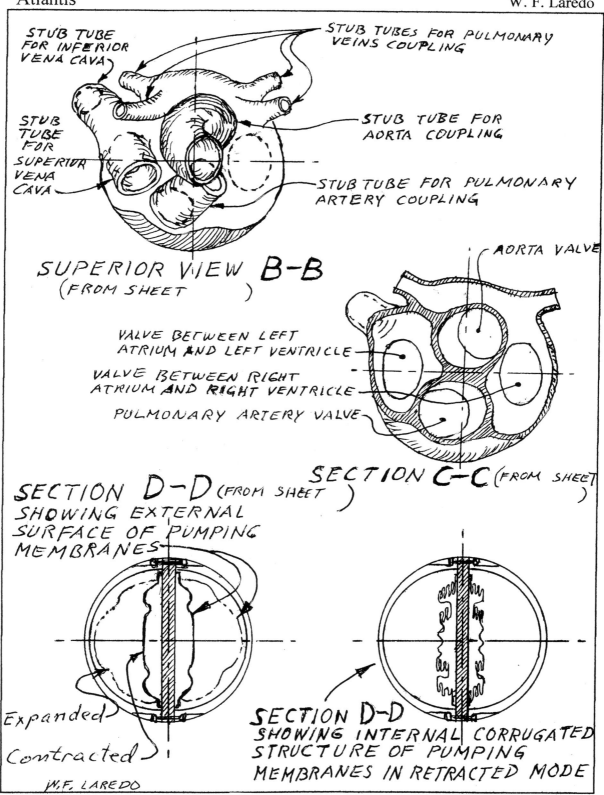

STUB TUBE FOR INFERIOR VENA CAVA

STUB TUBES FOR PULMONARY VEINS COUPLING

STUB TUBE FOR SUPERIOR VENA CAVA

STUB TUBE FOR AORTA COUPLING

STUB TUBE FOR PULMONARY ARTERY COUPLING

SUPERIOR VIEW B-B
(FROM SHEET        )

AORTA VALVE

VALVE BETWEEN LEFT ATRIUM AND LEFT VENTRICLE

VALVE BETWEEN RIGHT ATRIUM AND RIGHT VENTRICLE

PULMONARY ARTERY VALVE

SECTION C-C (FROM SHEET        )

SECTION D-D (FROM SHEET        )
SHOWING EXTERNAL SURFACE OF PUMPING MEMBRANES

Expanded

Contracted

SECTION D-D
SHOWING INTERNAL CORRUGATED STRUCTURE OF PUMPING MEMBRANES IN RETRACTED MODE

W.F. LAREDO

# INTERNAL STRUCTURE OF THE BLOOD PUMPING DIAPHRAGM

STRUCTURE IN CONTACT WITH THE PUMPING HYDRAULIC FLUID; IT IS
MADE FROM SPECIAL ALLOY TO WITHSTAND ONE BILLION CYCLES. THIS
STRUCTURE AND ITS MATERIAL ARE DESIGNED TO WITHSTAND FATIGUE,
DESIGNED IN SUCH WAY THAT MOST DEFLECTION IS BY BENDING AND
NOT BY STRETCHING.

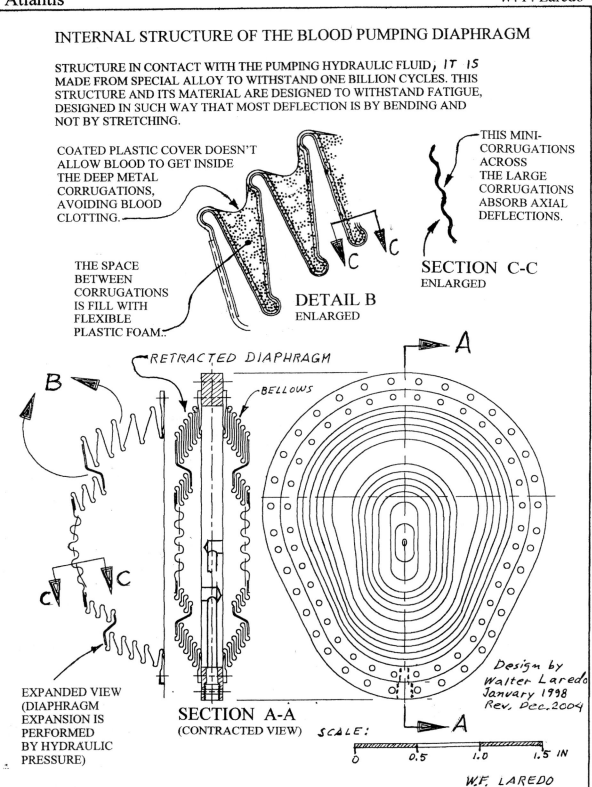

COATED PLASTIC COVER DOESN'T
ALLOW BLOOD TO GET INSIDE
THE DEEP METAL
CORRUGATIONS,
AVOIDING BLOOD
CLOTTING.

THIS MINI-
CORRUGATIONS
ACROSS
THE LARGE
CORRUGATIONS
ABSORB AXIAL
DEFLECTIONS.

THE SPACE
BETWEEN
CORRUGATIONS
IS FILL WITH
FLEXIBLE
PLASTIC FOAM.

DETAIL B
ENLARGED

SECTION C-C
ENLARGED

RETRACTED DIAPHRAGM

BELLOWS

B

C    C

EXPANDED VIEW
(DIAPHRAGM
EXPANSION IS
PERFORMED
BY HYDRAULIC
PRESSURE)

SECTION A-A
(CONTRACTED VIEW)

A

A

Design by
Walter Laredo
January 1998
Rev. Dec. 2004

SCALE:

0        0.5        1.0        1.5 IN

W.F. LAREDO

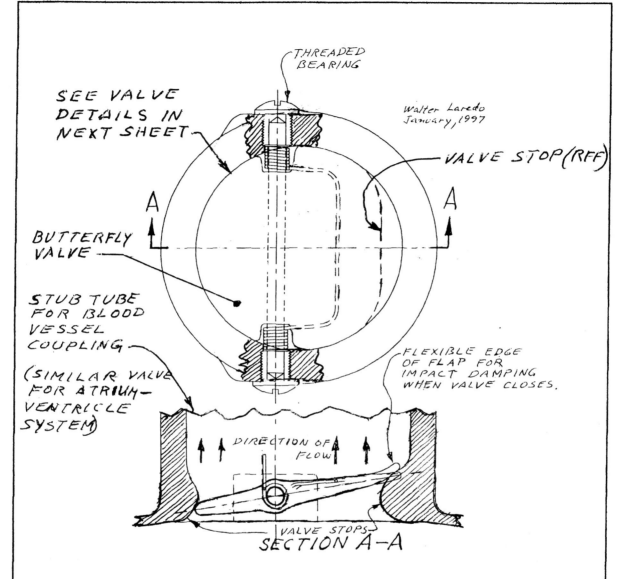

SEE VALVE DETAILS IN NEXT SHEET

THREADED BEARING

Walter Laredo January, 1997

VALVE STOP (REF)

BUTTERFLY VALVE

STUB TUBE FOR BLOOD VESSEL COUPLING

(SIMILAR VALVE FOR ATRIUM-VENTRICLE SYSTEM)

FLEXIBLE EDGE OF FLAP FOR IMPACT DAMPING WHEN VALVE CLOSES.

DIRECTION OF FLOW

VALVE STOPS
SECTION A-A

VALVE ASSEMBLY SYSTEM
FOR ARTIFICIAL HEART

INTERNAL DUCT AND VALVE SURFACES ARE COATED WITH A SUBSTANCE THAT DOESN'T ALLOW BLOOD TO CLOTH.

W.F. LAREDO

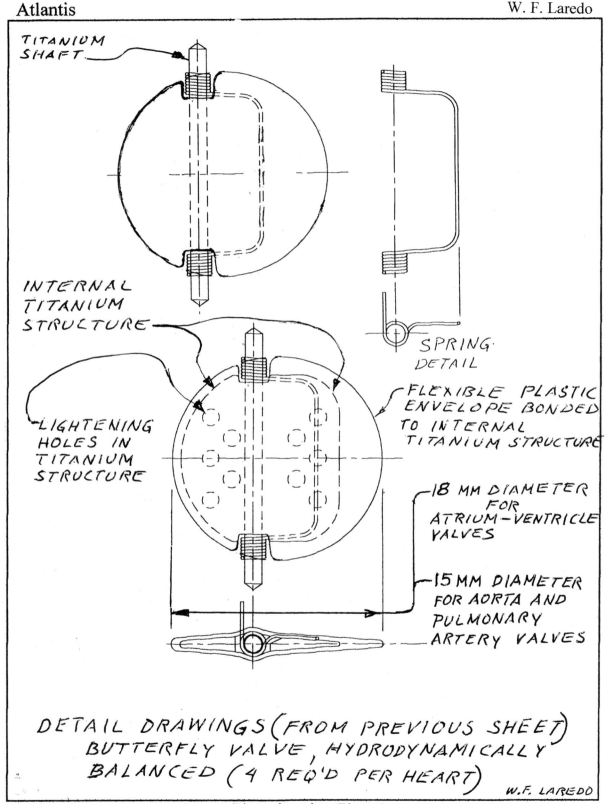

TITANIUM SHAFT

INTERNAL TITANIUM STRUCTURE

LIGHTENING HOLES IN TITANIUM STRUCTURE

SPRING DETAIL

FLEXIBLE PLASTIC ENVELOPE BONDED TO INTERNAL TITANIUM STRUCTURE

18 MM DIAMETER FOR ATRIUM-VENTRICLE VALVES

15 MM DIAMETER FOR AORTA AND PULMONARY ARTERY VALVES

DETAIL DRAWINGS (FROM PREVIOUS SHEET) BUTTERFLY VALVE, HYDRODYNAMICALLY BALANCED (4 REQ'D PER HEART)

W.F. LAREDO

Bioengineering Plate 8

---

Atlantis — W. F. Laredo

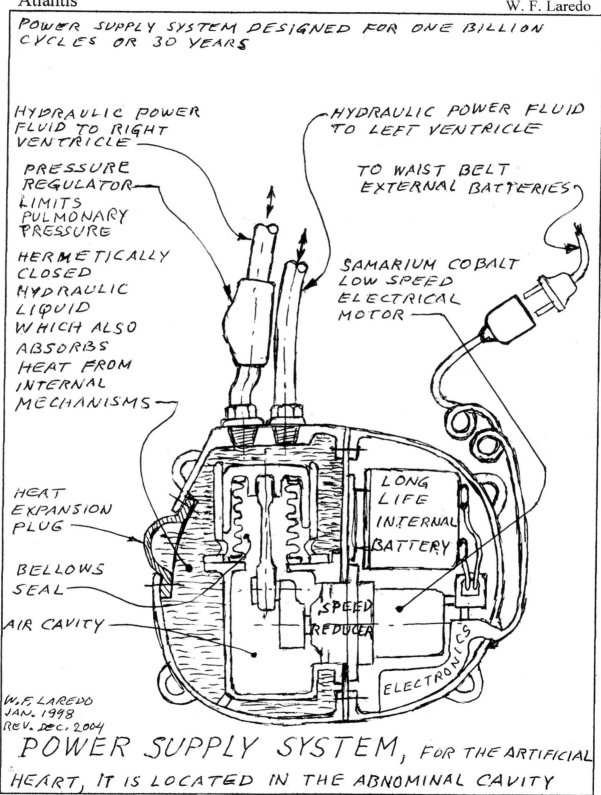

POWER SUPPLY SYSTEM DESIGNED FOR ONE BILLION CYCLES OR 30 YEARS

HYDRAULIC POWER FLUID TO RIGHT VENTRICLE
HYDRAULIC POWER FLUID TO LEFT VENTRICLE
PRESSURE REGULATOR LIMITS PULMONARY PRESSURE
TO WAIST BELT EXTERNAL BATTERIES
HERMETICALLY CLOSED HYDRAULIC LIQUID WHICH ALSO ABSORBS HEAT FROM INTERNAL MECHANISMS
SAMARIUM COBALT LOW SPEED ELECTRICAL MOTOR
HEAT EXPANSION PLUG
LONG LIFE INTERNAL BATTERY
BELLOWS SEAL
SPEED REDUCER
AIR CAVITY
ELECTRONICS

W.F. LAREDO JAN. 1998 REV. DEC. 2004

POWER SUPPLY SYSTEM, FOR THE ARTIFICIAL HEART, IT IS LOCATED IN THE ABNOMINAL CAVITY

Bioengineering Plate 9

# MECHANICAL HEART, PUMPING POWER CALCULATION

70 pulses a minute with cycles of 0.86 seconds.

To simplify calculations assume that blood density and its relative density is equal to that of water, 62.4 lb/cu ft and 1 respectively.

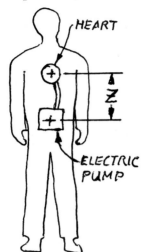

$Z = 15$ in. $= 1.25$ ft

$h_1 =$ Systolic blood pressure of 120 mm of mercury.

$h_2 =$ Occasional blood pressure rise of 50.28 mm of mercury, when artificial sensors detects an state of emergency or emotional state.

$F =$ Force to overcome the stiffness of the deflecting steel diaphragm.

$h_1 = 120$ mm Hg $= 1636.8$ mm water $= 5.37$ ft

$h_2 = 50.28$ mmHg $= 685.8$ mm water $= 2.25$ ft

Head    $H = h_1 + h_2 + Z = 8.87$ ft

Pressure at point A $=$ Head $\times$ Density

   $(8.87$ ft$) \times (62.4$ lb/cu ft$) = 553.5$ lb/sq ft

Ventricle volume $= 78.33$ cu cm
Blood pumped volume (both ventricles)
  $2 (78.33) = 156.66$ cu cm $= .005232$ cu ft
Per min. $0.005232 \times 70 = 0.36624$ cu ft/min
Per sec. $0.36624 / 60 = .0061$ cu ft / sec.

Power $=$ (Pressure $\times$ Volume)$/$t
   $553.5$ lb/sq ft $\times .0061$ cu ft/ sec
   $= 3.38$ lb. ft/sec

Hydraulic HP
   WHP $= 3.38/550 = .0061$
Break HP required for motor,
with a motor-pump efficiency of 0.7
   bHP $= .0061/ 0.7 = .0087$

ADDITIONAL OPERATING POWER TO DEFLECT THE HEART PUMPING DIAPHRAGMS

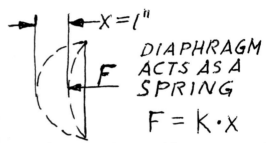

DIAPHRAGM ACTS AS A SPRING

$F = K \cdot X$

70 pulses per minute, with 0.86 sec cycles
$K = 2$ lb/in $= 24$ lb/ft,
average deflection $= 1$ inch

Energy for a cycle of 0.86 sec
$F = k \cdot x = 24$ lb/ft $\times x$

$$\text{Energy} = \int_0^1 F \cdot dx = \int_0^1 k \cdot x \cdot dx = 24 \left[ \frac{x^2}{2} \right]_0^1 = 12 \text{ ft. lb}$$

Energy per minute,   $12 \times 70 = 840$ ft. lb
Energy per second,   $840/60 = 14$ ft. lb
   For 2 springs $= 28$ ft.lb
The diaphragms' springs return most of this energy to the system, assuming the system absorbs only 20 per cent of it.
   Energy $= 0.20 \times 28 = 5.60$ ft. lb/sec
HP spring $= 5.60/550 = 0.010$ HP

Total pump HP $=$ breakHP $+$ HP spring
   $0.87 + 0.010 = 0.0187$ HP
Better use a,

## 0.03 HP  or  17.16 watts
electric motor.     W.F. LAREDO
                    JAN 1997

National Aeronautics and
Space Administration

**Lewis Research Center**
Cleveland, OH 44135-3191

APR 1 7 1998

Attn of:  6000

Mr. Walter F. Laredo
780 Oak Grove Rd
Apt. C-216
Concord, CA 94518-2708

Dear Mr. Laredo:

I have had several members of my staff review your
unsolicited proposal for design of bionic heart pump and for
a reusable Earth-to-Orbit launch vehicle. Obviously, your
proposals in both areas are very detailed, and contain some
thoughtful engineering ideas. I thank you very much for your
interest. The assessment and suggestions follow.

Bionic Heart:

NASA Reviewer:   Joseph P. Veres
Org Code:        2900
Telephone:       (216) 433-2436
E-mail:          joseph.veres@lerc.nasa.gov

The concept has numerous interesting features that appear to
address some fundamental design criteria for artificial heart
pumps. However, there appears to be unresolved mechanical,
as well as biological, issues that need to be addressed by
technology development programs. A summary of the challenges
to the proposed bionic heart concept include the following:

1.  There are many mechanical moving parts in the proposed
    "bionic heart" pumping device. The numerous moving parts
    in this concept may be prone to increased risk of failure
    over time. (Note: other artificial heart pumps that are
    currently under development are simpler in concept, with
    significantly fewer moving parts, and reduced risk of
    failure.)

2.  Long-term lubrication of the motor bearing is not
    addressed in the bionic heart concept. If the motor were
    to use conventional rolling element bearings, they would
    be prone to failure over long periods of time.

3.  The speed reduction gear is also a complex mechanical
    part. The proposal states that the pump pulsations would
    simulate the human heart at 70 beats per minute.

---

2

If the electric motor were to rotate at 3000RPM, the
corresponding speed reduction gear ratio would be about
50:1. A high gear ratio such as this may also have
correspondingly high losses. The gear and its bearings
would need lubrication and a cooling scheme for heat
removal. Similarly, the linkage driving the
reciprocating piston pump has the same lubrication and
cooling requirements for its bearings or bushings.

4.  The special durable metallic alloy of the flexible
    pumping bellows, and the expandable pumping membrane, are
    both materials that need to be developed. The proposal
    refers to this yet to be discovered material as "tireless
    devil" because of its resistance to fatigue.

5.  The system operation of the bionic heart does not
    completely simulate the human heart. The two halves of
    the human heart pump in series; that is, the right side
    pulses while the left side is at rest, and the left side
    pulses while the right side is at rest. The bionic heart
    proposes to pressurize both the right and left ventricles
    simultaneously, and this difference from the operation of
    the human heart may be biologically significant. In
    addition, the left side of the human heart does most of
    the work, creating a pressure rise of approximately 100mm
    of mercury, while the right side creates a 25mm pressure
    rise.

6.  The design of long life mechanical valves that are
    acceptable for blood flow is an area that is currently
    the subject of research in the medical community.
    Movement of the valve may cause damage to the blood
    cells.

7.  Uneven flow swirling and vortices within the large
    cavities of the bionic heart can create areas of stagnant
    flow. The residence time of blood within the pump is a
    known key parameter that is responsible for the onset of
    coagulation. With partially stagnant flow in the
    cavities and bellows, the time the blood is in contact
    with the foreign material increases and triggers the
    blood to coagulate, and in time collect on the internal
    walls.

8.  The proposed "grommet seal" in the human diaphragm muscle
    may be a challenge.

9.  The bio compatibility of all of the materials that are in
    contact with blood is an issue on all blood pump
    development projects. This proposal has a large variety
    of materials that contact the blood, and for each of them
    the bio compatibility issue has to be addressed.

---

3

In closing, Mr. Laredo's proposal has numerous novel concepts
for blood pumps. Some of these concepts appear to be low
risk and can be pursued in a routine design and development
program. However, some of the issues inherent to this
pumping system, such as long life flexible materials and high
potential for blood clotting, need to be addressed by long-
term technology development programs. My suggestion is for
Mr. Laredo to also contact a medical research institution,
such as the Cleveland Clinic or University Hospitals, that
can provide him more insight into the typical rheological
issues associated with blood.

Earth-to-Orbit Launch Vehicle:

Mr. Laredo's recent paper on the World Aerospace Center and
Space Plane concepts contains several very impressive
drawings and clearly indicates that he is aware of many of
the primary engineering issues and concerns associated with
reusable launch vehicles and their supporting infrastructure.
Advancing the longer term state of the art in space
transportation has always been part of the National
Aeronautics and Space Administration's plan for the future
development of space. His concept for enabling single and
two stage to orbit vehicles is generally consistent with
related concepts which NASA Headquarters and Marshall Space
Flight Center (MSFC) are studying under the Reusable Launch
Vehicle (RLV) program.

In particular, the set of nine detailed design drawings was
most impressive. I suggest that Mr. Laredo send a copy of
the proposal to the MSFC. MSFC is NASA's lead center for
Earth-to-Orbit and space propulsion vehicle concepts. NASA
Lewis has been largely devoted to propulsion systems (the
engine), not necessarily the entire vehicle or its supporting
infrastructure. I also recommend sending a copy to NASA
Headquarters, where much of what he is proposing has been in
the evaluation process over the last few years. Both
organizations are better positioned to evaluate and perhaps
act on your concept than the staff at NASA Lewis. Please
contact:

Garry Lyles
NASA Marshall Space Flight Center
Huntsville, AL
Telephone: (205)544-9203
E-mail    garry.lyles@msfc.nasa.gov

John Mankins
NASA Headquarters
Washington, DC
Telephone: (202)358-4659
E-mail:    john.mankins@hq.nasa.gov

---

I would like to make a suggestion to improve Mr. Laredo's
concept. The primary goal of the current major NASA effort
is to explore Earth-to-Orbit concepts that offer the
potential to significantly reduce, by one to two orders of
magnitude, the cost per pound of payload to low Earth orbit.
A comprehensive, total life cycle cost analysis would be a
powerful and essential addition to his work. This should
also include the cost of ground infrastructure, labor-
intensive maintenance, and cost of failure, i.e. replacement
cost. Such an analysis is needed to truly assess the merits
of any reusable infrastructure.

I hope our comments will be taken as constructive criticism
to improve your concepts in both areas. Again, we appreciate
your interest and the effort you expended in these proposals,
and wish you the best in your future endeavors.

Sincerely,

Donald J. Campbell
Director

*NASA'S REVIEW
OF THE ARTIFICIAL
HEART DESIGNED BY
W. F. LAREDO*

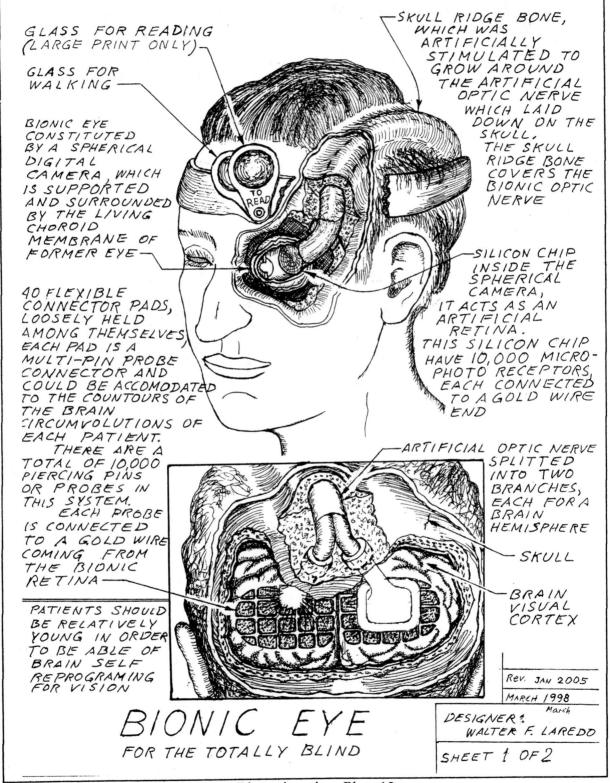

GLASS FOR READING
(LARGE PRINT ONLY)

GLASS FOR
WALKING

BIONIC EYE
CONSTITUTED
BY A SPHERICAL
DIGITAL
CAMERA, WHICH
IS SUPPORTED
AND SURROUNDED
BY THE LIVING
CHOROID
MEMBRANE OF
FORMER EYE

40 FLEXIBLE
CONNECTOR PADS,
LOOSELY HELD
AMONG THEMSELVES
EACH PAD IS A
MULTI-PIN PROBE
CONNECTOR AND
COULD BE ACCOMODATED
TO THE COUNTOURS OF
THE BRAIN
CIRCUMVOLUTIONS OF
EACH PATIENT.
    THERE ARE A
TOTAL OF 10,000
PIERCING PINS
OR PROBES IN
THIS SYSTEM.
    EACH PROBE
IS CONNECTED
TO A GOLD WIRE
COMING FROM
THE BIONIC
RETINA

PATIENTS SHOULD
BE RELATIVELY
YOUNG IN ORDER
TO BE ABLE OF
BRAIN SELF
REPROGRAMING
FOR VISION

TO READ

SKULL RIDGE BONE,
WHICH WAS
ARTIFICIALLY
STIMULATED TO
GROW AROUND
THE ARTIFICIAL
OPTIC NERVE
WHICH LAID
DOWN ON THE
SKULL.
THE SKULL
RIDGE BONE
COVERS THE
BIONIC OPTIC
NERVE

SILICON CHIP
INSIDE THE
SPHERICAL
CAMERA,
IT ACTS AS AN
ARTIFICIAL
RETINA.
THIS SILICON CHIP
HAVE 10,000 MICRO-
PHOTO RECEPTORS,
EACH CONNECTED
TO A GOLD WIRE
END

ARTIFICIAL OPTIC NERVE
SPLITTED
INTO TWO
BRANCHES,
EACH FOR A
BRAIN
HEMISPHERE

SKULL

BRAIN
VISUAL
CORTEX

# BIONIC EYE
## FOR THE TOTALLY BLIND

Rev. JAN 2005

MARCH 1998
                                March
DESIGNER:
WALTER F. LAREDO

SHEET 1 OF 2

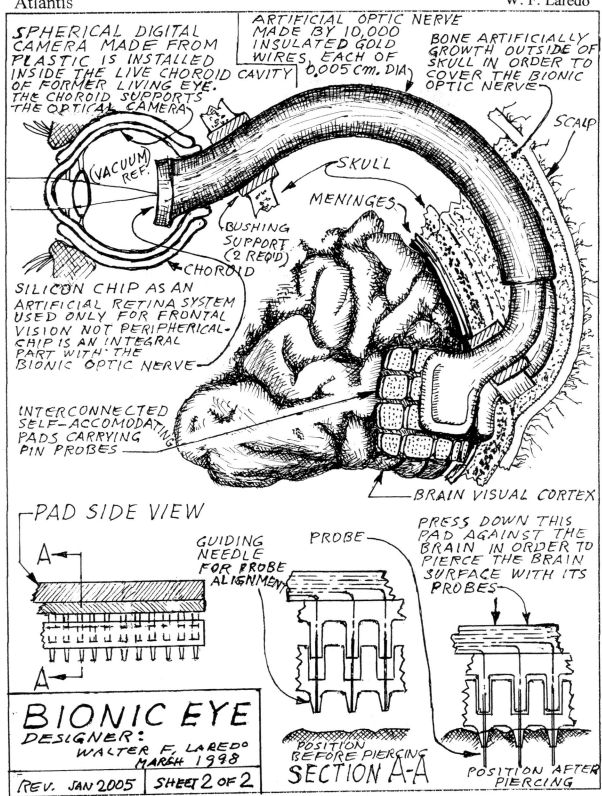

SPHERICAL DIGITAL CAMERA MADE FROM PLASTIC IS INSTALLED INSIDE THE LIVE CHOROID OF FORMER LIVING EYE. THE CHOROID SUPPORTS THE OPTICAL CAMERA

ARTIFICIAL OPTIC NERVE MADE BY 10,000 INSULATED GOLD WIRES, EACH OF 0.005 CM. DIA

BONE ARTIFICIALLY GROWTH OUTSIDE OF SKULL IN ORDER TO COVER THE BIONIC OPTIC NERVE

SCALP

(VACUUM) REF.

CAVITY

SKULL

MENINGES

BUSHING SUPPORT (2 REQ'D)

CHOROID

SILICON CHIP AS AN ARTIFICIAL RETINA SYSTEM USED ONLY FOR FRONTAL VISION NOT PERIPHERICAL- CHIP IS AN INTEGRAL PART WITH THE BIONIC OPTIC NERVE

INTERCONNECTED SELF-ACCOMODATING PADS CARRYING PIN PROBES

BRAIN VISUAL CORTEX

PAD SIDE VIEW

A

A

GUIDING NEEDLE FOR PROBE ALIGNMENT

PROBE

PRESS DOWN THIS PAD AGAINST THE BRAIN IN ORDER TO PIERCE THE BRAIN SURFACE WITH ITS PROBES

BIONIC EYE
DESIGNER:
WALTER F. LAREDO
MARCH 1998

REV. JAN 2005 | SHEET 2 OF 2

POSITION BEFORE PIERCING
SECTION A-A

POSITION AFTER PIERCING

MEDICAL WONDERS IN A GREAT CIVILIZATION.


THE PICTURE SHOWS ONE OF THE SEVERAL OFFICES FROM A FUTURISTIC
HOSPITAL.

OFFICES FROM WHERE SURGICAL OPERATIONS WAS PERFORMED BY
REMOTE CONTROL AND BY LOOKING AT A HUGE TELEVISION SCREEN
THAT OCCUPIED AN ENTIRE WALL, IN THE SCREEN WAS DISPLAYED THE
OPERATION THAT WAS PERFORMED IN THE MAIN ROOM, THE MAIN ROOM
WAS LOCATED AT THE CENTER OF THE BUILDING.
(continues in Plate 15)

Bioengineering  Plate 14

(Continues from Plate 14)

*This case concerns with the reconstruction of a new human being by using the* undamaged head of a person with a total damaged body and the undamaged body of another person with brain dead. Both passengers were the victims of an accident, when a space vehicle crash on the moon, fortunately parts of both persons were compatible between themselves for a major transplant. The operation was performed in a hospital in the moon. The low gravity of the moon helped to reduce body sores due to pressures against the cradle, a person on the moon weights only one sixth of what it weights on Earth.

In the screen is displayed a cross section of the spinal cord from the neck area, the image was enlarged 160 times. In the left upper corner are shown only for size comparison, a needle eye and a pinhead.

The projected picture shows special electromagnetic devices surrounding the spinal cord in the neck area, stimulating the growth of the neurons' axons from the head group of one person unto the tubes of myelin sheaths belonging to the other person body group, where the original axons died and disappeared.

In the same screen are shown the devices for the injection of stem cells ready to transform themselves into neurons. After lying with its respective life support systems for six months on the cradles, both spinal cords got joined and healed and step one was finish.

Next step included a series of operations performed by surgeons with other specialization, as for instance bringing back to its original position the removed vertebra, it was followed with the stitching of minute veins, arteries and other tissues in the neck area. All operations were performed by remote control from several offices where 40 surgeons and 90 nurses got involved in this complex series of surgical procedures, all together lasting for six months. A special long-term anesthesia that doesn't kill brain cells was discovered and used.

Two years of rehabilitation was required allowing enough time for the brain to self reprogram itself, mostly in its motor and sensory areas, compensating the errors of some axons of growing inside wrong sheath tubes.

# SUPPLEMENT II

## ATLANTIS ENGINEERING CHRONICLES

## Contents

### ENGINEERING CHRONICLE No. 1
Technical description of "Atlantis 2" spaceship
including its propulsion system

### ENGINEERING CHRONICLE No. 2
Commuter twin jet airliner for 30 passengers

### ENGINEERING CHRONICLE No. 3
Flying boat aircraft with nuclear propulsion system

# ENGINEERING CHRONICLE No. 1

## TECHNICAL DESCRIPTION OF "ATLANTIS 2" SPACESHIP INCLUDING ITS PROPULSION SYSTEM
(Also see Chapter 14)

The main structural support of the ship was a long heavy hollow shaft as a tube, around which everything else was attached. Near its mid length were mounted a group of huge fat rings like donuts, where the big one counter-rotated with respect to the others. In this way producing enough centrifugal force to act as an artificial force of gravity with a equivalent intensity as that of the moon, enough to make feel people comfortable during the long voyages.

The interior of the hollow shaft was used as an aisle for people, allowing passengers to visit other ship compartments. The main shaft ends were plugged with welded thick disk plates, strong enough to support other external structures as the head and the tail of the vehicle,. That tail called scorpion tail was a light structure, consisting of a truss 250 meters long made of slender bars. The spherical head of the vehicle and its neck was attached at the forward end of the main shaft. The spherical head of the ship, was constituted by three floor full of windows. The upper floor was the observation deck; it had a telescope. The next lower floor oof the same head was the bridge from where Captain Cronus gave his orders, and the third floor below was the dormitory only for the crew on duty. In the spherical head of the ship there was no artificial gravity, because it didn't rotate; for navigation purposes it was fixed with respect to the stars. Captain Cronus and his on-duty crew spent most of their time on the bridge and the living quarters of the sphere, where only trained astronauts could work in that environment of zero gravity.

The rotating donut-shaped structures contained most of the massive components of the ship, included the living quarters for passengers and the off-duty crew, the entertainment and sports rooms, the theater that doubled as a meeting place. The huge rotating donut structures contained the ship's life-support equipment, with air and water recycling systems, the hydroponics gardens, repair shops, laboratories, and one-room hospital. As a partial protection against external radiation, inside each of the fat rings was enclosed a smaller ring, it was as the inner tube of a giant tire, there were the living quarters with the bedrooms. Most of the equipment and accessories surrounded this inner tube. In this design the living quarters were surrounded with enough material thickness that acted as a shield protecting humans from cosmic radiation and occasional sun flares. With this design all bedrooms were kept away from the ship's external walls; another reason not to have real windows but artificial ones.

Because the bridge didn't rotate, and was fixed with respect to the stars, cameras mounted on the bridge transmitted TV images from the universe to the bedroom's faked windows.

For safety reasons, to protect crew and passengers from radiation, the nuclear power group was located away at the tip of the long tail called scorpion tail and behind a semi-spherical radiation shield umbrella.

The nuclear power group was constituted by the small nuclear fission reactors that supplied internal energy for the ship and by the fusion parabolic reactors the main components of the propulsion system that propelled the ship.

## PROPULSION SYSTEM

An hour or so after landing on an icy Saturn moonlet, teams of space workers descended to the surface and were doing their work. Among them was a team operating special equipment, with a sign that read HEAVY WATER SEPARATOR. Indeed, this was very complicated equipment used for the separation and extraction of heavy water from the moonlet's melted ice, then pumped to special tanks inside the ship.

Captain Cronus said, "Once we depart, we will have plenty of time to operate continuously our electrolysis devices, where the heavy water will be separated into its basic elements, deuterium (hydrogen's heavy isotope) and oxygen.

"The oxygen will be stored in aluminum bottles to later produce more breathable atmosphere inside the ship. The deuterium gas will flow into a special machine, where with pulverized lithium, will be synthesized into lithium deuteride, a white powder. In this new form it will be sent into another machine which will encapsulate it into millions of hollow microspheres, or miniature pellets.

"These pellets of lithium deuteride constitute the actual nuclear fuel for the fusion engines of the spaceship, and will be stored in a tank which will contain enough of this fuel to last for the rest of the trip."

The outer shell from each microsphere or pellet was covered with several coats, each from a different substance. The purpose of the pellet's outer coat was to be suspended electromagnetically, at the exact focus point from the parabolic chamber. Once the pellet was suspended at that focus point, several laser beams were fired simultaneously from the protruded ends of crystal rods, arranged around the interior of the parabolic chambers, and the pellet, which was a miniature hydrogen bomb, exploded, producing the necessary thrust that propelled the ship. See the corresponding engineering illustration in the appendix of this book, where it shows a mechanical method of pellet suspension, support that was also vaporized with each explosion.

The miniature factory carried inside the ship continuously produced millions of pellets. The pellets were sent, one by one, into the engine's open chambers for controlled fusion, (nuclear mini explosion). These were not actually chambers; chambers would melt. Instead they were like open gigantic rocket nozzles made from beryllium and coated like a mirror. Actually, they were parabolic reflectors of electromagnetic energy, with a coat that also reflected some neutrons. On the ship's tail were two side-by-side fusion engines looking like parabolic reflectors. In this design, the explosion chamber and the nozzle were integrated into a simple parabolic mirror. Its walls were continuously cooled by a serpentine system with circulating liquid. The explosive fusion reaction form each pellet took place at the focus of each parabolic reflector, and its energy was reflected away from the rear of the ship as a powerful beam, whose momentum effect was the thrust that propelled the ship.

Preliminary design drawings of this interplanetary spaceship are shown in the appendix of this book. In the zone concerning the nuclear fusion engine are shown some blank spaces without drawings. Many details and section views are missing, because I never got that fantastic information to develop it. I am not aware if somebody today already generated the necessary data to design a very small and compact, multi beam laser system, able to ignite each pellet made from lithium deuteride. Anyway, some components of the engine are shown, including a mechanical fuel feeding system and the parabolic nozzles.

By the time a modern spaceship will be entirely designed at the beginning of the twenty first century, probably no fusion engine would be available. So a more practical way would be to mount on this ship a less sophisticated electrical propulsion system. Although inadequate for round trips through the solar system, good enough to allow round trips to Mars, Jupiter and Saturn. The preliminary designs for this modern spaceship are shown in the appendix section of this book. Those drawings shows engine mounting provisions and adapter plate to be use for alternative different propulsion system, from the sophisticated fusion propulsion system, to the more realistic and simpler electric propulsion system. This last may prove satisfactory for round trips to Mars.

# ENGINEERING CHRONICLE No. 2

## COMMUTER TWIN JET AIRLINER FOR 30 PASSENGERS

PROJECT PERFORMED BY A GROUP OF TALENTED
HIGH SCHOOL STUDENTS
(See also Chapter 15)

The professor of the class acted as the chief project engineer. He was assisted by seven students, each student working in his own specialty and with his own computer. In order to stimulate the self-confidence of these youths, each got a temporary title of design engineer.

Their desks were numbered 1 through 7.

Prior to the initiation of the project, an airliner executive gave to the professor a list with all the desired characteristics and requirements the aircraft design should have, including performance and weights. On the first day of work the professor gave this package full of information to the student at desk number 1, whose title was of configuration engineer, who with the help of the professor became the architect for this aircraft. He was responsible to design the initial concept and the preliminary layouts and the drawings of the general arrangement of the aircraft, showing the entire aircraft but without too much detail.

In this preliminary design was shown the top, the side, the front view and the cross sections of the airplane. In another set of drawings was shown the aircraft interior including the plan view of the passengers seating arrangement, the cockpit arrangement, the cargo compartments, the doors, windows, the locations of toilets, galleys, engines, fuel tanks, and landing gear.

Several blueprint copies from this original set of plans created by student at desk number one, was made and distributed to his other six colleagues. Each of them would use these copies to revise, to correct and as guidance for further development adding more details in the field of his or hers expertise.

The first design cycle for this aircraft was completed, but it was not perfect yet.

The student at desk number two, whose specialty was aerodynamics and aerodynamic stability and control, analyzed many parameters for several flight conditions and speeds involving lift and drag. With this analysis and calculations, he found some mistakes in the design of the aircraft, then he made the required corrections of the external shape of the vehicle to its proper aerodynamic shape.

The student at desk number three acted as the structural engineer and designed the whole internal structure of the wings, body, tail and some mechanical systems and with the help of his computer he performed the calculations for the total structural analysis of the vehicle.

The student at desk number four, working as mechanical engineer, designed the landing gear, flap mechanisms, door locking systems, and various other mechanical systems inside the aircraft structure.

The student at desk number five, working as mechanical and propulsion engineer was in charge of choosing the type of engine to be purchased for this aircraft. He did the drawings for the fuel system and the installation of the propulsion system, including the design for the engine mountings, the engine cowlings and the installation of the oil coolers.

The student at desk number six worked as a chemist and as material properties specialist, providing technical support, consultation, and the required materials data including metals, alloys, plastics and composites to his colleagues.

At desk number seven was a student with two specialties, an Electrical and electronics engineer.

With each new review and corrections from the previous cycle started a new cycle. The project circulated again in between these students, becoming more refined. Then after two or more cycles of refinements, the project became perfect and was released. At this point the project was finish, the students had nothing else to do and left. However the student at desk number one, the architect of the project was re-assigned and got a different task much simpler than before, assigned to create a comfortable and aesthetic interior design of the passenger's cabin, which should be pleasant to the eye.

The project developed by these kids was completed. The design including all the construction drawings for the new commuter jet were shipped to the manufacturers in order to build the first two prototype aircraft, to be tested in flight for hundreds of hours. After passing all flying tests, the aircraft was certified to get mass produce for the airline. Two months later these seven students got their high school diploma and in addition, after the completion of the aircraft project, they received an aeronautical certificate and additional school credits, a useful practical engineering experience, and enough money to pay their entire career at the Atlantis University.

# ENGINEERING CHRONICLE No. 3

## FLYING BOAT AIRCRAFT WITH NUCLEAR PROPULSION

### AIR CARGO TRANSPORT, WITH ENOUGH NUCLEAR FUEL FOR TEN YEARS OF CONTINUOS OPERATION BEFORE IT GETS REFUELED AGAIN
(Also see Chapter 15)

Flying monsters, weighing hundreds of tons, were actually flying cargo boats. Flying boats able to fly with its nuclear propulsion for more than ten years of without the need of getting refueled. Aircraft called "geese" because of their canard shape. The vehicle had a long, thick hollow neck used as the compartment for cargo and passengers. The cockpit was at the head of the bird, and its nuclear engines were located inside its massive rear.

The principal consideration for the development of this aircraft was the extra heavy protective shielding system against radiation. Which was a cover used to protect the environment from the nuclear reactor radiation, it was a spherical container wrapped around the nuclear reactor, the outer case of the container was a thick lead shield and the inner case made from a thin reflective material. But because this kind of shielding would be too heavy, the airplane would not be able to fly.

The solution to reduce shielding weight was by using a partial shield container, the forward part of this spherical container would have full thickness walls, while the rear half should have only one-fourth the original thickness. The front part of the container could be compared with a thick umbrella, blocking the radiation mostly in the forward direction, such as the pilot's cockpit, the passenger cabin, and most equipment systems.

When this sea aircraft was parked in a pier, it was forbidden to walk close to its rear where the radioactive nuclear engines were located. After its arrival, to dock, the aircraft was pushed in reverse by tugboats, until its protruding rear end could enter and hide in a hole on the 20-foot thick concrete wall, protruding up from the waters. The external surface of the concrete wall was covered with lead to protect people and the environment from radiation. Aircraft built in Atlantis times, when the Earth population was small, and nobody objected to the construction of nuclear projects. This was in a time when pollution, including nuclear, was unnoticeable in affecting the environment.

For long trips, this aircraft flew not higher than 300 feet above the ocean, because the aircraft used to descend every thirty minutes, barely touching the surface of the ocean for few seconds in order to scoop enough water to load its water tank with seawater. In order to condense the clean steam exhaust of the turbines, some of the aircraft condensers were exposed to the free air stream. To cool the condensers, seawater was sprayed into them. This water was lost into the atmosphere. There was no reason to recycle it, because of the excessive weight of this system. Instead, to recuperate the lost water, periodically the aircraft descended close to the sea surface to scoop some water.

The clean steam from the closed circuit, after passing by the turbines, was condensed and brought back to the water system to be re-used to circulated again by the nuclear reactor and converted into the steam that moved the turbines.

# APPENDIX

## ENGINEERING DRAWINGS AND DESIGNS

In this appendix are displayed real engineering projects, which development was inspired in the dreams and tales of semi-utopian advanced civilizations including legendary Atlantis.

This is a pragmatic section of the book where dreams and dreamers are no longer considered.

This section is strictly dedicated to expose the preliminary designs of real advanced engineering projects, in which development was used the laws of physics and the latest-state-of-the-art in technology.

Those legendary science wonders, mentioned through the book, inspired the following preliminary designs for real engineering projects.

Through proper research, the preliminary designs listed below could be use as a guideline for further development of the same projects by the aerospace industry and the space agencies.

# LIST OF ENGINEERING PLATES
## ENGINEERING DRAWINGS AND DESIGNS

## CONTENTS

ENGINEERING PROJECTS
INSPIRED IN THE TALES
AND IN THE DREAMS OF
LEGENDARY ATLANTIS

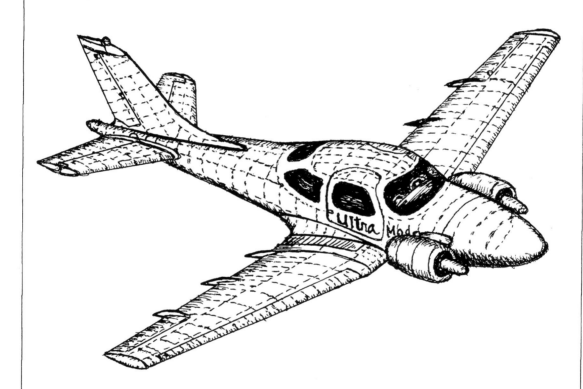

# THE MOST SOPHISTICATED SMALL PRESSURIZED JET OF THE WORLD

ATLANTIS, ADVANCED ENGINEERING PROJECTS

Name of project:
## "ULTRA MODERN" AIRCRAFT

| Designer and builder: | WALTER F. LAREDO | Date: |
| --- | --- | --- |
| Drawing Number: 800 SERIES | | Sheet 1 of 24 |

While working in the Structural Engineering Department of McDonnell Douglas Corp., where the Douglas DC-10 transport was developed, learned to design long life airframe structures with good fatigue resistance and applied to big jets. Then one day decided to design and build his own miniature executive aircraft named "ULTRA MODERN", although the size of a small Cessna its structure is much more sophisticated.

## "ULTRA MODERN " AIRCRAFT, A DREAM FOR THE SPORTLY RICH PILOT

An expensive leisure private plane, which cockpit surrounded with windows all around and with modern instruments is for 2 people, it resembles the cabin of a small sport car.

It is also a STOL aircraft for short takeoff and short landing as most big birds do. For landings or takeoffs could use grass fields or short dirt runways. Ideal private plane for picnics and camping, and because of its long range, ideal for long trips, safaris, and vacations to different places of the world, from the hot deserts to the polar caps regions.

It cruises at high altitude of around 36,000 feet, the cabin's structure and its pressure bulkheads are designed for pressurization, including the double pane windows and the two doors, each door with a double hinge and four sliding safe locks.

A special feature of this aircraft is the foldable wings for towing and easy storage. The wing box structure is also an integral fuel tank of great capacity. The span of the horizontal stabilizer was established in order its tips should clear by one inch a single car garage door for storage.

For short takeoffs and landings the wings are provided with double slotted flaps and with wing leading edge slats, all them similar to the Boeing 747 but in miniature.

The structure of this aircraft is so sophisticated that to build it will take the same number of man hours than to build an average size executive aircraft.

The aluminum structure is designed for long life span (30 years), made by a large number of components, each extremely light, highly elaborated and good against fatigue.

## CHARACTERISTICS AND PERFORMANCE
### GENERAL DESCRIPTION:

High performance STOL (Short Takeoff, and Landing) aircraft. Takeoff under 560 ft over 50 ft obstacle, pressurized for a service ceiling of 37,000 ft., and a speed of Mach 0.5 (332 mph) at 36,000 ft. with a range near to 800 miles.

Sophisticated structure, Very light but super strong at flight, designed for 50, 000 cycles (flights).

Wings are easy to fold, whenever fuel contained in each is less than 11 gallons.

The inboard constant section of the wing have a Supercritical NASA airfoil GA (W)-1, while the outboard trapezoidal section have a constant transition airfoil

| "ULTRA MODERN" AIRCRAFT | | |
|---|---|---|
| Designer and builder: WALTER F. LAREDO | | |
| Drawing Number: 800 series | | Sheet 2 of 24 |

between NASA GA (W)-1 and NACA 4412.

The NASA GA (W)-1 is a laminar flow and low drag airfoil. Because this airfoil is thicker than ordinary ones, the wing contains more fuel, also for a thicker wing the structural weight would be lighter than for a thin one, subject to the same loads.

## POWERPLANT

Turbojet engine, 2 required
Designer: WALTER F. LAREDO
Power output per engine, sea level, static, standard day

| | |
|---|---|
| Takeoff Thrust (lb.) | 326 |
| Max. Continuous Thrust (lb.) | 310 |
| Max. Cruise Thrust (lb.) | 290 |
| 75 % Max. Continuous (lb.) | 233 |
| Max. Cruise Thrust (lb.) | |
| at 36.089 ft. Mach 0.45 | 83 |

Fuel consumption per engine:

| | |
|---|---|
| Max Cruise, standard day, Sea level, static (lb./hr) | 184 |
| Max Cruise, at 35,000 ft., Standard day (lb./hr) | 98 |

Mechanical Speed limits:

| | |
|---|---|
| Spool speed (RPM) | 50,000 |
| Exhaust Gas temperature limit at Takeoff | 1090 deg. F |

Weight                    88 lb.
Power/ Weight Ratio        3.70 : 1
Fuels:        JP-4, JP-5, Jet A
Oils:         Mil-L-7808, Mil-L-23699
              Maximum oil consumption  0.10 pt/hr

## AIRCRAFT DIMENSIONS

| | |
|---|---|
| Overall length, ft. | 20' 8" |
| Height, ft. | 7' 1" |
| Seating Capacity | 2 |
| Cabin Door, h x w, in. | 38 x 29 |
| Headroom, sidewise front, in. | 35 |
| Legroom, front, in | 48 |
| Hiproom, front, in. | 40.5 |
| Elbow to elbow room front, in. | 41 |
| Baggage Capacity, lb | 100 |
| Size, in. | 24x24x30 |
| If air conditioning is removed, in. | 36x30x30 |
| Wheel base, in. | 79 |
| Thread, in. C/L Tires | 72 |

---

## "ULTRA MODERN" AIRCRAFT

Designer and builder: WALTER F. LAREDO

| Drawing Number: | 800 series | Sheet 3 of 24 |
|---|---|---|

| | |
|---|---|
| Main tire size, in. | 6.00 x 6 |
| Nose tire size, in | 5.00 x 5 |

## DESIGN DATA AND WEIGHTS

| | |
|---|---|
| Empty weight, lb. | 1150 |
| Useful load, lb. (payload plus fuel) | 900 |
| Gross weight, lb. | 2050 |
| G Limit Load, pos. | 7 (semi-aerobatic) |
| Neg. | 5 |
| Datum station | Perimeter of Fwd. Pressure Bulkhead |
| C.G. Limits, fore, in. | 35.50 |
| aft, in. | 39.00 |

## CONTROL SURFACES

| | |
|---|---|
| Aileron area, sq. ft. | 6.8 |
| Up deflection, degrees. | 25 |
| Down deflection, degrees. | 20 |
| Elevator area, sq.ft. | 6 |
| Up deflection, degrees. | 30 |
| Down deflection, degrees. | 25 |
| Horizontal stabilizer, sq. ft. | 9.3 |
| Up incidence travel, degrees | 5 |
| Down incidence travel, degrees | 8 |
| Rudder area, sq. ft. | 3.4 |
| Deflection, L & R, degrees | 30 |
| Slat, wing leading edge | most of the span |
| Double slotted flap, area, sq. ft. | 17 |
| No of positions | variable in between the two following positions |
| Takeoff setting, deg. | 30 |
| Landing setting, deg. | 45 |

## SYSTEMS OPERATION

| | |
|---|---|
| Double slotted flaps and leading edge slat | Electric |
| Oleopneumatic landing gear, retractable | Electric & manual (backup) |
| Brakes | Hydraulic |
| Air conditioning | Electric |
| Pressurization | Bleed air from engine compressor |
| PSI differential | 7.0 |

## FUEL SYSTEM

| | |
|---|---|
| Capacity, main tanks (standard) gal. | 75 |
| With auxiliary tanks, (over-gross-weight aircraft, requires long runway for takeoff, no landing is permitted for this weight condition) gal. | 104 |

## "ULTRA MODERN" AIRCRAFT

Designer and builder: WALTER F. LAREDO

| Drawing Number: | 800 series | sheet 4 of 24 |
|---|---|---|

## WING

| | |
|---|---|
| Wing loading, lb/sq ft | 21.23 |
| Wing Airfoil, section of constant chord | Supercritical NASA GA(W)-1 |
| Wing Airfoil, outboard trapezoidal section | Constant transition Airfoil between Between NASA GAW-1 and NACA 4412 |
| Airfoil, wing tip | NACA 4412 |
| Incidence angle, degrees | 2.5 |
| Dihedral, degrees | 5 |
| Wingspan, ft. | 30 |
| Wing Area, sq. ft. | 96.57 |
| Wing Chord, root, in. | 42 |
| Aspect Ratio | 9.32 |
| MAC, in. | 38.6 |

## PERFORMANCE

| | |
|---|---|
| Service ceiling, ft | 37000 |
| Glide ratio (flaps retracted) | 10.2 |
| Takeoff roll, ft. | 330 |
| Over 50 ft. | 650 |
| Landing roll, ft. | 310 |
| Over 50 ft. | 603 |

## SPEEDS

| | |
|---|---|
| Normal operating at 36,000 ft, mph | 332 |
| Economy cruising at 36,000 ft, mph | 301 |
| Max. Speed to extend flaps, IAS, mph | 120 |
| Max. Speed to extend gear, IAS, mph | 130 |
| Slow flight, IAS, mph (flaps and slat extended) | 35 |
| Best Rate of Climb, IAS, at sea level, ft/min | 1610 |
| Liftoff, IAS, mph | 40 |
| Touchdown, IAS, mph | 35 |
| Stall, flaps down, slat extended, IAS, mph | 30 |

## RANGE  (with no reserve)

| | |
|---|---|
| With only main tanks, at 36,089 ft. and Mach 0.45, miles | 794 |
| With main and auxiliary tanks, at 36,089 ft. and Mach 0.45 | 1100 |

## "ULTRA MODERN" AIRCRAFT

Designer and builder:  WALTER F. LAREDO

Drawing Number:  **800** series          Sheet 5 of *24*

TOWING VIEW OF THE "ULTRA MODERN"

FAA Inspections:
During the various steps of the structural construction for the "ULTRA MODERN"
aircraft and previous to the closure of each aerodynamic surface, it was inspected and
approved by the inspectors of the Federal Aviation Administration of The United States,
Long Beach branch, CA.

The construction of this aircraft stopped, after the builder injured his left arm in a traffic
accident.  In the aerospace industry, usually two specialists are required to do the
riveting, but for the rare case that there is only one, this person must use both of his hands
for a precise riveting with conventional rivets.  Grabbing simultaneously the pneumatic
riveter with the right hand and the bucking bar with the other.

## "ULTRA MODERN" AIRCRAFT

Designer and builder:   WALTER F. LAREDO

Drawing Number:      800   series                    Sheet  6  of  24

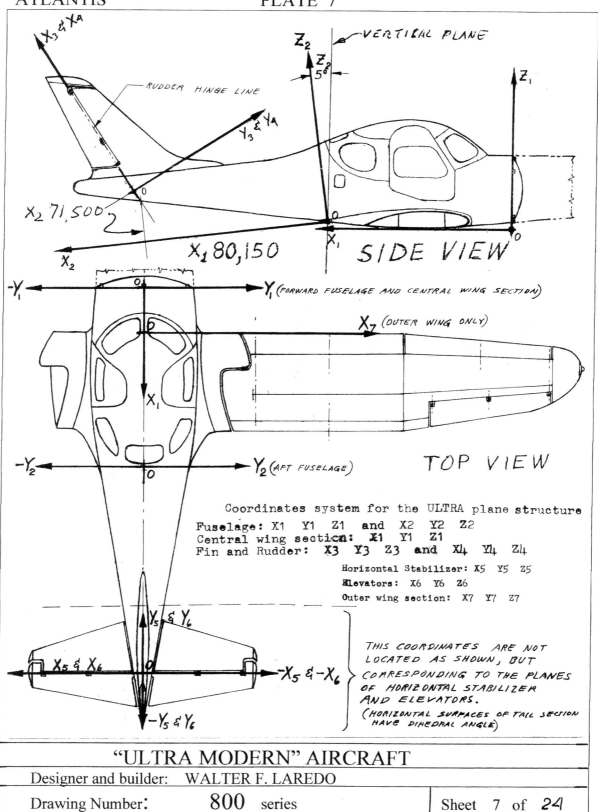

VERTICAL PLANE

RUDDER HINGE LINE

SIDE VIEW

$-Y_1$    $Y_1$ (FORWARD FUSELAGE AND CENTRAL WING SECTION)

$X_7$ (OUTER WING ONLY)

$-Y_2$    $Y_2$ (AFT FUSELAGE)

TOP VIEW

Coordinates system for the ULTRA plane structure
Fuselage: X1  Y1  Z1  and  X2  Y2  Z2
Central wing section:  X1  Y1  Z1
Fin and Rudder:  X3  Y3  Z3  and  X4  Y4  Z4

Horizontal Stabilizer: X5  Y5  Z5
Elevators:  X6  Y6  Z6
Outer wing section:  X7  Y7  Z7

THIS COORDINATES ARE NOT
LOCATED AS SHOWN, BUT
CORRESPONDING TO THE PLANES
OF HORIZONTAL STABILIZER
AND ELEVATORS.
(HORIZONTAL SURFACES OF TAIL SECTION
HAVE DIHEDRAL ANGLE)

## "ULTRA MODERN" AIRCRAFT

Designer and builder:   WALTER F. LAREDO

Drawing Number:    800   series      Sheet 7 of 24

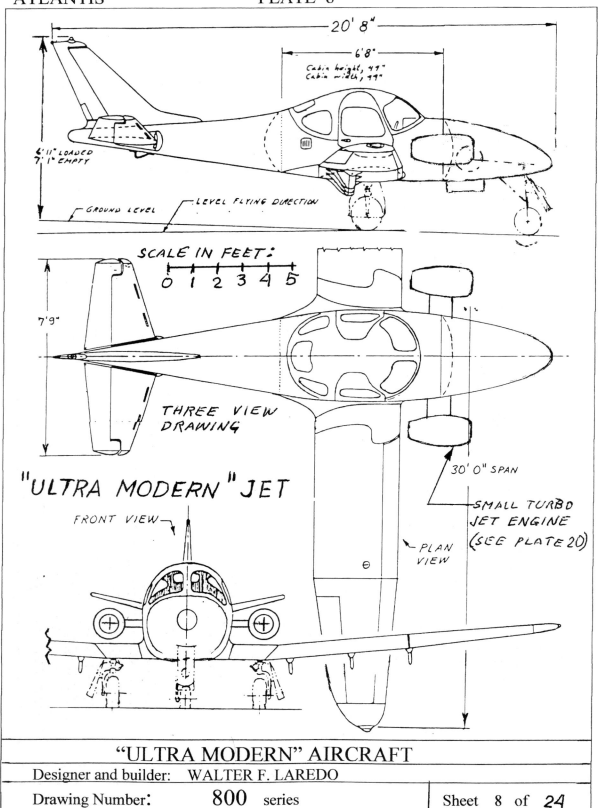

20' 8"

6' 8"

Cabin height, 49"
Cabin width, 49"

6' 11" LOADED
7' 1" EMPTY

GROUND LEVEL

LEVEL FLYING DIRECTION

SCALE IN FEET:

0 1 2 3 4 5

7' 9"

THREE VIEW DRAWING

"ULTRA MODERN" JET

FRONT VIEW

30' 0" SPAN

SMALL TURBO JET ENGINE (SEE PLATE 20)

PLAN VIEW

"ULTRA MODERN" AIRCRAFT

Designer and builder:   WALTER F. LAREDO

Drawing Number:        800   series

Sheet  8  of  24

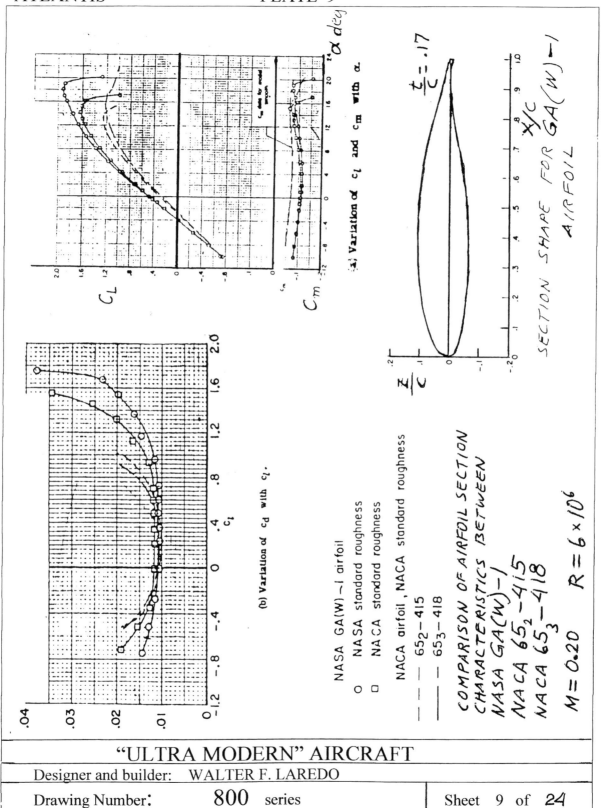

(a) Variation of $c_l$ and $c_m$ with $\alpha$.

(b) Variation of $c_d$ with $c_l$.

$\frac{t}{c} = .17$

SECTION SHAPE FOR GA(W)—1 AIRFOIL

NASA GA(W)—1 airfoil
o   NASA standard roughness
□   NACA standard roughness

NACA airfoil, NACA standard roughness

— — —   $65_2$—415
—  —   $65_3$—418

COMPARISON OF AIRFOIL SECTION
CHARACTERISTICS BETWEEN
NASA GA(W)—1
NACA $65_2$—415
NACA $65_3$—418
$M = 0.20$　　$R = 6 \times 10^6$

## "ULTRA MODERN" AIRCRAFT

Designer and builder:　WALTER F. LAREDO

| Drawing Number: | 800 series | Sheet 9 of 24 |

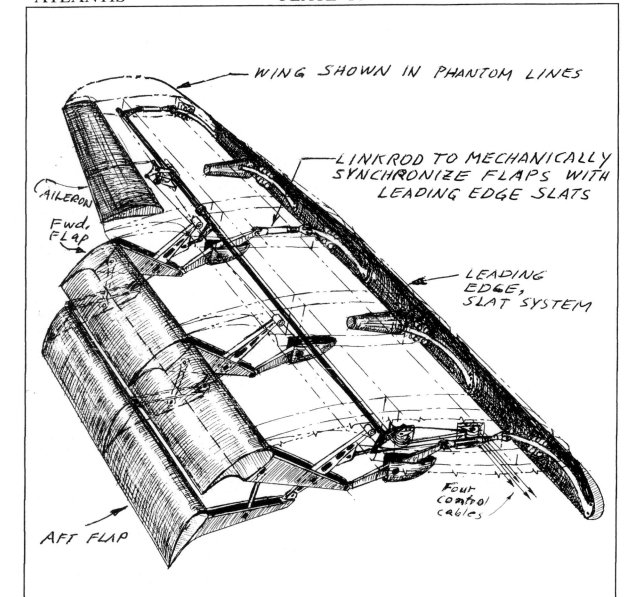

WING SHOWN IN PHANTOM LINES

LINKROD TO MECHANICALLY SYNCHRONIZE FLAPS WITH LEADING EDGE SLATS

LEADING EDGE, SLAT SYSTEM

AILERON

Fwd. FLAP

Four control cables

AFT FLAP

MECHANISM OF FLAPS AND SLATS
SHOWN DEPLOYED

## "ULTRA MODERN" AIRCRAFT

Designer and builder:   WALTER F. LAREDO

| Drawing Number: | 800 series | Sheet 10 of 24 |

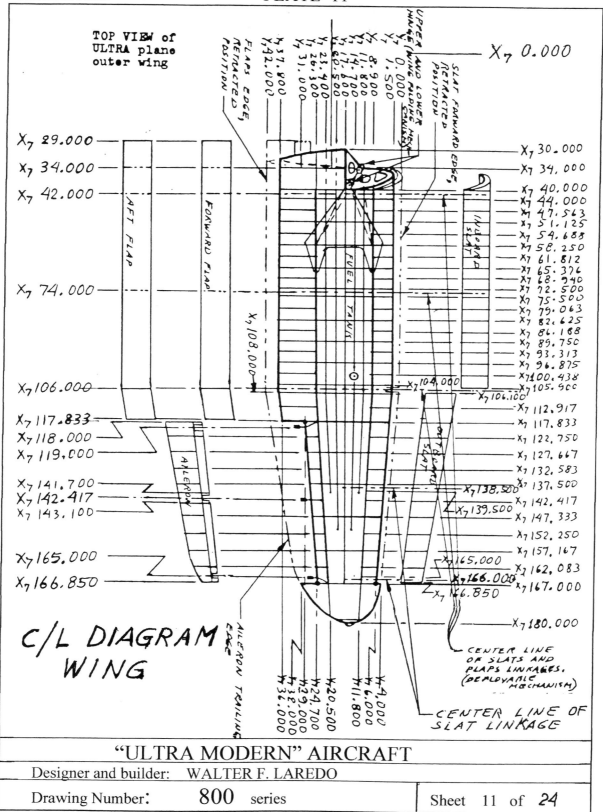

TOP VIEW of
ULTRA plane
outer wing

C/L DIAGRAM
WING

**"ULTRA MODERN" AIRCRAFT**

Designer and builder:   WALTER F. LAREDO

Drawing Number:   **800**  series

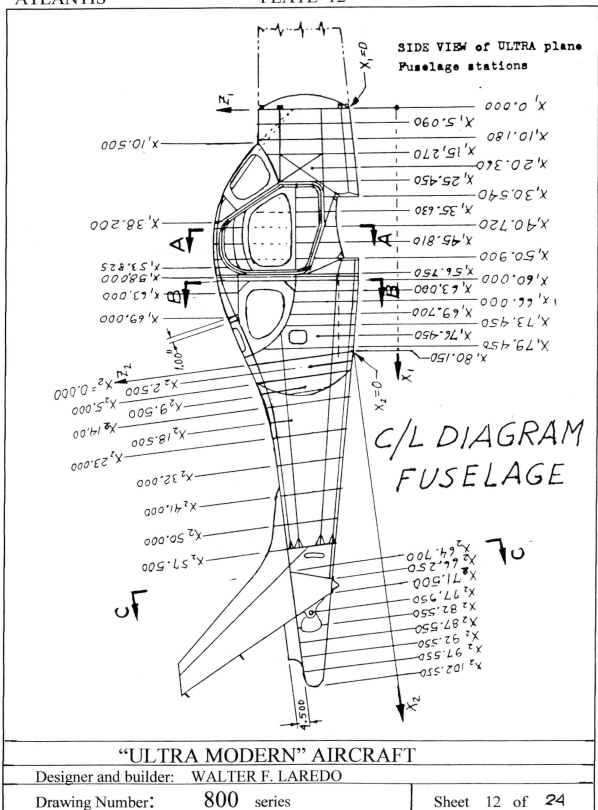

SIDE VIEW of ULTRA plane
Fuselage stations

C/L DIAGRAM
FUSELAGE

---

## "ULTRA MODERN" AIRCRAFT

Designer and builder:  WALTER F. LAREDO

| Drawing Number: | 800 series | Sheet 12 of 24 |

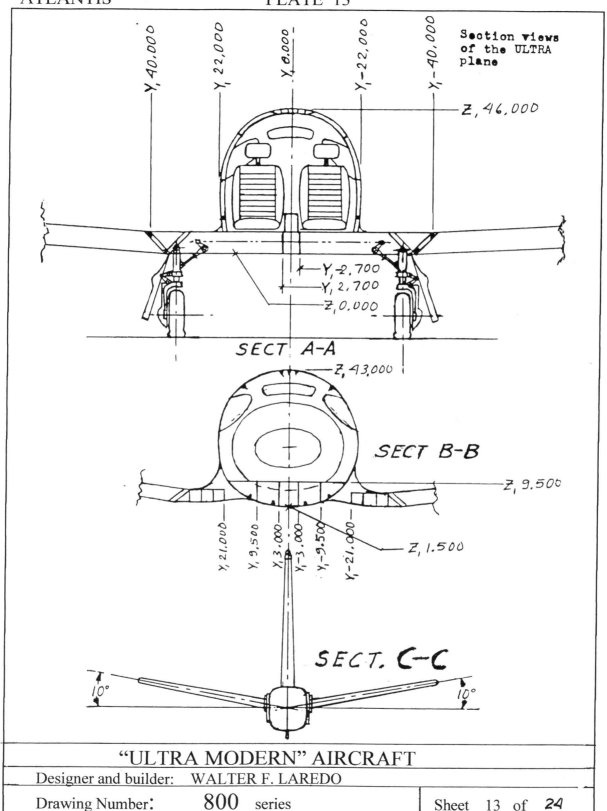

Section views
of the ULTRA
plane

$Y, 40.000$

$Y, 22.000$

$Y, 0.000$

$Y, -22.000$

$Y, -40.000$

$Z, 46.000$

$Y, -2.700$

$Y, 2.700$

$Z, 0.000$

SECT A-A

$Z, 43.000$

SECT B-B

$Z, 9.500$

$Y, 21.000$

$Y, 9.500$

$Y, 3.000$

$Y, -3.000$

$Y, -9.500$

$Y, -21.000$

$Z, 1.500$

SECT. C-C

10°        10°

## "ULTRA MODERN" AIRCRAFT

Designer and builder:    WALTER F. LAREDO

Drawing Number:    800  series

Sheet  13  of  24

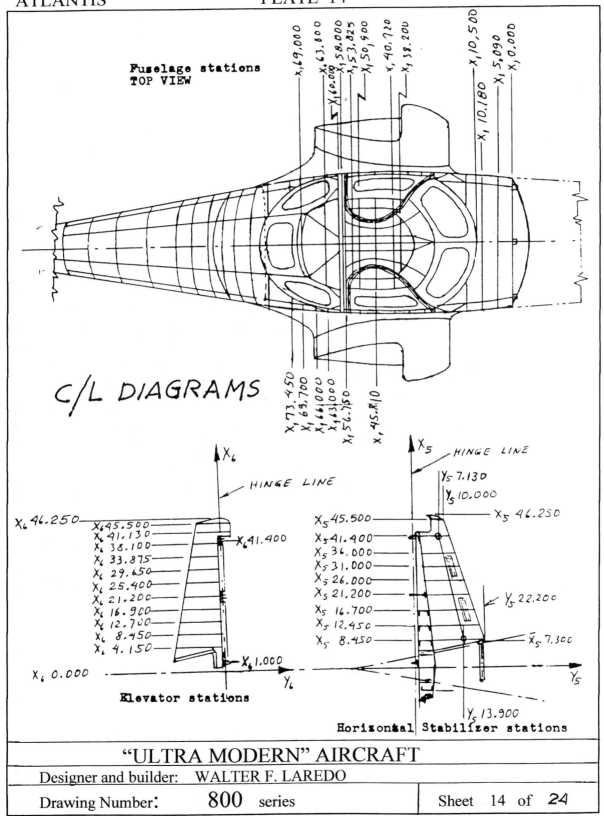

Fuselage stations
TOP VIEW

$x_1\,69.000$
$x_1\,63.600$
$x_1\,58.000$
$x_1\,60.000$
$x_1\,53.825$
$x_1\,50.900$
$x_1\,40.720$
$x_1\,38.200$
$x_1\,10.500$
$x_1\,10.180$
$x_1\,5.090$
$x_1\,0.000$

C/L DIAGRAMS

$x_1\,73.450$
$x_1\,69.700$
$x_1\,66.000$
$x_1\,63.000$
$x_1\,56.750$
$x_1\,45.810$

$X_6$

HINGE LINE

$x_6\,46.250$
$x_6\,45.500$
$x_6\,41.130$
$x_6\,38.100$
$x_6\,33.875$
$x_6\,29.650$
$x_6\,25.400$
$x_6\,21.200$
$x_6\,16.900$
$x_6\,12.700$
$x_6\,8.450$
$x_6\,4.150$
$x_6\,0.000$

$x_6\,41.400$

$X_6\,1.000$

$Y_6$

**Elevator stations**

$X_5$

HINGE LINE

$Y_5\,7.130$
$Y_5\,10.000$

$X_5\,45.500$
$X_5\,41.400$
$X_5\,36.000$
$X_5\,31.000$
$X_5\,26.000$
$X_5\,21.200$
$X_5\,16.700$
$X_5\,12.450$
$X_5\,8.450$

$X_5\,46.250$

$Y_5\,22.200$

$\bar{X}_5\,7.300$

$Y_5$

$Y_5\,13.900$

**Horizontal Stabilizer stations**

## "ULTRA MODERN" AIRCRAFT

Designer and builder:  WALTER F. LAREDO

Drawing Number:  **800**  series           Sheet  14  of  **24**

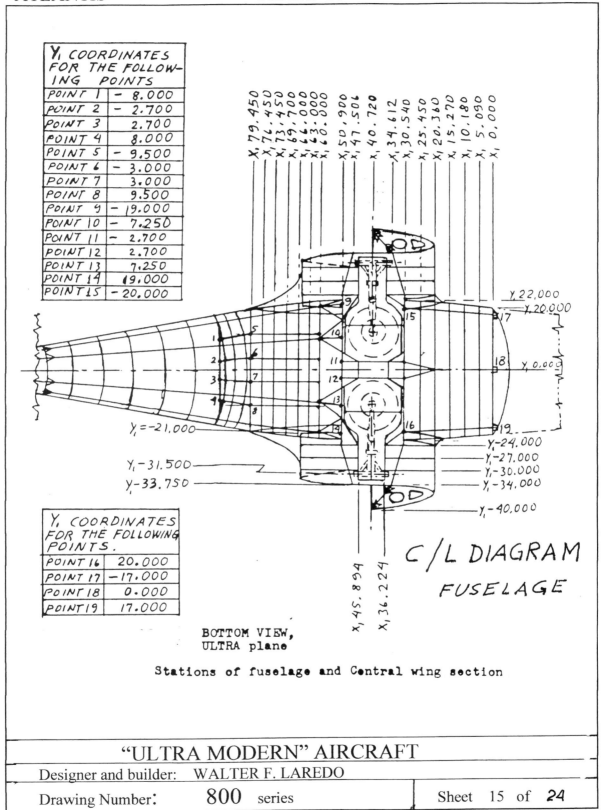

Y₁ COORDINATES FOR THE FOLLOWING POINTS

| POINT 1 | − 8.000 |
|---|---|
| POINT 2 | − 2.700 |
| POINT 3 | 2.700 |
| POINT 4 | 8.000 |
| POINT 5 | − 9.500 |
| POINT 6 | − 3.000 |
| POINT 7 | 3.000 |
| POINT 8 | 9.500 |
| POINT 9 | − 19.000 |
| POINT 10 | − 7.250 |
| POINT 11 | − 2.700 |
| POINT 12 | 2.700 |
| POINT 13 | 7.250 |
| POINT 14 | 19.000 |
| POINT 15 | − 20.000 |

Y₁ COORDINATES FOR THE FOLLOWING POINTS.

| POINT 16 | 20.000 |
|---|---|
| POINT 17 | −17.000 |
| POINT 18 | 0.000 |
| POINT 19 | 17.000 |

C/L DIAGRAM
FUSELAGE

BOTTOM VIEW, ULTRA plane

Stations of fuselage and Central wing section

## "ULTRA MODERN" AIRCRAFT

Designer and builder:   WALTER F. LAREDO

Drawing Number:   800   series          Sheet   15  of  24

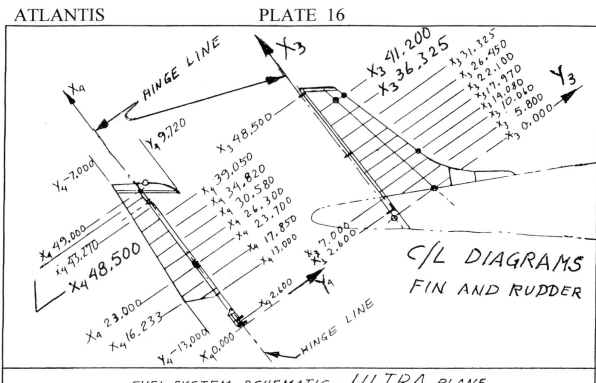

C/L DIAGRAMS
FIN AND RUDDER

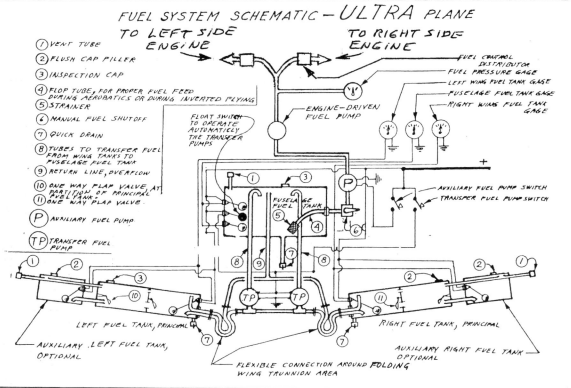

FUEL SYSTEM SCHEMATIC—ULTRA PLANE

TO LEFT SIDE ENGINE

TO RIGHT SIDE ENGINE

① VENT TUBE
② FLUSH CAP FILLER
③ INSPECTION CAP
④ FLOP TUBE, FOR PROPER FUEL FEED DURING AEROBATICS OR DURING INVERTED FLYING
⑤ STRAINER
⑥ MANUAL FUEL SHUTOFF
⑦ QUICK DRAIN
⑧ TUBES TO TRANSFER FUEL FROM WING TANKS TO FUSELAGE FUEL TANK
⑨ RETURN LINE, OVERFLOW
⑩ ONE WAY FLAP VALVE, AT PARTITION OF PRINCIPAL FUEL TANK.
⑪ ONE WAY FLAP VALVE.
Ⓟ AUXILIARY FUEL PUMP.
Ⓣⓟ TRANSFER FUEL PUMP

FLOAT SWITCH TO OPERATE AUTOMATICLY THE TRANSFER PUMPS

ENGINE—DRIVEN FUEL PUMP

FUSELAGE FUEL TANK

FUEL CONTROL DISTRIBUTOR
FUEL PRESSURE GAGE
LEFT WING FUEL TANK GAGE
FUSELAGE FUEL TANK GAGE
RIGHT WING FUEL TANK GAGE

AUXILIARY FUEL PUMP SWITCH
TRANSFER FUEL PUMP SWITCH

LEFT FUEL TANK, PRINCIPAL
RIGHT FUEL TANK, PRINCIPAL
AUXILIARY LEFT FUEL TANK, OPTIONAL
AUXILIARY RIGHT FUEL TANK OPTIONAL
FLEXIBLE CONNECTION AROUND FOLDING WING TRUNNION AREA

## "ULTRA MODERN" AIRCRAFT

Designer and builder:  WALTER F. LAREDO

Drawing Number:  **800** series

Sheet 16 of **24**

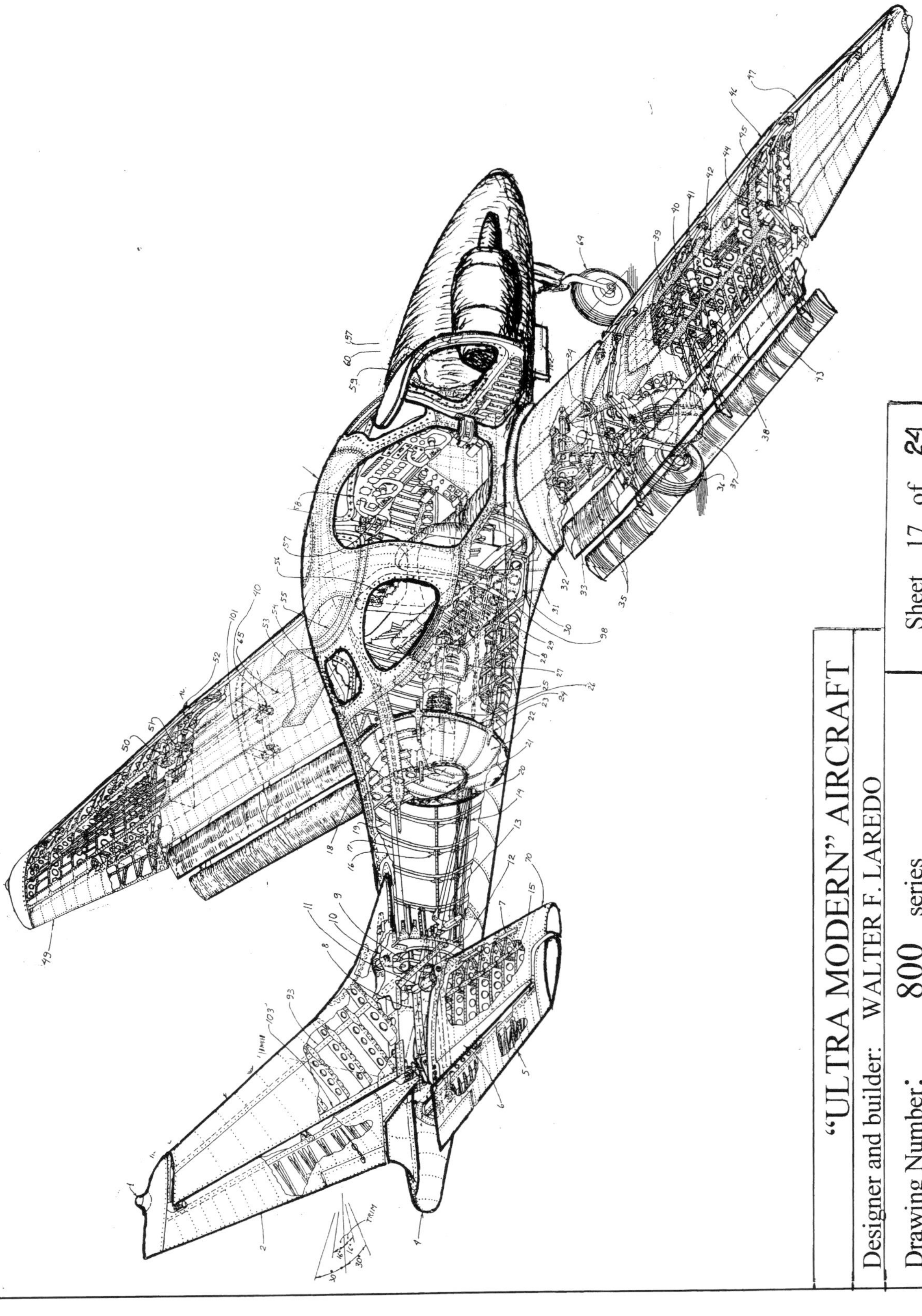

"ULTRA MODERN" AIRCRAFT

Designer and builder: WALTER F. LAREDO

Drawing Number: 800 series

Sheet 17 of 24

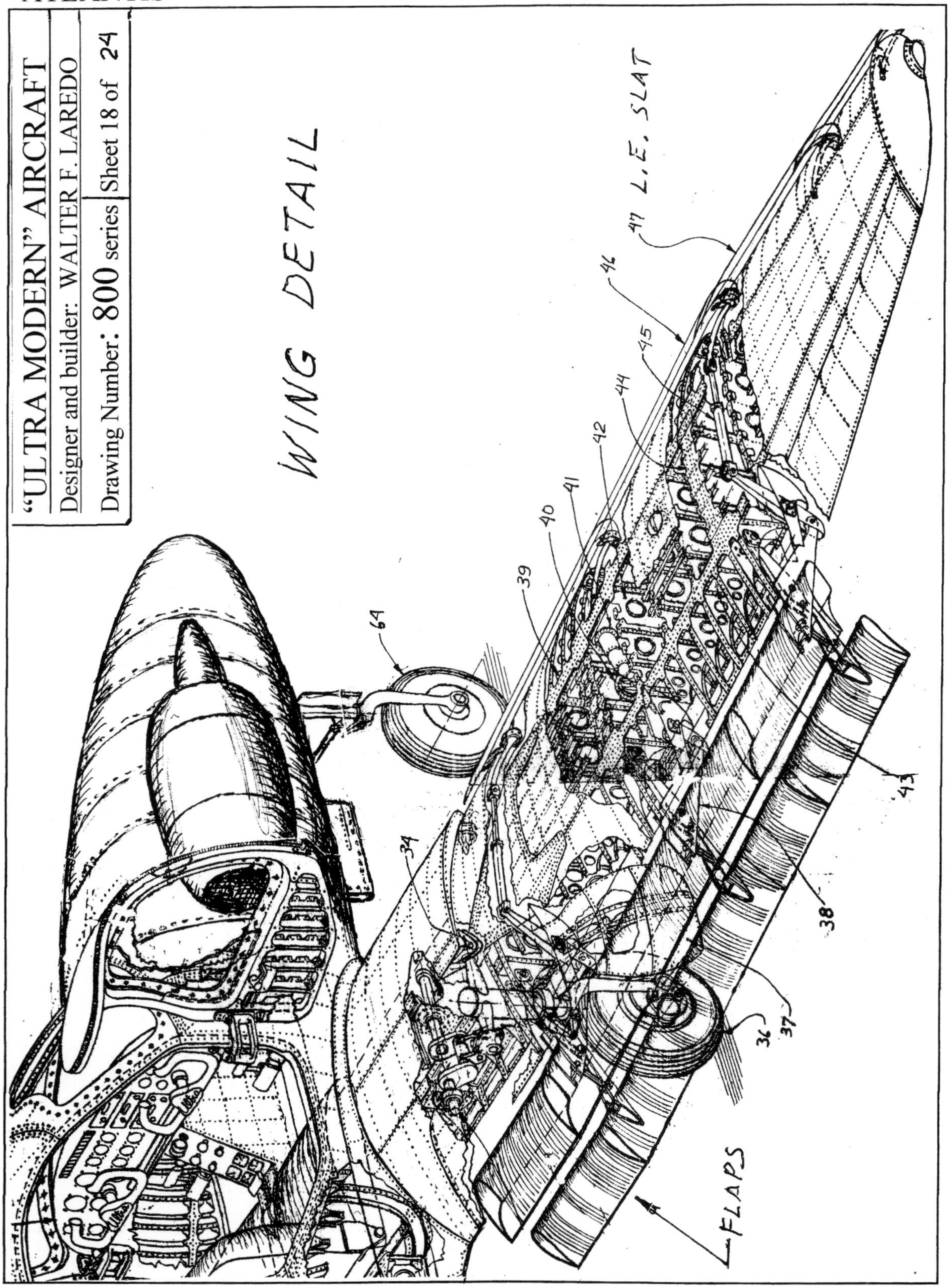

"ULTRA MODERN" AIRCRAFT

Designer and builder: WALTER F. LAREDO

Drawing Number: 800 series | Sheet 18 of 24

WING DETAIL

L.E. SLAT

47

46

45

44

42

41

40

39

64

34

43

38

36

37

FLAPS

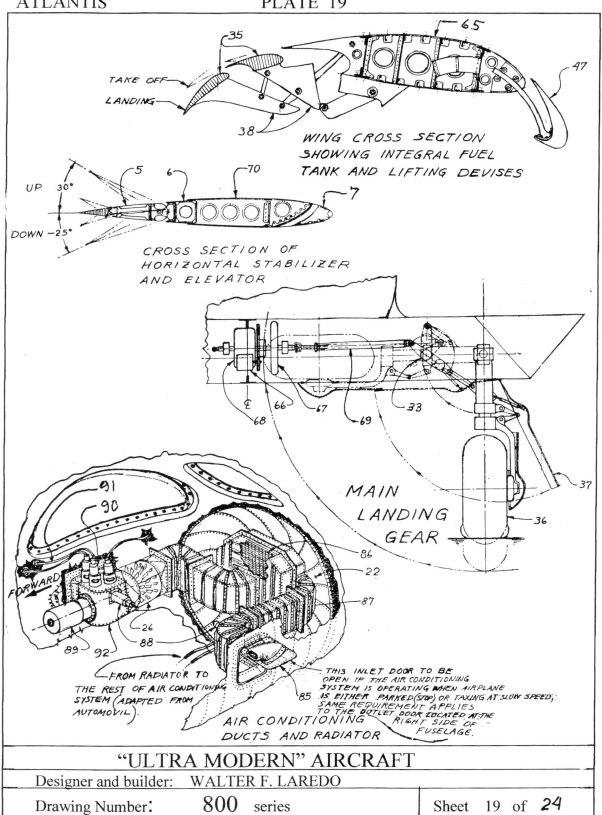

35

65

47

TAKE OFF

LANDING

38

WING CROSS SECTION
SHOWING INTEGRAL FUEL
TANK AND LIFTING DEVISES

UP 30°

5   6   70

7

DOWN -25°

CROSS SECTION OF
HORIZONTAL STABILIZER
AND ELEVATOR

C
68   66   67   33   69

MAIN
LANDING
GEAR

37

36

91
90

86

22

87

FORWARD

26
88

89   92

85

FROM RADIATOR TO
THE REST OF AIR CONDITIONING
SYSTEM (ADAPTED FROM
AUTOMOVIL).

THIS INLET DOOR TO BE
OPEN IF THE AIR CONDITIONING
SYSTEM IS OPERATING WHEN AIRPLANE
IS EITHER PARKED (STOP) OR TAXING AT SLOW SPEED;
SAME REQUIREMENT APPLIES
TO THE OUTLET DOOR LOCATED AT THE
RIGHT SIDE OF
FUSELAGE.

AIR CONDITIONING
DUCTS AND RADIATOR

# "ULTRA MODERN" AIRCRAFT

Designer and builder:   WALTER F. LAREDO

Drawing Number:   **800** series          Sheet  19  of  **24**

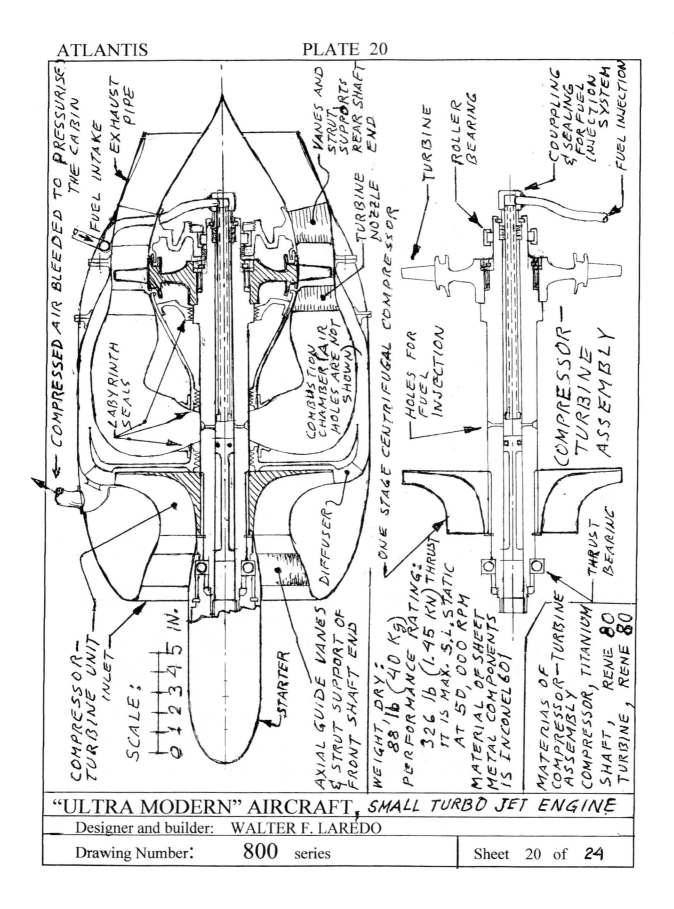

"ULTRA MODERN" AIRCRAFT, SMALL TURBO JET ENGINE

Designer and builder: WALTER F. LAREDO

| Drawing Number: | 800 series | | Sheet 20 of 24 |

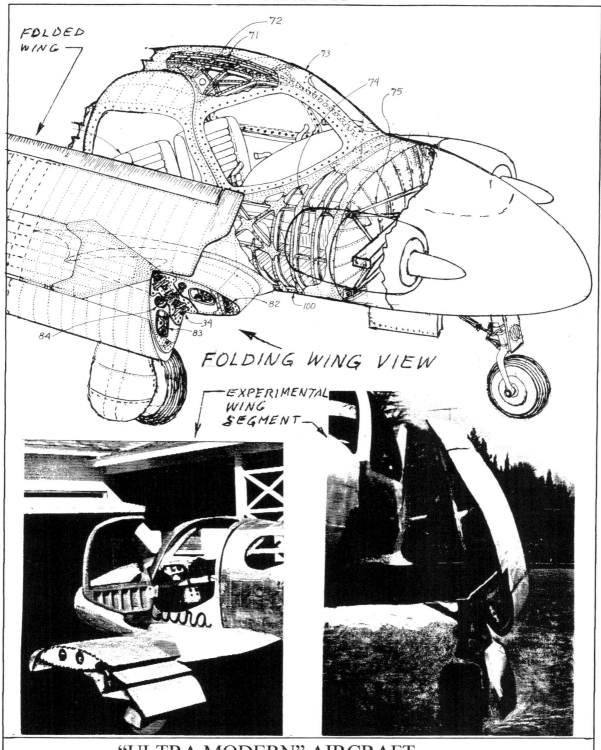

FOLDED WING

FOLDING WING VIEW

EXPERIMENTAL WING SEGMENT

## "ULTRA MODERN" AIRCRAFT

Designer and builder:   WALTER F. LAREDO

Drawing Number:   800 series

# CUSTOM MADE PARTS, FORMED FROM ALUMINUM ALLOY SHEET ON HARD WOOD DIES

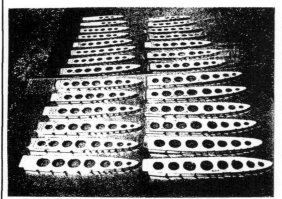

RIBS FOR THE STABILIZERS

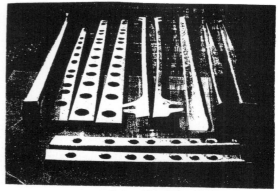

TAIL SECTION SPARS

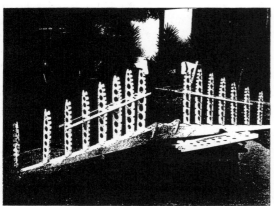

CONSTRUCTION VIEW OF HORIZONTAL STABILIZER

FITTINGS STAMPED FROM ALUMINUM SHEET

HORIZONTAL STABILIZER READY FOR RIVETING (AL. SKIN HOLD BY CLICOS)

CONSTRUCTION OF VERTICAL STABILIZER

## "ULTRA MODERN" AIRCRAFT

Designer and builder: WALTER F. LAREDO

| Drawing Number: 800 series | Sheet 22 of 24 |

AFT
FUSELAGE
AIRFRAME

AIRCRAFT
STRUCTURE
IS HALF
COMPLETED

PRESSURE
BULKHEAD
AFT OF
PRESSURIZED
AREA

## "ULTRA MODERN" AIRCRAFT

Designer and builder:   WALTER F. LAREDO

Drawing Number:    800   series

Sheet  23  of  24

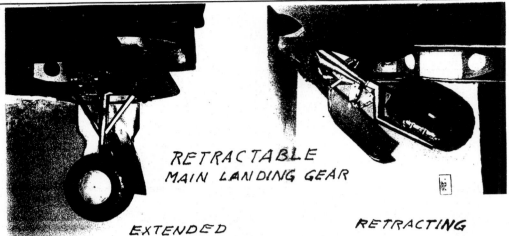

RETRACTABLE
MAIN LANDING GEAR

EXTENDED                    RETRACTING

L.E. SLAT

MAIN LANDING GEAR

FUSELAGE CONSTRUCTION

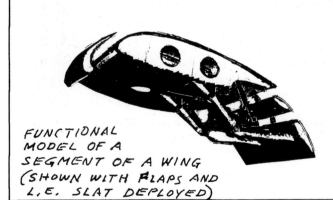

FUNCTIONAL
MODEL OF A
SEGMENT OF A WING
(SHOWN WITH FLAPS AND
L.E. SLAT DEPLOYED)

BUILDING A WOOD CRADDLE
MAIN TOOL TO ASSEMBLY
THE AIRFRAME

## "ULTRA MODERN" AIRCRAFT

| Designer and builder: WALTER F. LAREDO | |
|---|---|
| Drawing Number: 800 series | Sheet 24 of 24 |

ENGINEERING PROJECTS
INSPIRED IN THE TALES
AND IN THE DREAMS OF
LEGENDARY ATLANTIS

TWIN TURBOFAN TRANSPORT FOR 30 PASSENGERS

| ATLANTIS, ADVANCED ENGINEERING PROJECTS | | |
|---|---|---|
| Name of project: "ULTRA TWIN JET" AIRCRAFT | | |
| Design Engineer:    WALTER F. LAREDO | | Date: |
| Drawing Number:    900 SERIES | Sheet 1 of 14 | |

## INTRODUCCION

The "Ultra Twin Jet " is a thirty passenger twin-turbofan aircraft. Though its primary role is as commercial transport, it can be suited to other roles included commuter, business, VIP and express cargo. The aircraft have high by pass ratio engines, advanced airframe, swept wing design, advanced composite structure and digital avionics will enable this new aircraft to achieve better quietness and fuel efficiency. Aircraft sized effectively for profitably entry in variety of markets without the burden of surplus seats.

Designed to meet future demand in high or low-density routes, the Ultra Twin Jet of advanced technology could be implemented to serve routes of average flight time up to six continuous hours. For later production models, structural materials such as aluminum-lithium will replace to conventional aluminum alloys. With those considerations, the Ultra Twin Jet will become one of the most advanced aircraft ever built by any aircraft industries in to-day's and future short-to-medium and long range twin jet standards for durability, reliability, maintainability and profitability.

## FLIGHT TEST OF PROTOTYPE AND FLIGHT CERTIFICATION

Fight test of prototype and flight certification for a thirty (30) passenger commercial twin jet aircraft shall meet the normal category requirements of the United States Federal Aviation Administration.

## GENERAL DESCRIPTION

The Ultra Twin Jet will be a fuel efficient airplane and will have lower cost per passenger-mile than most passenger jets flying today, efficiency will be the result of its aerodynamics, an advanced wing design and high-bypass-ratio engines will provide excellent performance. In fact the Ultra Twin Jet will operate from most general airfields. The innovative wing will give the plane more lift with less drag and less weight, this last as a result of improved aluminum alloys and lightweight composites.

Ailerons, spoilers, elevators and rudder will be build as a sandwich structure with woven or with tape form graphite skins over a Du Pond "Nomex" honeycomb. Parts exposed to small foreign object impact as landing gear doors, nacelle-cowl components and wing body fairing which will be covered with an additional outer layer of extremely thought woven Du Pond "Kevlar" fibers imbedded in an epoxy matrix.

This medium range aircraft will have integral fuel tanks in the wings and in the medium long configuration, probably will have extra fuel tanks in its body. Carrying additional fuel in external wing tip tanks to extend range as in many executive airplanes was not considered as acceptable alternative, wing tanks present problems as high roll inertia with detrimental effects on lateral and directional handling qualities. Conventional wings could not have the volume to hold the required amount of fuel, but the advanced technology wing is about 20 per cent thicker, increasing in this way its fuel volume.

| "ULTRA TWIN JET", aircraft for 30 passengers | | |
|---|---|---|
| Design Engineer:   WALTER F. LAREDO | | |
| Drawing number:         900    series | | Sheet  2  of  14 |

The advanced-technology-wing with supercritical airfoils will be able to retain the high critical number and reasonable drag-rise characteristics. This wing will be thicker, less swept with advanced high lift devices as double slotted Fowler flaps and full-span leading-edge devices will be incorporated in this airplane to compensate for its relative higher wing loading that offers good ride. Lifting heavy loads from high hot fields, because its leading edge devices the airplane will require about 30 per cent less runway length in addition to that will also reduce its stalling speed. Good wing for higher cruising efficiency and higher cruising altitudes where the thin air will produce less drag, faster climbing, quieter approaches and all that was indicated will result in excellent fuel savings.

A good maximum lift capability will be obtain, by incorporating to this wing full-span leading-edge devices, plus double slotted Fowler flaps, with all this considerations this airplane will offer good a good ride because its high wing loading per square feet at cruise.

## STRUCTURES DESIGN PHILOSOPHY
Safety will be the prime consideration in structural design of the Ultra Twin Jet airplane, the primary structure of wing and fuselage are of conventional semi-monocoque construction. Every part, every assembly will be designed to minimize corrosion and fatigue and for fail-safe.

Latest-State-of-the-Art in fatigue-resistance design, airframe designed for fatigue life in excess of 40 000 hours. Damage-tolerant Structure, corrosion resistance and low maintenance aircraft.

## WINGS
One piece wing utilizes a two-spar box for strength, full span leading edge slats and two section double-slotted flaps, two spoilers used concurrently with the ailerons. A low swept wing design with supercritical airfoil enable me to design a more efficient and lighter structure than for a wing of conventional design. The wing box have Zee and Jay stringers, fastened to a constant tapered machine skins(*), spar caps are also machined (*), spar webs are chemically milled(*).

Materials for wing components:
       Upper Wing Panels: Aluminum alloys 7000 series. (*)
       Lower Wing Panels: Aluminum alloys 2000 series. (*)
       The upper and lower panels are Machine tapered and shot peen formed. (*)
       (*) At the beginning of production, for low budget construction could be use
       build-up parts by riveting constant thickness stock, build this way instead of
       machined tapered parts, sacrificing a little payload.
       Stringers: Zee and jay extrusion sections, 7000 series aluminum alloys.
       Spar caps, spar web, ribs and rib chords are from series 2000 and 7000 to meet special
       Requirements.
       Leading edge slats and its tracks cover or fairing, trailing edge flaps, flaps veins, aileron
       and spoilers are built from advanced composites, by using some of the following
       materials:

## "ULTRA TWIN JET", aircraft for 30 passengers
Design Engineer:   WALTER F. LAREDO

| Drawing number: | 900 series | Sheet 3 of 14 |
| --- | --- | --- |

Graphite, Kevlar, fiberglass and "Nomex" core, all embedded with epoxy resin. By using advanced technology materials, wing will become 20 per cent lighter.

## BODY

Damage-tolerant, Fail-safe type of construction, semi-monocoque design. The body is of circular cross section. Skins from 2024-T3 aluminum clad, stringers from 7075-T6 or 2024-T3511 aluminum alloys, the bonded tear straps are of 7075-T6 aluminum alloy. In later production airplanes of more advanced technology the skins could be made by employing mechanically or chemically milled aluminum alloys.

Body pressurization to a maximum differential pressure of 8.5 psi.

## EMPENAGE

The T tail configuration design, uses an incident-adjustable horizontal stabilizer with inverted airfoil is made by a two-spar box structure and skins with zee stringers.

The vertical stabilizer box is a multiple-spar structure, with fittings at its upper end which houses the bearings that supports the horizontal stabilizer hinges. The leading edge and the trailing edge of the elevator and rudder structure are made from graphite-epoxy.

The aft end of the fuselage behind the pressure bulkhead is not pressurized and contains the air conditioning pack, bleeding-ducts from the engines, accessories and parts of the fuel system. The forward spars of the engine struts are integral with the pressure bulkhead structure.

## FLIGHT CONTROLS

Ailerons, rudder and elevators are driven by hydraulic servo-actuators combined with push-pull rod linkages, backed by a mechanical cable system. A motor jack is attached to the stabilizer for pitch trim. Full span leading edge slats, double slotted flaps and spoilers are actuated by an electric motor or as alternative by a hydraulic motor.

## HYDRAULIC SYSTEM

Two independent 3000 psi systems powered by the two pumps mounted on the two engines. System 1 and system 2, both independently powers the flight controls, Leading Edge Slats, Trailing Edge Flaps, Main and Nose Landing Gears, Landing Gear Doors (which could be actuated by hydraulic power or by a direct mechanical linkage connected to the landing gear struts). Hydraulic system number 1, also powers the brakes.

## ENVIRONMENT CONTROL SYSTEM

Pressurization in climb and cruise flight conditions are obtained by bleeding air from an intermediate compressor stage. During idle, descend and other low flight conditions, pressurization is obtained from the last compressor stage.
Engine bleed air powers the Air Cycle Machine, then this air passes through the Ram Heat Exchanger to be cool, then to a dehumidifier and other processes. At 36000 ft (10800 m) is maintained an equivalent cabin pressure of 8000 ft (2400 m).

## "ULTRA TWIN JET", aircraft for 30 passengers

Design Engineer:    WALTER F. LAREDO

| Drawing number: | 900 series | Sheet 4 of 14 |

OXYGEN SYSTEM:   Conventional Gaseous System
FIRE EXTINGUISHER:   Conventional
ELECTRIC SYSTEM:   Conventional
ELECTRONICS:   Small Radar
ANTI-ICING SYSTEM:   Will prevent the formation of ice on the Engine Nose Cone.  The
engine inlet Anti-Icing System uses hot engine air bleed.  Pitot Static and Probes are heated by
Electric Heaters.
PRESSURIZATION:   Normal cabin pressure differential is 8.6 psi.

## EXPECTED PERFORMANCE AND WEIGHTS DATA

PERFORMANCE

SPEEDS
Maximum cruise..............528  mph   (850 km/hr)     (0.80 Mach)
Normal Cruise................501  mph   (806 km/hr)     (0.76 Mach)
Long-Range Cruise...........469  mph   (754 km/hr)     (0.71 Mach)

CEILING
Maximum Operating Altitude........42,000 ft.   (12,802  m)

CLIMB
Time of Climb to Initial Cruise Altitude......23 minutes

AIRFIELD PERFORMANCE
Balance Field Length at Max. Takeoff Weight.......5500 ft.  (1676 m.)
Landing Distance at Max. Landing Weight...........3800 ft.  (1158 m.)

RANGE
2095  nautical miles   (2408 miles)  (3874  km) with 30 passengers and a crew of two.

WEIGHTS
Maximum ramp weight.....................39100 lb.  (17735 kg.)
Maximum takeoff weight..................39000 lb.  (17689 kg.)
Maximum landing weight.................36000 lb.  (16329 kg.)
Maximum zero fuel weight...............25500 lb.  (11566 kg.)
Approximate weight empty.................17500 lb.  ( 7938 kg.)
Typical operating weight empty...........22450 lb.  (10183 kg.)
Maximum fuel load........................... 9771 lb.  ( 4432 kg.)
Payload with full fuel....................... 6879 lb.  ( 3120 kg.)
Maximum payload weight................. 8000 lb.  ( 3629 kg.)

FWD  C.G.  LIMIT (% MAC)............17 inch  (0.432 m.)
AFT  C.G.  LIMIT (% MAC)............34 inch  (0.864 m.)

## "ULTRA TWIN JET", aircraft for 30 passengers

Design Engineer:   WALTER F. LAREDO

| Drawing number: | 900 series | Sheet 5 of 14 |

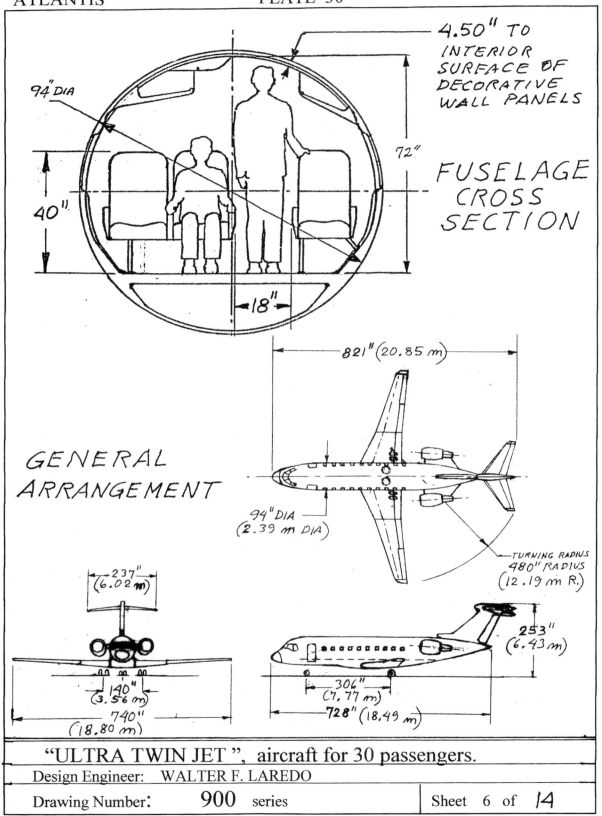

4.50" TO INTERIOR SURFACE OF DECORATIVE WALL PANELS

94" DIA

72"

40"

18"

FUSELAGE CROSS SECTION

GENERAL ARRANGEMENT

821" (20.85 m)

94" DIA (2.39 m DIA)

TURNING RADIUS 480" RADIUS (12.19 m R.)

237" (6.02 m)

253" (6.43 m)

140" (3.56 m)

740" (18.80 m)

306" (7.77 m)

728" (18.49 m)

"ULTRA TWIN JET", aircraft for 30 passengers.

Design Engineer: WALTER F. LAREDO

Drawing Number: 900 series

Sheet 6 of 14

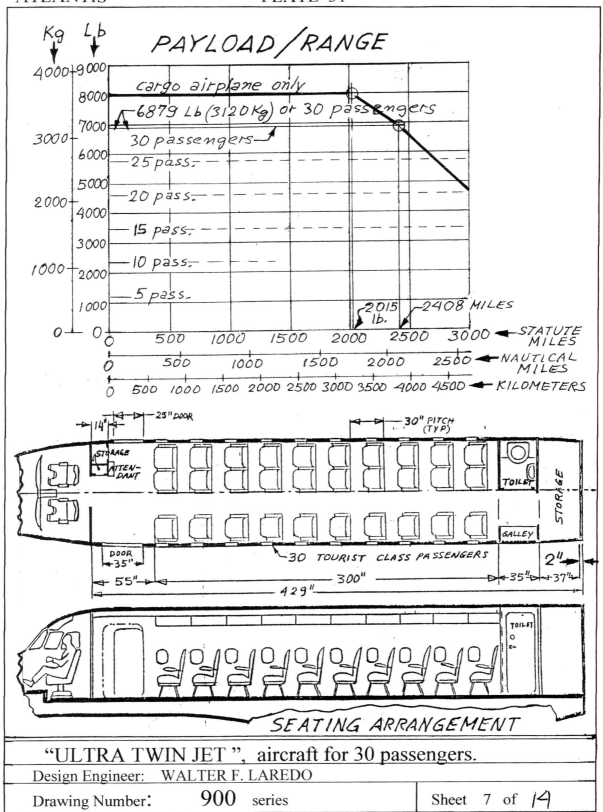

# PAYLOAD/RANGE

cargo airplane only

6879 Lb (3120 Kg) or 30 passengers

30 passengers

25 pass.

20 pass.

15 pass.

10 pass.

5 pass.

2015 lb.   2408 MILES

STATUTE MILES

NAUTICAL MILES

KILOMETERS

25" DOOR          30" PITCH (TYP)

14"

STORAGE
ATTEN-DANT

TOILET

STORAGE

GALLEY

DOOR 35"

30 TOURIST CLASS PASSENGERS

2"

55"          300"          35"  37"

429"

TOILET

## SEATING ARRANGEMENT

## "ULTRA TWIN JET", aircraft for 30 passengers.

Design Engineer:   WALTER F. LAREDO

Drawing Number:   **900** series          Sheet  7  of  14

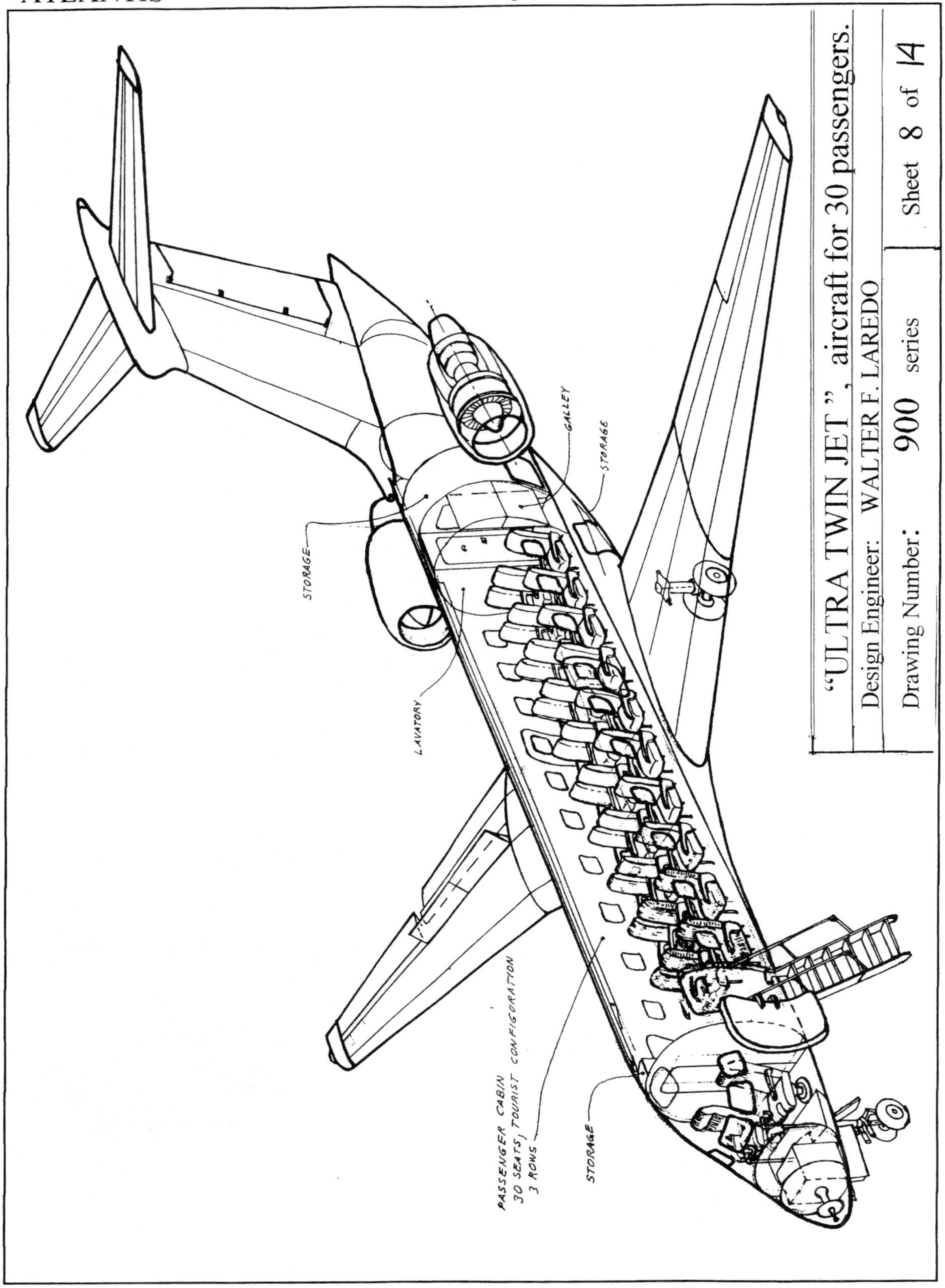

"ULTRA TWIN JET", aircraft for 30 passengers.

Design Engineer: WALTER F. LAREDO

Drawing Number: 900 series

Sheet 8 of 14

STORAGE

GALLEY

STORAGE

LAVATORY

PASSENGER CABIN
30 SEATS, TOURIST CONFIGURATION
3 ROWS

STORAGE

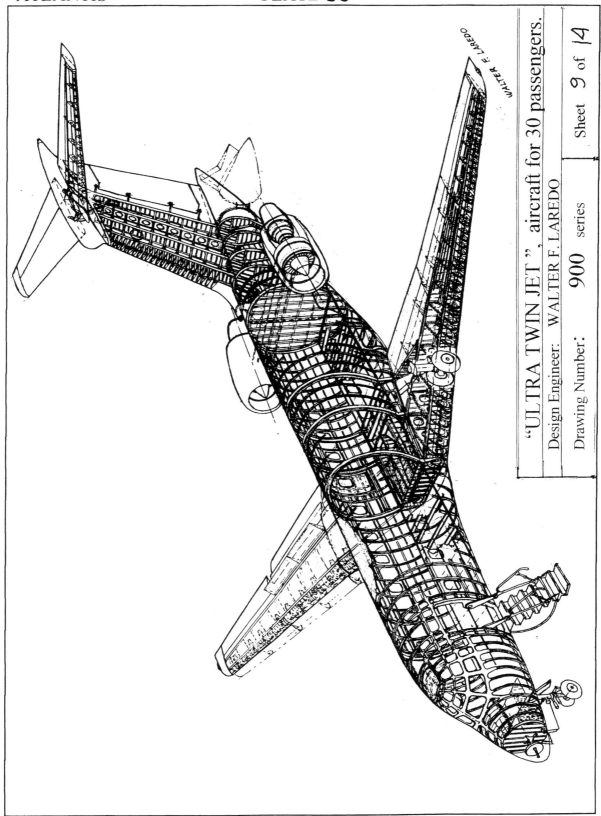

"ULTRA TWIN JET", aircraft for 30 passengers.

| Design Engineer: WALTER F. LAREDO | | Sheet 9 of 14 |
| Drawing Number: 900 series | | |

WALTER F. LAREDO

GENERAL ELECTRIC *CF 34* HIGH BYPASS TURBOFAN ENGINE TO BE USE IN THE "ULTRA TWINJET" AIRCRAFT

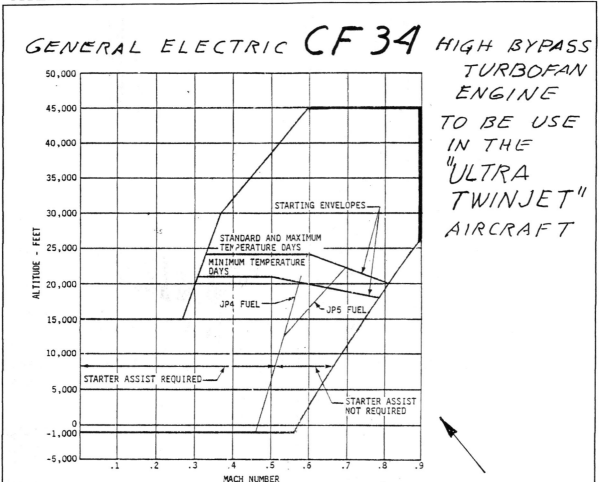

STARTING ENVELOPES

STANDARD AND MAXIMUM TEMPERATURE DAYS

MINIMUM TEMPERATURE DAYS

JP4 FUEL

JP5 FUEL

STARTER ASSIST REQUIRED

STARTER ASSIST NOT REQUIRED

MACH NUMBER

ALTITUDE - FEET

*Flight Envelope Altitude/Mach No. Extremes*

## SPECIFICATIONS _____

| | |
|---|---|
| Takeoff Thrust (lb) | 7990 |
| 7990 (flat rated to 73°F) | |
| Max Continuous Thrust (.8M/36K) (lb) | 1760 |
| Specific Fuel Consumption at Takeoff | .359 |
| Max Continuous Specific Fuel Consumption (.8M/36K) | .687 |
| Weight (lb) | 1525 |
| Length (in.) | 100 |
| Max Diameter (in.) | 49 |

"ULTRA TWIN JET ", aircraft for 30 passengers.

Design Engineer: WALTER F. LAREDO

Drawing Number: 900 series      Sheet 10 of 14

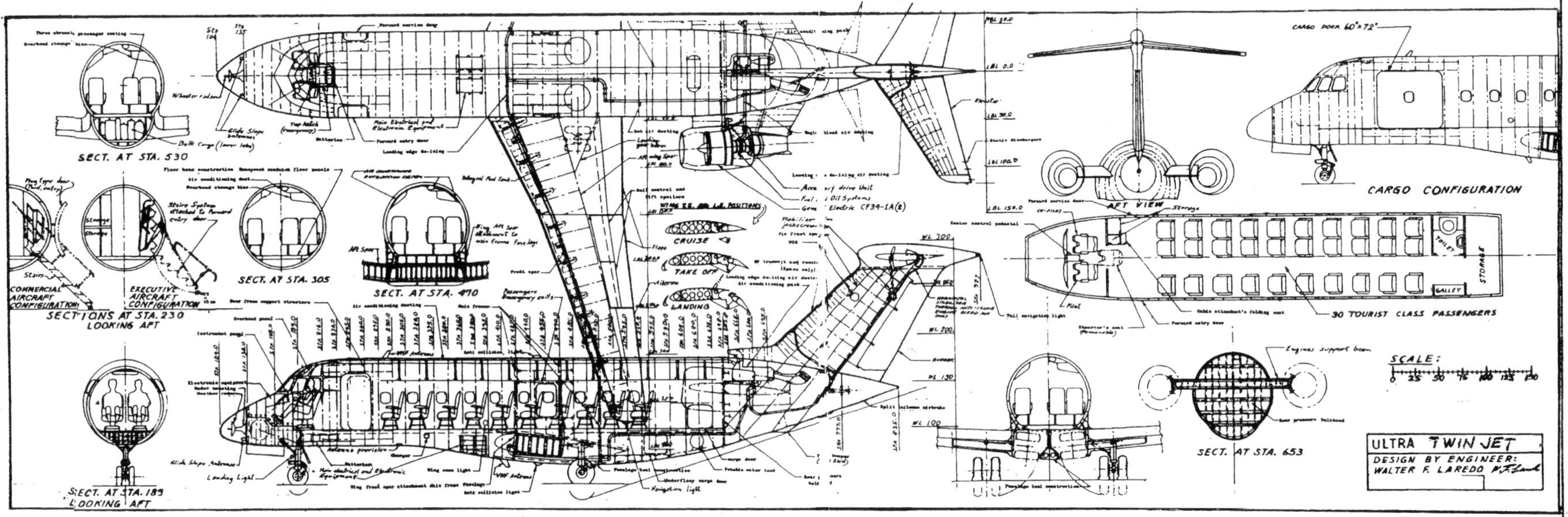
SECT. AT STA. 530
SECT. AT STA. 305
SECT. AT STA. 470
COMMERCIAL AIRCRAFT CONFIGURATION
EXECUTIVE AIRCRAFT CONFIGURATION
SECTIONS AT STA. 230 LOOKING AFT
SECT. AT STA. 189 LOOKING AFT
CRUISE
TAKE OFF
LANDING
AFT VIEW
CARGO CONFIGURATION
30 TOURIST CLASS PASSENGERS
SECT. AT STA. 653
SCALE:
ULTRA TWIN JET
DESIGN BY ENGINEER:
WALTER F. LAREDO

See plate 37

See plate 36

See plate 38

"ULTRA TWIN JET", aircraft for 30 passengers.

Design Engineer: WALTER F. LAREDO

Drawing Number: 900 series

Sheet 11 of 14

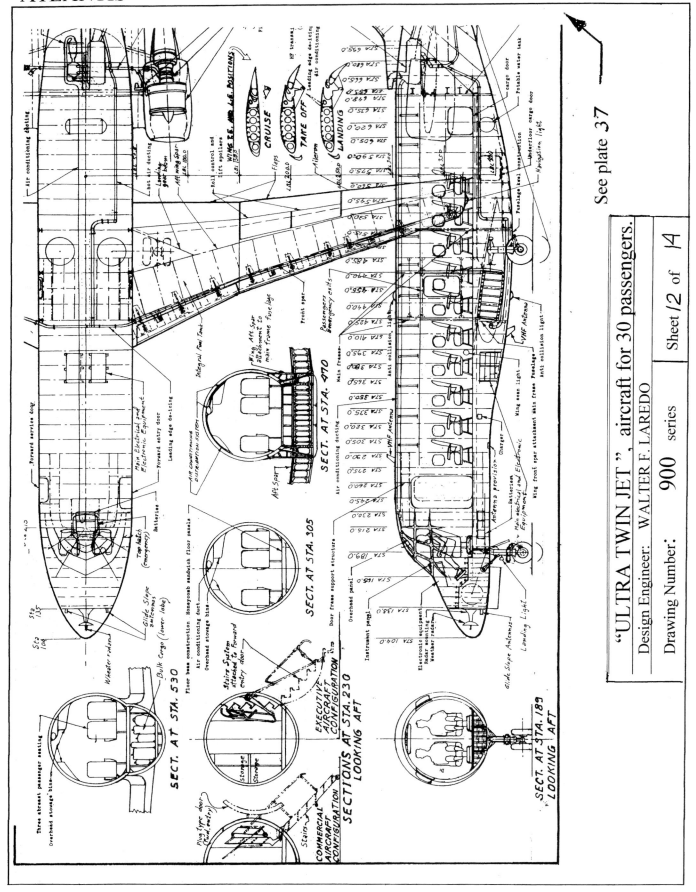

See plate 37

"ULTRA TWIN JET", aircraft for 30 passengers.

Design Engineer: WALTER F. LAREDO

Drawing Number: 900 series | Sheet 12 of 14

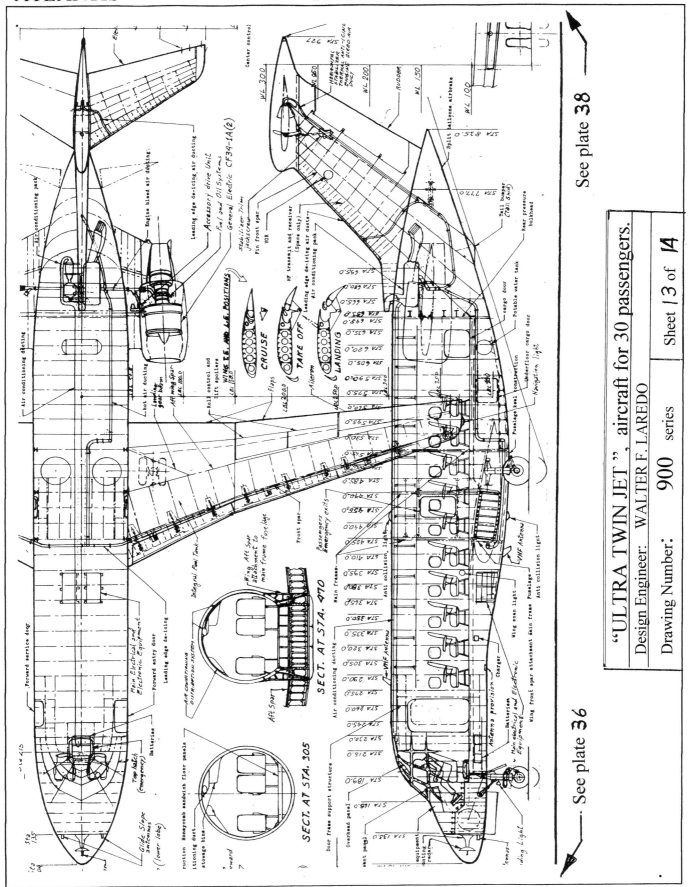

See plate **38**

See plate **36**

"ULTRA TWIN JET", aircraft for 30 passengers.

| Design Engineer: | WALTER F. LAREDO | |
| --- | --- | --- |
| Drawing Number: | **900** series | Sheet 13 of **14** |

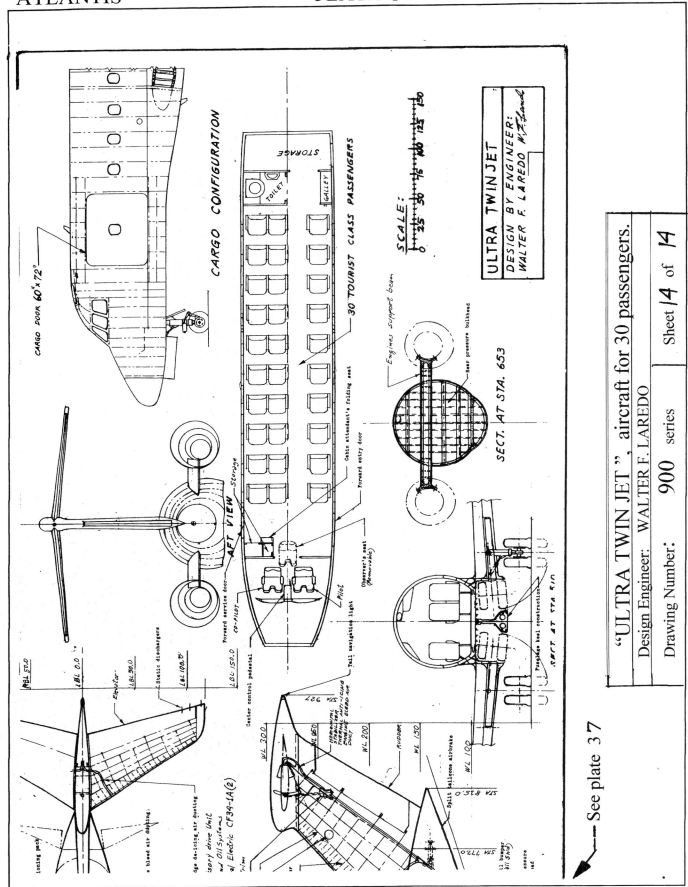

CARGO CONFIGURATION

CARGO DOOR 60"x72"

30 TOURIST CLASS PASSENGERS

STORAGE

TOILET

GALLEY

Cabin attendant's folding seat

Forward entry door

Observer's seat (Removable)

PILOT

CO-PILOT

Forward service door

Storage

AFT VIEW

Tail navigation light

Center control pedestal

Engines support beam

Rear pressure bulkhead

SECT. AT STA. 653

SECT. AT STA. ___

Fuselage keel construction

Split balloons airbrake

WL 100
WL 150
WL 200
WL 300
WL 250

RUDDER

STA 835.0
STA 772.0

HORIZONTAL STABILIZER THERMAL ANTI-ICING ENGINE BLEED AIR DUCT

STA 927

SCALE:
0  25  50  75  100  125  150

ULTRA TWIN JET

DESIGN BY ENGINEER:
WALTER F. LAREDO

Sheet 14 of 14

Elevator
Static dischargers

RBL 50.0
LBL 0.0
LBL 50.0
LBL 100.0
LBL 150.0

de-icing air ducting
drive Unit
Oil Systems
Electric CF34-1A(2)

bleed air duct

oning pack

See plate 37

"ULTRA TWIN JET", aircraft for 30 passengers.

Design Engineer:    WALTER F. LAREDO

Drawing Number:    900    series

ENGINEERING PROJECTS
INSPIRED IN THE TALES
AND IN THE DREAMS OF
LEGENDARY ATLANTIS

HALCON WLI

FOR ADDITIONAL INFORMATION SEE
"HALCON WLI" PROPOSAL BOOK
BY W.F. LAREDO

ATLANTIS, ADVANCED ENGINEERING PROJECTS

| Name of project: | PRELIMINARY DESIGN | |
|---|---|---|
| "HALCON WF1", Lightweight fighter | | |
| Design Engineer:  WALTER F. LAREDO | | Date:  May 1987 |
| Drawing Number:   1000  SERIES | | Sheet 1 of 34 |

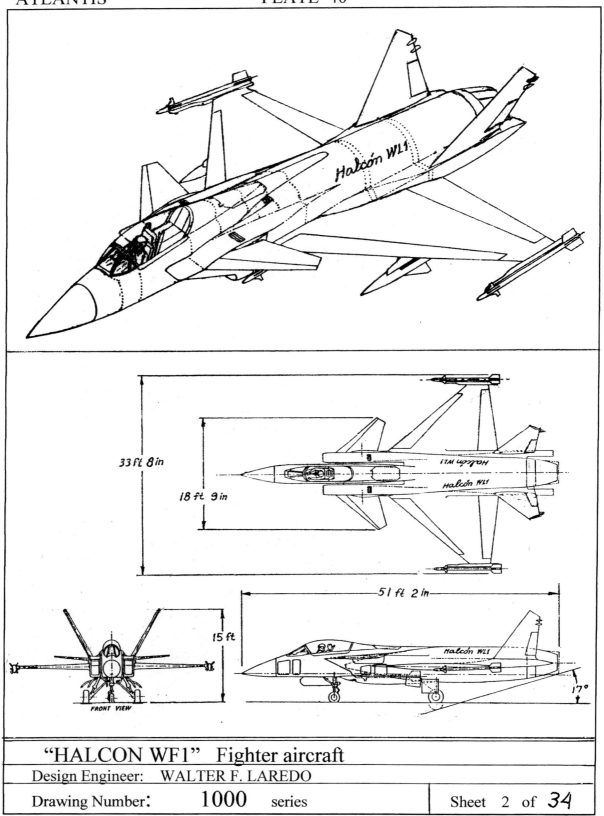

33 ft 8 in

18 ft 9 in

51 ft 2 in

15 ft

17°

FRONT VIEW

Halcón WL1

# "HALCON WF1"   Fighter aircraft

Design Engineer:   WALTER F. LAREDO

Drawing Number:      **1000**    series

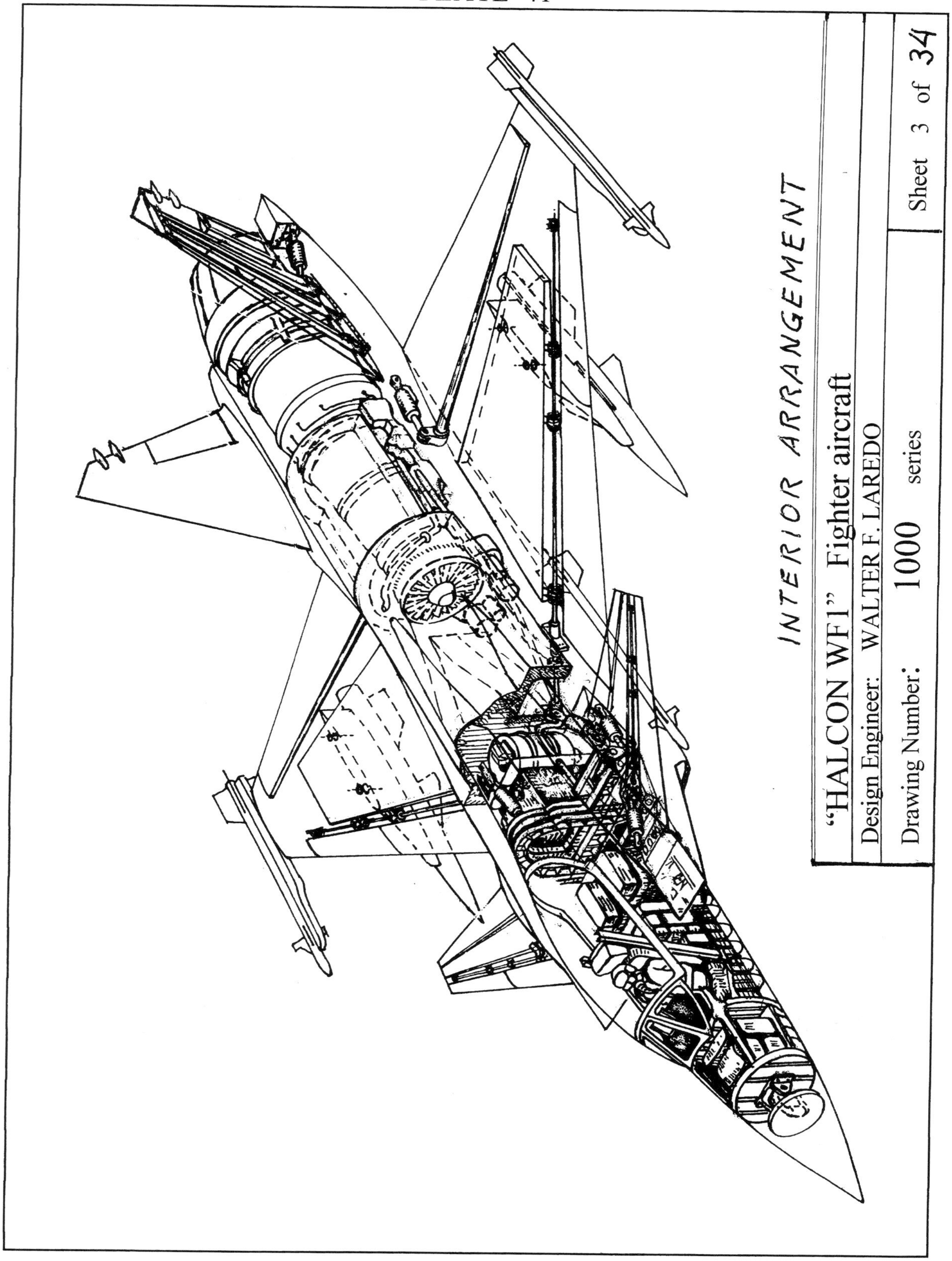

INTERIOR ARRANGEMENT

"HALCON WF1" Fighter aircraft

Design Engineer:  WALTER F. LAREDO

Drawing Number:  1000  series

Sheet 3 of 34

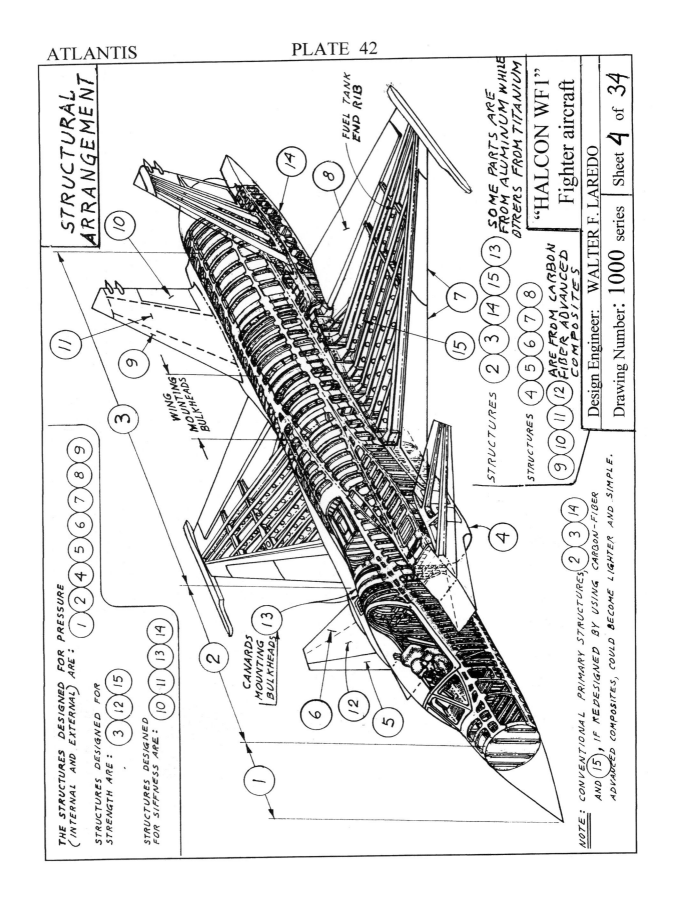

STRUCTURAL ARRANGEMENT

FUEL TANK END RIB

WING MOUNTING BULKHEADS

CANARDS MOUNTING BULKHEADS

THE STRUCTURES DESIGNED FOR PRESSURE (INTERNAL AND EXTERNAL) ARE: ① ② ④ ⑤ ⑥ ⑦ ⑧ ⑨

STRUCTURES DESIGNED FOR STRENGTH ARE: ③ ⑫ ⑮

STRUCTURES DESIGNED FOR STIFFNESS ARE: ⑩ ⑪ ⑬ ⑭

STRUCTURES ② ③ ⑭ ⑮ ⑬ ARE FROM CARBON FIBER ADVANCED COMPOSITES

STRUCTURES ④ ⑤ ⑥ ⑦ ⑧ ⑨ ⑩ ⑪ ⑫ ARE FROM CARBON FIBER ADVANCED COMPOSITES

SOME PARTS ARE FROM ALUMINUM WHILE OTHERS FROM TITANIUM

NOTE: CONVENTIONAL PRIMARY STRUCTURES, ② ③ ⑭ AND ⑮, IF REDESIGNED BY USING CARBON-FIBER ADVANCED COMPOSITES, COULD BECOME LIGHTER AND SIMPLE.

"HALCON WF1" Fighter aircraft

Design Engineer: WALTER F. LAREDO

Drawing Number: 1000 series | Sheet 4 of 34

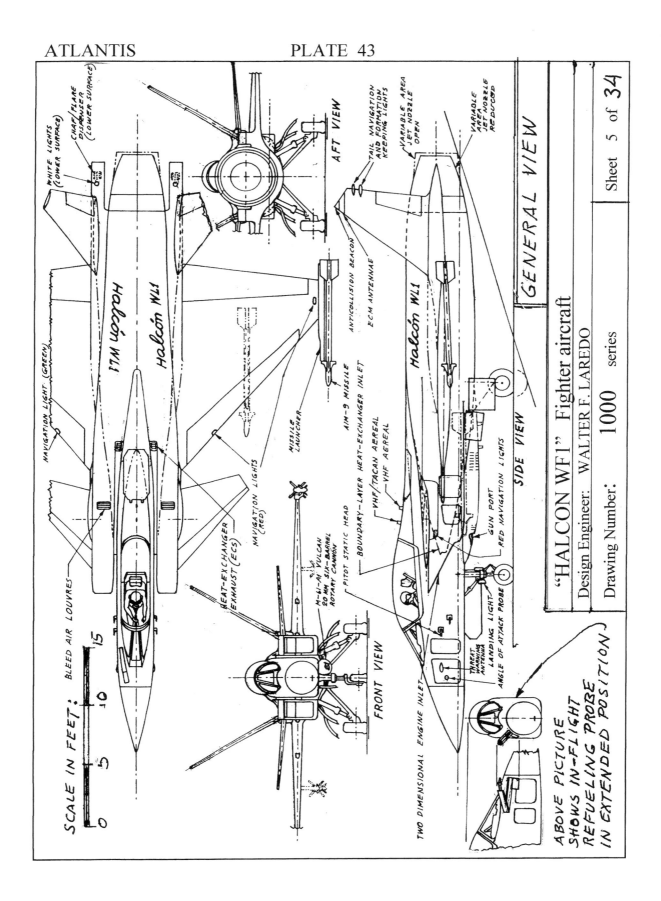

SCALE IN FEET:

AFT VIEW

WHITE LIGHTS (LOWER SURFACE)

CHAFF/FLARE DISPENSER (LOWER SURFACE)

NAVIGATION LIGHT (GREEN)

Halcón WL1

Halcón WL1

BLEED AIR LOUVRES

HEAT-EXCHANGER EXHAUST (ECS)

NAVIGATION LIGHTS (RED)

MISSILE LAUNCHER

AIM-9 MISSILE

ANTICOLLISION BEACON

ECM ANTENNAE

TAIL NAVIGATION AND FORMATION KEEPING LIGHTS

VARIABLE AREA JET NOZZLE OPEN

VARIABLE AREA JET NOZZLE REDUCED

BOUNDARY-LAYER HEAT-EXCHANGER INLET

VHF/TACAN AERIAL

VHF AERIAL

PITOT STATIC HEAD

M-61-A1 VULCAN 20 MM SIX-BARREL ROTARY CANNON

GUN PORT

RED NAVIGATION LIGHTS

LANDING LIGHT

ANGLE OF ATTACK PROBE

THREAT WARNING ANTENNA

TWO DIMENSIONAL ENGINE INLET

FRONT VIEW

SIDE VIEW

GENERAL VIEW

ABOVE PICTURE SHOWS IN-FLIGHT REFUELING PROBE IN EXTENDED POSITION

"HALCON WF1" Fighter aircraft

Design Engineer: WALTER F. LAREDO

Drawing Number: 1000 series

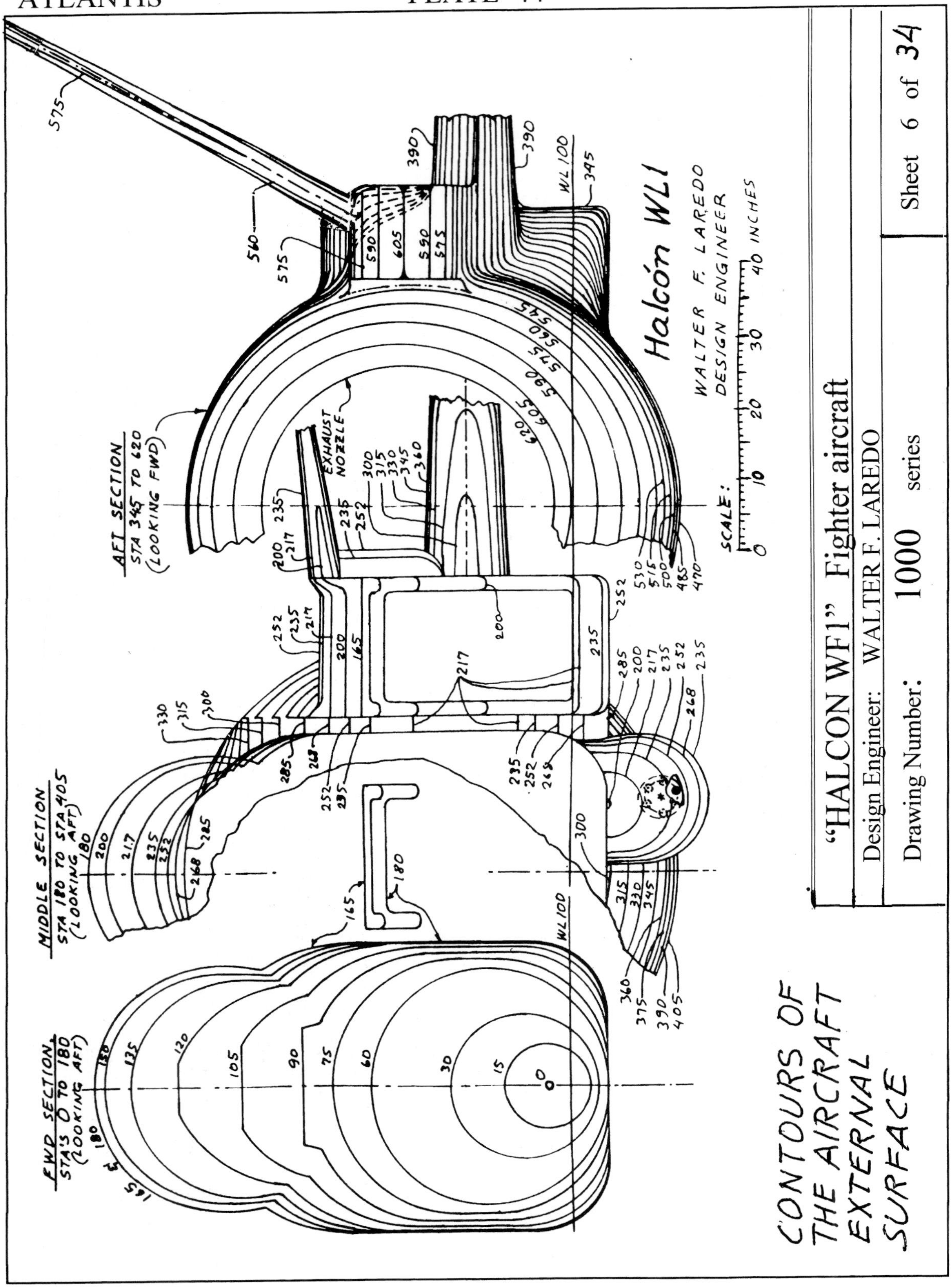

AFT SECTION
STA 345 TO 620
(LOOKING FWD)

EXHAUST NOZZLE

MIDDLE SECTION
STA 180 TO STA 405
(LOOKING AFT)

FWD SECTION
STAS 0 TO 180
(LOOKING AFT)

Halcón WL1

WALTER F. LAREDO
DESIGN ENGINEER

SCALE:
0    10    20    30    40 INCHES

"HALCON WF1"  Fighter aircraft

Design Engineer:  WALTER F. LAREDO

Drawing Number:  1000  series

Sheet 6 of 34

CONTOURS OF
THE AIRCRAFT
EXTERNAL
SURFACE

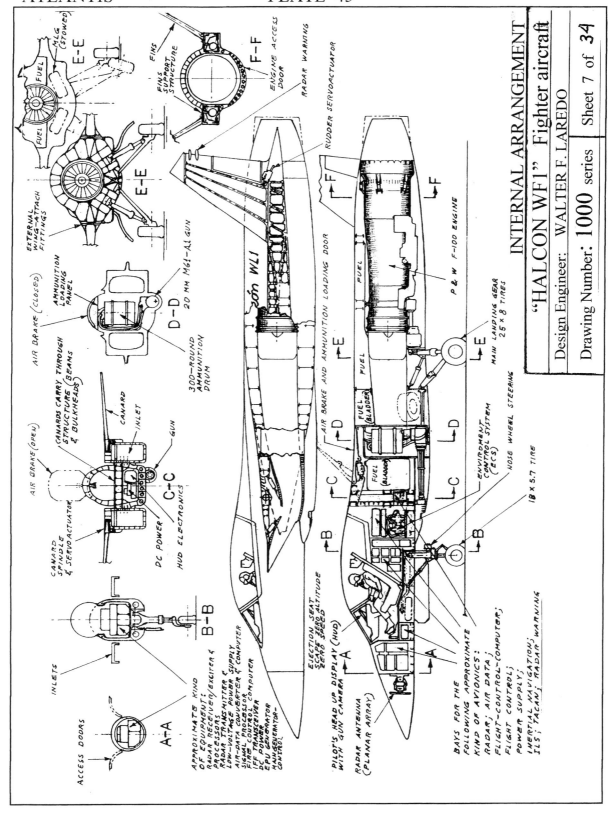

INTERNAL ARRANGEMENT
"HALCON WF1" Fighter aircraft
Design Engineer: WALTER F. LAREDO
Drawing Number: 1000 series | Sheet 7 of 34

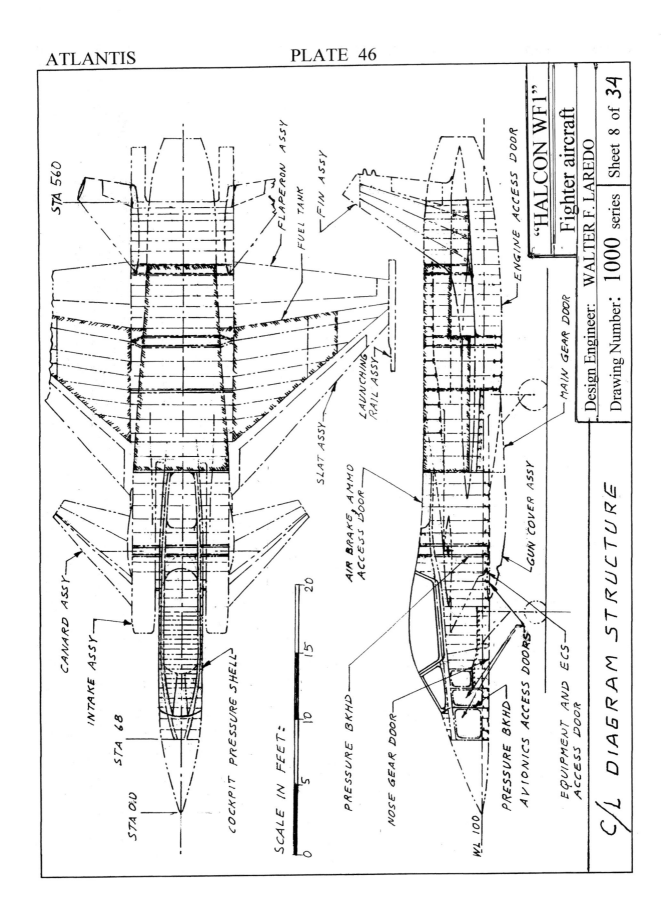

STA 560

FLAPERON ASSY

FUEL TANK

FIN ASSY

STA 00

STA 68

INTAKE ASSY

CANARD ASSY

COCKPIT PRESSURE SHELL

SCALE IN FEET:

0  5  10  15  20

SLAT ASSY

LAUNCHING RAIL ASSY

AIR BRAKE AMMO ACCESS DOOR

PRESSURE BKHD

NOSE GEAR DOOR

PRESSURE BKHD

AVIONICS ACCESS DOORS

EQUIPMENT AND ECS ACCESS DOOR

WL 100

GUN COVER ASSY

MAIN GEAR DOOR

ENGINE ACCESS DOOR

"HALCON WF1"

Fighter aircraft

Design Engineer: WALTER F. LAREDO

Drawing Number: 1000 series | Sheet 8 of 34

C/L DIAGRAM STRUCTURE

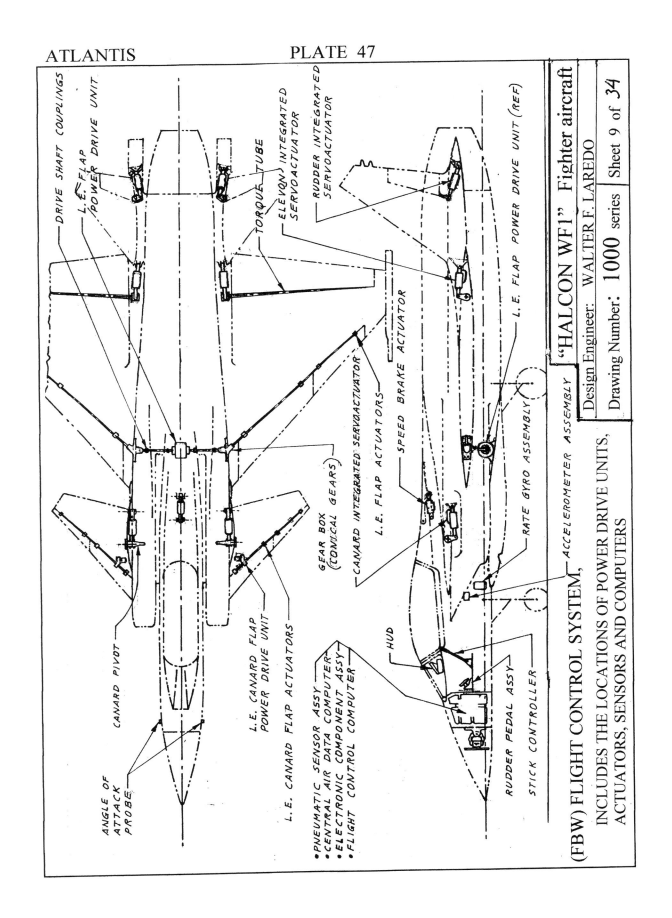

(FBW) FLIGHT CONTROL SYSTEM,
INCLUDES THE LOCATIONS OF POWER DRIVE UNITS,
ACTUATORS, SENSORS AND COMPUTERS

"HALCON WF1" Fighter aircraft

Design Engineer: WALTER F. LAREDO

Drawing Number: 1000 series | Sheet 9 of 34

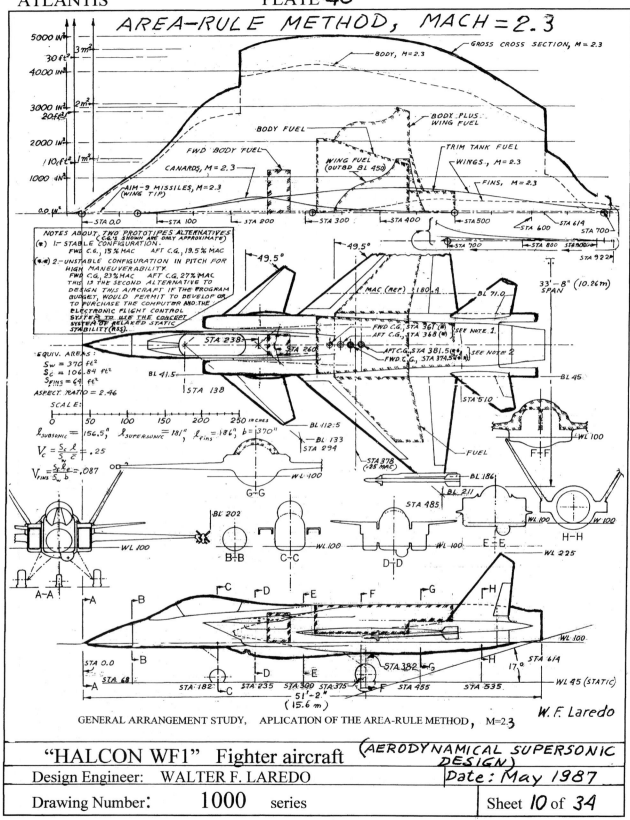

# AREA-RULE METHOD, MACH = 2.3

GROSS CROSS SECTION, M = 2.3
BODY, M = 2.3
BODY PLUS WING FUEL
BODY FUEL
FWD BODY FUEL
WING FUEL (OUTBD BL 450)
TRIM TANK FUEL
WINGS, M = 2.3
CANARDS, M = 2.3
AIM-9 MISSILES, M = 2.3 (WING TIP)
FINS, M = 2.3

STA 0.0, STA 100, STA 200, STA 300, STA 400, STA 500, STA 600, STA 614, STA 700
STA 700, STA 800, STA 900, STA 922

NOTES ABOUT TWO PROTOTIPES ALTERNATIVES (C.G.'s SHOWN ARE ONLY APPROXIMATE)
(*) 1- STABLE CONFIGURATION.
FWD C.G. 15% MAC    AFT C.G. 19.5% MAC
(**) 2- UNSTABLE CONFIGURATION IN PITCH FOR HIGH MANEUVERABILITY.
FWD C.G. 23% MAC   AFT C.G. 27% MAC
THIS IS THE SECOND ALTERNATIVE TO DESIGN THIS AIRCRAFT IF THE PROGRAM BUDGET, WOULD PERMIT TO DEVELOP OR TO PURCHASE THE COMPUTER AND THE ELECTRONIC FLIGHT CONTROL SYSTEM TO USE THE CONCEPT SYSTEM OF RELAXED STATIC STABILITY (RSS).

EQUIV. AREAS:
$S_w = 370$ ft²
$S_c = 106.84$ ft²
$S_{FINS} = 69$ ft²
ASPECT RATIO = 2.46

SCALE:
0    50    100    150    200    250 INCHES

$\ell_{SUBSONIC} = 156.5"$, $\ell_{SUPERSONIC} = 181"$, $\ell_{fins} = 186"$, $b = 370"$

$V_c = \frac{S_c \ell}{S_w \bar{c}} = .25$

$V_{FINS} = \frac{S_c \ell}{S_w b} = .087$

49.5°    49.5°
MAC (REF.) 180.4
BL 71.0
33'-8" (10.26 m) SPAN
FWD C.G. STA 361 (*)
AFT C.G. STA 368 (*)    SEE NOTE 1.
AFT C.G. STA 381.5 (**)    SEE NOTE 2
FWD C.G. STA 374.5 (**)
STA 238
STA 260
BL 41.5
STA 138
BL 45
STA 510
BL 112.5
BL 133
STA 294
STA 378 (.25 MAC)
FUEL
WL 100
F-F
G-G
WL 100
BL 186
BL 211
STA 485
A-A
WL 100
BL 202
B-B
C-C
WL 100
D-D
WL 100
E-E
WL 225
H-H
WL 100    W 100

C    D    E    F    G    H
WL 100
STA 0.0
STA 68
STA 182    STA 235    STA 300    STA 375    STA 382    STA 455    STA 535    STA 614
17°
WL 45 (STATIC)
51'-2" (15.6 m)

W. F. Laredo

GENERAL ARRANGEMENT STUDY,    APLICATION OF THE AREA-RULE METHOD, M = 2.3

| "HALCON WF1"  Fighter aircraft | (AERODYNAMICAL SUPERSONIC DESIGN) |
|---|---|
| Design Engineer:  WALTER F. LAREDO | Date: May 1987 |
| Drawing Number:    1000    series | Sheet 10 of 34 |

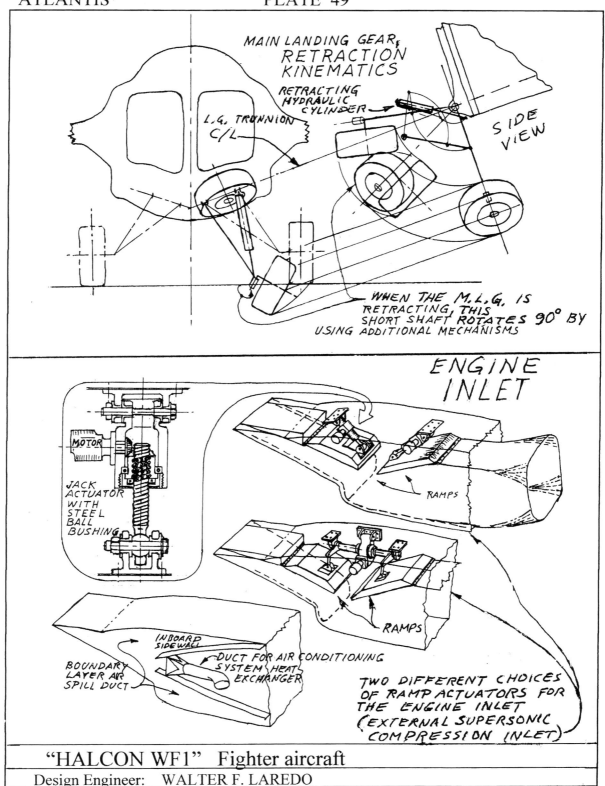

MAIN LANDING GEAR
RETRACTION
KINEMATICS

RETRACTING
HYDRAULIC
CYLINDER

L.G. TRUNNION
C/L

SIDE
VIEW

WHEN THE M.L.G. IS
RETRACTING, THIS
SHORT SHAFT ROTATES 90° BY
USING ADDITIONAL MECHANISMS

ENGINE
INLET

MOTOR

JACK
ACTUATOR
WITH
STEEL
BALL
BUSHING

RAMPS

RAMPS

INBOARD
SIDEWALL

DUCT FOR AIR CONDITIONING
SYSTEM HEAT
EXCHANGER

BOUNDARY
LAYER AIR
SPILL DUCT

TWO DIFFERENT CHOICES
OF RAMP ACTUATORS FOR
THE ENGINE INLET
(EXTERNAL SUPERSONIC
COMPRESSION INLET)

"HALCON WF1"   Fighter aircraft

Design Engineer:   WALTER F. LAREDO

| Drawing Number: | 1000 series | Sheet 11 of 34 |

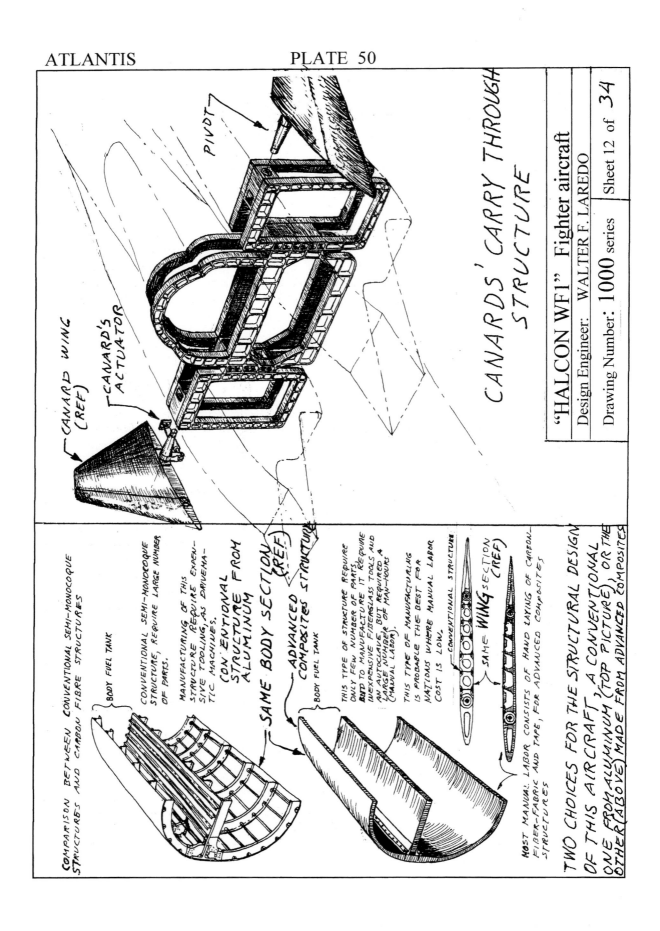

CANARD WING (REF)

CANARD'S ACTUATOR

PIVOT

CANARDS' CARRY THROUGH STRUCTURE

"HALCON WF1" Fighter aircraft

Design Engineer: WALTER F. LAREDO

Drawing Number: 1000 series | Sheet 12 of 34

COMPARISON BETWEEN CONVENTIONAL SEMI-MONOCOQUE STRUCTURES AND CARBON FIBRE STRUCTURES

BODY FUEL TANK

CONVENTIONAL SEMI-MONOCOQUE STRUCTURE, REQUIRE LARGE NUMBER OF PARTS.

MANUFACTURING OF THIS STRUCTURE REQUIRE EXPENSIVE TOOLING, AS DRIVE-MATIC MACHINES.

CONVENTIONAL STRUCTURE FROM ALUMINUM

SAME BODY SECTION (REF)

ADVANCED COMPOSITES STRUCTURE

BODY FUEL TANK

THIS TYPE OF STRUCTURE REQUIRE ONLY FEW NUMBER OF PARTS, AND TO MANUFACTURE IT REQUIRE INEXPENSIVE FIBERGLASS TOOLS AND AN AUTOCLAVE, BUT REQUIRED A LARGE NUMBER OF MAN-HOURS (MANUAL LABOR).

THIS TYPE OF MANUFACTURING IS PROBABLE THE BEST FOR NATIONS WHERE MANUAL LABOR COST IS LOW.

CONVENTIONAL STRUCTURE

SAME WING SECTION (REF)

MOST MANUAL LABOR CONSISTS OF HAND LAYING OF CARBON FIBER-FABRIC AND TAPE, FOR ADVANCED COMPOSITES STRUCTURES

TWO CHOICES FOR THE STRUCTURAL DESIGN OF THIS AIRCRAFT, A CONVENTIONAL ONE FROM ALUMINUM (TOP PICTURE), OR THE OTHER (ABOVE) MADE FROM ADVANCED COMPOSITES

# "HALCON WF1", AN ADVANCED LIGHTWEIGHT FIGHTER
(FOR MORE DETAIL SEE "PROPOSAL FOR THE DEVELOPMENT OF THE HALCON WL1", PREPARED BY WALTER F. LAREDO)

The Halcon WF1 is a high performance lightweight advanced fighter Mach 2.3, designed with the latest-state- of-the-art.  An aircraft developed as a new-generation lightweight supersonic combat aircraft, using new technologies, considering its high degree of readiness, mobility and striking power.

In this decade of the 1980's the Halcon WF1 will be develop as a competitor to other modern fighters in process of development as the Soviet's MIG 2000 and MIG 29, the multinational European fighter EFA, French's Rafale, Sweden's Gripen and the American Advanced Tactical Fighter (ATF).  Also competitor to existing aircraft as the Mirage III, Mirage 2000, MIG 21 and F-16.

Maintenance of the Halcon WF1 will be easy, because its good accessibility through many inspections doors, at suitable location of equipment.

This aircraft configuration is basically a Delta wing with sweptback Canards, which spigots are supported by bushings inserted in the main titanium bulkhead, a structure across the fuselage and the two-dimensional air inlets.  This aircraft have two vertical stabilizers.  Large portions of the aircraft structure is made from advanced composites materials, in the form of graphite fibers imbedded in epoxy resin, as well as Kevlar fibers in zones requiring impact resistance.

This aircraft will be design basically for the Pratt & Whitney F100-PW-100 engine (Max. Sea Level Static Thrust = 23000 lb.), other alternate engines are the F100-PW-200 and The F100-PW-220 (both, Max. Sea Level Static Thrust 25000 lb.), engines currently in use by the F-15 and the F-16 aircraft, another alternate engine with slightly different characteristics and flight envelopes would be the General Electric F404 currently used in the F-18 with an afterburner thrust of 16000 lb. at Sea Level, Standard day.  In this aircraft also could be installed equivalent European engines with a minimum of engine mountings modification.  In most Halcons WL1 aircraft will use the low bypass 20 years old F100-PW-100 engine with the following characteristics:
Length (including nozzle),  190 in (4.83 m)
Weight (bare),  2310 lb. (1050 kg)
Bypass Ratio,  0.71
Afterburner Thrust, Sea Level Static, 23000 lb. (uninstalled).
Sea Level Thrust Specific Fuel Consumption (TSFC) of 2.48 lb. fuel/lb. thrust per hour with afterburner.

The Halcon WF1 aircraft, with the F100-PW-100 engine, have a thrust : weight ratio of 1.04 at combat weight.  This aircraft have a combination of the four most wanted

| | "HALCON WF1"  Fighter aircraft | | . |
|---|---|---|---|
| . | Design Engineer:          WALTER F. LAREDO | | . |
| | Drawing number:    **1000 series** | Sheet   13   of   34 | . |

characteristics, as high top speed, low sensitivity to turbulent air, and great maneuverability at typical combat speeds, plus exceptional low speed performance for short takeoff and landing.

For pilots, the maneuverability of changing the flight paths mainly in the pitch plane is considered of primary importance.  The Halcon WF1 will be designed as a highly maneuvering fighter with short Turn Radius and a high Sustained Turn Rate, so that it could hold a turn without loosing speed and slip inside the adversary's arc to get in his tail.
During the studies and the design phase of the Halcon WF1 will be charted its Energy Maneuverability as plots of Turn Rate vs. Velocity for given altitudes as well as for small changes in configuration.

The pilot will have all around excellent visibility.  The propulsion system will have lateral inlets of special design to obtain "LOW DISTORTION FLOW" and good "PRESSURE RECOVERY" at high angles of attack during air combat and maneuvers.

The cockpit Display System will have one Head Up Display (HUD), where vital information is presented in the line of sight of the pilot, as he looks into the forward direction.  The cockpit instrument panel located next to the radar display will have either conventional instruments or more modern head down electronic display as preferred by most fighter pilots.

The Halcon WF1 as a modern supersonic aircraft will use hydraulic servoactuators, controlled by ALL ELECTRONIC FLY-BY-WIRE FLIGHT-CONTROL SYSTEM COMMAND AND STABILITY-AUGMENTATION SYSTEM.   SINCE THE HALCON WL1 CENTER OF GRAVITY IS CLOSE TO THE CENTER OF PRESSURE, RELAXED STABILITY DESIGN FOR MINIMUM TRIM DRAG, WAS POSSIBLE TO REDUCE THE SIZE OF THE ELEVATORS AND FLAPERONS.

Unstable full fly-by-wire aircraft, with new generation of computers and more advanced radar, allowed using the concept of relaxed stability for minimum trim drag.  Its maneuverability and controllability together will comprise good agility, hence an agile aircraft.  Vital for survival in the air defense role are its maneuverability and turning capability, advantages to which should be add its full all-weather, and all-altitude defense capability.

Infrared-seeking missiles have made the tail chase of enemy aircraft unnecessary.  The Halcon WF1 when followed by a seeking enemy missile, as in some modern fighters, will be alerted by their tail warning system.    The basic Halcon WF1 will be armed with the following weapons:
• Infrared and radar homing air-to-air  missiles as the American AIM-9 Sidewinder also could be adapted to use equivalent European missiles.
• A build-in, high performance M-61 six barrel, 20 mm cannon with 300 rounds of ammunition.
The aircraft have provisions to be used for other roles, as for ground attack, carrying laser guided missiles, bombs or anti-ship missiles.

"HALCON WF1"  Fighter aircraft

Design Engineer:        WALTER F. LAREDO

Drawing number:   1000 series                    Sheet  14 of  34

The main landing gear will be designed to resist an impact at a descent rate of 13 ft per second (3.9 m/sec), good for direct short landing without flare. It will use either, conventional or carbon brakes, probably with an antiskid system.

Its modular design facilitates major repairs, re-design, and quick replacement of equipment. Major aircraft modifications and adaptations may happens sometime during the next twenty years, such as future variable cycle engines with two dimensional vectoring nozzles, better avionics, better radar and other advanced systems.

DESIGN AND DEVELOPMENTAL PHASES FOR THE HALCON WL1 AIRCRAFT

Testing with wind tunnel models will require hundreds or thousands of hours. By using CAD-CAM equipment could be produced all the drawings required to build the airplane. Applying the Area Rule for Mach 2.3 created the external geometrical design. For the development of this aircraft was used several engineering specialties as Aerodynamics, Aerodynamic Stability and Control, Structures (Stress, Aeroelasticity, Fatigue and Flutter), Electronics, Flight Control System. Materials and Processes, Electric and Hydraulic Systems, Armament and Operational equipment, Cockpit Display System, Fuel System, Propulsion, Fire Extinguishing System, Environmental Control System and Miscellaneous.

In addition to the early data obtained from wind tunnel models, the full size actual flying demonstrator will provide excellent aerodynamic representation of the flow field around the aircraft. Flying tests will provide more realistic data concerning different flight conditions, than can be obtain from wind tunnel models. An additional and important wind tunnel model test would be the launching and dropping of various stores shapes from the aircraft model and later from the actual flight tests of the demonstrator.

The ejection seat will be operable from zero to an equivalent air speed of 690 mph at zero altitude. The pilot will control the aircraft with a central conventional stick. A disadvantage of the side-stick control as in the F-16 is that it increases the frontal cross section area of the cockpit design.

The Halcon WF1 will be pressurizing with bleed air from the engine, air that will be cool with a combination of cycle machine with ram air radiators.

Fuel tanks should be inert, either, Halon or nitrogen gas.

The Maneuverability and Controllability of this aircraft will comprise Agility, with high Sustained Turn Rate, able to hold a "turn without loosing speed" and slip inside the adversary's arc to get on his tail. Good Energy Maneuverability will be charter as plots of "Turn Rate vs. Velocity" for a given Altitude and Configuration. Also will be charted the Energy Maneuver Performance in terms of specific excess power (Ps), and persistence (fuel flow).

| "HALCON WF1"  Fighter aircraft | | |
|---|---|---|
| Design Engineer:        WALTER F. LAREDO | | |
| Drawing number:  **1000 series** | Sheet  15  of   34 | |

## HALCON WL1, PERFORMANCE AND CHARACTERISTICS
Primary role: Lightweight fighter. Secondary role; attack

**DIMENSIONS:**

| | | |
|---|---|---|
| Wing span | 33 ft 8 in | 10.26 m |
| Max. length | 51 ft 2 in | 15.60 m |
| Wheel track | 8 ft 4 in | 2.54 m |
| Wheel base | 16 ft 8 in | 5.08 m |
| Height (static) | 15 ft 2 in | 4.62 m |

**WEIGHTS:**

| | | |
|---|---|---|
| Empty | 14058 lb | 6376.7 Kg |
| Loaded (clean), fighting mission | 22200 lb | 10070 Kg |
| Max. takeoff gross weight | 32000 lb | 14515 Kg |
| Payload, fighting mission | 1800 lb | 816.5 Kg |
| Max. armament load | 6000 lb | 2722 Kg |
| Internal fuel | 9060 lb | 4110 Kg |
| 70 % internal fuel, fighting mission | 6342 lb | 2877 Kg |
| Total fuel capacity, includes external tanks | 11242 lb | 5099 Kg |

**WING:**

| | | |
|---|---|---|
| Wing area | 370 sq ft | 34.37 sq. m. |
| Aspect Ratio | 2.46 | |
| Sweep Leading Edge | 49 degrees | |
| MAC | 181 in | 4.60 m |
| T/C SOB / T/C TIP | 5 % / 3.5 % | |
| Wing Angle of incidence and the Dihedral | To be determinate | |

**CANARD WINGS:**

| | | |
|---|---|---|
| Area | 46 sq ft | 4.27 sq. m. |
| Area, plus fuselage lift Contributing sect. | 106.8 sq ft | 9.93 sq. m. |

$V_c = (L_c)(S_c) / (c)(S_w)$

| | | |
|---|---|---|
| $V_c$ (for $S_c$=46 sq ft) | 0.107 | |
| $V_c$ (for $S_c$=106.8 sq ft) | 0.25 | |
| Aspect Ratio | 3.32 | |
| T/C SOB / T/C tip | 4.5 % / 3 % | |
| Sweep L.E. | 49 degrees | |

**VERTICAL TAILS:**

| | | |
|---|---|---|
| Sweep L.E. | 36 degrees | |
| Area (both fins) | 64 sq ft | 5.95 sq. m. |
| $V_v = (L_v)(S_v) / (b)(S_w)$ | = 0.087 | |
| T/C root / T/C tip | 4.5 % / 3.5 % | |

## "HALCON WF1" Fighter aircraft

Design Engineer: WALTER F. LAREDO

Drawing Number: **1000 series**

WING LOADING  (for 22200 lb G.W.)        60 lb/sq ft                293 Kg/sq.m.
UNINSTALLED THRUST/WEIGHT  (SLS)       1.04
LOAD FACTOR  (for 22200 lb G.W.)         +7.33 and –3    G's limits

PERFORMANCE:
    SPEEDS
    Max. Mach No. at Sea Level (interceptor)     1.2
    Max. Mach No. at 40000 ft  (interceptor)      2.2
    Cruise Mach No.  at 36000 ft                  0.85
    Takeoff safety speed (22200 lb G.W.)         140 mph        225 kph
    Takeoff safety speed (Max. TOW)              168 mph        270.4 kph
    Approach speed                               142 mph        228.5 kph
    Landing (touchdown)                          135 mph        217 kph

    CEILING
    Service ceiling                          62000 ft        18898 m.
    Absolute ceiling (no weapons)            90000 ft        27432 m.

    CLIMB
    Rate of Climb (with afterburner)       To be determinate
    Initial  Climb                          48000 ft/min              14630 m/min
    RANGE
    Combat radius,  internal fuel (20 min. reserve)    400 miles      644 Km
    Interceptor radius (70 % internal fuel)            280 miles      450 Km
    Interceptor radius, high speed interception
        with full Afterburner, Mach 2.2             84 miles       135 Km
    Ferry range, without refueling in the air        1800 miles      2897 Km

TAKEOFF AND LANDING DISTANCES
    Takeoff distance (clean aircraft)        1400 ft          427 m
    Takeoff distance at Max. TOW             3800 ft          1158 m
    Landing distance at SL  (no flare)       1600 ft          488 m
    Landing distance at ST (conventional)    2600 ft          792.5 m
    Rate of sink  (at landing)               14 ft/sec        4.27 m/sec

TURING RATE AT 15000 FT
    Sustaining turning rate at M.8              13.4 deg/sec
    Sustaining turning rate at M.9              13.5 deg/sec
    Instantaneous turning rate at M.5           21.6 deg/sec
    Instantaneous turning rate at M.9           17.4 deg/sec

SPECIFIC EXCESS POWER,  at M.8,  1G and  GW=22200 lb      (GW=10070 Kg)
    At Sea Level,              $Ps = 863$ ft/sec      (263 m/sec)
    At 15000 ft  (4572 m),     $Ps = 654$ ft/sec      (199 m/sec)

## "HALCON WF1"  Fighter aircraft

Design Engineer:   WALTER F. LAREDO

| Drawing Number:  **1000 series** | Sheet  17  of  34 . |

# PERFORMANCE CALCULATIONS

AIR TO AIR FIGHTING MISSION WITH A TAKEOFF GROSS WEIGHT OF 22200 LB (70 % INTERNAL FUEL), BASIC FLIGHT MISSION TO DESIGN THE HALCON WF1 AIRCRAFT

Aircraft designed with a limit load factor $n = 7.33$ (subsonic) and $n = 6.5$ (supersonic)

To find the following, for Mach numbers 0.9, 0.8 & 0.5 and an altitude of 15000 Ft:

- Sustained Load Factor
- Sustained Turn Rate
- Instantaneous Load Factor
- Instantaneous Turn Rate
- Acceleration Level Flight
- Excess of Specific Power for :
    1. Mach 0.9 & 0.8 at an altitude of 15000 Ft
    2. Mach 0.8 at sea level

WEIGHT CHANGE CALCULATION AFTER BURNING FUEL DURING EACH MISSION PHASE, PHASES 1 THROUGH 7

| | |
|---|---|
| Phase 1: | Takeoff |
| Phase 2: | Climbing |
| Phase 3: | Cruise and Range, between 36000 Ft to 47000 Ft |
| Phase 4: | Dash acceleration to combat arena |
| Phase 5: | Combat (4 minutes, 25000 Ft, Mach 0.9) |
| Phase 6: | Cruise return |
| Phase 7: | Loiter at sea level |

Calculation of the Instantaneous Turn Rate, Continuous Turn Rate and its Radius for a safe load factor.

Calculate Total Takeoff Distance at sea level

Calculate Total Landing Distance with 50 % internal fuel.

## "HALCON WF1"  Fighter aircraft

| Design Engineer:  WALTER F. LAREDO | |
|---|---|
| Drawing Number:  **1000 series** | Sheet 18 of 34 |

FOR THE $Halcón \ WL1$ FLYING AT AN ALTITUDE OF 15000 FT, TO FIND FOR EACH ONE OF THE FOLLOWING MACH NUMBERS 0.9, 0.8 AND 0.5, THE FOLLOWING:

- SUSTAINED LOAD FACTOR = $n_{sust}$
- SUSTAINED TURN RATE = $\dot{\psi}_{sust}$
- INSTANTANEOUS LOAD FACTOR = $n_{inst}$
- INSTANTANEOUS TURN RATE = $\dot{\psi}_{inst}$
- ACCELERATION LEVEL FLIGHTS $\frac{dV}{dt}$ FOR $n = 5$

DATA

ALTITUDE = 15000 FT
$P = 1194.17 \ Lb/ft^2$
$\rho = .0015 \ Lb \cdot sec^2/ft^4$
$a = 1057.23 \ ft/sec$
$\gamma = C_P/C_V = 1.40$
$S_w = 370 \ ft^2$
$C_{D_o} = .018$ (MACH NUMBERS 0.9, 0.8 AND 0.5) DATA FROM SIMILAR AIRPLANES
$K = .16$ (MACH NOS. 0.9, 0.8 AND 0.5) DATA FROM SIMILAR AIRCRAFT
$W = 22200 \ Lb$
$C_{L_{max}} = 0.8$ FOR SERIES 64, 65 AND 66 AIRFOILS, 5% T/C, NO FLAPS DEPLOYED

MACH NUMBER 0.9, ALTITUD 15000 FT

F-100-PW ENGINE, INSTALLED THRUST WITH MAXIMUM AFTERBURNER = $T_{max}$ = 20000 Lbs
$V = 951.54 \ Ft/sec$
$\frac{1}{2}\rho V^2 = q = 677.04 \ Lb/ft^2$

SUSTAINED LOAD FACTOR
$$n_{sust} = \frac{q}{W/S_w}\sqrt{\frac{1}{K}\left(\frac{T_{max}}{qS_w} - C_{D_o}\right)} = 7.0150$$

SUSTAINED TURN RATE
$$\dot{\psi} = \frac{g\sqrt{n_{sust}^2 - 1}}{V} \times (57.3) = 13.46 \ \frac{DEG}{SEC}$$

$n$ INSTANTANEOUS:
$C_{L_{max}} = .8$
$$n_{inst} = \frac{q \ C_{L_{max}}}{W/S} = 9.03$$

INSTANTANEOUS TURN RATE:
$$\dot{\psi}_{INST} = \frac{g\sqrt{n_{inst}^2 - 1}}{V} \times (57.3) = 17.39 \ \frac{DEGREES}{SEC}$$

MACH NUMBER 0.8, ALTITUDE 15000 FT

F-100-PW ENGINE, INSTALLED THRUST WITH MAXIMUM AFTERBURNER = $T_{max}$ = 18800 Lb
$V = 845.78 \ Ft/sec$
$q = \frac{1}{2}\rho V^2 = 539.93 \ Lb/ft^2$

$n$ SUSTAINED:
$$n_{sust} = \frac{q}{W/S}\sqrt{\frac{1}{K}\left(\frac{T_{max}}{qS_w} - C_{D_o}\right)} = 6.21$$

SUSTAINED TURN RATE:
$$\dot{\psi} = \frac{g\sqrt{n_{sust}^2 - 1}}{V} \times (57.3) = 13.36 \ \frac{DEG}{SEC}$$

$n$ INSTANTANEOUS:
$C_{L_{max}} = .8$
$$n_{inst} = \frac{q \ C_{L_{max}}}{W/S} = 7.2$$

INSTANTANEOUS TURN RATE:
$$\dot{\psi}_{INST} = \frac{g\sqrt{n_{inst}^2 - 1}}{V} \times (57.3) = 15.55 \ \frac{DEG}{SEC}$$

MACH NUMBER 0.5, ALTITUDE 15000 FT

F-100-PW ENGINE INSTALLED THRUST WITH MAXIMUM AFTERBURNING = $T_{max}$ = 15000 Lb
$V = 528.62 \ FT/SEC$
$q = \frac{1}{2}\rho V^2 = 208.97 \ LB/FT^2$

$n$ SUSTAINED:
$$n_{sust} = \frac{q}{W/S_w}\sqrt{\frac{1}{K}\left(\frac{T_{max}}{qS_w} - C_{D_o}\right)} = 3.65$$

SUSTAINED TURN RATE:
$$\dot{\psi} = \frac{g\sqrt{n_{sust}^2 - 1}}{V} \times (57.3) = 12.26 \ \frac{DEG}{SEC}$$

$n$ INSTANTANEOUS:
$C_{L_{max}} = 1.8$ WITH LEADING EDGE FLAPS DEFLECTED DOWN
$$n_{inst} = \frac{q \ C_{L_{max}}}{W/S} = 6.27$$

INSTANTANEOUS TURN RATE:
$$\dot{\psi}_{INST} = \frac{g\sqrt{n_{inst}^2 - 1}}{V} \times (57.3) = 21.6 \ \frac{DEG}{SEC}$$

TO FIND THE EXCESS SPECIFIC POWER $P_s = \frac{dh_e}{dt}$

FOR MACH 0.9, $n = 5$ AT AN ALTITUDE OF 15000 ft
$C_L = \frac{nW}{qS} = .4431$
$C_D = C_{D_o} + KC_L^2 = .049$
$D = \frac{\gamma}{2}PM^2 S_w C_D = 12379.44 \ Lbs$
$P_s = \frac{dh_e}{dt} = \frac{V(T-D)}{W} = 326.62 \ ft/sec$

FOR MACH 0.8, $n = 5$ AT AN ALTITUDE OF 15000 ft
$C_L = \frac{nW}{qS} = .5556$
$C_D = C_{D_o} + KC_L^2 = .0673$
$D = \frac{\gamma}{2}PM^2 S_w C_D = 5478.26 \ Lbs$
$P_s = \frac{dh_e}{dt} = \frac{V(T-D)}{W} = 208.71 \ ft/sec$

FOR MACH .8 $n = 1$ AT AN ALTITUDE OF 15000 ft
$C_L = \frac{nW}{qS} = .1112$
$C_D = C_{D_o} + KC_L^2 = .02$
$D = \frac{\gamma}{2}PM^2 S_w C_D = 1628 \ Lbs$
$P_s = \frac{dh_e}{dt} = \frac{V(T-D)}{W} = 654.2 \ ft/sec$

AND THE ACCELERATION IN LEVEL FLIGHT $\frac{dV}{dt}$ IS
$\frac{dV}{dt} = \frac{g \ P_s}{V} = 24.9 \ ft/sec^2$

FOR MACH .8 $n = 1$ AT SEA LEVEL
INSTALLED THRUST WITH AFTERBURNER = 28000 Lbs
$C_L = \frac{nW}{qS} = .0633$ then $C_D = C_{D_o} + KC_L^2 = .01864$
$D = \frac{\gamma}{2}PM^2 S_w C_D = 6539 \ Lbs$
$P_s = \frac{dh_e}{dt} = \frac{V(T-D)}{W} = \boxed{863 \ ft/sec} = \text{INSTANTANEOUS RATE OF CLIMB}$

| "HALCON WF1"   Fighter aircraft | |
|---|---|
| Design Engineer:   WALTER F. LAREDO | |
| Drawing Number:   **1000** series | Sheet 19 of **34** |

COMPARISON OF SUSTAINED TURNING RATE PERFORMANCE AND THE INSTANTANEOUS TURNING RATE PERFORMANCE, BETWEEN THE FOLLOWING AIRCRAFTS, INCLUDING THE HALCON WF1.

| AIRCRAFT → | MC DONNELL DOUGLAS F-15 EAGLE | Halcón WF1 | MIG-21 | GENERAL DYNAMICS F-16 FALCON | NORTHROP F-5A | LAVI | MC DONNELL DOUGLAS F-4 PHANTOM |
|---|---|---|---|---|---|---|---|
| SUSTAINED TURNING RATE AT MACH NUMBER .8 | 11.8 DEG/SEC | 13.36 DEG/SEC | | | | 13.2 DEG/SEC | |
| SUSTAINED TURNING RATE AT M. 9 | | 13.46 DEG/SEC | 7.5 DEG/SEC | 12.8 DEG/SEC | 7.8 DEG/SEC | | 9 DEG/SEC |
| INSTANTANEOUS TURNING RATE AT M. 9 | 14.1 DEG/SEC | 17.39 DEG/SEC | 13.4 DEG/SEC | 17.3 DEG/SEC | 14 DEG/SEC | | 13.5 DEG/SEC |
| INSTANTANEOUS TURNING RATE AT M. 5 | 16.5 DEG/SEC | 21.6 DEG/SEC | 11.1 DEG/SEC | 15.6 DEG/SEC | 11.4 DEG/SEC | | 7.8 DEG/SEC |
| INST. TURNING RATE AT M. 8 | | 15.55 DEG/SEC | | | | 24.3 DEG/SEC | |

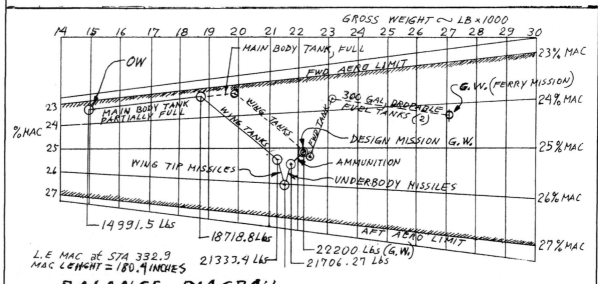

BALANCE DIAGRAM
AIRCRAFT CONFIGURATION USING ARTIFICIAL GRAVITY

| "HALCON WF1"  Fighter aircraft | |
|---|---|
| Design Engineer:  WALTER F. LAREDO | |
| Drawing Number:  **1000** series | Sheet 20 of 34 |

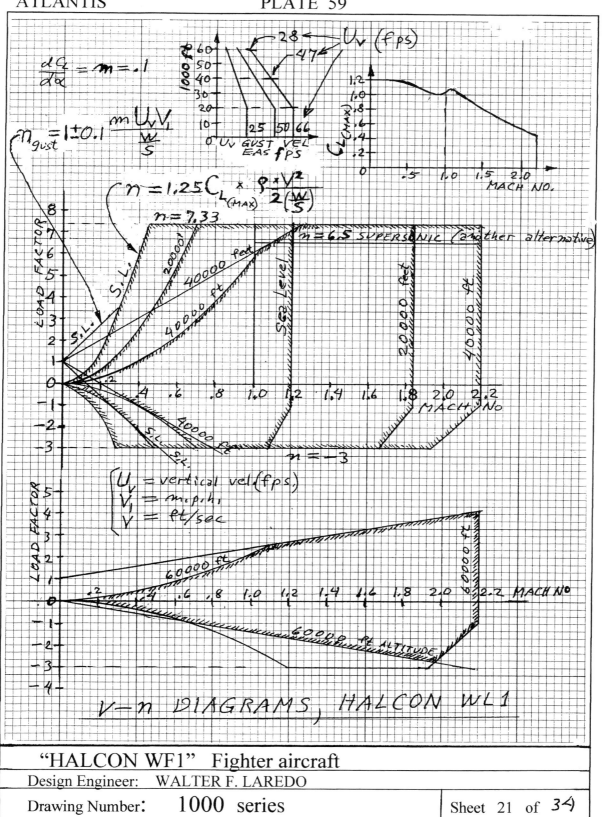

$$\frac{dC_L}{d\alpha} = m = .1$$

$$n_{gust} = 1 \pm 0.1 \frac{m\, U_v V_i}{\frac{W}{S}}$$

$$n = 1.25 \, C_{L(MAX)} \times \frac{\rho * V^2}{2 \left(\frac{W}{S}\right)}$$

$$n = 7.33$$

$m = 6.5$ SUPERSONIC (another alternative)

$n = -3$

$\begin{cases} U_v = \text{vertical vel.(fps.)} \\ V_i = \text{m.p.h.} \\ V = \text{ft/sec} \end{cases}$

V-n DIAGRAMS, HALCON WL1

"HALCON WF1"  Fighter aircraft

Design Engineer:  WALTER F. LAREDO

Drawing Number:  **1000** series

Sheet 21 of 34

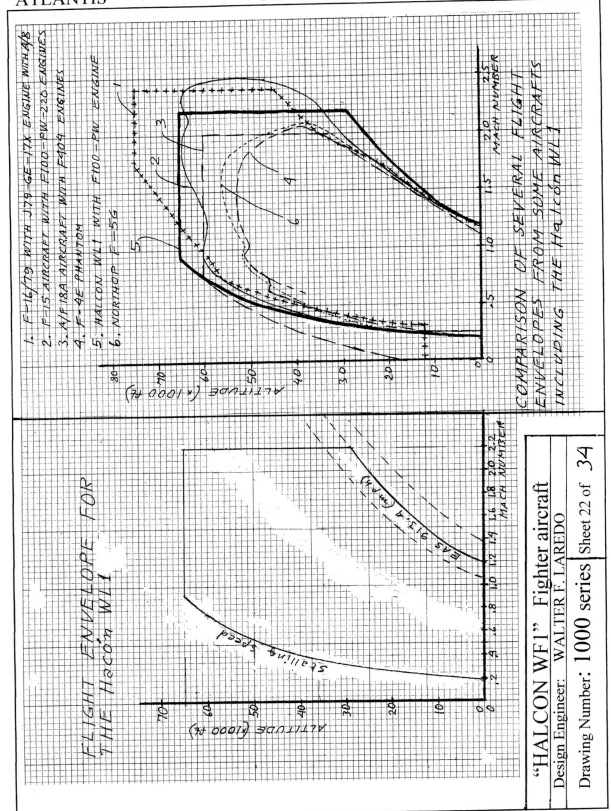

1. F-16/79 WITH J79-GE-17X ENGINE WITH A/B
2. F-15 AIRCRAFT WITH F100-PW-220 ENGINES
3. A/F 18A AIRCRAFT WITH F404 ENGINES
4. F-4E PHANTOM
5. HALCON WL1 WITH F100-PW ENGINE
6. NORTHOP F-5G

COMPARISON OF SEVERAL FLIGHT
ENVELOPES FROM SOME AIRCRAFTS
INCLUDING THE Halcón WL1

ALTITUDE (x 1000 ft)

MACH NUMBER

FLIGHT ENVELOPE FOR
THE Halcón WL1

Stalling speed

ALTITUDE (x1000 ft)

MACH NUMBER

"HALCON WF1"  Fighter aircraft

Design Engineer:   WALTER F. LAREDO

Drawing Number: 1000 series | Sheet 22 of 34

*HALCON WL1*
*AIR TO AIR FIGHTING MISSION*

WITH THE GROSS WEIGHT (70% INTERNAL FUEL) OF 22,200 LBS, THE AIRCRAFT IS GOING TO BE DESIGNED WITH A LIMIT LOAD FACTOR, $n = 7.3$
$W_1 = W_{TO} = 22200$ Lbs.

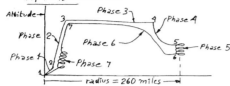

Fixed Weights:

Pilot plus gear ............................. = 200 Lbs
4 AIM missiles plus racks ........ = 944 Lbs
M-61 cannon plus accessories .. = 485 Lbs
300 rounds of 20mm shells ....... = 171.43 Lbs
                                                      1800.43 Lbs

$W_{fixed} = 1800$ lbs

Radius using 70% fill fuel tanks = 280 miles
Max. speed for this mission = M 1.6
cruising between 36000 ft and 47000 ft

PHASE 1

$W_{TO} = W_1 =$ GROSS weight before start and before start and before takeoff. The aircraft burns 3% of $W_{TO}$ fuel

$$\frac{W_2}{W_1} = .97$$

Aspect ratio $AR = 2.46$
$\bar{e} = .8$ is used for swept thin wing aircraft, with thicknesses from 3% to 8% chord.

$K = \frac{1}{\pi \, AR \, \bar{e}} = .1617$ subsonic

| | | |
|---|---|---|
| Range mission for jet aircraft | $C_L = \sqrt{C_{D_0}/3K}$ ←constant altitude condition. | |
| | $C_L = \sqrt{C_{D_0}/2K}$ ←constant throttle setting condition (cruse climb) | |
| Endurance mission for jet aircraft | $C_L = \sqrt{C_{D_0}/K}$ ←minimum thrust required | |

$C_L = \sqrt{C_{D_0}/2K}$

$\frac{L}{D} = \frac{C_L}{C_D} = \frac{C_L}{C_{D_0} + KC_L^2} = \frac{\sqrt{C_{D_0}/2K}}{C_{D_0} + K(C_{D_0}/2K)} = \sqrt{\frac{8}{9}}\left(\frac{L}{D}\right)_{max}$

where $\left(\frac{L}{D}\right)_{max} = \frac{1}{2\sqrt{C_{D_0}K}} = 9.27$

So $\frac{L}{D} = \sqrt{\frac{8}{9}}(9.27) = 8.74$

To find $\frac{W_3}{W_4}$ using the Breguet Range equation

$Range = \left(\frac{V}{TSFC}\right)\left(\frac{L}{D}\right)\left(\ln\frac{W_3}{W_4}\right)$

$\ln\frac{W_3}{W_4} = \frac{(R)(TSFC)}{(V)\left(\frac{L}{D}\right)} = \frac{(280)(.91)}{(685)(8.74)} = .04256$

$\frac{W_3}{W_4} = e^{.04256} = 1.05$

or $\boxed{\frac{W_4}{W_3} = .953}$

PHASE 2 Climbing, from fig. below $\frac{W_3}{W_2} = .975$

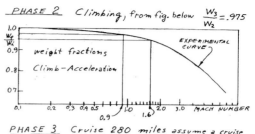

PHASE 3 Cruise 280 miles assume a cruise assume a cruise between 36000 to 47000,

ALTITUDE: 36089
F-100 ENGINE
TSFC FOR PARTIAL POWER SETTINGS (NON AFTER-BURNING)

FROM PICTURES AT LEFT FOR MACH NUMBER .9

$TSFC = .91$ lb/lb-hr

and

$C_{D_0} = .018$

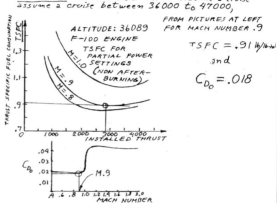

PHASE 4. Dash acceleration to high speed (combat), acceleration to Mach 1.6 at 25000 ft of altitude.

$W_f = \frac{W_5}{W_2} = .950,$ (Going from $M_{(5)} = .1$ to $M_{(5)} = 1.6$)

$W_i = \frac{W_3}{W_2} = .975,$ (Going from $M_{(5)} = .1$ to $M_{(5)} = .9$)

BUT IN PHASE 4, INICIAL MACH NO IS .9, SO.

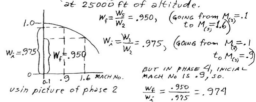

usin picture of phase 2

$\frac{W_f}{W_i} = \frac{.950}{.975} = .974$

PHASE 5. Four minutes of combat turns at 25000 ft of altitude and Mach Number = .9 use diagram about Installed Thrust vs. Mach Number for the F-100 Engine.

Maximum thrust with afterburner at 25000 ft = 13700 Lbs

$TSFC = 2.185$

Fuel burn in combat
$= T \times TSFC \times time$
$= (13700)(2.185)\left(\frac{4}{60}\right)$
$= 1996$ lbs.

combat fuel = $W_{fuel} = 1996$ lbs

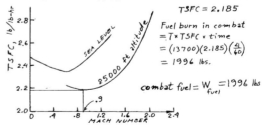

"HALCON WF1"   Fighter aircraft

Design Engineer:   WALTER F. LAREDO

Drawing Number:   1000 series                Sheet 23 of 34

**PHASE 6** _Cruise return, same as phase 3_

$$\frac{W_6}{W_7} = \frac{W_3}{W_4} = 1.05 \qquad \frac{W_7}{W_6} = .9524$$

**PHASE 7** _Loiter at sea level, 20 minutes_

To find $C_L$ from range and endurance chart in phase 3.

$$C_L = \sqrt{C_{D_o}/K}$$
$$C_D = C_{D_o} + K C_L^2$$

so $\dfrac{L}{D} = \dfrac{C_L}{C_D} = \dfrac{\sqrt{C_{D_o}/K}}{C_{D_o}+K C_L^2} = \dfrac{\sqrt{C_{D_o}/K}}{C_{D_o}+K(C_{D_o}/K)} = \dfrac{1}{2\sqrt{C_{D_o}K}}$

$$= 9.2678$$

$$Endurance = E = \frac{L}{D}\frac{1}{TSFC}\ln\frac{W_7}{W_8}$$

From F-100 engine data, for low subsonic flight TSFC = .84

$$E = \frac{20}{60} = (9.2678)\left(\frac{1}{.84}\right)\ln\frac{W_7}{W_8}$$

$$\frac{W_7}{W_8} = 1.03 \quad or \quad \frac{W_8}{W_7} = .970$$

---

**TO FIND:**

- THE AIRCRAFT WEIGHT AT THE BEGINNING OF COMBAT ($W_5$).
- THE WEIGHT AT THE END OF COMBAT ($W_6$).
- LANDING WEIGHT ($W_8$).
- MISSION FUEL WEIGHT.
- AIRCRAFT EMPTY WEIGHT
- FEASIBILITY OF TAKEOFF WEIGHT VS. EMPTY WEIGHT

MISSION PHASES:
- Phase 1, $\frac{W_2}{W_1} = .97$ Lbs
- Phase 2, $\frac{W_3}{W_2} = .975$ Lbs
- Phase 3, $\frac{W_4}{W_3} = .9524$ Lbs
- Phase 4, $\frac{W_5}{W_4} = .974$ Lbs
- Phase 5, $\frac{W_{fuel}}{combat} = 1996$ Lbs
- Phase 6, $\frac{W_7}{W_6} = .9524$ Lbs
- Phase 7, $\frac{W_8}{W_7} = .970$ Lbs

AIRCRAFT TAKEOFF WEIGHT = $W_{TO} = W_1$ = 22200 Lbs

- AIRCRAFT WEIGHT AT THE BEGINNING OF COMBAT.

$$W_5 = \left(\frac{W_2}{W_1}\right)\left(\frac{W_3}{W_2}\right)\left(\frac{W_4}{W_3}\right)\left(\frac{W_5}{W_4}\right)W_1 = (.877)(22200) = 19476 \text{ Lbs}$$

- WEIGHT AT THE END OF COMBAT = $W_6 = W_5 -$ EXPENDABLE FIXED WEIGHTS

EXPENDABLE FIXED WEIGHTS
- FUEL (4 MINUTES OF COMBAT) ...... 1996 Lbs
- 4 AIM MISSILES ........ 696 Lbs
- 300 ROUNDS OF 20 MM AMMUNITION ...... 171.43 Lbs
  _____
  2863.43 Lbs

$$W_6 = 19476 \text{ Lbs} - 2863.43 \text{ Lbs} = 16612.57 \text{ Lbs}$$

---

To cruise back use $W_6$ as the new initial weight.

- The weight at landing is $W_8$

$$W_8 = \left(\frac{W_7}{W_6}\right)\left(\frac{W_8}{W_7}\right)W_6 = (.9524)(.970)(16612.57) = 15350 \text{ Lbs}$$

- Fuel weight required for the mission, $W_{fuel}$

$$W_{fuel}_{mission} = W_{TO} - W_8 - missile - ammo = 5982.6 \text{ Lbs}$$

The total fuel required, includes 5% reserve fuel plus 1% trapped fuel.

$$W_{fuel} = 1.06\, W_{fuel}_{mission} = 6341.5 \text{ Lbs}$$

- Empty weight

$$W_{empty} = W_{TO} - W_{fuel} - W_{FIXED} = 22200 - 6341.5 - 1880$$
$$= 14058.5 \text{ Lbs} \quad (I)$$

Comparing this result with the one obtained by using a formula which was obtained from historical data and applies when $\frac{T}{W_{TO}} > 0.9$ and $\frac{W}{S} < 70$

$$W_{empty}_{with conventional structure} = 1.605 (W_{TAKEOFF})^{0.916} = 15372 \text{ Lbs}$$

some parts of the aircraft structure will be made using advanced composites materials, so the aircraft will be 10% lighter.

$$W_{empty}_{(advanced technology materials)} = (15372)(.90) = 13835 \text{ Lbs} \quad (II)$$

$(I) > (II)$, it is acceptable

- so this mission relation between $W_{empty}$ and $W_{TO}$ is feasible.

---

_HALCON WL1_

At the end of phase 4 (Dash operation), the aircraft will be flying horizontally at the following conditions:
altitude = 25000 ft.
Mach number = 1.6, (V = 1625 ft/sec)
Max. Thrust = 21000 Lb
GROSS WEIGHT = (.8773)($W_1$) = 19476 Lb
$C_D$ = .04092 (from similar aircraft) SUPERSONIC.
$\gamma = \frac{C_P}{C_V} = 1.4$ for air
P = pressure at 25000 ft (air)
S = 370 ft²

$$D = \frac{\gamma}{2}PM^2 S C_D = 21046 \text{ Lb}$$

$$P_s = \frac{dh_s}{dt} = \frac{V(T-D)}{W} = \frac{(1625)(21000-21046)}{19476}$$

$$P_s = -3.85 \text{ ft/sec}$$

desacceleration in horizontal flight = $\frac{gP_s}{V}$ ft/sec²

$$\frac{gP_s}{V} = \frac{(32.2)(-3.85)}{(1625)} = -.076 \approx 0 \text{ (negligible)}$$

so that the airplane will be on a level flight, its maximum sustained turn rate $\dot\psi$ and n are:

$$n_{sustained} = \frac{q}{W/S}\sqrt{\frac{1}{K}\left(\frac{T_{max}}{qS}-C_{D_o}\right)} \qquad where: \begin{cases} M=1.6 \\ V = 1625 \text{ ft/sec} \\ \rho = .001065 \text{ slugs/ft}^3 \\ K = .25 \\ C_{D_o} = .04 \\ S = 370 \\ T_{max} = 21000 \text{ Lb} \end{cases}$$

$$= 1.0189$$

$$\dot\psi = \frac{g\sqrt{n^2-1}}{V} = .039 \frac{rad}{sec} = .22 \frac{degree}{sec}$$

$R \approx \infty$, straight line flight

Calculate $\dot\psi$ and n for .9M, at an altitude of 25000 ft

$$n_{sustained} = \frac{q}{W/S}\sqrt{\frac{1}{K}\left(\frac{T_{max}}{qS}-C_{D_o}\right)} \qquad \begin{cases} V = 1015.74 \text{ ft/sec} \\ \rho = .001065 \text{ slugs/ft}^3 \\ K = .16 \\ C_{D_o} = .018 \\ T_{max} = 21000 \text{ Lb} \end{cases}$$

$$= 7.61 \text{ which is a high load factor for the pilot and the aircraft above the limit strength of the structure.}$$

$$\dot\psi = \frac{g\sqrt{n^2-1}}{V} = .239 \frac{rad}{sec} = 13.7 \text{ degrees/sec}.$$

---

**"HALCON WF1"   Fighter aircraft**

Design Engineer:   WALTER F. LAREDO

Drawing Number:   **1000** series                    Sheet 24 of **34**

$Radius = \dfrac{V^2}{g\sqrt{n^2-1}} = 4250\ ft$

$wing\ tilt\ angle,\quad \phi = arc\cos\left(\dfrac{1}{n}\right) = 82.2°$

To calculate the instantaneous turn rate for $C_{L_{max}} = .8$

$n_{inst} = \dfrac{q\, C_{L_{max}}}{W/S} = 8.35$

$\dot\psi = \dfrac{g\sqrt{n^2-1}}{V}(57.3) = 15\ degrees\ per\ second$

The n g's of the sustained turn rate and the instantaneous turn rate are too high and could damage or destroy the aircraft structure. So using a lower value of $n = 5$, is calculated the new Thrust setting ($T$).

$P_S = \dfrac{dh_e}{dt} = 0 = V\left[\dfrac{T}{W} - \dfrac{q\,C_{D_o}}{W/S} - \dfrac{K}{q}\,n^2\dfrac{W}{S}\right]$

$T = 11589\ lbs$

max. sustained turn rate $\dot\psi = \dfrac{g\sqrt{n^2-1}}{V}(57.3) = 8.9\ degrees/sec$

$Radius = \dfrac{V^2}{g\sqrt{n^2-1}} = 6540\ feet$

---

## HALCON WL1
### TOTAL TAKEOFF DISTANCE AT SEA LEVEL

mission: Air to air combat, 4 AIM missiles, M-61 300 RNDS 20 mm, partially fill internal fuel tanks.
Takeoff weight = 22200 lbs

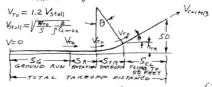

$Total\ Takeoff\ distance = S_G + S_R + S_{TR} + S_{CL}$  $\;(\text{I})$

$S_G = \left(\dfrac{1}{2}V_{TO}^2\right)\dfrac{1}{a}$, acceleration $a$ is at $.7\,V_{TO}$

$S_R = t\,V_{TO}$, $t = 3$, (3 seconds of rotation)

$S_{TR} = R\sin\theta$; $\quad R = \dfrac{V_{TO}^2}{n\,g}$

$n = \dfrac{L}{W} = 1.15$  $\Big\}\,(*)$

$\sin\theta = \dfrac{T-D}{W_{TO}}$

$S_{CL} = \dfrac{50 - h_{TR}}{\tan\theta}$ where $h_{TR} = R(1-\cos\theta)$

$(*)\quad L = W_{TO} + (\text{centrifugal force}) = W_{TO} + \dfrac{W_{TO}}{g}\dfrac{V_{TO}^2}{R}$ divide by $W_{TO}$

$n = \dfrac{L}{W_{TO}} = 1 + \dfrac{V_{TO}^2}{Rg} = \dfrac{\frac{1}{2}\rho\left(1.2\,V_{stall}\right)^2 S_w(.8\,C_{L_{max}})}{\frac{1}{2}\rho\left(V_{stall}^2\right) S_w\, C_{L_{max}}}$

$n = 1.15$ the airplane is rotated to an angle of attack, such that $C_L = .8\,C_{L_{max}}$

---

EQUATION $(\text{I})$ BECOME:

TOTAL TAKEOFF DISTANCE =

$$\dfrac{1.44\,\dfrac{W_{TO}}{S_w}}{g\rho\,C_{L_{max}}\left[\dfrac{T}{W_{TO}} - \dfrac{D}{W_{TO}} - \mu\left(1 - \dfrac{L_a}{W_{TO}}\right)\right]} + 3V_{TO} + \left(\dfrac{V_{TO}^2}{1.15g}\right)\left(\dfrac{T-D}{W_{TO}}\right) + \dfrac{50 - h_{TR}}{\tan\theta}\qquad (\text{II})$$

where:

$W_{TO} = 22200\ lbs$
$S_w = 370\ ft^2$
$\rho = .002377$
$g = 32.2$
$\mu = .025$
$T = 20000\ lbs$, F-100 engine (installed)
$C_{L_{max}} = 1.7$ considered deflected flaps and ground effect
$AR = 2.46$
$\bar e = .8$ for swept thin wings aircraft
$K = .162$, from $K = \dfrac{1}{\pi\cdot AR\cdot\bar e}$

$V_{stall} = 172.3\ ft/sec$ where $V_{stall} = \sqrt{\dfrac{W_{TO}}{S_w}\dfrac{2}{\rho\,C_{L_{max}}}}$

$V_{TO} = 206.8\ ft/sec$ where $V_{TO} = 1.2\,V_{stall}$

$L_a = 4922.9\ lbs$ = Average lift in ground running where $V = .7\,V_{TO}$

$L_a = \dfrac{1}{2}\rho V^2 S_w\, C_L$

$D = 5163.76\ lbs$

from $D = \dfrac{1}{2}\rho V^2 S_w\, C_D$

(see next page for $C_D$)

---

$C_D = .2746$ from $C_D = \left[C_{D_o} + K\cdot C_{L_G}^2\right] + \Delta C_{D_{flaps}} + \Delta C_{D_{gear}} + etc.$

where:

$C_{D_o} = .016$ (for supersonic fighters in subsonic cruise $C_{D_o}$ from .014 to .022)

$C_{L_G} = .42$ (flaps deployed and $\alpha_{wing} = 0$)

$\Delta C_{D_{flaps}} = .04$ from charts

$\Delta C_{D_{gear}} = .19$   $\Delta C_D$ was obtained from
$D = C_D\cdot S_w\cdot q = \Delta f_{gear}\cdot A_{f_{gear}}\cdot q$
$A_{f_{gear}}$ is frontal area = 4.7 ft²
and $\Delta f_{gear} = 15$ from diagram shown below

curve for tricycle landing gear

Replacing all the indicated values from Equation $(\text{II})$

$S_G = 1024.25\ ft$
$S_R = 620.4\ ft$
$S_{TR} = 771.82\ ft$

The value of $S_{TR}$ should be decrease to 336.11 ft because $h_{TR} = 296\ ft$, which is higher than the required 50 ft obstacle.

TOTAL TAKEOFF DISTANCE = __1981__ ft

The actual Takeoff Distance will be by far less, because in this calculation was not considered, the aditional lifting by the canards.

---

## "HALCON WF1"   Fighter aircraft

Design Engineer:   WALTER F. LAREDO

Drawing Number:   **1000** series

Sheet 25 of **34**

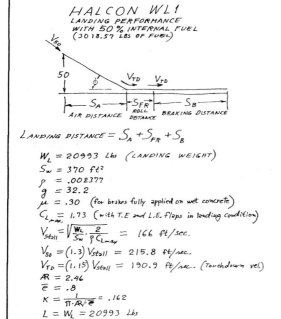

HALCON WL1
LANDING PERFORMANCE
WITH 50 % INTERNAL FUEL
(3018.57 LBS OF FUEL)

$\text{LANDING DISTANCE} = S_A + S_{FR} + S_B$

$W_L = 20993 \text{ Lbs} \quad (\text{LANDING WEIGHT})$

$S_w = 370 \text{ ft}^2$

$\rho = .002377$

$g = 32.2$

$\mu = .30 \quad (\text{for brakes fully applied on wet concrete})$

$C_{L_{max}} = 1.73 \quad (\text{with T.E and L.E. flaps in landing condition})$

$V_{stall} = \sqrt{\frac{W_L}{S_w} \cdot \frac{2}{\rho C_{L_{max}}}} = 166 \text{ ft/sec.}$

$V_{50} = (1.3) V_{stall} = 215.8 \text{ ft/sec.}$

$V_{TD} = (1.15) V_{stall} = 190.9 \text{ ft/sec.} \quad (\text{Touchdown vel.})$

$AR = 2.46$

$\bar{e} = .8$

$K = \frac{1}{\pi \cdot AR \cdot \bar{e}} = .162$

$L = W_L = 20993 \text{ Lbs}$

---

$C_{D_0} = .016$

$C_{L(SA)} = (.8) C_{L_{max}} = 1.73$

$C_{L_G} = .42$

$\Delta C_{D_{flaps}} = .041$

$\Delta C_{D_{gear}} = .19$

$C_{D(SA)} = \left[ C_{D_0} + K C_{L(SA)}^2 \right] + \Delta C_{D_{flap}} + \Delta C_{D_{gear}} = .7318$

$V_{(SA)} = 208 \quad \text{where} \quad V_{50} > V_{(SA)} > V_{TD}$

$D_{(SA)} = \frac{1}{2} \rho V_{(SA)}^2 S_w C_{D(SA)} = 13923. \text{ Lbs.}$

$S_A = \frac{L}{D_{(SA)}} \times \left[ \frac{V_{50}^2 - V_{TD}^2}{2g} + 50 \right] = 312.5 \text{ ft}$

$S_{FR} = t \, V_{TD} = (3)(190.9) = 572.7 \text{ ft} \quad (t = 3 \text{ seconds})$

$S_B = \frac{W_L}{g \mu \rho S_w \left( \frac{C_D}{\mu} - C_{L_G} \right)} \ln \left[ 1 + \frac{\rho S_w}{W_L} \left( \frac{C_D}{\mu} - C_{L_G} \right) V_{TD}^2 \right]$

So $S_B = 2805 \quad$ where: $\left[ C_D = \left[ C_{D_0} + K C_{L_k}^2 \right] + \Delta C_{D_{flap}} + \Delta C_{D_{gear}} = .2756 \right]$

$\text{TOTAL LANDING DISTANCE} = S_A + S_{FR} + S_B = \underline{3690 \text{ ft}}$

The actual landing distance will be considereble less than indicated; because in this calculation was not considered neither the air brake flap (above the fuselage), nor the canards which will increase lift reducing the approach speed.

---

## "HALCON WF1"   Fighter aircraft

Design Engineer:   WALTER F. LAREDO

Drawing Number:   **1000** series

"HALCON WF1" Fighter aircraft

Design Engineer: WALTER F. LAREDO

Drawing Number: 1000 series | Sheet 27 of 34

**Top graphs:**

CANARD OFF
CANARD ON

CG RANGE (CANARD ON)

$M$ — 2.9M, 2.0, 1.5, 1.0, 0.5, 0

AIRCRAFT AERODYNAMIC CENTER (% MAC)
60, 50, 40, 30, 20, 10

ZERO LIFT ANGLE OF ATTACK $\alpha_{OL}$ (+) (−)

CANARD ON
CANARD OFF

$C_{L\alpha}$ (1/DEG) — (+) 0.04, 0.02, 0
2.5M, 2.0, 1.5, 1.0, 0.5, 0

PITCHING MOMENT COEFFICIENT AT ZERO LIFT $C_{m_0}$ (+)

MACH NUMBER (M) — 0.5, 1.0, 1.5, 2.0, 2.5, 0

**Lower diagram:**

$D_{i(total)}$ = Total Config. Drag-Due-to-Lift

$D_{i(wing)}$ = Drag-Due-to-Lift of optimum isolated wing ($e_w = 1$)

TRIM LIMIT WITH $C_{L_H} = C_{L_W}$

MINIMUM DRAG FOR STABLE AIRPLANE

STABLE / UNSTABLE

$\dfrac{D_{i(total)}}{D_{i(wing)}}$ — 2.0, 1.5, 1.0, .5, 0.0

$\dfrac{L_c}{L_{TOTAL}}$ — 1.0, 0.6, 0.4, 0.2, 0.0, −0.2, −0.5

TRIM LOCUS

NEGATIVE C.G. SPREAD

TRIM LIMIT (FWD C.G. LIMIT)

C.G. LOCATION

$\left(\dfrac{X}{\ell}\right)$ — 0.4, 0.3, 0.2, 0.1, 0.0, −0.2, −0.4, −0.6, −0.8, −1.0

A.C. wing
A.C. canard

Neutral point (approx. aft C.G. Limit for stable airplane)

$b_w$
$b_c$
$x$  $+x$

$c$

$\ell$

DRAG-DUE-TO-LIFT, TRIM LOCUS AND NEUTRAL POINT OF A CANARD CONFIGURATION WITH VERTICAL SEPARATION $\dfrac{h}{b_w} = 0.043$

and $\dfrac{b_c}{b_w} = 0.6$

## STABILITY AND CONTROL

The delta wing is relatively large, reducing wing loading providing better low-speed performance, and permitting higher turn-rates at high altitude.  The wing has almost no camber, but leading-edge flaps (very rare in deltas) and large trailing-edge elevons, which drops as flaps during maneuvers, can produce more lift per unit area than the inefficient conventional delta wing.

The Halcon WL1 aircraft will use a sophisticated electronic control system, using a concept called Relaxed Static Stability (RSS), such instability will require active controls, the aircraft will employ canard surfaces for gust alleviation, maneuvering, and trimmed lift enhancement. A canard configuration offers advantages of less rearward aerodynamic center travel than a conventional tail arrangement; also the wing-canard combination is of load sharing.  The wing and the canard variable camber controlled by the computer will be use to optimize the body-wing lift to drag ratio, at lift coefficients up to maximum sustained maneuver levels.  Beyond that point the wing flaps will be deflected for stability and control demands.

The Halcon WL1 will have an autopilot and use triple-redundant, digital fly-by-wire flight-control system command and stability-augmentation.  This aircraft also will carry a mechanical backup for the flight control systems.

The addition of canards, slightly ahead of and above the wing, increases the lift available at a given angle of attack.  Canards allows the aircraft to operate over a greater range of angles of attack, and reduces stability because the center of lift and center of gravity are moved closer together.  A very important purpose of the canards is to improve maneuverability in combat, also to operate from shorter runways.

The aircraft has an electronic fly-by-wire flight control system, which allows the aircraft center of gravity range to be extended further aft than on a conventional aircraft.  This will produce less basic stability.  Without the FBW system, it could not be possible to position the aircraft center of gravity behind the center of pressure to give a reduced or negative static margin.

For the halcon all-electronic fly-by-wire (FBW) Flight-control system is used, where electrical circuits replace the conventional hydromechanical system with linkages and cables.

The control configured vehicle (CCV) concept is related to the ratio of the aircraft balance to the aircraft static longitudinal stability, allowing the CG to be moved further aft than in conventional configurations.  With the CG near the center of pressure, drag is reduced especially at high load factors and at supersonic speeds, this aft CG location also reduces trim drag.  Because the center of gravity is so close to the center of pressure, therefore is used relaxed stability design, which allowed reducing de size of canards and flaperons.

As in all jet fighters, the control surfaces of the Halcon WF1 will be actuated by servos, using. CCV (Control Configured Vehicle) technology, which uses FBW (Fly-by-Wire) Flight Control

| "HALCON WF1"  Fighter aircraft | | |
|---|---|---|
| Design Engineer:     WALTER F. LAREDO | | |
| Drawing number     1000  series | | Sheet 28 of  34 |

System. A flight control system with instant response to pilot input, which computer, will accept, refuse or modify the pilot's command to prevent the aircraft from exceeding its maneuvering structural limits, then the FBW will send the pilot input directly to servomotors that operates the control surfaces. The movable surfaces are continuously adjusted to let the aircraft follows it's required trajectory. The unstable aircraft is prevented from divergent accelerations by continuous positive control. CCV technology is ideal for this type of aircraft configuration, because it reduces the severe trim drag. The system will use a Flight Control Computer and a Central Air Data Computer. The Fly-by-Wire Control System will be integrated with the engine control and link with the weapons system, in order to relieve the pilot from many monitoring tasks, letting him to concentrate in dogfighting.

Electronic wire pulses command small, light, high-pressure (preferable 4000 psi) actuators for the control surfaces. Computer control of elevons and all-moving canard independent from the pilot maintains the aircraft stability.

The short coupled canard configuration of the Halcon WF1 will have good longitudinal aerodynamic and lateral-directional characteristics. The wing efficiency is highly increased by the canard, particularly at high angles of attack, by deflecting the airflow on the wing; the canard also will allow large movements of the center of gravity, which could be handle by a simple autopilot.

On most fighters today roll rate is automatically limited when the aircraft flies below a certain speed, pulling g's, this prevents an inertial coupling from raising angle of attack to where the aircraft becomes unstable in yaw. On the other hand if there were no roll limiter, pilots would put on a margin of safety, ending up with problems. The designers would like to increase roll rates while maintaining high angle of attack stability.

For the HALCON WF1 will be develop charts with a variety family of curves to represent the approximate performance of this aircraft, for example one important family of curves are the dog-house shaped curves, where the left wall is determined by MAXIMUM LIFT, the roof by MAXIMUM G's, and the right wall by MAXIMUM SPEED. These curves will be used to compare one fighter aircraft to another by superposing their doghouse curves. Other family of curves will show TURNS AT CONSTANT G's, when speed is lost or gained, and SUSTAINED, WHICH IS THE MAXIMUM TURN RATE AT ANY CONSTANT SPEED.

Approximate values for the wing-body-canard configuration of the Halcon WF1, using the concept of Relaxed Static Stability will be as indicated below, but need to be recalculated:

Transonic aerodynamic center shift from the subsonic......12 % MAC
Subsonic aerodynamic center at................................32 % MAC
Supersonic aerodynamic center, varies from.........40 % to 44 % MAC
If a 5 % MAC static margin is designed too,
    the aft C.G. limit will be................................27 % MAC
At supersonic speeds with the C.G. at the aft limit,
    the static margin will be usually less than.............17 %

Low stability couples with positive values of $(C_{m,o})$, pitching moment at zero lift will result in "GOOD MANEUVER CAPABILITY AND LOW TRIM DRAG". At high dynamic pressure conditions, the airplane will trim at a negative angle of attack, probably caused by the large pitching moment at zero lift $(C_{m,o})$. This aircraft will require a new, more accurate analysis of Stability Control, including trimming and other flight conditions. Will be created charts for canard and elevon trim requirements, which must cover most of the flight envelope, curves that will reflect the "Natural Longitudinal Static Stability" of the airplane, assuming no thrust effect.

## "HALCON WF1" Fighter aircraft

| Design Engineer: | WALTER F. LAREDO | |
|---|---|---|
| Drawing number | 1000 series | Sheet 29 of 34 |

Just for a preliminary estimation could be assume that the wing's elevons are fix and that the airplane could employ the canards for trimming and maneuvering, although wing leading edge flaps and elevons will be also use to decamber the wing at supersonic speed.

The lift curve slope per degree of $\alpha$, and the pitching moment coefficient at zero lift is maximum at Mach 1. The zero lift angle of attack increases negatively as Mach number increases, the aerodynamic center shift aft by 12 % MAC at transonic and supersonic speeds.  At the aft C.G. the airplane will be unstable over most of the flight envelope, (the rate of change of the canard angle is positive and the rate of change of the wing's elevon angle is negative). Subsonically the aft center of gravity is 5 % ahead of the aerodynamic center, and the airplane is still unstable. Supersonically the aft center of gravity will be in between 13 and 17 % ahead of the aerodynamic center and the configuration will become more stable, but not too stable because this unstability is caused by the rate of change of $(Cm,o)$ with respect to Mach number, $\delta Cm / \delta$ Mach is some small negative number at supersonic speeds.  This is a destabilizing effect because the elevon must deflect in a negative direction, as speed is increased to compensate for it, and the canards must deflect increasing its angle of attack.  At low supersonic stability levels, the speed effect is dominating static stability characteristics.  The canard's area was designed for the forward C.G. at transonic and supersonic speeds.

Optimum $(Cm,o)$ for an aircraft with relaxed stability is different than for a conventional aircraft.  Canard and elevon deflection required to maneuver at the aft C.G. condition, for an additional "g" required that additional canard angles are small, and the required wing elevon angles are smaller yet, positive or negative.  This is one of the primary benefits of RELAXED STABILITY.

The increase in vertical tail area by using two vertical tails will give to the Halcon WF1 aircraft a good lateral directional stability for a variety of angles of attack as long as they are not too large.  Fins better exposed to the air stream increasing its rudder effectiveness.  The redundancy of using two vertical tails increases survivability.   If there will be some decrease in wing-body directional stability at Mach numbers greater than 2, then this problem can be alleviated by small design changes in the wing Strake.

The Roll Power is provided from differentially operated elevons, with one second or less time to bank from 0 to 90 degrees, could exist throughout most of the flight envelope.  Data that will be gathered from the wind tunnel test plus the prototype flying tests, Data used to reprogram the software of the flight control system until the aircraft could perform in very efficient way under all kinds of flight conditions.

## STRUCTURAL ARRANGEMENT

Early in this proposal, the primary structure of this aircraft was designed from aluminum lithium alloy, and the rest including the secondary structure from advanced composites.  However this concept changed, because it seems more promising that in order to reduce weight and to reduce the number of parts, the whole aircraft should be build from advanced composites, using the latest state-of-the-art in structural design, considering this material is good for long fatigue life.  Materials ways of arrangement would be selected to limit crack growth/time.

Materials using carbon fibers, kevlar (an aramid fiber) and fiberglass, all them imbedded in an epoxy resin matrix would be use in honeycomb sandwich shell form or in laminar form.

Both, conventional and advanced composite structures will be designed with sufficient load path redundancy to prevent catastrophic failure due to a 23-mm shell hit on the primary airframe structure.

This structure will be analyze for several load conditions using Matrix computer analysis of structures to find Static and Dynamic loads, Stresses, deflection and flutter.

### WING:

The wing structure consists of the wing box, leading edge and trailing edge flaps.  The leading edge and the trailing edge flaps are made from full depth honeycomb because of its thinness. A honeycomb sandwich structure made from advanced composites would be lighter than a similar conventional from aluminum alloy.  The composite wing box structure is multispar, where at the wing-body join, each spar end is bolted to its corresponding extension from a body frame, so wing spars became extensions of body frames.  The wing box section outboard  BL 45 serves as support structure for the variable camber leading and trailing edge components, the wing box is also an integral fuel tank. Integral stringers stiffen the skin to prevent buckling prior to limit load. For a wing box from advanced

| "HALCON WF1"  Fighter aircraft | | . |
|---|---|---|
| . | Design Engineer:      WALTER F. LAREDO | . |
| . | Drawing number    1000  series | Sheet 30 of 34  . |

composites, the skin ply orientation are + & - 45 degrees Gp/Ep to carry shear with some 0.0 degrees added to improve their crack stopping capability.

## VERTICAL FINS:

The fins are assembled structures of several honeycomb core skins sandwich components, which includes spars, ribs to support the rudder hinges and a root rib to contribute the transfer of loads from the fin to the body support structure. The fins are full depth honeycomb due to its thinness.
The skin fiber orientation are + & - 45 degrees Gr/Ep to carry shear loads.

## FOREBODY

The forebody contains the pressurized cockpit, avionics packages and radar system, part of the avionics are located below the pressure deck and other part behind the pilot's seat, they are accessible through a non-structural access door. The radar system is contained within the radome, which is mounted on Sta. 68 bulkhead. A load-carrying frame at Sta. 188 supports the nose landing gear.

## AFT-BODY

A load carrying frame, Sta.390 supports the main landing gear. The aft body structure supports the wing and fin spars, which load carrying frames are located in between Sta's 364 & 440 and Sta's 510 & 575 respectively, it also serves as the support structure for the M61 gun.

The ammunition storage and the environmental control equipment are located in the non-pressurized area of the aft-body and are accessible through non-structural doors. The aft-body includes the engine intake duct, body fuel tanks, two external semi-submerged missile systems and the mechanical equipment.

The duct penetrates the body frames and becomes part of the body structure. The ducts, the outer skin and the body side rib provides the boundaries for the body fuel tank between Sta's 315 and 500. Two AIM-9 missiles or similar are stored in external conformal pockets located at the lower outboard corner of the inlets external surfaces. The fuselage have four pairs of fail-safe longerons, to carry fuselage bending loads prior to limit load, designed by pairs for redundancy to avoid catastrophic failure due to a shell hit. For the fighter aircraft version with conventional aluminum structure, the skins are stiffened by close spaced fuselage frames, but in the advanced composites sandwich structural version, the skin faces (internal and external) are stiffened by the honeycomb core, the fiber orientation in such skins are primarily + & - 45 degrees to carry the shear loads.

The upper temperature limit for the 305 degrees F cure for graphite-epoxy systems was established to be 250 to 275 degrees F. The 275 degrees F temperature is the maximum temperature encountered during any flight condition.

For the basic aircraft, its engine will be supported at four points, the front mount is a vertical link and a rail, which is hung at the top of intercostals; this support reacts only vertical loads allowing the engine to expand. The other two mounts are trunnions that reacts engine axial, vertical and torsion loads, while allowing engine radial expansion, this radial expansion is allowed by the trunnions sliding inside spherical bearings. Side loads at the rear mount probable will be reached by a horizontal link between the body of the engine and the aft body frames. Access to the engine equipment for normal maintenance is provided by a lower structural access door, which carry shear loads when it is lock closed, a major engine maintenance require its removal from the aircraft.

An interface between the engine and the exhaust or afterburner system is located aft of the rear mount but forward of the flameholder location and sealed by a gas tight rolling-bellows. A fan discharge air-cools all surfaces of the afterburner exhaust system, upstream of the nozzle exit plane.

# PROPULSION

The Halcon WF1 will use the popular low bypass Pratt & Whitney F100-PW-100, A/B engine:

| | |
|---|---|
| Area of each two-dimensional inlet | To be determinate |
| Nozzle Area | Same as in the F-15 or F-16 fighters |
| Length (including nozzle) | 190 in (4.83 m) |
| Weight (bare) | 2737 lb. (1242 Kg) |
| Sea Level Static Airflow | 217 lb./sec (98 Kg/sec) |
| Bypass Ratio | 0.71 |

| "HALCON WF1" Fighter aircraft | | . |
|---|---|---|
| . Design Engineer:    WALTER F. LAREDO | | . |
| . Drawing number    1000 series | Sheet 31 of 34 | . |

Thrust with afterburner
Sea Level Static (uninstalled) 23 000 lb.  (102 000 KN)

Specific Fuel Consumption (TSFC), Sea Level
2.48 lb. fuel/lb. thrust per second with afterburner
(70.46 mg fuel /Newton per second with reheat)

This cycle was selected as a compromise between high altitude supersonic dash and low altitude subsonic cruise mission. The Halcon WF1 will have in interceptor configuration a thrust-to-weight ratio at takeoff greater than one.

Also to this aircraft could be adapt equivalent American or European engines, where the designs of the aircraft inlet and exhaust may or may not be changed. As alternate engines are: Snecmas M53, -2, -5 & P2, F100-PW-220, TF30-P-100 and the latest F404-GE.

This aircraft will have two variable geometry air intakes, one at each side of the forward fuselage, each with two dimensional inlets for external compression with movable ramps, throat bleed system and auxiliary doors for takeoff.

The propulsion system, it will consist of the engine, the variable geometry air intakes and the exhaust system. A variety of tests will be required to cover all flight conditions.  Test that can be performed by renting testing facilities in America or in Europe.

## WEAPONS

The combat arena could be divided into regions having different requirements for both, the aircraft and the weapons.  Flying at high altitude and speed is for fighting beyond visual range.  At high cruise speed but fuel-efficient, the aircraft radar can search a broad area of the sky, and once the target is detected and identified to turn into it and launch preferable an Active Radar Homing Missile then leave.  A Semiactive Radar Missile requires, staying locked into the target and for a while illuminating it with its radar.  Active Radar Homing missiles are AMRAAM, Phoenix and others, and among the Semiactive Radar guided missiles is the SPARROW.

Witting visual range (3 to 5 miles), pointing all-aspect Infrared Missiles and leave, or get engaged in gun battle (perhaps maneuvering to the aircraft limit for short time).  Since a decade ago, short-range, all-aspect-attack infrared seeking missiles have made the tail chase of an enemy aircraft unnecessary, and also was innovation of warning systems installed in the aircraft's tails to alert them of coming missiles.

A very maneuverable canard configuration aircraft.  In addition to the internal gun and the electronic countermeasures and despite its small size the Halcon WF1 will have seven hard points for mounting weapons, it will have two at the wing tips, two under the wing and two semisubmerged on both sides of the lower fuselage.   The Halcon WF1 can carry an arrangement combination of infrared seeking missiles and radar homing missiles, in interception configuration can carry six short range infrared guided missiles as the AIM-9 Sidewinders, and for the international version aircraft, the Matra R.550 Magic or any other of the same equivalent characteristics.  For a Mach 2.3 interception mission it could carry two AIM-9,  conformally in a semi-submerged arrangement at both sides of the fuselage to reduce drag, and to reduce also radar, infrared and optical signatures.

Pylons will allow the Halcon WF1 to carry many different weapons and sensors for its diverse missions, including dropable fuel tanks.

The aircraft will carry one internal 20 mm M61 six-barrel gun, with 300 rounds of ammunition.
Maximum armament load (attack mission)        6000 lb.  (2722 Kg)
Stores, Hard Points:
    Fuselage  3        (two conformal and one underneath)
    Under wing      2
    Wing tips 2

## MATERIALS

The Halcon WF1 could be designed with either two kinds of structures, the first one from conventional aluminum alloy and the other, perhaps the best one from advanced composites materials with some titanium fittings. Some steel hardware as the landing gears to be use on both types of structures.

| "HALCON WF1"  Fighter aircraft | |
|---|---|
| Design Engineer:      WALTER F. LAREDO | |
| Drawing number      1000  series | Sheet 32 of  34 |

For both choices of structures, the wing leading edge, the wing trailing edge flaps, the canard surfaces, the fins, the landing gear doors, the inlets and the radome structural components will be made from advanced composites materials.

In the conventional structural construction of aluminum, cold be saved more weight by using aluminum-lithium alloy, however still more weight would be saved as much as 20 % by using advanced composites materials, enabling fighters to takeoff and land on runways less than 1500 ft. long. The size of autoclave for curing composite parts is important, the larger the autoclave, the larger the components to be cure and less the number of production brakes (splicing joins) to be made, which also translates into weight savings. The largest part of the aircraft structure probable is the wing skins with its bonded spars and the aft fuselage skins.

The materials for the composite parts are: carbon fibers, Kevlar, fiberglass, boron, could be use a single material or a combination of them as required, materials that could be obtained in the form of tape, imbedded in epoxy resin. For the prototype aircraft, the honeycomb sandwich panels and the skin lay-ups would be made by hand on long wood tables. The wing bottom skin and the wing spars will be bonded together and put to get cured in the autoclave, later this integral skin-spar unit will be mechanically fastened to the upper skin and sealed, since this wing is also an integral fuel tank.

The major structural splicing in the Halcon WF1 aircraft will employ small titanium attachment fittings, made by superplastic forming and diffusion bonding. Bonding of titanium fittings to carbon composites structures are more effective than the bonding of aluminum fittings to the same structure, mostly because titanium have smaller differential thermoexpansion and is good for corrosion resistance.

Canopy and windshield materials are primary polycarbonate, and for economical reasons could be build as an assembly of several parts. A single unit canopy windshield structure would be the best, but very expensive.

## AVIONICS

The avionics and its characteristics, will be established by a group of experts. Here is only described the rough preliminary idea. For the Halcon WF1 aircraft probably will be choose an efficient radar system, small enough to be accommodated in the radome small room available there.

The cockpit instrumentation includes a head-up display (HUD) where vital information is presented to the pilot's line of vision. The Halcon WF1 may have either a conventional arrangement of instruments or a head-down system of electronic displays, controlled by programmable computers, the company producing these aircraft, the pilots and the engineers would decide the type of cockpit instrumentation arrangement. The pilot could allow the Digital Automatic Flight Control System, take over a broad or a narrow part of the controls, reducing the pilot's workload. This enables the pilot to concentrate on other work such as in radar observation or in dog fighting. Avionics, cockpit displays, radar, computers and the rest of all electronics could be purchase from countries that produce them. Combat avionics for the Halcon WF1 most probably would be: RADAR, HUD, UHF, ECM, UHF/IFF, RWR, and TACAN.

## FUEL SYSTEM

The internal fuel capacity for this aircraft is 9060 lb. (4109 Kg).

For a fighting mission of a Gross Weight of 22200 lb. and with 70 % of internal fuel, the weight of this amount of fuel is 6342 lb. (2877 Kg).

The fuel from the wing tanks will flow first to the feed tanks located in the body, and from there to the engine. The maximum flow of the fuel system is of 40 000 lb./hr. The fuel pressure at the inlet of the engine fuel pump should be more than 5 gpsi and less than 50 gpsi. Positive pressure should be maintain in all flight conditions at the inlet of the engine driven pumps, included maneuvers and inverted flight, by electrical boost pumps mounted inside a negative "g" housing located at the bottom of the main tank.

Because fuels are volatile, all fuel tanks including the external, will be pressurized to operate the aircraft at high altitude, pressure obtained by bleeding air from the engine compressor, this air will flow through a system that includes also a dehumidifier then to the tanks.

The aircraft will have a single point ground refuel receptacle connected internally with the air refuel probe manifold.

The Halcon WF1 fuel tanks will be inert depending on threat, the aircraft will be design with either system, one that uses halon or the other that uses nitrogen to inert the fuel tanks, also a bottle will be located inside the nose gear well and will provide 30 minutes of inerting at near empty fuel tank level. Additional survivability and vulnerability

| "HALCON WF1" Fighter aircraft | | |
|---|---|---|
| Design Engineer: WALTER F. LAREDO | | |
| Drawing number 1000 series | | Sheet 33 of 34 |

protection is giving by a self-sealing blanket between fuel and inlet duct and around the engine in the area of the body fuel tank. Some redundant fuel ducting system will be required for combat survivability.

## ELECTRIC POWER GENERATION AND DIDTRIBUTION SYSTEM

Normal power generation system is achieved from the engine's takeoff shaft driving probable two separate accessories gear boxes, where in each is mounted a variable frequency (VSCF) 60 KVA main generator and a hydraulic pump. The cycle-converters convert the variable frequency output of the generator to the fix required number of HZ power of the aircraft. A central Starting/APU unit will provide engine-starting power.

There will be Generator's control breakers. Redundant AC buses will be required for combat survivability.

## HYDRAULIC SYSTEM. Two or three independent hydraulic systems will supply hydraulic

power for the Flight Controls and other systems. Variable displacement, constant pressure preferable 4000-psi pumps, installed in the accessory drive units. Two pumps will supply hydraulic power to elevons, rudders, canards, landing gear retraction, steering, brakes, inlet ramps, gun drive and other systems. The wing leading edge flaps could be designed to be actuated either, hydraulically or electrically.

## ENVIRONMENTAL CONTROL SYSTEM. The Environmental Control System

provides air-conditioned for the pilot, for cooling the Avionics Equipment and for the fuel tank pressurization system.

The system extracts engine bleed air from an intermediate compressor stage for all climbs and cruise conditions. Last stage compressor bleed air is required for the cockpit pressurization and equipment operation during Idle descent and other Low Power flight conditions.

Engine bleed air, powers the Air Cycle Machine through the dual nozzle drive turbine when ram air pressure is insufficient. Will be study if in addition to the ram air cooled heat exchanger will be necessary a second heat exchanger cooled by tank fuel.

## SONIC ENVIRONMENT. Sonic fatigue is nor considered a problem for the wing, fuselage,

canards, fins and other critical components. In the critical structural areas, the sonic environment will not be severe, the highest sound pressure levels are confined to aft nozzles sections, followed by the fins and its neighborhood areas, but will not be a problem for the aircraft critical components.

Some time during the development of the program with the obtained data will be made a preliminary jet noise analysis for static, and takeoff thrust conditions with afterburner, then to made a drawing of the external view of the aircraft showing lines of constant sound pressure levels.

## ANTI-ICING. On the Halcon WF1, anti-icing will prevent the formation of ice on the engine nose

cone, engine inlet and its guide vanes, pitot static, total temperature sensor, angle-of-attack and other probes. The engine inlet anti-icing could use regulated compressor bleed air from each engine, and 115-volt AC electrical heaters will heat the probes. Also should be study how convenient would be if most of the systems are heated electrically.

## OXYGEN SYSTEM. The oxygen system for the Halcon WF1 will be designed either, as a

gaseous system or as a liquid oxygen system. Located either, in the forward fuselage or behind the pilot seat.

## WEIGHT AND BALANCE. At the time I made this proposal for the Halcon WF1 aircraft, I

did a quick weight and balance estimation (see diagram). However before starting the aircraft final detail design stage, will be required to do a new precise weight and balance analysis.

## ENGINE. See propulsion information in forward pages, in the last twenty years, engineers have

developed engines providing the same thrust while weighting about half as much, having 30 % fewer parts and significantly lower fuel consumption.

| "HALCON WF1" Fighter aircraft | |
|---|---|
| Design Engineer: WALTER F. LAREDO | |
| Drawing number 1000 series | Sheet 34 of 34 |

## POWER PLANT

Two 200 lb.-thrust turbojet engines power this VSTOL, jet aircraft.
For liftoff the efflux is diverted to drive two fans housed in the wings.  Each
fan augments the jet thrust by 300 per cent, hence the liftoff thrust of each
fan is 600 lb., giving a total lift of 1200 lb.

## SPECIFICATIONS

| | |
|---|---|
| Accommodation | 2 tandem  (as in a motorcycle) |
| Wing's span,   (b) | 23.42  ft |
| Wing's gross area,   (Sw) | 131.7  sq. ft. |
| Airfoil | Supercritical |
| Wing chord,   root/ tip | 6.2 ft  /  4.0 ft |
| MAC | 5.6 ft |
| Wing aspect Ratio,   AR= (b  square)/ Sw | 4.16 |

( Continues in next page)

## ATLANTIS, ADVANCED ENGINEERING PROJECTS

Name of project:

# MECHANICAL FLYING HORSE, VSTOL MACHINE

## GODIN'S FIRST PROTOTYPE

| Design Engineer:  Walter F. Laredo  *WFLaredo* | Date: March 15, 2002 |
|---|---|

Areas of Development:
Aerodynamics ✔, Stability Control ✔, Thermodynamics ✔, Materials ✔,
Structures (Design and Analysis) ✔, Mechanisms & Systems ✔,

NOTE 1:   This is the PRELIMINARY DESIGN for a real engineering
project.  A project inspired by the legendary dreams and tales of the semi-
utopian highly advanced civilization, called Atlantis.

NOTE 2:   Godin is an imaginary character,  he represents a legendary
Atlantis Engineer.

| Drawing Number:   1100 | Sheet  1   of  26 |
|---|---|

( Continues from page 1 )

| | |
|---|---|
| Horizontal tail area  (Sc) | 24 sq. ft. |
| Vertical tail area  (Sv) | 8.2  sq. ft. |
| Tail arm for hor. tail  (Lc) | 8 ft. |
| Tail arm for ver. tail  (Lv) | 7.18  ft. |

Tail volume:

Horizontal tail

$$Vc = (Lc \times Sc) \ / \ (M.A.C. \ \times \ Sw) \qquad 0.26$$

Vertical tail

$$Vv = (Lv \times Sv) \ / \ ( b \ \times \ Sw) \qquad 0.02$$

| | |
|---|---|
| Weight empty | 420 lb. |
| Weight max. takeoff | 840 lb. |
| Max. wing loading | 6.38  lb. / sq. ft. |
| Max. power loading | 2.1 lb. / thrust lb. |

Ratio of Fans liftoff thrust to gross weight

$$L/W = 1200 \ lb. \ T. \ / \ 840 \ lb. \ G. \ W. \qquad 1.43$$

---

**PERFORMANCE**

| | |
|---|---|
| Max. Level speed at SL | 130 mph |
| Service ceiling | 15 000  ft |
| Range | 200 mile |

---

**NOTE:**

SHEET NUMBERING SYSTEM FOR DRAWINGS

| | |
|---|---|
| Airframe drawings | sheets  3  through  16 |
| Propulsion system drawings | sheets 17 through  26 |

---

## ATLANTIS, ADVANCED ENGINEERING PROJECTS

Name of project:  MECHANICAL FLYING HORSE
(GODIN'S FIRST PROTOTYPE)

| | |
|---|---|
| Design Engineer:  Walter F. Laredo  *W.F.Laredo* | Date:  March 15,  2002 |
| Drawing Number:  1100 | Sheet **2**  of  **26** |

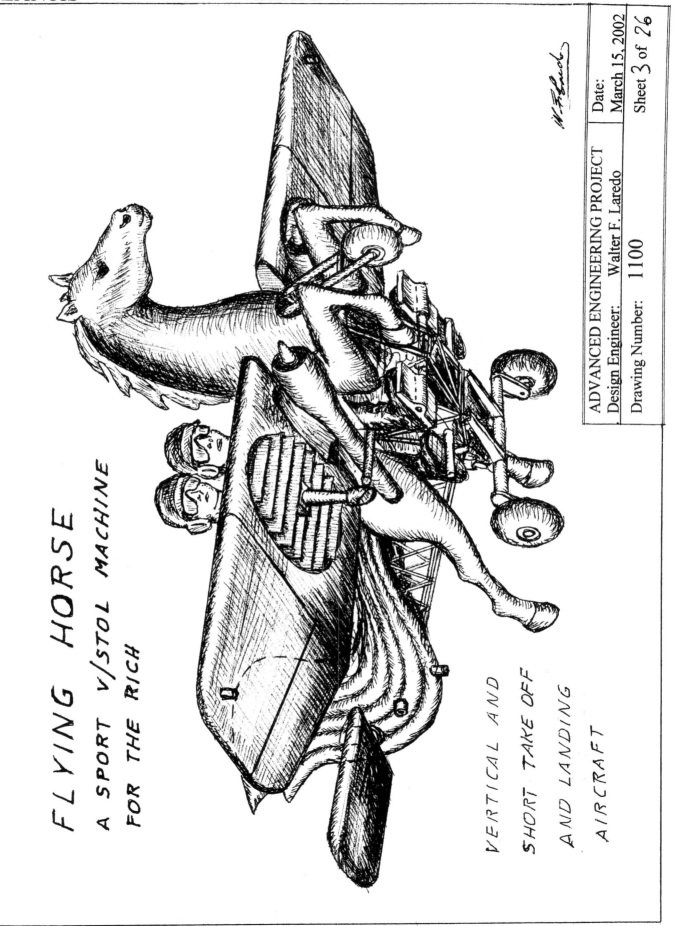

# FLYING HORSE
## A SPORT V/STOL MACHINE
### FOR THE RICH

VERTICAL AND

SHORT TAKE OFF

AND LANDING

AIRCRAFT

| | | |
|---|---|---|
| ADVANCED ENGINEERING PROJECT | | Date: |
| Design Engineer: | Walter F. Laredo | March 15, 2002 |
| Drawing Number: | 1100 | Sheet 3 of 26 |

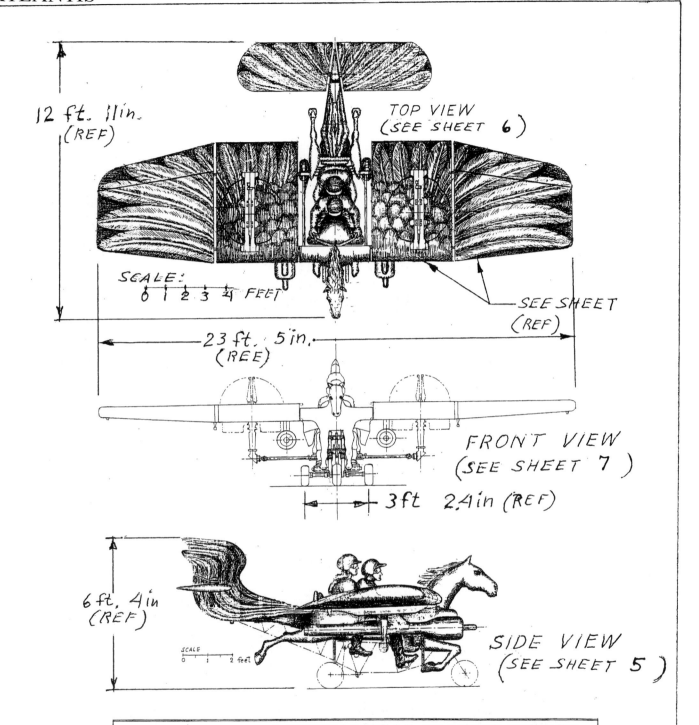

12 ft. 11in.
(REF)

TOP VIEW
(SEE SHEET 6)

SCALE:
0 1 2 3 4 FEET

SEE SHEET
(REF)

23 ft. 5 in.
(REF)

FRONT VIEW
(SEE SHEET 7)

3 ft 2.4 in (REF)

6 ft. 4 in
(REF)

SCALE
0 1 2 feet

SIDE VIEW
(SEE SHEET 5)

| Name of project: | **MECHANICAL FLYING HORSE** | |
|---|---|---|
| ADVANCED ENGINEERING PROJECT Design Engineer:   Walter F. Laredo   *W.F.Laredo* | | Date: March 15, 2002 |
| Drawing Number:   1100 | | Sheet 4 of 26 |

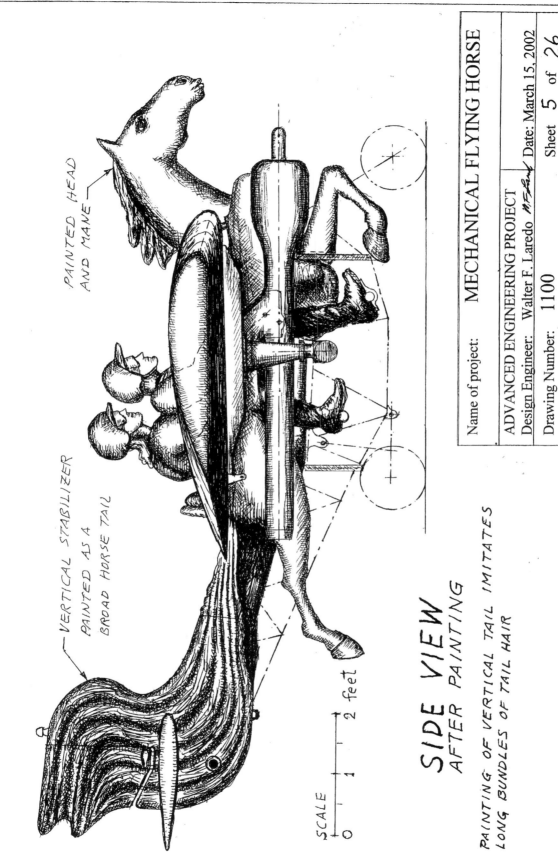

PAINTED HEAD AND MANE

VERTICAL STABILIZER PAINTED AS A BROAD HORSE TAIL

SIDE VIEW
AFTER PAINTING

PAINTING OF VERTICAL TAIL IMITATES LONG BUNDLES OF TAIL HAIR

SCALE
0    1    2 feet

Name of project:     MECHANICAL FLYING HORSE

ADVANCED ENGINEERING PROJECT
Design Engineer:   Walter F. Laredo    Date: March 15, 2002

Drawing Number:   1100              Sheet  5  of  26

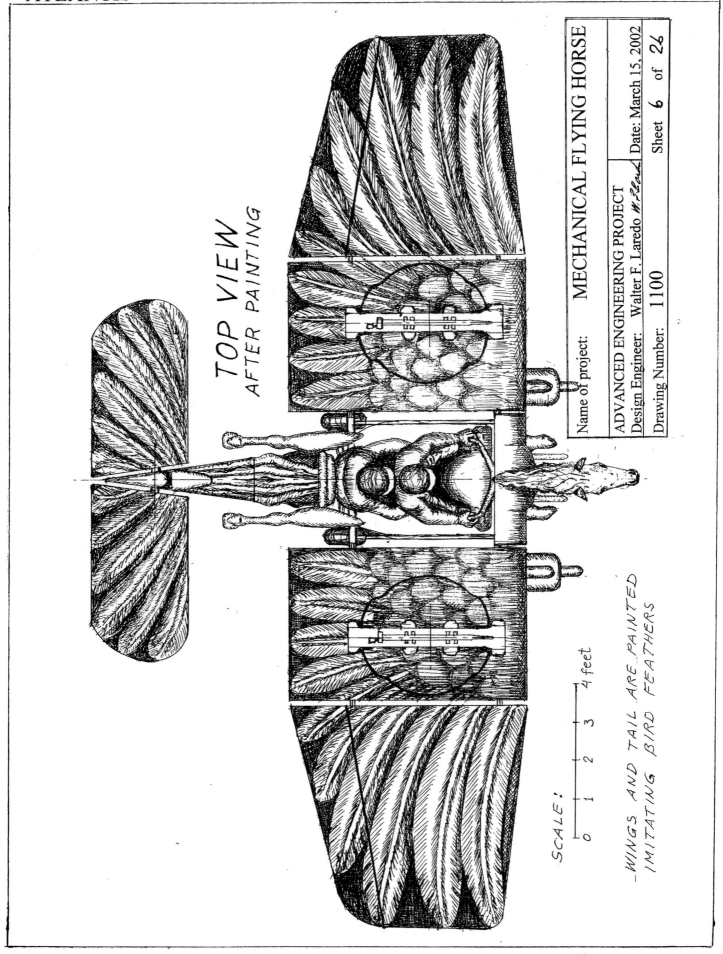

TOP VIEW
AFTER PAINTING

SCALE:

0   1   2   3   4 feet

WINGS AND TAIL ARE PAINTED
IMITATING BIRD FEATHERS

| Name of project: | MECHANICAL FLYING HORSE | |
|---|---|---|
| ADVANCED ENGINEERING PROJECT | | |
| Design Engineer: Walter F. Laredo | Date: March 15, 2002 | |
| Drawing Number: 1100 | Sheet 6 of 26 | |

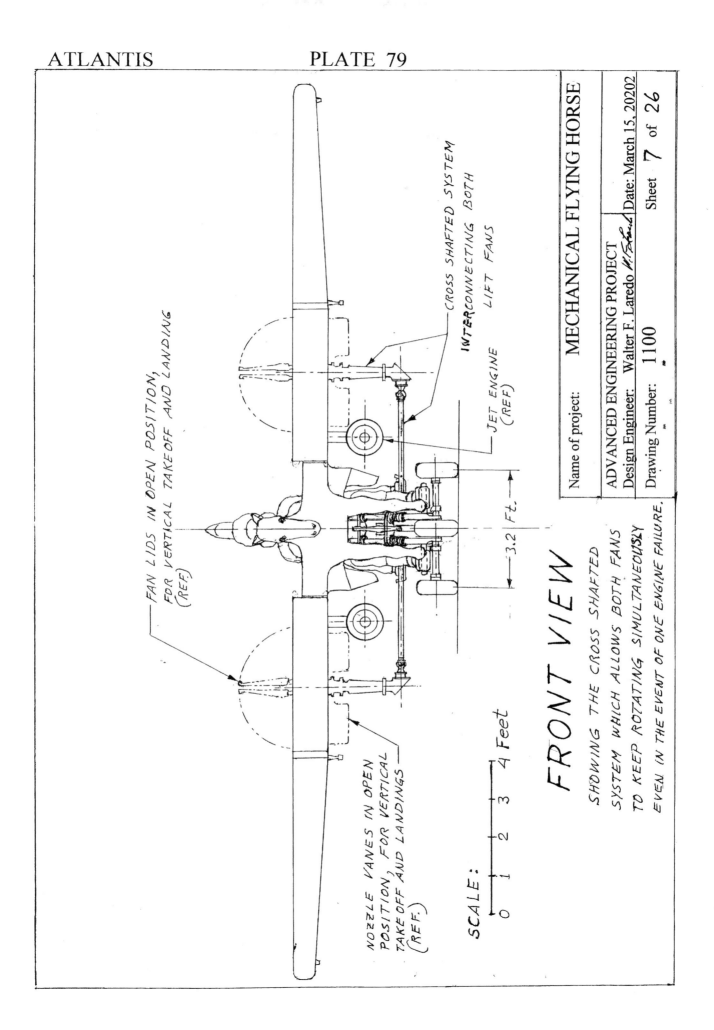

FAN LIDS IN OPEN POSITION, FOR VERTICAL TAKE OFF AND LANDING (REF.)

CROSS SHAFTED SYSTEM

INTERCONNECTING BOTH LIFT FANS

JET ENGINE (REF.)

NOZZLE VANES IN OPEN POSITION, FOR VERTICAL TAKE OFF AND LANDINGS (REF.)

3.2 Ft.

# FRONT VIEW

SHOWING THE CROSS SHAFTED SYSTEM WHICH ALLOWS BOTH FANS TO KEEP ROTATING SIMULTANEOUSLY EVEN IN THE EVENT OF ONE ENGINE FAILURE.

SCALE:

0 1 2 3 4 Feet

| Name of project: | MECHANICAL FLYING HORSE | |
|---|---|---|
| ADVANCED ENGINEERING PROJECT | | |
| Design Engineer: Walter F. Laredo | Date: March 15, 20202 | |
| Drawing Number: 1100 | Sheet 7 of 26 | |

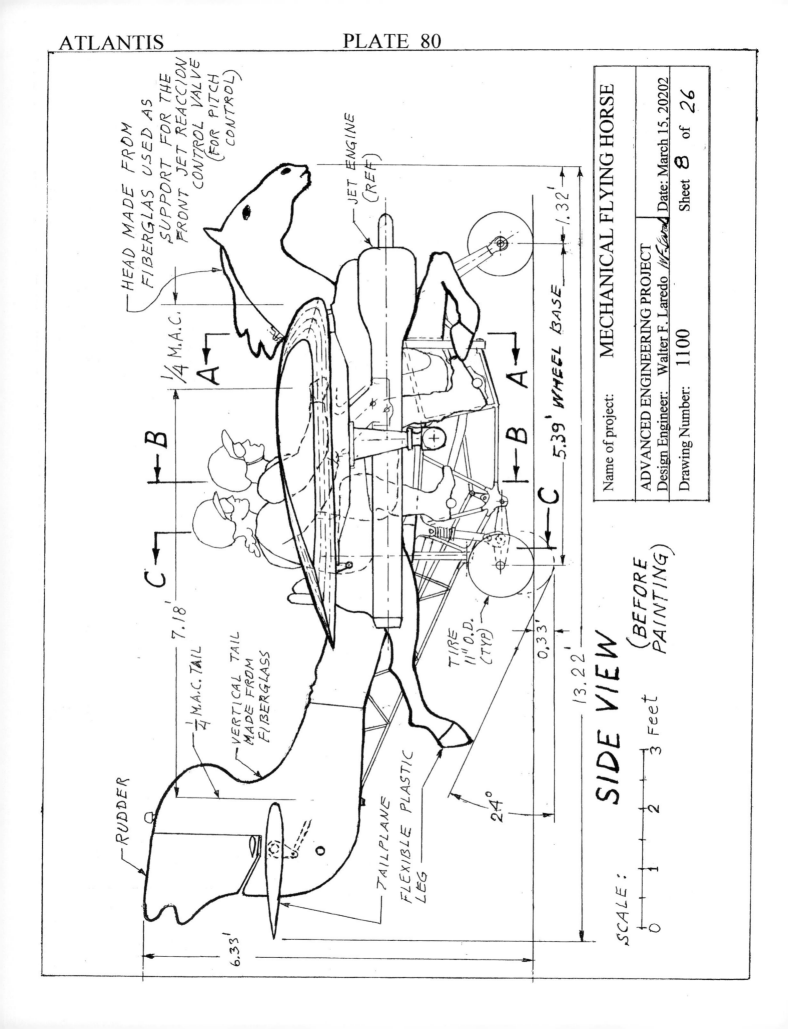

HEAD MADE FROM FIBERGLAS USED AS SUPPORT FOR THE FRONT JET REACCION CONTROL VALVE (FOR PITCH CONTROL)

JET ENGINE (REF)

1/4 M.A.C.

A

B

C

7.18'

1/4 M.A.C. TAIL

VERTICAL TAIL MADE FROM FIBERGLASS

RUDDER

TAILPLANE

FLEXIBLE PLASTIC LEG

24°

TIRE 11" O.D. (TYP)

0.33'

13.22'

5.39' WHEEL BASE

1.32'

6.33'

SIDE VIEW

(BEFORE PAINTING)

SCALE:
0 1 2 3 Feet

| Name of project: | MECHANICAL FLYING HORSE | |
|---|---|---|
| ADVANCED ENGINEERING PROJECT | | |
| Design Engineer: | Walter F. Laredo | Date: March 15, 20202 |
| Drawing Number: | 1100 | Sheet 8 of 26 |

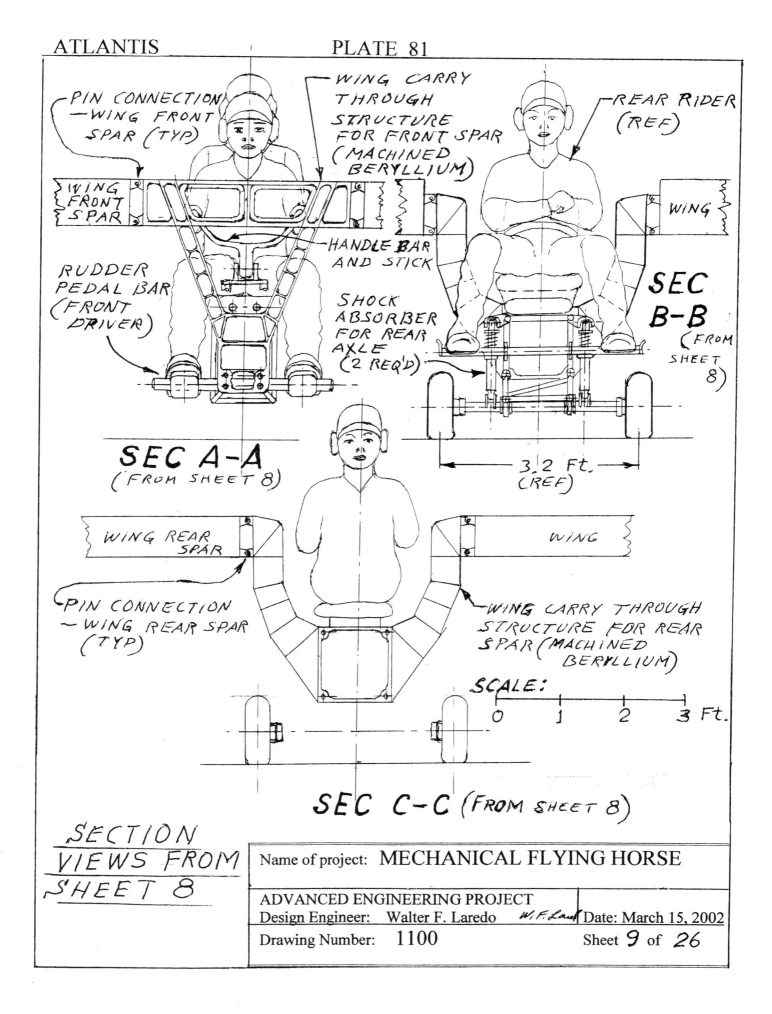

PIN CONNECTION — WING FRONT SPAR (TYP)

WING CARRY THROUGH STRUCTURE FOR FRONT SPAR (MACHINED BERYLLIUM)

REAR RIDER (REF)

WING FRONT SPAR

WING

HANDLE BAR AND STICK

RUDDER PEDAL BAR (FRONT DRIVER)

SEC B-B (FROM SHEET 8)

SHOCK ABSORBER FOR REAR AXLE (2 REQ'D)

SEC A-A (FROM SHEET 8)

3.2 Ft. (REF)

WING REAR SPAR

WING

PIN CONNECTION — WING REAR SPAR (TYP)

WING CARRY THROUGH STRUCTURE FOR REAR SPAR (MACHINED BERYLLIUM)

SCALE:
0    1    2    3 Ft.

SEC C-C (FROM SHEET 8)

SECTION VIEWS FROM SHEET 8

| Name of project: | MECHANICAL FLYING HORSE | |
|---|---|---|
| ADVANCED ENGINEERING PROJECT | | |
| Design Engineer: Walter F. Laredo | W.F. Laud | Date: March 15, 2002 |
| Drawing Number: 1100 | | Sheet 9 of 26 |

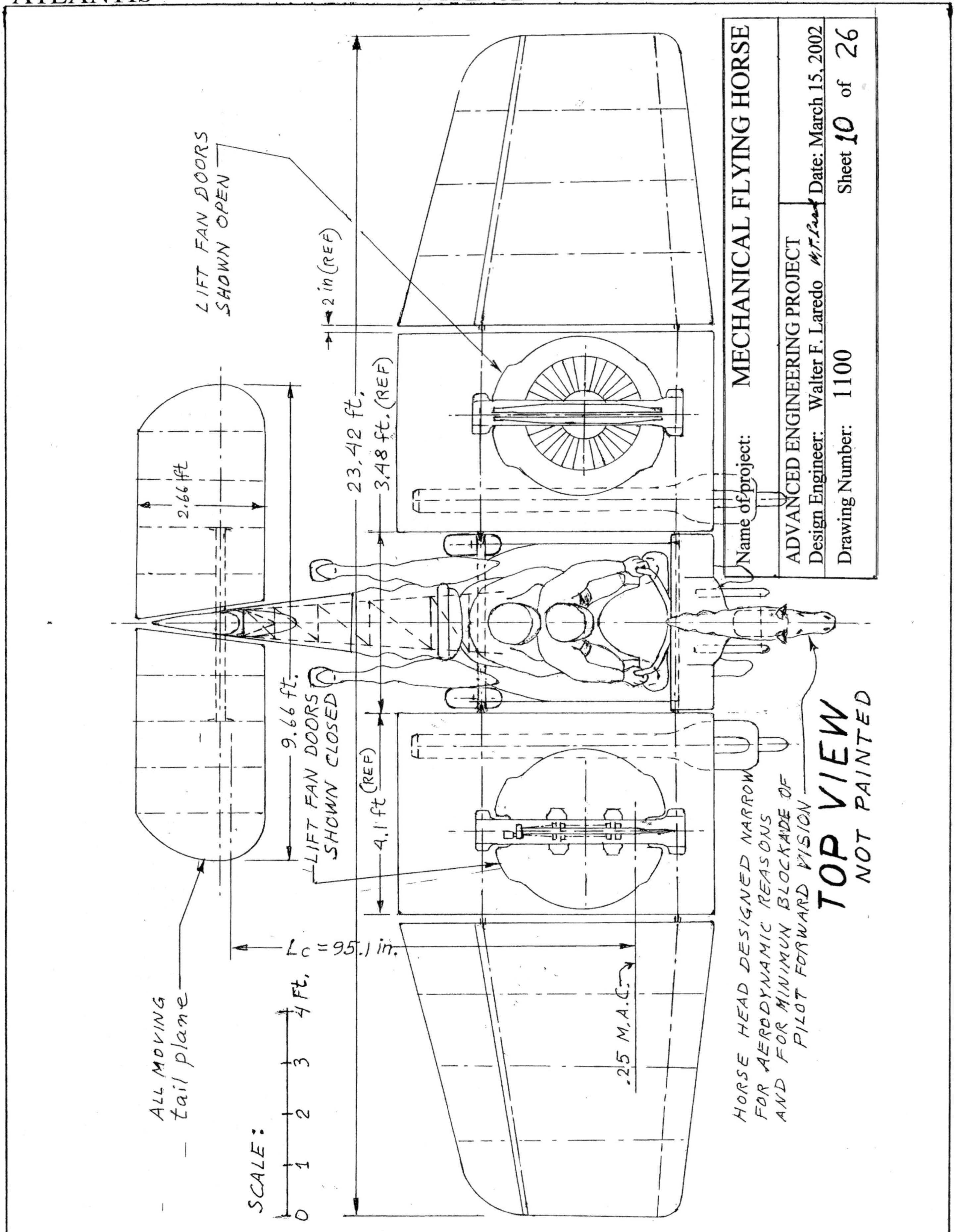

LIFT FAN DOORS SHOWN OPEN

2 in (REF)

23.42 ft.

3.48 ft. (REF)

2.66 ft

9.66 ft.

LIFT FAN DOORS SHOWN CLOSED

4.1 ft (REF)

$L_c$ = 95.1 in.

.25 M.A.C.

ALL MOVING tail plane

SCALE:

0   1   2   3   4 Ft.

HORSE HEAD DESIGNED NARROW FOR AERODYNAMIC REASONS AND FOR MINIMUN BLOCKADE OF PILOT FORWARD VISION

**TOP VIEW**
NOT PAINTED

Name of project:    **MECHANICAL FLYING HORSE**

ADVANCED ENGINEERING PROJECT

Design Engineer:   Walter F. Laredo   W.F.Laredo   Date: March 15, 2002

Drawing Number:   1100      Sheet 10 of 26

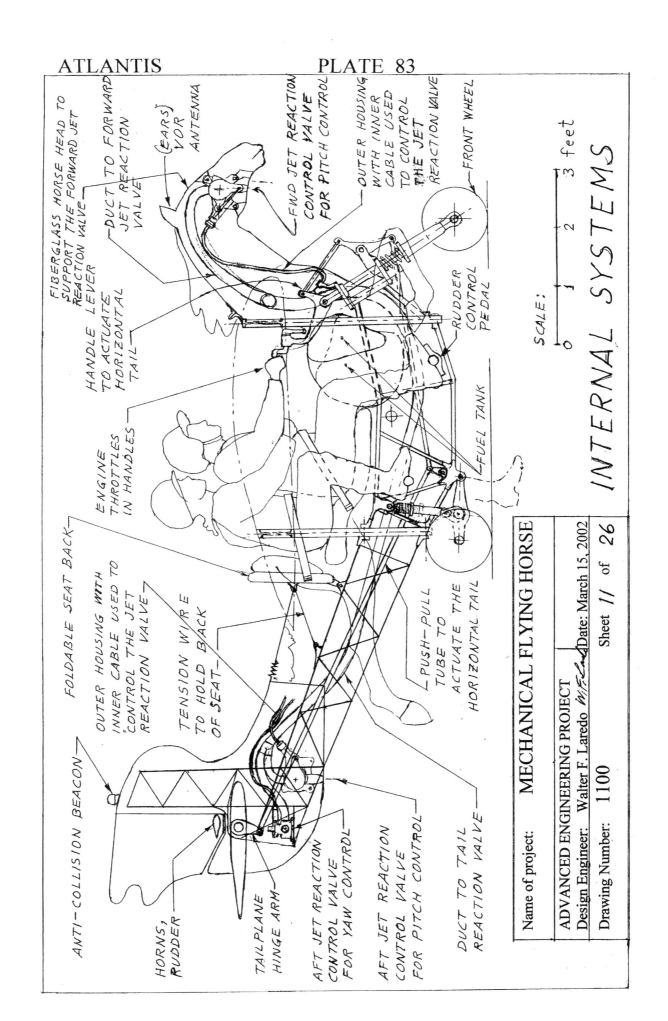

FIBERGLASS HORSE HEAD TO SUPPORT THE FORWARD JET REACTION VALVE

DUCT TO FORWARD JET REACTION VALVE

(EARS) VOR ANTENNA

FWD JET REACTION CONTROL VALVE FOR PITCH CONTROL

OUTER HOUSING WITH INNER CABLE USED TO CONTROL THE JET REACTION VALVE

FRONT WHEEL

HANDLE LEVER TO ACTUATE HORIZONTAL TAIL

ENGINE THROTTLES IN HANDLES

RUDDER CONTROL PEDAL

FUEL TANK

ANTI-COLLISION BEACON

FOLDABLE SEAT BACK

OUTER HOUSING WITH INNER CABLE USED TO CONTROL THE JET REACTION VALVE

TENSION WIRE TO HOLD BACK OF SEAT

PUSH-PULL TUBE TO ACTUATE THE HORIZONTAL TAIL

HORNS, RUDDER

TAILPLANE HINGE ARM

AFT JET REACTION CONTROL VALVE FOR YAW CONTROL

AFT JET REACTION CONTROL VALVE FOR PITCH CONTROL

DUCT TO TAIL REACTION VALVE

INTERNAL SYSTEMS

SCALE:

0  1  2  3 feet

| Name of project: | MECHANICAL FLYING HORSE | |
|---|---|---|
| ADVANCED ENGINEERING PROJECT | | |
| Design Engineer: | Walter F. Laredo  W. F. Lml | Date: March 15, 2002 |
| Drawing Number: | 1100 | Sheet 11 of 26 |

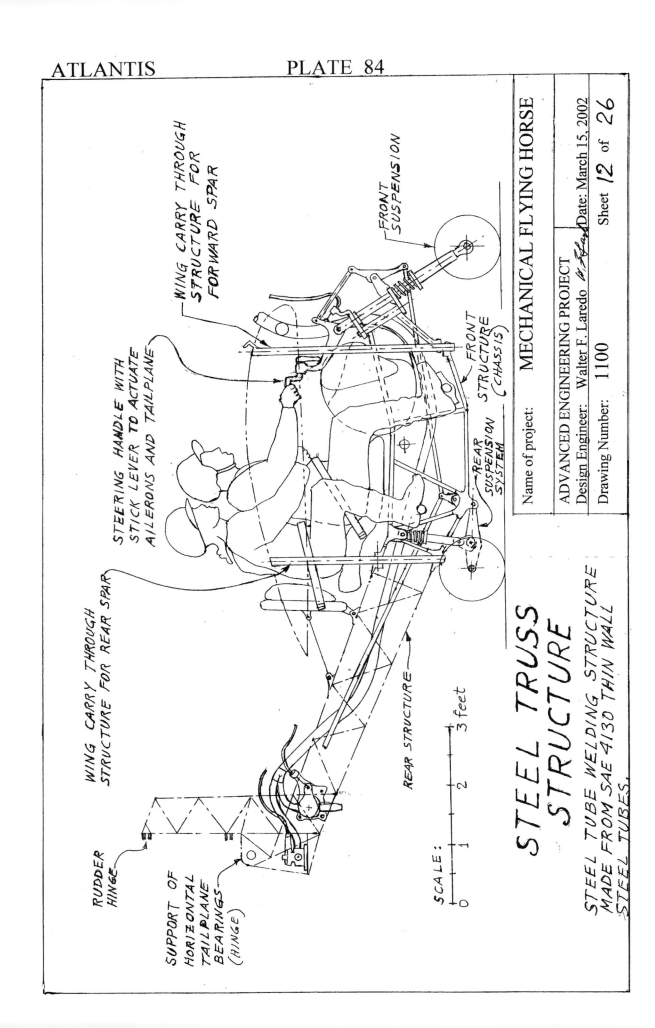

WING CARRY THROUGH STRUCTURE FOR FORWARD SPAR

FRONT SUSPENSION

STEERING HANDLE WITH STICK LEVER TO ACTUATE AILERONS AND TAILPLANE

FRONT STRUCTURE (CHASSIS)

REAR SUSPENSION SYSTEM

WING CARRY THROUGH STRUCTURE FOR REAR SPAR

REAR STRUCTURE

RUDDER HINGE

SUPPORT OF HORIZONTAL TAILPLANE BEARINGS (HINGE)

SCALE:
0    1    2    3 feet

STEEL TRUSS STRUCTURE

STEEL TUBE WELDING STRUCTURE MADE FROM SAE 4130 THIN WALL STEEL TUBES.

| Name of project: | MECHANICAL FLYING HORSE |
| --- | --- |
| ADVANCED ENGINEERING PROJECT | |
| Design Engineer: | Walter F. Laredo    Date: March 15, 2002 |
| Drawing Number: | 1100    Sheet 12 of 26 |

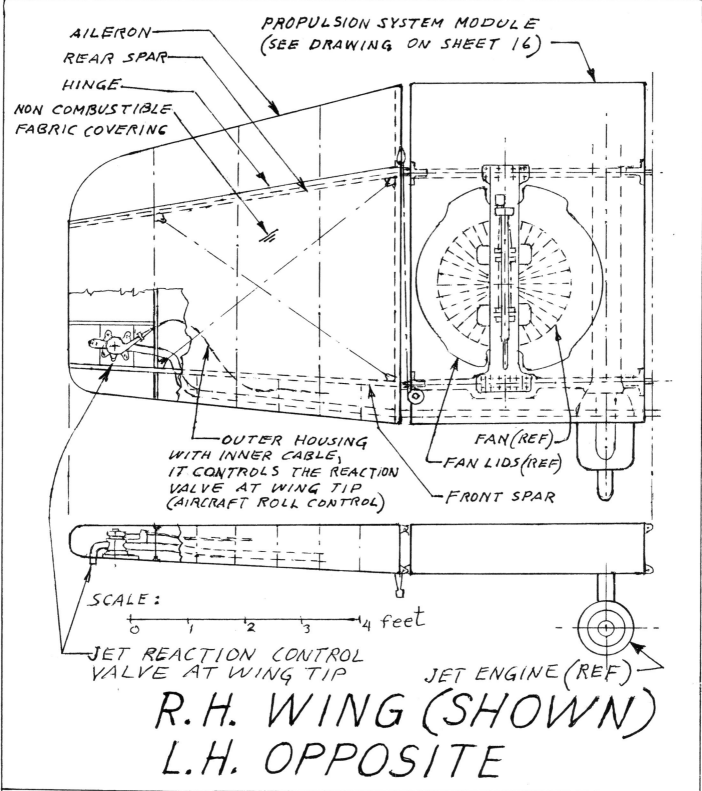

AILERON

REAR SPAR

HINGE

NON COMBUSTIBLE
FABRIC COVERING

PROPULSION SYSTEM MODULE
(SEE DRAWING ON SHEET 16)

OUTER HOUSING
WITH INNER CABLE,
IT CONTROLS THE REACTION
VALVE AT WING TIP
(AIRCRAFT ROLL CONTROL)

FAN (REF)

FAN LIDS (REF)

FRONT SPAR

SCALE:

0   1   2   3   4 feet

JET REACTION CONTROL
VALVE AT WING TIP

JET ENGINE (REF)

# R.H. WING (SHOWN)
# L.H. OPPOSITE

WING STRUCTURAL
MATERIAL

STEEL TUBING
SAE 4130
SPARS:
3/4 O.D. × .040" WALL
RIBS:
1/4 O.D. × .010" WALL

Name of project: **MECHANICAL FLYING HORSE**

ADVANCED ENGINEERING PROJECT

Design Engineer:   Walter F. Laredo   *W.F.Laredo*

Date: March 15, 2002

Drawing Number:   1100

Sheet 13 of 26

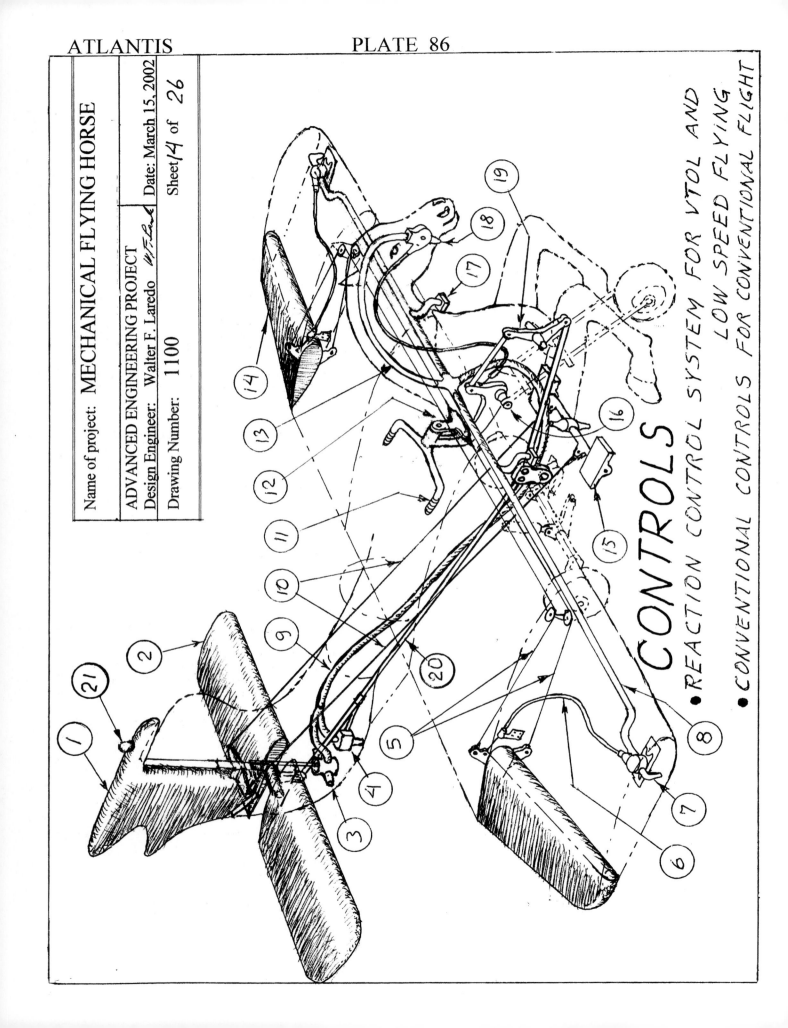

Name of project: MECHANICAL FLYING HORSE

ADVANCED ENGINEERING PROJECT
Design Engineer: Walter F. Laredo   WFLad   Date: March 15, 2002
Drawing Number: 1100     Sheet 14 of 26

CONTROLS
• REACTION CONTROL SYSTEM FOR VTOL AND LOW SPEED FLYING
• CONVENTIONAL CONTROLS FOR CONVENTIONAL FLIGHT

(Continuation from CONTROLS, sheet 14)

1    Rudder
2    Horizontal tail
3    Yaw-control reaction jet
4    Pitch-control reaction jet
5    Cables to actuate ailerons
6    Outer housing with inner cable system controls wing tip reaction control valve.  Inner cables are actuated by aileron movements
7    Roll-control reaction jet (wing tip)
8    Lateral duct, supplies compressed air for roll-control reaction jets
9    Duct to tail reaction control jets
10   Steel cables to actuate rudder
11   Pilot's handlebar, it steers front wheel, also actuates ailerons and tail plane, the throttles controls are located at handles
12   Crank, pulls ailerons control cables
13   Duct to forward control reaction jet
14   Aileron
15   Pedals, controls rudder
16   Pin, hold handlebar
17   Connector with one way valve, supplies compressed air from engine air bleed hole to reaction jets control system
18   Fwd. Pitch-control reaction jet
19   Rocker connected to pilot's handlebar lever, actuates horizontal tail
20   Push-pull tube, actuates horizontal tail
21   Tail strobe light.

| Name of project: | **MECHANICAL FLYING HORSE** | |
|---|---|---|
| ADVANCED ENGINEERING PROJECT | | |
| Design Engineer:   Walter F. Laredo | | Date: March 15, 2002 |
| Drawing Number:   1100 | | Sheet 15 of  26 |

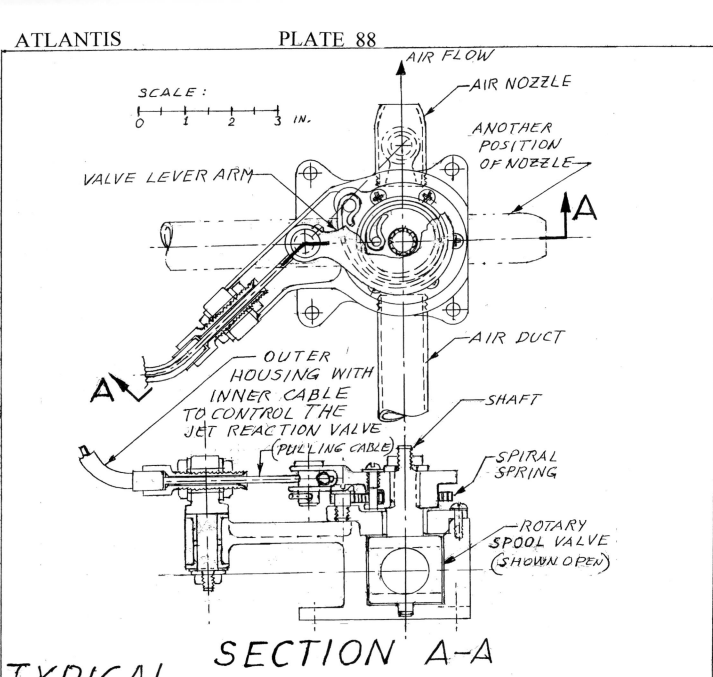

SCALE:
0 1 2 3 IN.

AIR FLOW

AIR NOZZLE

ANOTHER POSITION OF NOZZLE

VALVE LEVER ARM

A

A

AIR DUCT

OUTER HOUSING WITH INNER CABLE TO CONTROL THE JET REACTION VALVE (PULLING CABLE)

SHAFT

SPIRAL SPRING

ROTARY SPOOL VALVE (SHOWN OPEN)

SECTION A-A

TYPICAL REACTION JET CONTROL VALVE

(REACTION CONTROL SYSTEM)

| Name of project: | MECHANICAL FLYING HORSE | |
| --- | --- | --- |
| ADVANCED ENGINEERING PROJECT | | |
| Design Engineer: Walter F. Laredo | | Date: March 15, 2002 |
| Drawing Number: 1100 | | Sheet 16 of 26 |

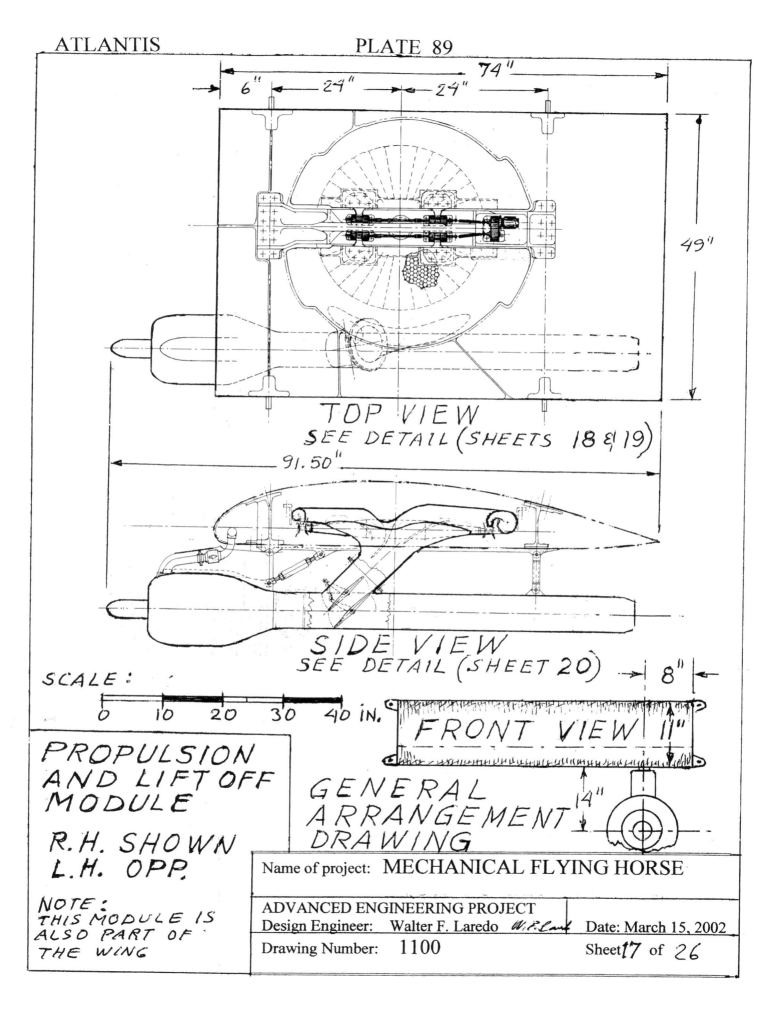

74"

6"   24"   24"

49"

## TOP VIEW
SEE DETAIL (SHEETS 18 & 19)

91.50"

## SIDE VIEW
SEE DETAIL (SHEET 20)   8"

SCALE:

0   10   20   30   40 IN.

## FRONT VIEW 11"

## PROPULSION AND LIFT OFF MODULE

## R.H. SHOWN L.H. OPP.

NOTE:
THIS MODULE IS ALSO PART OF THE WING

## GENERAL ARRANGEMENT DRAWING

14"

Name of project: **MECHANICAL FLYING HORSE**

ADVANCED ENGINEERING PROJECT
Design Engineer:   Walter F. Laredo   *W.F.Laredo*    Date: March 15, 2002

Drawing Number:   1100      Sheet 17 of 26

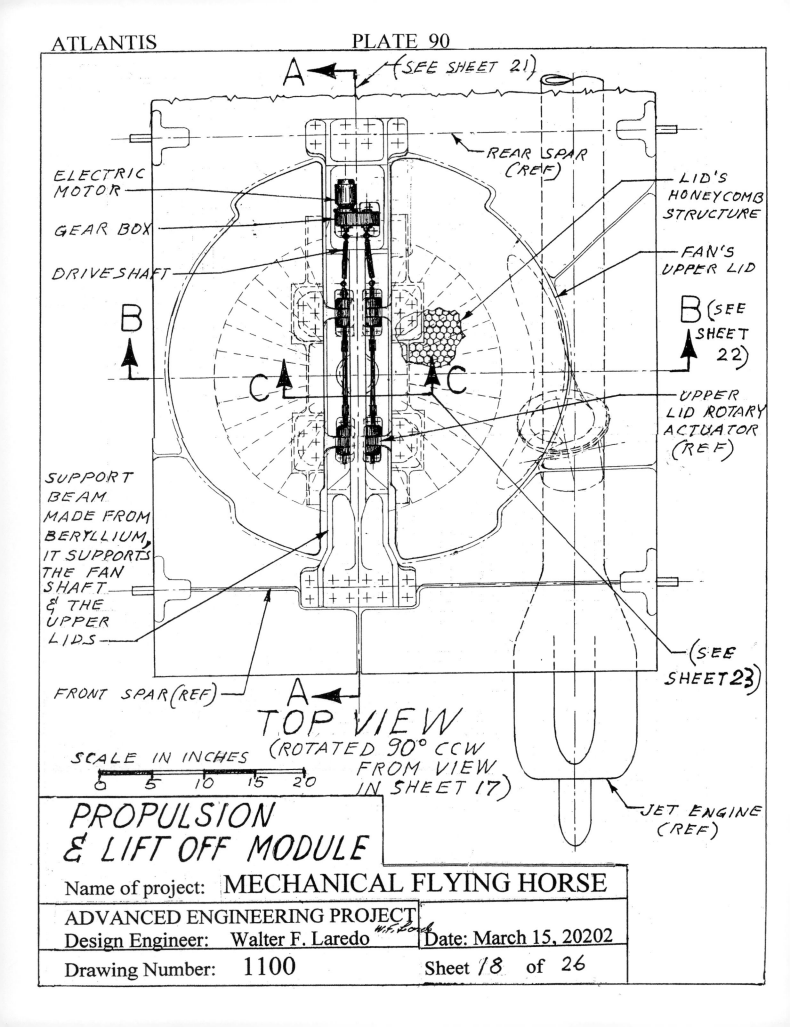

(SEE SHEET 21)

A

REAR SPAR (REF)

ELECTRIC MOTOR

LID'S HONEYCOMB STRUCTURE

GEAR BOX

FAN'S UPPER LID

DRIVESHAFT

B

B (SEE SHEET 22)

C

C

UPPER LID ROTARY ACTUATOR (REF)

SUPPORT BEAM MADE FROM BERYLLIUM, IT SUPPORTS THE FAN SHAFT & THE UPPER LIDS

(SEE SHEET 23)

FRONT SPAR (REF)

A

TOP VIEW
(ROTATED 90° CCW FROM VIEW IN SHEET 17)

SCALE IN INCHES
0   5   10   15   20

JET ENGINE (REF)

# PROPULSION & LIFT OFF MODULE

Name of project: **MECHANICAL FLYING HORSE**

ADVANCED ENGINEERING PROJECT
Design Engineer: Walter F. Laredo    Date: March 15, 20202

Drawing Number: 1100    Sheet 18 of 26

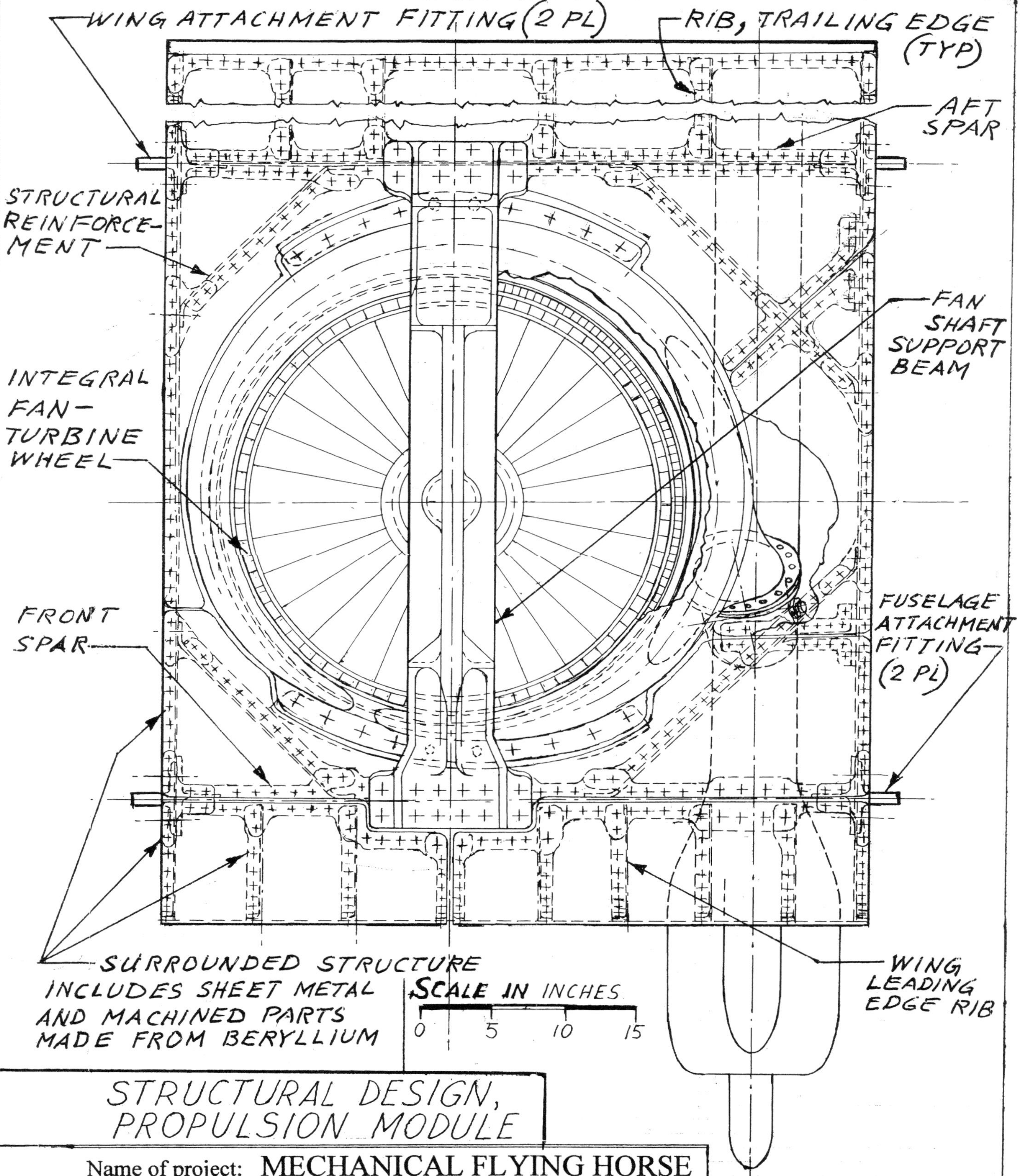

WING ATTACHMENT FITTING (2 PL)

RIB, TRAILING EDGE (TYP)

AFT SPAR

STRUCTURAL REINFORCE-MENT

FAN SHAFT SUPPORT BEAM

INTEGRAL FAN-TURBINE WHEEL

FRONT SPAR

FUSELAGE ATTACHMENT FITTING (2 PL)

SURROUNDED STRUCTURE INCLUDES SHEET METAL AND MACHINED PARTS MADE FROM BERYLLIUM

SCALE IN INCHES

0    5    10    15

WING LEADING EDGE RIB

STRUCTURAL DESIGN, PROPULSION MODULE

Name of project: MECHANICAL FLYING HORSE

ADVANCED ENGINEERING PROJECT

Design Engineer: Walter F. Laredo   *W. F. Laredo*   Date: March 15, 2002

Drawing Number: 1100      Sheet 19 of 26

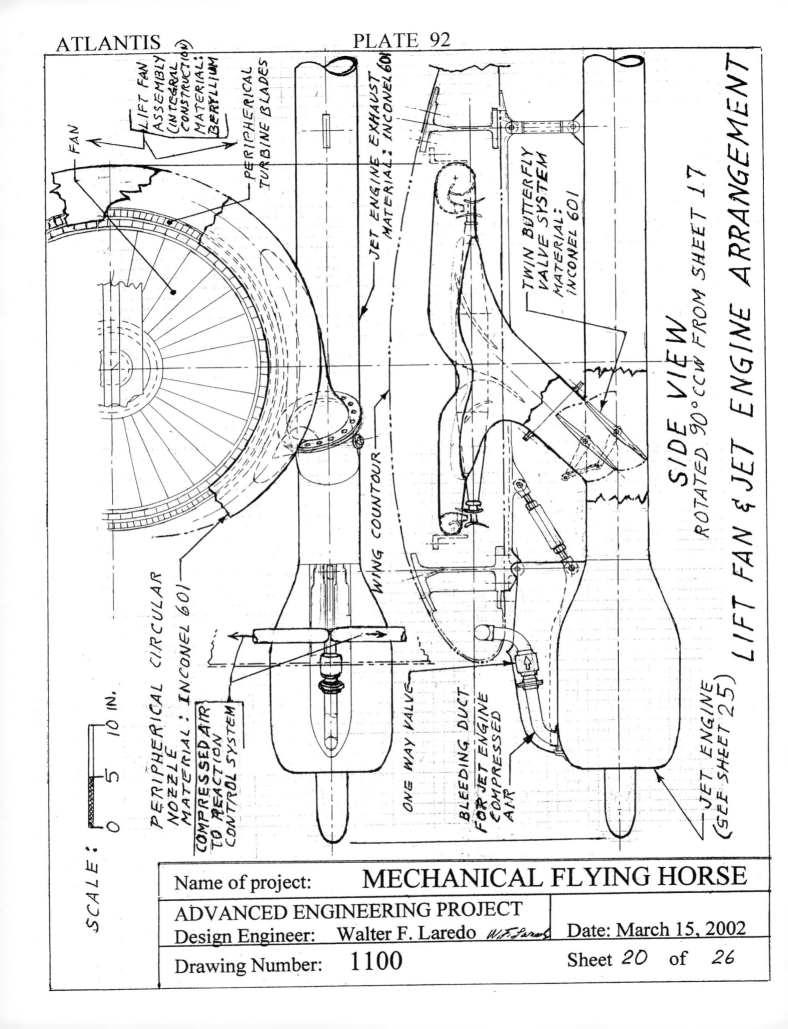

FAN

LIFT FAN ASSEMBLY (INTEGRAL CONSTRUCTION) MATERIAL: BERYLLIUM

PERIPHERICAL TURBINE BLADES

JET ENGINE EXHAUST MATERIAL: INCONEL 601

TWIN BUTTERFLY VALVE SYSTEM MATERIAL: INCONEL 601

PERIPHERICAL CIRCULAR NOZZLE MATERIAL: INCONEL 601

COMPRESSED AIR TO REACTION CONTROL SYSTEM

WING COUNTOUR

ONE WAY VALVE

BLEEDING DUCT FOR JET ENGINE COMPRESSED AIR

JET ENGINE (SEE SHEET 25)

SIDE VIEW
ROTATED 90° CCW FROM SHEET 17

LIFT FAN & JET ENGINE ARRANGEMENT

SCALE:
0   5   10 IN.

| Name of project: | **MECHANICAL FLYING HORSE** | |
|---|---|---|
| ADVANCED ENGINEERING PROJECT | | |
| Design Engineer:   Walter F. Laredo   *W.F. Laredo* | | Date: March 15, 2002 |
| Drawing Number:   **1100** | | Sheet 20 of 26 |

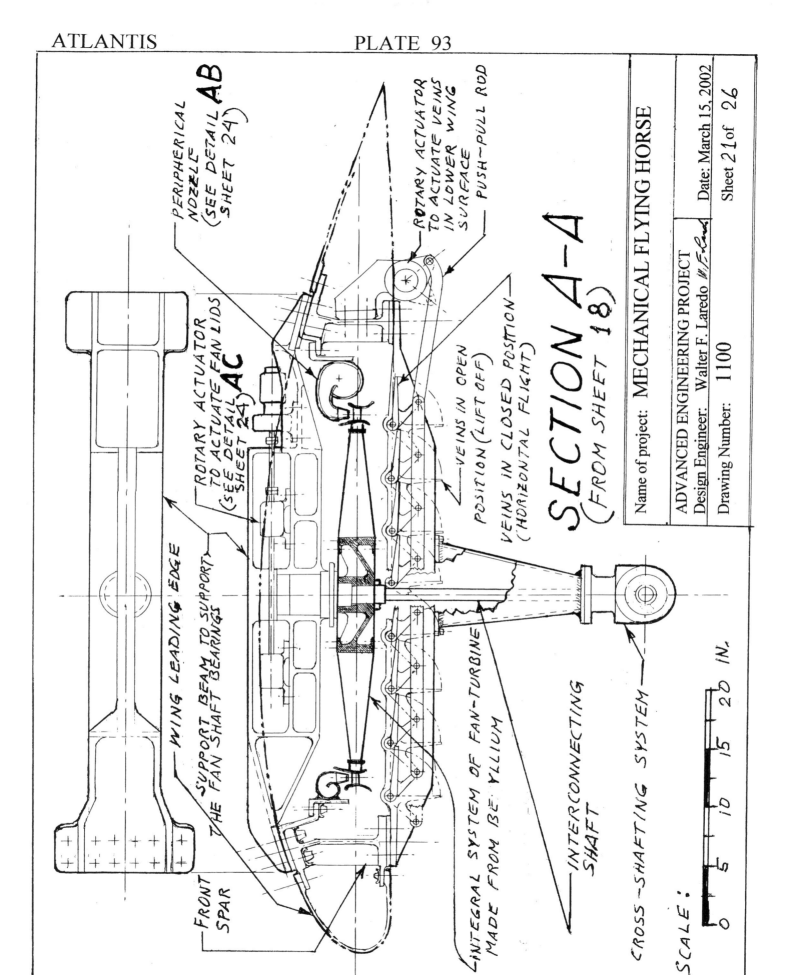

PERIPHERICAL NOZZLE (SEE DETAIL **AB** SHEET 24)

ROTARY ACTUATOR TO ACTUATE VEINS IN LOWER WING SURFACE

PUSH-PULL ROD

ROTARY ACTUATOR TO ACTUATE FAN LIDS (SEE DETAIL **AC** SHEET 24)

WING LEADING EDGE

SUPPORT BEAM TO SUPPORT THE FAN SHAFT BEARINGS

FRONT SPAR

VEINS IN OPEN POSITION (LIFT OFF)

VEINS IN CLOSED POSITION ("HORIZONTAL FLIGHT")

*SECTION A-A*
(FROM SHEET 18)

INTEGRAL SYSTEM OF FAN-TURBINE MADE FROM BERYLLIUM

INTERCONNECTING SHAFT

CROSS-SHAFTING SYSTEM

SCALE:   0   5   10   15   20 IN.

| Name of project: | MECHANICAL FLYING HORSE | |
|---|---|---|
| ADVANCED ENGINEERING PROJECT | | Date: March 15, 2002 |
| Design Engineer: | Walter F. Laredo | |
| Drawing Number: | 1100 | Sheet 21 of 26 |

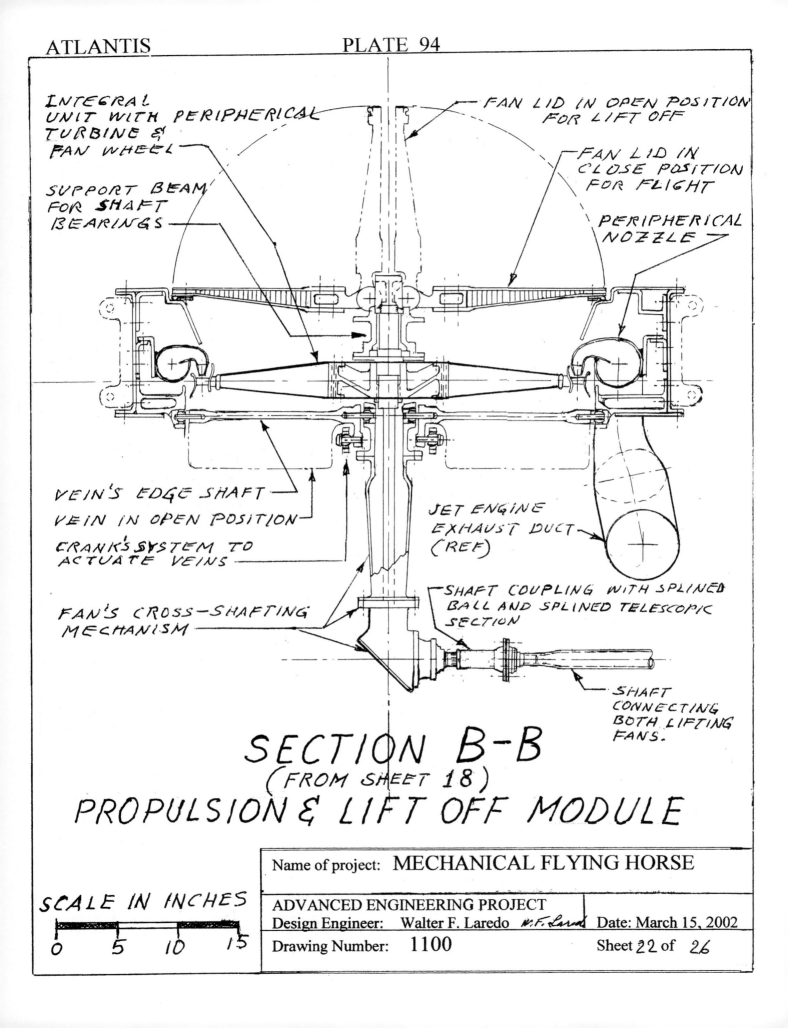

INTEGRAL UNIT WITH PERIPHERICAL TURBINE & FAN WHEEL

SUPPORT BEAM FOR SHAFT BEARINGS

FAN LID IN OPEN POSITION FOR LIFT OFF

FAN LID IN CLOSE POSITION FOR FLIGHT

PERIPHERICAL NOZZLE

VEIN'S EDGE SHAFT

VEIN IN OPEN POSITION

CRANK'S SYSTEM TO ACTUATE VEINS

JET ENGINE EXHAUST DUCT (REF)

FAN'S CROSS-SHAFTING MECHANISM

SHAFT COUPLING WITH SPLINED BALL AND SPLINED TELESCOPIC SECTION

SHAFT CONNECTING BOTH LIFTING FANS.

# SECTION B-B
(FROM SHEET 18)
## PROPULSION & LIFT OFF MODULE

SCALE IN INCHES

0   5   10   15

| Name of project: | MECHANICAL FLYING HORSE | |
| --- | --- | --- |
| ADVANCED ENGINEERING PROJECT | | |
| Design Engineer: Walter F. Laredo   *W.F. Laredo* | | Date: March 15, 2002 |
| Drawing Number: 1100 | | Sheet 22 of 26 |

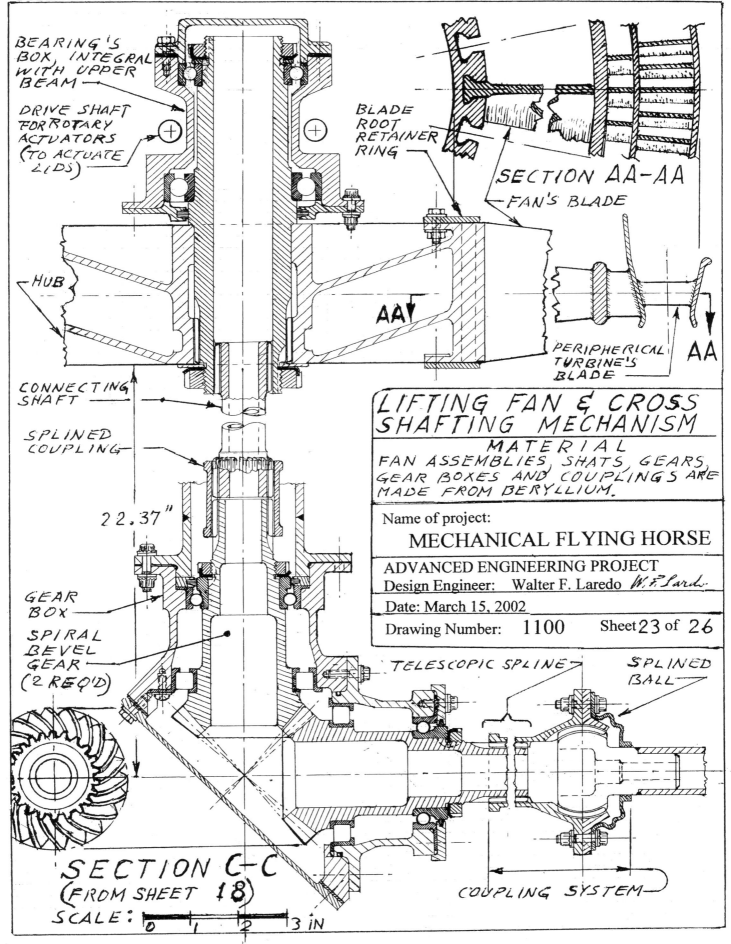

BEARING'S BOX, INTEGRAL WITH UPPER BEAM

DRIVE SHAFT FOR ROTARY ACTUATORS (TO ACTUATE LIDS)

HUB

BLADE ROOT RETAINER RING

SECTION AA-AA
FAN'S BLADE

AA

PERIPHERICAL TURBINE'S BLADE

AA

CONNECTING SHAFT

SPLINED COUPLING

22.37"

GEAR BOX

SPIRAL BEVEL GEAR (2 REQ'D)

TELESCOPIC SPLINE

SPLINED BALL

SECTION C-C
(FROM SHEET 18)
SCALE: 0 1 2 3 IN

COUPLING SYSTEM

**LIFTING FAN & CROSS SHAFTING MECHANISM**

MATERIAL
FAN ASSEMBLIES, SHATS, GEARS, GEAR BOXES AND COUPLINGS ARE MADE FROM BERYLLIUM.

Name of project:
**MECHANICAL FLYING HORSE**

ADVANCED ENGINEERING PROJECT
Design Engineer: Walter F. Laredo   W.F.Laredo

Date: March 15, 2002

Drawing Number: 1100     Sheet 23 of 26

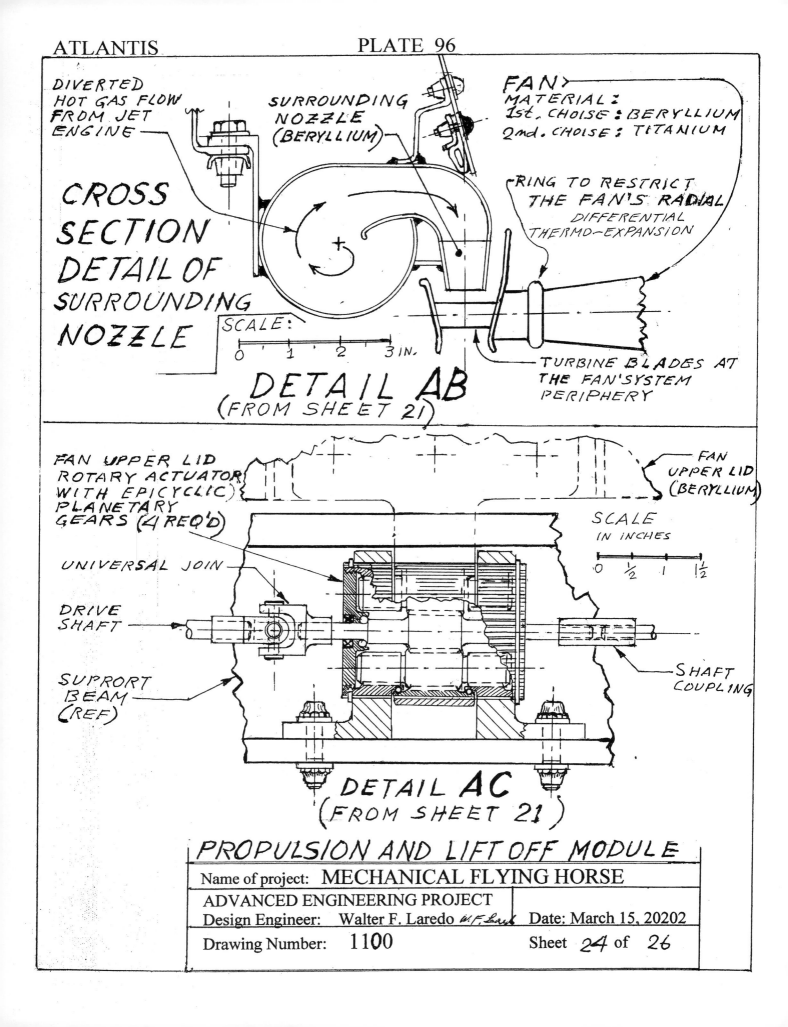

DIVERTED HOT GAS FLOW FROM JET ENGINE

SURROUNDING NOZZLE (BERYLLIUM)

FAN>
MATERIAL:
1st. CHOISE : BERYLLIUM
2nd. CHOISE : TITANIUM

CROSS SECTION DETAIL OF SURROUNDING NOZZLE

RING TO RESTRICT THE FAN'S RADIAL DIFFERENTIAL THERMO-EXPANSION

SCALE:
0  1  2  3 IN.

TURBINE BLADES AT THE FAN'SYSTEM PERIPHERY

## DETAIL AB
(FROM SHEET 21)

FAN UPPER LID ROTARY ACTUATOR WITH EPICYCLIC) PLANETARY GEARS (4 REQ'D)

FAN UPPER LID (BERYLLIUM)

SCALE IN INCHES
0  ½  1  1½

UNIVERSAL JOIN

DRIVE SHAFT

SHAFT COUPLING

SUPPORT BEAM (REF)

## DETAIL AC
(FROM SHEET 21)

PROPULSION AND LIFT OFF MODULE

| Name of project: MECHANICAL FLYING HORSE | |
|---|---|
| ADVANCED ENGINEERING PROJECT | |
| Design Engineer: Walter F. Laredo | Date: March 15, 20202 |
| Drawing Number: 1100 | Sheet 24 of 26 |

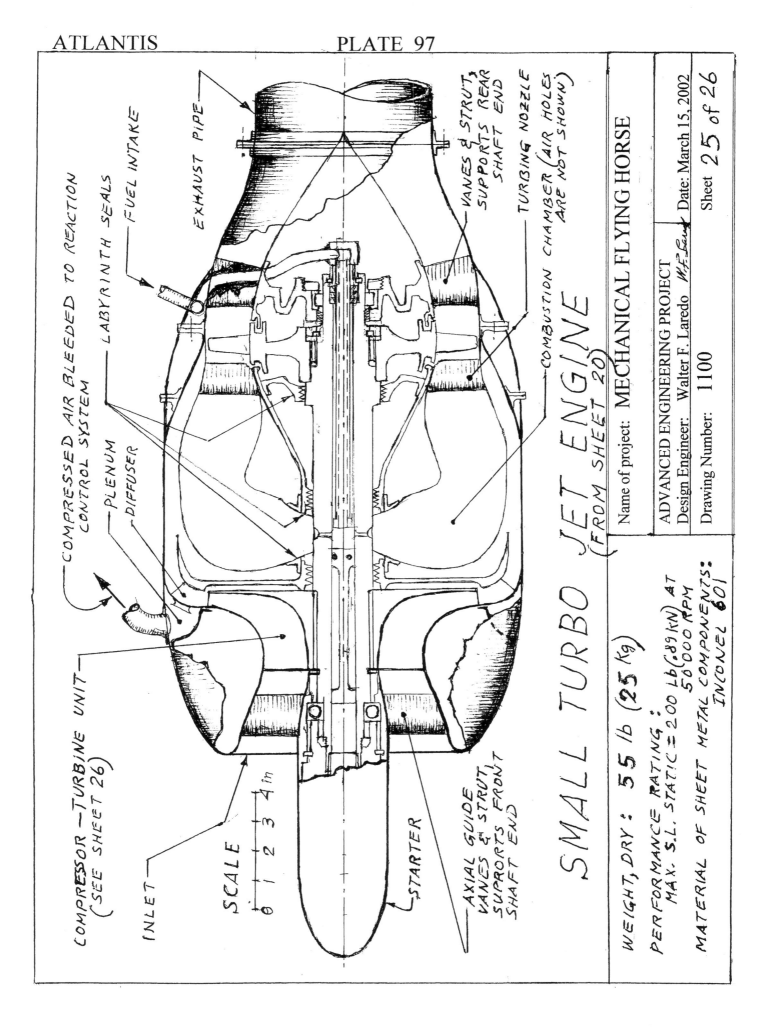

COMPRESSED AIR BLEEDED TO REACTION CONTROL SYSTEM

LABYRINTH SEALS

FUEL INTAKE

EXHAUST PIPE

VANES & STRUT, SUPPORTS REAR SHAFT END

TURBING NOZZLE

COMBUSTION CHAMBER (AIR HOLES ARE NOT SHOWN)

PLENUM

DIFFUSER

COMPRESSOR—TURBINE UNIT (SEE SHEET 26)

INLET

SCALE

0  1  2  3  4 in

STARTER

AXIAL GUIDE VANES & STRUT, SUPPORTS FRONT SHAFT END

SMALL TURBO JET ENGINE
(FROM SHEET 20)

WEIGHT, DRY: 55 lb (25 kg)

PERFORMANCE RATING:
MAX. S.L. STATIC = 200 Lb (.89 kN) AT 50,000 RPM

MATERIAL OF SHEET METAL COMPONENTS: INCONEL 601

| | |
|---|---|
| Name of project: | MECHANICAL FLYING HORSE |
| ADVANCED ENGINEERING PROJECT | |
| Design Engineer:   Walter F. Laredo | Date: March 15, 2002 |
| Drawing Number:   1100 | Sheet 25 of 26 |

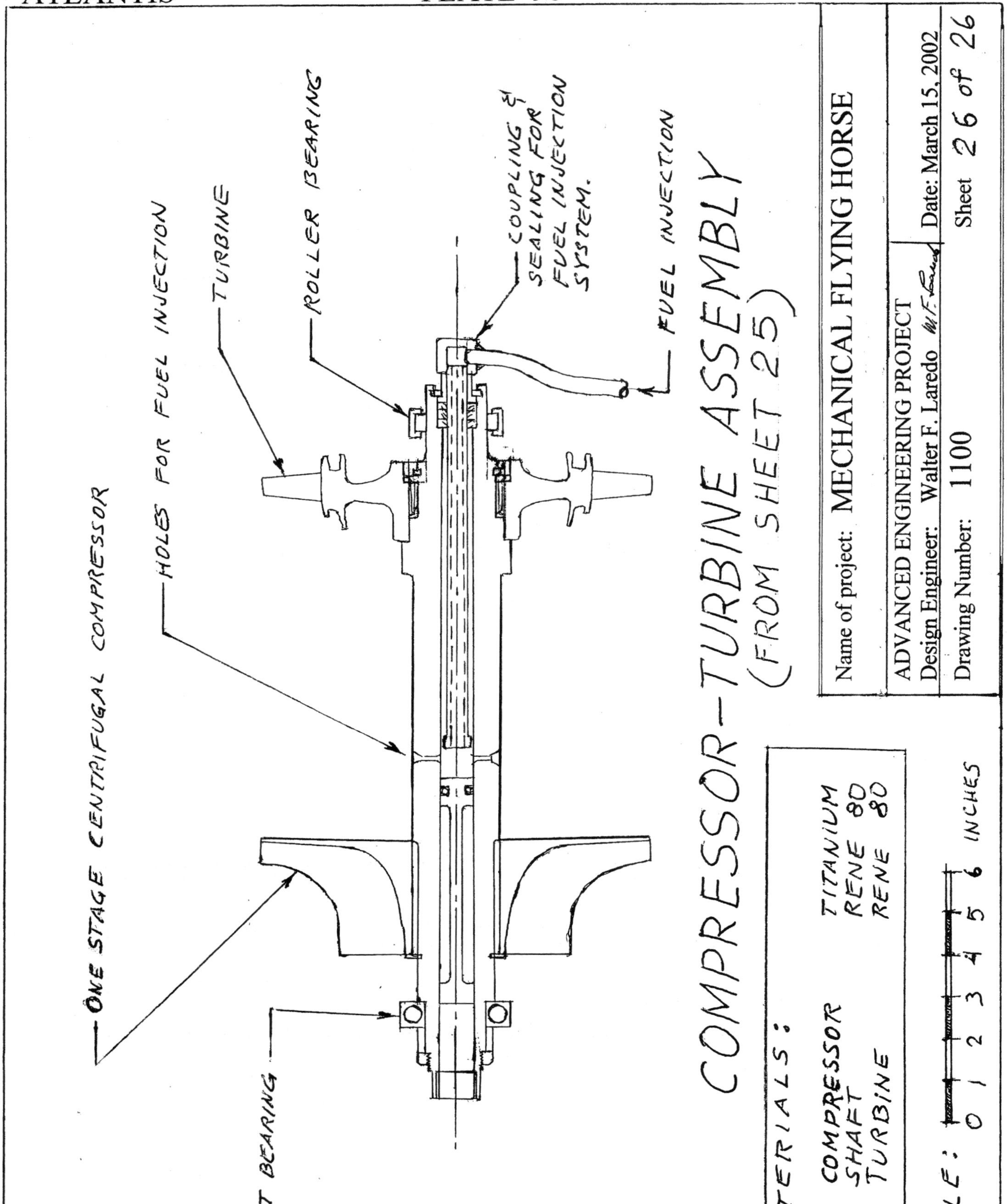

COMPRESSOR-TURBINE ASSEMBLY
(FROM SHEET 25)

ONE STAGE CENTRIFUGAL COMPRESSOR

HOLES FOR FUEL INJECTION

TURBINE

ROLLER BEARING

COUPLING & SEALING FOR FUEL INJECTION SYSTEM.

FUEL INJECTION

THRUST BEARING

MATERIALS:

| COMPRESSOR | TITANIUM |
| SHAFT | RENE 80 |
| TURBINE | RENE 80 |

SCALE:  0  1  2  3  4  5  6  INCHES

| Name of project: | MECHANICAL FLYING HORSE |
|---|---|
| ADVANCED ENGINEERING PROJECT | |
| Design Engineer: Walter F. Laredo  W.F. Laredo | Date: March 15, 2002 |
| Drawing Number:  1100 | Sheet 26 of 26 |

## POWER PLANT (BOTH CONFIGURATIONS)

65 HP, air cooled Hirth engine,
Limited to 15 HP in road-ridden mode.

## SPECIFICATIONS (WING TYPE)

| | | |
|---|---|---|
| Accommodation | 2 tandem | (as in a motorcycle) |
| Wing's span,   (b) | | 24 ft  8in |
| Wing's gross area,   (Sw) | | 23.3  sq. ft. |
| Airfoil | | High lift (see Supl. Inf.) |
| Wing chord, | | 5.0 ft |
| MAC | | 5.0 ft |
| Wing aspect Ratio,    AR= b/a | | 4.93 |
| Canard Area (Sc) | | 25.32  sq. ft. |
| Canard MAC | | 2  ft. |

( Continues in next page)

## ATLANTIS, ADVANCED ENGINEERING PROJECTS

Name of project:

# FLYING CAR   (AIRCRAFT-CAR, VEHICLE)

PROJECT INCLUDES THE FOLLOWING TWO CONFIGURATIONS:
   I.  RETRACTABLE WING TYPE
   II.  POWERED PARACHUTE TYPE

Design Engineer:  Walter F. Laredo  *WFLaredo*  | Date: March 15, 2002

Areas of Development:
Aerodynamics ✓, Stability Control ✓, Thermodynamics ✓, Materials ✓,
Structures (Design and Analysis) ✓ , Mechanisms & Systems ✓ ,

NOTE: This is the PRELIMINARY DESIGN for a real engineering project.
A project inspired by the legendary dreams and tales of the semi-utopian
highly advanced civilization, called Atlantis.

| Drawing Number:   1200 | Sheet  1   of   18 |
|---|---|

( Continues from page 1 )

| | |
|---|---|
| Vertical tail area  (Sv) | 12  sq. ft. |
| Canard arm  (Lc) | 7 ft.  4in |
| Tail arm for ver. tail (Lv) | 11 ft.  3in |
| Vertical tail volume: | |
| $Vv = (Lv \times Sv) / (b \times Sw)$ | 0.044 |
| | |
| Weight empty | 515 lb. |
| Weight max. takeoff | 910 lb. |
| Max. wing loading | 7.38 lb. / sq. ft. |
| Max. power loading | 14.0 lb. / HP |

## PERFORMANCE  (WING TYPE CONFIGURATION)

| | |
|---|---|
| Max. flying level speed at SL | 130 mph |
| Stall speed | 46 mph |
| Max. Road ridden speed in car mode | 30 mph |
| Service ceiling | 15 000  ft |
| Range | 250 miles |

## PERFORMANCE  (POWERED PARACHUTE TYPE)

| | |
|---|---|
| Cruise speed | 33 mph |
| Stall speed | 26 mph |

**NOTE:**
SHEET NUMBERING SYSTEM FOR DRAWINGS

| | |
|---|---|
| Airframe drawings | sheets  3  through  13 |
| Propulsion system drawings | sheets 14 through  18 |

## ATLANTIS, ADVANCED ENGINEERING PROJECTS

Name of project:

# FLYING CAR
### (INCLUDES TWO DIFFERENT CONFIGURATIONS)

| Design Engineer:   Walter F. Laredo   *W.F. Laredo* | Date:   March 15, 2002 |
|---|---|
| Drawing Number:   1200 | Sheet 2    of   18 |

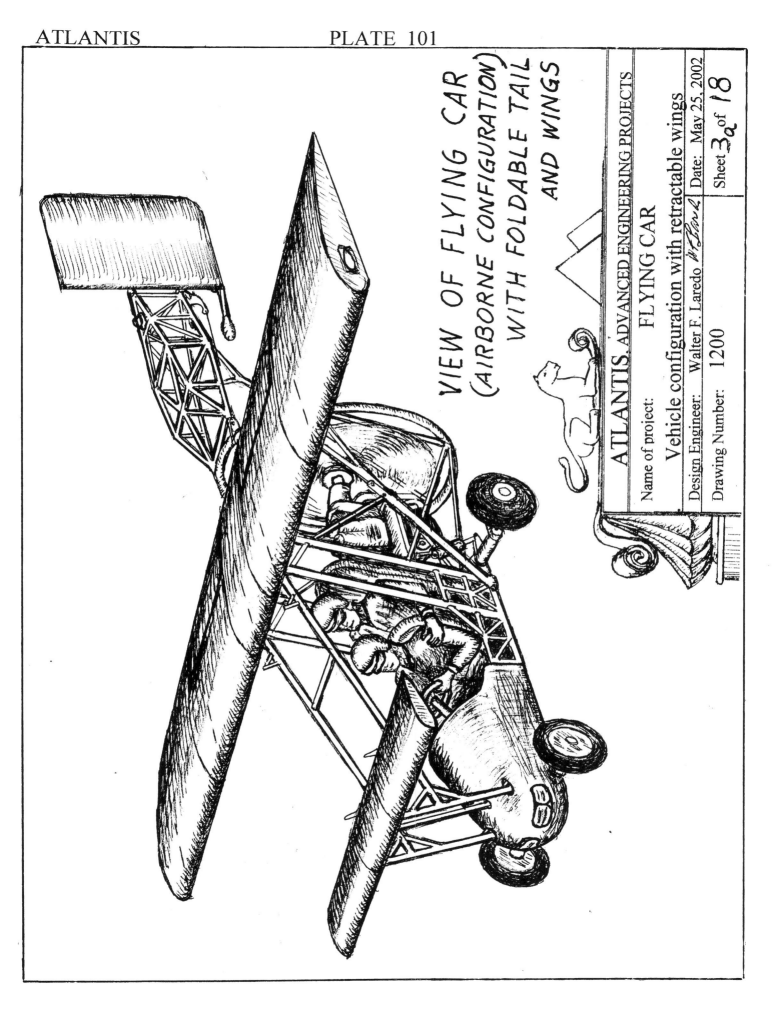

VIEW OF FLYING CAR
(AIRBORNE CONFIGURATION)
WITH FOLDABLE TAIL
AND WINGS

ATLANTIS ADVANCED ENGINEERING PROJECTS

| Name of project: | FLYING CAR | | Date: | May 25, 2002 |
|---|---|---|---|---|
| Design Engineer: | Vehicle configuration with retractable wings | | | |
| | Walter F. Laredo | | | |
| Drawing Number: | 1200 | | Sheet | 3a of 18 |

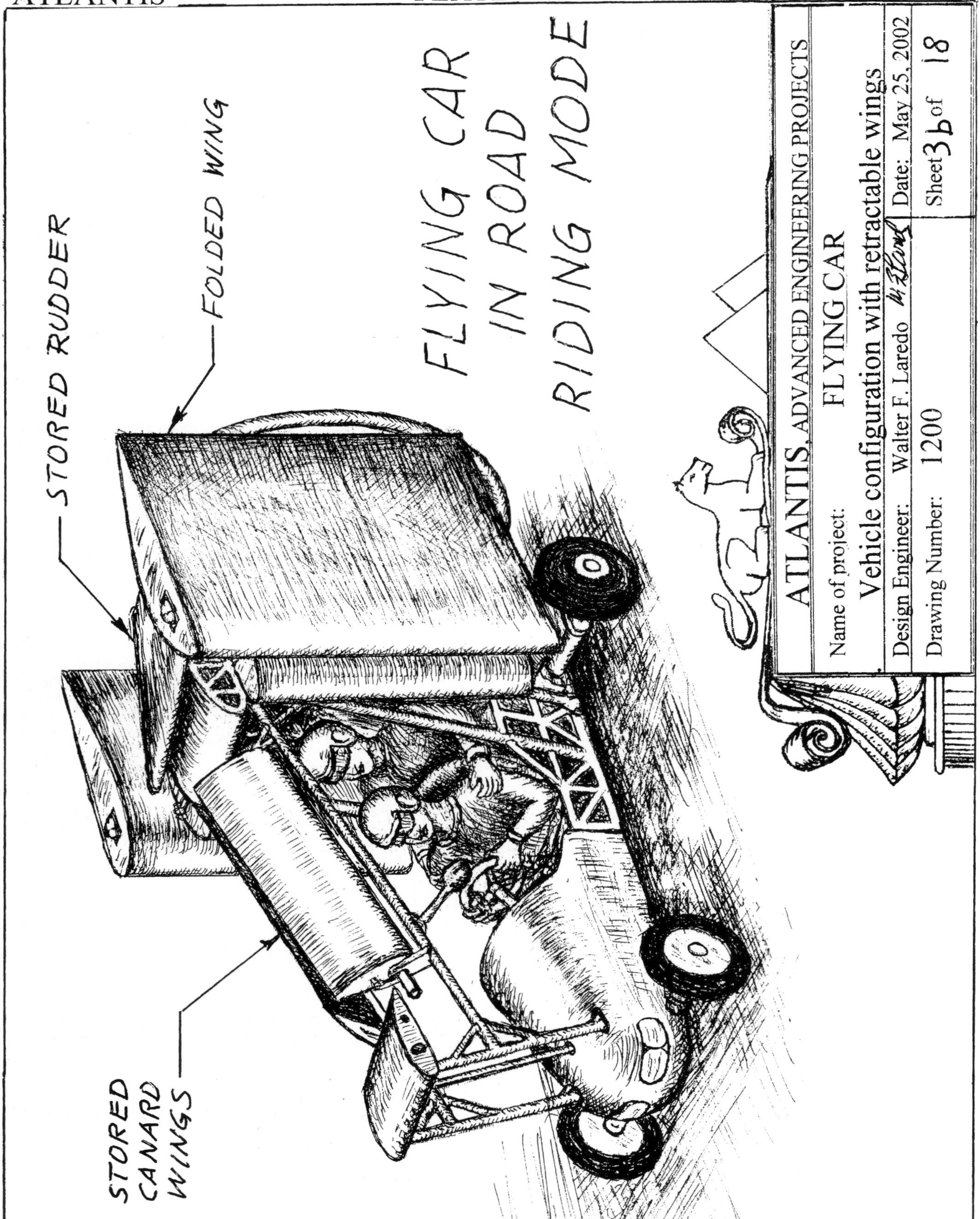

STORED RUDDER

FOLDED WING

FLYING CAR
IN ROAD
RIDING MODE

STORED
CANARD
WINGS

| ATLANTIS, ADVANCED ENGINEERING PROJECTS | | |
|---|---|---|
| FLYING CAR | | |
| Name of project: | Vehicle configuration with retractable wings | |
| Design Engineer: | Walter F. Laredo | Date: May 25, 2002 |
| Drawing Number: | 1200 | Sheet 3b of 18 |

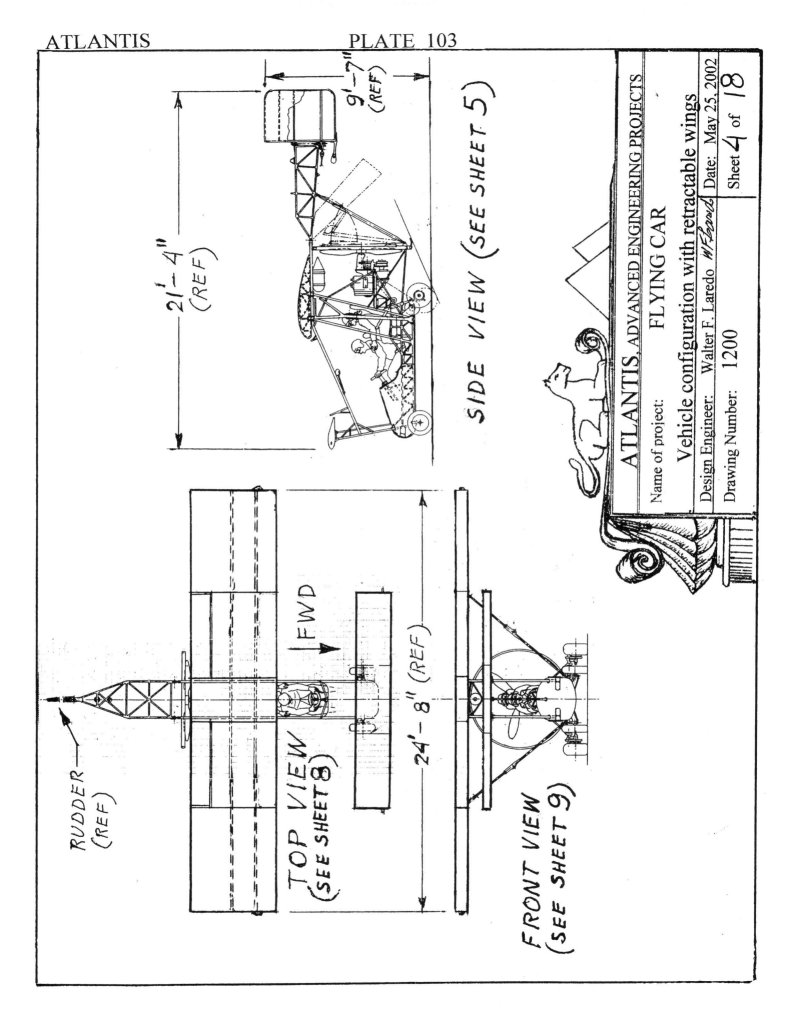

9' – 7" (REF)

21' – 4" (REF)

SIDE VIEW (SEE SHEET 5)

RUDDER (REF)

FWD

24' – 8" (REF)

TOP VIEW (SEE SHEET 8)

FRONT VIEW (SEE SHEET 9)

| ATLANTIS, ADVANCED ENGINEERING PROJECTS | | |
|---|---|---|
| FLYING CAR | | |
| Name of project: | Vehicle configuration with retractable wings | |
| Design Engineer: | Walter F. Laredo  W.F.Laredo | Date: May 25, 2002 |
| Drawing Number: 1200 | | Sheet 4 of 18 |

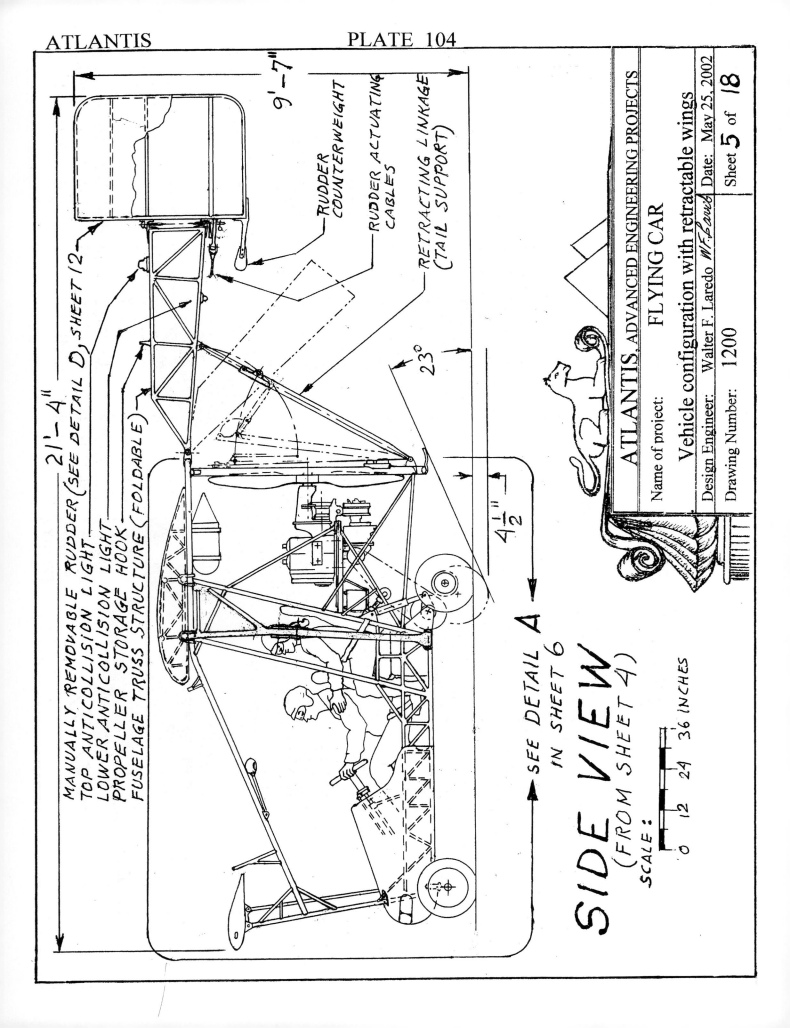

SIDE VIEW
(FROM SHEET 4)
SCALE:

0  12  24  36 INCHES

9'-7"
21'-4"

23°
4 1/2"

RUDDER COUNTERWEIGHT
RUDDER ACTUATING CABLES
RETRACTING LINKAGE (TAIL SUPPORT)

MANUALLY REMOVABLE RUDDER (SEE DETAIL D, SHEET 12)
TOP ANTICOLLISION LIGHT
LOWER ANTICOLLISION LIGHT
PROPELLER STORAGE HOOK
FUSELAGE TRUSS STRUCTURE (FOLDABLE)

SEE DETAIL A IN SHEET 6

ATLANTIS, ADVANCED ENGINEERING PROJECTS
FLYING CAR
Vehicle configuration with retractable wings
Name of project:
Design Engineer: Walter F. Laredo    W.F.Laredo    Date: May 25, 2002
Drawing Number: 1200    Sheet 5 of 18

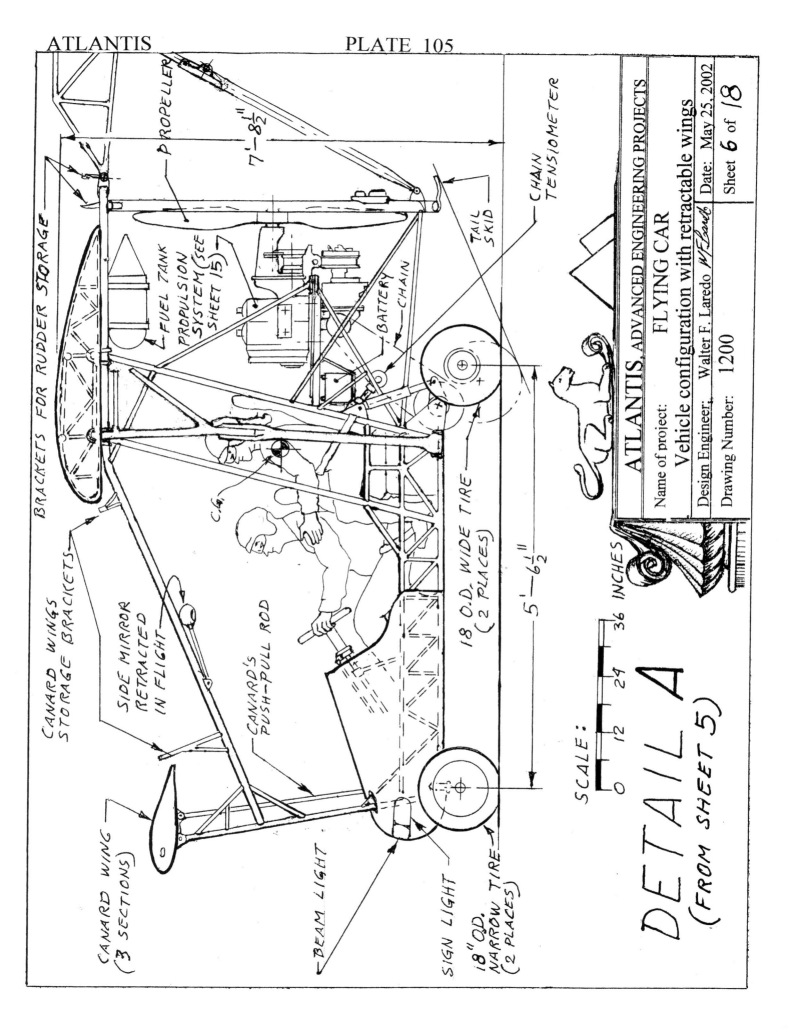

DETAIL A
(FROM SHEET 5)

SCALE:
0  12  24  36  INCHES

BRACKETS FOR RUDDER STORAGE

PROPELLER

7'-8½"

CHAIN TENSIOMETER

TAIL SKID

FUEL TANK

PROPULSION SYSTEM (SEE SHEET 15)

BATTERY

CHAIN

C.G.

CANARD WINGS STORAGE BRACKETS

SIDE MIRROR RETRACTED IN FLIGHT

CANARD'S PUSH-PULL ROD

18 O.D. WIDE TIRE (2 PLACES)

5'-6½"

CANARD WING (3 SECTIONS)

BEAM LIGHT

SIGN LIGHT

18" O.D. NARROW TIRE (2 PLACES)

| ATLANTIS, ADVANCED ENGINEERING PROJECTS | | |
|---|---|---|
| FLYING CAR | | |
| Name of project: Vehicle configuration with retractable wings | | |
| Design Engineer: Walter F. Laredo WFLaredo | Date: May 25, 2002 | |
| Drawing Number: 1200 | Sheet 6 of 18 | |

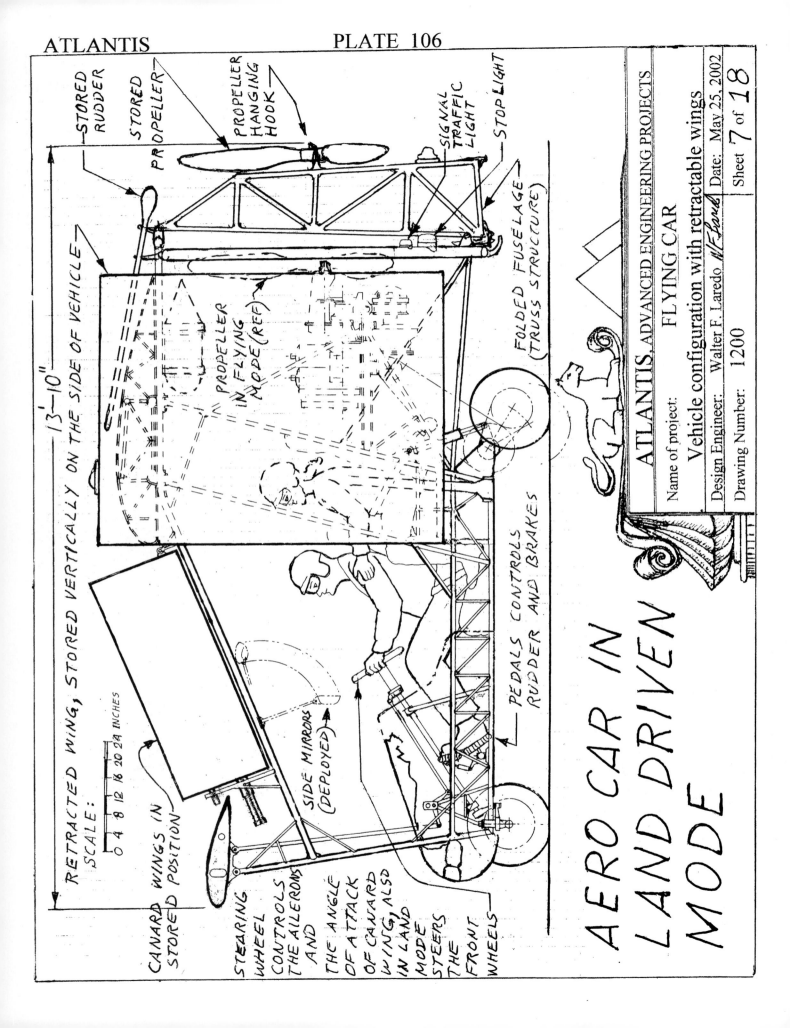

STORED RUDDER

STORED PROPELLER

PROPELLER HANGING HOOK

SIGNAL TRAFFIC LIGHT

STOP LIGHT

FOLDED FUSELAGE (TRUSS STRUCTURE)

PROPELLER IN FLYING MODE (REF)

13'-10"

RETRACTED WING, STORED VERTICALLY ON THE SIDE OF VEHICLE

SCALE:
0 4 8 12 16 20 24 INCHES

CANARD WINGS IN STORED POSITION

STEARING WHEEL CONTROLS THE AILERONS AND THE ANGLE OF ATTACK OF CANARD WING, ALSO IN LAND MODE STEERS THE FRONT WHEELS

SIDE MIRRORS (DEPLOYED)

PEDALS CONTROLS RUDDER AND BRAKES

AERO CAR IN LAND DRIVEN MODE

ATLANTIS, ADVANCED ENGINEERING PROJECTS

FLYING CAR

Name of project:

Vehicle configuration with retractable wings

Design Engineer: Walter F. Laredo    Date: May 25, 2002

Drawing Number: 1200    Sheet 7 of 18

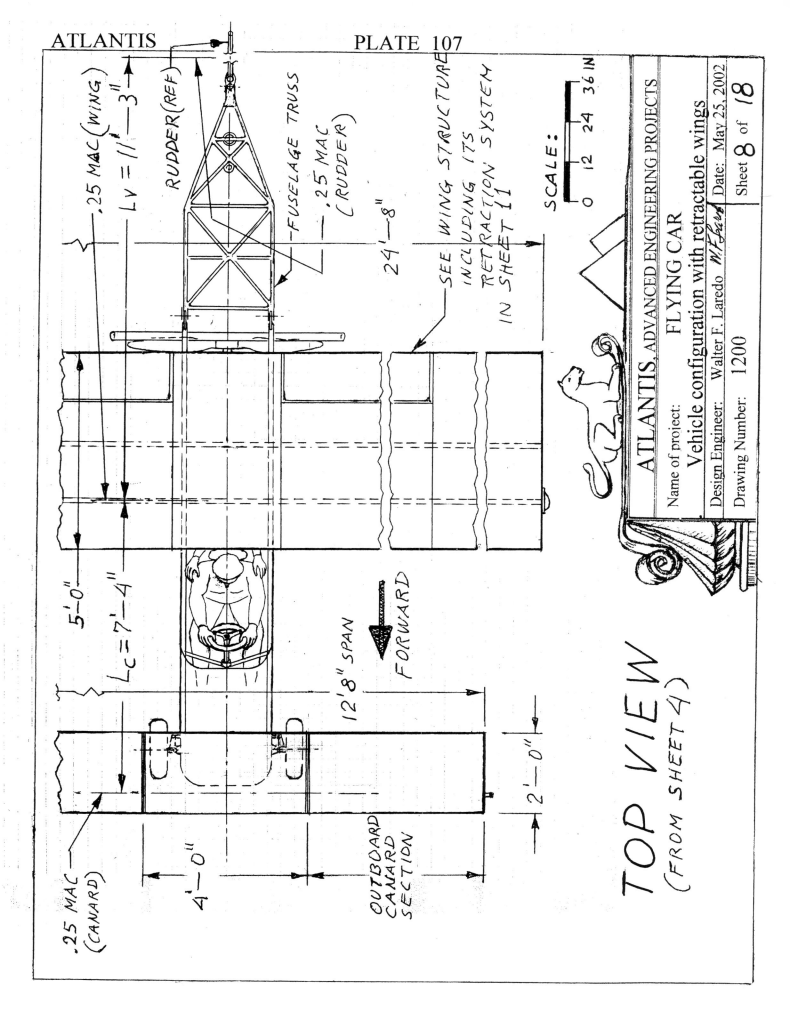

.25 MAC (WING)

LV = 11'—3"

RUDDER (REF)

FUSELAGE TRUSS

.25 MAC (RUDDER)

24'—8"

SEE WING STRUCTURE INCLUDING ITS RETRACTION SYSTEM IN SHEET 11

SCALE:

0   12   24   36 IN

5'—0"

$L_C = 7'—4"$

12'8" SPAN

FORWARD

2'—0"

.25 MAC (CANARD)

4'—0"

OUTBOARD CANARD SECTION

TOP VIEW
(FROM SHEET 4)

| ATLANTIS, ADVANCED ENGINEERING PROJECTS | |
|---|---|
| FLYING CAR | |
| Name of project: | |
| Vehicle configuration with retractable wings | |
| Design Engineer: Walter F. Laredo | Date: May 25, 2002 |
| Drawing Number: 1200 | Sheet 8 of 18 |

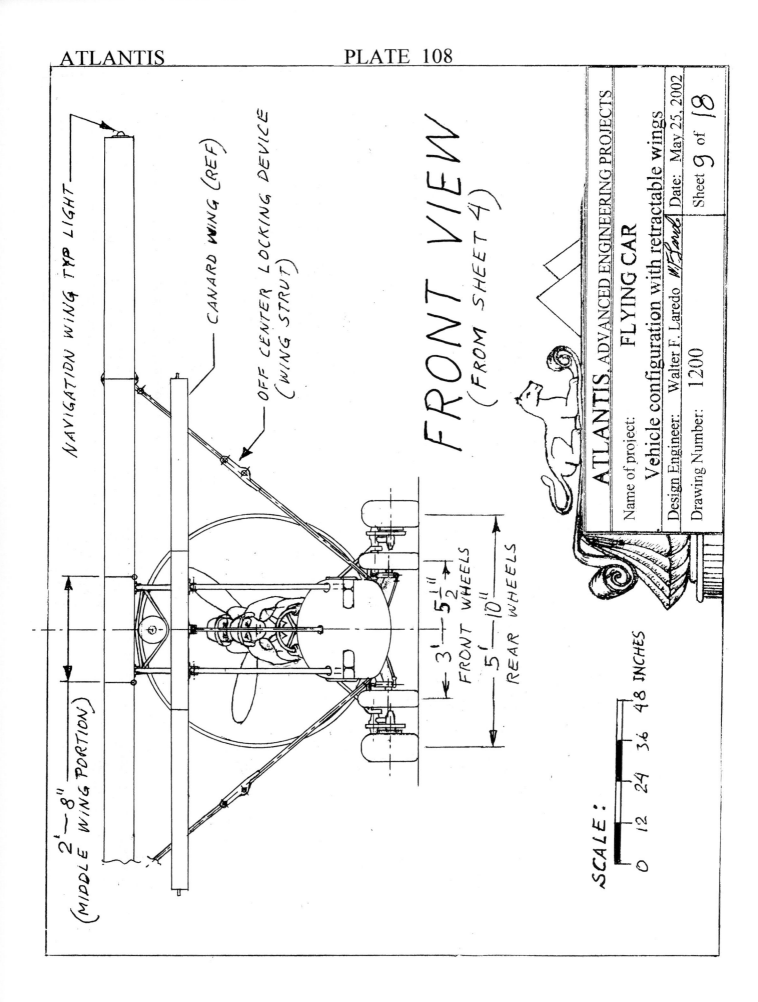

NAVIGATION WING TYP LIGHT

CANARD WING (REF)

OFF CENTER LOCKING DEVICE
(WING STRUT)

FRONT VIEW
(FROM SHEET 4)

2'—8" (MIDDLE WING PORTION)

3'—5½" FRONT WHEELS

5'—10" REAR WHEELS

SCALE:
0  12  24  36  48 INCHES

| ATLANTIS ADVANCED ENGINEERING PROJECTS | | |
|---|---|---|
| FLYING CAR | | |
| Vehicle configuration with retractable wings | | |
| Name of project: | | |
| Design Engineer: | Walter F. Laredo | Date: May 25, 2002 |
| Drawing Number: | 1200 | Sheet 9 of 18 |

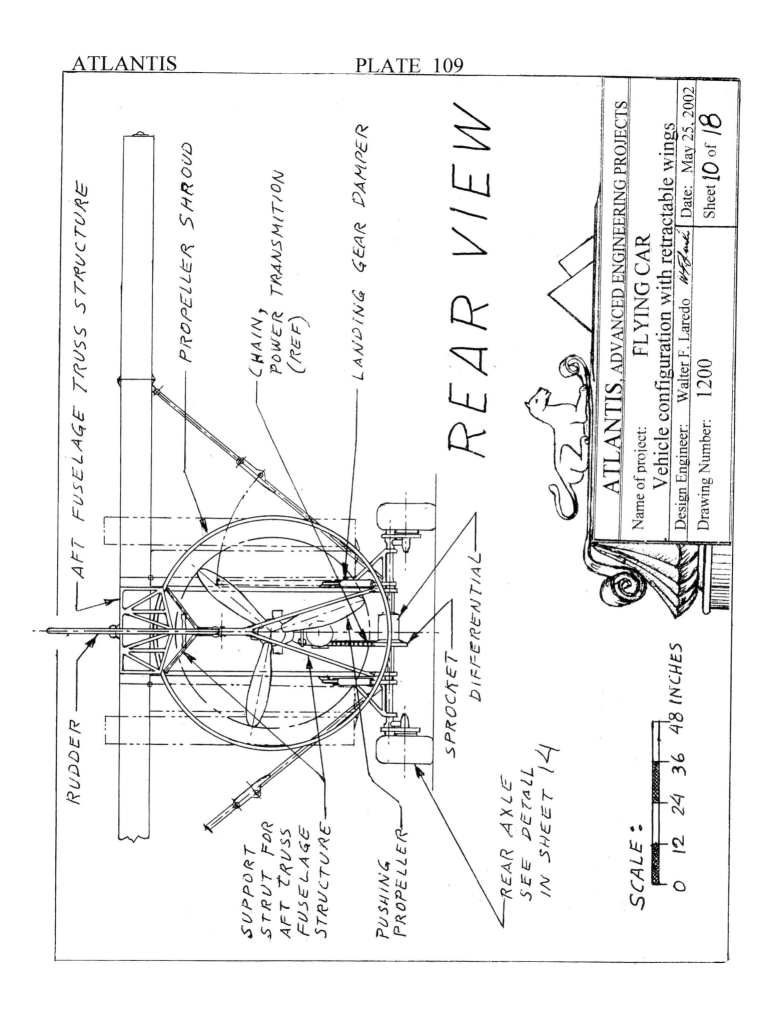

REAR VIEW

AFT FUSELAGE TRUSS STRUCTURE

PROPELLER SHROUD

CHAIN, POWER TRANSMITION (REF)

LANDING GEAR DAMPER

RUDDER

SUPPORT STRUT FOR AFT TRUSS FUSELAGE STRUCTURE

PUSHING PROPELLER

SPROCKET

DIFFERENTIAL

REAR AXLE SEE DETAIL IN SHEET 14

SCALE:

0   12   24   36   48 INCHES

| ATLANTIS, ADVANCED ENGINEERING PROJECTS | | |
|---|---|---|
| Name of project: FLYING CAR | | |
| Vehicle configuration with retractable wings | | |
| Design Engineer: Walter F. Laredo | | Date: May 25, 2002 |
| Drawing Number: 1200 | | Sheet 10 of 18 |

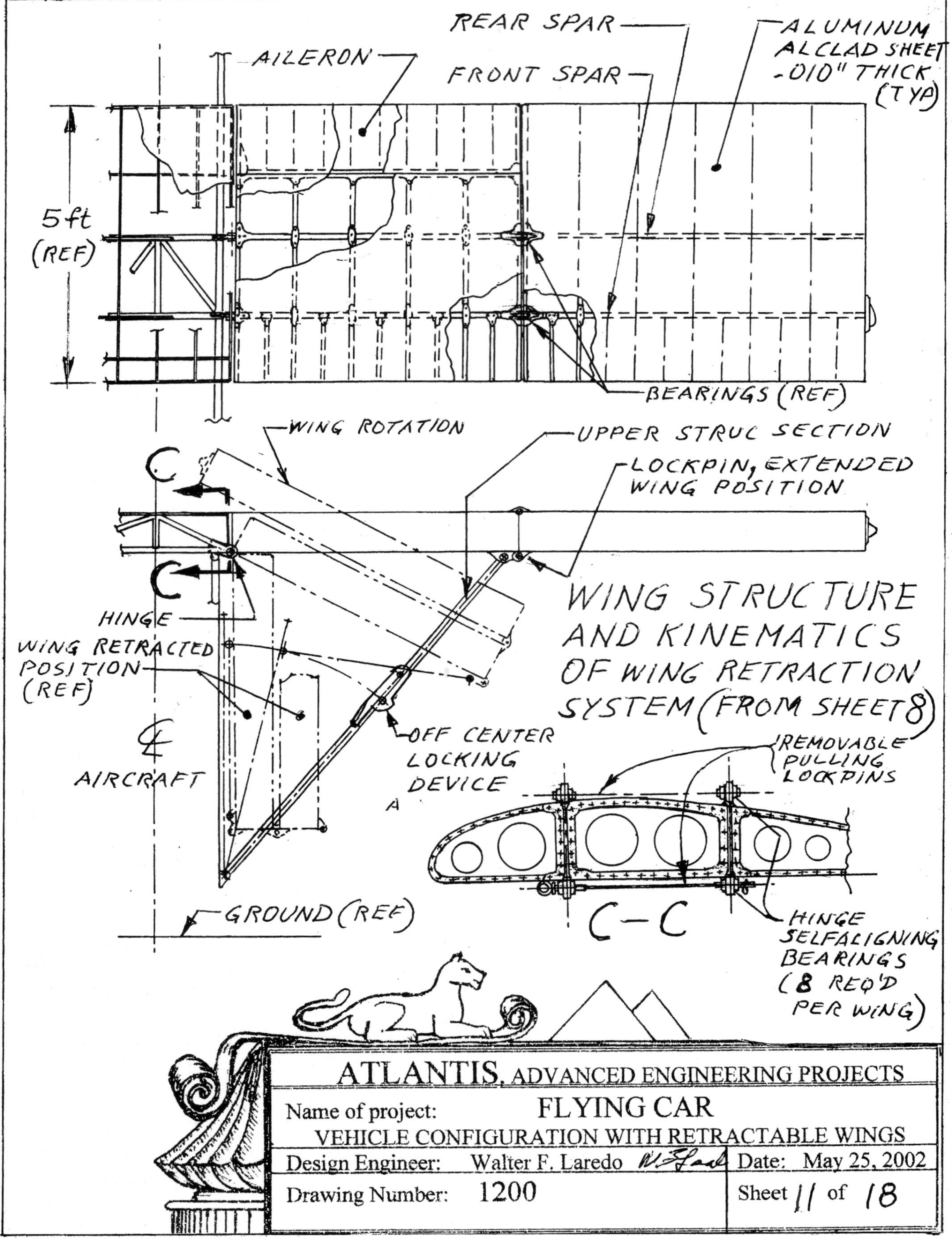

AILERON

REAR SPAR

FRONT SPAR

ALUMINUM ALCLAD SHEET .010" THICK (TYP)

5 ft (REF)

BEARINGS (REF)

WING ROTATION

UPPER STRUC SECTION

LOCKPIN, EXTENDED WING POSITION

C

C

HINGE

WING RETRACTED POSITION (REF)

WING STRUCTURE AND KINEMATICS OF WING RETRACTION SYSTEM (FROM SHEET 8)

℄ AIRCRAFT

OFF CENTER LOCKING DEVICE

A

REMOVABLE PULLING LOCKPINS

C — C

HINGE SELFALIGNING BEARINGS (8 REQ'D PER WING)

GROUND (REF)

ATLANTIS, ADVANCED ENGINEERING PROJECTS

| | |
|---|---|
| Name of project: | **FLYING CAR** |
| VEHICLE CONFIGURATION WITH RETRACTABLE WINGS | |
| Design Engineer: Walter F. Laredo | Date: May 25, 2002 |
| Drawing Number: 1200 | Sheet 11 of 18 |

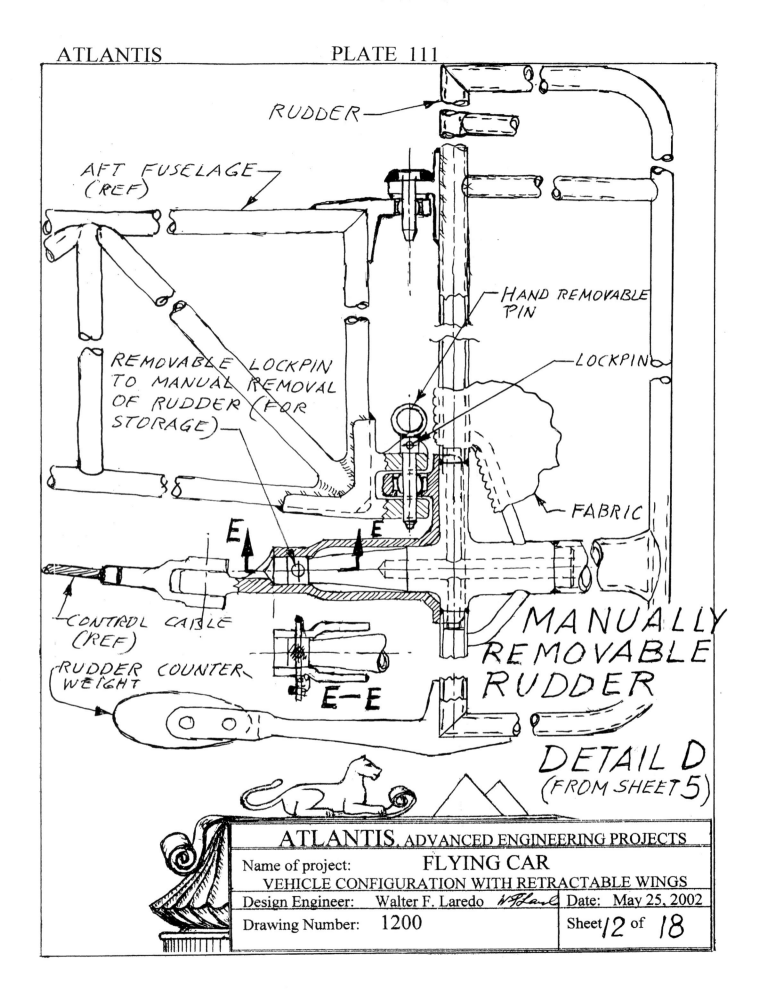

RUDDER

AFT FUSELAGE
(REF)

HAND REMOVABLE
PIN

LOCKPIN

REMOVABLE LOCKPIN
TO MANUAL REMOVAL
OF RUDDER (FOR
STORAGE)

FABRIC

E      E

CONTROL CABLE
(REF)

RUDDER COUNTER
WEIGHT

E-E

MANUALLY
REMOVABLE
RUDDER

DETAIL D
(FROM SHEET 5)

| ATLANTIS, ADVANCED ENGINEERING PROJECTS | | |
|---|---|---|
| Name of project:    **FLYING CAR** | | |
| VEHICLE CONFIGURATION WITH RETRACTABLE WINGS | | |
| Design Engineer:   Walter F. Laredo | | Date:   May 25, 2002 |
| Drawing Number:   1200 | | Sheet 12 of 18 |

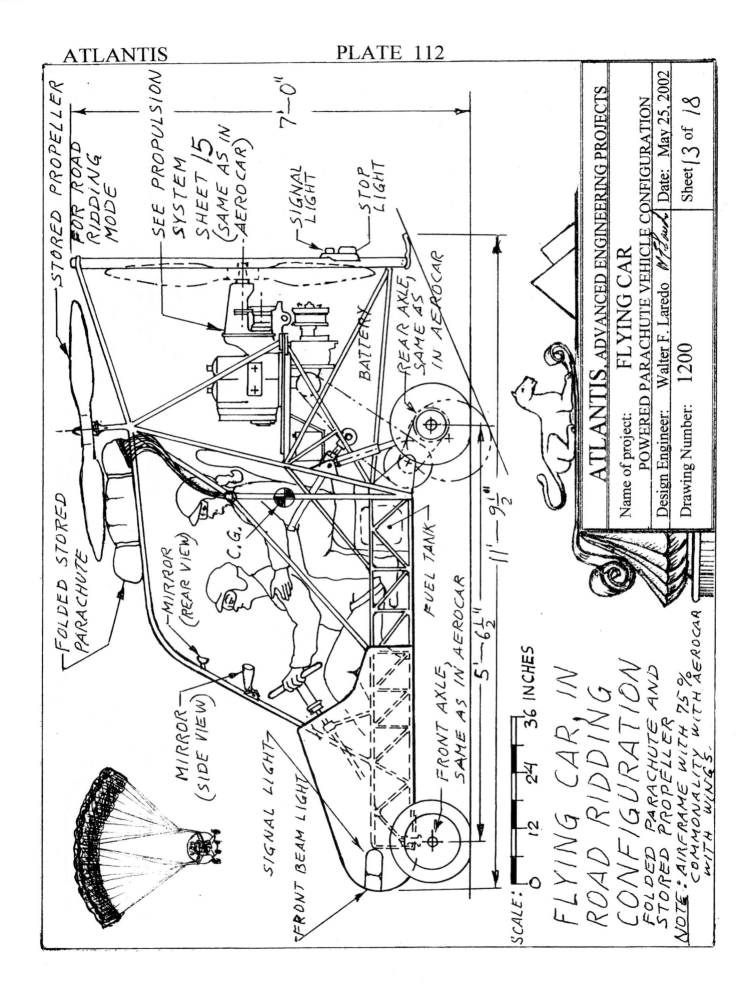

STORED PROPELLER

FOR ROAD RIDDING MODE

SEE PROPULSION SYSTEM SHEET 15 (SAME AS IN AEROCAR)

SIGNAL LIGHT

STOP LIGHT

7'-0"

BATTERY

REAR AXLE, SAME AS IN AEROCAR

FOLDED STORED PARACHUTE

MIRROR (REAR VIEW)

C.G.

MIRROR (SIDE VIEW)

SIGNAL LIGHT

FRONT BEAM LIGHT

FUEL TANK

FRONT AXLE, SAME AS IN AEROCAR

5'-6½"

11'-9½"

SCALE:
0    12    24    36 INCHES

FLYING CAR IN ROAD RIDDING CONFIGURATION

FOLDED PARACHUTE AND STORED PROPELLER

NOTE: AIRFRAME WITH 75% COMMONALITY WITH AEROCAR WITH WINGS.

| ATLANTIS ADVANCED ENGINEERING PROJECTS | | |
|---|---|---|
| Name of project: FLYING CAR POWERED PARACHUTE VEHICLE CONFIGURATION | | Date: May 25, 2002 |
| Design Engineer: Walter F. Laredo | | Sheet 13 of 18 |
| Drawing Number: 1200 | | |

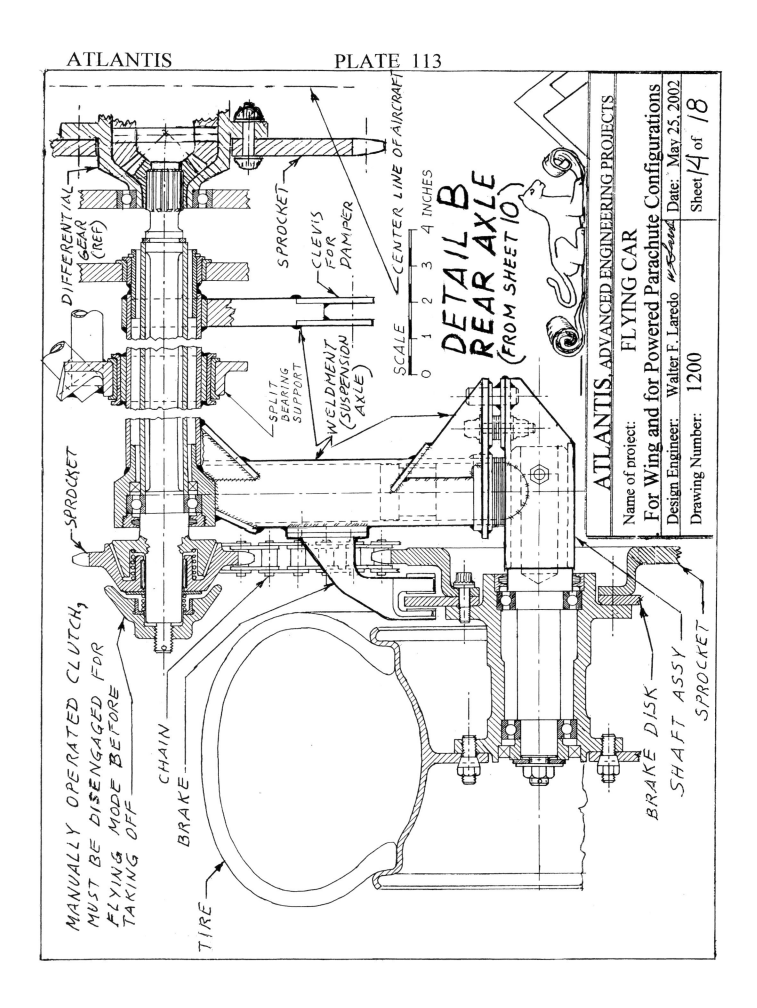

DIFFERENTIAL GEAR (REF)

SPROCKET

CLEVIS FOR DAMPER

CENTER LINE OF AIRCRAFT

SPLIT BEARING SUPPORT

WELDMENT (SUSPENSION AXLE)

SCALE 0 1 2 3 4 INCHES

## DETAIL B REAR AXLE
(FROM SHEET 10)

SPROCKET

MANUALLY OPERATED CLUTCH, MUST BE DISENGAGED FOR FLYING MODE BEFORE TAKING OFF

CHAIN

BRAKE

TIRE

BRAKE DISK

SHAFT ASSY

SPROCKET

ATLANTIS, ADVANCED ENGINEERING PROJECTS

FLYING CAR

Name of project:
For Wing and for Powered Parachute Configurations

Design Engineer: Walter F. Laredo    Date: May 25, 2002

Drawing Number: 1200    Sheet 14 of 18

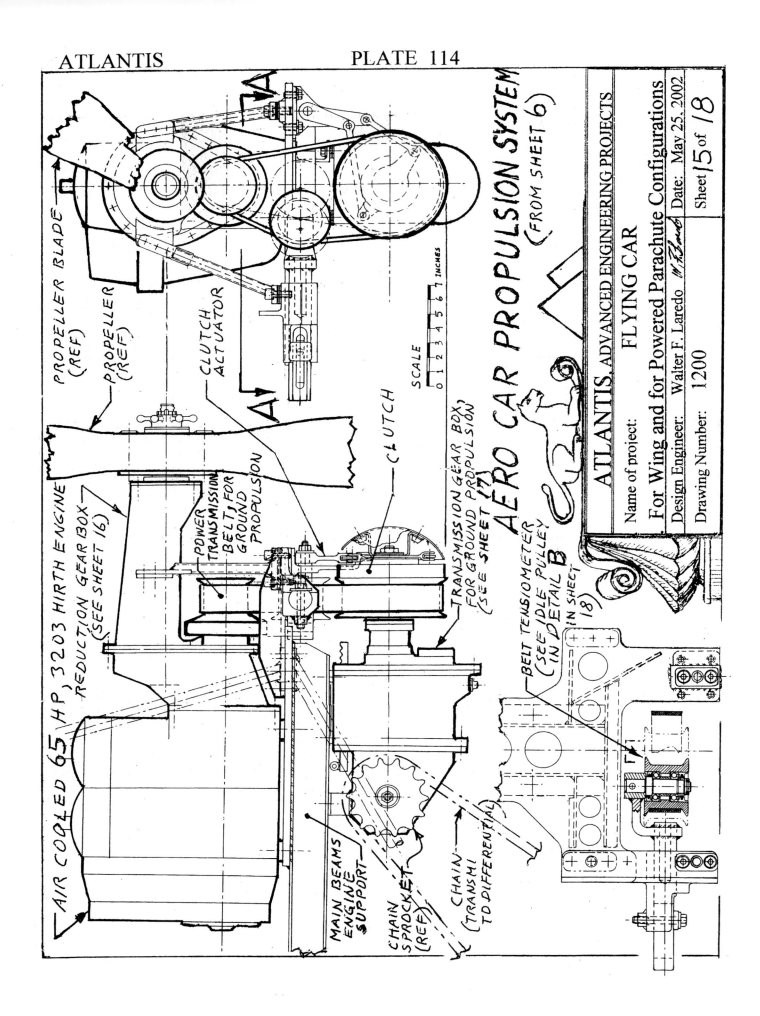

AIR COOLED 65 HP, 3203 HIRTH ENGINE

PROPELLER BLADE (REF)

PROPELLER (REF)

CLUTCH ACTUATOR

REDUCTION GEAR BOX (SEE SHEET 16)

POWER TRANSMISSION BELTS FOR GROUND PROPULSION

CLUTCH

TRANSMISSION GEAR BOX, FOR GROUND PROPULSION (SEE SHEET 17)

BELT TENSIOMETER (SEE IDLE PULLEY IN DETAIL B IN SHEET 18)

MAIN BEAMS ENGINE SUPPORT

CHAIN SPROCKET (REF)

CHAIN (TRANSMI TO DIFFERENTIAL)

SCALE

0 1 2 3 4 5 6 7 INCHES

AERO CAR PROPULSION SYSTEM (FROM SHEET 6)

ATLANTIS, ADVANCED ENGINEERING PROJECTS

FLYING CAR

Name of project:
For Wing and for Powered Parachute Configurations

Design Engineer: Walter F. Laredo     Date: May 25. 2002

Drawing Number: 1200     Sheet 15 of 18

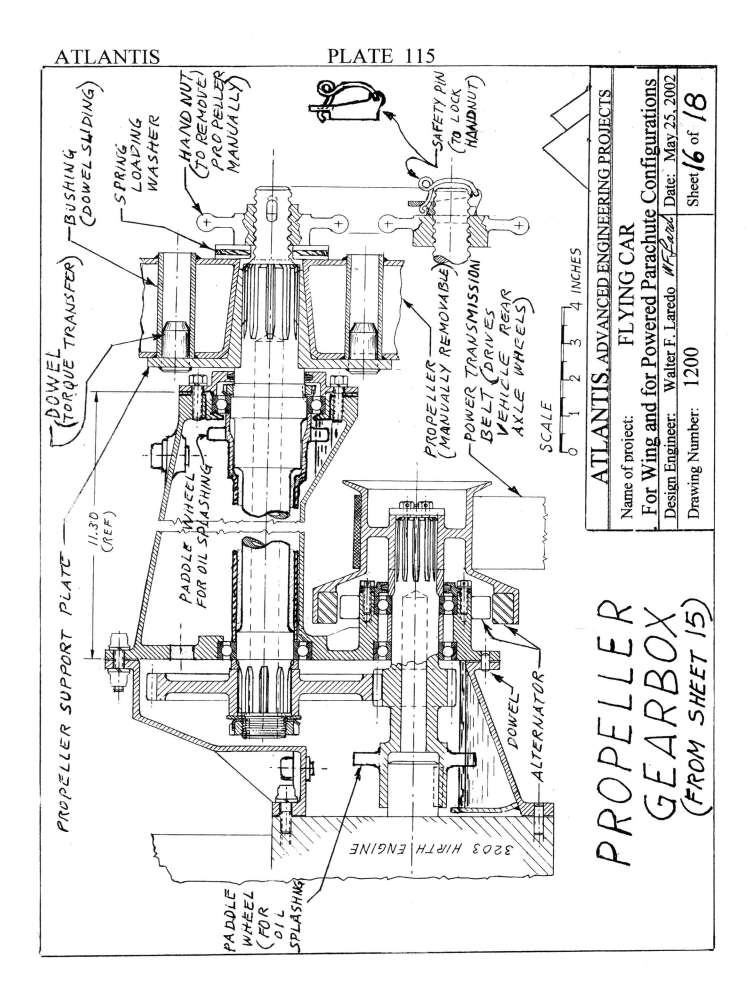

DOWEL
(TORQUE TRANSFER)

BUSHING
(DOWEL SLIDING)

SPRING
LOADING
WASHER

HAND NUT
(TO REMOVE)
PROPELLER
MANUALLY)

SAFETY PIN
(TO LOCK
HANDNUT)

PROPELLER
(MANUALLY REMOVABLE)

POWER TRANSMISSION
BELT (DRIVES
VEHICLE REAR
AXLE WHEELS)

DOWEL
(TORQUE TRANSFER)

PROPELLER SUPPORT PLATE

11.30
(REF)

PADDLE WHEEL
FOR OIL SPLASHING

DOWEL

ALTERNATOR

3203 HIRTH ENGINE

PADDLE
WHEEL
(FOR
OIL
SPLASHING)

SCALE

0   1   2   3   4 INCHES

PROPELLER
GEARBOX
(FROM SHEET 15)

ATLANTIS, ADVANCED ENGINEERING PROJECTS

Name of project:                  FLYING CAR

For Wing and for Powered Parachute Configurations

| Design Engineer: | Walter F. Laredo | W F Laredo | Date: | May 25, 2002 |
|---|---|---|---|---|

| Drawing Number: | 1200 | | Sheet 16 of 18 |

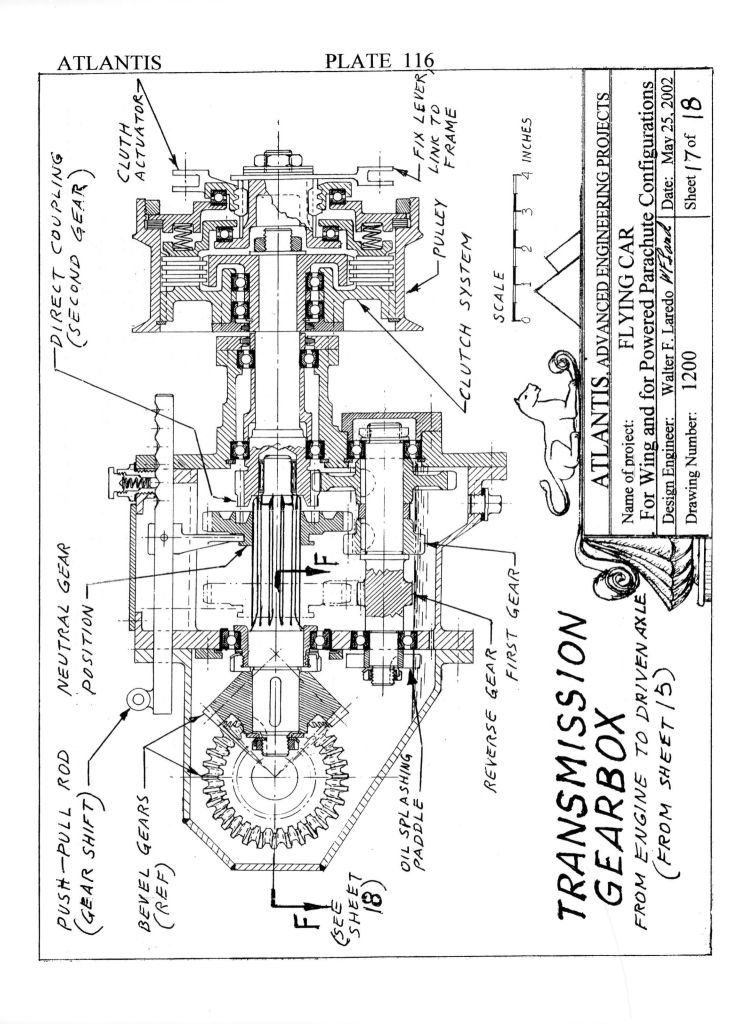

DIRECT COUPLING
(SECOND GEAR)

CLUTH ACTUATOR

FIX LEVER,
LINK TO
FRAME

PULLEY

CLUTCH SYSTEM

PUSH-PULL ROD
(GEAR SHIFT)

NEUTRAL GEAR
POSITION

BEVEL GEARS
(REF)

OIL SPLASHING
PADDLE

REVERSE GEAR

FIRST GEAR

F

F
(SEE
SHEET
18)

TRANSMISSION
GEARBOX

FROM ENGINE TO DRIVEN AXLE
(FROM SHEET 15)

SCALE

0 1 2 3 4 INCHES

ATLANTIS ADVANCED ENGINEERING PROJECTS

FLYING CAR

| Name of project: | FLYING CAR | | |
| --- | --- | --- | --- |
| | For Wing and for Powered Parachute Configurations | | |
| Design Engineer: | Walter F. Laredo | W.F.Lord | Date: May 25, 2002 |
| Drawing Number: | 1200 | | Sheet 17 of 18 |

18

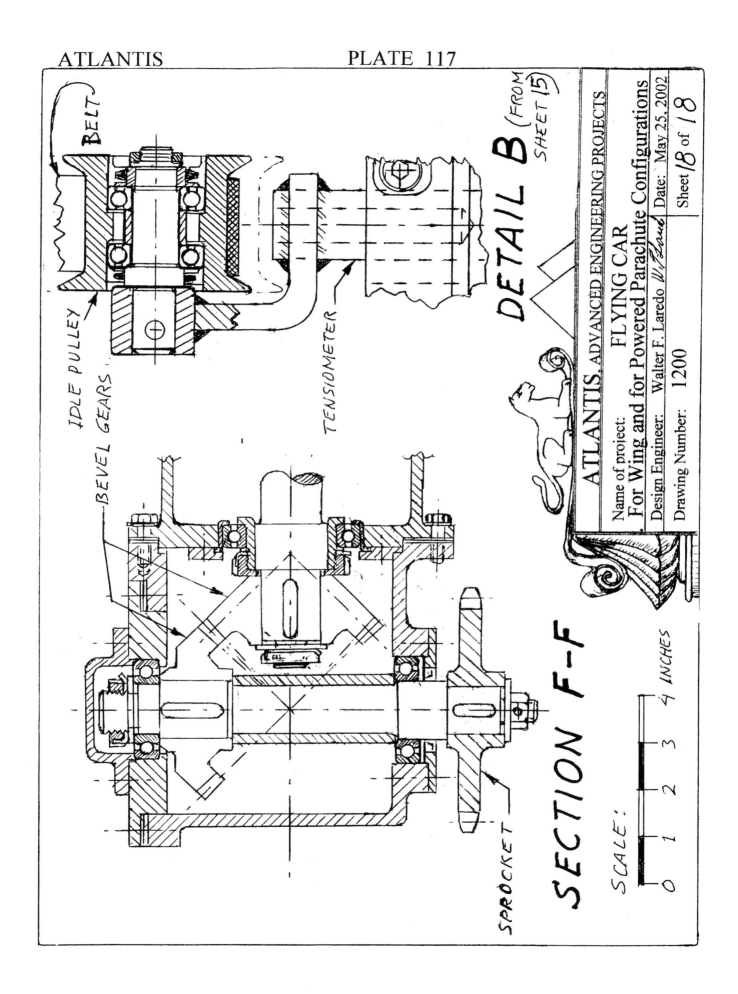

BELT

IDLE PULLEY

BEVEL GEARS

TENSIOMETER

DETAIL B (FROM SHEET 15)

SECTION F-F

SPROCKET

SCALE:
0  1  2  3  4 INCHES

| ATLANTIS. ADVANCED ENGINEERING PROJECTS | | |
|---|---|---|
| FLYING CAR | | |
| Name of project: For Wing and for Powered Parachute Configurations | | Date: May 25, 2002 |
| Design Engineer: Walter F. Laredo W. Laud | | Sheet 18 of 18 |
| Drawing Number: 1200 | | |

| Sheet No. | Name | Quantity | Material |
|---|---|---|---|
| Sheet 17 | ARM, FOREARM & HAND ASSEMBLY | R.H. (1)  L.H. (1) | STEEL |
| Sheets 14 & 16 | ROBOT'S FOOT | R.H. (1)  L.H. (1) | STEEL |
| Sheets 13 & 15 | ROBOT HIP AND PIVOTS | 1 | STEEL |
| Sheet 12 | HYDRAULIC POWER SYSTEM | R.H. (1)  L.H. (1) | — |
| Sheet 11 | LEG SYSTEM ASSEMBLY | RIGHT HAND (1)  LEFT HAND (1) | STEEL |
| Sheet 10 | ROBOT'S STRUCTURAL ARRANGEMENT | 1 | — |
| Sheet 9 | ROBOT'S GENERAL ARRANGEMENT | 1 | — |
| Sheet 8 | WALKING CONTROL SYSTEM | 1 | — |

## ATLANTIS, ADVANCED ENGINEERING PROJECTS

Name of project:

# GIANT ROBOT WORKER

MECHANICAL BEAST USED TO TRANSPORT HEAVY CARGO, BY
CARRYING IT THROUGH MOUNTAINS WITH NO ROADS.
CARGO INCLUDES BOULDERS AND MARBLE COLUMNS, TO BE USE TO
BUILD TEMPLES AND BUILDINGS .

| Design Engineer:  Walter F. Laredo | Date: August 8, 2002 |
|---|---|

Areas of Development:   Stability Control ✓, Thermodynamics __, Materials ✓
Structures (Design and Analysis) ✓, Mechanisms & Systems ✓,

NOTE: This is the PRELIMINARY DESIGN for a real engineering project.
Project inspired by the legendary dreams and tales of the semi-utopian and
highly advanced legendary civilization, called Atlantis.

| Drawing Number:   1300 | Sheet  1  of   17 |
|---|---|

W. F. Laredo
8-8-03

| ATLANTIS, ADVANCED ENGINEERING PROJECTS | |
|---|---|
| Name of project:          **GIANT ROBOT** | |
| It can transport heavy structures above mountains with no roads | |
| Design Engineer:   Walter F. Laredo | Date: August 8, 2002 |
| Drawing Number:   **1300** | Sheet **2** of **17** |

# GIANT WALKING ROBOT
## STABILITY AND CONTROL SYSTEM

This robot operates automatically by its own electronic brain, however if necessary it could be operated by a human operator seating inside its head, but always with the help of the robot's computers.

The robot has three laser scanners, each act as a special eye, the one located on top of the robot's head is for distant scanning, 25 feet and beyond, it have 340 degrees field of view. It is also a laser range finder, which warns the robot's electronic brain of approaching dangers as trees, rocky walls or precipice edges. The other two, are short-range laser scanners located one forward of the robot's belly and the other behind the robot's hip. Both facing down to scan the ground, one scans few feet in front of the robot and the other few feet behind, scanning a piece of terrain not larger than the robot's footprint, the area where the robot will step next.

With an artificial intelligence of an insect, this robot has an artificial nervous system, which works as follows:

After scanning a miniature terrain either forward or behind the robot, the laser scanner transfers this 3D mapping information to the robot's brain, which with this DATA will order one of the legs to move, it depends, one step forward or one aft. Then the leg will move first up, then as it moves forward will rotate its foot to the proper angle in order that its underneath surface will match exactly the same average slope of the terrain it will step next.

The kinematics sequence of each robot's step begins at the moment when the robot raises its leg followed by a forward movement. When this leg is still in the air the foot rotates an angle that should match the same average slope of the terrain where it will step next. As the robot steps on this terrain, thick hairy sensors sticking out from its legs would sense the terrain characteristics such as softness, hardness, humid or dry or muddy. After that step, the robot will stand on both feet, one foot forward and the other behind, then without moving its feet the robot body will move (Continues in next sheet)

## ATLANTIS, ADVANCED ENGINEERING PROJECTS

Name of project:  **GIANT ROBOT**

It can transport heavy structures above mountains with no roads

| Design Engineer: Walter F. Laredo | Date: August 8, 2002 |
|---|---|
| Drawing Number:  **1300** | Sheet  3  of  17 |

(Continues from preceding sheet)
forward, then rise vertically, with the body the position of the center of gravity will rise along a stable vertical theoretical line.

Here CG means center of gravity of a system that includes robot plus cargo or payload. The CG position is constantly corrected, in order for the robot to remain stable. This is done by the robot's stability and control system, which consist of a computer, a guidance system and load or pressure sensors located under the robot feet. The robot's feet are broad and rectangular, underneath each of the four-foot corner's there is a protrusion, all used to support the robot's weight and inside each protrusion there is a load sensor. When the robot stands on one foot only, its electronic brain receives signs of the feet load sensors. With this DATA, stability is computed several times per second and the robot position with its center of gravity is changed continuously by the Hydraulic power system, until the robot weight will be evenly distributed on the four protrusions of the standing foot. This stable condition will happen only if the vertical projection of the center of gravity falls inside the footprint or inside the area made by the four load sensors.

Each step of the robot represents a complete cycle of a set of operations, after this cycle was completed; the robot is ready to start the step, a new cycle, operation that could be repeated over and over.

The robot walking kinematics and its stability are controlled by the stability control and guidance systems, which consist of computers, load distribution, terrain pressure sensors, laser scanners range finders, a guidance system with gyros and two accelerometers. The guidance system considers the robot's platform as the theoretical horizontal plane of reference. Another plane of reference is a vertical one used for navigation purposes along the robot's trip, it extends from the point of the robot's departure to the point of its arrival.

The robot feet are designed in such way, when the robot is standing on both feet, the toes of one foot penetrates the toes spaces of the other foot, as interlocked combs, so both feet rest at the same time on the same surface or on a single footprint. Something similar as if both feet blended into a single-foot resting on a single footprint, a very stable structure.

## ATLANTIS, ADVANCED ENGINEERING PROJECTS

| Name of project: | GIANT ROBOT | |
| --- | --- | --- |
| It can transport heavy structures above mountains with no roads | | |
| Design Engineer: Walter F. Laredo | | Date: August 8, 2002 |
| Drawing Number: 1300 | | Sheet 4 of 17 |

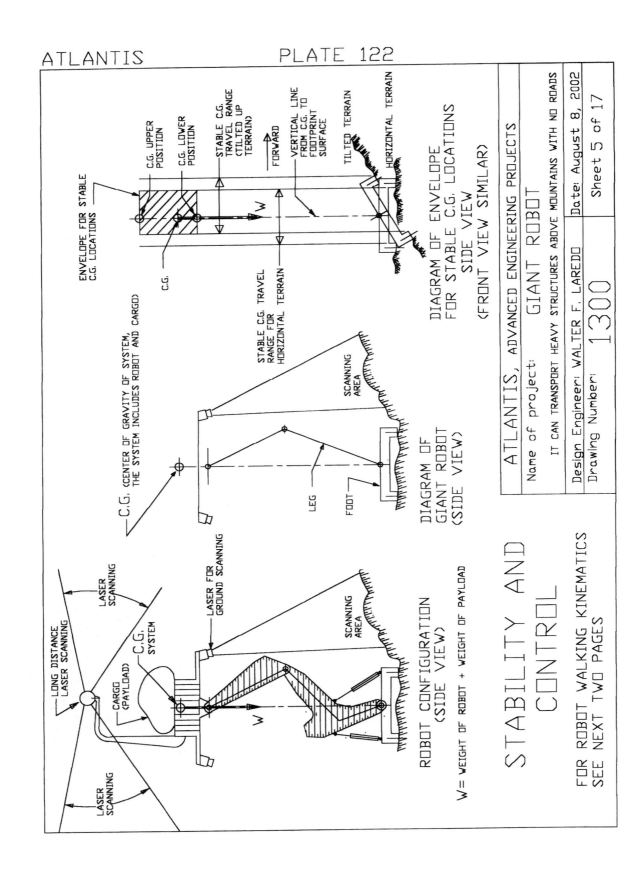

ENVELOPE FOR STABLE
C.G. LOCATIONS

C.G. UPPER POSITION

C.G. LOWER POSITION

STABLE C.G. TRAVEL RANGE (TILTED UP TERRAIN)

FORWARD

VERTICAL LINE FROM C.G. TO FOOTPRINT SURFACE

TILTED TERRAIN

HORIZONTAL TERRAIN

C.G.

W

DIAGRAM OF ENVELOPE
FOR STABLE C.G. LOCATIONS
SIDE VIEW
(FRONT VIEW SIMILAR)

STABLE C.G. TRAVEL RANGE FOR HORIZONTAL TERRAIN

C.G. (CENTER OF GRAVITY OF SYSTEM, THE SYSTEM INCLUDES ROBOT AND CARGO)

SCANNING AREA

LEG

FOOT

DIAGRAM OF
GIANT ROBOT
(SIDE VIEW)

LONG DISTANCE LASER SCANNING

LASER SCANNING

LASER FOR GROUND SCANNING

C.G. SYSTEM

CARGO (PAYLOAD)

W

SCANNING AREA

LASER SCANNING

ROBOT CONFIGURATION
(SIDE VIEW)

W = WEIGHT OF ROBOT + WEIGHT OF PAYLOAD

STABILITY AND
CONTROL

FOR ROBOT WALKING KINEMATICS
SEE NEXT TWO PAGES

| ATLANTIS, ADVANCED ENGINEERING PROJECTS | |
|---|---|
| Name of project:  GIANT ROBOT | |
| IT CAN TRANSPORT HEAVY STRUCTURES ABOVE MOUNTAINS WITH NO ROADS | |
| Design Engineer: WALTER F. LAREDO | Date: August 8, 2002 |
| Drawing Number:  1300 | Sheet 5 of 17 |

# ROBOT WALKING KINEMATICS (CONTINUES IN NEXT SHEET)

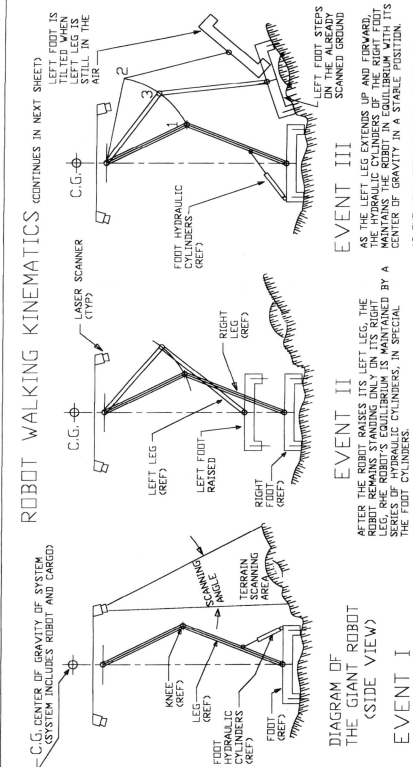

LEFT FOOT IS TILTED WHEN LEFT LEG IS STILL IN THE AIR

LEFT FOOT STEPS ON THE ALREADY SCANNED GROUND

LASER SCANNER (TYP)

FOOT HYDRAULIC CYLINDERS (REF)

C.G.

RIGHT LEG (REF)

LEFT LEG (REF)

LEFT FOOT RAISED

RIGHT FOOT (REF)

C.G. CENTER OF GRAVITY OF SYSTEM (SYSTEM INCLUDES ROBOT AND CARGO)

SCANNING ANGLE

TERRAIN SCANNING AREA

KNEE (REF)

LEG (REF)

FOOT HYDRAULIC CYLINDERS (REF)

FOOT (REF)

## EVENT III

AS THE LEFT LEG EXTENDS UP AND FORWARD, THE HYDRAULIC CYLINDERS OF THE RIGHT FOOT MAINTAINS THE ROBOT IN EQUILIBRIUM WITH ITS CENTER OF GRAVITY IN A STABLE POSITION.

AS THE LEFT FOOT IS STILL IN THE AIR, THE PLANE OF ITS LOWER SURFACE TILTS TO MATCH THE SAME ORIENTATION OF THE TERRAIN WHERE THE FOOT WILL STEP NEXT.

## EVENT II

AFTER THE ROBOT RAISES ITS LEFT LEG, THE ROBOT REMAINS STANDING ONLY ON ITS RIGHT LEG. RHE ROBOT'S EQUILIBRIUM IS MAINTAINED BY A SERIES OF HYDRAULIC CYLINDERS, IN SPECIAL THE FOOT CYLINDERS.

## DIAGRAM OF THE GIANT ROBOT (SIDE VIEW)

## EVENT I

INITIALLY THE ROBOT STANDS WITH ITS LEGS SIDE BY SIDE, THE ROBOT'S GROUND LASER SCANNER SCANS THE SMALL TERRAIN AREA WHERE ITS LEFT FOOT WILL STEP NEXT.

## STABILITY AND CONTROL

STABILITY AND CONTROL IS PROVIDED BY THE ROBOT'S WALKING CONTROL AND GUIDANCE SYSTEM WHICH INCLUDES RATE GYROS, ACCELEROMETERS, SENSORS AND COMPUTERS, THIS SYSTEM CONTROLS THE OPERATION OF ALL HYDRAULIC CYLINDERS AND MOTORS, NECESSARY FOR THE MOTION OF THE ROBOT.

---

ATLANTIS, ADVANCED ENGINEERING PROJECTS

Name of project: GIANT ROBOT

IT CAN TRANSPORT HEAVY STRUCTURES ABOVE MOUNTAINS WITH NO ROADS

| Design Engineer: WALTER F. LAREDO | Date:August 8, 2002 |
| Drawing Number: 1300 | Sheet 6 of 17 |

# ROBOT WALKING KINEMATICS (CONTINUATION OF PRIOR SHEET)

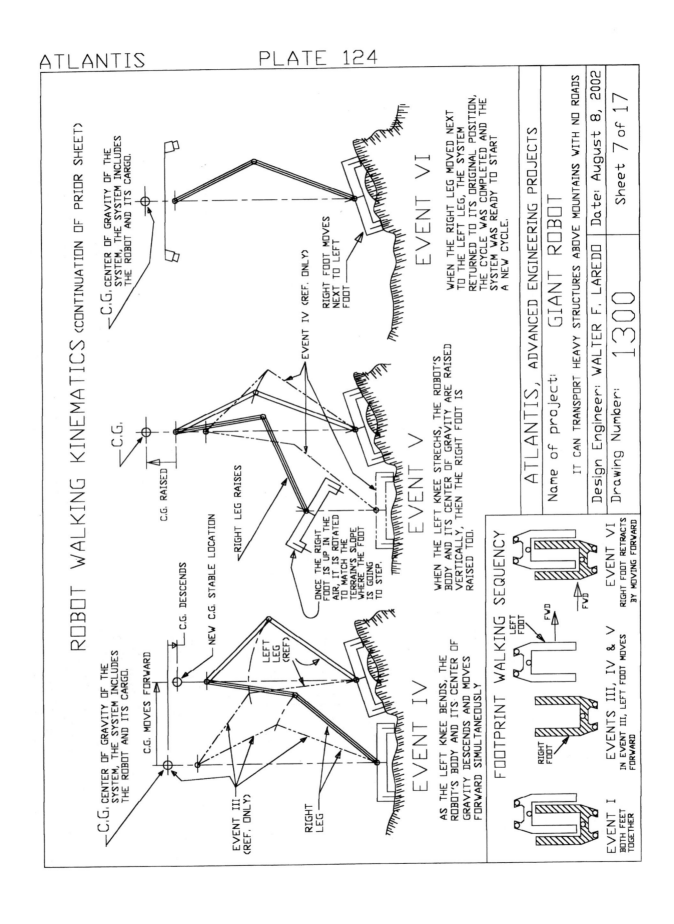

C.G. CENTER OF GRAVITY OF THE SYSTEM, THE SYSTEM INCLUDES THE ROBOT AND ITS CARGO.

## EVENT VI

WHEN THE RIGHT LEG MOVED NEXT TO THE LEFT LEG, THE SYSTEM RETURNED TO ITS ORIGINAL POSITION, THE CYCLE WAS COMPLETED AND THE SYSTEM WAS READY TO START A NEW CYCLE.

RIGHT FOOT MOVES NEXT TO LEFT FOOT

EVENT IV (REF. ONLY)

C.G.

C.G. RAISED

RIGHT LEG RAISES

ONCE THE RIGHT FOOT IS UP IN THE AIR, IT IS ROTATED TO MATCH THE TERRAIN'S SLOPE WHERE THE FOOT IS GOING TO STEP.

## EVENT V

WHEN THE LEFT KNEE STRECHS, THE ROBOT'S BODY AND ITS CENTER OF GRAVITY ARE RAISED VERTICALLY, THEN THE RIGHT FOOT IS RAISED TOO.

C.G. CENTER OF GRAVITY OF THE SYSTEM, THE SYSTEM INCLUDES THE ROBOT AND ITS CARGO.

C.G. MOVES FORWARD

C.G. DESCENDS

NEW C.G. STABLE LOCATION

LEFT LEG (REF)

EVENT III (REF. ONLY)

RIGHT LEG

## EVENT IV

AS THE LEFT KNEE BENDS, THE ROBOT'S BODY AND ITS CENTER OF GRAVITY DESCENDS AND MOVES FORWARD SIMULTANEOUSLY.

## FOOTPRINT WALKING SEQUENCE

LEFT FOOT

FWD

FWD

RIGHT FOOT

EVENT I
BOTH FEET TOGETHER

EVENTS III, IV & V
IN EVENT III, LEFT FOOT MOVES FORWARD

EVENT VI
RIGHT FOOT RETRACTS BY MOVING FORWARD

| ATLANTIS, ADVANCED ENGINEERING PROJECTS |
|---|
| Name of project: GIANT ROBOT |
| IT CAN TRANSPORT HEAVY STRUCTURES ABOVE MOUNTAINS WITH NO ROADS |
| Design Engineer: WALTER F. LAREDO        Date: August 8, 2002 |
| Drawing Number: 1300        Sheet 7 of 17 |

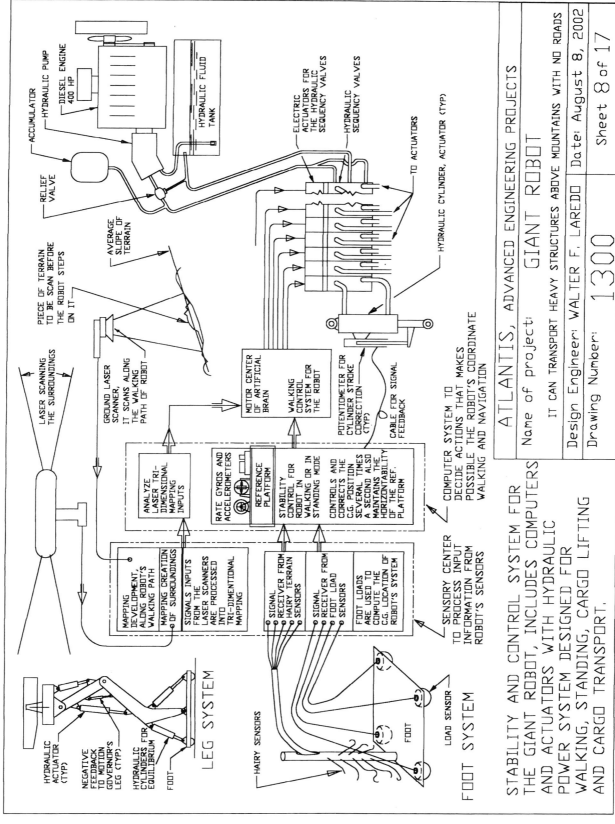

ACCUMULATOR
HYDRAULIC PUMP
DIESEL ENGINE 400 HP
HYDRAULIC FLUID TANK
RELIEF VALVE
ELECTRIC ACTUATORS FOR THE HYDRAULIC SEQUENCE VALVES
HYDRAULIC SEQUENCE VALVES
TO ACTUATORS
HYDRAULIC CYLINDER, ACTUATOR (TYP)

AVERAGE SLOPE OF TERRAIN
PIECE OF TERRAIN TO BE SCAN BEFORE THE ROBOT STEPS ON IT
LASER SCANNING THE SURROUNDINGS
GROUND LASER SCANNER, IT SCANS ALONG THE WALKING PATH OF ROBOT

MOTOR CENTER OF ARTIFICIAL BRAIN
WALKING CONTROL SYSTEM FOR THE ROBOT
POTENTIOMETER FOR CYLINDER STROKE CORRECTION (TYP)
CABLE FOR SIGNAL FEEDBACK
COMPUTER SYSTEM TO DECIDE ACTIONS THAT MAKES POSSIBLE THE ROBOT'S COORDINATE WALKING AND NAVIGATION

ANALYZE LASER TRI-DIMENSIONAL MAPPING INPUTS
RATE GYROS AND ACCELEROMETERS
REFERENCE PLATFORM
STABILITY CONTROL FOR ROBOT IN WALKING OR IN STANDING MODE
CONTROLS AND CORRECTS THE C.G. POSITION SEVERAL TIMES A SECOND ALSO MAINTAINS THE HORIZONTABILITY OF THE REF. PLATFORM

MAPPING DEVELOPMENT, ALONG ROBOT'S WALKING PATH
MAPPING CREATION OF SURROUNDINGS
SIGNALS INPUTS FROM THE LASER SCANNERS ARE PROCESSED INTO TRI-DIMENTIONAL MAPPING
SIGNAL RECEIVER FROM HAIRY TERRAIN SENSORS
SIGNAL RECEIVER FROM FOOT LOAD SENSORS
FOOT LOADS ARE USED TO COMPUTE THE C.G. LOCATION OF ROBOT'S SYSTEM
SENSORY CENTER TO PROCESS INPUT INFORMATION FROM ROBOT'S SENSORS

HAIRY SENSORS
FOOT
LOAD SENSOR
FOOT SYSTEM

HYDRAULIC ACTUATOR (TYP)
NEGATIVE FEEDBACK TO MOTION GOVERNOR'S LEG (TYP)
HYDRAULIC CYLINDERS FOR EQUILIBRIUM
FOOT
LEG SYSTEM

ATLANTIS, ADVANCED ENGINEERING PROJECTS

Name of project: GIANT ROBOT

IT CAN TRANSPORT HEAVY STRUCTURES ABOVE MOUNTAINS WITH NO ROADS

Design Engineer: WALTER F. LAREDO   Date: August 8, 2002

Drawing Number: 1300          Sheet 8 of 17

STABILITY AND CONTROL SYSTEM FOR THE GIANT ROBOT, INCLUDES COMPUTERS AND ACTUATORS WITH HYDRAULIC POWER SYSTEM DESIGNED FOR WALKING, STANDING, CARGO LIFTING AND CARGO TRANSPORT.

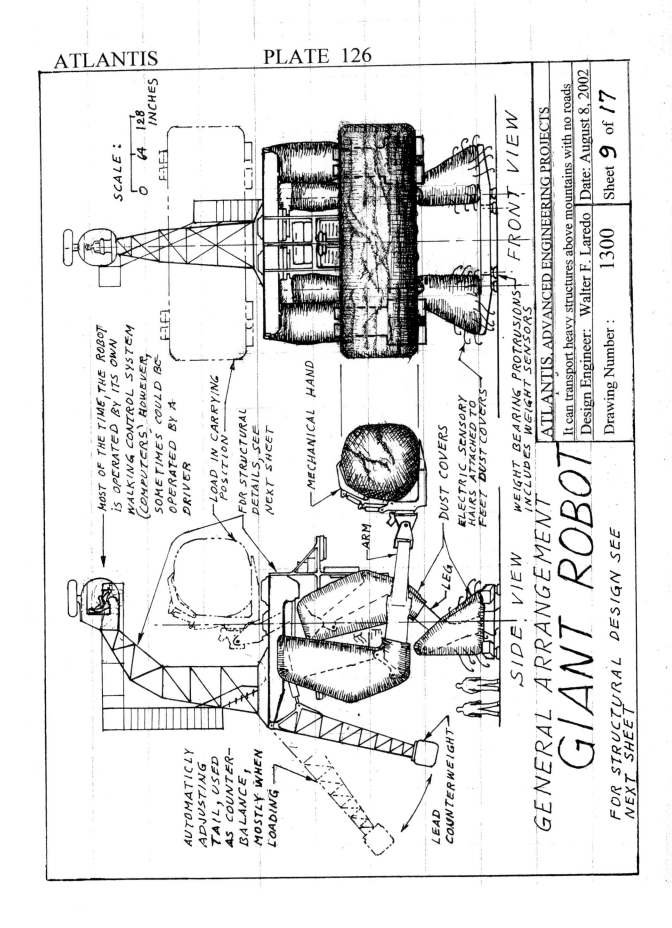

SCALE :

0   64   128

INCHES

MOST OF THE TIME, THE ROBOT IS OPERATED BY ITS OWN WALKING CONTROL SYSTEM (COMPUTERS) HOWEVER, SOMETIMES COULD BE OPERATED BY A DRIVER

LOAD IN CARRYING POSITION

FOR STRUCTURAL DETAILS, SEE NEXT SHEET

MECHANICAL HAND

ARM

LEG

DUST COVERS

ELECTRIC SENSORY HAIRS ATTACHED TO FEET DUST COVERS

AUTOMATICLY ADJUSTING TAIL, USED AS COUNTER-BALANCE, MOSTLY WHEN LOADING

LEAD COUNTERWEIGHT

SIDE VIEW

FRONT VIEW

WEIGHT BEARING PROTRUSIONS

WEIGHT SENSORS INCLUDES WEIGHT SENSORS

GENERAL ARRANGEMENT

GIANT ROBOT

FOR STRUCTURAL DESIGN SEE NEXT SHEET

ATLANTIS ADVANCED ENGINEERING PROJECTS

It can transport heavy structures above mountains with no roads

Design Engineer:   Walter F. Laredo     Date: August 8, 2002

Drawing Number:   1300     Sheet **9** of *17*

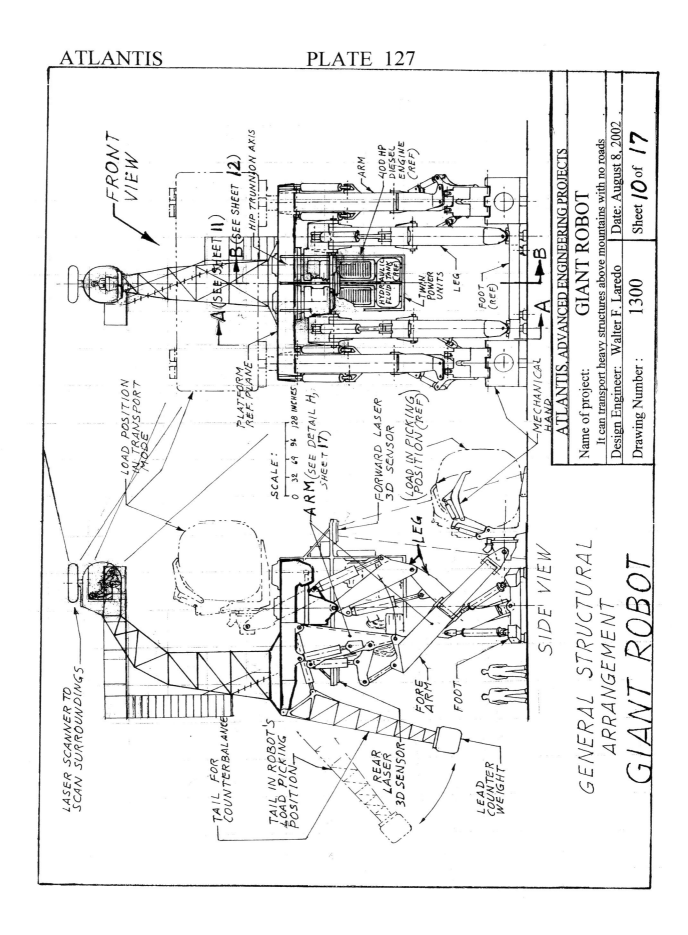

FRONT VIEW

A (SEE SHEET 11)

B (SEE SHEET 12)

HIP TRUNNION AXIS

ARM

400 HP DIESEL ENGINE (REF)

HYDRAULIC FLUID TANK (REF)

TWIN POWER UNITS

LEG

FOOT (REF)

PLATFORM REF. PLANE

LOAD POSITION IN TRANSPORT MODE

SCALE: 0  32  64  96  128 INCHES

ARM (SEE DETAIL H, SHEET 17)

FORWARD LASER 3D SENSOR

(LOAD IN PICKING POSITION) (REF)

MECHANICAL HAND

LEG

FORE ARM

FOOT

LASER SCANNER TO SCAN SURROUNDINGS

TAIL FOR COUNTERBALANCE

TAIL IN ROBOT'S LOAD PICKING POSITION

REAR LASER 3D SENSOR

LEAD COUNTER WEIGHT

SIDE VIEW

GENERAL STRUCTURAL ARRANGEMENT

GIANT ROBOT

ATLANTIS ADVANCED ENGINEERING PROJECTS

GIANT ROBOT

Name of project: It can transport heavy structures above mountains with no roads

Design Engineer: Walter F. Laredo    Date: August 8, 2002

Drawing Number: 1300    Sheet 10 of 17

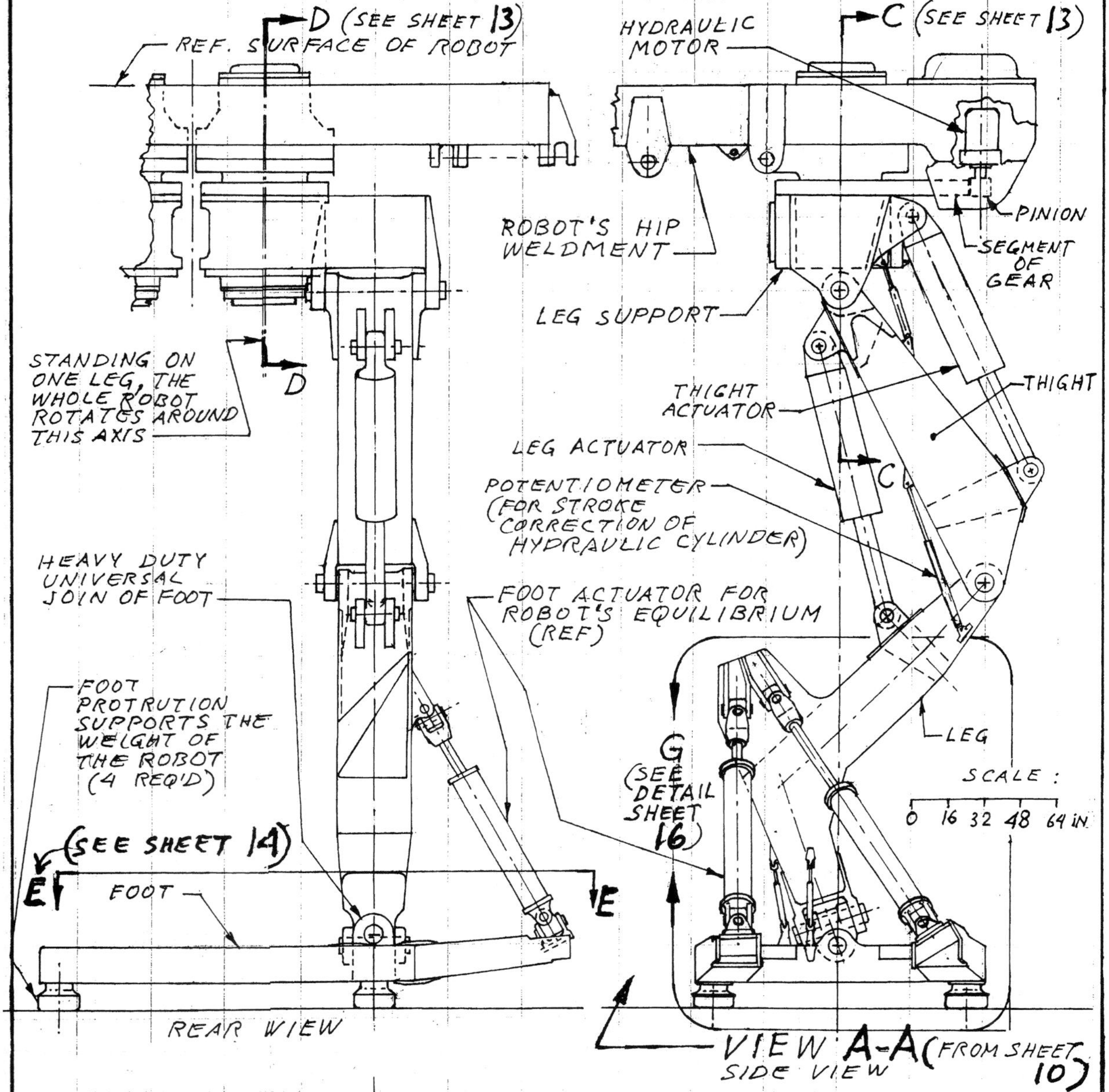

D (SEE SHEET 13)

REF. SURFACE OF ROBOT

HYDRAULIC MOTOR

C (SEE SHEET 13)

ROBOT'S HIP WELDMENT

LEG SUPPORT

PINION

SEGMENT OF GEAR

THIGHT ACTUATOR

THIGHT

LEG ACTUATOR

POTENTIOMETER (FOR STROKE CORRECTION OF HYDRAULIC CYLINDER)

STANDING ON ONE LEG, THE WHOLE ROBOT ROTATES AROUND THIS AXIS

HEAVY DUTY UNIVERSAL JOIN OF FOOT

FOOT ACTUATOR FOR ROBOT'S EQUILIBRIUM (REF)

FOOT PROTRUTION SUPPORTS THE WEIGHT OF THE ROBOT (4 REQ'D)

G (SEE DETAIL SHEET 16)

LEG

SCALE :
0  16  32  48  64 IN.

(SEE SHEET 14)

E

FOOT

E

REAR WIEW

VIEW A-A (FROM SHEET 10)
SIDE VIEW

# LEG SYSTEM ASS'Y

| ATLANTIS, ADVANCED ENGINEERING PROJECTS | |
|---|---|
| Name of project: **GIANT ROBOT** | |
| It can transport heavy structures above mountains with no roads | |
| Design Engineer:  Walter F. Laredo | Date: August 8, 2002 |
| Drawing Number:  **1300** | Sheet **11** of **17** |

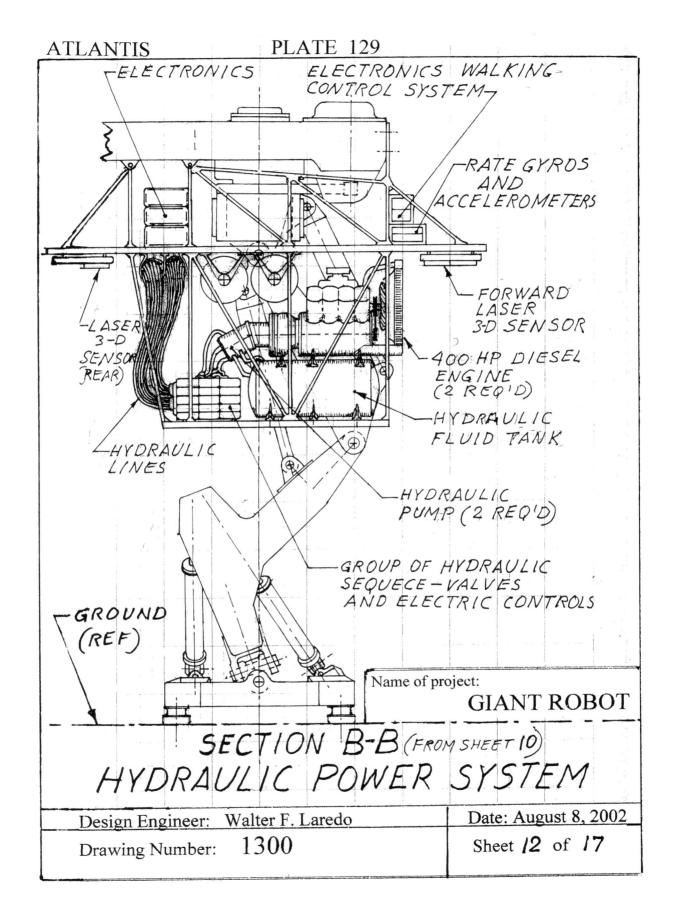

ELECTRONICS

ELECTRONICS WALKING
CONTROL SYSTEM

RATE GYROS
AND
ACCELEROMETERS

LASER
3-D
SENSOR
(REAR)

FORWARD
LASER
3-D SENSOR

400 HP DIESEL
ENGINE
(2 REQ'D)

HYDRAULIC
LINES

HYDRAULIC
FLUID TANK

HYDRAULIC
PUMP (2 REQ'D)

GROUND
(REF)

GROUP OF HYDRAULIC
SEQUECE-VALVES
AND ELECTRIC CONTROLS

Name of project:

**GIANT ROBOT**

*SECTION B-B* (FROM SHEET 10)
*HYDRAULIC POWER SYSTEM*

| Design Engineer: Walter F. Laredo | Date: August 8, 2002 |
|---|---|
| Drawing Number: 1300 | Sheet 12 of 17 |

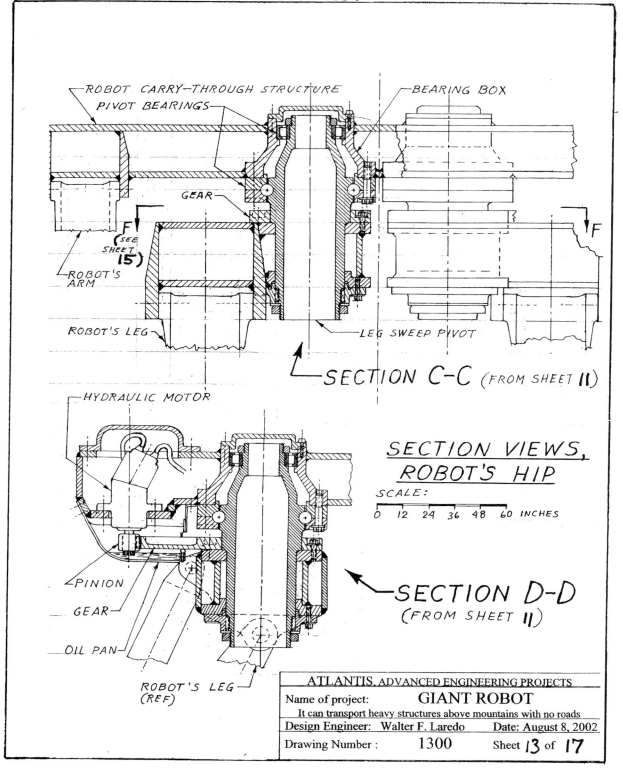

ROBOT CARRY-THROUGH STRUCTURE
PIVOT BEARINGS
BEARING BOX
GEAR
F (SEE SHEET 15)
ROBOT'S ARM
ROBOT'S LEG
LEG SWEEP PIVOT
F

**SECTION C-C** (FROM SHEET 11)

HYDRAULIC MOTOR

**SECTION VIEWS, ROBOT'S HIP**

SCALE:

0   12   24   36   48   60 INCHES

PINION
GEAR
OIL PAN
ROBOT'S LEG (REF)

**SECTION D-D**
(FROM SHEET 11)

| ATLANTIS, ADVANCED ENGINEERING PROJECTS | | |
|---|---|---|
| Name of project: | **GIANT ROBOT** | |
| It can transport heavy structures above mountains with no roads | | |
| Design Engineer: Walter F. Laredo | | Date: August 8, 2002 |
| Drawing Number : | 1300 | Sheet 13 of 17 |

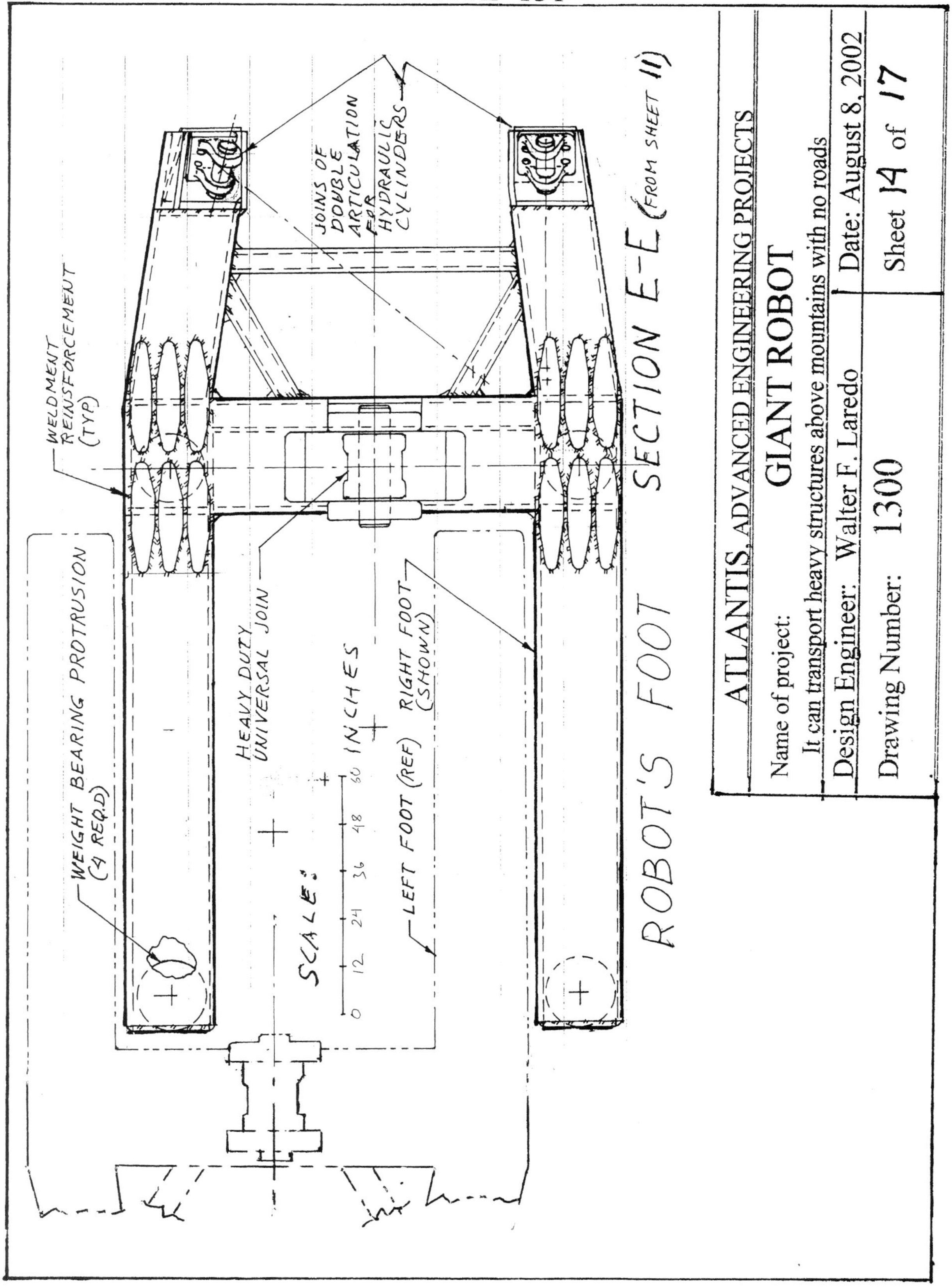

JOINS OF
DOUBLE
ARTICULATION
FOR
HYDRAULIC
CYLINDERS

WELDMENT
REINSFORCEMENT
(TYP)

WEIGHT BEARING PROTRUSION
(4 REQ.D)

HEAVY DUTY
UNIVERSAL JOIN

SCALE:

0  12  24  36  48  60  INCHES

LEFT FOOT (REF)   RIGHT FOOT
(SHOWN)

SECTION E-E (FROM SHEET 11)

ROBOT'S FOOT

| ATLANTIS, ADVANCED ENGINEERING PROJECTS | |
|---|---|
| GIANT ROBOT | |
| Name of project: It can transport heavy structures above mountains with no roads | |
| Design Engineer:   Walter F. Laredo | Date: August 8, 2002 |
| Drawing Number:   1300 | Sheet 14 of 17 |

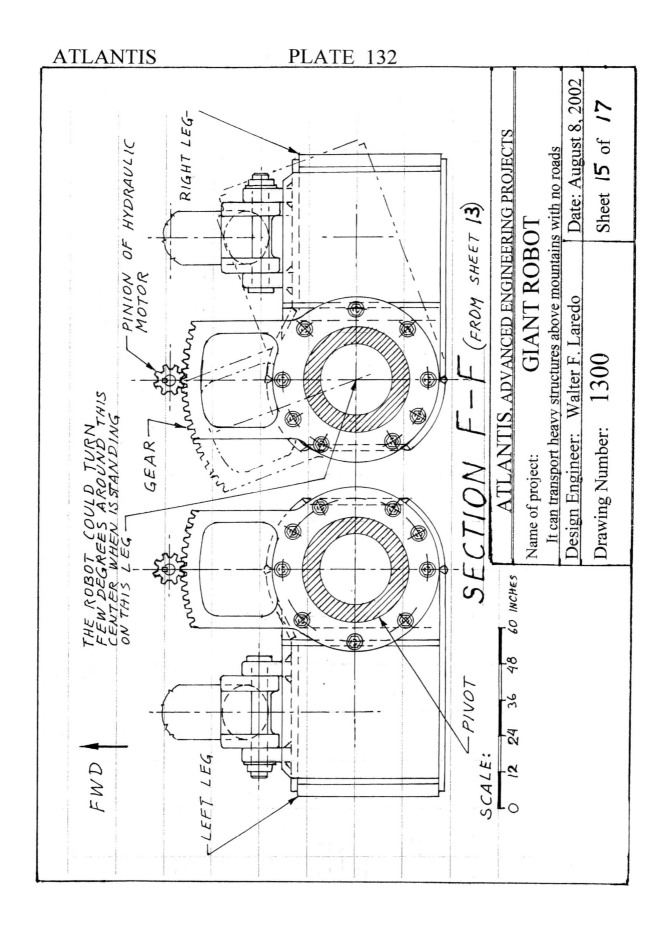

RIGHT LEG

PINION OF HYDRAULIC
MOTOR

THE ROBOT COULD TURN
FEW DEGREES AROUND THIS
CENTER WHEN IS STANDING
ON THIS LEG

GEAR

FWD

LEFT LEG

PIVOT

SCALE:

0   12   24   36   48   60 INCHES

SECTION F—F (FROM SHEET 13)

| ATLANTIS, ADVANCED ENGINEERING PROJECTS | |
|---|---|
| GIANT ROBOT | |
| Name of project: | |
| It can transport heavy structures above mountains with no roads | |
| Design Engineer:   Walter F. Laredo | Date: August 8, 2002 |
| Drawing Number:   1300 | Sheet 15 of 17 |

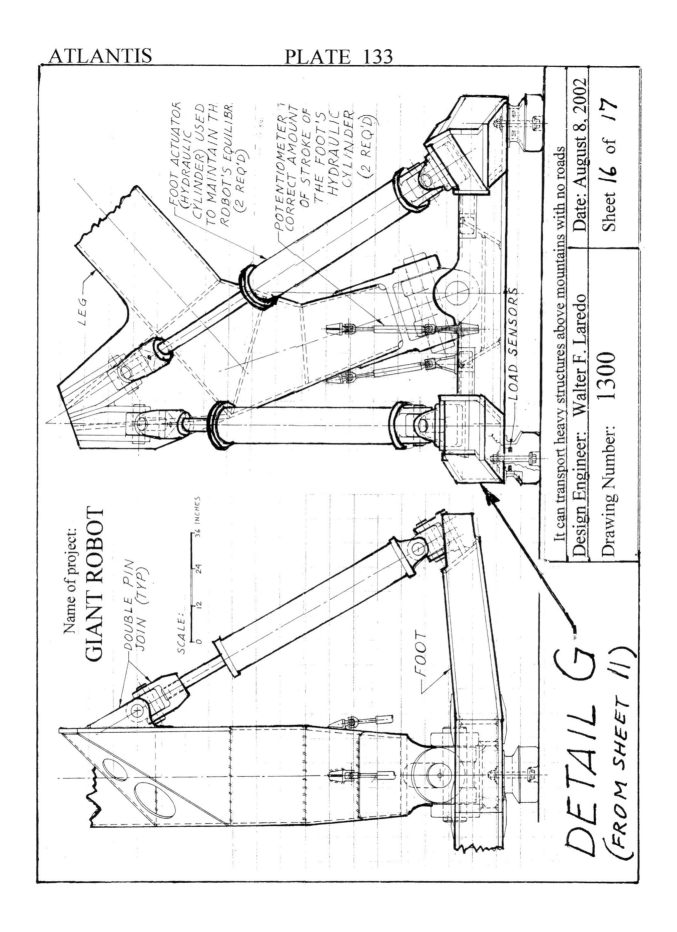

Name of project:
# GIANT ROBOT

DOUBLE PIN JOIN (TYP)

SCALE:
0   12   24   36 INCHES

LEG

FOOT ACTUATOR (HYDRAULIC CYLINDER) USED TO MAINTAIN TH ROBOT'S EQUILIBR. (2 REQ'D)

POTENTIOMETER CORRECT AMOUNT OF STROKE OF THE FOOT'S HYDRAULIC CYLINDER (2 REQ'D)

LOAD SENSORS

FOOT

# DETAIL G
(FROM SHEET 11)

It can transport heavy structures above mountains with no roads

| Design Engineer: Walter F. Laredo | Date: August 8, 2002 |
|---|---|
| Drawing Number: 1300 | Sheet 16 of 17 |

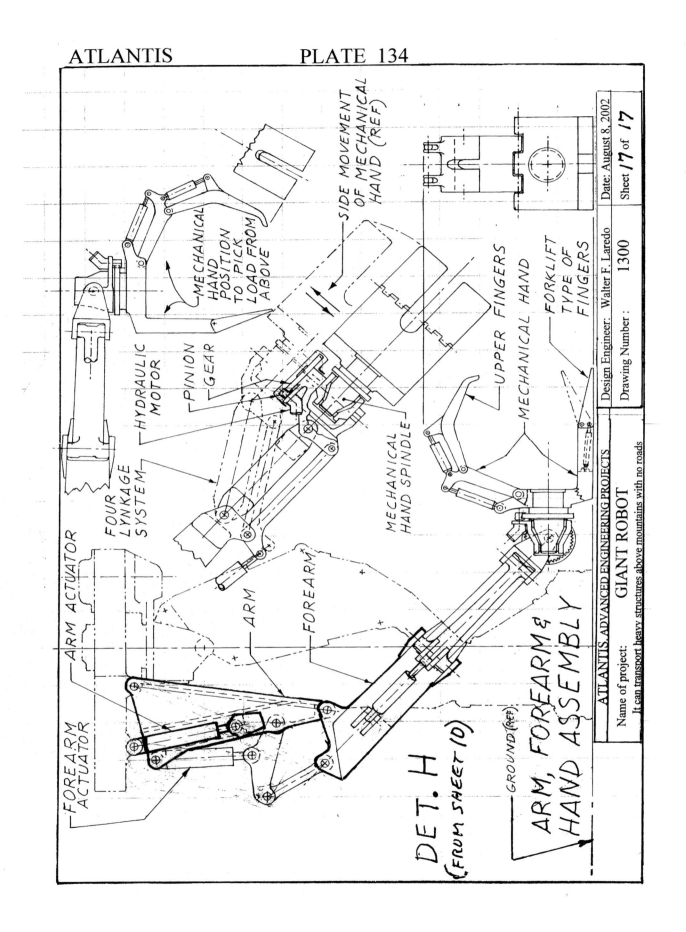

SIDE MOVEMENT OF MECHANICAL HAND (REF)

MECHANICAL HAND POSITION TO PICK LOAD FROM ABOVE

PINION GEAR

HYDRAULIC MOTOR

FOUR LYNKAGE SYSTEM

ARM ACTUATOR

FOREARM ACTUATOR

ARM

FOREARM

MECHANICAL HAND SPINDLE

UPPER FINGERS

MECHANICAL HAND

FORKLIFT TYPE OF FINGERS

GROUND (REF)

DET. H
(FROM SHEET 10)

ARM, FOREARM & HAND ASSEMBLY

| ATLANTIS ADVANCED ENGINEERING PROJECTS | Design Engineer: Walter F. Laredo | Date: August 8, 2002 |
|---|---|---|
| GIANT ROBOT | Drawing Number: 1300 | Sheet 17 of 17 |
| Name of project: | | |
| It can transport heavy structures above mountains with no roads | | |

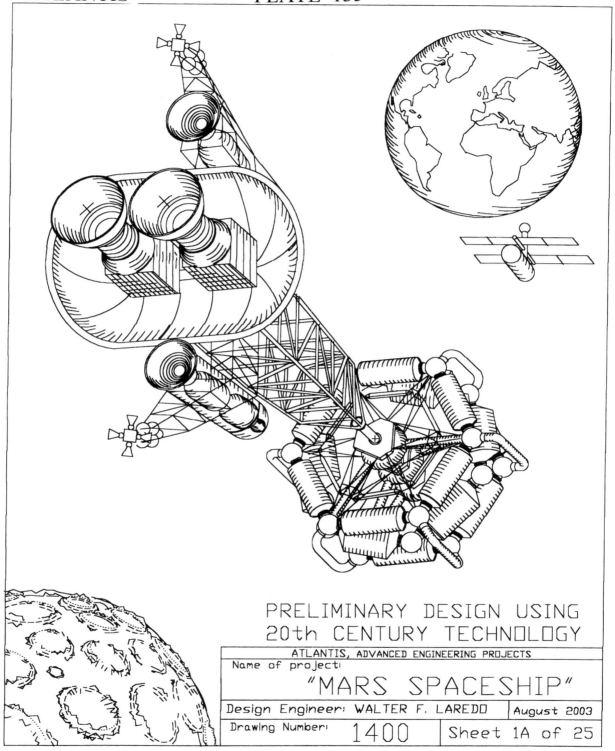

PRELIMINARY DESIGN USING
20th CENTURY TECHNOLOGY

| ATLANTIS, ADVANCED ENGINEERING PROJECTS | | |
|---|---|---|
| Name of project: | | |
| "MARS SPACESHIP" | | |
| Design Engineer: WALTER F. LAREDO | | August 2003 |
| Drawing Number: 1400 | | Sheet 1A of 25 |

# MARS SPACESHIP

## VEHICLE GROSS WEIGHT: 1,000 METRIC TONS

## PERFORMANCE

THE CRUISING SPEED OF THIS SHIP WITH RESPECT TO THE EARTH WILL VARY
ACCORDING TO THE TYPE OF PROPULSION SYSTEM USED. FROM 38,000 MPH TO
ABOVE. THE DESIRED ONE WAY TRANSIT TIME BETWEEN EARTH AND MARS WILL
BE LESS THAN FIVE MONTHS, HOWEVER IT COULD TAKE MORE TIME DEPENDING
OF THE THRUST OF THE PROPULSION SYSTEM USED BY THIS SPACECRAFT.   A
PROPULSION SYSTEM WITH A SPECIFIC IMPULSE OF 4,000 SECONDS OR MORE
WILL BE DESIRABLE TO EXPLORE PART OF THIS SOLAR SYSTEM, HOWEVER A
LESS SPECIFIC IMPULSE WOULD BE ACCEPTABLE AS MORE REALISTIC.

THE ACCELERATION AFTER DEPARTING FROM AN ORBIT AROUND A CELESTIAL BODY AND THE
DECELERATION WHEN APPROACHING AND ARRIVING TO AN ORBIT OF ANOTHER ONE DEPENDS ON
THE THRUST PROVIDED BY THE TYPE OF SPACE PROPULSION SYSTEM THAT WOULD BE USED
ON THIS SPACESHIP.   THE NUCLEAR FUSION PROPULSION SYSTEM WOULD BE THE BEST, HOWEVER
THE DEVELOPMENT OF VARIOUS TYPES  OF ELECTRICAL PROPULSION SYSTEM SEEMS MORE
FEASABLE FOR THE NEAR FUTURE.

SOME PROPULSION INFORMATION IS SHOWN IN SHEET 20 FROM THIS PRELIMINARY DESIGN PACKAGE.

## TEST FLIGHTS

PRIOR TO THE VOYAGE TO MARS, IT WOULD BE NECESSARY TO PERFORM TWO SHORT TEST
FLIGHTS, DEPARTING EITHER FROM A SPACE STATION, OR DIRECTLY FROM AN EARTH PARKING
ORBIT TO AN ORBIT AROUND THE MOON AND BACK.  THIS IS A SPACECRAFT THAT WOULD TRAVEL
AT HIGH INTERPLANETARY CRUISING SPEED HOWEVER ITS ACCELERATION AFTER DEPARTING FROM
A PARKING ORBIT AND ITS DECELERATION WHEN APPROACHING TO THE OTHER PLANET ORBIT,
WOULD BE RELATIVELY SLOW DUE TO ITS PROPULSION SYSTEM WITH A SMALL THRUST, BUT
WITH THE GREAT ADVANTAGE OF ACCELERATING FOR LONG PERIODS OF TIME.

## ARTIFICIAL GRAVITY

THE CIRCULAR ROTATING BODIES OF THIS SPACESHIP (WITH AN AVERAGE RADIUS OF 40 FEET)
WILL PROVIDE TO THE CREW AND PASSENGERS INSIDE IT WITH A CENTRIFUGAL FORCE
(ARTIFICIAL GRAVITY) EQUIVALENT TO SOMEWHERE BETWEEN ONE THIRD AND ONE QUARTER OF
THE ACCELERATION OF GRAVITY AT THE EARTH'S SURFACE.  A CENTRIPETAL FORCE IS PRODUCED
BY ROTATING THESE BODIES BETWEEN 5 AND 4.38 RPM RESPECTIVELY.  THE ROTATION OF THESE
BODIES WILL START FROM ZERO AND SLOWLY BUILD UP TO THE FULL RPM'S IN FOUR HOURS,
AN OPERATION THAT SHOULD BE PERFORMED PRIOR TO BOARDING THE SHIP.

## NOTES:

FOR CONSTRUCTION MATERIALS, INSULATION INSTALLATION, STRUCTURAL ASSEMBLY, INSTALLATION
OF SYSTEMS, MATERIALS PROCESSES, ETC., SEE THE ACTUAL PROPOSAL BOOK.

## FLIGHT PROFILE FOR THE "MARS SPACESHIP" MISSION

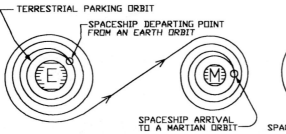

TERRESTRIAL PARKING ORBIT

SPACESHIP DEPARTING POINT
FROM AN EARTH ORBIT

MARTIAN PARKING ORBIT

SPACESHIP ARRIVAL
TO A MARTIAN ORBIT

SPACESHIP ARRIVAL

SPACESHIP DEPARTING

EARTH-MARS TRIP                MARS-EARTH RETURN TRIP

| ATLANTIS, ADVANCED ENGINEERING PROJECTS | |
|---|---|
| Name of project: "MARS SPACESHIP" | |
| Design Engineer: WALTER F. LAREDO | Date: August 2003 |
| Drawing Number: 1400 | Sheet 1B of 25 |

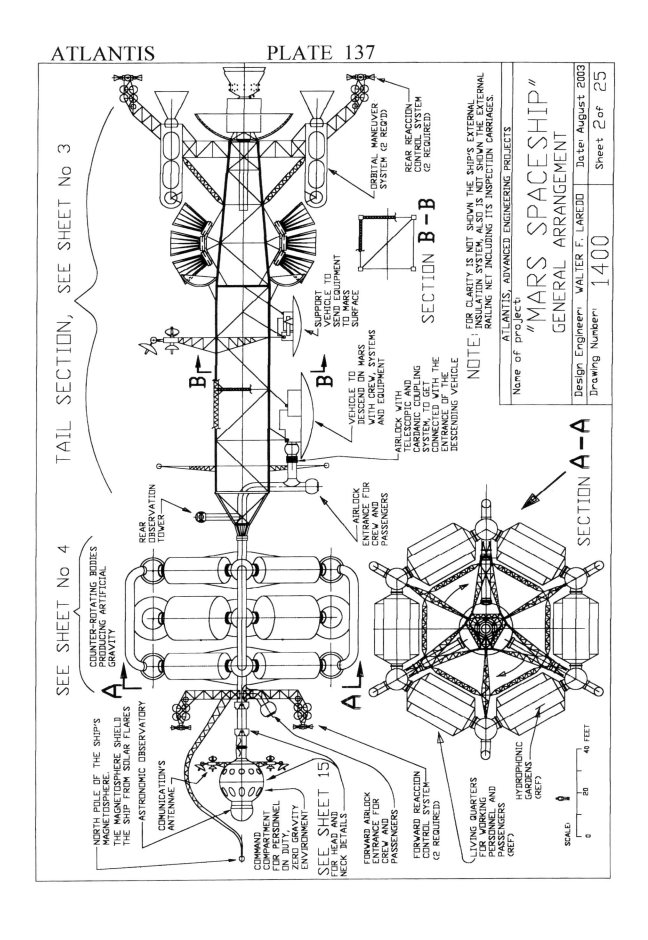

TAIL SECTION, SEE SHEET No 3

SEE SHEET No 4

COUNTER-ROTATING BODIES PRODUCING ARTIFICIAL GRAVITY

NORTH POLE OF THE SHIP'S MAGNETOSPHERE.
THE MAGNETOSPHERE SHIELD THE SHIP FROM SOLAR FLARES

ASTRONOMIC OBSERVATORY

REAR OBSERVATION TOWER

COMUNICATION'S ANTENNAE

SEE SHEET 15 FOR HEAD AND NECK DETAILS

COMMAND COMPARTMENT FOR PERSONNEL ON DUTY, ZERO GRAVITY ENVIRONMENT

FORWARD AIRLOCK ENTRANCE FOR CREW AND PASSENGERS

FORWARD REACCION CONTROL SYSTEM (2 REQUIRED)

LIVING QUARTERS FOR WORKING PERSONNEL AND PASSENGERS (REF)

HYDROPHONIC GARDENS (REF)

SCALE:  0   20   40 FEET

SECTION A-A

SECTION B-B

ORBITAL MANEUVER SYSTEM (2 REQ'D)

REAR REACCION CONTROL SYSTEM (2 REQUIRED)

SUPPORT VEHICLE TO SEND EQUIPMENT TO MARS SURFACE

VEHICLE TO DESCEND ON MARS WITH CREW, SYSTEMS AND EQUIPMENT

AIRLOCK WITH TELESCOPIC AND CARDANIC COUPLING SYSTEM, TO GET CONNECTED WITH THE ENTRANCE OF THE DESCENDING VEHICLE

AIRLOCK ENTRANCE FOR CREW AND PASSENGERS

NOTE: FOR CLARITY IS NOT SHOWN THE SHIP'S EXTERNAL INSULATION SYSTEM, ALSO IS NOT SHOWN THE EXTERNAL RAILING NET INCLUDING ITS INSPECTION CARRIAGES.

Name of project:
"MARS SPACESHIP"
GENERAL ARRANGEMENT

ATLANTIS, ADVANCED ENGINEERING PROJECTS

Design Engineer: WALTER F. LAREDO     Date: August 2003

Drawing Number: 1400     Sheet 2 of 25

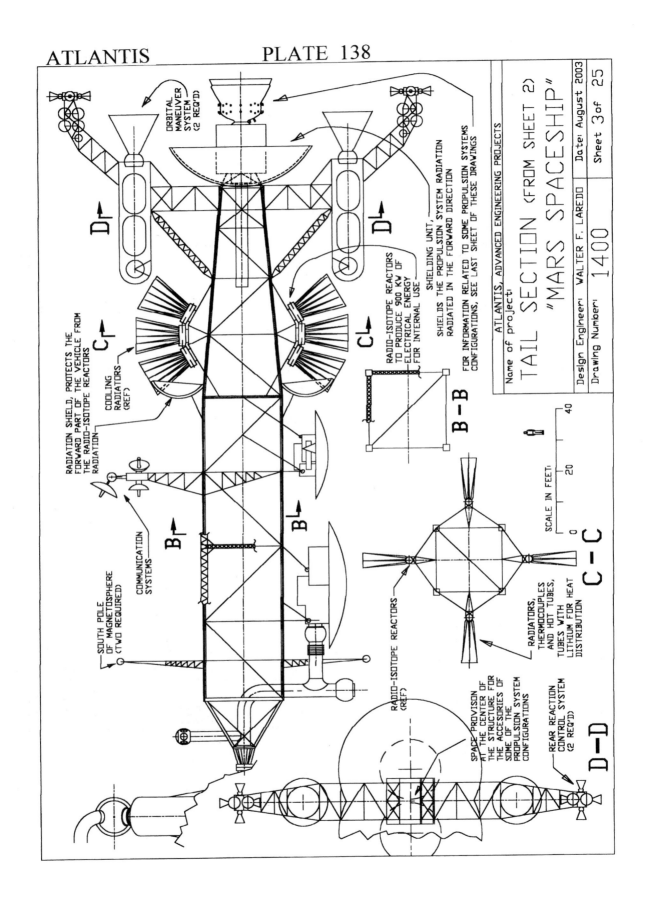

ATLANTIS, ADVANCED ENGINEERING PROJECTS

Name of project:
TAIL SECTION (FROM SHEET 2)
"MARS SPACESHIP"

Design Engineer: WALTER F. LAREDO    Date: August 2003

Drawing Number: 1400    Sheet 3 of 25

ORBITAL MANEUVER SYSTEM (2 REQ'D)

RADIO-ISOTOPE REACTORS TO PRODUCE 900 KW OF ELECTRICAL ENERGY FOR INTERNAL USE

SHIELDING UNIT, SHIELDS THE PROPULSION SYSTEM RADIATION RADIATED IN THE FORWARD DIRECTION

FOR INFORMATION RELATED TO SOME PROPULSION SYSTEMS CONFIGURATIONS, SEE LAST SHEET OF THESE DRAWINGS

RADIATION SHIELD, PROTECTS THE FORWARD PART OF THE VEHICLE FROM THE RADIO-ISOTOPE REACTORS RADIATION

COOLING RADIATORS (REF)

D
D

C
C

B-B

COMMUNICATION SYSTEMS

SOUTH POLE OF MAGNETOSPHERE (TWO REQUIRED)

B
B

RADIO-ISOTOPE REACTORS (REF)

SCALE IN FEET:
0   20   40

C-C

RADIATORS, THERMOCOUPLES AND HOT TUBES, TUBES WITH LITHIUM FOR HEAT DISTRIBUTION

SPACE PROVISION AT THE CENTER OF THE STRUCTURE FOR THE ACCESORIES OF SOME OF THE PROPULSION SYSTEM CONFIGURATIONS

REAR REACTION CONTROL SYSTEM (2 REQ'D)

D-D

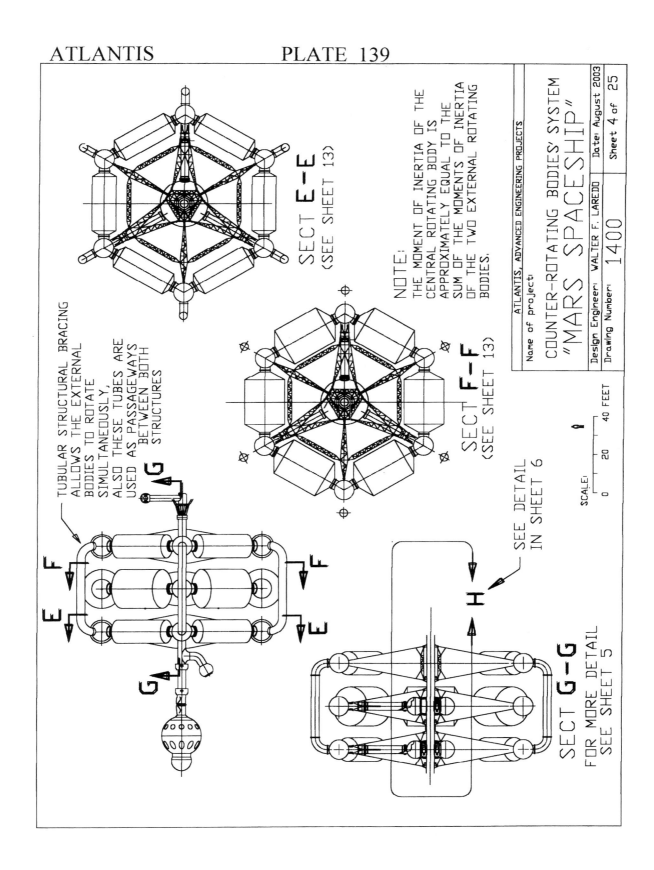

SECT **E-E**
(SEE SHEET 13)

SECT **F-F**
(SEE SHEET 13)

SECT **G-G**

FOR MORE DETAIL
SEE SHEET 5

NOTE:
THE MOMENT OF INERTIA OF THE CENTRAL ROTATING BODY IS APPROXIMATELY EQUAL TO THE SUM OF THE MOMENTS OF INERTIA OF THE TWO EXTERNAL ROTATING BODIES.

TUBULAR STRUCTURAL BRACING ALLOWS THE EXTERNAL BODIES TO ROTATE SIMULTANEOUSLY, ALSO THESE TUBES ARE USED AS PASSAGEWAYS BETWEEN BOTH STRUCTURES

SEE DETAIL IN SHEET 6

SCALE:
0    20    40 FEET

| ATLANTIS, ADVANCED ENGINEERING PROJECTS | | |
|---|---|---|
| Name of project: | | |
| COUNTER-ROTATING BODIES' SYSTEM "MARS SPACESHIP" | | |
| Design Engineer: WALTER F. LAREDO | | Date: August 2003 |
| Drawing Number: 1400 | | Sheet 4 of 25 |

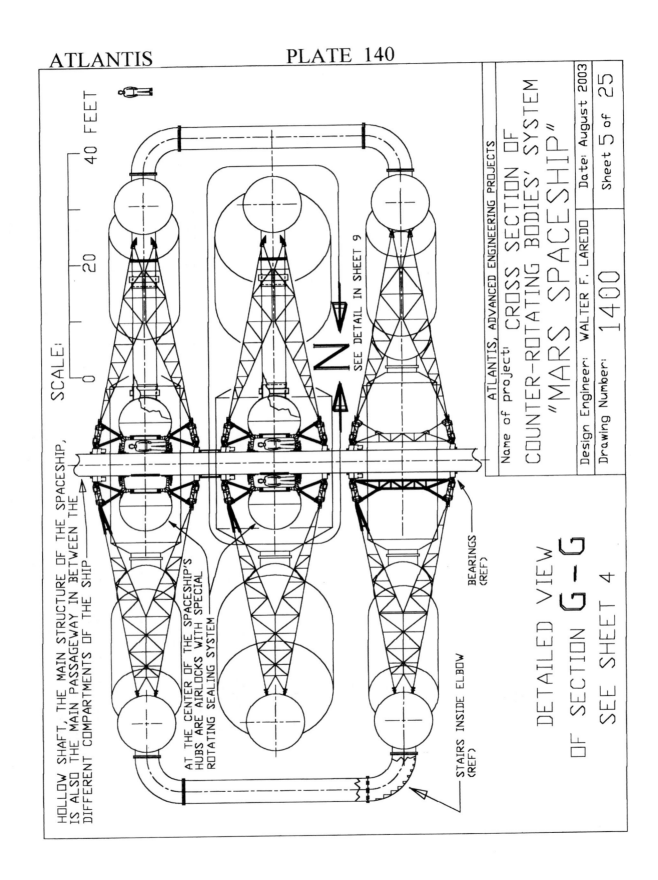

SCALE:
0          20          40 FEET

HOLLOW SHAFT, THE MAIN STRUCTURE OF THE SPACESHIP, IS ALSO THE MAIN PASSAGEWAY IN BETWEEN THE DIFFERENT COMPARTMENTS OF THE SHIP

AT THE CENTER OF THE SPACESHIP'S HUBS ARE AIRLOCKS WITH SPECIAL ROTATING SEALING SYSTEM

SEE DETAIL IN SHEET 9

BEARINGS (REF)

STAIRS INSIDE ELBOW (REF)

DETAILED VIEW OF SECTION G-G
SEE SHEET 4

Name of project: CROSS SECTION OF COUNTER-ROTATING BODIES' SYSTEM "MARS SPACESHIP"

ATLANTIS, ADVANCED ENGINEERING PROJECTS

Design Engineer: WALTER F. LAREDO

Date: August 2003

Drawing Number: 1400

Sheet 5 of 25

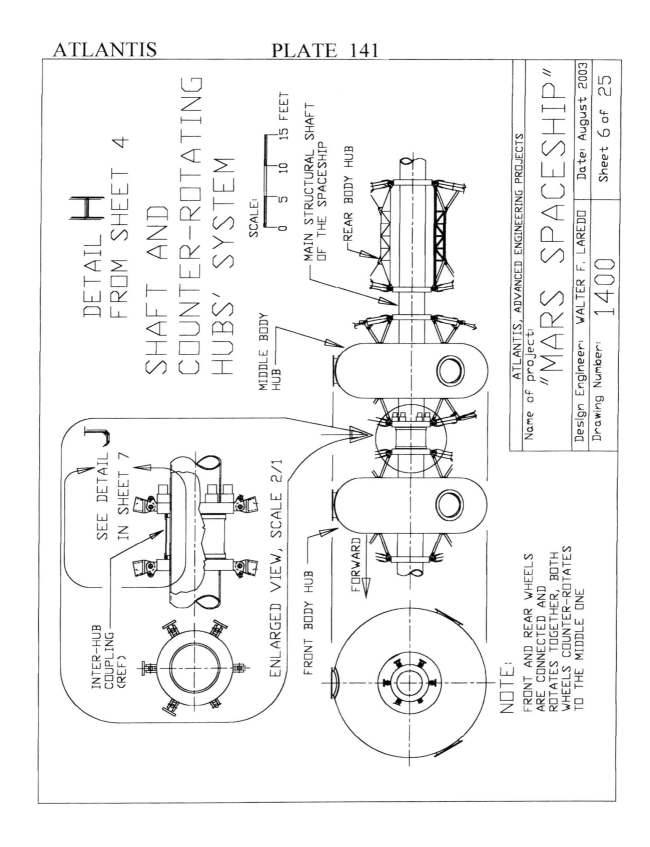

DETAIL H
FROM SHEET 4

SHAFT AND
COUNTER-ROTATING
HUBS' SYSTEM

SCALE:

0   5   10   15 FEET

MAIN STRUCTURAL SHAFT
OF THE SPACESHIP

REAR BODY HUB

MIDDLE BODY
HUB

DETAIL J

SEE DETAIL
IN SHEET 7

INTER-HUB
COUPLING
(REF)

ENLARGED VIEW, SCALE 2/1

FRONT BODY HUB

FORWARD

NOTE:
FRONT AND REAR WHEELS
ARE CONNECTED AND
ROTATES TOGETHER, BOTH
WHEELS COUNTER-ROTATES
TO THE MIDDLE ONE

Name of project:
"MARS SPACESHIP"

ATLANTIS, ADVANCED ENGINEERING PROJECTS

Design Engineer: WALTER F. LAREDO       Date: August 2003

Drawing Number: 1400          Sheet 6 of 25

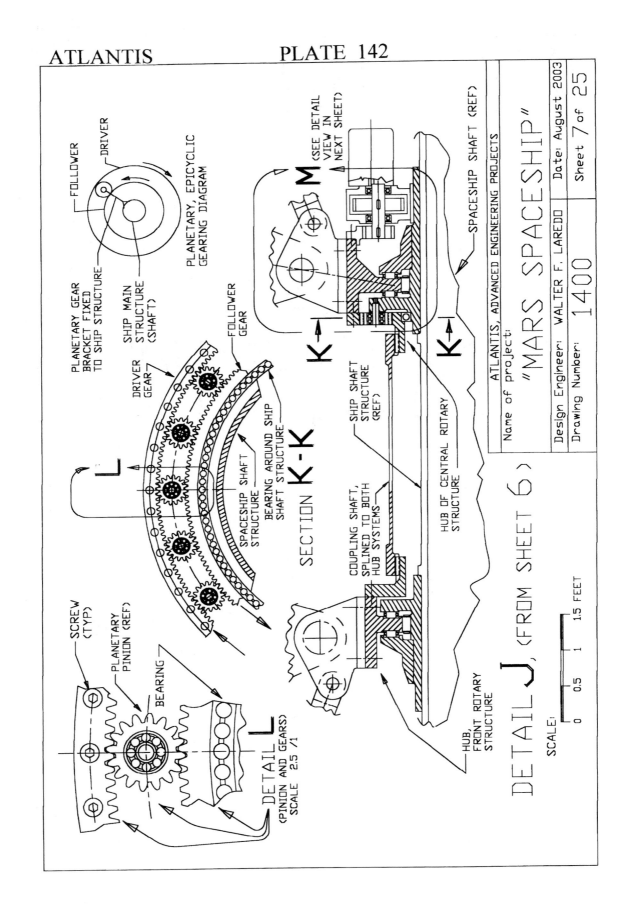

FOLLOWER

DRIVER

PLANETARY, EPICYCLIC
GEARING DIAGRAM

PLANETARY GEAR
BRACKET FIXED
TO SHIP STRUCTURE

SHIP MAIN
STRUCTURE
(SHAFT)

DRIVER
GEAR

FOLLOWER
GEAR

SPACESHIP SHAFT
STRUCTURE

BEARING AROUND SHIP
SHAFT STRUCTURE

SECTION K-K

SCREW
(TYP)

PLANETARY
PINION (REF)

BEARING

DETAIL L
(PINION AND GEARS)
SCALE 2.5 /1

M (SEE DETAIL
VIEW IN
NEXT SHEET)

SPACESHIP SHAFT (REF)

SHIP SHAFT
STRUCTURE
(REF)

COUPLING SHAFT,
SPLINED TO BOTH
HUB SYSTEMS

HUB OF CENTRAL ROTARY
STRUCTURE

HUB,
FRONT ROTARY
STRUCTURE

DETAIL J, (FROM SHEET 6)

SCALE:

0   0.5   1   1.5 FEET

Name of project:

"MARS SPACESHIP"

ATLANTIS, ADVANCED ENGINEERING PROJECTS

| Design Engineer: WALTER F. LAREDO | Date: August 2003 |
|---|---|
| Drawing Number: 1400 | Sheet 7 of 25 |

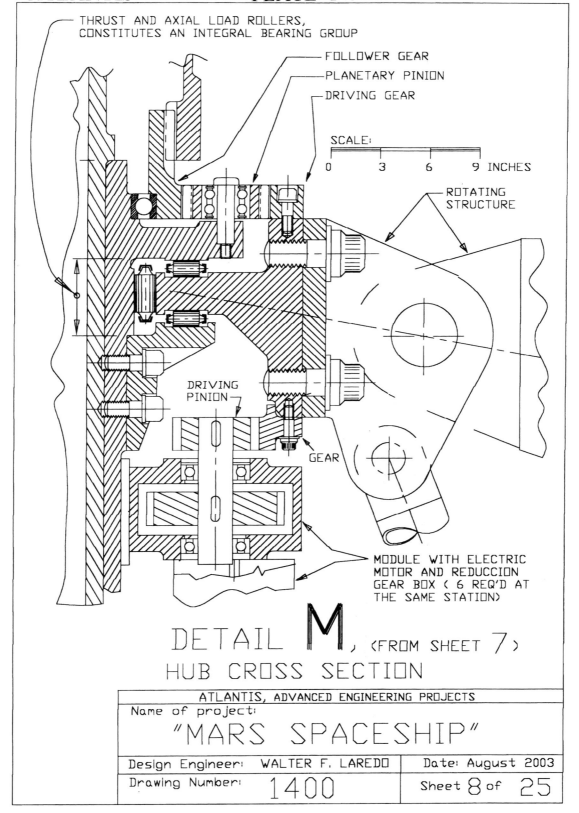

THRUST AND AXIAL LOAD ROLLERS,
CONSTITUTES AN INTEGRAL BEARING GROUP

FOLLOWER GEAR
PLANETARY PINION
DRIVING GEAR

SCALE:

0    3    6    9 INCHES

ROTATING
STRUCTURE

DRIVING
PINION

GEAR

MODULE WITH ELECTRIC
MOTOR AND REDUCCION
GEAR BOX ( 6 REQ'D AT
THE SAME STATION)

DETAIL **M**, (FROM SHEET 7)
HUB CROSS SECTION

| ATLANTIS, ADVANCED ENGINEERING PROJECTS | | |
|---|---|---|
| Name of project: "MARS SPACESHIP" | | |
| Design Engineer: WALTER F. LAREDO | Date: August 2003 | |
| Drawing Number: 1400 | Sheet 8 of 25 | |

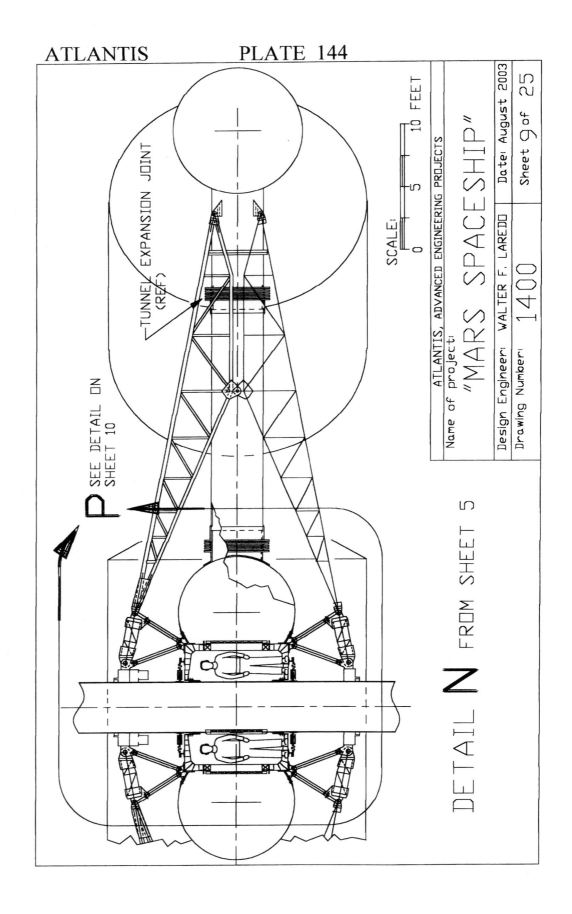

DETAIL N FROM SHEET 5

TUNNEL EXPANSION JOINT (REF)

P SEE DETAIL ON SHEET 10

SCALE:

0   5   10 FEET

ATLANTIS, ADVANCED ENGINEERING PROJECTS

Name of project:

"MARS SPACESHIP"

| Design Engineer: WALTER F. LAREDO | Date: August 2003 |
| Drawing Number: 1400 | Sheet 9 of 25 |

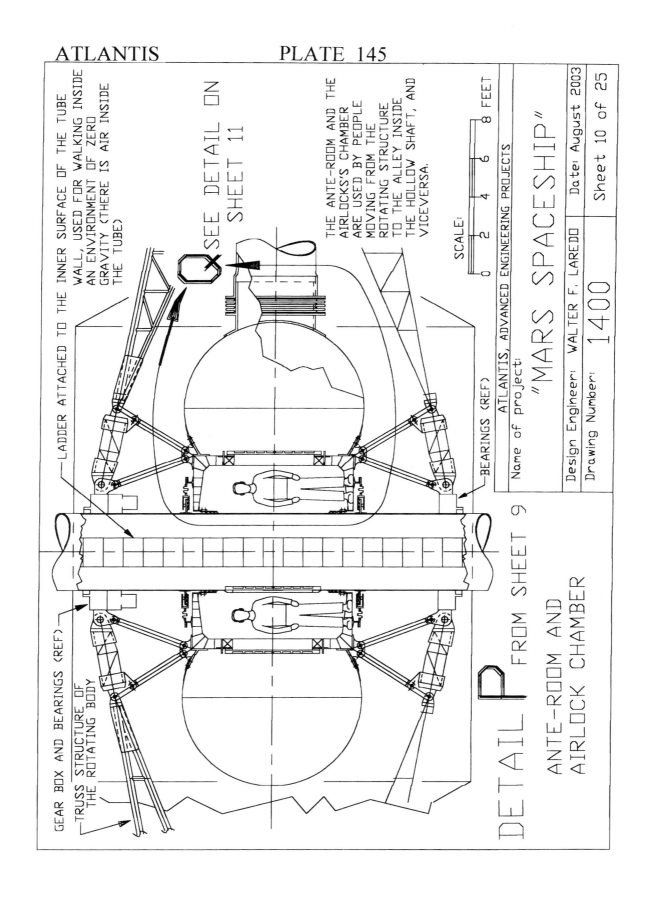

LADDER ATTACHED TO THE INNER SURFACE OF THE TUBE WALL, USED FOR WALKING INSIDE AN ENVIRONMENT OF ZERO GRAVITY (THERE IS AIR INSIDE THE TUBE)

SEE DETAIL ON SHEET 11

THE ANTE-ROOM AND THE AIRLOCKS'S CHAMBER ARE USED BY PEOPLE MOVING FROM THE ROTATING STRUCTURE TO THE ALLEY INSIDE THE HOLLOW SHAFT, AND VICEVERSA.

BEARINGS (REF)

GEAR BOX AND BEARINGS (REF)

TRUSS STRUCTURE OF THE ROTATING BODY

DETAIL P FROM SHEET 9

ANTE-ROOM AND AIRLOCK CHAMBER

SCALE:

0   2   4   6   8 FEET

ATLANTIS, ADVANCED ENGINEERING PROJECTS

Name of project:

"MARS SPACESHIP"

Design Engineer: WALTER F. LAREDO     Date: August 2003

Drawing Number: 1400     Sheet 10 of 25

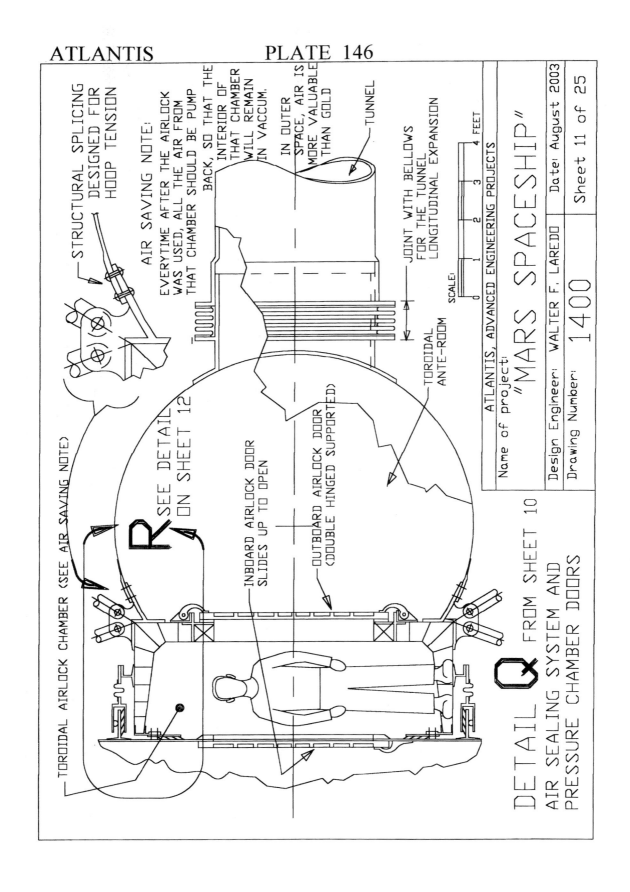

STRUCTURAL SPLICING DESIGNED FOR HOOP TENSION

AIR SAVING NOTE:
EVERYTIME AFTER THE AIRLOCK WAS USED, ALL THE AIR FROM THAT CHAMBER SHOULD BE PUMP BACK, SO THAT THE INTERIOR OF THAT CHAMBER WILL REMAIN IN VACCUM.

IN OUTER SPACE, AIR IS MORE VALUABLE THAN GOLD

TUNNEL

JOINT WITH BELLOWS FOR THE TUNNEL LONGITUDINAL EXPANSION

TOROIDAL ANTE-ROOM

SCALE:
0    1    2    3    4 FEET

TOROIDAL AIRLOCK CHAMBER (SEE AIR SAVING NOTE)

SEE DETAIL ON SHEET 12

INBOARD AIRLOCK DOOR SLIDES UP TO OPEN

OUTBOARD AIRLOCK DOOR (DOUBLE HINGED SUPPORTED)

DETAIL Q FROM SHEET 10

AIR SEALING SYSTEM AND PRESSURE CHAMBER DOORS

Name of project: "MARS SPACESHIP"

ATLANTIS, ADVANCED ENGINEERING PROJECTS

Design Engineer: WALTER F. LAREDO     Date: August 2003

Drawing Number: 1400     Sheet 11 of 25

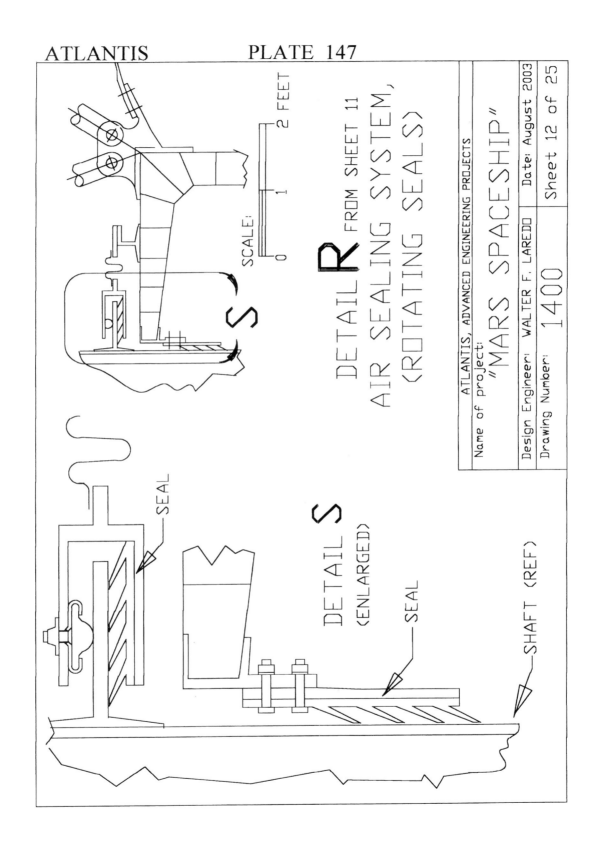

SCALE:
0    1    2 FEET

DETAIL R FROM SHEET 11
AIR SEALING SYSTEM,
(ROTATING SEALS)

DETAIL S
(ENLARGED)

SEAL

SEAL

SHAFT (REF)

| | |
|---|---|
| Name of project: | ATLANTIS, ADVANCED ENGINEERING PROJECTS |
| | "MARS SPACESHIP" |
| Design Engineer: WALTER F. LAREDO | Date: August 2003 |
| Drawing Number: 1400 | Sheet 12 of 25 |

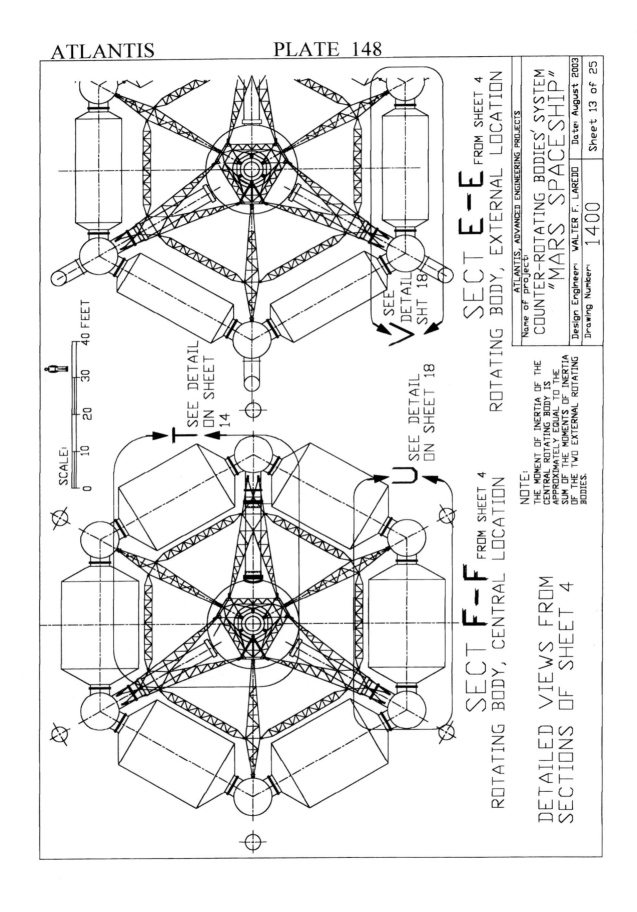

SECT **E-E** FROM SHEET 4

ROTATING BODY, EXTERNAL LOCATION

SEE DETAIL SHT 18

SEE DETAIL ON SHEET 14

SEE DETAIL ON SHEET 18

SECT **F-F** FROM SHEET 4

ROTATING BODY, CENTRAL LOCATION

SCALE:

0   10   20   30   40 FEET

NOTE:
THE MOMENT OF INERTIA OF THE
CENTRAL ROTATING BODY IS
APPROXIMATELY EQUAL TO THE
SUM OF THE MOMENTS OF INERTIA
OF THE TWO EXTERNAL ROTATING
BODIES.

DETAILED VIEWS FROM
SECTIONS OF SHEET 4

Name of project:
ATLANTIS, ADVANCED ENGINEERING PROJECTS
COUNTER-ROTATING BODIES' SYSTEM
"MARS SPACESHIP"

| Design Engineer: WALTER F. LAREDO | Date: August 2003 |
| Drawing Number: 1400 | Sheet 13 of 25 |

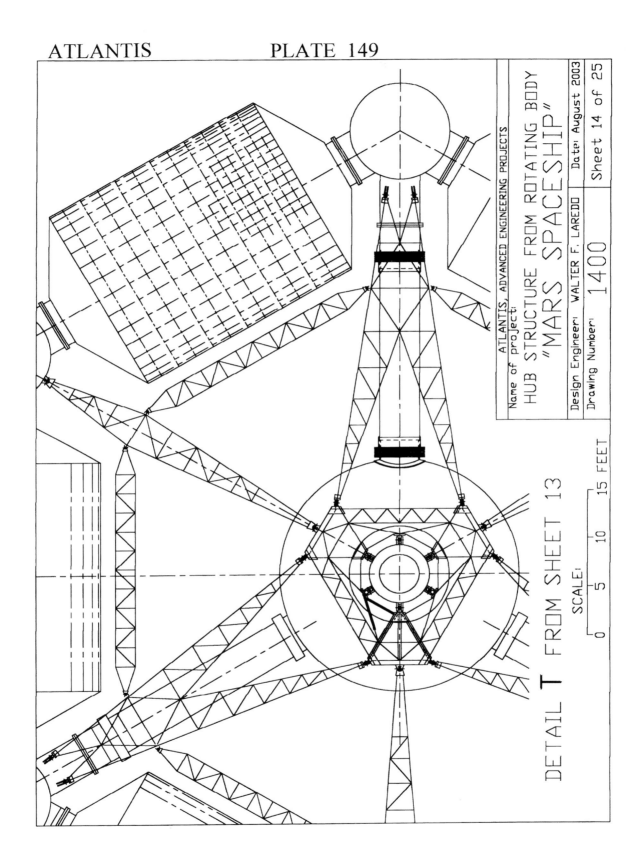

DETAIL T FROM SHEET 13

SCALE:

0   5   10   15 FEET

Name of project:
ATLANTIS, ADVANCED ENGINEERING PROJECTS
HUB STRUCTURE FROM ROTATING BODY
"MARS SPACESHIP"

Design Engineer: WALTER F. LAREDO   Date: August 2003

Drawing Number: 1400   Sheet 14 of 25

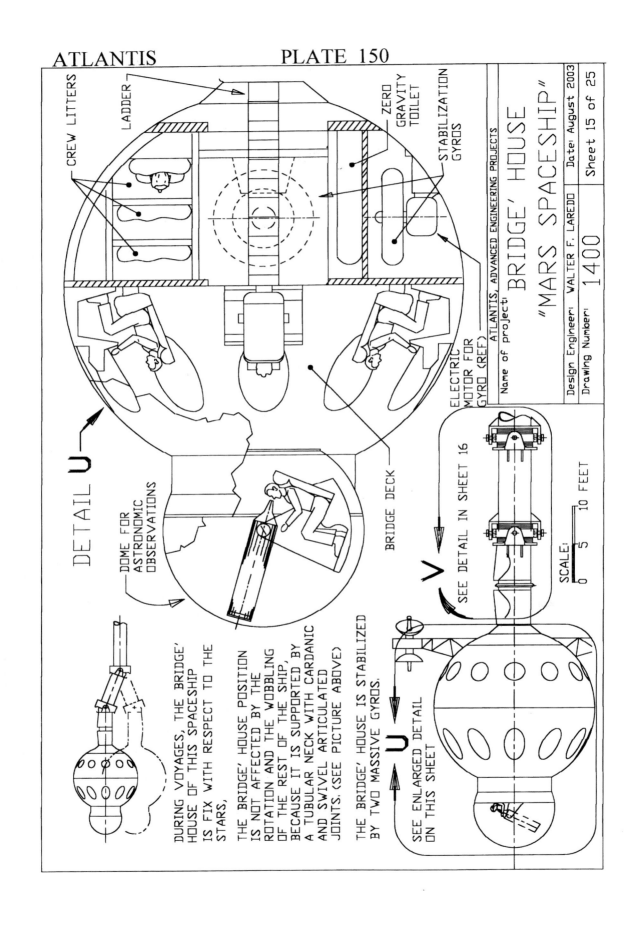

CREW LITTERS

LADDER

ZERO
GRAVITY
TOILET

STABILIZATION
GYROS

DETAIL U

DOME FOR
ASTRONOMIC
OBSERVATIONS

ELECTRIC
MOTOR FOR
GYRO (REF)

BRIDGE DECK

SEE DETAIL IN SHEET 16

DURING VOYAGES, THE BRIDGE'
HOUSE OF THIS SPACESHIP
IS FIX WITH RESPECT TO THE
STARS,

THE BRIDGE' HOUSE POSITION
IS NOT AFFECTED BY THE
ROTATION AND THE WOBBLING
OF THE REST OF THE SHIP,
BECAUSE IT IS SUPPORTED BY
A TUBULAR NECK WITH CARDANIC
AND SWIVEL ARTICULATED
JOINTS. (SEE PICTURE ABOVE)

THE BRIDGE' HOUSE IS STABILIZED
BY TWO MASSIVE GYROS.

SEE ENLARGED DETAIL
ON THIS SHEET

U

SCALE:
0    5    10 FEET

ATLANTIS, ADVANCED ENGINEERING PROJECTS

Name of project: BRIDGE' HOUSE
"MARS SPACESHIP"

| Design Engineer: WALTER F. LAREDO | Date: August 2003 |
| Drawing Number: 1400 | Sheet 15 of 25 |

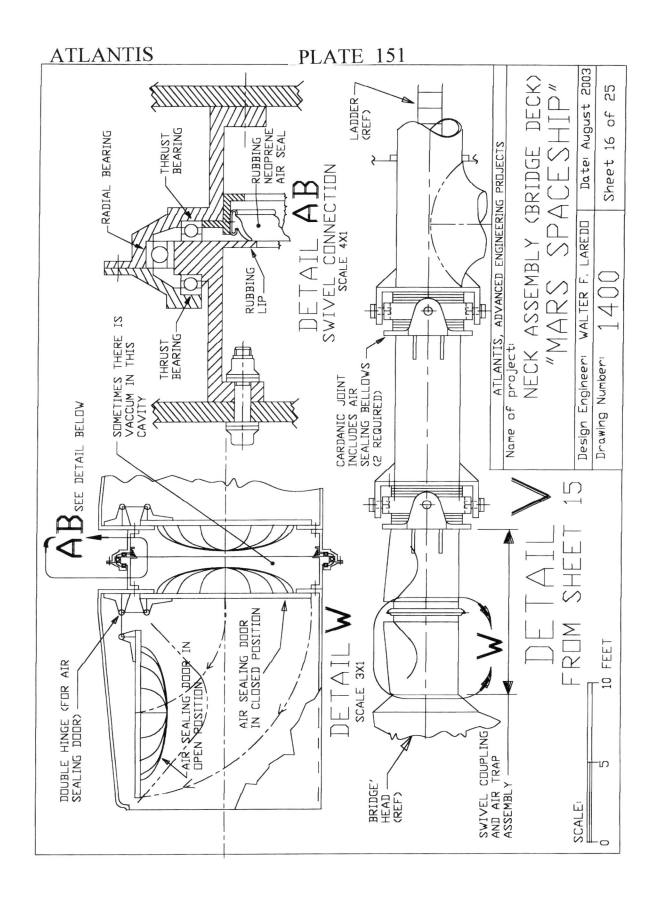

RADIAL BEARING

THRUST BEARING

RUBBING NEOPRENE AIR SEAL

RUBBING LIP

THRUST BEARING

DETAIL AB
SWIVEL CONNECTION
SCALE 4X1

LADDER (REF)

CARDANIC JOINT INCLUDES AIR SEALING BELLOWS (2 REQUIRED)

AB SEE DETAIL BELOW

SOMETIMES THERE IS VACCUM IN THIS CAVITY

DOUBLE HINGE (FOR AIR SEALING DOOR)

AIR SEALING DOOR IN OPEN POSITION

AIR SEALING DOOR IN CLOSED POSITION

DETAIL W
SCALE 3X1

BRIDGE' HEAD (REF)

SWIVEL COUPLING AND AIR TRAP ASSEMBLY

DETAIL V
FROM SHEET 15

W

SCALE:
0    5    10 FEET

Name of project:
ATLANTIS, ADVANCED ENGINEERING PROJECTS
NECK ASSEMBLY (BRIDGE DECK)
"MARS SPACESHIP"

| Design Engineer: WALTER F. LAREDO | Date: August 2003 |
|---|---|
| Drawing Number: 1400 | Sheet 16 of 25 |

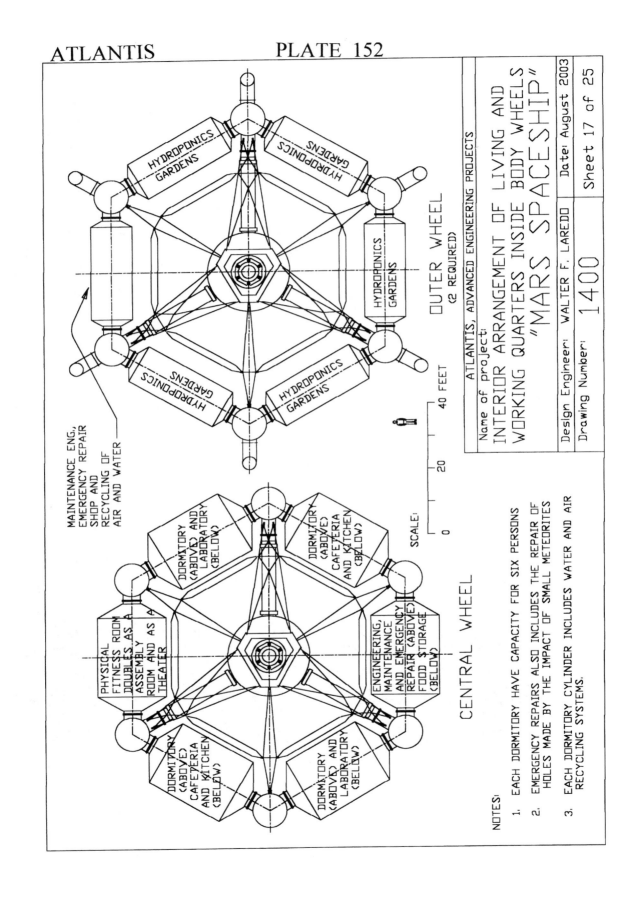

OUTER WHEEL
(2 REQUIRED)

HYDROPONICS GARDENS

HYDROPONICS GARDENS

HYDROPONICS GARDENS

HYDROPONICS GARDENS

HYDROPONICS GARDENS

MAINTENANCE ENG.,
EMERGENCY REPAIR
SHOP AND
RECYCLING OF
AIR AND WATER

CENTRAL WHEEL

DORMITORY (ABOVE) AND LABORATORY (BELOW)

DORMITORY (ABOVE) CAFETERIA AND KITCHEN (BELOW)

PHYSICAL FITNESS ROOM DOUBLES AS A ASSEMBLY ROOM AND AS A THEATER

ENGINEERING, MAINTENANCE AND EMERGENCY REPAIR (ABOVE) FOOD STORAGE (BELOW)

DORMITORY (ABOVE) CAFETERIA AND KITCHEN (BELOW)

DORMITORY (ABOVE) AND LABORATORY (BELOW)

SCALE:

0          20          40 FEET

ATLANTIS, ADVANCED ENGINEERING PROJECTS

Name of project:
INTERIOR ARRANGEMENT OF LIVING AND WORKING QUARTERS INSIDE BODY WHEELS "MARS SPACESHIP"

Date: August 2003

Sheet 17 of 25

Design Engineer: WALTER F. LAREDO

Drawing Number: 1400

NOTES:

1. EACH DORMITORY HAVE CAPACITY FOR SIX PERSONS

2. EMERGENCY REPAIRS ALSO INCLUDES THE REPAIR OF HOLES MADE BY THE IMPACT OF SMALL METEORITES

3. EACH DORMITORY CYLINDER INCLUDES WATER AND AIR RECYCLING SYSTEMS.

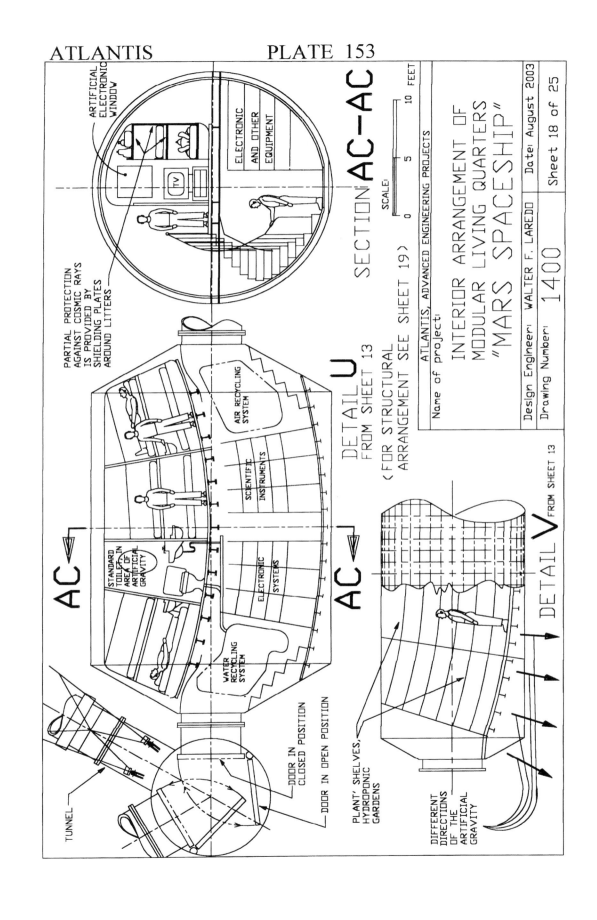

ARTIFICIAL ELECTRONIC WINDOW

PARTIAL PROTECTION AGAINST COSMIC RAYS IS PROVIDED BY SHIELDING PLATES AROUND LITTERS

ELECTRONIC AND OTHER EQUIPMENT

SECTION AC-AC

SCALE:
0    5    10 FEET

DETAIL U FROM SHEET 13

< FOR STRUCTURAL ARRANGEMENT SEE SHEET 19 >

AIR RECYCLING SYSTEM

SCIENTIFIC INSTRUMENTS

ELECTRONIC SYSTEMS

WATER RECYCLING SYSTEM

STANDARD TOILET IN AREA OF ARTIFICIAL GRAVITY

AC

AC

TUNNEL

DOOR IN CLOSED POSITION

DOOR IN OPEN POSITION

PLANT' SHELVES, HYDROPONIC GARDENS

DIFFERENT DIRECTIONS OF THE ARTIFICIAL GRAVITY

DETAIL V FROM SHEET 13

Name of project: ATLANTIS, ADVANCED ENGINEERING PROJECTS

INTERIOR ARRANGEMENT OF MODULAR LIVING QUARTERS "MARS SPACESHIP"

Design Engineer: WALTER F. LAREDO        Date: August 2003

Drawing Number: 1400                     Sheet 18 of 25

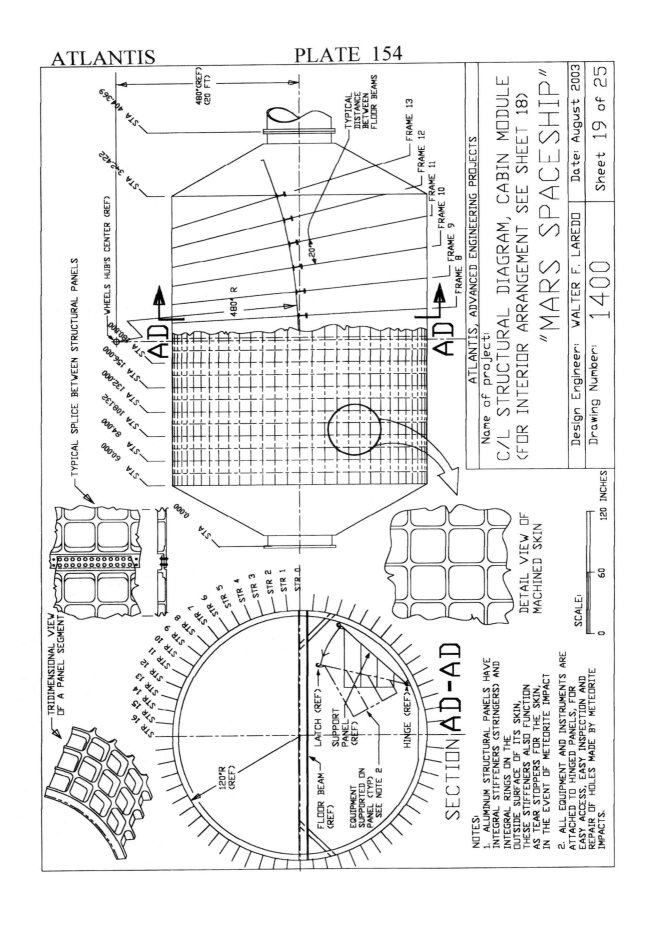

Name of project:
ATLANTIS, ADVANCED ENGINEERING PROJECTS
C/L STRUCTURAL DIAGRAM, CABIN MODULE
(FOR INTERIOR ARRANGEMENT SEE SHEET 18)
"MARS SPACESHIP"

| Design Engineer: | WALTER F. LAREDO | Date: August 2003 |
| --- | --- | --- |
| Drawing Number: | 1400 | Sheet 19 of 25 |

TRIDIMENSIONAL VIEW OF A PANEL SEGMENT

TYPICAL SPLICE BETWEEN STRUCTURAL PANELS

480"(REF) (20 FT)

TYPICAL DISTANCE BETWEEN FLOOR BEAMS

FRAME 13
FRAME 12
FRAME 11
FRAME 10
FRAME 9
FRAME 8

WHEELS HUB'S CENTER (REF)

STA 404.369
STA 342.422
STA 180.000
STA 156.000
STA 132.000
STA 108.132
STA 84.000
STA 60.000
STA 0.000
STA

480" R
20°

DETAIL VIEW OF MACHINED SKIN

SECTION AD-AD

STR 0
STR 1
STR 2
STR 3
STR 4
STR 5
STR 6
STR 7
STR 8
STR 9
STR 10
STR 11
STR 12
STR 13
STR 14
STR 15
STR 16

120"R (REF)

FLOOR BEAM (REF)
LATCH (REF)
SUPPORT PANEL (REF)
HINGE (REF)
EQUIPMENT SUPPORTED ON PANEL (TYP) SEE NOTE 2

NOTES:
1. ALUMINUM STRUCTURAL PANELS HAVE INTEGRAL STIFFENERS (STRINGERS) AND INTEGRAL RINGS ON THE OUTSIDE SURFACE OF ITS SKIN. THESE STIFFENERS ALSO FUNCTION AS TEAR STOPPERS FOR THE SKIN, IN THE EVENT OF METEORITE IMPACT

2. ALL EQUIPMENT AND INSTRUMENTS ARE ATTACHED TO HINGED PANELS, FOR EASY ACCESS, EASY INSPECTION AND REPAIR OF HOLES MADE BY METEORITE IMPACTS.

SCALE:
0    60    120 INCHES

# MARS SPACESHIP PROPULSION SYSTEMS

AT PRESENT TIME THERE IS NO PROPULSION SYSTEM WITH A SPECIFIC IMPULSE OF 4,000 SECONDS OR MORE. A SYSTEM IS NEEDED FOR THE LONG VOYAGES NECESSARY FOR EXPLORING PART OF THIS SOLAR SYSTEM, ONE THAT HAVE MUCH HIGHER SPECIFIC IMPULSE THAN CHEMICAL ROCKETS.

UNIVERSITIES, AEROSPACE INSTITUTIONS AND AEROSPACE AGENCIES OF MOST DEVELOPED COUNTRIES HAVE BEEN DOING RESEARCH ON SPACE PROPULSION CONCEPTS FOR MORE THAN TWENTY YEARS. PERHAPS IT WOULD NOT BE A BAD IDEA TO CREATE AN INTERNATIONAL ORGANIZATION SIMILAR TO THE ONE CREATED FOR THE INTERNATIONAL SPACE STATION TO DEVELOP AND DESIGN THE PROPULSION SYSTEM FOR THIS SPACESHIP, WHICH GROSS WEIGHT IS APPROXIMATELY 2,210,000 POUNDS (ONE MILLION KILOGRAMS).

INSTEAD OF A PROPULSION SYSTEM WITH ONE BIG SINGLE ENGINE, A SAFER ALTERNATIVE WOULD BE A SHIP WITH TWO OR THREE SMALLER PROPULSION SYSTEMS INSTALLED IN PARALLEL.

PROPULSION OPTIONS FOR THIS SPACESHIP ARE ELECTRIC ROCKETS AND NUCLEAR FUSION. THESE OPTIONS WILL BE CHOSEN NOT NECESSARILY FOR THE ENGINE WITH THE HIGHEST PERFORMANCE, BUT FOR THE ONE THAT WILL BECOME FIRST AVAILABLE, AFTER IT HAS BEEN DEVELOPED AND TESTED.

PROPULSION OPTIONS FOR THIS SPACESHIP ARE:

I.  ELECTRICAL ROCKETS:
        ARCJET
        ION ENGINE
        MDP
        SUPERCONDUCTING PROYECTILE (MACROPARTICLE)

II. NUCLEAR FUSION:
        INERTIAL CONFINEMENT FUSION

FOR THE INERTIAL CONFINEMENT FUSION ENGINE IT WOULD BE NECESSARY FOR SCIENTISTS AND AEROSPACE INSTITUTIONS OF THE WORLD TO DEVELOP A COMPACT, RELATIVELY SMALL AND VERY POWERFULL LASER TRIGGER SYSTEM INCLUDING ITS LASER RODS COMPONENTS. THE ONLY INFORMATION THAT I KNOW, AND WOULD SUPPLY TO THE PROPULSION ENGINEERS ARE THE DIMENSIONS OF THE MOUNTING PLATE WHERE THOSE ENGINES SHOULD BE INSTALLED AND ITS BOLTS.

## SUPPLEMENTARY INFORMATION,   AS REFERENCE ONLY

WHEN I WAS A SMALL CHILD, I OVERHEARD A CONVERSATION BETWEEN MY FATHER AND A TOURIST, A SWISS ENGINEER. THE ENGINEER COMMENTED THAT IF THERE ARE ADVANCED CIVILIZATIONS IN THE UNIVERSE THAT HAVE ALREADY ATTAINED SPACE FLIGHT, THE CROSS SECTION OF THEIR ENGINES PROBABLY WOULD LOOK LIKE A CRESCENT MOON. IT WAS A CONCEPT THAT YEARS LATER APPEARED LOGICAL TO ME. THIS IS TRUE BECAUSE AN OPEN EXHAUST WILL NOT CONFINE THE ENERGY YIELD BY THE FUSION OF THE LITHIUM DEUTERIDE PELLETS, IN A CLOSED CHAMBER OR IN A CONVERGING-DIVERGING ROCKET NOZZLE, THE WALLS WOULD MELT. ALSO IT SEEMS LOGICAL THAT THE THICK HOLLOW WALLS FROM AN ENGINE, (WHICH CROSS SECTIONS APPEAR TO BE AS THE SILHOUETTE OF A CRESCENT MOON) WILL ALLOW MORE VOLUME FOR THE REFRIGERATING FLUID. THIS DESIGN WILL OPERATE AS A MODIFIED PUSHER PLATE OF MINIATURE HYDROGEN BOMBS.

I USED THESE CONCEPTS TO DO QUICK SKETCHES OF A FUSION INERTIAL CONFINEMENT REACTOR AS SHOWN IN THE DRAWINGS OF SHEETS 21, 22, 23 AND 24 OF THIS PROJECT, WHICH SHOWS A PARABOLIC FUSION CHAMBER INTEGRATED WITH A SHORT ALSO PARABOLIC EXHAUST.

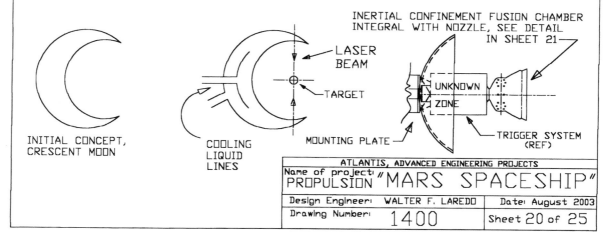

INITIAL CONCEPT, CRESCENT MOON

COOLING LIQUID LINES

LASER BEAM

TARGET

MOUNTING PLATE

INERTIAL CONFINEMENT FUSION CHAMBER INTEGRAL WITH NOZZLE, SEE DETAIL IN SHEET 21

UNKNOWN ZONE

TRIGGER SYSTEM (REF)

| ATLANTIS, ADVANCED ENGINEERING PROJECTS | | |
|---|---|---|
| Name of project: PROPULSION "MARS SPACESHIP" | | |
| Design Engineer: WALTER F. LAREDO | | Date: August 2003 |
| Drawing Number: 1400 | | Sheet 20 of 25 |

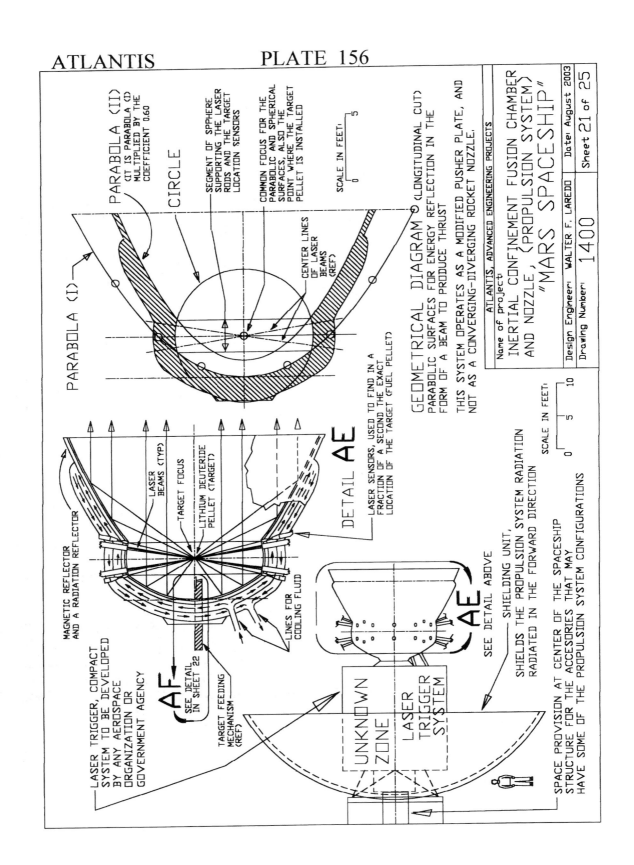

PARABOLA (I)

PARABOLA (II)
(IT IS PARABOLA (I) MULTIPLIED BY THE COEFFICIENT 0.60)

CIRCLE

SEGMENT OF SPPHERE SUPPORTING THE LASER RODS AND THE TARGET LOCATION SENSORS

COMMON FOCUS FOR THE PARABOLIC AND SPHERICAL SURFACES, ALSO THE POINT WHERE THE TARGET PELLET IS INSTALLED

CENTER LINES OF LASER BEAMS (REF)

SCALE IN FEET:
0                    5

GEOMETRICAL DIAGRAM (LONGITUDINAL CUT)
PARABOLIC SURFACES FOR ENERGY REFLECTION IN THE FORM OF A BEAM TO PRODUCE THRUST

THIS SYSTEM OPERATES AS A MODIFIED PUSHER PLATE, AND NOT AS A CONVERGING-DIVERGING ROCKET NOZZLE.

Name of project:
INERTIAL CONFINEMENT FUSION CHAMBER AND NOZZLE, (PROPULSION SYSTEM) "MARS SPACESHIP"

ATLANTIS, ADVANCED ENGINEERING PROJECTS

| Design Engineer: | WALTER F. LAREDO | Date: August 2003 |
| Drawing Number: | 1400 | Sheet 21 of 25 |

MAGNETIC REFLECTOR AND A RADIATION REFLECTOR

LASER BEAMS (TYP)

TARGET FOCUS

LITHIUM DEUTERIDE PELLET (TARGET)

LINES FOR COOLING FLUID

DETAIL AE

LASER SENSORS, USED TO FIND IN A FRACTION OF A SECOND THE EXACT LOCATION OF THE TARGET (FUEL PELLET)

LASER TRIGGER, COMPACT SYSTEM TO BE DEVELOPED BY ANY AEROSPACE ORGANIZATION OR GOVERNMENT AGENCY

AF

SEE DETAIL IN SHEET 22

TARGET FEEDING MECHANISM (REF)

UNKNOWN ZONE

LASER TRIGGER SYSTEM

AE

SEE DETAIL ABOVE

SHIELDING UNIT, SHIELDS THE PROPULSION SYSTEM RADIATION RADIATED IN THE FORWARD DIRECTION

SCALE IN FEET:
0        5        10

SPACE PROVISION AT CENTER OF THE SPACESHIP STRUCTURE FOR THE ACCESORIES THAT MAY HAVE SOME OF THE PROPULSION SYSTEM CONFIGURATIONS

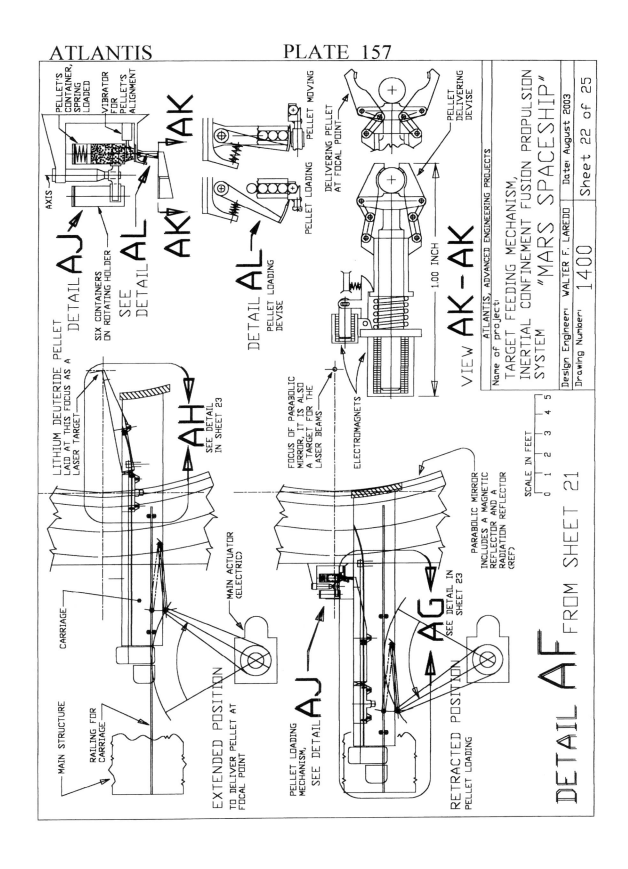

PELLET'S CONTAINER, SPRING LOADED

VIBRATOR FOR PELLET'S ALIGNMENT

AXIS

DETAIL AJ

SEE DETAIL AL

SIX CONTAINERS ON ROTATING HOLDER

DETAIL AK

AK

PELLET LOADING

PELLET MOVING

DELIVERING PELLET AT FOCAL POINT

PELLET DELIVERING DEVISE

DETAIL AL

PELLET LOADING DEVISE

VIEW AK-AK

1.00 INCH

ELECTROMAGNETS

FOCUS OF PARABOLIC MIRROR, IT IS ALSO A TARGET FOR THE LASER BEAMS

LITHIUM DEUTERIDE PELLET LAID AT THIS FOCUS AS A LASER TARGET

AH

SEE DETAIL IN SHEET 23

MAIN STRUCTURE

CARRIAGE

RAILING FOR CARRIAGE

MAIN ACTUATOR (ELECTRIC)

EXTENDED POSITION TO DELIVER PELLET AT FOCAL POINT

PELLET LOADING MECHANISM, SEE DETAIL AJ

AJ

AG

SEE DETAIL IN SHEET 23

PARABOLIC MIRROR INCLUDES A MAGNETIC REFLECTOR AND A RADIATION REFLECTOR (REF)

RETRACTED POSITION PELLET LOADING

DETAIL AF FROM SHEET 21

SCALE IN FEET
0 1 2 3 4 5

Name of project:
TARGET FEEDING MECHANISM, INERTIAL CONFINEMENT FUSION PROPULSION SYSTEM "MARS SPACESHIP"

| Design Engineer: WALTER F. LAREDO | Date: August 2003 |
| Drawing Number: 1400 | Sheet 22 of 25 |

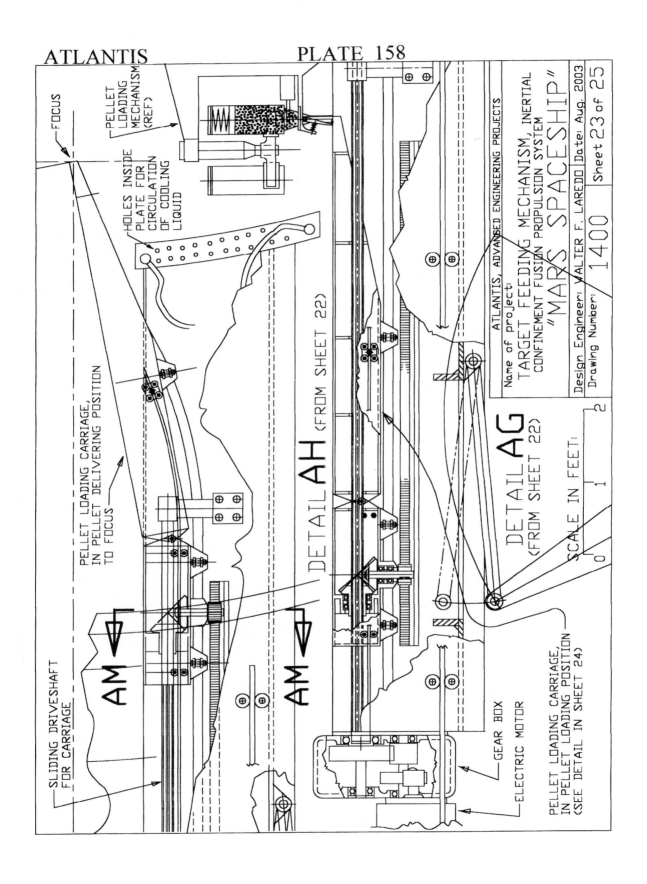

FOCUS

PELLET LOADING MECHANISM (REF)

HOLES INSIDE PLATE FOR CIRCULATION OF COOLING LIQUID

PELLET LOADING CARRIAGE, IN PELLET DELIVERING POSITION TO FOCUS

SLIDING DRIVESHAFT FOR CARRIAGE

AM

AM

DETAIL AH (FROM SHEET 22)

DETAIL AG (FROM SHEET 22)

SCALE IN FEET:

0    1    2

GEAR BOX

ELECTRIC MOTOR

PELLET LOADING CARRIAGE, IN PELLET LOADING POSITION (SEE DETAIL IN SHEET 24)

Name of project:
TARGET FEEDING MECHANISM, INERTIAL CONFINEMENT FUSION PROPULSION SYSTEM
"MARS SPACESHIP"

ATLANTIS, ADVANCED ENGINEERING PROJECTS

Design Engineer: WALTER F. LAREDO | Date: Aug. 2003

Drawing Number: 1400 | Sheet 23 of 25

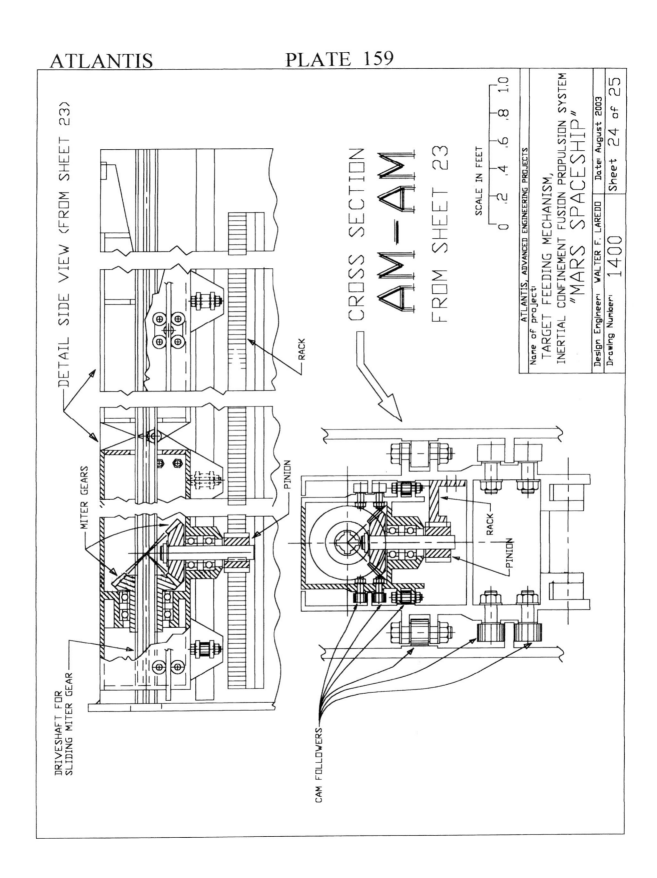

DETAIL SIDE VIEW (FROM SHEET 23)

RACK

MITER GEARS

PINION

DRIVESHAFT FOR SLIDING MITER GEAR

CROSS SECTION AM–AM FROM SHEET 23

RACK

PINION

CAM FOLLOWERS

SCALE IN FEET

0 .2 .4 .6 .8 1.0

ATLANTIS, ADVANCED ENGINEERING PROJECTS

Name of project:
TARGET FEEDING MECHANISM,
INERTIAL CONFINEMENT FUSION PROPULSION SYSTEM
"MARS SPACESHIP"

Design Engineer: WALTER F. LAREDO    Date: August 2003
Drawing Number: 1400    Sheet 24 of 25

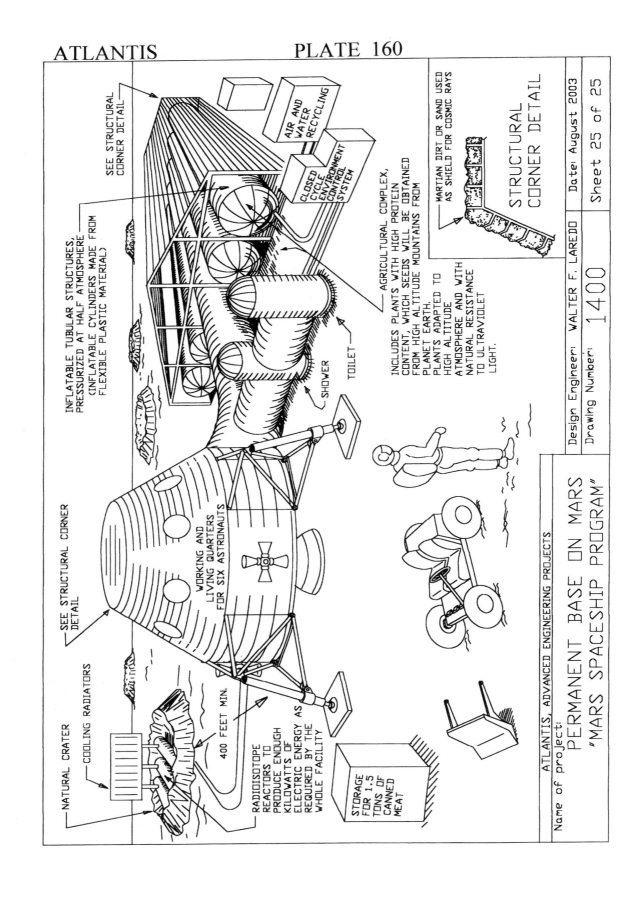

SEE STRUCTURAL CORNER DETAIL

INFLATABLE TUBULAR STRUCTURES, PRESSURIZED AT HALF ATMOSPHERE (INFLATABLE CYLINDERS MADE FROM FLEXIBLE PLASTIC MATERIAL)

AIR AND WATER RECYCLING

CLOSED CYCLE ENVIRONMENT CONTROL SYSTEM

AGRICULTURAL COMPLEX, INCLUDES PLANTS WITH HIGH PROTEIN CONTENT, WHICH SEEDS WILL BE OBTAINED FROM HIGH ALTITUDE MOUNTAINS FROM PLANET EARTH. PLANTS ADAPTED TO HIGH ALTITUDE ATMOSPHERE AND WITH NATURAL RESISTANCE TO ULTRAVIOLET LIGHT.

SHOWER

TOILET

MARTIAN DIRT OR SAND USED AS SHIELD FOR COSMIC RAYS

STRUCTURAL CORNER DETAIL

Date: August 2003

Sheet 25 of 25

Design Engineer: WALTER F. LAREDO

Drawing Number: 1400

SEE STRUCTURAL CORNER DETAIL

WORKING AND LIVING QUARTERS FOR SIX ASTRONAUTS

NATURAL CRATER

COOLING RADIATORS

400 FEET MIN.

RADIOISOTOPE REACTORS TO PRODUCE ENOUGH KILOWATTS OF ELECTRIC ENERGY AS REQUIRED BY THE WHOLE FACILITY

STORAGE FOR 1.5 TONS OF CANNED MEAT

Name of project:

ATLANTIS, ADVANCED ENGINEERING PROJECTS

PERMANENT BASE ON MARS
"MARS SPACESHIP PROGRAM"

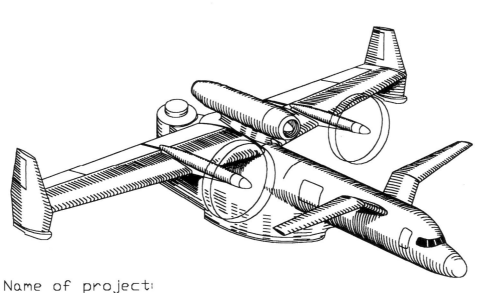

Name of project:

PRELIMINARY DESIGN OF
# CARGO AIRCRAFT WITH NUCLEAR PROPULSION

| | |
|---|---|
| CRUISING SPEED | 292 MPH |
| SERVICE CEILING | FROM 15 TO 5,000 FT |
| RANGE | LIMITLESS, REACTOR HAVE FUEL FOR 10 YEARS OF CONTINUOUS USE |
| OVERALL LENGHT | 108 FEET |
| WING SPAN | 120 FEET |
| WING AREA | 3,180 SQ FT |
| GROSS WEIGHT | 254,400 LB |
| WING LOADING | 80 LB/SQ FT |
| POWER LOADING | 8.48 PER SHP |
| TURBINE OUTPUT POWER | 30,000 SHP = 22,371 KW |
| REACTOR THERMAL POWER | 67,000 KW |
| EFFICIENCY | 33 % |
| REACTOR SHIELDING WEIGHT | 70,000 LB |

FLIGHT
PROFILE:

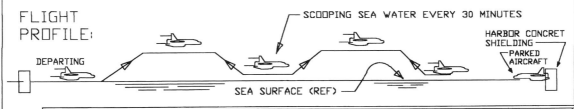

SCOOPING SEA WATER EVERY 30 MINUTES

HARBOR CONCRET SHIELDING

PARKED AIRCRAFT

DEPARTING

SEA SURFACE (REF)

| ATLANTIS, ADVANCED ENGINEERING PROJECTS | |
|---|---|
| Design Engineer: Walter F. Laredo | Date: August 2003 |
| Drawing Number: 1500 | Sheet 1 of 9 |

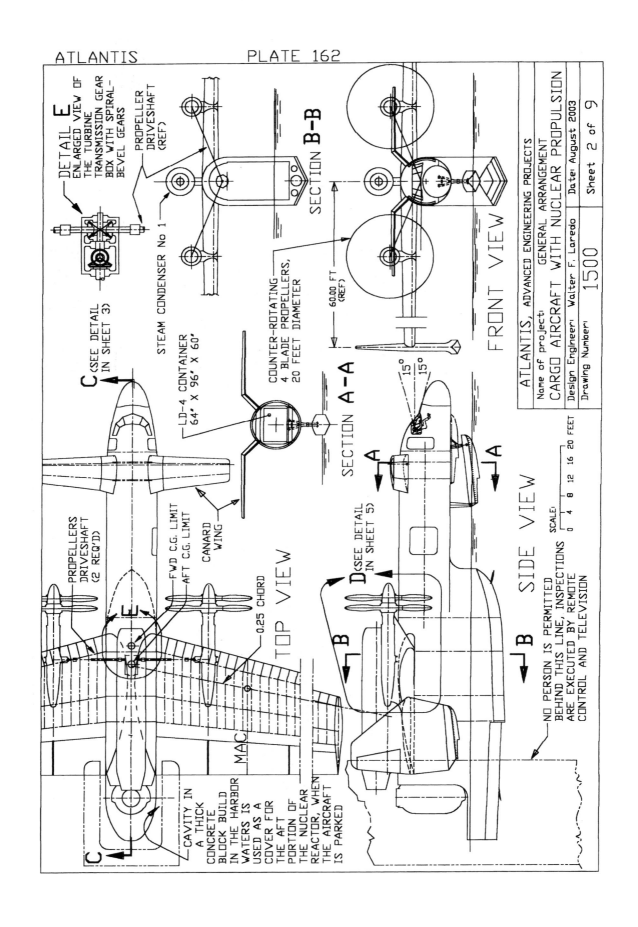

DETAIL E
ENLARGED VIEW OF THE TURBINE TRANSMISSION GEAR BOX WITH SPIRAL-BEVEL GEARS

PROPELLER DRIVESHAFT (REF)

SECTION B-B

STEAM CONDENSER No 1

C (SEE DETAIL IN SHEET 3)

LD-4 CONTAINER 64' X 96' X 60'

COUNTER-ROTATING 4 BLADE PROPELLERS, 20 FEET DIAMETER

60.00 FT (REF)

FRONT VIEW

PROPELLERS DRIVESHAFT (2 REQ'D)

FWD C.G. LIMIT
AFT C.G. LIMIT

CANARD WING

0.25 CHORD

MAC

TOP VIEW

SECTION A-A

D (SEE DETAIL IN SHEET 5)

15°
15°

SIDE VIEW

SCALE:
0   4   8   12   16   20 FEET

NO PERSON IS PERMITTED BEHIND THIS LINE, INSPECTIONS ARE EXECUTED BY REMOTE CONTROL AND TELEVISION

CAVITY IN A THICK CONCRETE BLOCK BUILD IN THE HARBOR WATERS IS USED AS A COVER FOR THE AFT PORTION OF THE NUCLEAR REACTOR, WHEN THE AIRCRAFT IS PARKED

ATLANTIS, ADVANCED ENGINEERING PROJECTS
Name of project: GENERAL ARRANGEMENT
CARGO AIRCRAFT WITH NUCLEAR PROPULSION
Design Engineer: Walter F. Laredo    Date: August 2003
Drawing Number:   1500              Sheet 2 of 9

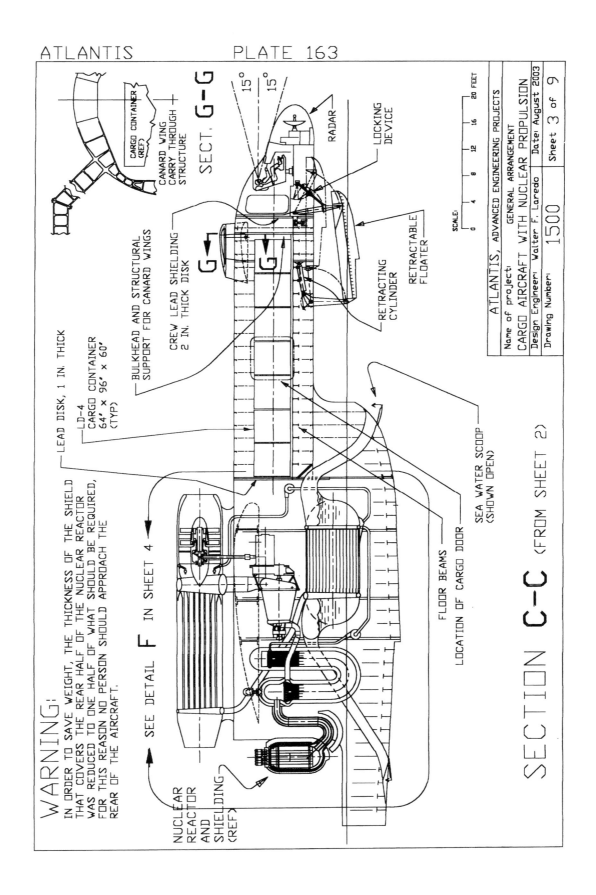

WARNING:
IN ORDER TO SAVE WEIGHT, THE THICKNESS OF THE SHIELD THAT COVERS THE REAR HALF OF THE NUCLEAR REACTOR WAS REDUCED TO ONE HALF OF WHAT SHOULD BE REQUIRED, FOR THIS REASON NO PERSON SHOULD APPROACH THE REAR OF THE AIRCRAFT.

SEE DETAIL F IN SHEET 4

NUCLEAR REACTOR AND SHIELDING (REF)

CARGO CONTAINER (REF)

CANARD WING CARRY THROUGH STRUCTURE

SECT. G-G

15°
15°

RADAR

LOCKING DEVICE

RETRACTABLE FLOATER

RETRACTING CYLINDER

SEA WATER SCOOP (SHOWN OPEN)

LOCATION OF CARGO DOOR

FLOOR BEAMS

BULKHEAD AND STRUCTURAL SUPPORT FOR CANARD WINGS

CREW LEAD SHIELDING 2 IN. THICK DISK

LEAD DISK, 1 IN. THICK

LD-4 CARGO CONTAINER 64" x 96" x 60" (TYP)

SECTION C-C (FROM SHEET 2)

SCALE:
0   4   8   12   16   20 FEET

ATLANTIS, ADVANCED ENGINEERING PROJECTS
Name of project: GENERAL ARRANGEMENT
CARGO AIRCRAFT WITH NUCLEAR PROPULSION
Design Engineer: Walter F. Laredo    Date: August 2003
Drawing Number: 1500    Sheet 3 of 9

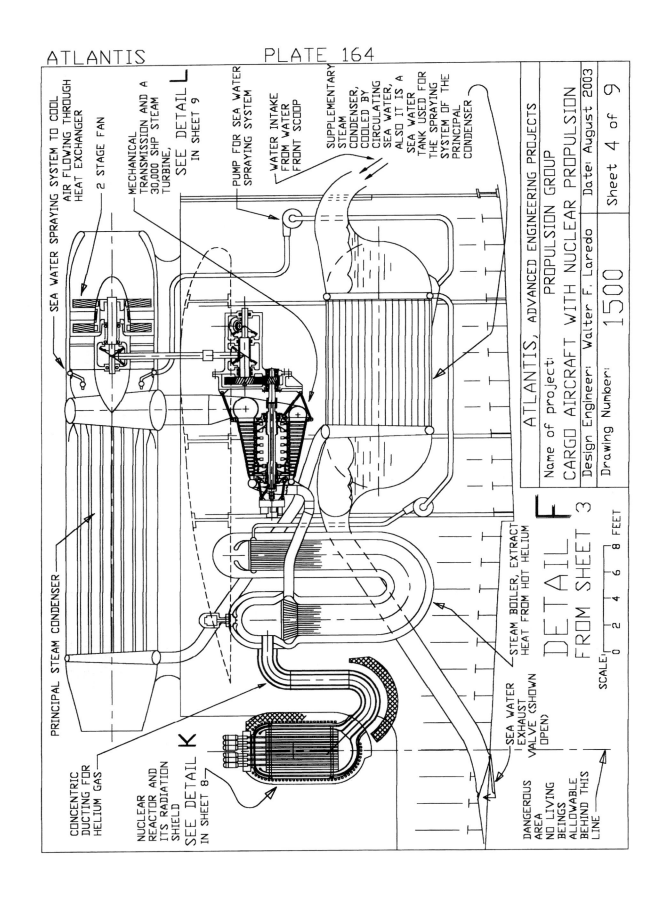

SEA WATER SPRAYING SYSTEM TO COOL AIR FLOWING THROUGH HEAT EXCHANGER

2 STAGE FAN

MECHANICAL TRANSMISSION AND A 30,000 SHP STEAM TURBINE.

SEE DETAIL L IN SHEET 9

PUMP FOR SEA WATER SPRAYING SYSTEM

WATER INTAKE FROM WATER FRONT SCOOP

SUPPLEMENTARY STEAM CONDENSER, COOLED BY CIRCULATING SEA WATER, ALSO IT IS A SEA WATER TANK USED FOR THE SPRAYING SYSTEM OF THE PRINCIPAL CONDENSER

PRINCIPAL STEAM CONDENSER

CONCENTRIC DUCTING FOR HELIUM GAS

NUCLEAR REACTOR AND ITS RADIATION SHIELD

SEE DETAIL K IN SHEET 8

SEA WATER EXHAUST VALVE (SHOWN OPEN)

STEAM BOILER, EXTRACT HEAT FROM HOT HELIUM

DANGEROUS AREA NO LIVING BEINGS ALLOWABLE BEHIND THIS LINE

DETAIL F FROM SHEET 3

SCALE: 0 2 4 6 8 FEET

ATLANTIS, ADVANCED ENGINEERING PROJECTS

Name of project: PROPULSION GROUP
CARGO AIRCRAFT WITH NUCLEAR PROPULSION

Design Engineer: Walter F. Laredo    Date: August 2003

Drawing Number: 1500    Sheet 4 of 9

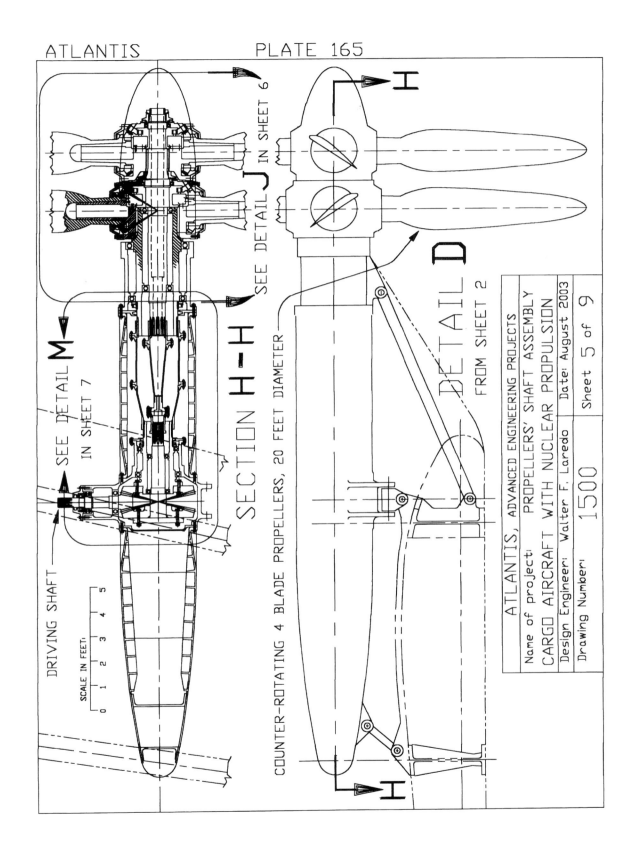

SEE DETAIL J IN SHEET 6

SECTION H-H

SEE DETAIL M IN SHEET 7

DRIVING SHAFT

DETAIL D

FROM SHEET 2

COUNTER-ROTATING 4 BLADE PROPELLERS, 20 FEET DIAMETER

SCALE IN FEET:
0  1  2  3  4  5

| ATLANTIS, ADVANCED ENGINEERING PROJECTS | |
| --- | --- |
| Name of project: PROPELLERS' SHAFT ASSEMBLY | |
| CARGO AIRCRAFT WITH NUCLEAR PROPULSION | |
| Design Engineer: Walter F. Laredo | Date: August 2003 |
| Drawing Number: 1500 | Sheet 5 of 9 |

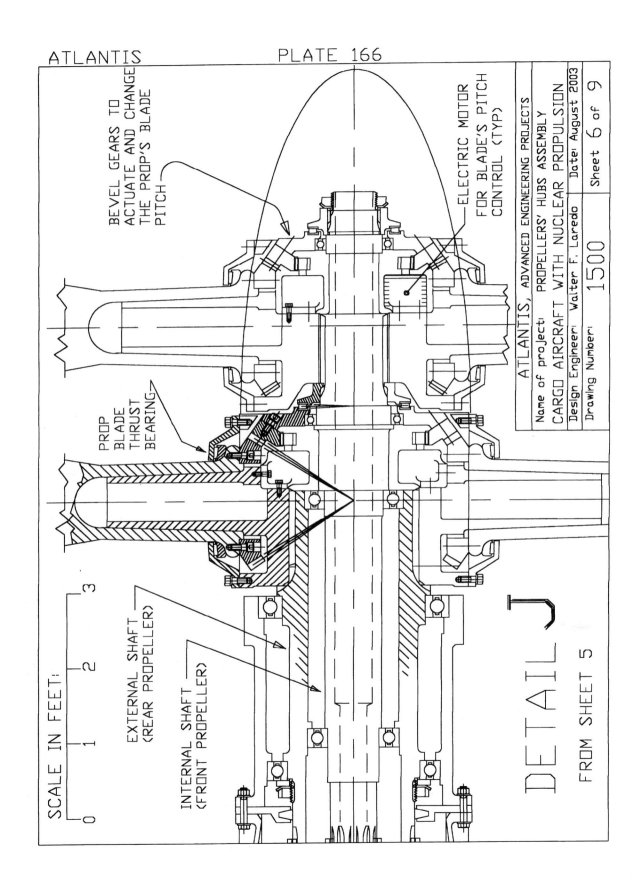

BEVEL GEARS TO ACTUATE AND CHANGE THE PROP'S BLADE PITCH

ELECTRIC MOTOR FOR BLADE'S PITCH CONTROL (TYP)

PROP BLADE THRUST BEARING

SCALE IN FEET:

0   1   2   3

EXTERNAL SHAFT (REAR PROPELLER)

INTERNAL SHAFT (FRONT PROPELLER)

DETAIL J

FROM SHEET 5

ATLANTIS, ADVANCED ENGINEERING PROJECTS

Name of project: PROPELLERS' HUBS ASSEMBLY

CARGO AIRCRAFT WITH NUCLEAR PROPULSION

Design Engineer: Walter F. Laredo          Date: August 2003

Drawing Number:  1500                       Sheet 6 of 9

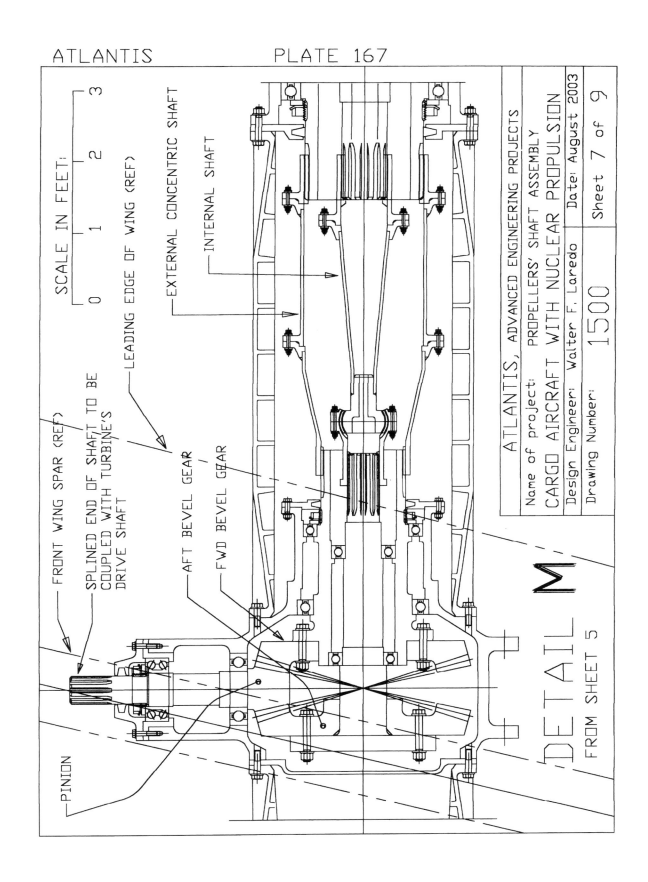

SCALE IN FEET:

3   2   1   0

LEADING EDGE OF WING (REF)

EXTERNAL CONCENTRIC SHAFT

INTERNAL SHAFT

FRONT WING SPAR (REF)

SPLINED END OF SHAFT TO BE COUPLED WITH TURBINE'S DRIVE SHAFT

AFT BEVEL GEAR

FWD BEVEL GEAR

PINION

DETAIL M

FROM SHEET 5

ATLANTIS, ADVANCED ENGINEERING PROJECTS

Name of project: PROPELLERS' SHAFT ASSEMBLY

CARGO AIRCRAFT WITH NUCLEAR PROPULSION

Design Engineer: Walter F. Laredo    Date: August 2003

Drawing Number: 1500     Sheet 7 of 9

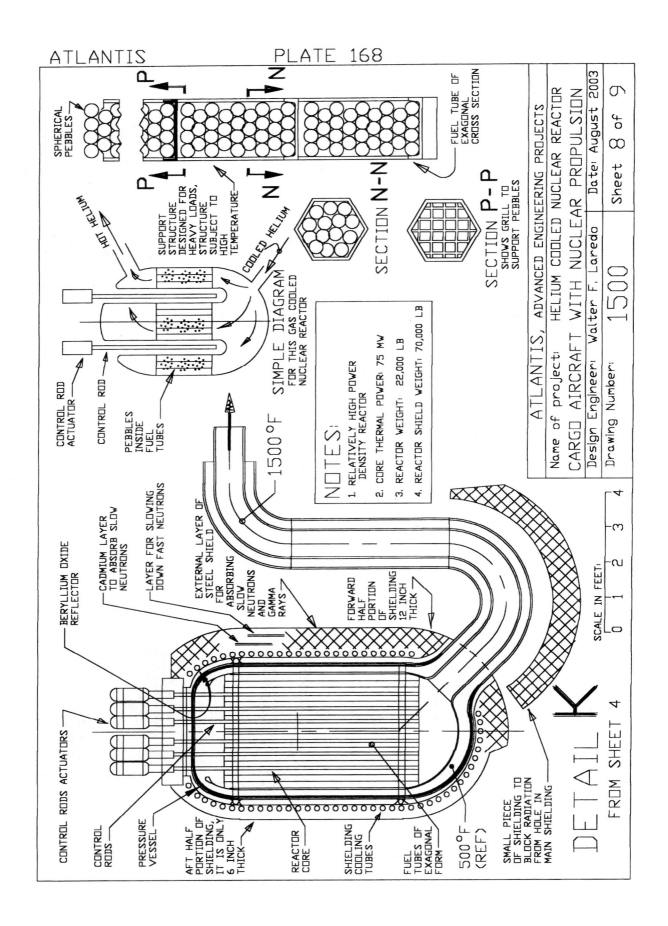

ATLANTIS                    PLATE 168

SPHERICAL PEBBLES

HOT HELIUM

COOLED HELIUM

SUPPORT STRUCTURE DESIGNED FOR HEAVY LOADS, STRUCTURE SUBJECT TO HIGH TEMPERATURE

CONTROL ROD ACTUATOR

CONTROL ROD

PEBBLES INSIDE FUEL TUBES

SIMPLE DIAGRAM FOR THIS GAS COOLED NUCLEAR REACTOR

1500°F

FUEL TUBE OF EXAGONAL CROSS SECTION

SECTION N-N

SECTION P-P
SHOWS GRILL TO SUPPORT PEBBLES

NOTES:

1. RELATIVELY HIGH POWER DENSITY REACTOR
2. CORE THERMAL POWER: 75 MW
3. REACTOR WEIGHT: 22,000 LB
4. REACTOR SHIELD WEIGHT: 70,000 LB

BERYLLIUM OXIDE REFLECTOR

CADMIUM LAYER TO ABSORB SLOW NEUTRONS

LAYER FOR SLOWING DOWN FAST NEUTRONS

EXTERNAL LAYER OF STEEL SHIELD FOR ABSORBING SLOW NEUTRONS AND GAMMA RAYS

FORWARD HALF PORTION OF SHIELDING 12 INCH THICK

CONTROL RODS ACTUATORS

CONTROL RODS

PRESSURE VESSEL

AFT HALF PORTION OF SHIELDING, IT IS ONLY 6 INCH THICK

REACTOR CORE

SHIELDING COOLING TUBES

FUEL TUBES OF EXAGONAL FORM

500°F (REF)

SMALL PIECE OF SHIELDING TO BLOCK RADIATION FROM HOLE IN MAIN SHIELDING

DETAIL K
FROM SHEET 4

SCALE IN FEET:
0 1 2 3 4

ATLANTIS, ADVANCED ENGINEERING PROJECTS

Name of project: HELIUM COOLED NUCLEAR REACTOR
CARGO AIRCRAFT WITH NUCLEAR PROPULSION

Design Engineer: Walter F. Laredo     Date: August 2003

Drawing Number: 1500     Sheet 8 of 9

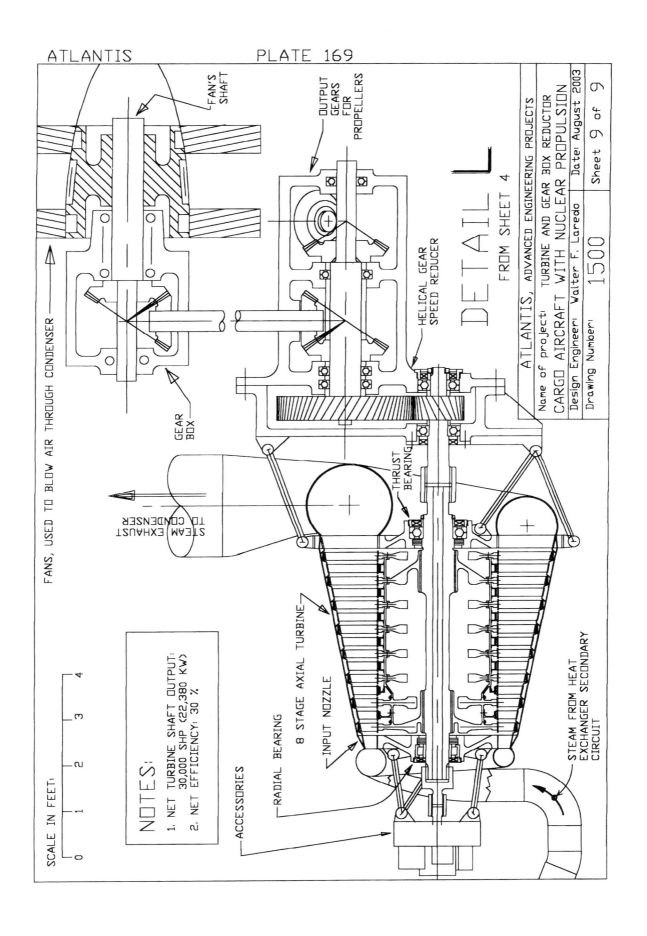

ATLANTIS                    PLATE 169

FAN'S SHAFT

OUTPUT GEARS FOR PROPELLERS

FANS, USED TO BLOW AIR THROUGH CONDENSER

HELICAL GEAR SPEED REDUCER

GEAR BOX

STEAM EXHAUST TO CONDENSER

THRUST BEARING

DETAIL L
FROM SHEET 4

8 STAGE AXIAL TURBINE

INPUT NOZZLE

RADIAL BEARING

ACCESSORIES

STEAM FROM HEAT EXCHANGER SECONDARY CIRCUIT

SCALE IN FEET:
0   1   2   3   4

NOTES:
1. NET TURBINE SHAFT OUTPUT: 30,000 SHP (22,380 KW)
2. NET EFFICIENCY: 30 %

Name of project: TURBINE AND GEAR BOX REDUCTOR
ATLANTIS, ADVANCED ENGINEERING PROJECTS
CARGO AIRCRAFT WITH NUCLEAR PROPULSION
Design Engineer: Walter F. Laredo    Date: August 2003
Drawing Number: 1500              Sheet 9 of 9

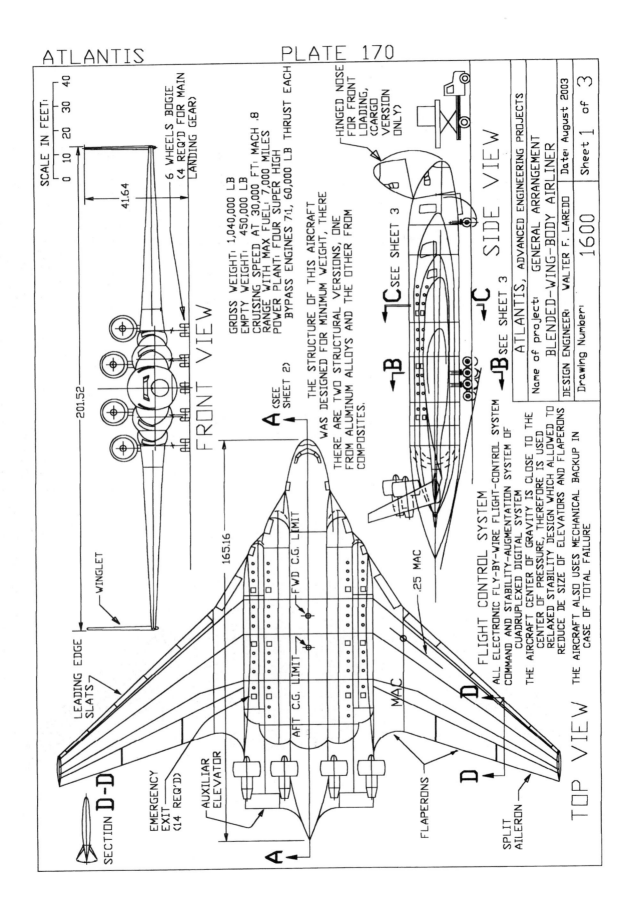

SCALE IN FEET:
0  10  20  30  40

41.64

6 WHEELS BOGIE
(4 REQ'D FOR MAIN
LANDING GEAR)

201.52

WINGLET

165.16

FRONT VIEW

GROSS WEIGHT: 1,040,000 LB
EMPTY WEIGHT: 450,000 LB
CRUISING SPEED AT 30,000 FT: MACH .8
RANGE WITH MAX FUEL: 7,000 MILES
POWER PLANT: FOUR SUPER HIGH
BYPASS ENGINES 71, 60,000 LB THRUST EACH

A (SEE SHEET 2)

THE STRUCTURE OF THIS AIRCRAFT
WAS DESIGNED FOR MINIMUM WEIGHT, THERE
THERE ARE TWO STRUCTURAL VERSIONS, ONE
FROM ALUMINUM ALLOYS AND THE OTHER FROM
COMPOSITES.

HINGED NOSE
FOR FRONT
LOADING,
(CARGO
VERSION
ONLY)

B  C SEE SHEET 3

C

B SEE SHEET 3

SIDE VIEW

ATLANTIS, ADVANCED ENGINEERING PROJECTS

| Name of project: | GENERAL ARRANGEMENT |
|---|---|
| | BLENDED-WING-BODY AIRLINER |
| DESIGN ENGINEER: | WALTER F. LAREDO | Date: August 2003 |
| Drawing Number: | 1600 | Sheet 1 of 3 |

LEADING
EDGE
SLATS

FWD C.G. LIMIT

AFT C.G. LIMIT

.25 MAC

MAC

FLIGHT CONTROL SYSTEM
ALL ELECTRONIC FLY-BY-WIRE FLIGHT-CONTROL SYSTEM
COMMAND AND STABILITY-AUGMENTATION SYSTEM OF
CUADRUPLEXED DIGITAL SYSTEM
THE AIRCRAFT CENTER OF GRAVITY IS CLOSE TO THE
CENTER OF PRESSURE, THEREFORE IS USED
RELAXED STABILITY DESIGN WHICH ALLOWED TO
REDUCE DE SIZE OF ELEVATORS AND FLAPERONS

D

D

THE AIRCRAFT ALSO USES MECHANICAL BACKUP IN
CASE OF TOTAL FAILURE

SECTION D-D

EMERGENCY
EXIT
(14 REQ'D)

AUXILIAR
ELEVATOR

FLAPERONS

SPLIT
AILERON

A

TOP VIEW

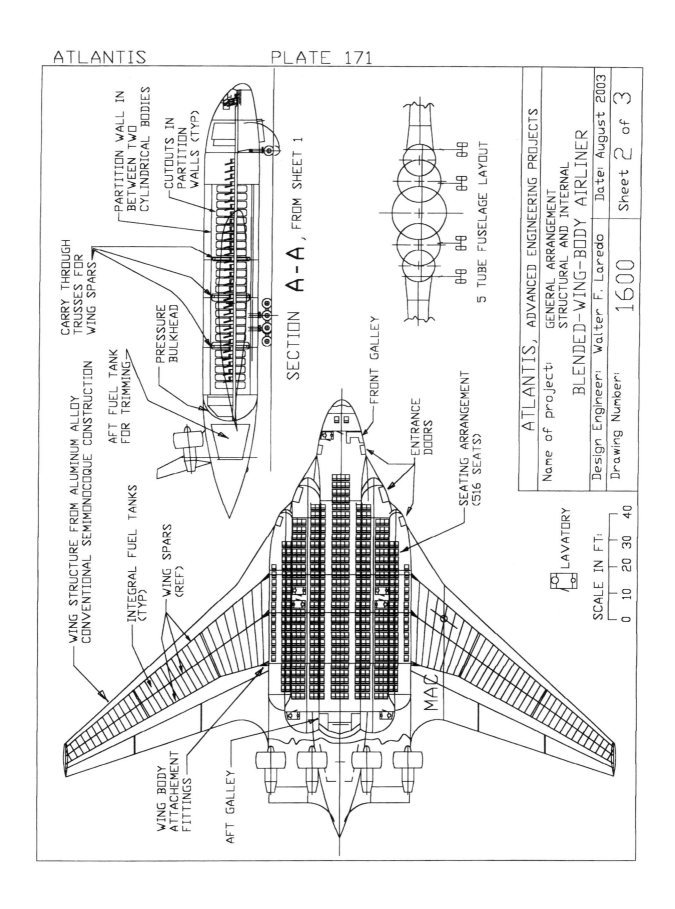

PARTITION WALL IN BETWEEN TWO CYLINDRICAL BODIES

CUTOUTS IN PARTITION WALLS (TYP)

CARRY THROUGH TRUSSES FOR WING SPARS

PRESSURE BULKHEAD

AFT FUEL TANK FOR TRIMMING

SECTION A-A, FROM SHEET 1

5 TUBE FUSELAGE LAYOUT

FRONT GALLEY

ENTRANCE DOORS

SEATING ARRANGEMENT (516 SEATS)

WING STRUCTURE FROM ALUMINUM ALLOY CONVENTIONAL SEMIMONOCOQUE CONSTRUCTION

INTEGRAL FUEL TANKS (TYP)

WING SPARS (REF)

WING BODY ATTACHEMENT FITTINGS

AFT GALLEY

MAC

LAVATORY

SCALE IN FT:

0   10   20   30   40

ATLANTIS, ADVANCED ENGINEERING PROJECTS

Name of project:   GENERAL ARRANGEMENT STRUCTURAL AND INTERNAL

BLENDED-WING-BODY AIRLINER

Design Engineer: Walter F. Laredo    Date: August 2003

Drawing Number:   1600          Sheet 2 of 3

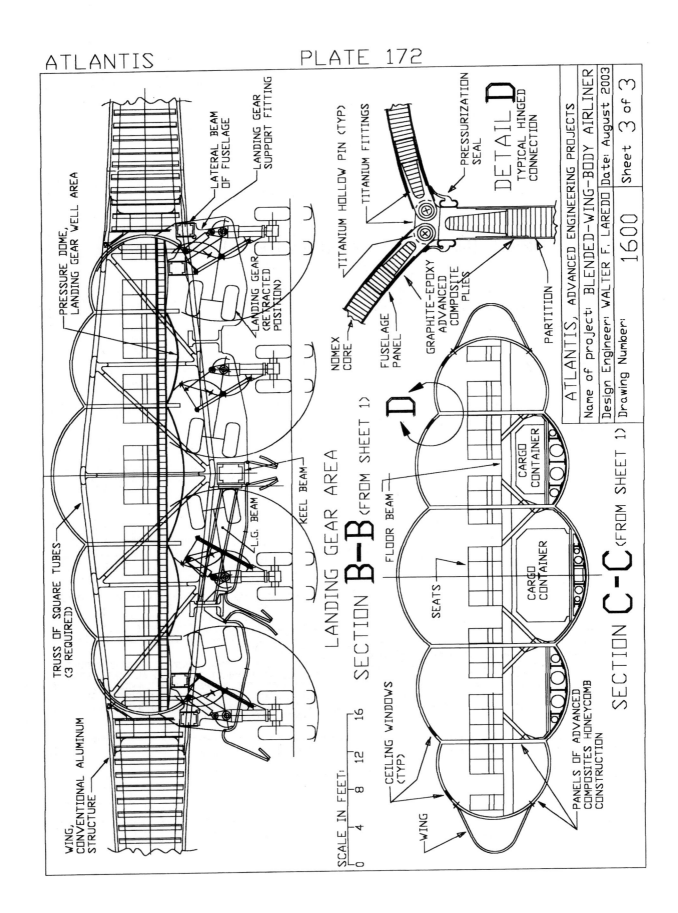

LATERAL BEAM OF FUSELAGE

LANDING GEAR SUPPORT FITTING

PRESSURE DOME, LANDING GEAR WELL AREA

LANDING GEAR (RETRACTED POSITION)

TRUSS OF SQUARE TUBES (3 REQUIRED)

WING, CONVENTIONAL ALUMINUM STRUCTURE

L.G. BEAM

KEEL BEAM

LANDING GEAR AREA

SECTION B-B (FROM SHEET 1)

SCALE IN FEET:
0  4  8  12  16

TITANIUM HOLLOW PIN (TYP)

TITANIUM FITTINGS

PRESSURIZATION SEAL

DETAIL D
TYPICAL HINGED CONNECTION

NOMEX CORE

FUSELAGE PANEL

GRAPHITE-EPOXY ADVANCED COMPOSITE PLIES

PARTITION

D

CARGO CONTAINER

CARGO CONTAINER

FLOOR BEAM

SEATS

CEILING WINDOWS (TYP)

WING

PANELS OF ADVANCED COMPOSITES HONEYCOMB CONSTRUCTION

SECTION C-C (FROM SHEET 1)

ATLANTIS, ADVANCED ENGINEERING PROJECTS
Name of project: BLENDED-WING-BODY AIRLINER
Design Engineer: WALTER F. LAREDO   Date: August 2003
Drawing Number:   1600   Sheet 3 of 3

ENGINEERING PROJECTS
INSPIRED IN THE TALES
AND DREAMS OF
LEGENDARY ATLANTIS

# AEROSPACE PROJECT
## COMMUTING SYSTEM BETWEEN EARTH AND THE INTERNATIONAL SPACE STATION

IN THE 21 CENTURY, SPACE AIRPORTS WILL BE BUSY PLACES WHERE COMMUTING FLIGHTS BETWEEN EARTH AND THE SPACE STATION WILL BECOME ROUTINE WITH THE USE OF EFFICIENT SPACE SHUTTLES AND SCRAM-JET SPACE PLANES, THIS CONMUTING SYSTEM WILL BE USED BY THE SPACE AGENCIES, GOVERNMENTS, SPACE TOURISTS, EXPLORERS, SCIENTISTS AND SPACE INDUSTRIALISTS.

IN THIS PROJECT ARE INCLUDED A SERIES OF DESIGNS, THE FIRST AND SECOND SHEETS SHOWS A SPACE AIRPORT DESIGNED FOR CONTINUOUS OPERATION, WHERE SPACECRAFT COULD BE LAUNCH ONE EVERY TWO HOURS.

A LARGE SPACE STATION WOULD BE NECESSARY TO USE AS AN OUTER-SPACE PORT, USED FOR THE DEPARTURE AND ARRIVAL OF INTERPLANETARY SPACESHIPS, TO OR FROM DIFFERENT DESTINATIONS OF OUR SOLAR SYSTEM, SPACESHIPS THAT ALWAYS WILL REMAIN IN OUTER-SPACE, EITHER, WHEN TRAVELING IN DEEP SPACE OR WHEN ACHORED TO A SPACE STATION. SHIPS THAT NEVER DESCENDS TO THE SURFACE FROM EARTH OR ANY OTHER CELESTIAL BODY.

OUR CIVILIZATION SHOULD CONTINUE WITH EXPLORATION, MOSTLY TO OUR MOON AND MARS, IN ORDER TO LEARN MORE ABOUT OUR SOLAR SYSTEM.

A WORLD CATACLYSM IS DUE, BUT NOBODY KNOWS WHEN IT WILL HAPPENS, MOST LIKELY IT WILL BE LINK WITH THOSE EARTH PERIODIC EXTINCTIONS CAUSED BY COMETS, METEORS AND ASTEROIDS, EVENTS THAT IN THE PAST HAD OBLITERATED MOST EARTH SPECIES, NEXT TIME WHEN A FOREIGN OBJECT WILL APPROACH TO STRIKE EARTH AGAIN, WILL BE THE FIRST TIME WITNESSED BY HUMANS BEINGS,

AND PERHAPS THE LAST TIME BEFORE OUR SPECIES DESAPPEARS.

SOME DAY, THE CONFIRMATION OF AN APPROACHING OBJECT OR COMET MAY DRIVE THE DESPERATE HUMANITY TO ORGANIZE AN INTERPLANETARY EXODUS IN ORDER TO PERPETUATE OUR SPECIES, SENDING THOUSANDS OF HUMAN COUPLES AND WITH THEM SURVIVAL EQUIPMENT, SEEDS OF EDIBLE PLANTS AND FRUITS TO BE PLANTED LATER ON ALIEN LAND, AND ALSO TO SEND ANIMALS THAT COULD MULTIPLY TO BE USED AS SOURCE OF FOOD.

THOSE VOYAGES MAY LAST FROM FEW MONTHS TO MANY YEARS, FINALLY ARRIVING INTO AUTONOMOUS SELF SUPPORTING BASES, LOCATED IN MARS AND IN OTHER MOONS FROM OUR SOLAR SYSTEM, WITH BASES BUILT IN ADVANCED BY ASTRONAUTS SENT IN PREVIOUS MISSIONS.

THE POWERS OF THE WORLD SHOULD JOIN, IN ORDER TO BUILD TWO INTERNATIONAL SPACE-PORTS (ANTE-ROOMS OF THE UNIVERSE) LOCATED IN THE TWO HIGHEST PLATEAUS OF THE WORLD, ONE ON THE TIBET REGION OF THE HIMALAYAS AND THE OTHER IN THE ALTIPLANO PLATEAU OF THE ANDES MOUNTAINS OF SOUTH AMERICA, SPACE-PORTS WHICH SHOULD INCLUDE TILTTED UP LAUNCHING RAMPS WITH EXTRA LONG 2 STAGES CATAPULTS, STEAM GENERATION PLANTS, AND IF GEOTHERMAL SOURCES ARE AVAILABLE, TAPPING HIGH PRESSURE STEAM, THE SPACE BASE SHOULD ALSO INCLUDE LONG LANDING STRIPS LOCATED ON THE SALTED DRY LAKES OF THE PLATEAUS.

HIGH SPEED HANGING MONORAIL TRAINS SHOULD BE USE TO CONNECT THE HIGH ALTITUDE SPACE-PORT WITH THE NEAREST LOW LANDS AND OCEAN PORT WHERE THE LIQUID OXYGEN AND LIQUID HYDROGEN PROCESS AND STORAGE PLANTS ARE LOCATED.

---

## ATLANTIS, ADVANCED ENGINEERING PROJECTS

| | |
|---|---|
| Name of project: | LAUNCHING FACILITY |
| COMMUTING SYSTEM BETWEEN EARTH AND THE SPACE STATION | |
| Design Engineer: WALTER F. LAREDO | Date: Feb. 1997 |
| Drawing Number: 1700 | Sheet 1 of 11 |

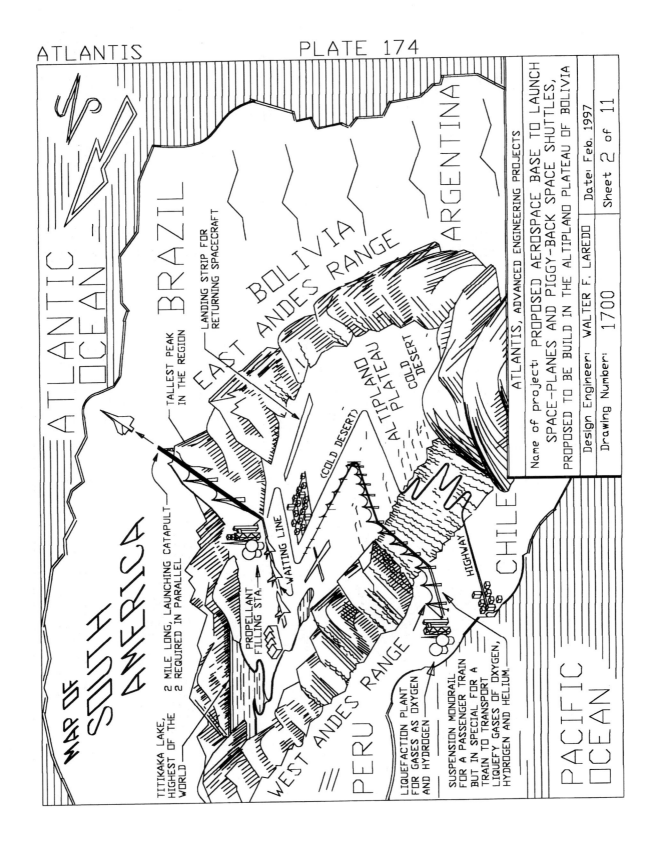

ATLANTIS                    PLATE 174

MAP OF SOUTH AMERICA

ATLANTIC OCEAN

BRAZIL

BOLIVIA

EAST ANDES RANGE

ARGENTINA

CHILE

PERU RANGE

WEST ANDES RANGE

PACIFIC OCEAN

TITICAKA LAKE, HIGHEST OF THE WORLD

2 MILE LONG, LAUNCHING CATAPULT 2 REQUIRED IN PARALLEL

TALLEST PEAK IN THE REGION

LANDING STRIP FOR RETURNING SPACECRAFT

ALTIPLANO PLATEAU

COLD DESERT

(COLD DESERT)

WAITING LINE

PROPELLANT FILLING STA.

HIGHWAY

LIQUEFACTION PLANT FOR GASES AS OXYGEN AND HYDROGEN

SUSPENSION MONORAIL FOR A PASSENGER TRAIN BUT IN SPECIAL FOR A TRAIN TO TRANSPORT LIQUEFY GASES OF OXYGEN, HYDROGEN AND HELIUM.

ATLANTIS, ADVANCED ENGINEERING PROJECTS

Name of project: PROPOSED AEROSPACE BASE TO LAUNCH SPACE-PLANES AND PIGGY-BACK SPACE SHUTTLES, PROPOSED TO BE BUILD IN THE ALTIPLANO PLATEAU OF BOLIVIA

| Design Engineer: WALTER F. LAREDO | Date: Feb. 1997 |
| Drawing Number:  1700 | Sheet 2 of 11 |

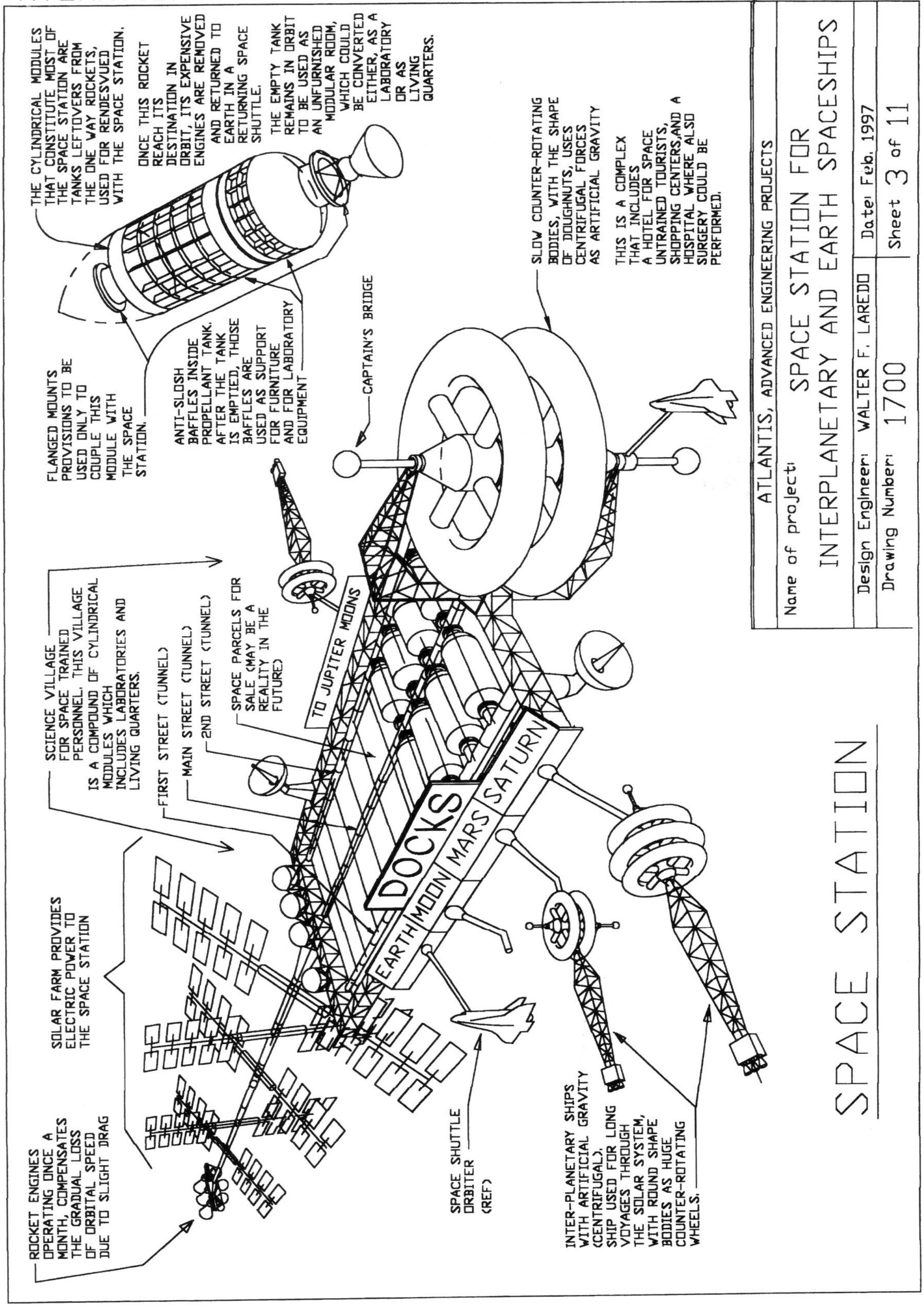

# SPACE STATION

THE CYLINDRICAL MODULES THAT CONSTITUTE MOST OF THE SPACE STATION ARE TANKS LEFTOVERS FROM THE ONE WAY ROCKETS, USED FOR RENDESVUED WITH THE SPACE STATION.

ONCE THIS ROCKET REACH ITS DESTINATION IN ORBIT, ITS EXPENSIVE ENGINES ARE REMOVED AND RETURNED TO EARTH IN A RETURNING SPACE SHUTTLE.

THE EMPTY TANK REMAINS IN ORBIT TO BE USED AS AN UNFURNISHED MODULAR ROOM, WHICH COULD BE CONVERTED EITHER, AS A LABORATORY OR AS LIVING QUARTERS.

FLANGED MOUNTS PROVISIONS TO BE USED ONLY TO COUPLE THIS MODULE WITH THE SPACE STATION.

ANTI-SLOSH BAFFLES INSIDE PROPELLANT TANK. AFTER THE TANK IS EMPTIED, THOSE BAFFLES ARE USED AS SUPPORT FOR FURNITURE AND FOR LABORATORY EQUIPMENT

CAPTAIN'S BRIDGE

SLOW COUNTER-ROTATING BODIES, WITH THE SHAPE OF DOUGHNUTS, USES CENTRIFUGAL FORCES AS ARTIFICIAL GRAVITY

THIS IS A COMPLEX THAT INCLUDES A HOTEL FOR SPACE UNTRAINED TOURISTS, SHOPPING CENTERS,AND A HOSPITAL WHERE ALSO SURGERY COULD BE PERFORMED.

SCIENCE VILLAGE FOR SPACE TRAINED PERSONNEL. THIS VILLAGE IS A COMPOUND OF CYLINDRICAL MODULES WHICH INCLUDES LABORATORIES AND LIVING QUARTERS.

FIRST STREET (TUNNEL)

MAIN STREET (TUNNEL)

2ND STREET (TUNNEL)

SPACE PARCELS FOR SALE (MAY BE A REALITY IN THE FUTURE)

TO JUPITER MOONS

DOCKS

EARTH MOON MARS SATURN

SOLAR FARM PROVIDES ELECTRIC POWER TO THE SPACE STATION

ROCKET ENGINES OPERATING ONCE A MONTH, COMPENSATES THE GRADUAL LOSS OF ORBITAL SPEED DUE TO SLIGHT DRAG

SPACE SHUTTLE ORBITER (REF)

INTER-PLANETARY SHIPS WITH ARTIFICIAL GRAVITY (CENTRIFUGAL), SHIP USED FOR LONG VOYAGES THROUGH THE SOLAR SYSTEM, WITH ROUND SHAPE BODIES AS HUGE COUNTER-ROTATING WHEELS.

| | | |
|---|---|---|
| Name of project: | SPACE STATION FOR INTERPLANETARY AND EARTH SPACESHIPS | |
| Design Engineer: WALTER F. LAREDO | | Date: Feb. 1997 |
| Drawing Number: 1700 | | Sheet 3 of 11 |

ATLANTIS, ADVANCED ENGINEERING PROJECTS

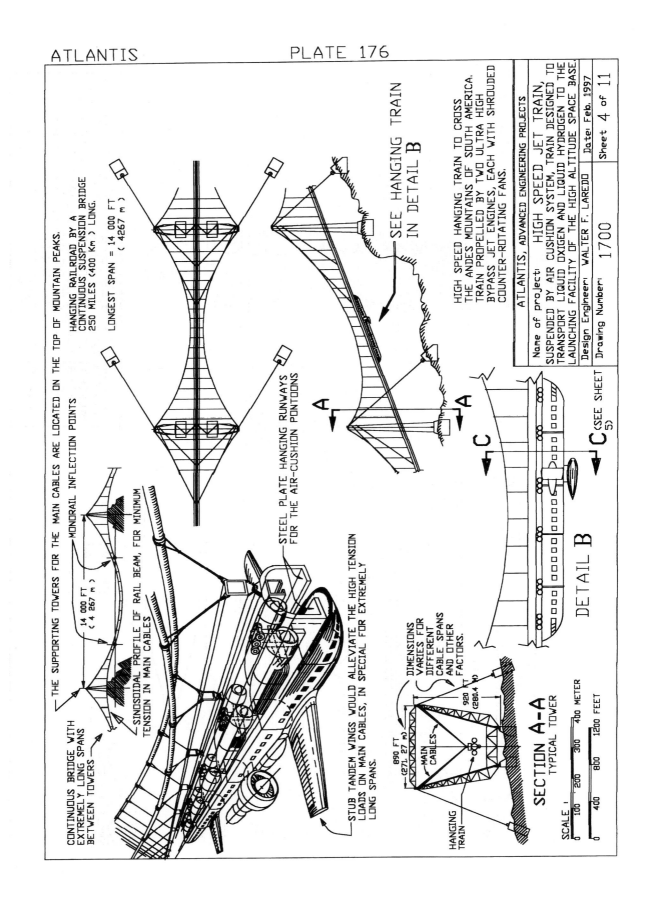

THE SUPPORTING TOWERS FOR THE MAIN CABLES ARE LOCATED ON THE TOP OF MOUNTAIN PEAKS.

MONORAIL INFLECTION POINTS

HANGING RAILROAD BY A
CONTINUOUS SUSPENSION BRIDGE
250 MILES (400 Km) LONG.

LONGEST SPAN = 14 000 FT
( 4267 m )

SEE HANGING TRAIN
IN DETAIL B

HIGH SPEED HANGING TRAIN TO CROSS
THE ANDES MOUNTAINS OF SOUTH AMERICA.
TRAIN PROPELLED BY TWO ULTRA HIGH
BYPASS JET ENGINES, EACH WITH SHROUDED
COUNTER-ROTATING FANS.

14 000 FT
( 4 267 m )

CONTINUOUS BRIDGE WITH
EXTREMELY LONG SPANS
BETWEEN TOWERS

SINUSOIDAL PROFILE OF RAIL BEAM, FOR MINIMUM
TENSION IN MAIN CABLES

STEEL PLATE HANGING RUNWAYS
FOR THE AIR-CUSHION PONTOONS

STUB TANDEM WINGS WOULD ALLEVIATE THE HIGH TENSION
LOADS ON MAIN CABLES, IN SPECIAL FOR EXTREMELY
LONG SPANS.

HANGING
TRAIN

DIMENSIONS
VARIES FOR
DIFFERENT
CABLE SPANS
AND OTHER
FACTORS.

920 FT
(280.4 m)

890 FT
(271. 27 m)

MAIN
CABLES

SECTION A-A
TYPICAL TOWER

SCALE :

| 0 | 100 | 200 | 300 | 400 METER |
| 0 | 400 | 800 | 1200 FEET |

DETAIL B

C (SEE SHEET 5)

ATLANTIS, ADVANCED ENGINEERING PROJECTS

Name of project:  HIGH SPEED JET TRAIN,
SUSPENDED BY AIR CUSHION SYSTEM, TRAIN DESIGNED TO
TRANSPORT LIQUID OXIGEN AND LIQUID HYDROGEN TO THE
LAUNCHING FACILITY OF THE HIGH ALTITUDE SPACE BASE.

Design Engineer:  WALTER F. LAREDO      Date: Feb. 1997

Drawing Number:  1700             Sheet 4 of 11

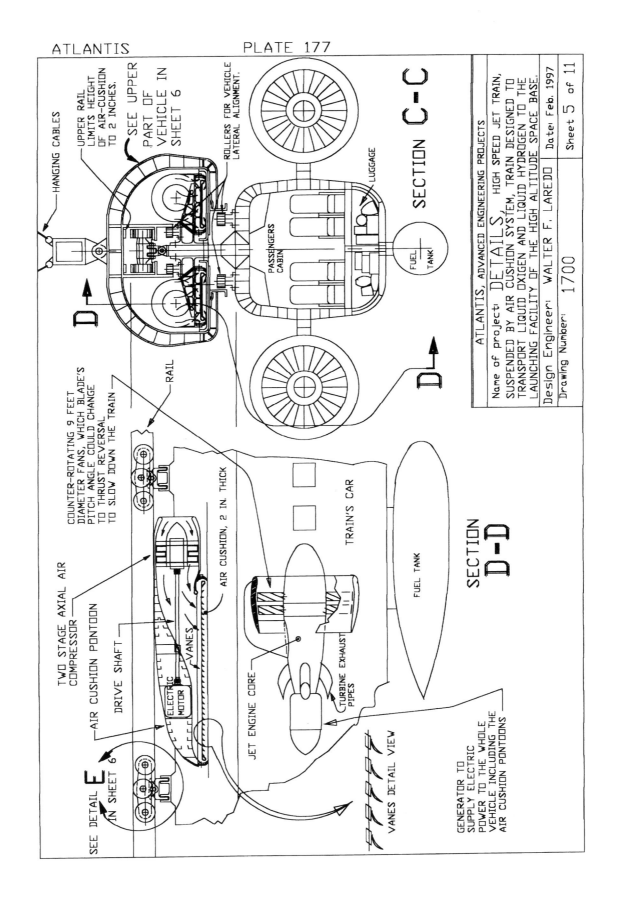

HANGING CABLES

UPPER RAIL LIMITS HEIGHT OF AIR-CUSHION TO 2 INCHES.

SEE UPPER PART OF VEHICLE IN SHEET 6

ROLLERS FOR VEHICLE LATERAL ALIGNMENT.

LUGGAGE

PASSENGERS CABIN

FUEL TANK

SECTION C-C

COUNTER-ROTATING 9 FEET DIAMETER FANS, WHICH BLADE'S PITCH ANGLE COULD CHANGE TO THRUST REVERSAL TO SLOW DOWN THE TRAIN

RAIL

TWO STAGE AXIAL AIR COMPRESSOR

AIR CUSHION PONTOON

DRIVE SHAFT

ELECTRIC MOTOR

VANES

AIR CUSHION, 2 IN. THICK

TRAIN'S CAR

FUEL TANK

JET ENGINE CORE

TURBINE EXHAUST PIPES

SECTION D-D

SEE DETAIL E IN SHEET 6

VANES DETAIL VIEW

GENERATOR TO SUPPLY ELECTRIC POWER TO THE WHOLE VEHICLE INCLUDING THE AIR CUSHION PONTOONS

ATLANTIS, ADVANCED ENGINEERING PROJECTS

Name of project: DETAILS. HIGH SPEED JET TRAIN, SUSPENDED BY AIR CUSHION SYSTEM, TRAIN DESIGNED TO TRANSPORT LIQUID OXIGEN AND LIQUID HYDROGEN TO THE LAUNCHING FACILITY OF THE HIGH ALTITUDE SPACE BASE.

Design Engineer: WALTER F. LAREDO    Date: Feb. 1997

Drawing Number: 1700                 Sheet 5 of 11

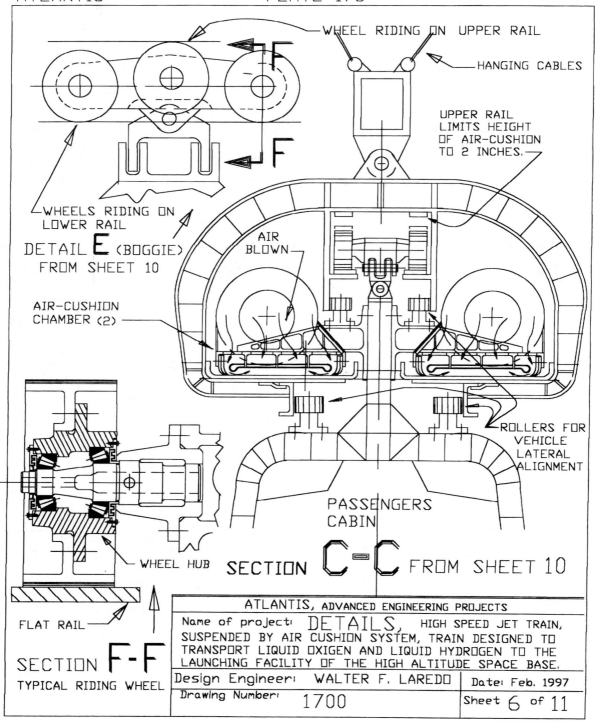

WHEEL RIDING ON UPPER RAIL

HANGING CABLES

UPPER RAIL
LIMITS HEIGHT
OF AIR-CUSHION
TO 2 INCHES.

WHEELS RIDING ON
LOWER RAIL

DETAIL E (BOGGIE)
FROM SHEET 10

AIR
BLOWN

AIR-CUSHION
CHAMBER (2)

ROLLERS FOR
VEHICLE
LATERAL
ALIGNMENT

PASSENGERS
CABIN

WHEEL HUB    SECTION C-C FROM SHEET 10

FLAT RAIL

SECTION F-F

TYPICAL RIDING WHEEL

| ATLANTIS, ADVANCED ENGINEERING PROJECTS | | |
|---|---|---|
| Name of project: DETAILS, HIGH SPEED JET TRAIN, SUSPENDED BY AIR CUSHION SYSTEM, TRAIN DESIGNED TO TRANSPORT LIQUID OXIGEN AND LIQUID HYDROGEN TO THE LAUNCHING FACILITY OF THE HIGH ALTITUDE SPACE BASE. | | |
| Design Engineer: WALTER F. LAREDO | | Date: Feb. 1997 |
| Drawing Number: 1700 | | Sheet 6 of 11 |

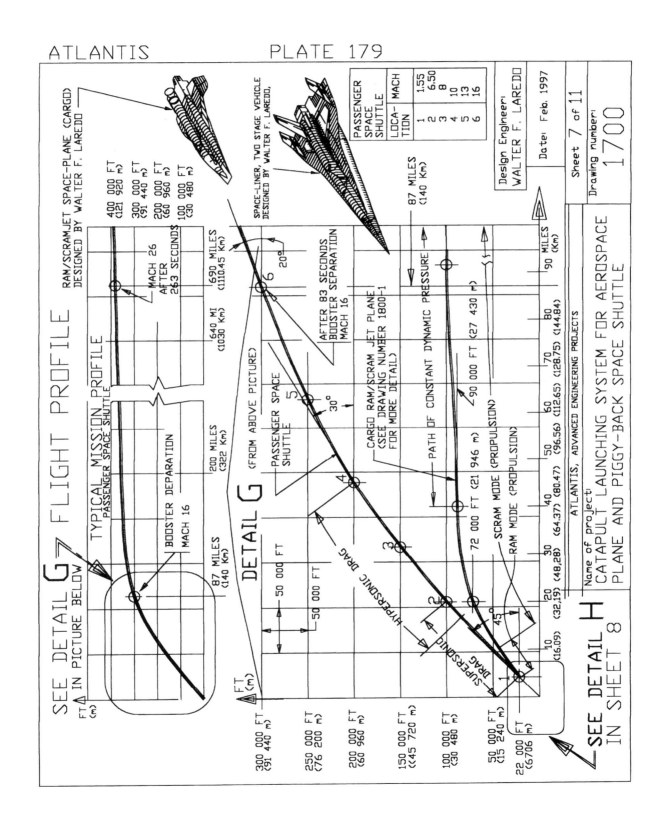

# FLIGHT PROFILE

RAM/SCRAMJET SPACE-PLANE (CARGO)
DESIGNED BY WALTER F. LAREDO

SPACE-LINER, TWO STAGE VEHICLE
DESIGNED BY WALTER F. LAREDO,

SEE DETAIL G IN PICTURE BELOW

TYPICAL MISSION PROFILE
PASSENGER SPACE SHUTTLE

DETAIL G

| PASSENGER SPACE SHUTTLE | |
|---|---|
| LOCA-TION | MACH |
| 1 | 1.55 |
| 2 | 6.50 |
| 3 | 8 |
| 4 | 10 |
| 5 | 13 |
| 6 | 16 |

MACH 26 AFTER 263 SECONDS

690 MILES (1110.45 Km)

640 MI (1030 Km)

BOOSTER DEPARATION
MACH 16

200 MILES (322 Km)

87 MILES (140 Km)

400 000 FT (121 920 m)
300 000 FT (91 440 m)
200 000 FT (60 960 m)
100 000 FT (30 480 m)

(FROM ABOVE PICTURE)

20°

6

5   30°

4

PASSENGER SPACE SHUTTLE

3

2

45°

1

AFTER 83 SECONDS BOOSTER SEPARATION MACH 16

CARGO RAM/SCRAM JET PLANE (SEE DRAWING NUMBER 1800-1 FOR MORE DETAIL)

PATH OF CONSTANT DYNAMIC PRESSURE

90 000 FT (27 430 m)

87 MILES (140 Km)

72 000 FT (21 946 m)

SCRAM MODE (PROPULSION)

RAM MODE (PROPULSION)

HYPERSONIC DRAG

SUPERSONIC DRAG

300 000 FT (91 440 m)
250 000 FT (76 200 m)
200 000 FT (60 960 m)
150 000 FT (45 720 m)
100 000 FT (30 480 m)
50 000 FT (15 240 m)
22 000 FT (6706 m)

FT (m)

50 000 FT

50 000 FT

FT (m)

10  (16.09)
20  (32.19)
30  (48.28)
40  (64.37)
50  (80.47)
60  (96.56)
70  (112.65)
80  (128.75)
90  (144.84)
MILES (Km)

SEE DETAIL H IN SHEET 8

ATLANTIS, ADVANCED ENGINEERING PROJECTS

Name of project:
CATAPULT LAUNCHING SYSTEM FOR AEROSPACE PLANE AND PIGGY-BACK SPACE SHUTTLE

Design Engineer:
WALTER F. LAREDO

Date: Feb. 1997

Sheet 7 of 11

Drawing number:
1700

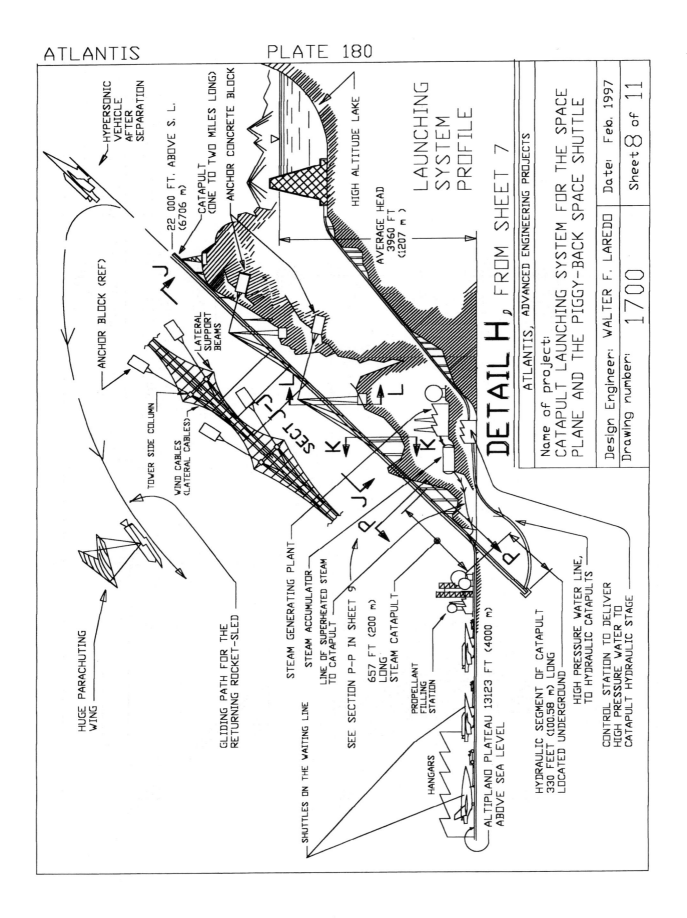

HYPERSONIC VEHICLE AFTER SEPARATION

22 000 FT. ABOVE S. L. (6706 m)

CATAPULT (ONE TO TWO MILES LONG)

ANCHOR CONCRETE BLOCK

HIGH ALTITUDE LAKE

AVERAGE HEAD 3960 FT (1207 m)

ANCHOR BLOCK (REF)

LATERAL SUPPORT BEAMS

TOWER SIDE COLUMN

WIND CABLES (LATERAL CABLES)

HUGE PARACHUTING WING

GLIDING PATH FOR THE RETURNING ROCKET-SLED

STEAM GENERATING PLANT

STEAM ACCUMULATOR

LINE OF SUPERHEATED STEAM TO CATAPULT

SEE SECTION P-P IN SHEET 9

657 FT (200 m) LONG STEAM CATAPULT

PROPELLANT FILLING STATION

SHUTTLES ON THE WAITING LINE

HANGARS

ALTIPLANO PLATEAU 13123 FT (4000 m) ABOVE SEA LEVEL

HYDRAULIC SEGMENT OF CATAPULT 330 FEET (100.58 m) LONG LOCATED UNDERGROUND

HIGH PRESSURE WATER LINE, TO HYDRAULIC CATAPULTS

CONTROL STATION TO DELIVER HIGH PRESSURE WATER TO CATAPULT HYDRAULIC STAGE

SECT. J-J

K

K

J

J

P

P

# DETAIL H, FROM SHEET 7

## LAUNCHING SYSTEM PROFILE

| | |
|---|---|
| Name of project: CATAPULT LAUNCHING SYSTEM FOR THE SPACE PLANE AND THE PIGGY-BACK SPACE SHUTTLE | |
| ATLANTIS, ADVANCED ENGINEERING PROJECTS | |
| Design Engineer: WALTER F. LAREDO | Date: Feb. 1997 |
| Drawing number: 1700 | Sheet 8 of 11 |

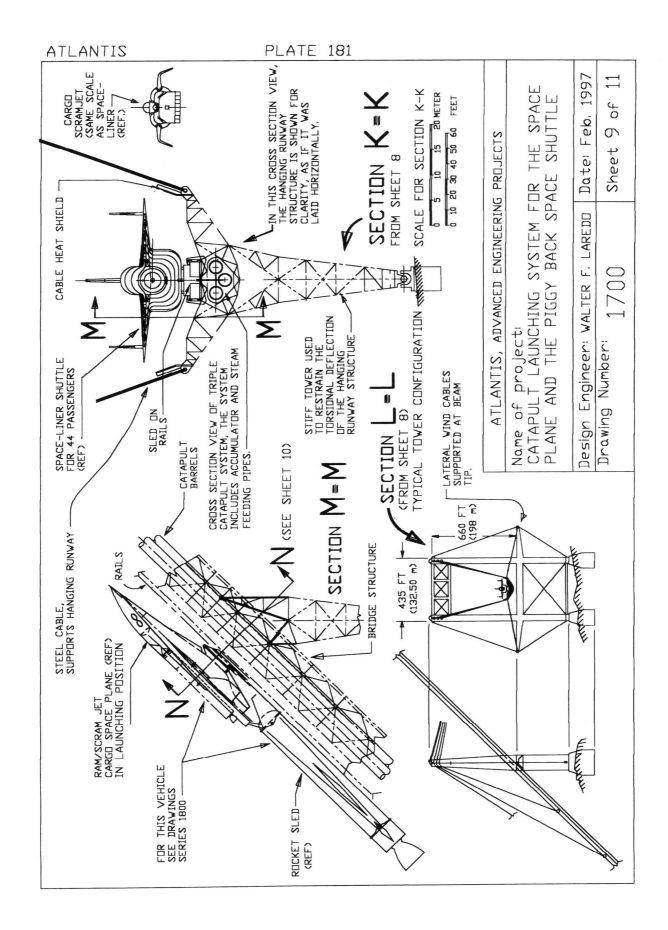

CARGO SCRAMJET (SAME SCALE AS SPACE-LINER (REF.)

CABLE HEAT SHIELD

IN THIS CROSS SECTION VIEW, THE HANGING RUNWAY STRUCTURE IS SHOWN FOR CLARITY, AS IF IT WAS LAID HORIZONTALLY.

SECTION K-K
FROM SHEET 8

SCALE FOR SECTION K-K

SPACE-LINER SHUTTLE FOR 44 PASSENGERS (REF)

SLED ON RAILS

CATAPULT BARRELS

CROSS SECTION VIEW OF TRIPLE CATAPULT SYSTEM, THE SYSTEM INCLUDES ACCUMULATOR AND STEAM FEEDING PIPES.

(SEE SHEET 10)

SECTION M-M

STIFF TOWER USED TO RESTRAIN THE TORSIONAL DEFLECTION OF THE HANGING RUNWAY STRUCTURE

SECTION L-L
(FROM SHEET 8)
TYPICAL TOWER CONFIGURATION

LATERAL WIND CABLES SUPPORTED AT BEAM TIP.

STEEL CABLE, SUPPORTS HANGING RUNWAY

RAILS

RAM/SCRAM JET CARGO SPACE PLANE (REF) IN LAUNCHING POSITION

BRIDGE STRUCTURE

FOR THIS VEHICLE SEE DRAWINGS SERIES 1800

ROCKET SLED (REF)

660 FT (198 m)

435 FT (132.50 m)

ATLANTIS, ADVANCED ENGINEERING PROJECTS

Name of project:
CATAPULT LAUNCHING SYSTEM FOR THE SPACE PLANE AND THE PIGGY BACK SPACE SHUTTLE

Design Engineer: WALTER F. LAREDO    Date: Feb. 1997

Drawing Number:   1700    Sheet 9 of 11

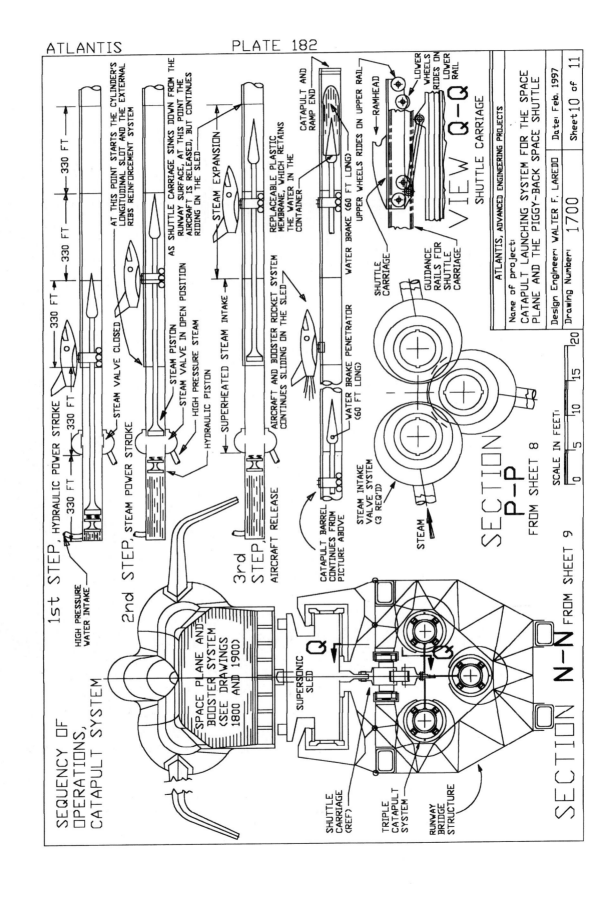

SEQUENCY OF OPERATIONS, CATAPULT SYSTEM

1st STEP, HYDRAULIC POWER STROKE

330 FT
330 FT
330 FT
330 FT
330 FT
330 FT

HIGH PRESSURE WATER INTAKE

AT THIS POINT STARTS THE CYLINDER'S LONGITUDINAL SLOT AND THE EXTERNAL RIBS REINFORCEMENT SYSTEM

STEAM VALVE CLOSED

2nd STEP, STEAM POWER STROKE

STEAM PISTON
STEAM VALVE IN OPEN POSITION
HIGH PRESSURE STEAM
HYDRAULIC PISTON

AS SHUTTLE CARRIAGE SINKS DOWN FROM THE RUNWAY SURFACE, AT THIS POINT THE AIRCRAFT IS RELEASED, BUT CONTINUES RIDING ON THE SLED

STEAM EXPANSION

SUPERHEATED STEAM INTAKE

3rd STEP, AIRCRAFT RELEASE

AIRCRAFT AND BOOSTER ROCKET SYSTEM CONTINUES SLIDING ON THE SLED

CATAPULT BARREL CONTINUES FROM PICTURE ABOVE

WATER BRAKE PENETRATOR (60 FT LONG)

STEAM INTAKE VALVE SYSTEM (3 REQ'D)

REPLACEABLE PLASTIC MEMBRANE, WHICH RETAINS THE WATER IN THE CONTAINER

CATAPULT AND RAMP END

WATER BRAKE (60 FT LONG)
UPPER WHEELS RIDES ON UPPER RAIL

RAMHEAD
LOWER WHEELS RIDES ON LOWER RAIL

VIEW Q-Q
SHUTTLE CARRIAGE

SHUTTLE CARRIAGE

GUIDANCE RAILS FOR SHUTTLE CARRIAGE

STEAM

SECTION P-P
FROM SHEET 8

SCALE IN FEET
0  5  10  15  20

SPACE PLANE AND BOOSTER SYSTEM (SEE DRAWINGS 1800 AND 1900)

SUPERSONIC SLED

Q

SHUTTLE CARRIAGE (REF)

TRIPLE CATAPULT SYSTEM

RUNWAY BRIDGE STRUCTURE

SECTION N-N FROM SHEET 9

ATLANTIS, ADVANCED ENGINEERING PROJECTS

Name of project:
CATAPULT LAUNCHING SYSTEM FOR THE SPACE PLANE AND THE PIGGY-BACK SPACE SHUTTLE

Design Engineer: WALTER F. LAREDO    Date: Feb. 1997

Drawing Number: 1700                 Sheet 10 of 11

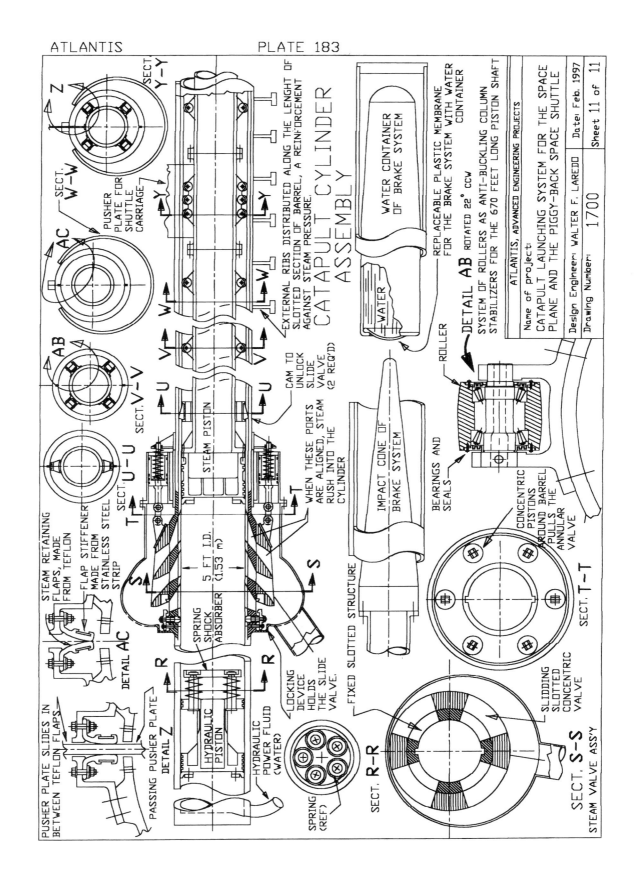

# CATAPULT CYLINDER ASSEMBLY

SECT. Y–Y

SECT. W–W

PUSHER PLATE FOR SHUTTLE CARRIAGE

SECT. V–V

SECT. U–U

EXTERNAL RIBS DISTRIBUTED ALONG THE LENGHT OF SLOTTED SECTION OF BARREL, A REINFORCEMENT AGAINST STEAM PRESSURE.

STEAM PISTON

CAM TO UNLOCK SLIDE VALVE (2 REQ'D)

WHEN THESE PORTS ARE ALIGNED, STEAM RUSH INTO THE CYLINDER

5 FT I.D. (1.53 m)

STEAM RETAINING FLAPS, MADE FROM TEFLON

FLAP STIFFENER MADE FROM STAINLESS STEEL STRIP

DETAIL AC

SPRING SHOCK ABSORBER

LOCKING DEVICE HOLDS THE SLIDE VALVE.

PUSHER PLATE SLIDES IN BETWEEN TEFLON FLAPS

PASSING PUSHER PLATE

DETAIL Z

HYDRAULIC PISTON

HYDRAULIC POWER FLUID (WATER)

SPRING (REF)

SECT. R–R

FIXED SLOTTED STRUCTURE

WATER CONTAINER OF BRAKE SYSTEM

WATER

REPLACEABLE PLASTIC MEMBRANE FOR THE BRAKE SYSTEM WITH WATER CONTAINER

DETAIL AB  ROTATED 22° CCW

SYSTEM OF ROLLERS AS ANTI-BUCKLING COLUMN STABILIZERS FOR THE 670 FEET LONG PISTON SHAFT

ROLLER

IMPACT CONE OF BRAKE SYSTEM

BEARINGS AND SEALS

CONCENTRIC PISTONS AROUND BARREL PULLS THE ANNULAR VALVE

SECT. T–T

SLIDDING SLOTTED CONCENTRIC VALVE

SECT. S–S STEAM VALVE ASS'Y

| Name of project: | | |
|---|---|---|
| ATLANTIS, ADVANCED ENGINEERING PROJECTS | | |
| CATAPULT LAUNCHING SYSTEM FOR THE SPACE PLANE AND THE PIGGY-BACK SPACE SHUTTLE | | |
| Design Engineer: WALTER F. LAREDO | | Date: Feb. 1997 |
| Drawing Number: 1700 | | Sheet 11 of 11 |

## AEROSPACE PROJECT

### DUAL-MODE RAMJET/SCRAMJET VEHICLE

#### PRELIMINARY DESIGN

ENGINEERING PROJECTS
INSPIRED IN THE TALES
AND DREAMS OF
LEGENDARY ATLANTIS

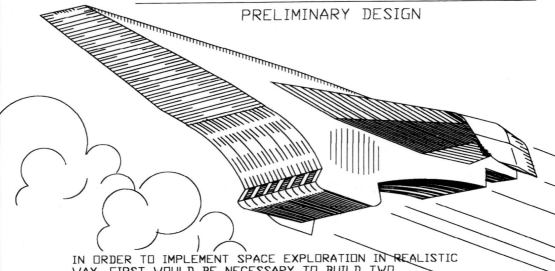

IN ORDER TO IMPLEMENT SPACE EXPLORATION IN REALISTIC
WAY, FIRST WOULD BE NECESSARY TO BUILD TWO
INTERNATIONAL SPACE BASES ON THE TWO HIGHEST PLATEAUS
OF THE WORLD, EACH BASE SHOULD INCLUDE PLANTS TO SUPPLY
STEAM FOR THE CATAPULTS, ALSO SHOULD HAVE LONG LANDING
STRIPS ON THE PLATEAUS' DRIED SALTED LAKES, ALSO EACH
BASE SHOULD INCLUDE A TILTED LAUNCHING RAMP WITH AN
EXTRALONG TWO STAGED CATAPULT, A HYDRAULIC STAGE
FOLLOWED BY A STEAM ONE.

NOTE: FOR CLARITY IN THE FOLLOWING DRAWINGS WAS NOT SHOWN THE
INTERNAL INSULATION OF THE EXTERNAL STRUCTURE AND THE FOAM INSULATION
THAT COVERS THE TANKS AND OTHER CRYOGENIC COMPONENTS.

ATLANTIS, ADVANCED ENGINEERING PROJECTS

Name of project:

# HYPERSONIC SPACE PLANE (SCRAMJET)

FOR CARGO TRANSPORTATION SYSTEM IN BETWEEN EARTH AND THE SPACE STATION

| Design Engineer: WALTER F. LAREDO | Date: Feb. 1997 |
|---|---|
| Drawing Number: 1800 | Sheet 1 of 21 |

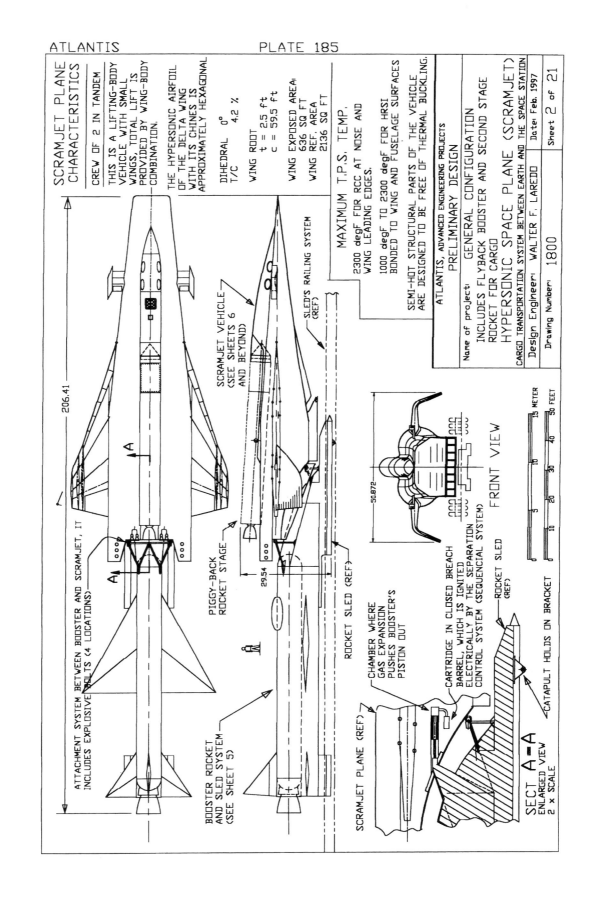

## SCRAMJET PLANE CHARACTERISTICS

CREW OF 2 IN TANDEM

THIS IS A LIFTING-BODY VEHICLE WITH SMALL WINGS. TOTAL LIFT IS PROVIDED BY WING-BODY COMBINATION.

THE HYPERSONIC AIRFOIL OF THE DELTA WING WITH ITS CHINES IS APPROXIMATELY HEXAGONAL.

DIHEDRAL      0°
T/C           4.2 %

WING ROOT
t = 2.5 ft
c = 59.5 ft

WING EXPOSED AREA: 636 SQ FT
WING REF. AREA    2136 SQ FT

MAXIMUM T.P.S. TEMP.

2300 degF FOR RCC AT NOSE AND WING LEADING EDGES.

1000 degF TO 2300 degF FOR HRSI BONDED TO WING AND FUSELAGE SURFACES

SEMI-HOT STRUCTURAL PARTS OF THE VEHICLE ARE DESIGNED TO BE FREE OF THERMAL BUCKLING.

ATLANTIS, ADVANCED ENGINEERING PROJECTS

PRELIMINARY DESIGN

Name of project: GENERAL CONFIGURATION

INCLUDES FLYBACK BOOSTER AND SECOND STAGE ROCKET FOR CARGO

HYPERSONIC SPACE PLANE (SCRAMJET)

CARGO TRANSPORTATION SYSTEM BETWEEN EARTH AND THE SPACE STATION

Design Engineer: WALTER F. LAREDO    Date: Feb. 1997

Drawing Number: 1800    Sheet 2 of 21

206.41

ATTACHMENT SYSTEM BETWEEN BOOSTER AND SCRAMJET, IT INCLUDES EXPLOSIVE BOLTS (4 LOCATIONS)

A

A

SCRAMJET VEHICLE (SEE SHEETS 6 AND BEYOND)

SLED'S RAILING SYSTEM (REF)

PIGGY-BACK ROCKET STAGE

29.54

BOOSTER ROCKET AND SLED SYSTEM (SEE SHEET 5)

ROCKET SLED (REF)

CHAMBER WHERE GAS EXPANSION PUSHES BOOSTER'S PISTON OUT

CARTRIDGE IN CLOSED BREACH BARREL, WHICH IS IGNITED ELECTRICALLY BY THE SEPARATION CONTROL SYSTEM (SEQUENCIAL SYSTEM)

SCRAMJET PLANE (REF)

50.872

ROCKET SLED (REF)

CATAPULT HOLDS ON BRACKET

FRONT VIEW

SECT A-A
ENLARGED VIEW
2 x SCALE

15 METER
50 FEET

## WEIGHTS

| | |
|---|---|
| PAYLOAD | 4 000 LB |
| PIGGY-BACK ROCKET WITH PAYLOAD | 31 000 LB |
| EMPTY WEIGHT OF SCRAMJET PLANE AT LANDING | 170 511 LB |
| LAUNCHING WEIGHT OF SCRAMJET PLANE WITH PIGGY-BACK ROCKET AND PAYLOAD | 246 000 LB |
| WEIGHT OF THE SRB | 270 000 LB |
| WEIGHT OF SLED INCLUDING SRB | 290 000 LB |
| TOTAL LAUNCHING WEIGHT OF COMPOUND VEHICLE | 536 000 LB |

### PROPELLANT WEIGHT

| | | |
|---|---|---|
| SCRAMJET PLANE | LH2 | 38 489 LB |
| AUX.TANK | LO2 | 6 000 LB |
| | | 44 489 LB |
| ROCKET (SECOND STAGE) | LH2 | 3 090 LB |
| | LO2 | 18 435 LB |
| | | 21 525 LB |

L/W AT LAUNCHING IS APPROXIMATELY 1.2

---

ATLANTIS, ADVANCED ENGINEERING PROJECTS

## PRELIMINARY DESIGN

Name of project:
GENERAL ARRANGEMENT, INCLUDES FLYBACK BOOSTER AND SECOND STAGE CARGO ROCKET

### HYPERSONIC SPACE PLANE (SCRAMJET)

CARGO TRANSPORTATION SYSTEM BETWEEN EARTH AND THE SPACE STATION

Design Engineer: WALTER F. LAREDO

Date: Feb. 1997

Drawing Number: 1800    Sheet 3 of 21

---

## FLIGHT CONTROL SYSTEM

ALL ELECTRONIC FLY-BY-WIRE FLIGHT-CONTROL SYSTEM.
COMMAND AND STABILITY-AUGMENTATION SYSTEM OF CUADRUPLEXED DIGITAL SYSTEM.
THE AIRCRAFT CENTER OF GRAVITY IS CLOSE TO THE CENTER OF PRESSURE, THEREFORE IS USED RELAXED STABILITY DESIGN WHICH WILL ALLOW

THE USE OF RELATIVELY SMALL SIZE ELEVATORS AND FLAPERONS.

THE FLIGHT CONTROL SYSTEM ALSO CONTROLS THE REACTION CONTROL SYSTEM AT HIGH ALTITUDE WHERE AERODYNAMIC CONTROL SURFACES ARE NOT EFFICIENT.

THIS SCRAMJET PLANE ALSO USES SOME MECHANICAL BACKUP IN CASE OF TOTAL FAILURE.
MOST MECHANISMS AND AERODYNAMIC SURFACES ARE OPERATED BY ROTARY ACTUATORS.

## PROPULSION SYSTEM AND SPECIFIC IMPULSES

AT TAKE-OFF THE VEHICLE SLIDES ON A SLED, ON A TILT 1.5 TO 2 MILES LONG RAMP, THE VEHICLE IS INITIALLY LAUNCH BY A HYDRAULIC CATAPULT, THEN FOLLOWED BY THE STEAM CATAPULT, THE LAUNCHING STARTS AFTER THE SRB WAS IGNITED.

THE BOOSTER HAVE A THRUST OF 650 000 LB AND A SPECIFIC IMPULSE OF 260 SECONDS.

THE MAIN PROPULSION SYSTEM OF THE HYPERSONIC PLANE IS PROVIDED BY A CLUSTER OF 8 DUAL-MODE RAMJET/SCRAMJET ENGINE MODULES, WITH A TOTAL THRUST OF 460 000 LB AT LIFT-OFF FROM A HIGH ALTITUDE BASE AT THE ALTIPLANO PLATEAU IN THE ANDES MOUNTAINS.

THEORETICAL SPECIFIC IMPULSE OF THE AEROSPACE PLANE.

RAMJET MODE AT 40 000 FT AND M3, $Isp = 3300$ SEC.
SCRAMJET MODE:
AT 100 000 FT AND MACH 5, $Isp = 3000$ SEC
AT 100 000 FT AND MACH 12, $Isp = 1900$ SEC

HOWEVER IN PRACTICE WITH THE REAL VEHICLE
$Isp = 1500$ to $2000$ SEC.

SECOND STAGE ROCKET
THRUST IN VACCUM : 55 000 LB.
SPECIFIC IMPULSE : 450 SECONDS

---

## VERTICAL STABILIZERS

TWIN TYPE WITH DOUBLE WEDGE CROSS SECTIONS.

AREA, EACH =131.25 SQ FT
TOTAL AREA = 262.50 SQ FT
MOMENT ARM = $lvs$ = 25 FT

$\bar{V}s$ = VOLUME COEFFICIENT (VERT. STABILIZER)

$$\bar{V}s = \frac{lvs \times Svs}{b \times Sw} = 0.06$$

DESIGN C.G. RANGE FROM       TO       % M.A.C.

## DESIGN SPEEDS

AT LAUNCHING FROM CATAPULT (A SPECIAL CATAPULT 1650 FT LONG)       300 MPH

AT THE POINT WHEN SCRAMJET PLANE SEPARATES FROM BOOSTER       MACH 3.3

AT THE POINT WHEN PIGGY-BACK ROCKET SEPARATES FROM SCRAMJET PLANE       MACH 12

ROCKET MAX. MACH       MACH 26

MINIMUM LANDING SPEED OF SCRAMJET PLANE (0.0 FUEL)       175 MPH

## RANGE FACTOR

(M x (L/D))/ S.F.C.

25 TO 35

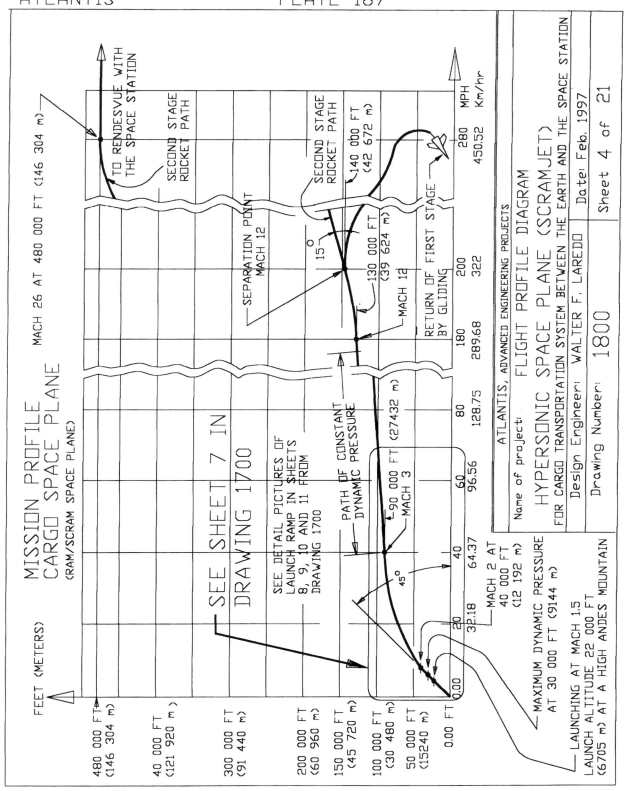

MISSION PROFILE
CARGO SPACE PLANE
(RAM/SCRAM SPACE PLANE)

MACH 26 AT 480 000 FT (146 304 m)

TO RENDESVUE WITH
THE SPACE STATION

SECOND STAGE
ROCKET PATH

SEPARATION POINT
MACH 12

SECOND STAGE
ROCKET PATH

140 000 FT
(42 672 m)

15°

130 000 FT
(39 624 m)

MACH 18

RETURN OF FIRST STAGE
BY GLIDING

SEE SHEET 7 IN
DRAWING 1700

SEE DETAIL PICTURES OF
LAUNCH RAMP IN SHEETS
8, 9, 10 AND 11 FROM
DRAWING 1700

PATH OF CONSTANT
DYNAMIC PRESSURE

90 000 FT (27432 m)
MACH 3

45°

MACH 2 AT
40 000 FT
(12 192 m)

MAXIMUM DYNAMIC PRESSURE
AT 30 000 FT (9144 m)

LAUNCHING AT MACH 1.5
LAUNCH ALTITUDE 22 000 FT
(6705 m) AT A HIGH ANDES MOUNTAIN

FEET (METERS)

480 000 FT
(146 304 m)

40 000 FT
(121 920 m )

300 000 FT
(91 440 m)

200 000 FT
(60 960 m)

150 000 FT
(45 720 m)

100 000 FT
(30 480 m)

50 000 FT
(15240 m)

0.00 FT

| | | MPH | | |
|---|---|---|---|---|
| 0.00 | 20 | 40 | 60 | 80 | 180 | 200 | 280 |
| | 32.18 | 64.37 | 96.56 | 128.75 | 289.68 | 322 | 450.52 Km/hr |

ATLANTIS, ADVANCED ENGINEERING PROJECTS

| Name of project: | FLIGHT PROFILE DIAGRAM |
|---|---|
| | HYPERSONIC SPACE PLANE (SCRAMJET) |
| | FOR CARGO TRANSPORTATION SYSTEM BETWEEN THE EARTH AND THE SPACE STATION |
| Design Engineer: WALTER F. LAREDO | Date: Feb. 1997 |
| Drawing Number: 1800 | Sheet 4 of 21 |

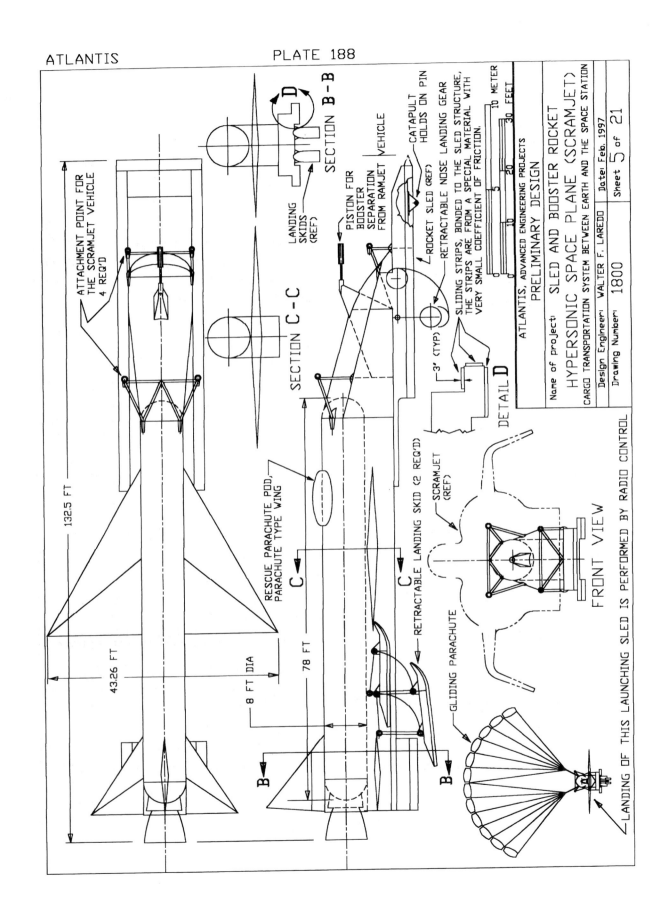

SECTION B-B

SECTION C-C

LANDING SKIDS (REF)

PISTON FOR BOOSTER SEPARATION FROM RAMJET

VEHICLE

CATAPULT HOLDS ON PIN

ROCKET SLED (REF)

RETRACTABLE NOSE LANDING GEAR

SLIDING STRIPS, BONDED TO THE SLED STRUCTURE, THE STRIPS ARE FROM A SPECIAL MATERIAL WITH VERY SMALL COEFFICIENT OF FRICTION.

3' (TYP)

DETAIL D

10 METER

5        20      30   FEET

ATTACHMENT POINT FOR THE SCRAMJET VEHICLE 4 REQ'D

132.5 FT

43.26 FT

8 FT DIA

78 FT

RESCUE PARACHUTE POD, PARACHUTE TYPE WING

RETRACTABLE LANDING SKID (2 REQ'D)

SCRAMJET (REF)

GLIDING PARACHUTE

FRONT VIEW

LANDING OF THIS LAUNCHING SLED IS PERFORMED BY RADIO CONTROL

| | |
|---|---|
| Name of project: | SLED AND BOOSTER ROCKET |

ATLANTIS, ADVANCED ENGINEERING PROJECTS

PRELIMINARY DESIGN

HYPERSONIC SPACE PLANE (SCRAMJET)

CARGO TRANSPORTATION SYSTEM BETWEEN EARTH AND THE SPACE STATION

| | | |
|---|---|---|
| Design Engineer: WALTER F. LAREDO | Date: Feb. 1997 | Sheet 5 of 21 |
| Drawing Number: 1800 | | |

ATLANTIS PLATE 189

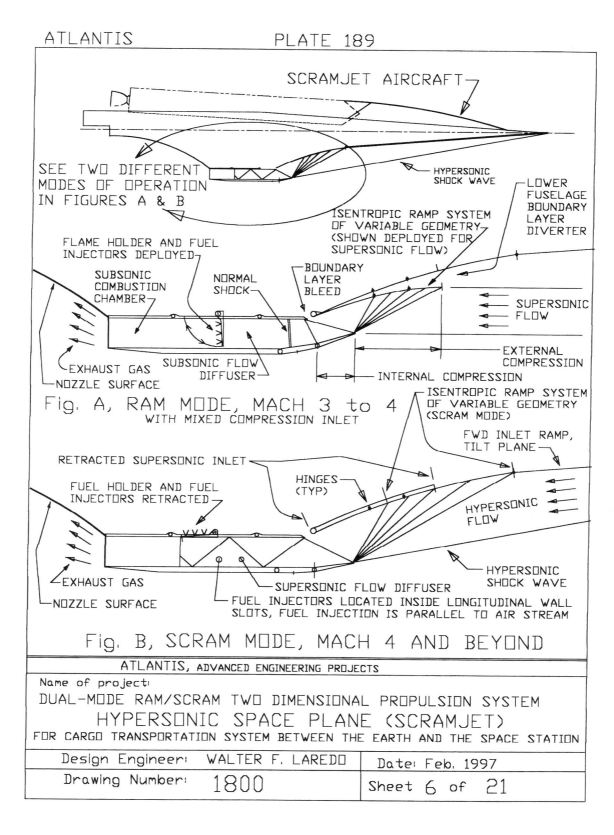

SCRAMJET AIRCRAFT

SEE TWO DIFFERENT
MODES OF OPERATION
IN FIGURES A & B

HYPERSONIC
SHOCK WAVE

LOWER
FUSELAGE
BOUNDARY
LAYER
DIVERTER

ISENTROPIC RAMP SYSTEM
OF VARIABLE GEOMETRY
(SHOWN DEPLOYED FOR
SUPERSONIC FLOW)

FLAME HOLDER AND FUEL
INJECTORS DEPLOYED

SUBSONIC
COMBUSTION
CHAMBER

NORMAL
SHOCK

BOUNDARY
LAYER
BLEED

SUPERSONIC
FLOW

EXHAUST GAS
NOZZLE SURFACE

SUBSONIC FLOW
DIFFUSER

EXTERNAL
COMPRESSION

INTERNAL COMPRESSION

Fig. A, RAM MODE, MACH 3 to 4
WITH MIXED COMPRESSION INLET

ISENTROPIC RAMP SYSTEM
OF VARIABLE GEOMETRY
(SCRAM MODE)

FWD INLET RAMP,
TILT PLANE

RETRACTED SUPERSONIC INLET

FUEL HOLDER AND FUEL
INJECTORS RETRACTED

HINGES
(TYP)

HYPERSONIC
FLOW

EXHAUST GAS

NOZZLE SURFACE

SUPERSONIC FLOW DIFFUSER

FUEL INJECTORS LOCATED INSIDE LONGITUDINAL WALL
SLOTS, FUEL INJECTION IS PARALLEL TO AIR STREAM

HYPERSONIC
SHOCK WAVE

Fig. B, SCRAM MODE, MACH 4 AND BEYOND

ATLANTIS, ADVANCED ENGINEERING PROJECTS

Name of project:
DUAL-MODE RAM/SCRAM TWO DIMENSIONAL PROPULSION SYSTEM
HYPERSONIC SPACE PLANE (SCRAMJET)
FOR CARGO TRANSPORTATION SYSTEM BETWEEN THE EARTH AND THE SPACE STATION

Design Engineer: WALTER F. LAREDO

Date: Feb. 1997

Drawing Number: 1800

Sheet 6 of 21

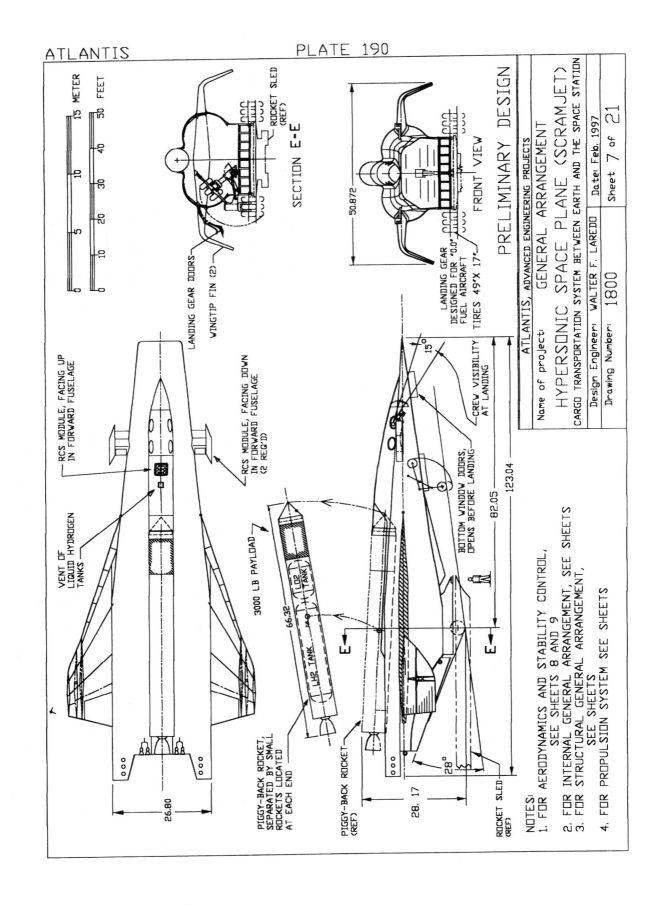

SECTION E-E

FRONT VIEW

50.872

LANDING GEAR DOORS

WINGTIP FIN (2)

ROCKET SLED (REF)

METER
FEET

LANDING GEAR DESIGNED FOR "0.0" FUEL AIRCRAFT
TIRES 49"X 17"

PRELIMINARY DESIGN

ATLANTIS, ADVANCED ENGINEERING PROJECTS

Name of project: GENERAL ARRANGEMENT

HYPERSONIC SPACE PLANE (SCRAMJET)

CARGO TRANSPORTATION SYSTEM BETWEEN EARTH AND THE SPACE STATION

| Design Engineer: WALTER F. LAREDO | Date: Feb. 1997 |
| Drawing Number: 1800 | Sheet 7 of 21 |

RCS MODULE, FACING UP IN FORWARD FUSELAGE

RCS MODULE, FACING DOWN IN FORWARD FUSELAGE (2 REQ'D)

VENT OF LIQUID HYDROGEN TANKS

3000 LB PAYLOAD

PIGGY-BACK ROCKET, SEPARATED BY SMALL ROCKETS LOCATED AT EACH END

PIGGY-BACK ROCKET (REF)

PIGGY-BACK ROCKET (REF)

CREW VISIBILITY AT LANDING

BOTTOM WINDOW DOORS, OPENS BEFORE LANDING

ROCKET SLED (REF)

15°

28°

26.80

66.32

LO2 TANK

LH2 TANK

28.17

82.05

123.04

NOTES:
1. FOR AERODYNAMICS AND STABILITY CONTROL, SEE SHEETS 8 AND 9
2. FOR INTERNAL GENERAL ARRANGEMENT, SEE SHEETS
3. FOR STRUCTURAL GENERAL ARRANGEMENT, SEE SHEETS
4. FOR PROPULSION SYSTEM SEE SHEETS

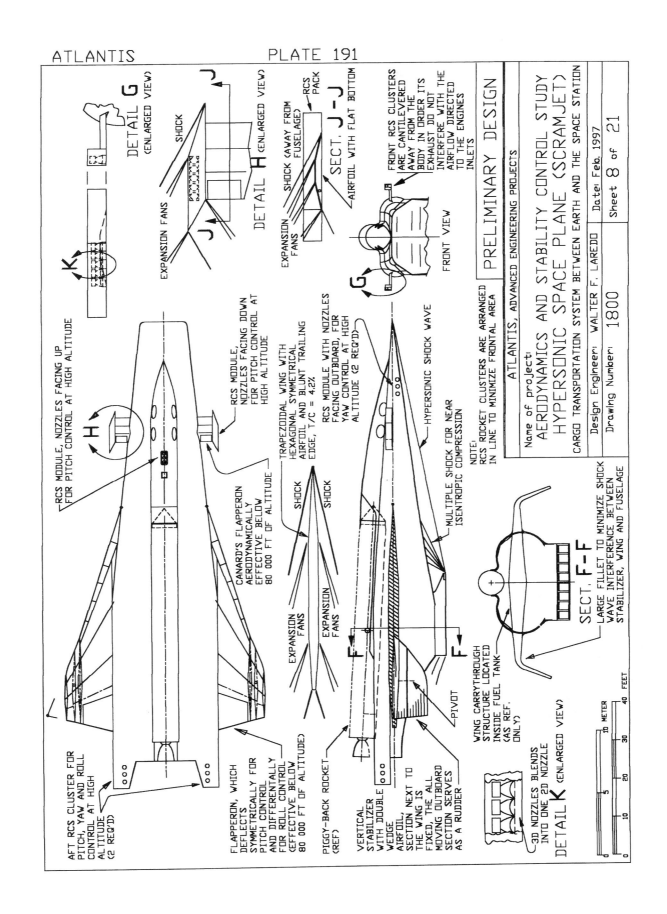

DETAIL G (ENLARGED VIEW)

SHOCK

EXPANSION FANS

DETAIL H (ENLARGED VIEW)

SHOCK (AWAY FROM FUSELAGE)

RCS PACK

EXPANSION FANS

SECT. J-J
AIRFOIL WITH FLAT BOTTOM

FRONT RCS CLUSTERS ARE CANTILEVERED AWAY FROM THE BODY IN ORDER ITS EXHAUST DO NOT INTERFERE WITH THE AIRFLOW DIRECTED TO THE ENGINES INLETS

FRONT VIEW

NOTE:
RCS ROCKET CLUSTERS ARE ARRANGED IN LINE TO MINIMIZE FRONTAL AREA

PRELIMINARY DESIGN

ATLANTIS, ADVANCED ENGINEERING PROJECTS

Name of project:
AERODYNAMICS AND STABILITY CONTROL STUDY
HYPERSONIC SPACE PLANE (SCRAMJET)
CARGO TRANSPORTATION SYSTEM BETWEEN EARTH AND THE SPACE STATION

| Design Engineer: WALTER F. LAREDO | Date: Feb. 1997 |
| Drawing Number: 1800 | Sheet 8 of 21 |

RCS MODULE, NOZZLES FACING UP FOR PITCH CONTROL AT HIGH ALTITUDE

RCS MODULE, NOZZLES FACING DOWN FOR PITCH CONTROL AT HIGH ALTITUDE

CANARD'S FLAPPERON AERODYNAMICALLY EFFECTIVE BELOW 80 000 FT OF ALTITUDE

TRAPEZOIDAL WING WITH HEXAGONAL SYMMETRICAL AIRFOIL AND BLUNT TRAILING EDGE, T/C = 4.2%

SHOCK

SHOCK

RCS MODULE WITH NOZZLES FACING OUTBOARD, FOR YAW CONTROL AT HIGH ALTITUDE (2 REQ'D)

HYPERSONIC SHOCK WAVE

MULTIPLE SHOCK FOR NEAR ISENTROPIC COMPRESSION

AFT RCS CLUSTER FOR PITCH, YAW AND ROLL CONTROL AT HIGH ALTITUDE (2 REQ'D)

FLAPPERON, WHICH DEFLECTS SYMMETRICALLY FOR PITCH CONTROL AND DIFFERENTIALLY FOR ROLL CONTROL (EFFECTIVE BELOW 80 000 FT OF ALTITUDE)

PIGGY-BACK ROCKET (REF)

VERTICAL STABILIZER WITH DOUBLE WEDGE AIRFOIL, SECTION NEXT TO THE WING IS FIXED, THE ALL MOVING OUTBOARD SECTION SERVES AS A RUDDER

EXPANSION FANS

EXPANSION FANS

PIVOT

WING CARRYTHROUGH STRUCTURE LOCATED INSIDE FUEL TANK (AS REF. ONLY)

SECT. F-F

LARGE FILLET TO MINIMIZE SHOCK WAVE INTERFERENCE BETWEEN STABILIZER, WING AND FUSELAGE

3D NOZZLES BLENDS INTO ONE 2D NOZZLE

DETAIL K (ENLARGED VIEW)

METER
FEET
0   5   10
0   10   20   30   40

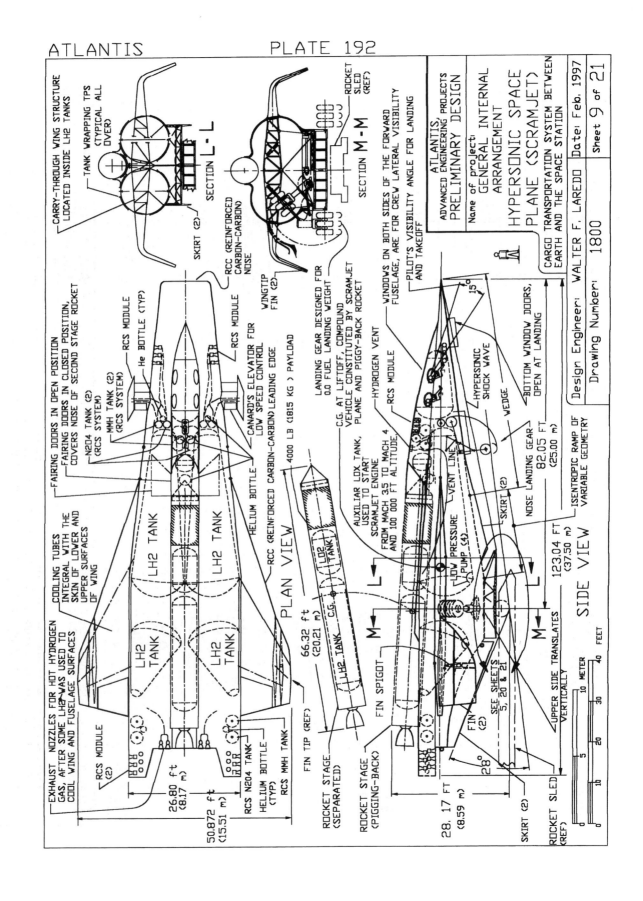

SECTION L-L

CARRY-THROUGH WING STRUCTURE LOCATED INSIDE LH2 TANKS

TANK WRAPPING TPS (TYPICAL ALL OVER)

SKIRT (2)

SECTION M-M

RCC (REINFORCED CARBON-CARBON) NOSE

WINGTIP FIN (2)

ROCKET SLED (REF)

RCS MODULE

RCS MODULE

RCS MODULE (RCS SYSTEM)

He BOTTLE (TYP)

N2O4 TANK (2) (RCS SYSTEM)

MMH TANK (2) (RCS SYSTEM)

CANARD'S ELEVATOR FOR LOW SPEED CONTROL

HELIUM BOTTLE

RCC (REINFORCED CARBON-CARBON) LEADING EDGE

FAIRING DOORS IN OPEN POSITION

FAIRING DOORS IN CLOSED POSITION, COVERS NOSE OF SECOND STAGE ROCKET

COOLING TUBES INTEGRAL WITH THE SKIN OF LOWER AND UPPER SURFACES OF WING

EXHAUST NOZZLES FOR HOT HYDROGEN GAS, AFTER SOME LH2 WAS USED TO COOL WING AND FUSELAGE SURFACES

RCS MODULE (2)

26.80 ft (8.17 m)

50.872 ft (15.51 m)

RCS N2O4 TANK

HELIUM BOTTLE (TYP)

RCS MMH TANK

LH2 TANK

LH2 TANK

LH2 TANK

LH2 TANK

PLAN VIEW

FIN TIP (REF)

66.32 ft (20.21 m)

4000 LB (1815 KG ) PAYLOAD

LANDING GEAR DESIGNED FOR 0.0 FUEL LANDING WEIGHT

C.G. AT LIFTOFF, COMPOUND VEHICLE CONSTITUTED BY SCRAMJET PLANE AND PIGGY-BACK ROCKET

AUXILIAR LOX TANK, USED TO START SCRAMJET ENGINE FROM MACH 3.5 TO MACH 4 AND 100 000 FT ALTITUDE

HYDROGEN VENT

RCS MODULE

WINDOWS ON BOTH SIDES OF THE FORWARD FUSELAGE, ARE FOR CREW LATERAL VISIBILITY

PILOT'S VISIBILITY ANGLE FOR LANDING AND TAKEOFF

15°

VENT LINE

HYPERSONIC SHOCK WAVE

WEDGE

BOTTOM WINDOW DOORS, OPEN AT LANDING

82.05 FT (25.00 m)

NOSE LANDING GEAR

SKIRT (2)

LOW PRESSURE PUMP (4)

LH2 TANK C.G.

LH2 TANK

FIN SPIGOT

ROCKET STAGE (SEPARATED)

ROCKET STAGE (PIGGING-BACK)

28.17 FT (8.59 m)

28°

SKIRT (2)

ROCKET SLED (REF)

FIN (2)

SEE SHEETS 5, 20 & 21

UPPER SIDE TRANSLATES VERTICALLY

ISENTROPIC RAMP OF VARIABLE GEOMETRY

123.04 FT (37.50 m)

SIDE VIEW

METER
10   5
FEET
40  30  20  10  0

ADVANCED ENGINEERING PROJECTS

PRELIMINARY DESIGN

Name of project:
GENERAL INTERNAL ARRANGEMENT

HYPERSONIC SPACE PLANE (SCRAMJET)

ATLANTIS,

CARGO TRANSPORTATION SYSTEM BETWEEN EARTH AND THE SPACE STATION

Design Engineer: WALTER F. LAREDO   Date: Feb. 1997

Drawing Number: 1800    Sheet 9 of 21

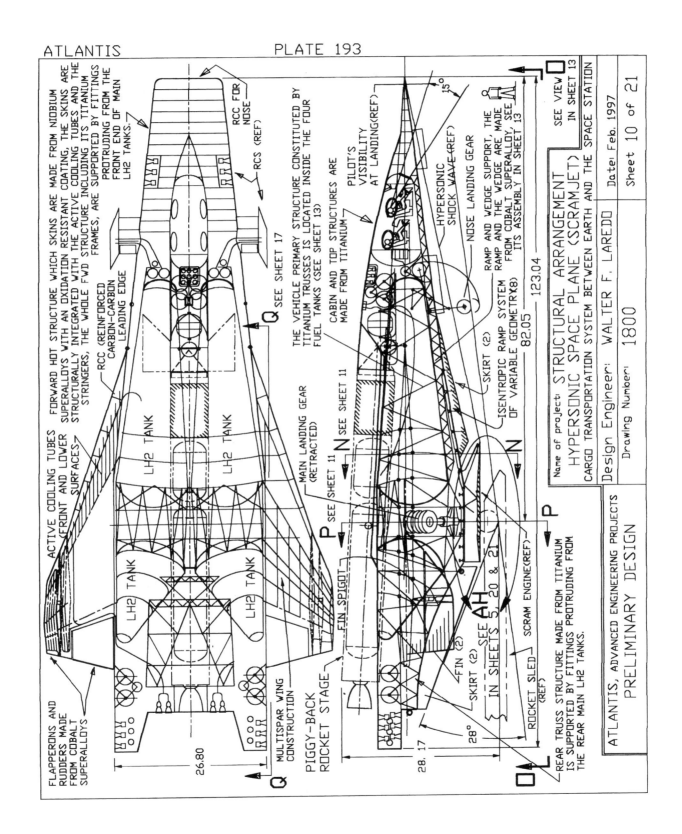

FLAPPERONS AND RUDDERS MADE FROM COBALT SUPERALLOYS

ACTIVE COOLING TUBES (FRONT AND LOWER SURFACES)

FORWARD HOT STRUCTURE WHICH SKINS ARE MADE FROM NIOBIUM SUPERALLOYS WITH AN OXIDATION RESISTANT COATING. THE SKINS ARE STRUCTURALLY INTEGRATED WITH THE ACTIVE COOLING TUBES AND THE STRINGERS. THE WHOLE FWD STRUCTURE INCLUDING ITS TITANIUM FRAMES, ARE SUPPORTED BY FITTINGS PROTRUDING FROM THE FRONT END OF MAIN LH2 TANKS.

RCC FOR NOSE (REF)

RCS (REF)

RCC (REINFORCED CARBON-CARBON LEADING EDGE

Q SEE SHEET 17

THE VEHICLE PRIMARY STRUCTURE CONSTITUTED BY TITANIUM TRUSSES IS LOCATED INSIDE THE FOUR FUEL TANKS (SEE SHEET 13)

CABIN AND TOP STRUCTURES ARE MADE FROM TITANIUM

PILOT'S VISIBILITY AT LANDING(REF)

15°

HYPERSONIC SHOCK WAVE(REF)

NOSE LANDING GEAR

RAMP AND WEDGE SUPPORT, THE RAMP AND THE WEDGE ARE MADE FROM COBALT SUPERALLOY, SEE ITS ASSEMBLY IN SHEET 13

SEE VIEW ☐ IN SHEET 13

LH2 TANK

LH2 TANK

MAIN LANDING GEAR (RETRACTED)

N SEE SHEET 11

ISENTROPIC RAMP SYSTEM OF VARIABLE GEOMETRY(8)

82.05

123.04

P SEE SHEET 11

LH2 TANK

LH2 TANK

MULTISPAR WING CONSTRUCTION

PIGGY-BACK ROCKET STAGE

Q

26.80

FIN SPIGOT

P

N

SKIRT (2)

FIN (2)

SKIRT (2)

AH SEE SHEETS 5, 20 & 21 IN SHEETS 5, 20 & 21

SCRAM ENGINE(REF)

28°

28.17

ROCKET SLED (REF)

REAR TRUSS STRUCTURE MADE FROM TITANIUM IS SUPPORTED BY FITTINGS PROTRUDING FROM THE REAR MAIN LH2 TANKS.

L

Name of project: STRUCTURAL ARRANGEMENT HYPERSONIC SPACE PLANE (SCRAMJET) CARGO TRANSPORTATION SYSTEM BETWEEN EARTH AND THE SPACE STATION

Date: Feb. 1997

Design Engineer: WALTER F. LAREDO

Drawing Number: 1800

Sheet 10 of 21

ATLANTIS, ADVANCED ENGINEERING PROJECTS
PRELIMINARY DESIGN

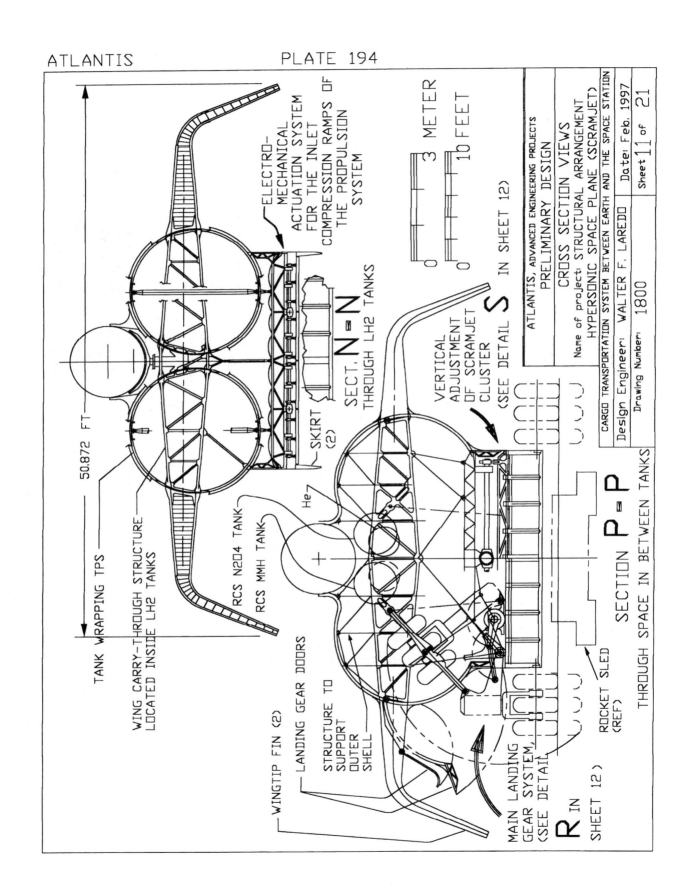

50.872 FT

ELECTRO-MECHANICAL ACTUATION SYSTEM FOR THE INLET COMPRESSION RAMPS OF THE PROPULSION SYSTEM

3 METER

10 FEET

SECT. N-N
THROUGH LH2 TANKS

SKIRT (2)

VERTICAL ADJUSTMENT OF SCRAMJET CLUSTER (SEE DETAIL S IN SHEET 12)

He

TANK WRAPPING TPS

WING CARRY-THROUGH STRUCTURE LOCATED INSIDE LH2 TANKS

RCS N2O4 TANK

RCS MMH TANK

WINGTIP FIN (2)

LANDING GEAR DOORS

STRUCTURE TO SUPPORT OUTER SHELL

MAIN LANDING GEAR SYSTEM, (SEE DETAIL R IN SHEET 12 )

ROCKET SLED (REF)

SECTION P-P
THROUGH SPACE IN BETWEEN TANKS

ATLANTIS, ADVANCED ENGINEERING PROJECTS
PRELIMINARY DESIGN
CROSS SECTION VIEWS
Name of project: STRUCTURAL ARRANGEMENT HYPERSONIC SPACE PLANE (SCRAMJET)
CARGO TRANSPORTATION SYSTEM BETWEEN EARTH AND THE SPACE STATION

| Design Engineer: WALTER F. LAREDO | Date: Feb. 1997 |
| Drawing Number: 1800 | Sheet 11 of 21 |

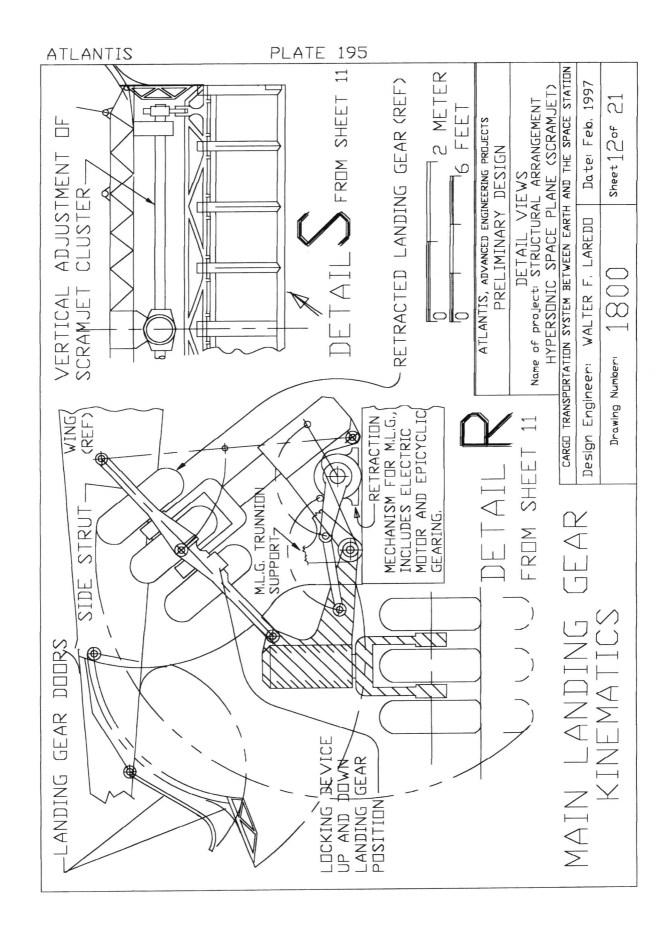

VERTICAL ADJUSTMENT OF SCRAMJET CLUSTER

DETAIL S  FROM SHEET 11

RETRACTED LANDING GEAR (REF)

2 METER

6 FEET

WING (REF)

SIDE STRUT

LANDING GEAR DOORS

M.L.G. TRUNNION SUPPORT

RETRACTION MECHANISM FOR M.L.G., INCLUDES ELECTRIC MOTOR AND EPICYCLIC GEARING.

DETAIL R  FROM SHEET 11

LOCKING DEVICE UP AND DOWN LANDING GEAR POSITION

MAIN LANDING GEAR KINEMATICS

ATLANTIS, ADVANCING ENGINEERING PROJECTS
PRELIMINARY DESIGN
DETAIL VIEWS
Name of project: STRUCTURAL ARRANGEMENT
HYPERSONIC SPACE PLANE (SCRAMJET)

CARGO TRANSPORTATION SYSTEM BETWEEN EARTH AND THE SPACE STATION

Design Engineer: WALTER F. LAREDO        Date: Feb. 1997

Drawing Number: 1800        Sheet 12 of 21

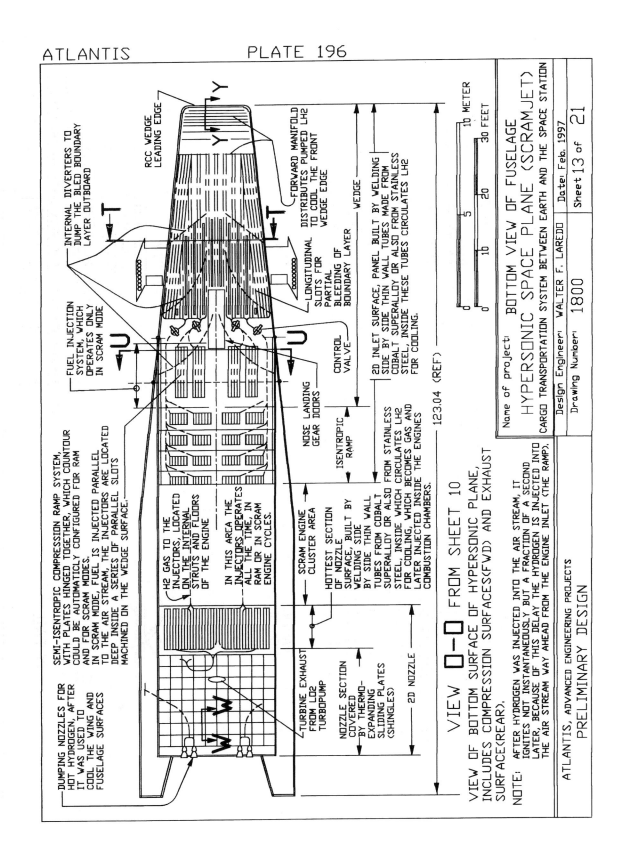

ATLANTIS      PLATE 196

DUMPING NOZZLES FOR HOT HYDROGEN, AFTER IT WAS USED TO COOL THE WING AND FUSELAGE SURFACES

SEMI-ISENTROPIC COMPRESSION RAMP SYSTEM, WITH PLATES HINGED TOGETHER, WHICH COUNTOUR COULD BE AUTOMATICLY CONFIGURED FOR RAM AND FOR SCRAM MODES. IN SCRAM MODE, FUEL IS INJECTED PARALLEL TO THE AIR STREAM, THE INJECTORS ARE LOCATED DEEP INSIDE A SERIES OF PARALLEL SLOTS MACHINED ON THE WEDGE SURFACE.

RCC WEDGE LEADING EDGE

INTERNAL DIVERTERS TO DUMP THE BLED BOUNDARY LAYER OUTBOARD

FORWARD MANIFOLD DISTRIBUTES PUMPED LH2 TO COOL THE FRONT WEDGE EDGE

WEDGE

LONGITUDINAL SLOTS FOR PARTIAL BLEEDING OF BOUNDARY LAYER

FUEL INJECTION SYSTEM, WHICH OPERATES ONLY IN SCRAM MODE

CONTROL VALVE

2D INLET SURFACE, PANEL BUILT BY WELDING SIDE BY SIDE THIN WALL TUBES MADE FROM COBALT SUPERALLOY OR ALSO FROM STAINLESS STEEL, INSIDE THESE TUBES CIRCULATES LH2 FOR COOLING.

H2 GAS TO THE INJECTORS, LOCATED ON THE INTERNAL STRUTS AND FLOORS OF THE ENGINE

IN THIS AREA THE INJECTORS OPERATES ALL THE TIME, IN RAM OR IN SCRAM ENGINE CYCLES.

NOSE LANDING GEAR DOORS

ISENTROPIC RAMP

SCRAM ENGINE CLUSTER AREA

HOTTEST SECTION OF NOZZLE SURFACE, BUILT BY WELDING SIDE BY SIDE THIN WALL TUBES FROM COBALT SUPERALLOY OR ALSO FROM STAINLESS STEEL, INSIDE WHICH CIRCULATES LH2 FOR COOLING, WHICH BECOMES GAS AND LATER INJECTED INSIDE THE ENGINES COMBUSTION CHAMBERS.

TURBINE EXHAUST FROM LO2 TURBOPUMP

NOZZLE SECTION COVERED BY THERMO-EXPANDING SLIDING PLATES (SHINGLES)

2D NOZZLE

123.04 (REF)

1 METER
30 FEET
5
20
10
10
0
0

VIEW □-□ FROM SHEET 10

VIEW OF BOTTOM SURFACE OF HYPERSONIC PLANE, INCLUDES COMPRESSION SURFACES(FWD) AND EXHAUST SURFACE(REAR).

NOTE: AFTER HYDROGEN WAS INJECTED INTO THE AIR STREAM, IT IGNITES NOT INSTANTANEOUSLY BUT A FRACTION OF A SECOND LATER, BECAUSE OF THIS DELAY THE HYDROGEN IS INJECTED INTO THE AIR STREAM WAY AHEAD FROM THE ENGINE INLET (THE RAMP).

Name of project: BOTTOM VIEW OF FUSELAGE
HYPERSONIC SPACE PLANE (SCRAMJET)
CARGO TRANSPORTATION SYSTEM BETWEEN EARTH AND THE SPACE STATION

Design Engineer: WALTER F. LAREDO  Date: Feb. 1997
Drawing Number: 1800  Sheet 13 of 21

ATLANTIS, ADVANCED ENGINEERING PROJECTS
PRELIMINARY DESIGN

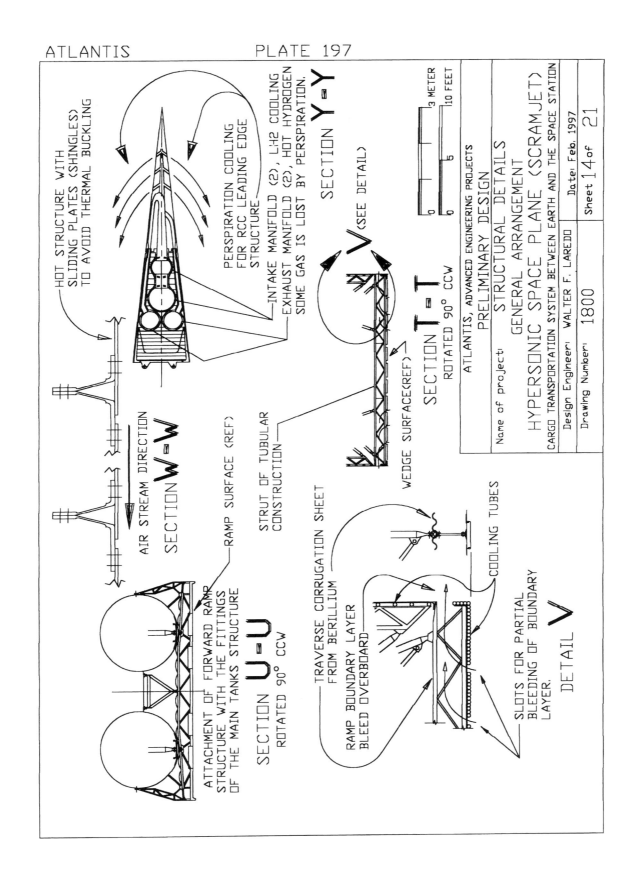

HOT STRUCTURE WITH SLIDING PLATES (SHINGLES) TO AVOID THERMAL BUCKLING

PERSPIRATION COOLING FOR RCC LEADING EDGE STRUCTURE

INTAKE MANIFOLD (2), LH2 COOLING EXHAUST MANIFOLD (2), HOT HYDROGEN SOME GAS IS LOST BY PERSPIRATION.

SECTION Y-Y

V (SEE DETAIL)

AIR STREAM DIRECTION

SECTION W-W

RAMP SURFACE (REF)

STRUT OF TUBULAR CONSTRUCTION

SECTION T-T
ROTATED 90° CCW

WEDGE SURFACE (REF)

ATTACHMENT OF FORWARD RAMP STRUCTURE WITH THE FITTINGS OF THE MAIN TANKS STRUCTURE

SECTION U-U
ROTATED 90° CCW

TRAVERSE CORRUGATION SHEET FROM BERILLIUM

RAMP BOUNDARY LAYER BLEED OVERBOARD

COOLING TUBES

SLOTS FOR PARTIAL BLEEDING OF BOUNDARY LAYER.

DETAIL V

3 METER

10 FEET

ATLANTIS, ADVANCED ENGINEERING PROJECTS

PRELIMINARY DESIGN
STRUCTURAL DETAILS
GENERAL ARRANGEMENT
HYPERSONIC SPACE PLANE (SCRAMJET)
CARGO TRANSPORTATION SYSTEM BETWEEN EARTH AND THE SPACE STATION

Name of project:

Design Engineer: WALTER F. LAREDO          Date: Feb. 1997

Drawing Number: 1800          Sheet 14 of 21

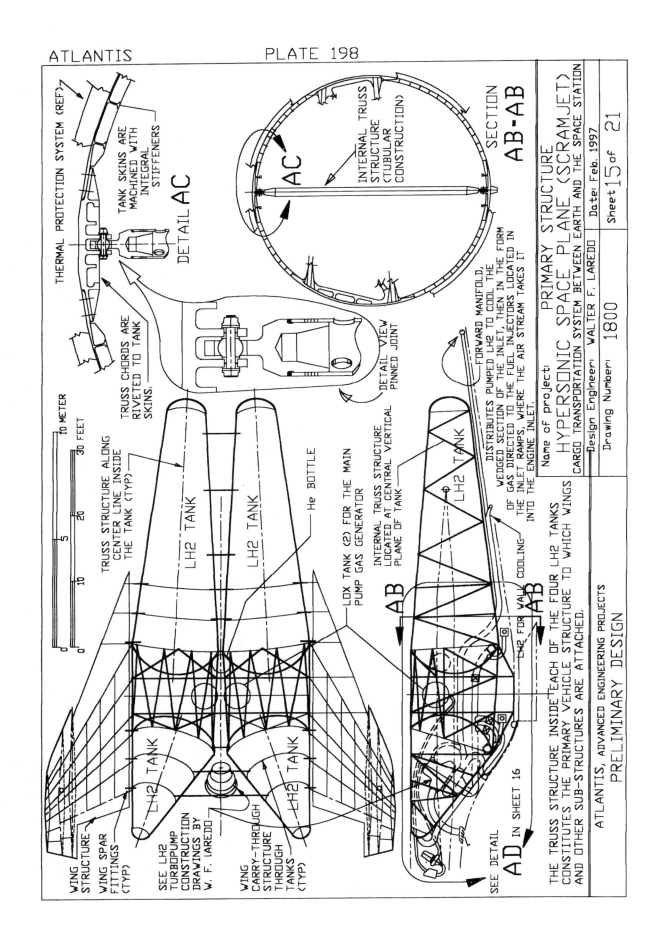

THERMAL PROTECTION SYSTEM (REF)

TANK SKINS ARE MACHINED WITH INTEGRAL STIFFENERS

DETAIL AC

AC

INTERNAL TRUSS STRUCTURE (TUBULAR CONSTRUCTION)

SECTION AB-AB

TRUSS CHORDS ARE RIVETED TO TANK SKINS.

DETAIL VIEW PINNED JOINT

FORWARD MANIFOLD, DISTRIBUTES PUMPED LH2 TO COOL THE WEDGED SECTION OF THE INLET, THEN IN THE FORM OF GAS DIRECTED TO THE FUEL INJECTORS LOCATED IN THE INLET RAMPS, WHERE THE AIR STREAM TAKES IT INTO THE ENGINE INLET.

10 METER
30 FEET

TRUSS STRUCTURE ALONG CENTER LINE INSIDE THE TANK (TYP)

LH2 TANK

LH2 TANK

He BOTTLE

LOX TANK (2) FOR THE MAIN PUMP GAS GENERATOR

INTERNAL TRUSS STRUCTURE LOCATED AT CENTRAL VERTICAL PLANE OF TANK

LH2 TANK

AB

LH2 FOR WALL COOLING

AB

WING STRUCTURE

WING SPAR FITTINGS (TYP)

SEE LH2 TURBOPUMP CONSTRUCTION DRAWINGS BY W. F. LAREDO

WING CARRY-THROUGH STRUCTURE THROUGH TANKS (TYP)

LH2 TANK

LH2 TANK

SEE DETAIL AD IN SHEET 16

THE TRUSS STRUCTURE INSIDE EACH OF THE FOUR LH2 TANKS CONSTITUTES THE PRIMARY VEHICLE STRUCTURE TO WHICH WINGS AND OTHER SUB-STRUCTURES ARE ATTACHED.

ATLANTIS, ADVANCED ENGINEERING PROJECTS

PRELIMINARY DESIGN

Name of project: PRIMARY STRUCTURE
HYPERSONIC SPACE PLANE (SCRAMJET)
CARGO TRANSPORTATION SYSTEM BETWEEN EARTH AND THE SPACE STATION

Design Engineer: WALTER F. LAREDO          Date: Feb. 1997

Drawing Number: 1800          Sheet 15 of 21

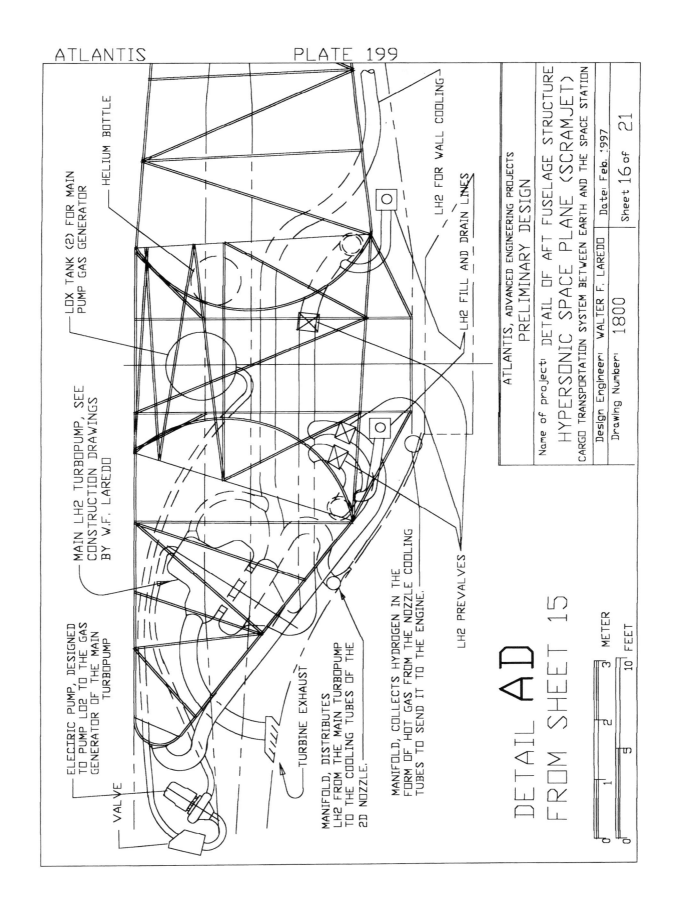

HELIUM BOTTLE

LOX TANK (2) FOR MAIN
PUMP GAS GENERATOR

LH2 FOR WALL COOLING

LH2 FILL AND DRAIN LINES

MAIN LH2 TURBOPUMP, SEE
CONSTRUCTION DRAWINGS
BY W.F. LAREDO

LH2 PREVALVES

ELECTRIC PUMP, DESIGNED
TO PUMP LO2 TO THE GAS
GENERATOR OF THE MAIN
TURBOPUMP

VALVE

TURBINE EXHAUST

MANIFOLD, DISTRIBUTES
LH2 FROM THE MAIN TURBOPUMP
TO THE COOLING TUBES OF THE
2D NOZZLE.

MANIFOLD, COLLECTS HYDROGEN IN THE
FORM OF HOT GAS FROM THE NOZZLE COOLING
TUBES TO SEND IT TO THE ENGINE.

# DETAIL AD
# FROM SHEET 15

Name of project: DETAIL OF AFT FUSELAGE STRUCTURE

ATLANTIS, ADVANCED ENGINEERING PROJECTS
PRELIMINARY DESIGN

HYPERSONIC SPACE PLANE (SCRAMJET)

CARGO TRANSPORTATION SYSTEM BETWEEN EARTH AND THE SPACE STATION

| Design Engineer: WALTER F. LAREDO | Date: Feb. 1997 |
| --- | --- |
| Drawing Number: 1800 | Sheet 16 of 21 |

METER

FEET

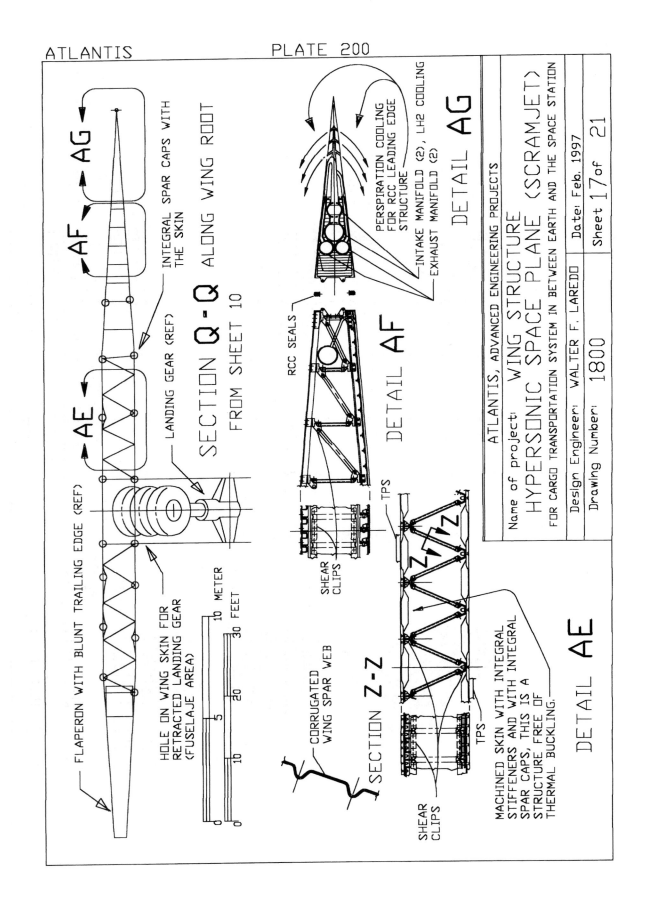

FLAPERON WITH BLUNT TRAILING EDGE (REF)

HOLE ON WING SKIN FOR RETRACTED LANDING GEAR (FUSELAJE AREA)

10 METER

10 FEET

30

20

5

10

INTEGRAL SPAR CAPS WITH THE SKIN

LANDING GEAR (REF)

AG

AF

AE

SECTION Q-Q ALONG WING ROOT

FROM SHEET 10

RCC SEALS

SHEAR CLIPS

TPS

DETAIL AF

PERSPIRATION COOLING FOR RCC LEADING EDGE STRUCTURE

INTAKE MANIFOLD (2), LH2 COOLING
EXHAUST MANIFOLD (2)

DETAIL AG

CORRUGATED WING SPAR WEB

SECTION Z-Z

Z

Z

SHEAR CLIPS

TPS

MACHINED SKIN WITH INTEGRAL STIFFENERS AND WITH INTEGRAL SPAR CAPS, THIS IS A STRUCTURE FREE OF THERMAL BUCKLING.

DETAIL AE

ATLANTIS, ADVANCED ENGINEERING PROJECTS

Name of project: WING STRUCTURE

HYPERSONIC SPACE PLANE (SCRAMJET)

FOR CARGO TRANSPORTATION SYSTEM IN BETWEEN EARTH AND THE SPACE STATION

| Design Engineer: WALTER F. LAREDO | Date: Feb. 1997 |
| --- | --- |
| Drawing Number: 1800 | Sheet 17 of 21 |

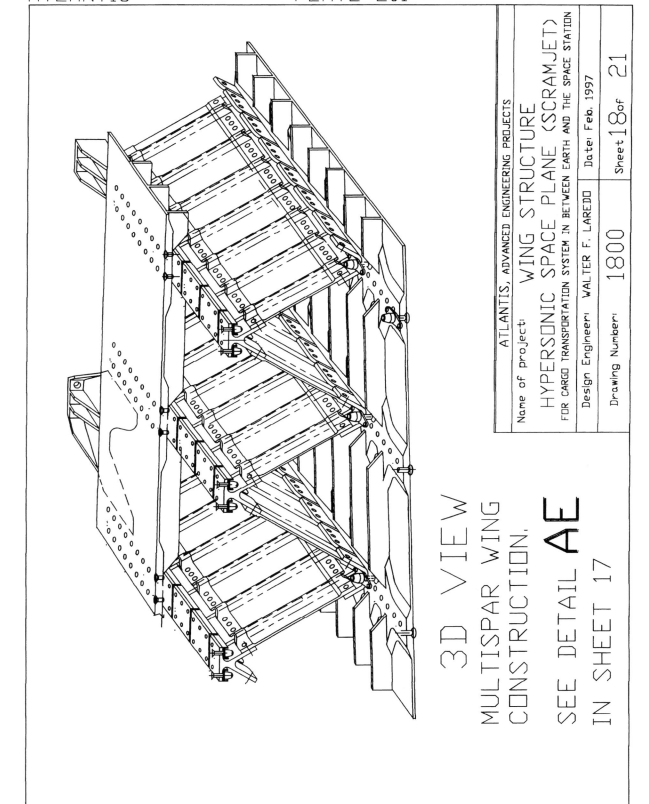

3D VIEW
MULTISPAR WING
CONSTRUCTION.
SEE DETAIL AE
IN SHEET 17

ATLANTIS, ADVANCED ENGINEERING PROJECTS

Name of project: WING STRUCTURE
HYPERSONIC SPACE PLANE (SCRAMJET)
FOR CARGO TRANSPORTATION SYSTEM IN BETWEEN EARTH AND THE SPACE STATION

| Design Engineer: WALTER F. LAREDO | Date: Feb. 1997 |
| Drawing Number: 1800 | Sheet 18 of 21 |

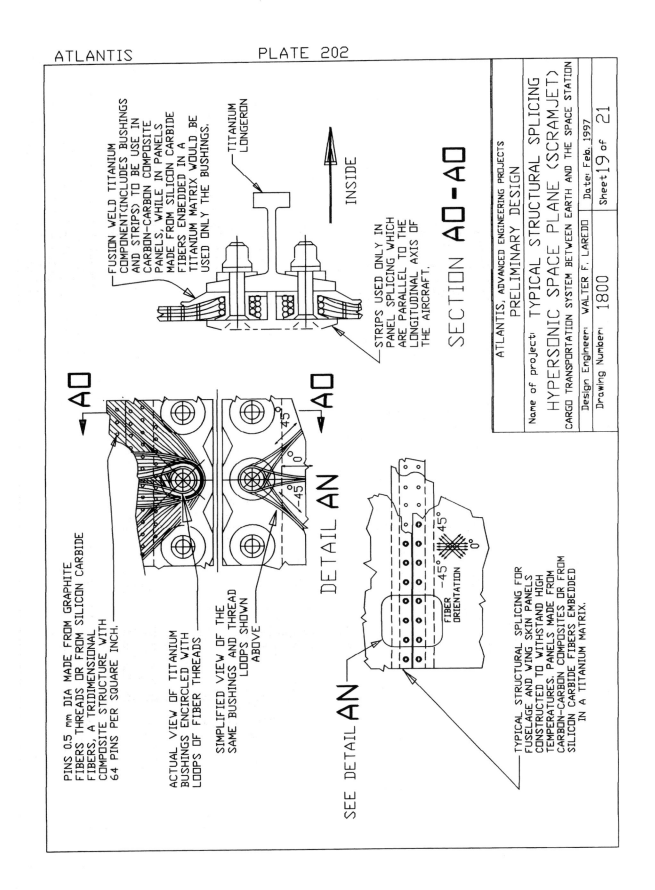

FUSION WELD TITANIUM COMPONENT(INCLUDES BUSHINGS AND STRIPS) TO BE USE IN CARBON-CARBON COMPOSITE PANELS, WHILE IN PANELS MADE FROM SILICON CARBIDE FIBERS EMBEDDED IN A TITANIUM MATRIX WOULD BE USED ONLY THE BUSHINGS.

TITANIUM LONGERON

INSIDE

STRIPS USED ONLY IN PANEL SPLICING WHICH ARE PARALLEL TO THE LONGITUDINAL AXIS OF THE AIRCRAFT.

SECTION AO-AO

PINS 0.5 mm DIA MADE FROM GRAPHITE FIBERS THREADS OR FROM SILICON CARBIDE FIBERS, A TRIDIMENSIONAL COMPOSITE STRUCTURE WITH 64 PINS PER SQUARE INCH.

ACTUAL VIEW OF TITANIUM BUSHINGS ENCIRCLED WITH LOOPS OF FIBER THREADS

SIMPLIFIED VIEW OF THE SAME BUSHINGS AND THREAD LOOPS SHOWN ABOVE

DETAIL AN

45°
0°
-45°

SEE DETAIL AN

-45°
45°
0°
FIBER ORIENTATION

TYPICAL STRUCTURAL SPLICING FOR FUSELAGE AND WING SKIN PANELS CONSTRUCTED TO WITHSTAND HIGH TEMPERATURES. PANELS MADE FROM CARBON-CARBON COMPOSITES OR FROM SILICON CARBIDE FIBERS EMBEDDED IN A TITANIUM MATRIX.

ATLANTIS, ADVANCED ENGINEERING PROJECTS
PRELIMINARY DESIGN
Name of project: TYPICAL STRUCTURAL SPLICING
HYPERSONIC SPACE PLANE (SCRAMJET)
CARGO TRANSPORTATION SYSTEM BETWEEN EARTH AND THE SPACE STATION
Design Engineer: WALTER F. LAREDO    Date: Feb. 1997
Drawing Number: 1800    Sheet 19 of 21

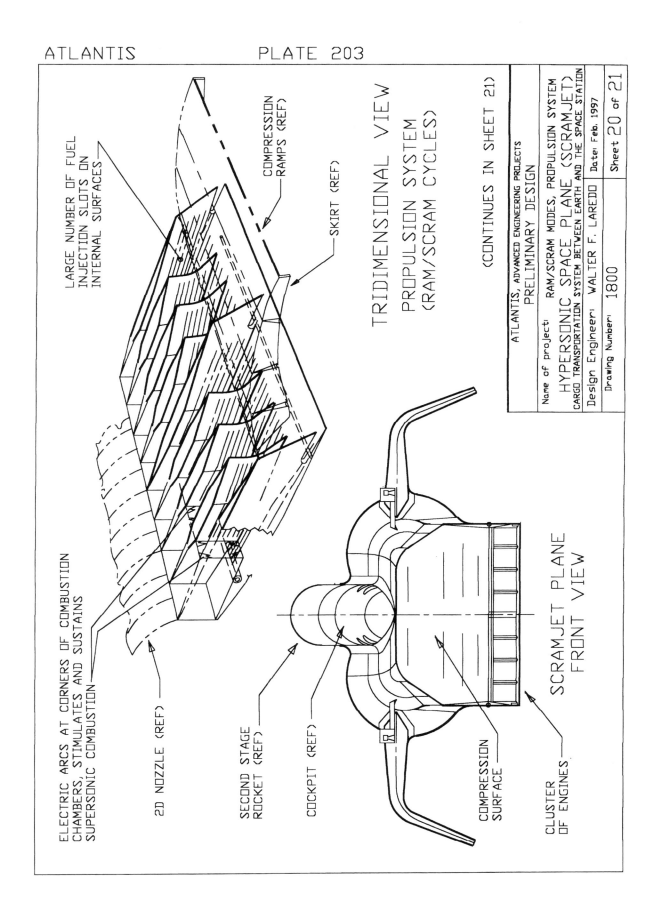

LARGE NUMBER OF FUEL
INJECTION SLOTS ON
INTERNAL SURFACES

COMPRESSION
RAMPS (REF)

SKIRT (REF)

TRIDIMENSIONAL VIEW
PROPULSION SYSTEM
(RAM/SCRAM CYCLES)

(CONTINUES IN SHEET 21)

ELECTRIC ARCS AT CORNERS OF COMBUSTION
CHAMBERS, STIMULATES AND SUSTAINS
SUPERSONIC COMBUSTION

2D NOZZLE (REF)

SECOND STAGE
ROCKET (REF)

COCKPIT (REF)

SCRAMJET PLANE
FRONT VIEW

COMPRESSION
SURFACE

CLUSTER
OF ENGINES

Name of project: RAM/SCRAM MODES, PROPULSION SYSTEM
ATLANTIS, ADVANCED ENGINEERING PROJECTS
PRELIMINARY DESIGN
HYPERSONIC SPACE PLANE (SCRAMJET)
CARGO TRANSPORTATION SYSTEM BETWEEN EARTH AND THE SPACE STATION
Design Engineer: WALTER F. LAREDO    Date: Feb. 1997
Drawing Number: 1800          Sheet 20 of 21

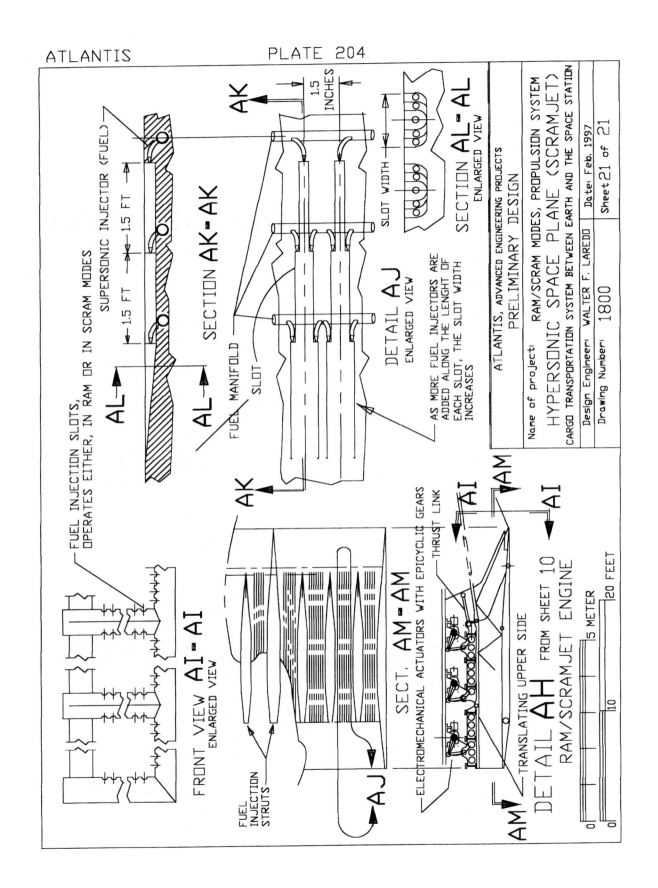

FUEL INJECTION SLOTS,
OPERATES EITHER, IN RAM OR IN SCRAM MODES

SUPERSONIC INJECTOR (FUEL)

1.5 FT — 1.5 FT — 1.5 FT

SECTION AK-AK

AK

1.5 INCHES

SLOT WIDTH

SECTION AL-AL
ENLARGED VIEW

AL

AL

FUEL MANIFOLD

SLOT

DETAIL AJ
ENLARGED VIEW

AS MORE FUEL INJECTORS ARE
ADDED ALONG THE LENGHT OF
EACH SLOT, THE SLOT WIDTH
INCREASES

AK

FRONT VIEW AI-AI
ENLARGED VIEW

FUEL
INJECTION
STRUTS

SECT. AM-AM

AJ

ELECTROMECHANICAL ACTUATORS WITH EPICYCLIC GEARS

THRUST LINK

AI

AM

AI

TRANSLATING UPPER SIDE

DETAIL AH FROM SHEET 10
RAM/SCRAMJET ENGINE

AM

5 METER

20 FEET

10

ATLANTIS, ADVANCED ENGINEERING PROJECTS
PRELIMINARY DESIGN

Name of project: RAM/SCRAM MODES, PROPULSION SYSTEM
HYPERSONIC SPACE PLANE (SCRAMJET)
CARGO TRANSPORTATION SYSTEM BETWEEN EARTH AND THE SPACE STATION

| Design Engineer: WALTER F. LAREDO | Date: Feb. 1997 |
| Drawing Number: 1800 | Sheet 21 of 21 |

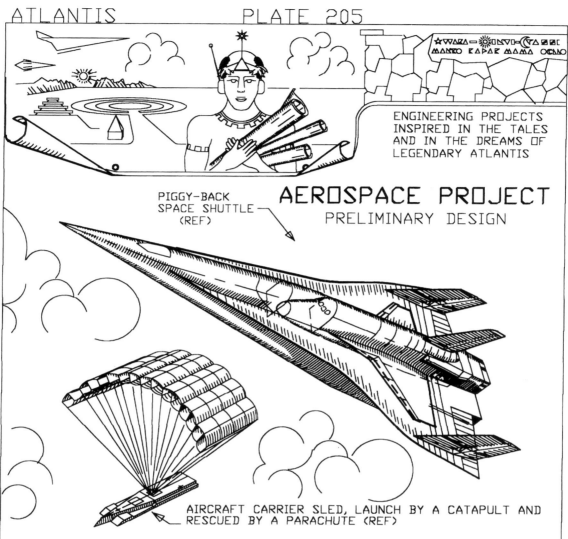

ENGINEERING PROJECTS
INSPIRED IN THE TALES
AND IN THE DREAMS OF
LEGENDARY ATLANTIS

PIGGY-BACK
SPACE SHUTTLE
(REF)

# AEROSPACE PROJECT
## PRELIMINARY DESIGN

AIRCRAFT CARRIER SLED, LAUNCH BY A CATAPULT AND
RESCUED BY A PARACHUTE (REF)

INTERNATIONAL SPACE BASES ON HIGH PLATEAUS OF THE WORLD SHOULD
INCLUDE TILTED LAUNCHING RAMPS WITH EXTRALONG TWO STAGGED CATAPULTS,
THE SAME BASES SHOULD HAVE ALSO LONG LANDING STRIPS ON THE DRIED
SALTED LAKES OF THE PLATEAU FOR THE RETURNING GLIDDING BOOSTER PLANE
AND LATER OF THE SPACE SHUTTLE.

NOTE: FOR CLARITY IN THE FOLLOWING DRAWINGS WAS NOT SHOWN THE
EXTERNAL THERMOPROTECCION SYSTEM OF THE SPACE VEHICLES, ALSO WAS
NOT SHOWN THE FOAM INSULATION THAT COVERS THE TANKS AND OTHER
CRYOGENIC COMPONENTS.

| ATLANTIS, ADVANCED ENGINEERING PROJECTS | | |
|---|---|---|
| Name of project: GENERAL ARRANGEMENT<br>HYPERSONIC PIGGYBACK PLANE<br>TRANSPORTATION SYSTEM BETWEEN EARTH AND THE SPACE STATION | | |
| Design Engineer: WALTER F. LAREDO | | Date: Feb. 1997 |
| Drawing Number: 1900 SERIES | | Sheet 1 of 12 |

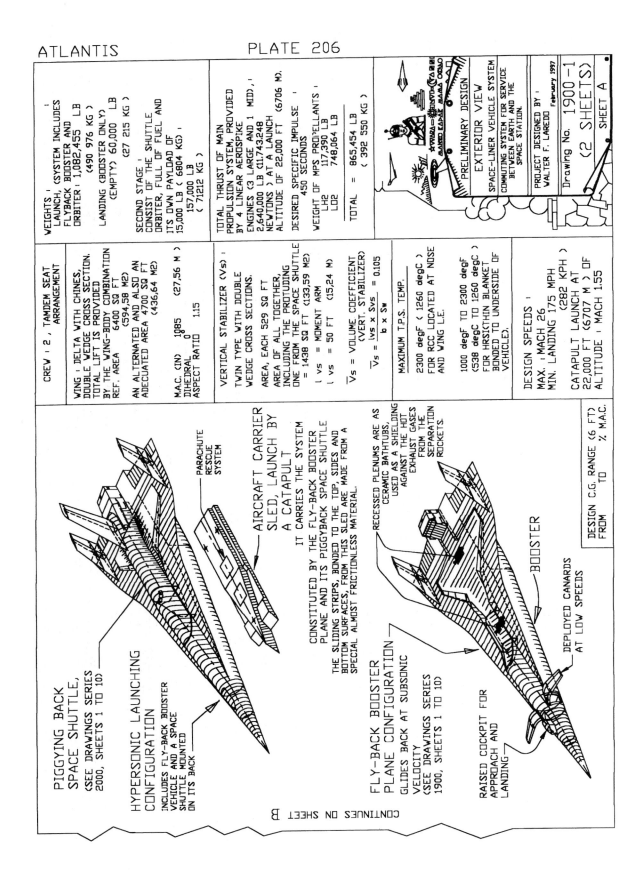

WEIGHTS:
LAUNCH, (SYSTEM INCLUDES FLYBACK BOOSTER AND ORBITER) 1,082,455 LB
(490 976 KG )
LANDING (BOOSTER ONLY)
(EMPTY) 60,000 LB
(27 215 KG )

SECOND STAGE:
CONSIST OF THE SHUTTLE ORBITER, FULL OF FUEL AND ITS OWN PAYLOAD OF
15,000 LB ( 6804 KG )
157,000 LB
( 71212 KG )

TOTAL THRUST OF MAIN PROPULSION SYSTEM, PROVIDED BY 4 LINEAR AEROSPIKE ENGINES (3 LARGE AND 1 MID),:
2,640,000 LB (11.743.248 NEWTONS ) AT A LAUNCH ALTITUDE OF 22,000 FT (6706 M).

DESIRED SPECIFIC IMPULSE:
450 SECONDS

WEIGHT OF MPS PROPELLANTS:
LH2    117,390 LB
LO2    748,064 LB
( 392 550 KG )

TOTAL = 865,454 LB

PRELIMINARY DESIGN
EXTERIOR VIEW
SPACE-LINER VEHICLE SYSTEM
COMMUTING SYSTEM FOR SERVICE BETWEEN EARTH AND THE SPACE STATION.

PROJECT DESIGNED BY:
WALTER F. LAREDO        February 1997

Drawing No. 1900-1
(2 SHEETS)
SHEET A

CREW: 2, TAMDEM SEAT ARRANGEMENT

WING: DELTA WITH CHINES, DOUBLE WEDGE CROSS SECTION. TOTAL LIFT IS PROVIDED BY THE WING-BODY COMBINATION
REF. AREA    6400 SQ FT
(594.58 M2)

AN ALTERNATED AND ALSO AN ADECUATED AREA 4700 SQ FT
(436.64 M2)

M.A.C. (IN)    1085    (27.56 M )
DIHEDRAL    0
ASPECT RATIO    1.15

VERTICAL STABILIZER (Vs):
TWIN TYPE WITH DOUBLE WEDGE CROSS SECTIONS.
AREA, EACH 529 SQ FT
AREA OF ALL TOGETHER, INCLUDING THE PROTUDING ONE FROM THE SPACE SHUTTLE
= 1438 SQ FT (133.59 M2)
( vs = MOMENT ARM
( vs = 50 FT    (15.24 M)

$\bar{V}s$ = VOLUME COEFFICIENT (VERT. STABILIZER)

$$\bar{V}s = \frac{(vs \times Svs}{b \times Sw} = 0.105$$

MAXIMUM T.P.S. TEMP.
2300 degF ( 1260 degC )
FOR RCC LOCATED AT NOSE AND WING L.E.

1000 degF TO 2300 degF (538 degC TO 1260 degC) FOR HRSI(THIN BLANKET BONDED TO UNDERSIDE OF VEHICLE).

DESIGN SPEEDS:
MAX.: MACH 26
MIN. LANDING 175 MPH
(282 KPH )
CATAPULT LAUNCH AT 22,000 FT (6707 M ) OF ALTITUDE : MACH 1.55

PIGGYING BACK SPACE SHUTTLE,
(SEE DRAWINGS SERIES 2000, SHEETS 1 TO 10)

HYPERSONIC LAUNCHING CONFIGURATION
INCLUDES FLY-BACK BOOSTER VEHICLE AND A SPACE SHUTTLE MOUNTED ON ITS BACK

PARACHUTE RESCUE SYSTEM

AIRCRAFT CARRIER SLED, LAUNCH BY A CATAPULT
IT CARRIES THE SYSTEM CONSTITUTED BY THE FLY-BACK BOOSTER PLANE AND ITS PIGGYBACK SPACE SHUTTLE
THE SLIDING STRIPS, BONDED TO THE TOP, SIDES AND BOTTOM SURFACES, FROM THIS SLED ARE MADE FROM A SPECIAL ALMOST FRICTIONLESS MATERIAL.

RECESSED PLENUMS ARE AS CERAMIC BATHTUBS, USED AS A SHIELDING AGAINST THE HOT EXHAUST GASES FROM THE SEPARATION ROCKETS.

FLY-BACK BOOSTER PLANE CONFIGURATION
GLIDES BACK AT SUBSONIC VELOCITY
(SEE DRAWINGS SERIES 1900, SHEETS 1 TO 10)

RAISED COCKPIT FOR APPROACH AND LANDING

BOOSTER

DEPLOYED CANARDS AT LOW SPEEDS

DESIGN C.G. RANGE (6 FT)
FROM    TO    % M.A.C.

CONTINUES ON SHEET B

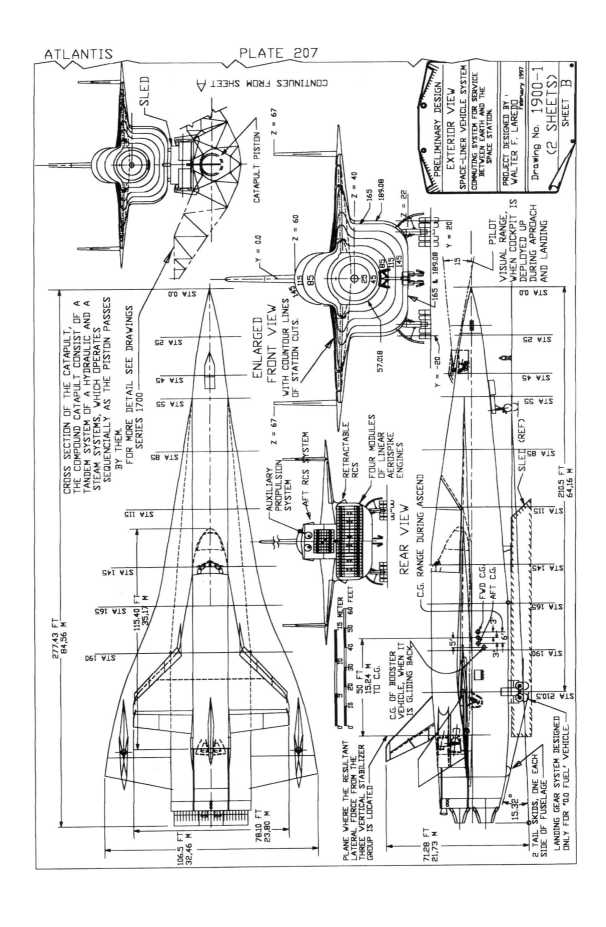

SLED

CONTINUES FROM SHEET A

CATAPULT PISTON

Z = 67

Y = 0.0

Z = 60

Z = 40

165

189.08

Z = 22

115
85

145
85
115

25
45
145

Y = 20

57.018

165 & 189.08

15

Y = -20

ENLARGED
FRONT VIEW
WITH CONTOUR LINES
OF STATION CUTS.

PILOT
VISUAL RANGE,
WHEN COCKPIT IS
DEPLOYED UP
DURING APPROACH
AND LANDING

Z = 67

AUXILIARY
PROPULSION
SYSTEM

AFT RCS SYSTEM

RETRACTABLE
RCS

FOUR MODULES
OF LINEAR
AEROSPIKE
ENGINES

REAR VIEW

C.G. RANGE DURING ASCEND

FWD C.G.
AFT C.G.

SLED (REF)

STA 0.0
STA 25
STA 45
STA 55
STA 85
STA 115
STA 145
STA 165
STA 190
STA 210.5

CROSS SECTION OF THE CATAPULT,
THE COMPOUND CATAPULT CONSIST OF A
TANDEM SYSTEM OF A HYDRAULIC AND A
STEAM SYSTEMS, WHICH OPERATES
SEQUENCIALLY AS THE PISTON PASSES
BY THEM.
FOR MORE DETAIL SEE DRAWINGS
SERIES 1700

STA 0.0
STA 25
STA 45
STA 55
STA 85
STA 115
STA 145
STA 165
STA 190

277.43 FT
84.56 M

115.40 FT
35.17 M

106.5 FT
32,46 M

78.10 FT
23,80 M

210.5 FT
64,16 M

PLANE WHERE THE RESULTANT
LATERAL FORCE FROM THE
THREE VERTICAL STABILIZER
GROUP IS LOCATED

15 METER    60 FEET
15.24 M     50
TO C.G.     40
            30
50 FT       20
15.24 M     10
TO C.G.

C.G. OF BOOSTER
VEHICLE, WHEN IT
IS GLIDING BACK

5'

3'
6'

3'

15.32°

71.28 FT
21,73 M

2 TAIL SKIDS, ONE EACH
SIDE OF FUSELAGE

LANDING GEAR SYSTEM DESIGNED
ONLY FOR '0.0 FUEL' VEHICLE.

PRELIMINARY DESIGN
EXTERIOR VIEW
SPACE-LINER VEHICLE SYSTEM
COMMUTING SYSTEM FOR SERVICE
BETWEEN EARTH AND THE
SPACE STATION.

PROJECT DESIGNED BY :
WALTER F. LAREDO     February 1997

Drawing No. 1900-1
(2 SHEETS)
SHEET B

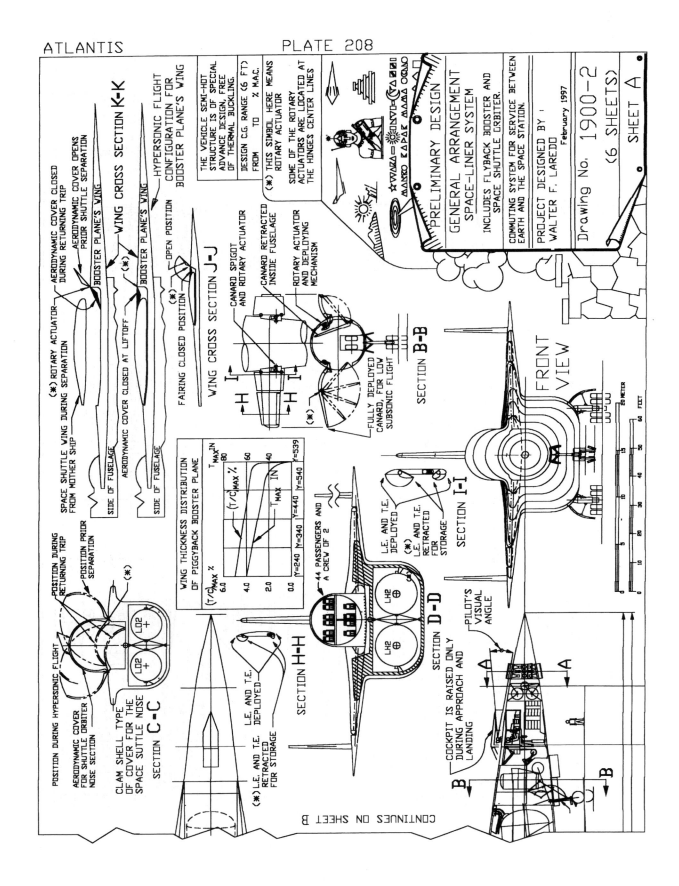

POSITION DURING HYPERSONIC FLIGHT

AERODYNAMIC COVER FOR SHUTTLE ORBITER NOSE SECTION

POSITION DURING RETURNING TRIP

POSITION PRIOR SEPARATION

CLAM SHELL TYPE OF COVER FOR THE SPACE SUTTLE NOSE

(*) L.E. AND T.E. RETRACTED FOR STORAGE

SECTION C-C

LO2 +   LO2 +

ROTARY ACTUATOR

AERODYNAMIC COVER CLOSED DURING RETURNING TRIP

AERODYNAMIC COVER OPENS PRIOR SHUTTLE SEPARATION

(*) ROTARY ACTUATOR

SPACE SHUTTLE WING DURING SEPARATION FROM MOTHER SHIP

AERODYNAMIC COVER CLOSED AT LIFTOFF

SIDE OF FUSELAGE

BOOSTER PLANE'S WING

WING CROSS SECTION K-K

BOOSTER PLANE'S WING

HYPERSONIC FLIGHT CONFIGURATION FOR BOOSTER PLANE'S WING

(*) OPEN POSITION

FAIRING CLOSED POSITION

WING CROSS SECTION J-J

SIDE OF FUSELAGE

THE VEHICLE SEMI-HOT STRUCTURE IS OF SPECIAL ADVANCE DESIGN, FREE OF THERMAL BUCKLING.

DESIGN C.G. RANGE (6 FT) FROM   TO   % M.A.C.

(*) THIS SIMBOL HERE MEANS ROTARY ACTUATOR

SOME OF THE ROTARY ACTUATORS ARE LOCATED AT THE HINGES CENTER LINES

PRELIMINARY DESIGN

GENERAL ARRANGEMENT SPACE-LINER SYSTEM

INCLUDES FLYBACK BOOSTER AND SPACE SHUTTLE ORBITER.

COMMUTING SYSTEM FOR SERVICE BETWEEN EARTH AND THE SPACE STATION.

PROJECT DESIGNED BY : WALTER F. LAREDO

February 1997

Drawing No. 1900-2 (6 SHEETS)

SHEET A

CANARD SPIGOT AND ROTARY ACTUATOR

CANARD RETRACTED INSIDE FUSELAGE

ROTARY ACTUATOR AND DEPLOYING MECHANISM

SECTION B-B

FULLY DEPLOYED CANARD, FOR LOW SUBSONIC FLIGHT

(*)

WING THICKNESS DISTRIBUTION OF PIGGYBACK BOOSTER PLANE

$(T/c)_{MAX}$ %    $T_{MAX}$ IN

6.0    80

4.0    60

$(T/c)_{MAX}$ %

2.0    40

$T_{MAX}$ IN

0.0

Y=240   Y=340   Y=440   Y=539
       Y=540

44 PASSENGERS AND A CREW OF 2

L.E. AND T.E. DEPLOYED

L.E. AND T.E. RETRACTED FOR STORAGE

(*) L.E. AND T.E. RETRACTED FOR STORAGE

SECTION I-I

LH2 +   LH2 +

SECTION D-D

SECTION H-H

PILOT'S VISUAL ANGLE

COCKPIT IS RAISED ONLY DURING APPROACH AND LANDING

FRONT VIEW

20 METER   FEET

60   50   40   15   30   20   10   5

A   A

B   B

CONTINUES ON SHEET B

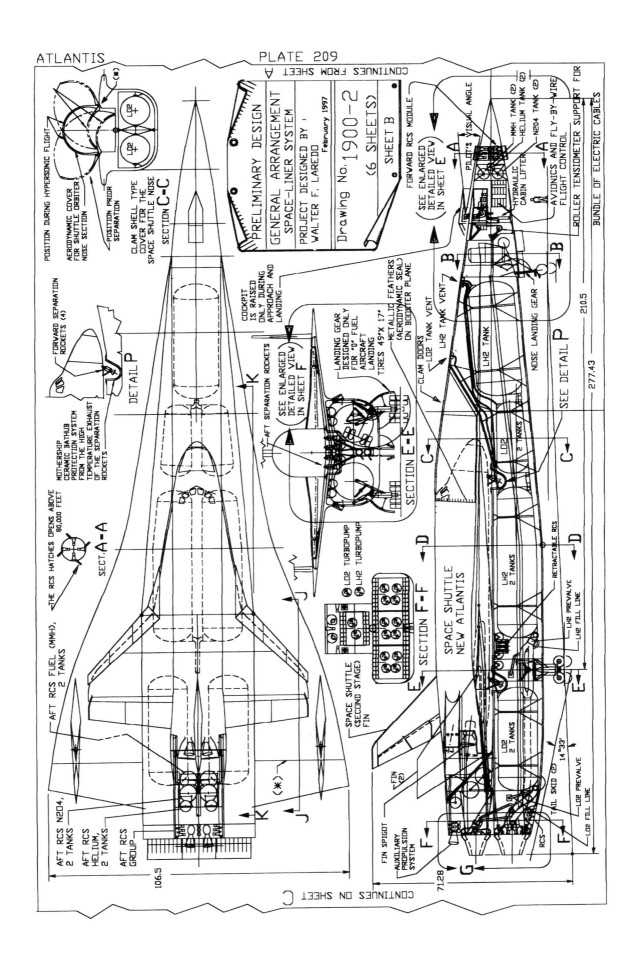

CONTINUES FROM SHEET A

POSITION DURING HYPERSONIC FLIGHT
AERODYNAMIC COVER FOR SHUTTLE ORBITER NOSE SECTION
POSITION PRIOR SEPARATION
CLAM SHELL TYPE COVER FOR THE SPACE SHUTTLE NOSE
SECTION C-C

PRELIMINARY DESIGN
GENERAL ARRANGEMENT SPACE-LINER SYSTEM
PROJECT DESIGNED BY :
WALTER F. LAREDO   February 1997
Drawing No.1900-2 (6 SHEETS)
SHEET B

FORWARD RCS MODULE
(SEE ENLARGED DETAILED VIEW IN SHEET E)

PILOT'S VISUAL ANGLE
MMH TANK (2)
HELIUM TANK (2)
N2O4 TANK (2)
HYDRAULIC CABIN LIFTER
AVIONICS AND FLY-BY-WIRE FLIGHT CONTROL
ROLLER TENSIOMETER SUPPORT FOR
BUNDLE OF ELECTRIC CABLES

FORWARD SEPARATION ROCKETS (4)
DETAIL P

MOTHERSHIP CERAMIC BATHUB PROTECTION SYSTEM FROM THE HIGH TEMPERATURE EXHAUST OF THE SEPARATION ROCKETS

COCKPIT IS RAISED ONLY DURING APPROACH AND LANDING

AFT SEPARATION ROCKETS
(SEE ENLARGED DETAILED VIEW IN SHEET F)

LANDING GEAR DESIGNED ONLY FOR "0" FUEL AIRCRAFT LANDING
TIRES 49"x 17"

METALLIC FEATHERS (AERODYNAMIC SEAL) ON BOOSTER PLANE

LH2 TANK VENT
LO2 TANK VENT
CLAM DOORS
LH2 TANK
LO2 2 TANKS
NOSE LANDING GEAR
SEE DETAIL P

210.5
277.43

THE RCS HATCHES OPENS ABOVE 80,000 FEET
SECT. A-A

SECTION E-E

LO2 TURBOPUMP
LH2 TURBOPUMP

SPACE SHUTTLE (SECOND STAGE) FIN
SECTION F-F

SPACE SHUTTLE NEW ATLANTIS

RETRACTABLE RCS
LH2 2 TANKS
LH2 PREVALVE
LH2 FILL LINE

AFT RCS FUEL (MMH), 2 TANKS
AFT RCS N2O4, 2 TANKS
AFT RCS HELIUM, 2 TANKS
AFT RCS GROUP

FIN SPIGOT
AUXILIARY PROPULSION SYSTEM
FIN (2)
LO2 2 TANKS
TAIL SKID (2) 14°33'
RCS
LO2 PREVALVE
LO2 FILL LINE

106.5
71.28

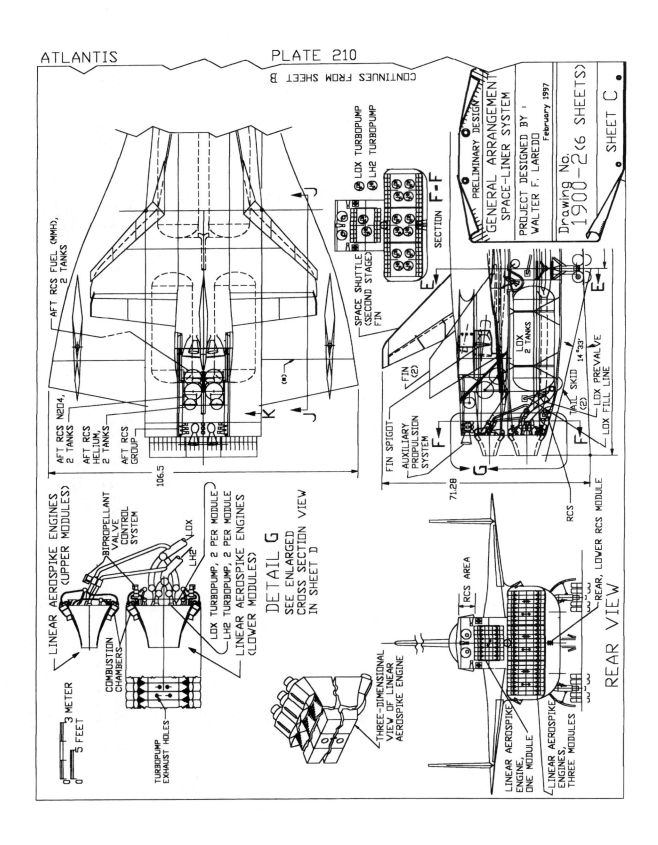

CONTINUES FROM SHEET B

PRELIMINARY DESIGN

GENERAL ARRANGEMENT
SPACE-LINER SYSTEM

PROJECT DESIGNED BY :
WALTER F. LAREDO
February 1997

Drawing No.
1900-2 (6 SHEETS)

SHEET C

AFT RCS FUEL (MMH),
2 TANKS

LOX TURBOPUMP
LH2 TURBOPUMP

SPACE SHUTTLE
(SECOND STAGE)
FIN

SECTION F-F

AFT RCS N2O4,
2 TANKS

AFT RCS
HELIUM,
2 TANKS

AFT RCS
GROUP

106.5

FIN
(2)

LOX
2 TANKS

14°33'

TAIL SKID
(2)

LOX PREVALVE

LOX FILL LINE

FIN SPIGOT

AUXILIARY
PROPULSION
SYSTEM

71.28

RCS

LINEAR AEROSPIKE ENGINES
(UPPER MODULES)

BIPROPELLANT
VALVE
CONTROL
SYSTEM

LOX

LH2

COMBUSTION
CHAMBERS

LOX TURBOPUMP, 2 PER MODULE
LH2 TURBOPUMP, 2 PER MODULE
LINEAR AEROSPIKE ENGINES
(LOWER MODULES)

DETAIL G
SEE ENLARGED
CROSS SECTION VIEW
IN SHEET D

3 METER
5 FEET

TURBOPUMP
EXHAUST HOLES

THREE-DIMENSIONAL
VIEW OF LINEAR
AEROSPIKE ENGINE

RCS AREA

REAR, LOWER RCS MODULE

LINEAR AEROSPIKE
ENGINE, ONE MODULE

LINEAR AEROSPIKE
ENGINES,
THREE MODULES

REAR VIEW

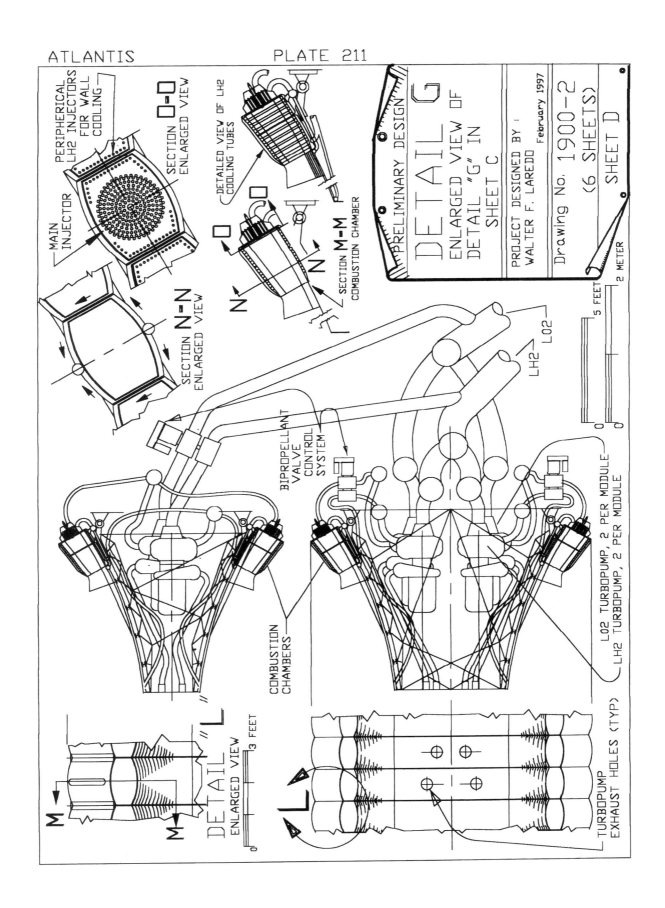

ATLANTIS     PLATE 211

PERIPHERICAL LH2 INJECTORS FOR WALL COOLING

SECTION □-□ ENLARGED VIEW

MAIN INJECTOR

DETAILED VIEW OF LH2 COOLING TUBES

SECTION N-N ENLARGED VIEW

SECTION M-M COMBUSTION CHAMBER

N

PRELIMINARY DESIGN

DETAIL G
ENLARGED VIEW OF DETAIL "G" IN SHEET C

PROJECT DESIGNED BY : WALTER F. LAREDO      February 1997

Drawing No. 1900-2
(6 SHEETS)

SHEET D

BIPROPELLANT VALVE CONTROL SYSTEM

LO2

LH2

5 FEET

2 METER

COMBUSTION CHAMBERS

LO2 TURBOPUMP, 2 PER MODULE
LH2 TURBOPUMP, 2 PER MODULE

DETAIL "L" ENLARGED VIEW

M

M

3 FEET

TURBOPUMP EXHAUST HOLES (TYP)

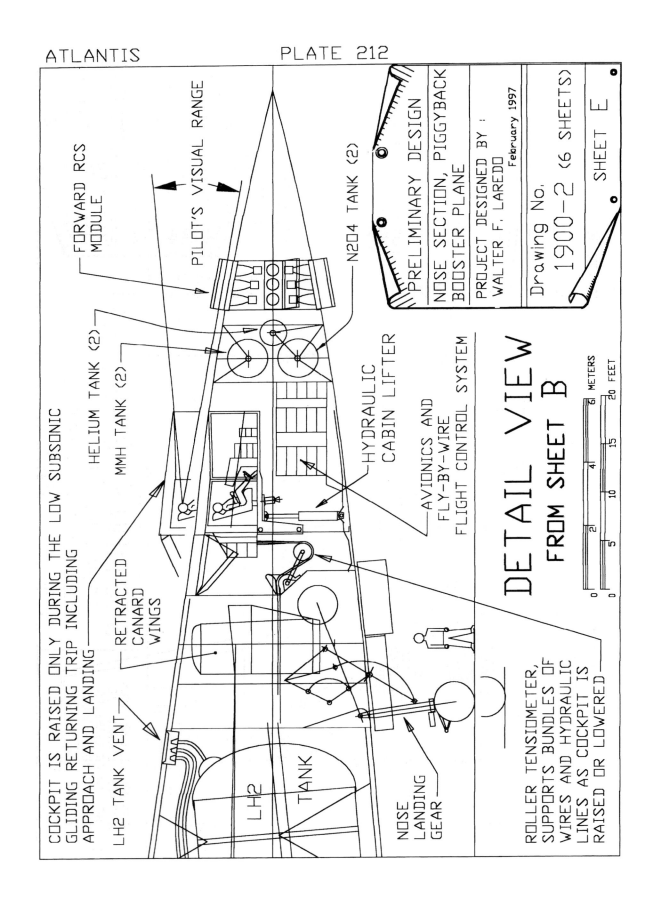

COCKPIT IS RAISED ONLY DURING THE LOW SUBSONIC
GLIDING RETURNING TRIP INCLUDING
APPROACH AND LANDING

FORWARD RCS
MODULE

PILOT'S VISUAL RANGE

HELIUM TANK (2)

MMH TANK (2)

N2O4 TANK (2)

LH2 TANK VENT

RETRACTED
CANARD
WINGS

HYDRAULIC
CABIN LIFTER

AVIONICS AND
FLY-BY-WIRE
FLIGHT CONTROL SYSTEM

LH2
TANK

NOSE
LANDING
GEAR

ROLLER TENSIOMETER,
SUPPORTS BUNDLES OF
WIRES AND HYDRAULIC
LINES AS COCKPIT IS
RAISED OR LOWERED

PRELIMINARY DESIGN

NOSE SECTION, PIGGYBACK
BOOSTER PLANE

PROJECT DESIGNED BY :
WALTER F. LAREDO
February 1997

Drawing No.
1900-2 (6 SHEETS)

SHEET E

DETAIL VIEW
FROM SHEET B

METERS
FEET

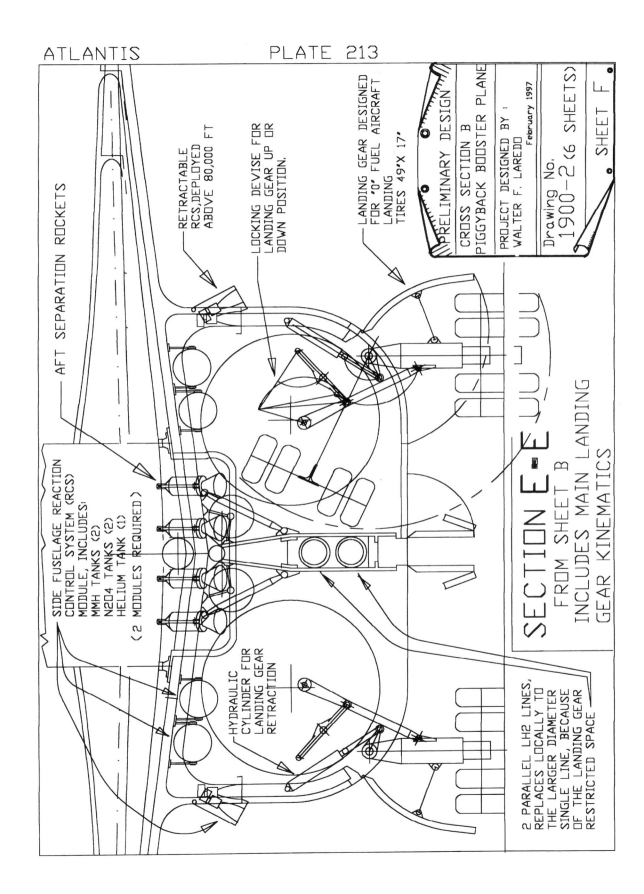

AFT SEPARATION ROCKETS

RETRACTABLE RCS, DEPLOYED ABOVE 80,000 FT

LOCKING DEVISE FOR LANDING GEAR UP OR DOWN POSITION.

LANDING GEAR DESIGNED FOR "0" FUEL AIRCRAFT LANDING
TIRES 49"X 17"

SIDE FUSELAGE REACTION CONTROL SYSTEM (RCS) MODULE, INCLUDES:
MMH TANKS (2)
N2O4 TANKS (2)
HELIUM TANK (1)
(2 MODULES REQUIRED)

HYDRAULIC CYLINDER FOR LANDING GEAR RETRACTION

2 PARALLEL LH2 LINES, REPLACES LOCALLY TO THE LARGER DIAMETER SINGLE LINE, BECAUSE OF THE LANDING GEAR RESTRICTED SPACE

SECTION E-E
FROM SHEET B
INCLUDES MAIN LANDING GEAR KINEMATICS

PRELIMINARY DESIGN

CROSS SECTION B
PIGGYBACK BOOSTER PLANE

PROJECT DESIGNED BY:
WALTER F. LAREDO
February 1997

Drawing No.
1900-2 (6 SHEETS)

SHEET F

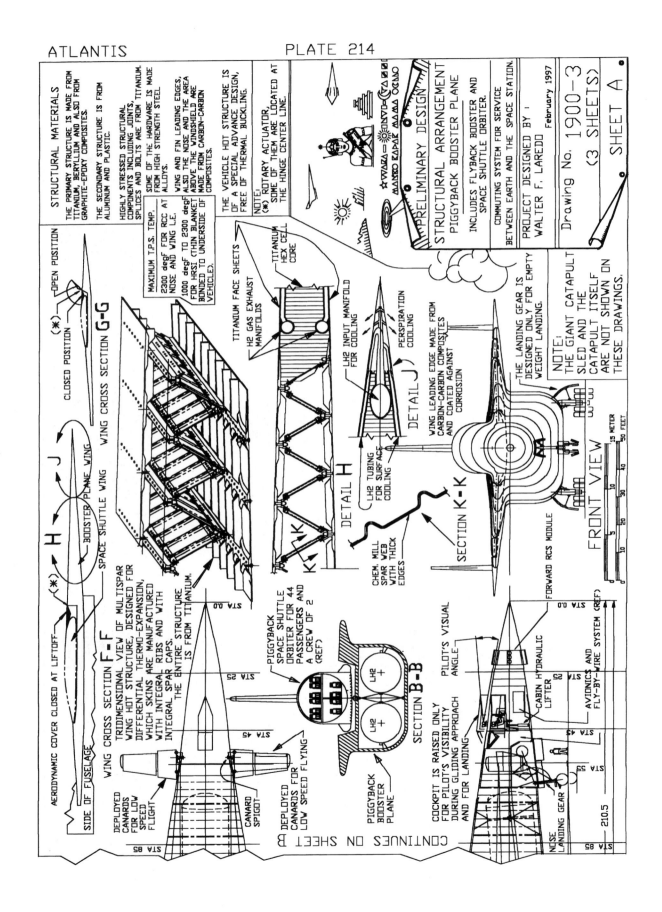

STRUCTURAL MATERIALS

THE PRIMARY STRUCTURE IS MADE FROM TITANIUM, BERYLLIUM AND ALSO FROM GRAPHITE-EPOXY COMPOSITES.

THE SECONDARY STRUCTURE IS FROM ALUMINUM AND PLASTIC.

HIGHLY STRESSED STRUCTURAL COMPONENTS INCLUDING JOINTS, SPLICES AND BOLTS ARE FROM TITANIUM.

SOME OF THE HARDWARE IS MADE FROM HIGH STRENGTH STEEL ALLOYS.

WING AND FIN LEADING EDGES, ALSO THE NOSE AND THE AREA ABOVE THE WINDSHIELD ARE MADE FROM CARBON-CARBON COMPOSITES.

THE VEHICLE HOT STRUCTURE IS OF A SPECIAL ADVANCE DESIGN, FREE OF THERMAL BUCKLING.

NOTE:
(*) ROTARY ACTUATOR, SOME OF THEM ARE LOCATED AT THE HINGE CENTER LINE.

PRELIMINARY DESIGN

STRUCTURAL ARRANGEMENT
PIGGYBACK BOOSTER PLANE

INCLUDES FLYBACK BOOSTER AND SPACE SHUTTLE ORBITER.

COMMUTING SYSTEM FOR SERVICE BETWEEN EARTH AND THE SPACE STATION.

PROJECT DESIGNED BY :
WALTER F. LAREDO          February 1997

Drawing No. 1900-3
(3 SHEETS)

SHEET A

AERODYNAMIC COVER CLOSED AT LIFTOFF

(*)          OPEN POSITION

CLOSED POSITION

WING CROSS SECTION G-G

SIDE OF FUSELAGE

BOOSTER PLANE WING
SPACE SHUTTLE WING

MAXIMUM T.P.S. TEMP.
2300 degF FOR RCC AT NOSE AND WING L.E.
1000 degF TO 2300 degF FOR HRSI (THIN BLANKET BONDED TO UNDERSIDE OF VEHICLE).

TITANIUM FACE SHEETS

TITANIUM HEX CELL CORE

H2 GAS EXHAUST MANIFOLDS

LH2 INPUT MANIFOLD FOR COOLING

PERSPIRATION COOLING

DETAIL J

WING LEADING EDGE MADE FROM CARBON-CARBON COMPOSITES AND COATED AGAINST CORROSION

LH2 TUBING FOR SURFACE COOLING

DETAIL H

THE LANDING GEAR IS DESIGNED ONLY FOR EMPTY WEIGHT LANDING.

NOTE:
THE GIANT CATAPULT SLED AND THE CATAPULT ITSELF ARE NOT SHOWN ON THESE DRAWINGS.

WING CROSS SECTION F-F

TRIDIMENSIONAL VIEW OF MULTISPAR WING HOT STRUCTURE, DESIGNED FOR DIFFERENTIAL THERMO-EXPANSION, WHICH SKINS ARE MANUFACTURED WITH INTEGRAL RIBS AND WITH INTEGRAL SPAR CAPS.
THE ENTIRE STRUCTURE IS FROM TITANIUM.

STA 0.0

CHEM. MILL SPAR WEB WITH THICK EDGES

SECTION K-K

AA

FRONT VIEW

15 METER
50 FEET
10    20    30    40    50
5    10    15    20
0

DEPLOYED CANARDS FOR LOW SPEED FLIGHT

CANARD SPIGOT

PIGGYBACK SPACE SHUTTLE ORBITER FOR 44 PASSENGERS AND A CREW OF 2 (REF)

STA 25
LH2 +
LH2 +

SECTION B-B

PIGGYBACK BOOSTER PLANE

STA 45

DEPLOYED CANARDS FOR LOW SPEED FLYING

FORWARD RCS MODULE

PILOT'S VISUAL ANGLE

COCKPIT IS RAISED ONLY FOR PILOT'S VISIBILITY DURING GLIDING APPROACH AND FOR LANDING.

CABIN HYDRAULIC LIFTER

AVIONICS AND FLY-BY-WIRE SYSTEM (REF)

STA 0.0
STA 25
STA 45
STA 55

NOSE LANDING GEAR

210.5

STA 85

CONTINUES ON SHEET B

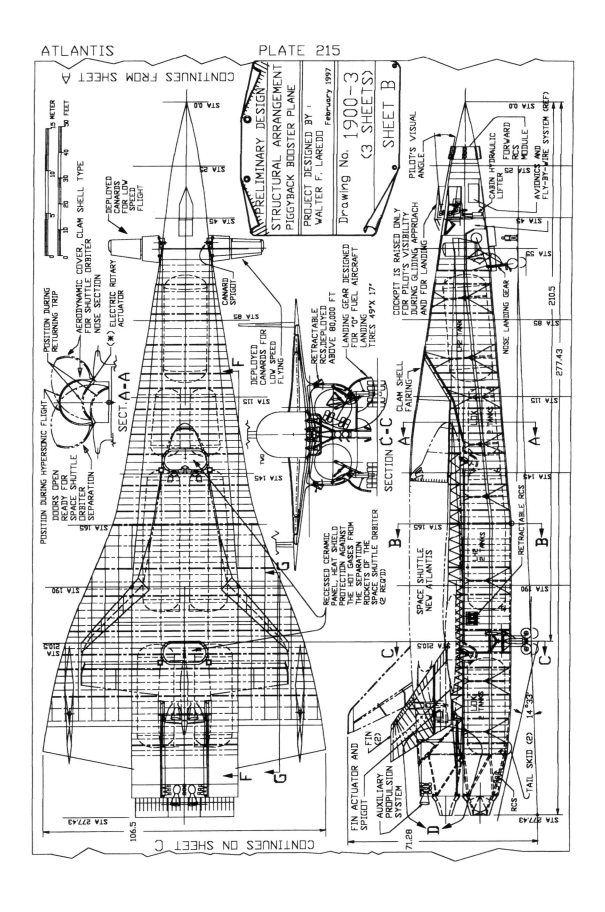

CONTINUES FROM SHEET A

PRELIMINARY DESIGN
STRUCTURAL ARRANGEMENT
PIGGYBACK BOOSTER PLANE

PROJECT DESIGNED BY :
WALTER F. LAREDO          February 1997

Drawing No. 1900-3
(3 SHEETS)
SHEET B

15 METER
50 FEET

DEPLOYED CANARDS FOR LOW SPEED FLIGHT

AERODYNAMIC COVER, CLAM SHELL TYPE FOR SHUTTLE ORBITER NOSE SECTION

(*) ELECTRIC ROTARY ACTUATOR

POSITION DURING RETURNING TRIP

POSITION DURING HYPERSONIC FLIGHT

DOORS OPEN READY FOR SPACE SHUTTLE ORBITER SEPARATION

SECT. A-A

CANARD SPIGOT

DEPLOYED CANARDS FOR LOW SPEED FLYING

RETRACTABLE RCS,DEPLOYED ABOVE 80,000 FT

LANDING GEAR DESIGNED FOR "0" FUEL AIRCRAFT LANDING TIRES 49"X 17'

SECTION C-C

RECESSED CERAMIC PANEL, HEAT SHIELD PROTECTION AGAINST THE HOT GASES FROM THE SEPARATION ROCKETS OF THE SPACE SHUTTLE ORBITER (2 REQ'D)

PILOT'S VISUAL ANGLE

FORWARD RCS MODULE

CABIN HYDRAULIC LIFTER

AVIONICS AND FLY-BY-WIRE SYSTEM (REF)

COCKPIT IS RAISED ONLY FOR PILOT'S VISIBILITY DURING GLIDING APPROACH AND FOR LANDING

CLAM SHELL FAIRING

NOSE LANDING GEAR

LHP TANK

LOX P.TANKS

RETRACTABLE RCS

SPACE SHUTTLE NEW ATLANTIS

LH2 P.TANKS

LOX TANKS

FIN (2)

FIN ACTUATOR AND SPIGOT

AUXILIARY PROPULSION SYSTEM

TAIL SKID (2)

RCS

14°33'

STA 0.0
STA 25
STA 45
STA 85
STA 115
STA 145
STA 165
STA 190
STA 210.5
STA 277.43

210.5
277.43
106.5
71.28

CONTINUES ON SHEET C

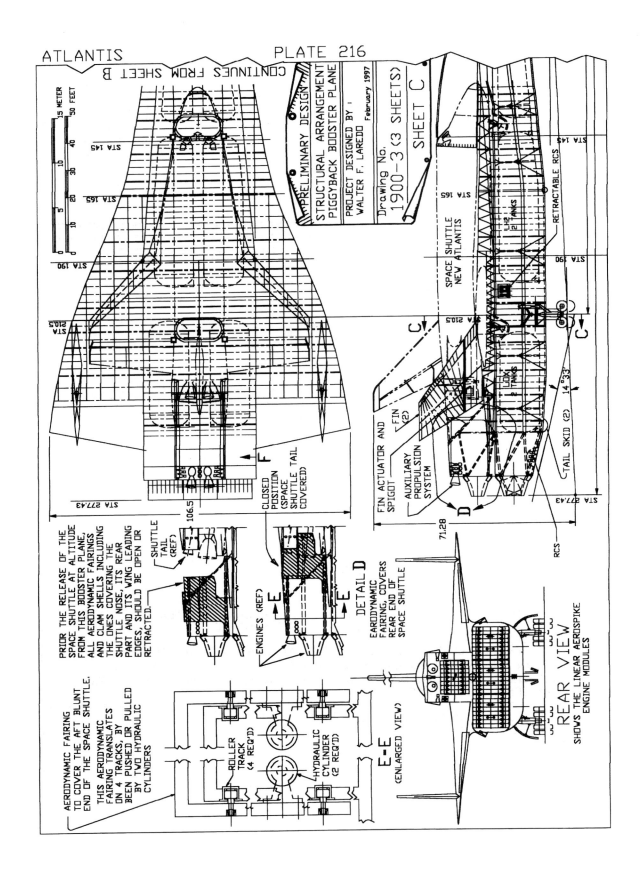

CONTINUES FROM SHEET B

PRELIMINARY DESIGN
STRUCTURAL ARRANGEMENT
PIGGYBACK BOOSTER PLANE

PROJECT DESIGNED BY :
WALTER F. LAREDO    February 1997

Drawing No.
1900-3 (3 SHEETS)
SHEET C

15 METER
50 FEET
40
10
30
5
20
10

STA 145
STA 165
STA 190
STA 210.5
STA 277.43

SPACE SHUTTLE
NEW ATLANTIS

LH2
TANKS

LOX
TANKS

RETRACTABLE RCS

FIN
(2)

FIN ACTUATOR AND
SPIGOT

AUXILIARY
PROPULSION
SYSTEM

14°33'

TAIL SKID (2)

RCS

106.5
71.28

CLOSED POSITION
(SPACE
SHUTTLE TAIL
COVERED)

SHUTTLE TAIL
(REF)

ENGINES (REF)

E    E

DETAIL D
AERODYNAMIC
FAIRING, COVERS
REAR END OF
SPACE SHUTTLE

ROLLER TRACK
(4 REQ'D)

HYDRAULIC
CYLINDER
(2 REQ'D)

E-E
(ENLARGED VIEW)

REAR VIEW
SHOWS THE LINEAR AEROSPIKE
ENGINE MODULES

AERODYNAMIC FAIRING
TO COVER THE AFT BLUNT
END OF THE SPACE SHUTTLE.

THIS AERODYNAMIC
FAIRING TRANSLATES
ON 4 TRACKS, BY
BEEN PUSHED OR PULLED
BY TWO HYDRAULIC
CYLINDERS

PRIOR THE RELEASE OF THE
SPACE SHUTTLE AT ALTITUDE
FROM THIS BOOSTER PLANE,
ALL AERODYNAMIC FAIRINGS
AND CLAM SHELLS INCLUDING
THE ONES COVERING THE
SHUTTLE NOSE, ITS REAR
PART AND ITS WING LEADING
EDGES, SHOULD BE OPEN OR
RETRACTED.

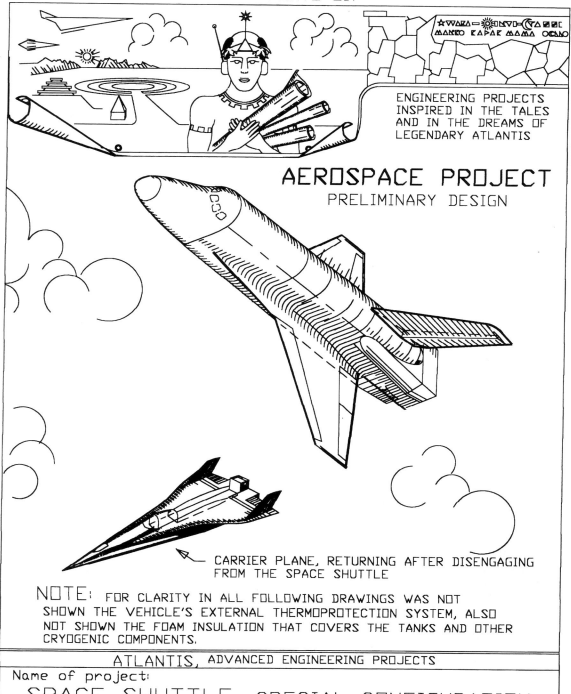

ENGINEERING PROJECTS
INSPIRED IN THE TALES
AND IN THE DREAMS OF
LEGENDARY ATLANTIS

# AEROSPACE PROJECT
## PRELIMINARY DESIGN

CARRIER PLANE, RETURNING AFTER DISENGAGING
FROM THE SPACE SHUTTLE

NOTE: FOR CLARITY IN ALL FOLLOWING DRAWINGS WAS NOT
SHOWN THE VEHICLE'S EXTERNAL THERMOPROTECTION SYSTEM, ALSO
NOT SHOWN THE FOAM INSULATION THAT COVERS THE TANKS AND OTHER
CRYOGENIC COMPONENTS.

| ATLANTIS, ADVANCED ENGINEERING PROJECTS | | |
|---|---|---|
| Name of project: SPACE SHUTTLE, SPECIAL CONFIGURATION TRANSPORTATION SYSTEM BETWEEN EARTH AND THE SPACE STATION | | |
| Design Engineer: WALTER F. LAREDO | | Date: Feb. 1997 |
| Drawing Number: 2000 | Sheet 1 | (TOTAL OF 11 SHEETS) |

MAIN PROPULSION SYSTEM
(2) ENGINES RATED AT :
115,080 LB THRUST IN THE VACUUM.
91,823 LB THRUST S.S.L.
DESIRED SPECIFIC IMPULSE = 450 SECONDS

PROPELLANT WEIGHT
LH2   13,138 LB
LO2   78,650 LB
TOTAL = 91,787 LB

RATIO OF TOTAL LIFTOFF WEIGHT TO 0.0 FUEL WEIGHT = 1.72

FOR FINAL DESIGN,
REDUCE WING AREA AS REQUIRED

PRELIMINARY DESIGN
GENERAL ARRANGEMENT
SHUTTLE ORBITER
"NEW ATLANTIS"

VEHICLE DESIGNED TO COMMUTE INTERPLANETARY TRAVELERS BETWEEN EARTH AND A SPACE STATION USED AS SPACEPORT FOR SPACESHIP

PROJECT DESIGNED BY :
WALTER F. LAREDO
February 1997

Drawing No.   TOTAL OF
2000   11 SHEETS

SHEET 2A

---

TOTAL NUMBER OF TRAVELLERS= 46
( 2 CREW + 44 PASSENGERS )

VERTICAL STABILIZER (Vs) :
AREA   380 SQ FT
lvs   20 FT
VOL. COEFFICIENT = $\overline{V}s$

$$\overline{V}s = \frac{lvs \times Svs}{b \times Sw} = 0.036$$

DESIGN C.G. RANGE
WITH 0 FUEL :
FROM 22 TO 28 % M.A.C.
BEFORE IGNITION :
FROM 33 TO 37 % M.A.C.

DESIGN SPEEDS :
MAX. MACH 26
MIN. LANDING 175 MPH

WING : COULD BE USE SAME WING AS NASA SPACE SHUTTLE,
ASPECT RATIO   2.26
AREA   2690 SQ FT
SWEEP   45 DEGREES
M.A.C. (IN.)   474.8
DIHEDRAL (T.E.)   3°  90'

ORBITER WEIGHTS :
LAUNCH   157,000 LB
LANDING   65,000 LB
DESIGN PAYLOAD 15,000 LB

MAXIMUM T.P.S. TEMPERATURES

2300 degF FOR RCC , USED AT NOSE AND WING L.E.

1200 degF TO 2300 degF FOR HRST TILES LOCATED AT UNDERSIZE OF VEHICLE

---

(COMPONENT'S LIST,
CONTINUES FROM SHEET 2B)

ORBITAL MANEUVERING SYSTEM (OMS)
18. OMS ENGINE (2)
19. OMS FUEL(MMH), 2 TANKS
20. OMS HELIUM, 2 TANKS
21. OMS N2O4, 2 TANKS

REACTION CONTROL SYSTEM (RCS)
22. AFT RCS MODULE (2)
23. AFT RCS HELIUM BOTTLE
24. AFT RCS N2O4, 2 TANKS
25. AFT RCS MMH, 2 TANKS
26. NOSE RCS MODULE

CABIN AREA
27. PRESSURIZED CHAMBER
28. AVIONIC BAY AND VARIOUS KINDS OF EQUIPMENT, INCLUDING THE ENVIRONMENT CONTROL SYSTEM.
29. AIR LOCK
30. INTERNAL AIR LOCK HATCH
31. EXTERNAL ACCESS, AIRLOCK HATCH
32. TOILET OF SPECIAL DESIGN
33. WARDROBE
34. AVIONIC BAY
35. COCKPIT
36. OUTER ACCESS HATCH
37. LADDER
38. FLOOR BEAM SUPPORT COLUMNS

39. MAIN LANDING GEAR
40. BODY FLAP
41. NOSE LANDING GEAR
42. BALLAST BLOCK FROM DEPLETED URANIUM, 2 REQ'D
43. NOSE CAP
44. EXPENDABLE AFT SEPARATION MOTORS, 4 REQ'D
45. EXPENDABLE FORWARD SEPARATION MOTORS, 4 REQUIRED
46. WING
47. FUSELAGE
48. TAIL SKID

CONTINUES ON SHEET 2B

CONTINUES FROM SHEET 2A

LIST OF COMPONENTS

## MAIN PROPULSION SYSTEM

1. MAIN ROCKET ENGINE (2)
2. LO2 FILL AND DRAIN AREA
3. LH2 MANIFOLD
4. LO2 MANIFOLD
5. LH2 LOW PRESSURE PUMP
6. LH2 FILL AND DRAIN LINE
7. LO2 PRE-VALVE
8. LO2 LOW PRESSURE PUMP
9. LH2 PRE-VALVE
10. LO2 LINE
11. LH2 TANK VENT
12. LO2 TANK VENT
13. MAIN LH2 TANK
14. MAIN LO2 TANK
15. 2 HELIUM TANKS
16. PITCH ACTUATOR
17. YAW ACTUATOR

(CONTINUES IN SHEET 2A)

"PRELIMINARY DESIGN"

GENERAL ARRANGEMENT
SHUTTLE ORBITER
"NEW ATLANTIS"

VEHICLE DESIGNED TO COMMUTE
INTERPLANETARY TRAVELERS
BETWEEN EARTH AND A
SPACE STATION (SPACEPORT)

February 1997

PROJECT DESIGNED BY :
WALTER F. LAREDO

Drawing No. 2000    TOTAL OF 11 SHEETS

SHEET 2B

## NOTES:

1. ENLARGED VIEWS FROM DETAIL DRAWINGS IN SHEET 1C ARE SHOWN IN FOLLOWING SHEETS.

2. FOR CLARITY WAS NOT SHOWN IN THESE DRAWINGS THE VEHICLE'S EXTERNAL THERMO PROTECTION SYSTEM AND THE INTERNAL HEAT INSULATION

3. TO AVOID DUPLICATION OF DEVELOPMENTAL WORK, FOR SOME COMPONENTS, COULD BE USE THE ONES FROM THE EXISTING NASA'S SPACE SHUTTLE ORBITERS, THOSE COMPONENTS ARE THE FOLLOWING:

   NOSE CAP, MAIN AND NOSE LANDING GEARS, NOSE REACTION CONTROL SYSTEM (RCS) AND THE OUTBOARD WING STRUCTURE, WITHOUT INCLUDING THE WING CARRY-THROUGH STRUCTURE.

4. THERE IS SOME RESEMBLANCE BETWEEN THE GENERAL ARRANGEMENT OF THIS VEHICLE AND THE GENERAL ARRANGEMENTE OF NASA'S SPACE SHUTTLE ORBITER. BOTH VEHICLES ARE ABOUT THE SAME SIZE. IN THIS VEHICLE THE WING AND THE MAIN LANDING GEAR WAS SHIFT TWO FEET FORWARD, IN ORDER TO IMPROVE ITS AERODYNAMIC STABILITY FOR SOME FLIGHT CONDITIONS, INCLUDING DURING THE RE-ENTRY, SUPERSONIC AND SUBSONIC GLIDING, FOLLOWED BY LOW SPEED APPROACH AND LANDING.

5. THE EXTERNAL COVER OF THE AFT RCS MODULE WAS DESIGNED FOR MINIMUM HYPERSONIC DRAG DURING ASCEND.

6. DEPLETED URANIUM IS USED AS A BALLAST TO BALANCE THE VEHICLE.

CONTINUES ON SHEET 2C

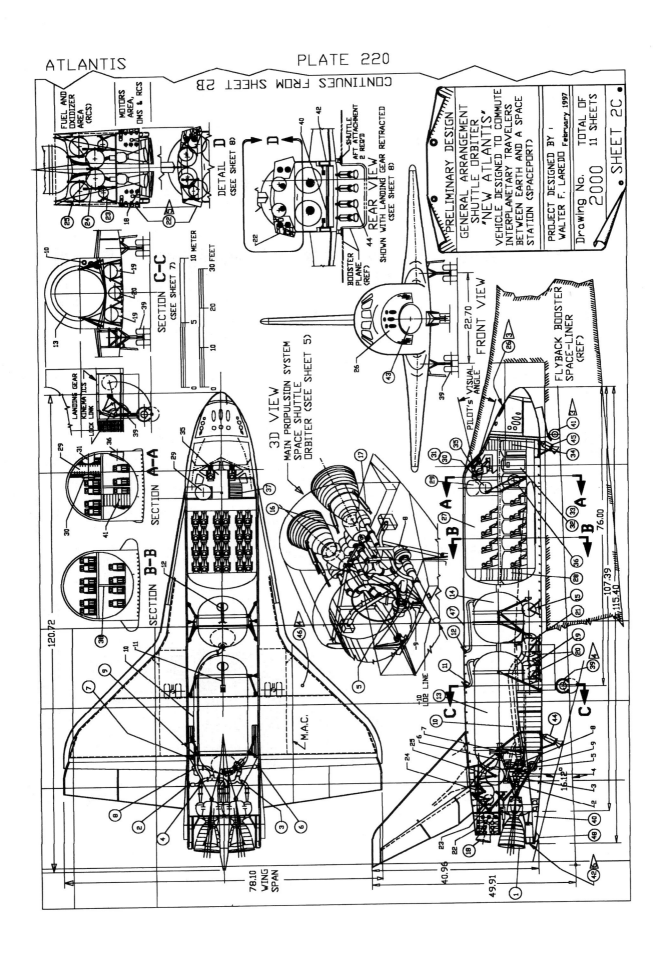

CONTINUES FROM SHEET 2B

FUEL AND OXIDIZER AREA (RCS)

MOTORS AREA, OMS & RCS

DETAIL D
(SEE SHEET 8)

REAR VIEW
SHOWN WITH LANDING GEAR RETRACTED
(SEE SHEET 8)

SHUTTLE AFT ATTACHMENT 2 REQ'D

BOOSTER PLANE (REF)

PRELIMINARY DESIGN
GENERAL ARRANGEMENT
SHUTTLE ORBITER
"NEW ATLANTIS"
VEHICLE DESIGNED TO COMMUTE
INTERPLANETARY TRAVELERS
BETWEEN EARTH AND A SPACE
STATION (SPACEPORT)

PROJECT DESIGNED BY :
WALTER F. LAREDO   February 1997

Drawing No.    TOTAL OF
2000           11 SHEETS

SHEET 2C

SECTION C-C
(SEE SHEET 7)

10 METER
30 FEET

3D VIEW

MAIN PROPULSION SYSTEM
SPACE SHUTTLE
ORBITER (SEE SHEET 5)

FRONT VIEW

22.70

PILOT'S VISUAL ANGLE

FLYBACK BOOSTER
SPACE-LINER
(REF)

LANDING GEAR
KINEMATICS
LOCK LINK

SECTION A-A

SECTION B-B

120.72

M.A.C.

76.00

107.39

115.40

WL 02 LINE

16.12°

78.10
WING SPAN

40.96

49.91

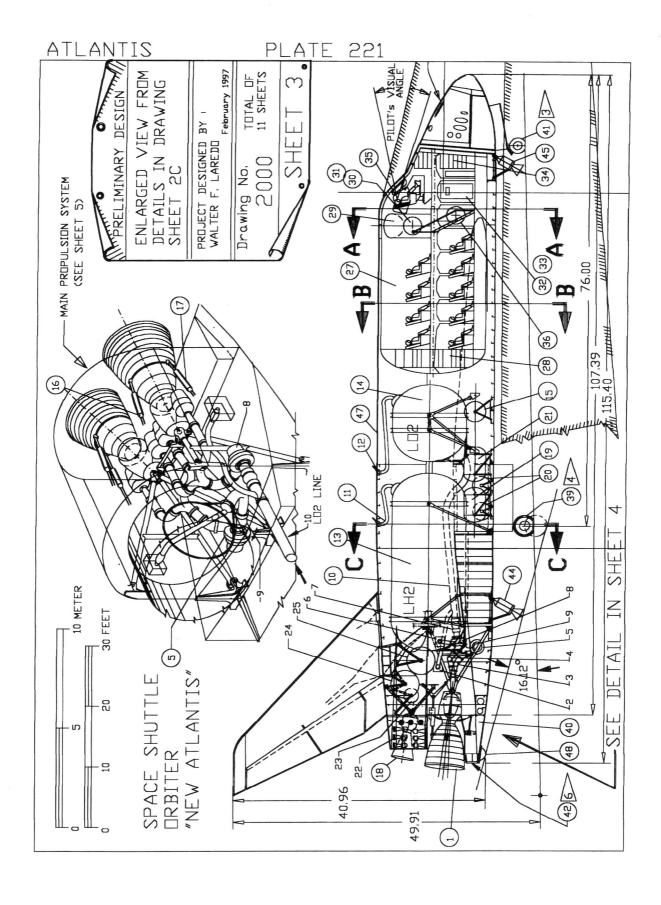

SPACE SHUTTLE
ORBITER
"NEW ATLANTIS"

MAIN PROPULSION SYSTEM
(SEE SHEET 5)

PRELIMINARY DESIGN

ENLARGED VIEW FROM
DETAILS IN DRAWING
SHEET 2C

PROJECT DESIGNED BY :
WALTER F. LAREDO      February 1997

Drawing No.      TOTAL OF
2000             11 SHEETS

SHEET 3

10 METER
30 FEET

PILOT's VISUAL ANGLE

SEE DETAIL IN SHEET 4

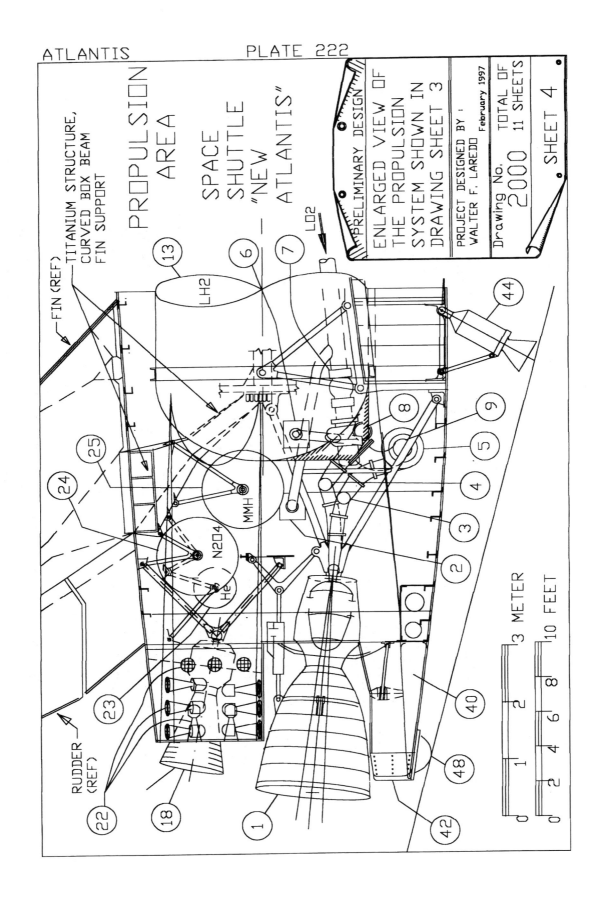

PROPULSION
AREA

SPACE
SHUTTLE
"NEW
ATLANTIS"

FIN (REF)

TITANIUM STRUCTURE,
CURVED BOX BEAM
FIN SUPPORT

RUDDER
(REF)

LH2

N2O4

He

MMH

LO2

PRELIMINARY DESIGN

ENLARGED VIEW OF
THE PROPULSION
SYSTEM SHOWN IN
DRAWING SHEET 3

PROJECT DESIGNED BY :
WALTER F. LAREDO          February 1997

Drawing No.          TOTAL OF
2000          11 SHEETS

SHEET 4

3 METER

10 FEET

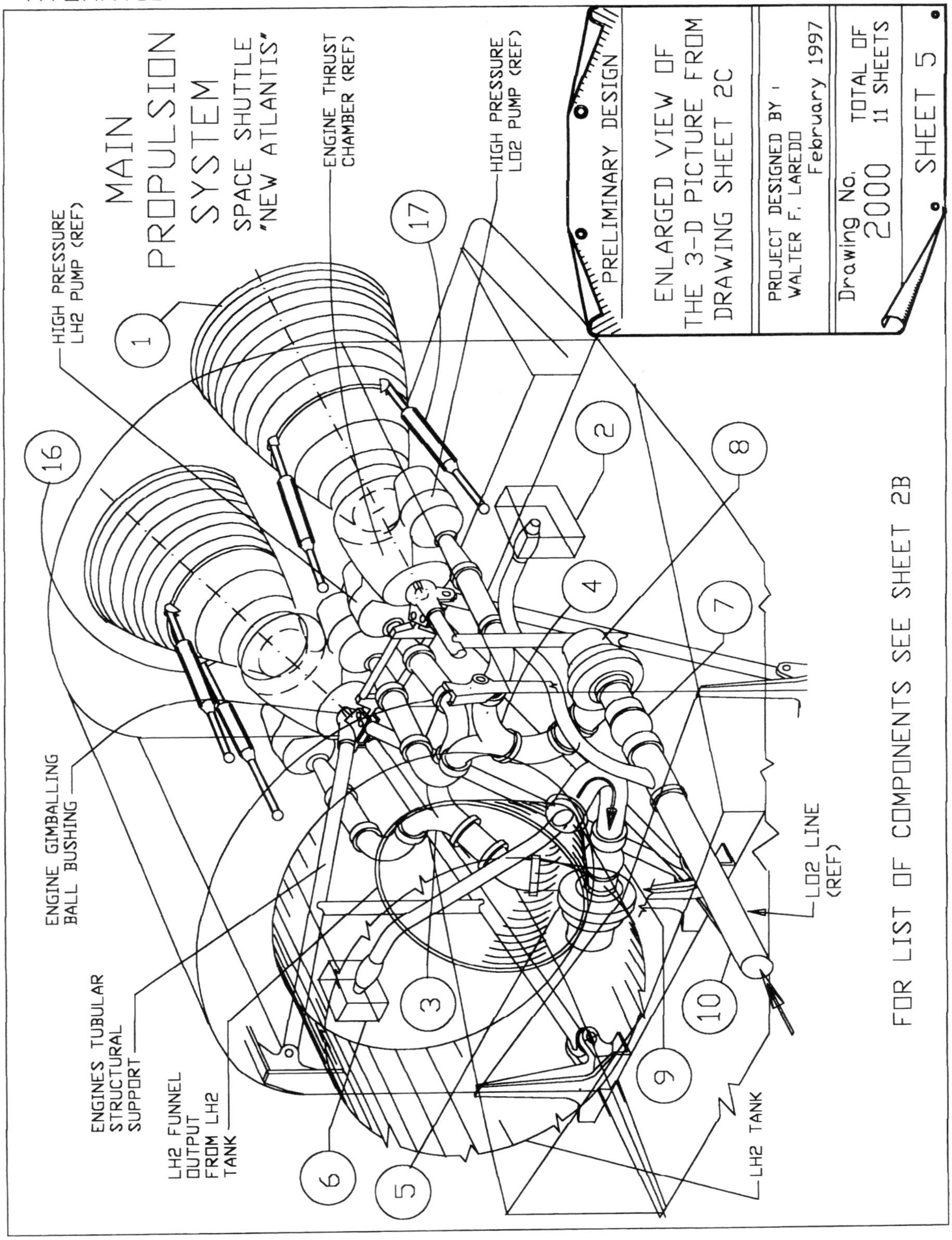
MAIN
PROPULSION
SYSTEM
SPACE SHUTTLE
"NEW ATLANTIS"
HIGH PRESSURE
LH2 PUMP (REF)
ENGINE THRUST
CHAMBER (REF)
HIGH PRESSURE
LO2 PUMP (REF)
PRELIMINARY DESIGN
ENLARGED VIEW OF
THE 3-D PICTURE FROM
DRAWING SHEET 2C
PROJECT DESIGNED BY :
WALTER F. LAREDO
February 1997
Drawing No.
2000
TOTAL OF
11 SHEETS
SHEET 5
1
16
17
2
8
4
7
3
10
9
6
5
ENGINE GIMBALLING
BALL BUSHING
ENGINES TUBULAR
STRUCTURAL
SUPPORT
LH2 FUNNEL
OUTPUT
FROM LH2
TANK
LO2 LINE
(REF)
LH2 TANK
FOR LIST OF COMPONENTS SEE SHEET 2B

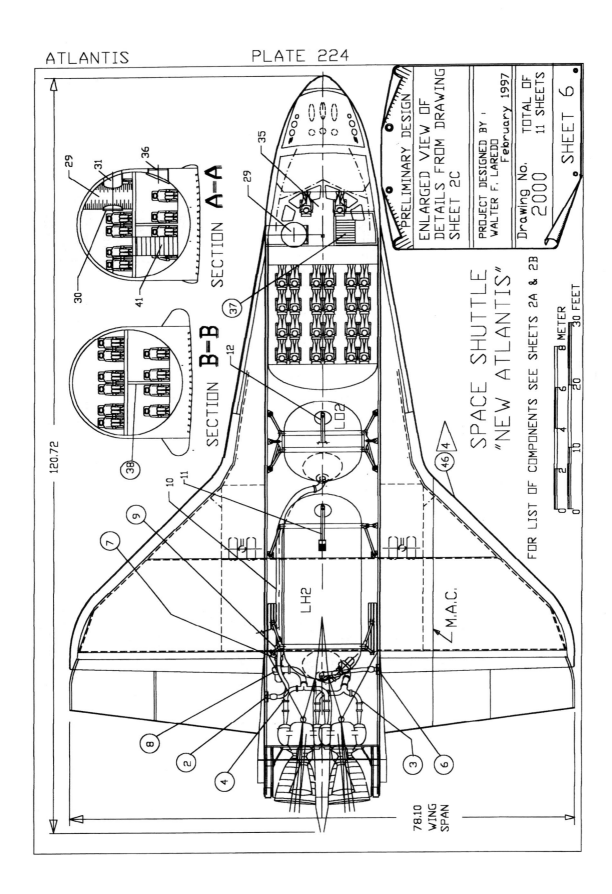

SECTION A-A

SECTION B-B

PRELIMINARY DESIGN

ENLARGED VIEW OF
DETAILS FROM DRAWING
SHEET 2C

PROJECT DESIGNED BY:
WALTER F. LAREDO          February 1997

Drawing No.          TOTAL OF
2000          11 SHEETS

SHEET 6

SPACE SHUTTLE
"NEW ATLANTIS"

FOR LIST OF COMPONENTS SEE SHEETS 2A & 2B

METER
30 FEET

120.72

LO2

LH2

M.A.C.

78.10
WING SPAN

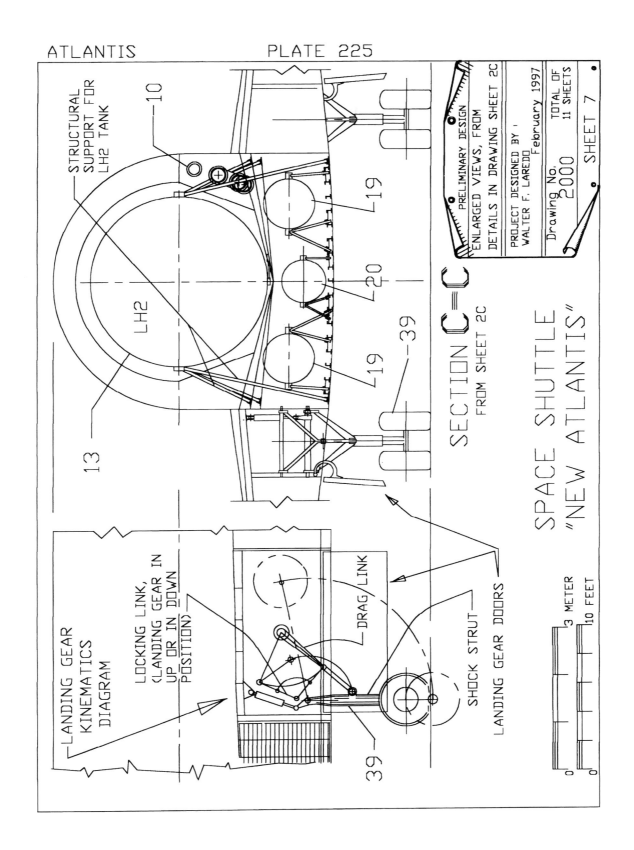

STRUCTURAL SUPPORT FOR LH2 TANK

10

LH2

13

19

20

39

19

LANDING GEAR KINEMATICS DIAGRAM

LOCKING LINK, (LANDING GEAR IN UP OR IN DOWN POSITION)

DRAG LINK

SHOCK STRUT

LANDING GEAR DOORS

39

SECTION C–C
FROM SHEET 2C

SPACE SHUTTLE
"NEW ATLANTIS"

PRELIMINARY DESIGN
ENLARGED VIEWS, FROM
DETAILS IN DRAWING SHEET 2C

PROJECT DESIGNED BY :
WALTER F. LAREDO
February 1997

Drawing No.          TOTAL OF
2000               11 SHEETS

SHEET 7

3 METER

10 FEET

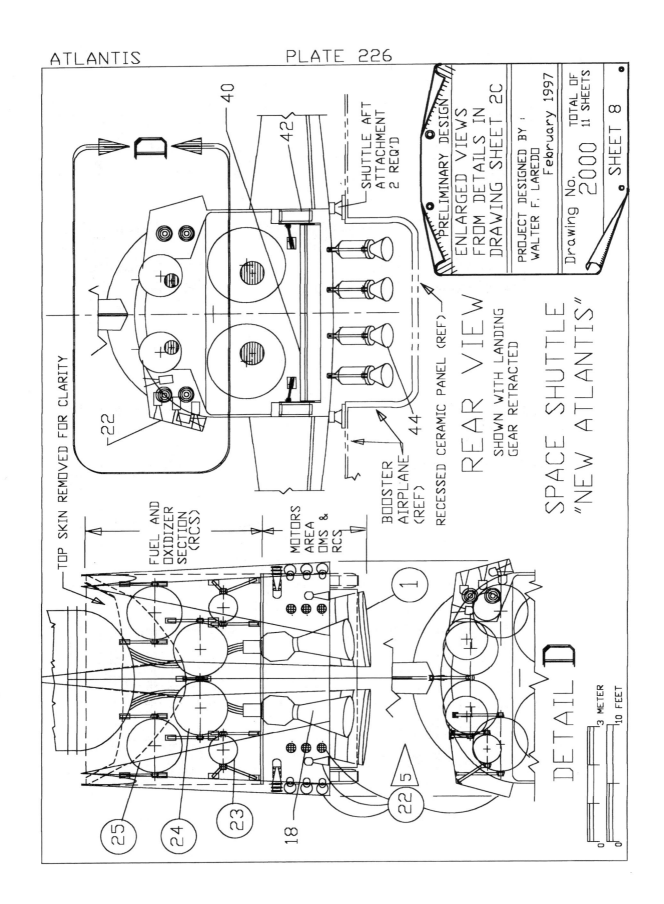

PRELIMINARY DESIGN

ENLARGED VIEWS
FROM DETAILS IN
DRAWING SHEET 2C

PROJECT DESIGNED BY :
WALTER F. LAREDO
February 1997

Drawing No. 2000    TOTAL OF 11 SHEETS

SHEET 8

SHUTTLE AFT
ATTACHMENT
2 REQ'D

TOP SKIN REMOVED FOR CLARITY

22

40

42

FUEL AND
OXIDIZER
SECTION (RCS)

MOTORS
AREA
OMS &
RCS

BOOSTER
AIRPLANE
(REF)

RECESSED CERAMIC PANEL (REF)

44

REAR VIEW

SHOWN WITH LANDING
GEAR RETRACTED

SPACE SHUTTLE
"NEW ATLANTIS"

DETAIL D

25

24

23

18

1

22

5

3 METER

10 FEET

0

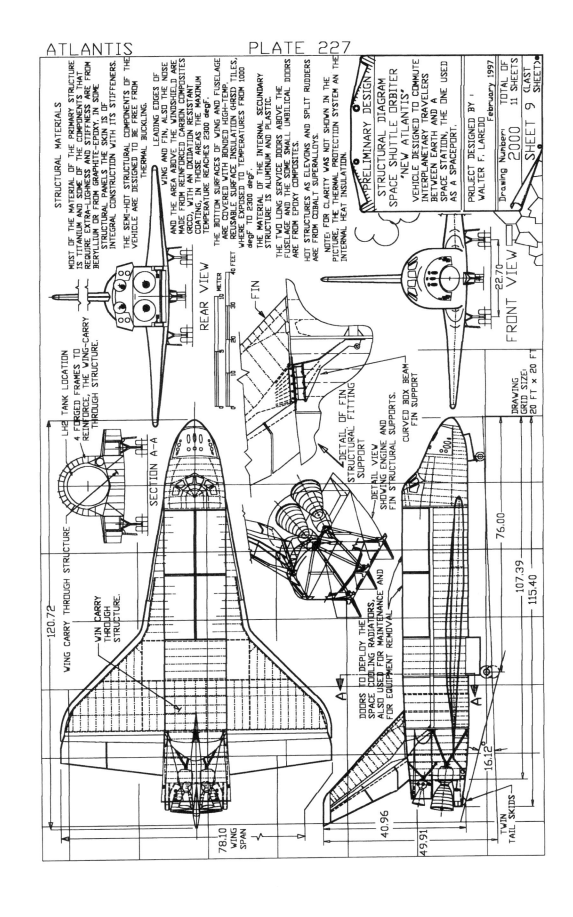

STRUCTURAL MATERIALS

MOST OF THE MATERIAL OF THE PRIMARY STRUCTURE IS TITANIUM AND SOME OF THE COMPONENTS THAT REQUIRE EXTRA-LIGHNESS AND STIFFNESS ARE FROM BERYLLIUM OR FROM GRAPHITE-EPOXY. IN SOME STRUCTURAL PANELS THE SKIN IS OF INTEGRAL CONSTRUCTION WITH ITS STIFFENERS.

THE SEMI-HOT STRUCTURAL COMPONENTS OF THE VEHICLE ARE DESIGNED TO BE FREE FROM THERMAL BUCKLING.

LEADING EDGES OF WING AND FIN, ALSO THE NOSE AND THE AREA ABOVE THE WINDSHIELD ARE MADE FROM REINFORCED CARBON COMPOSITES (RCC), WITH AN OXIDATION RESISTANT COATING, IN THOSE AREAS THE MAXIMUM TEMPERATURE REACHES 2300 degF.

THE BOTTOM SURFACES OF WING AND FUSELAGE ARE COVERED WITH BONDED HIGH-TEMP. REUSABLE SURFACE INSULATION (HRSI) TILES, WHERE EXPOSED TO TEMPERATURES FROM 1000 degF TO 2300 degF.

THE MATERIAL OF THE INTERNAL SECONDARY STRUCTURE IS ALUMINUM AND PLASTIC.

THE TWO LONG SERVICE DOORS ABOVE THE FUSELAGE AND THE SOME SMALL UMBILICAL DOORS ARE FROM EPOXY COMPOSITES.

HOT STRUCTURES AS ELEVONS AND SPLIT RUDDERS ARE FROM COBALT SUPERALLOYS.

NOTE: FOR CLARITY WAS NOT SHOWN IN THE PICTURE, THE THERMAL PROTECTION SYSTEM AN THE INTERNAL HEAT INSULATION.

PRELIMINARY DESIGN

STRUCTURAL DIAGRAM
SPACE SHUTTLE ORBITER
'NEW ATLANTIS'
VEHICLE DESIGNED TO COMMUTE INTERPLANETARY TRAVELERS BETWEEN EARTH AND A SPACE STATION, THE ONE USED AS A SPACEPORT.

PROJECT DESIGNED BY :
WALTER F. LAREDO

February 1997

Drawing Number:  TOTAL OF
2000            11 SHEETS

SHEET 9 (LAST SHEET)

REAR VIEW

FIN

40 FEET
METER
10
30
5
20
10

FRONT VIEW

22.70

DETAIL OF FIN STRUCTURAL FITTING SUPPORT

DETAIL VIEW SHOWING ENGINE AND FIN STRUCTURAL SUPPORTS.

CURVED BOX BEAM FIN SUPPORT

DRAWING GRID SIZE:
20 FT x 20 FT

LH2 TANK LOCATION

4 FORGED FRAMES TO REINFORCE, THE WING-CARRY THROUGH STRUCTURE.

SECTION A-A

WING CARRY THROUGH STRUCTURE

WIN CARRY THROUGH STRUCTURE.

120.72

A

A

DOORS TO DEPLOY THE SPACE COOLING RADIATORS, ALSO USED FOR MAINTENANCE AND FOR EQUIPMENT REMOVAL

76.00

107.39

115.40

16.12°

40.96

49.91

TWIN TAIL SKIDS

78.10 WING SPAN

# END OF APPENDIX

FUTURISTIC SEMI-STEALTH, MACH 1.5 TACTICAL FIGHTER, shown in pictures below, the aircraft carry a hydrogen fluorine chemical laser, its only weapon used for defense as well as for offence.

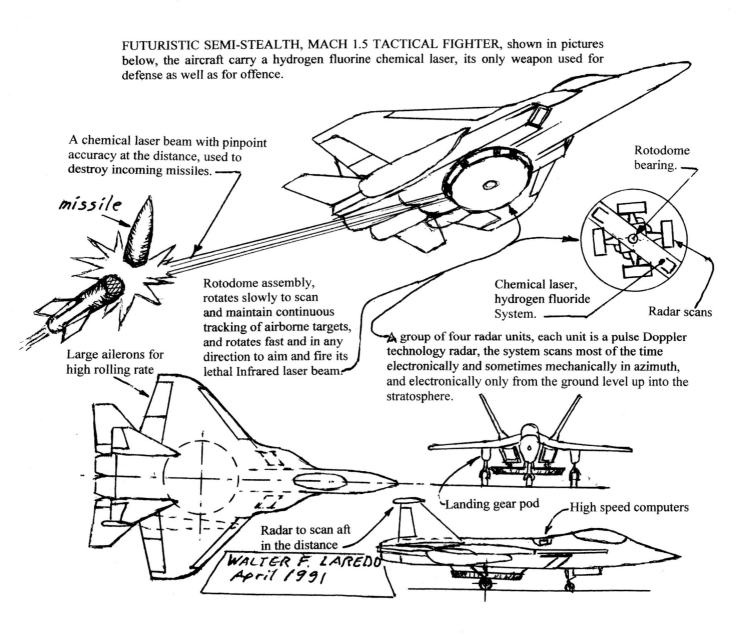

A chemical laser beam with pinpoint accuracy at the distance, used to destroy incoming missiles.

missile

Rotodome bearing.

Rotodome assembly, rotates slowly to scan and maintain continuous tracking of airborne targets, and rotates fast and in any direction to aim and fire its lethal Infrared laser beam.

Chemical laser, hydrogen fluoride System.

Radar scans

A group of four radar units, each unit is a pulse Doppler technology radar, the system scans most of the time electronically and sometimes mechanically in azimuth, and electronically only from the ground level up into the stratosphere.

Large ailerons for high rolling rate

Radar to scan aft in the distance

WALTER F. LAREDO
April 1991

Landing gear pod

High speed computers